RISE OF THE SILVAN

THE SILVAN BOOK V

R.K. LANDER

Edited by M.Y. LEIGH

Edited by ANDREA LUNDGREN

Illustrated by ASHA ZNAMENSKA

Illustrated by HECTOR AIRAGHI

Calrazia

Xeric Wood

Ea·Uaré

Sen·uar

Abiren·a   Sen·olei

L·an Taria
Ea·nanu

Everbinding Wood

Oran·dór

Sen·garay

Calin River

High Path

Court of
Thargoden

Pelagian Mountains

Port Helia

Glistening Fa

Pelagia

Dan·bar

Dan·sú

Pelagian Sea

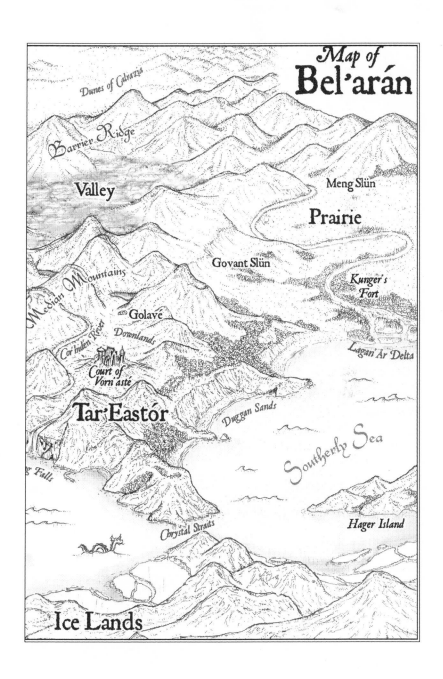

Map of
Bel'arán

Dunes of Cdraza

Barrier Ridge

Valley

Meng Slün

Prairie

Govant Slün

Median Mountains

Kunger's
Fort

Golavé

Downlands

Cor Inden River

Court of
Vorn'asté

Lagan'Ar Delta

Tar'Eastór

Dwggan Sands

Southerly Sea

Falls

Crystal Straits

Hager Island

Ice Lands

PART I

RESTORATION

1

BLIND FAITH

~

THE SILVAN ENCAMPMENT sprawled across the plains before the city gates of Ea Uaré.

It was a symbol of resistance against Alpine domination, a brave place where brave leaders had made their stand against injustice and won; in all but deed.

At the heart of the settlement, the command tent still stood. The Council of Elders had met with princes and captains, with a warlord too, and had decided great things, achieved great things; in all but deed.

It was quiet there, as one would expect it to be at this time of night. Everyone was inside, asleep or unwilling to know who had come in the dark. No one would think that just minutes away, there were hundreds of wounded, lying in makeshift beds under makeshift shelters that looked more like stables than any Healing Hall.

An elf lit candles which stood on long, decorative stands, laden with heavy drops of wax, like molten rock dried too quickly. Three wood-carved candelabras sat equidistant to each other down the long, rectangular table, where treaties had been signed, urgent missives penned and allies had shared worried words, angry words and then elated words.

Light slowly illuminated the tent, lending a sense of warmth to the place as the flame gathered strength and the wax began to melt. But none of that mattered to Fel'annár. His world was still as dark as the day Band'orán had blinded him.

They had not been expected, not at this time of night, not after what had happened just hours ago at the Healing Halls within the city walls.

The elf cast furtive glances at the cloaked and hooded newcomers who stood quietly by, waiting for him to finish his work, waiting for the Council of Elders to come. But he especially watched the one whose silvery hair had escaped the confines of his concealing garments, his ample hood casting his face into deep shadow.

"Warrior," a woman's voice from the centre of the group. The elf turned to her, stepping closer.

"Ask Tari Kristain to come, if you will."

"Of course. It may take a while. All our healers are busy."

"I know. Tell him Tari Llyniel is here."

He bowed to the tari he knew was the Warlord's wife, and then left to do her bidding, wishing he could stay and hear what news the visitors bore.

Fel'annár heard the elf's boots make for where he knew the tent flap was, saw his light as it winked out. But as the candles began to burn in earnest, the pitch black before his eyes lightened to a charcoal grey, except when an elf came into his sight, sight that was not his own.

The lights around him moved slowly, elves as they settled around him, not too far away, especially three of them. He was suddenly grateful for the blindfold across his eyes, for the peculiar sight that the forest lent him. Without it, with his eyes open, everything was dark. But closed, he was a tree contemplating the world on a moonless night.

The candles would be casting a comforting orange glow around him, illuminating the place as they flickered in the soft breeze he could feel coming through the tarpaulins. He yearned for a fire to warm his tired bones and soothe away the gnawing anxiety, but it pushed its way to the fore, again and again, despite his feeble attempts. He was so tired, needed a chair.

Would he ever regain his sight? See the world with his own eyes?

A hand at the small of his back, gentle pressure. He moved with the light that was Llyniel, his Connate, his healer tonight. His thighs pressed softly into an unyielding surface, the long, rectangular table he remembered from weeks before.

"Sit."

Fel'annár obeyed the murmured command, blind faith telling him there was a seat beneath him. He felt Llyniel sit beside him while to his left, another joined them.

"I'm here." It was loud enough only for him and perhaps Llyniel. Of all those who had come, Idernon was the one he needed the most beside him now. If he flailed in his logic, if his sluggish mind failed to explain what he desperately needed them to understand, then Idernon would do it for him.

Something thunked on the table before him, then the clink of a glass and the slosh of liquid. A pause and then a deep, accented voice from beside him.

"Drink." Something scraped over the surface of the table, touched his hand. A glass.

Had Tensári tested the water? He thought that she had, and he curled his hand around the cool surface, drinking sparingly.

His Ber'ator moved behind him, and Fel'annár knew that she would stay right there until his meeting with the Silvan Elders was over.

There were lights further away, not at the table. Ramien and Galadan, Galdith and Carodel. He flinched at the unexpected voice from behind.

"Don't try to get up and make an ass of yourself. Stay where you are and let's be done with this foolishness."

Sontúr. He was annoyed, almost as much as Llyniel was. Fel'annár had awoken just that morning after a five-day slumber. Aching body – no energy – no Dohai and eyes that scratched and burned like nails over raw skin.

But he had heard the distant song of the Nim'uán, and then Llyniel had told him how the Silvans had abandoned the Healing Halls in anger and indignation. He knew that he had to move fast, well-meaning healers be damned.

The rustle of oiled cloth, feet moving over the ground and the lights of three – no four – elves. One of them was distinctly Amareth. The smell of jasmine and the soft brush in his mind told him it was so. She came close but he didn't stand, just like Sontúr had warned him not to. Yet even if he had been hale, he wouldn't have. He was annoyed, would tell them so, as soon as they sat.

"You have come," said the light that was his aunt as it lowered onto a seat further along the table. The other lights also sat, one of them much brighter than the others. Narosén, he was sure. The other two would be Erthoron of Lan Taria, and Lorthil of Sen'oléi.

"Of course I've come." A quiet voice, careful and probing. "Did you think I wouldn't?"

"They said you were injured. They said you were blind."

Fel'annár turned to the voice he recognised from childhood. He had sat on this elf's knees, asked for stories, pulled on his many chocolatey-brown braids.

"I can see *you*, Lord Erthoron."

An odd silence enveloped the room. Fel'annár knew he had not been expected, not like this, at night and in secret. They would all be wondering what they should say to that because he surely *looked* blind. He quelled his irritation, pressed on.

"And even if I *were* blind, did you think that would stop me?"

Someone shuffled in their chair. "You are not well enough to be here, are you?" said Amareth.

"So they say. But there are priorities, and you did not come. None of you did. Tell me, why is that?"

"You have heard of the ... *incident*?"

Fel'annár sat back, took a moment to understand that Erthoron had not answered his question and instead, deflected it with his own. He half-turned to Llyniel when she spoke.

"I saw it with my own eyes. One act of discrimination by the Master Healer, an order that was obeyed at first. Outraged myself, I confronted Lestari Nestar in public, but the Silvans had already decided to leave the Halls, wouldn't wait for me to try and sort it. Those able enough helped and even carried the others away but there were not enough. An hour later, they came back with others, civilians with stretchers and blankets until there were no more Silvans in the Healing Halls of Ea Uaré.

"I and many others begged them to stop, to come back but they were adamant, and I had no choice but to follow them, with any who would accompany me. Yes, I saw it, Lord Erthoron, how our injured warriors turned their backs on Nestar, risked their own health for one act of discrimination, from *one* elf. Later, they said that you didn't discourage their actions at all – that you seconded them even. It seems that all you could see was Nestar's bigotry. You didn't consider the ten Alpine healers who followed me. You didn't consider the outrage on the faces of those *Alpine* warriors who occupied the beds. They stood, pushed away those who tried to help. They offered their places to the wounded Silvans, but it was too late. My people gave up and you applauded their surrender."

"We applaud those Alpine healers who heeded your call, and those warriors who would have relinquished their own comfort," said Erthoron. "But that vile act was obeyed by most other healers, and it was one insult too many. Most of our warriors would rather die before they allow themselves to be treated in such a way."

"I was there. I could have sorted it." Llyniel glared angrily at the Silvan leader.

Fel'annár spoke from where he leaned back against his chair, unwilling to give Erthoron a comeback to Llyniel's words. Handir had taught him that.

"I told you things would change. I told you to trust me, to give me the time I needed to bring equality to our people, to change the workings of the Inner Circle and the Royal Council. I asked you to have faith and ride with me into battle in the name of the king, and you did. We vanquished the true foe, Lord Erthoron. Will you throw all that away now, because of one elf and his foolish ways?"

"Band'orán's legacy endures, Warlord. That act of wanton hatred, to our wounded *warriors*, Fel'annár, is proof of that. After everything we did for that Alpine city, its master healer gives the order to prioritise the Alpine wounded." A gasp of utter disgust and frustration escaped him. "Everything we did hinged on promises, pledges from the king, grudging acceptance from Pan'assár – it is all *talk*. Five days, they have had five days to come and speak with us, and not one of them has bothered to do

so. No thanks, no signed documents. We have been taken for granted –
again."

"*I* promised you, Erthoron."

"A promise you cannot know will be honoured."

"You are sceptical."

"We have learned to be."

"I told you things would change. You wanted to believe me – but you
never really did, did you?" asked Fel'annár.

"We heeded your call to fight because your words gave us hope. We
are losing that hope now, and as my people lie injured, grieving over the
dead, they want *deeds*, Lord Fel'annár, not promises."

"And so you walked out. You choose to see Nestar's actions and you
ignored the others who shunned him for it. Were you waiting for me to
come and deliver it all on a platter then? And if I do, what next? Will you
walk out again when another act of discrimination occurs?"

"No. But now, it's time for the Alpines to reach out to *us*. They must
open the door for us, not wait for us to knock on it. We will not return to
barracks and city life until they do."

"Pride. That's what this is about then?"

"Pride, and justice." Narosén leaned forward. "It is all we have left."

"And what of faith, Ari'atór? What of faith?" Fel'annár watched as
Narosén leant back in his chair and said nothing.

"Our demands *will* be met. Simple words, yes, I know. But I believe
them, know that you doubt them, but you see, it matters little in the
greater scheme of things. I do not obey the Silvan Elders. I obey a higher
command."

That odd silence was back for a moment. They hadn't expected that,
had spent a lifetime raising Fel'annár for this very purpose, only for him
to now tell them that he was not beholden to their dictates. He was
reminding them of his duty to Aria, that it took priority over his duty to
the Silvan people.

"We're not asking for much, Warlord. Equality, respect. The same
opportunities as everyone else. These are not concessions but rights that
should never have been taken from us."

Fel'annár drew a heavy breath. They always came back to the same
arguments, the same reasoning. He understood it, of course he did, but

the battle was still fresh. There were dead to bury, every day. There were supplies to guarantee and manufacture, there were prisoners to interrogate and judge, debris everywhere ...

"Give me two days, lords. By the end of them, you will have your signed and sealed agreements. But know this. Danger is not far from these lands. True I cannot yet be sure, but the Nim'uán we fought in Tar'eastór was not alone. Another stirs in the north, its destination still unclear. But if our forest *is* its objective, you can be sure that all we have ever known will be obliterated, smashed into the ground and trampled underfoot. Alone, we don't have numbers. Alone, we don't have enough swords, horses or sufficient transport. Alone, we will be slaughtered. Warriors, civilians, *children*. But together, with the Alpines, we can work as one, defend ourselves from the real enemy, lords. Just as the real enemy was always Band'orán and his poisoning of an entire generation, now it is the threat of the Beautiful Monster. Yes, you want justice, and you want what is right, but remember the odds, lords. Remember them well. Only together can we survive."

"And if it comes to war ... who will command us?"

"We shall have to *see*, Lord Lorthil." Fel'annár's irritation was growing. The Elders were underestimating the threat of the Nim'uán, seeming only to care about who would command the army should it come to war. But there wouldn't *be* an army if the Silvan warriors didn't return to barracks. He clamped his jaw shut.

"And if you never regain your sight?"

A chair scraped jarringly over the floor. "Lord Erthoron." Idernon was on his feet beside him. "Fel'annár is not blind, and even if he were, he would still be our Warlord, our commander. Even had his eyes been gouged from his face he would charge into battle before us because Aria guides his hand and we, The Company, guard his back. This is not written on a signed and sealed scroll. This is fact, written upon the hearts of us all. Cold, hard reality. Do you understand, Lord Erthoron?"

Fel'annár saw the lights of The Company flare from where they had been standing towards the back of the tent. Idernon had stirred them with his words – had stirred *him*.

"We don't mean to be callous, Fel'annár," said Erthoron, holding an appeasing hand up at Idernon, eyes drifting from the angry Wise

Warrior to the expectant Warlord. Yet when Fel'annár answered him, it was sadness that impregnated his words, not anger.

"I know what you're thinking. That you made me what I am for a reason, for a purpose. I was your hope for a better future, the one who would bring liberation to our people. I disappoint you because I defy you, because I do not deliver signed documents, because I am blind and useless in a fight. You have never really seen me as anything other than an instrument made to fulfil a purpose."

The ensuing silence stretched on and Fel'annár's blind gaze rested on Amareth for a while before he stood. Llyniel joined him and behind, he heard Sontúr moving.

"I believe we understand one another quite well, lords. Two days then, to deliver the proof you require of the promises I have made. And when that happens, I expect you to fulfil your promises to *me*. I expect you to work hard to bring our people together, because if you don't, extinction may well be our only future, for Silvans and Alpines alike. Pan'assár knows this, accepts the challenge and the question is, will you?"

Fel'annár faltered, half bent over the table, one hand flat against it. Sontúr's hand was on his back, Llyniel's under his elbow. He straightened slowly, waited for the dizziness to pass.

A rustle of cloth, a slight breeze, a new light inside the tent and then beside Llyniel, murmuring words meant only for her.

"Llyniel."

"Kristain. How bad is it?"

"It's under control. Go home, rest if you can."

"I'll be back in the morning. What supplies do we need?"

"Here." The dry scrape of paper.

"Well done, Kristain. I'm proud of you all."

It was Tensári who led the way out of the tent, as if she knew her light would be stronger, or perhaps simply different. It was a beacon and Fel'annár followed, Llyniel and The Company around him. Cloaks were tied, hoods pulled further over heads. This was not the time to greet anyone. A hand clasped his forearm and he paused.

Amareth.

"You are not an instrument to me, Fel'annár. You are my son and I love you."

He wanted to believe her, ever since they had spoken in the woods, before Faron had betrayed him. But his doubts lingered.

He pulled his arm away softly and left. She wanted to shout out to him to come back, that he was wrong, that she would care for him, but The Company had gathered around him. She knew that he wouldn't look back, wouldn't see the hurt in her brimming eyes.

Clenched jaw and brow furrowed, she turned back into the tent, and faced her three companions. She wanted to say so many things to them, to rage at them for their cold disregard, for how they had not cared that he had been wounded and even so had come. Words were out of her mouth before she could check them.

"I am so very disappointed."

She turned, made to leave but Erthoron grasped her arm. She didn't look back, didn't want to see the hurt she knew would be swimming in his eyes. She yanked her arm away from him and left.

KING THARGODÉN STOOD in simple attire. A tunic and breeches, boots and a cloak. He was ready to work, just as he had been for the past week. Just another elf picking up the pieces after the battle, even though a crown sat upon his head.

He was still king, thanks to a handful of loyal Alpine warriors and the Silvans who had come to his aid.

He turned away from the Evergreen Wood before him and faced Gor'sadén, knowing that of all those present for this morning's briefing, he was the closest to his son; was more of a father to Fel'annár than he had ever been.

"Not yet fit enough to have ridden anonymously to the Silvan encampment last night, with no one but The Company to guard him."

"Llyniel was there too," said Handir.

"Was she now?" murmured Aradan from the king's side. Handir clasped his hands behind his back.

"If he went without telling *you*, Gor'sadén, it is because he felt there was no time to waste. That incident at the Healing Halls was far more significant than it may have seemed at the time."

"A last and intolerable step in the wrong direction," said Aradan. "We must speak with Fel'annár, now, if he can be found. The Silvans already have our assurances but what they need now are deeds."

Gor'sadén nodded. "He is resting now, and Llyniel and Sontúr are adamant he is not to be disturbed. After he wakes up, his presence is critical at the Inner Circle, but once we are finished, I will bring him here."

"And what of the fool healer?" asked Handir.

Thargodén turned to him, knew that he would be indignant with the Master Healer for his treatment of Llyniel. She had always been like a sister to Handir. Indeed, he couldn't remember a time when Handir had expressed himself in such terms in a formal setting such as this.

"Nestar has always been against the Silvans. It was why Band'orán presented his candidature for Lestari to the Royal Council. They approved his appointment, and I cannot even remember that happening. Melu'sán is another example of how Band'orán appointed those favourable to his plans to the most powerful of positions within my court and at the Inner Circle. Nestar has seriously hampered this nation's chances of peace."

"Do you think he did it on purpose?"

Thargodén frowned, turned to Handir, stepped towards him. "The thought hadn't occurred to me. It seems more like a spontaneous act of discrimination to me."

Handir nodded slowly, watched his father's gaze drift to Aradan. But *his* face was unreadable.

"Time will tell, I suppose. Still, whatever his reasons, Nestar must go. In his place, Llyniel will serve the crown, as Lestari." Thargodén allowed his gaze to drift to Rinon, to Aradan and Gor'sadén. "Let me be clear. This is *not* a political decision. It is based on credentials from Arané of Tar'eastór and Tanor of Pelagia. It is based on the respect of my Alpine and Silvan warriors, and on the singular perspective Nestar's successor will bring to my Halls."

Handir stood straighter, a soft smile tugging at the corners of his mouth and he turned to Aradan. His smile faltered, because his mentor was shocked, and Handir rather thought that he shouldn't be. He underestimated his daughter, had no idea of how skilled she was, how respected she was. But then he reminded himself that Llyniel had changed in the ten years she had been away, had become who she was today in that time. Aradan needed to see his daughter for who she had become and not who she had been.

"You will tell Nestar yourself, father?" asked Handir.

"I will." Thargodén turned back to Aradan. "Well then, congratulations are in order, Councillor. I hear Lady Miren will pay a visit to the Silvan encampment later and I feel sure they will all know about our new, half-Silvan Lestari by twilight."

"I am sure they will. But if they do not, I will hire a wagon, go there and stand upon it. I will proclaim it to them myself. You honour my family, sire."

Bright eyes, soft smile, no longer the king's daunting Chief Councillor but the proud father Handir had wanted to see before.

Thargodén turned to Gor'sadén, Handir and Rinon. "I will be absent until mid-morning. There are prisoners to judge and supplies to be guaranteed. The Royal Council must be addressed and our promises to the Silvan people must be signed and sealed before they lose their patience with us. It has taken us this long to stabilise the nation, to ensure our warriors receive the care and support they and their families need, to ensure no traitor walks free."

With a deep and steadying breath, Thargodén clasped his hands behind his back, walked towards where Gor'sadén stood. "Join Pan'assár and Turion at the Inner Circle, Commander. Bring Fel'annár here and then together, all of us must bring the Silvans back, to the place they should never have been excluded from. We must show them that we are grateful, that we are sorry and that we need them, as much as they may need us if this – Nim'uán – thinks to step foot inside this forest."

Gor'sadén regarded Thargodén, saw a spark of Or'Talán in the king's determination, in the clarity of his words. He smiled, fond memories of The Three stirring in the depths of his mind.

~

To the north-west of the Great Forest Belt, three Silvans sat around a small fire, resting after a long morning trekking through the forest on horseback.

The youngest of them sat caring for her bow. It was older than she was, had seen battle with Sand Lords and Deviants long before she had been born. It had been wielded by one of the best archers known to Abiren'á.

Nanor. Her mother.

Satisfied that it was clean and well-oiled as her father had taught her, she placed it carefully to one side and inspected the arrows in her quiver. One by one she held them up, eyes squinting at the metal tips and then sighting down the shafts. They were almost perfect.

"Vasanth."

She looked up at the powerful warrior, one-time captain of the Inner Circle. He towered over her, staring at her with his stubborn, weighty gaze.

"There's still time to turn back."

She regarded him coolly for a moment. "No."

The warrior turned, glancing at the other woman sitting before the fire, rubbing something dry between her hands. She threw it into her pot and then smelled her hands. She smiled as the scent of thyme infused the air.

The former captain said nothing. Instead, he sat and stared into the flames for a while. "These are uncertain times. With Yerái's report about the Warlord and his return, we all felt it was time to mend the errors of the past, meet the boy at last. Three weeks into our journey, we hear there's been a battle. We know of the Warlord's part in it, how the Silvans fought for the king, but what now? They say our army is shattered from the inside, that Pan'assár still commands what is left of it. We don't know if our Silvan brothers even wish to remain in that army and there are certainly no female soldiers, Vasanth."

"But the Warlord has returned. He'll change that. The women who once fought for this land will return to duty. Many of us believe that. And while some warriors won't serve under that Alpine, others will, if the Warlord asks it of them."

"*Pan'assár* is still Commander General as far as we know. And while he's there, things won't change, mark my words. I gave up my command because he and his purists treated my people like slaves. And you – you walk willingly into submission."

She stood, a scowl on her angular features. "I am slave to no one. I will find the Warlord. He will intervene, make things right for us."

"You don't know him."

"Then I must *meet* him. Isn't that what we came for?"

The warrior closed his eyes, let out a breath of frustration. "Can you not talk some sense into her, mother?"

The sitting woman smiled but still, she said nothing and the warrior turned back to his daughter.

"This boy is a mystery to us, Vasanth, and if Amareth has had her way he won't even know about us. We don't know if he's met his father, whether he even wants to meet him, or *us* for that matter. We've come to mend a wrong, meet the boy we should have known since his birth, would have known had it not been for Amareth. We can't expect him to welcome us with open arms or to grant all our wishes. Even if he wanted to, Pan'assár will be a serious impediment to your plans of warriorhood, daughter, as he surely is to Fel'annár's."

"But you heard what Yerái said in Abiren'á. He saw Fel'annár riding in the company of Prince Handir, and Pan'assár himself. He obviously knows about his father's side and Pan'assár must at least tolerate him. Yerái said they seemed on friendly terms."

"But Yerái didn't see his face, Vasanth. He can't know the boy's feelings. And even if it *was* him, even if he *does* know about us, it doesn't mean he'll want anything to do with us."

The ex-captain sighed, ran a hand through his hair. "I can't stop you, daughter, not anymore. But I can counsel you as your father. Don't assume he will want to help you. Don't assume you will even like him. Keep your mind as open as your eyes. Be *wary*, daughter."

He gestured to both women to pack up. It was time to continue their journey, and Vasanth watched her father prepare for their departure.

She knew the reasons that fuelled his words. Before she was born, he had been a mighty captain, one who had left because he refused to serve under Pan'assár. She had heard all about her father's exalted position at the Inner Circle, the respect he had boasted amongst Silvan and Alpine warriors alike. But her father had also been a husband, had lost his warrior wife to Sand Lords years ago while defending Abiren'á. He was frightened that if his daughter joined the army, the same fate awaited her. And maybe it did. But that is a warrior's lot. Yes, she was young, almost as young as Fel'annár had been when he had begun novice training. But she was ready. This was her vocation, just as it had been her mother's before her, her father's and her grandfather's, Zéndar the Ari'atór. It was in her blood. She would be a warrior, to hell with what anyone else thought.

She turned to her father. "If Dalú is there, if he asks it of you, will you return to the Inner Circle?" Slinging one leg over the saddle, she sat, cool gaze settling on her father.

"I'd hear what he has to say about the Warlord, if he truly has any power to change things, or whether he's nothing but a decoration to lure the Silvans back to barracks."

"If you leave, I will stay."

The warrior breathed deeply, pursed his lips.

"I know."

And well he did. She was too much like her blessed mother. Too much like her stubborn father, he reminded himself grudgingly.

They were soon on their way and he breathed in, foreign smells reminding him of his time in service and for a moment, only the good times prevailed.

He had been to Sen Garay many times, years ago when he had been younger, back in the days when he was proud to serve in the king's army. He'd been familiar with Pan'assár, had been named one of the mightiest Silvan captains there had ever been. But then Pan'assár had changed. He became absent, angry, unaware of the suffering he caused, unconcerned even.

And so, Bulan had relinquished his Golden Sun and returned to Abiren'á. He could not condone the discrimination, could no longer stand to watch Pan'assár's descent, the way he was slowly whittling away at their once glorious army. He had turned his back on what had been his entire life. All he had ever wanted to do was serve, his dream to become the best warrior he could be. He had achieved that. But it hadn't lasted. No, he had not set out to return to that life, but now that the possibility hung before his eyes, he wondered if there was any going back to the way things had been before.

Hours later, the three elves from Abiren'á stood alone amidst the bustling market village of Sen Garay, seat of the Silver Wolf. Some stared, just as they had done in the other villages they had passed through. It was not because they were strangers, but because Ar Zéndar had come, and upon his back, a legendary spear they had not seen in many years. There were two of them, so long they jutted past his shoulder, past his head and up into the air, half his length further. It made the warrior proud that they stared, and then sad because he was the only one left who could wield them.

With his mind on what awaited in the city, he did not hear the whispers of his return, nor did he see the spark in the eyes of the Silvans who said that their greatest captain would, perhaps, join forces with the newly returned Warlord, sit upon his seat at the Inner Circle once more. He did not see the queues at the swordsmith's anvils nor the watchful eyes of the Elders.

He had forgotten how much the warriors had loved him, was unaware of how much they remembered him and his spears no one else could wield.

He was Bulan, ex-captain of the Inner Circle, Spear Master, uncle of the Silvan Warlord. But he would have been a father to his sister son, had Amareth not stood in his way.

THE SEA WAS calm on the Island of Dan'bar, but Princess Maeneth's mind was not.

Her smile faltered and she looked down at the worn parchment in her rough hands, working hands that had long forgotten the creams and the massages of her ladies-in-waiting.

It was her brother's writing, passages she had read more times than she could count, and every time, she came to the same conclusion. The fool thought to keep her here, away from danger. Rinon the mule. Rinon the protector, *ass prince* as their father used to call him, Nuthead as Llyniel surely still did.

She chuckled, but then the familiar weight was back, and her humour faded into the silence. It was the weight of time and things left unsaid, but if time was her enemy, then she would stand before it, as the warrior she had once wanted to be. It *was* time to face the past, turn to the future, see Rinon and Handir, meet this Silvan boy that was her half-brother, the child of the woman who had always held the king's heart, in spite of Canusahéi, her mother.

She folded the paper, tucked it inside her bag and walked to the doors. She stopped, turned and for the last time, she cast her eyes over the rooms she had occupied for over fifty years.

The walls were covered in rough sketches and detailed diagrams, scrawling writing and arrows pointing to layers of soil, to water tanks, to renderings of seeds and their anatomy. There were drawings of mighty buildings, from which greenery hung in luscious waterfalls from the rooftops and balconies. Other sketches showed those same buildings from above, partitioned boxes full of vegetables and legumes. Somehow, Maeneth's love of all things growing had become this, the science of self-reliance. The ability to grow and eat, wherever you are, whatever weather you endure and however much coin is in your pocket. But it wasn't just about growing and enabling one to produce what they required. It was about respecting the land, the water, the forest and the sea. She had learned to grow things that could be eaten or admired while enhancing the land, replacing what was spent, magnifying its beauty.

Her eyes fell upon a painting gifted to her by Senairo of Dan'sú. It would be transported with the next supply caravan together with her books and her plans – all these sketches of past and future projects would soon grace the walls of her own quarters, on the last floor of her fortress home of Ea Uaré.

The soft hiss of salty foam, fizzling away over rock, the smell of the sea she would miss, always come back to.

She reached for the door handle, paused there as she remembered the extraordinary pair of boots that had resided right next to this door for so many years. Callan, a veteran of the Battle Under the Sun had made them for her, in exchange for her help in creating his food field and teaching him how to sustain it. He had no money, but he did have the knowledge to create excellent boots. She had packed them away for transport, would never think of working without them.

She navigated the art-lined corridors of the fortress palace of Dan'sú, passed renderings of the exalted ships of old, their celebrated captains standing proud upon the bows, staring out over the great expanse.

She took the stairs downwards and then stepped through the open doors and outside. There, her escort awaited, armed for the prospect of battle with pirates and Deviants. Behind them, the first building she had transformed here in the city, the one Senairo had captured in oil on canvas. She looked up in humble awe at the prototype while the people who had gathered there watched her, gestured to the building and their idyllic surroundings, as if to say behold what you have achieved, the legacy you leave behind.

This building was the Academics Guild, the only collective that had agreed to her experiment at first. It had taken fifteen years to make it what it was today, the centre of architectural admiration on the major island of Dan'sú.

Greenery fell from the rooftops in scandalous reams of colour, while rusty red leaves covered most of the rock faces. The hidden treasure lay at the very top where raised beds of produce were laden with vegetables ripe for late summer picking.

So many memories, so many moments she would treasure for the rest of her life. She wanted to stay, needed to return home, see Rinon. She knew the time was right, that she could stay away no longer.

The people of Pelagia watched her climb into the saddle under the watchful eye of the patrol captain. They would ride to the port, take ship and cover the short distance to Port Helia. From there, four more days' ride and she would be home, in a land she had left of her own volition, all but fleeing from a family she had both loved and hated. That had been fifty years ago. But if she could tell them now what lay in her heart, all she would say was sorrow – grief for the tidings messengers had brought about the battle. Worry, for what may have happened, for what those events may trigger later. Would her father take the Long Road at last, as she always thought he would? That would make Rinon king and if that did happen, he would need her. And if Rinon needed her, she would come.

Always.

It was time to lay the past to rest. It was time to forgive her mother for leaving, try to understand her father, meet her Silvan brother, the son of her mother's bane. Her father's tragic face danced before her mind's eye. On his right, Rinon, all ice and fire and on the king's left, Handir – calm intelligence, tempered prince.

The people raised their hands in silence as she passed, and her nod was slow and pensive. It was time to leave this beautiful place of ocean and song, this land of sea-faring elves that had beguiled her. But it was time to return to the wilder side, to the lands of her birth. She didn't know what awaited her there, but she would soon find out, in six days' time, when she would once more walk the forest she had so loved all her life, the forest that had inspired in her the desire to grow – grow things and consume them, admire them, never at the expense of the land and the trees.

The young princess who had left fifty years ago, would return a learned scholar, a wiser woman with a purpose stronger than ever. She would implement all that she had learned. She would create a paradise of green amongst the cold, unyielding stone of her fortress city. She would teach her people to sustain themselves, so that they would never be at the mercy of unscrupulous merchants who paid little and charged much.

But she wouldn't stop there. She would venture north, into the villages, provide them with a means of life and coin for themselves, so that hard labour was nothing but a choice, not a necessity.

She smiled, sad at what she was leaving behind, excited for the life that awaited her. She turned her eyes from the sea, spied the forest across the Crystal Straits. Home at last, to that familiar place, but she was utterly changed.

Accustomed though Sand Lords were to the heat, it was still taxing on the body and the mind. It made them short, irritable. All Key'hán could do was thank the powers that the Elven side of himself did not feel it quite so acutely.

But Key'hán was not just half-elf and half-Sand Lord. He was Deviant too. It was what made him special, unique in his features, his strength, the clarity of his intentions and the surety of his claims.

He was uniquely lucky, because although he was half-Deviant, he did not rot as they did. His part-elven soul impeded it in a way he would surely never understand. His physical integrity was a blessing under this blistering sun. Trying to imagine an army of Deviants here, in the southern reaches of Calrazia, was nothing short of sickening. Their stench would be eye-watering. Not even the Northerners would be able to endure it.

He peered into the distance. They were still weeks away from their destination.

Had it been just him and his twin brother Saz'nár, they would have made shorter work of the journey with their superior stamina and strength. He turned to his left, to the face that was almost identical to his own.

There was a delicate balance to ensure. They needed speed but so too did they need to travel safely. They had brought contraptions for mining water and Key'hán would not endanger their integrity. It was partly why they had come, to channel the waters into the sands, as far north as they could. This was the only reason he and his brother had been granted an army. The water they would mine and channel north was payment to the king for his investment, for his warriors and supplies. The king of Calrazia would found a new, southern outpost, an oasis from where water could continue to flow northwards, where other green spots would be established. Calrazia would no longer be under the doom of drought and the feuding for water that caused their never-ending border disputes.

But that was not the king's only motivation.

Key'hán, Saz'nár, Xar'dón and Gra'dón were lawful heirs to his throne, should have been kings had their mother not smuggled them away, had she not tried in vain to take them into Valley, into the Source. She had almost succeeded once, had almost passed the Last Markers, but the Ari'atór had come, sent them away. They had tried again, gone past that point of no return but their final destination had been cut off and they were forced to flee.

Key'hán sometimes wished that they had not escaped.

When their father had died, their uncle had taken the throne in the absence of heirs, but he had always known they existed somewhere - in Bel'arán or perhaps across the Veil. It was written in their history, recorded in the annals. Only recently had the current king come to understand that the half-elven heirs of Ebanuk had not crossed, that they were still alive after all these centuries and that they had a plan, one that would benefit them all.

And so, the need for water had outweighed the fear and rejection of the people – the very reason they had been exiled as children.

Sand Lords were superstitious, their beliefs a complex play of gods and demi-gods, of demons and reapers, and Key'hán and his brothers were not natural. They were half-elves – *immortals* – and that made them gods, dark lords to be feared and obeyed. Their mother always knew they would be assassinated long before they were old enough to defend themselves and take their rightful places.

Key'hán glanced to the left, beyond the ranks of his black-clad army. The sand undulated and he smiled. Their secret weapon, an invincible one he would unleash if the enemy proved a threat. He almost wanted them to, so that he could watch and marvel at the mesmerising power, their macabre existence, so like his own, in a strange sort of way. The Northerners who some called Reapers. They were feared and revered, shunned and yet respected. They would hold the southern oasis for the king, defend his most precious of assets – water – while Key'hán and his brothers pursued their own lands to rule over.

If only Xar'dón had waited before attacking Tar'eastór.

They had been mapping the northern reaches of the forest for many years, at the cost of hundreds, if not thousands of lives. Those brave scouts and cartographers had studied the lay of the land, traced the waters, even underground. Many never returned, perishing due to lack of supplies or attack from the elven patrols, but they eventually had what they had set out to achieve. A water map, every vein, where it ran, over the land and below it and now, they had the capacity to extract it, channel it. While the warriors defended them from any stupid enough to approach, his engineers would begin the process. And once they had tapped into those wells and piped their riches, the colonisation could truly begin.

Just the thought of cool, fresh air and pools of water, enough even to bathe in, took away the weeks of hardship still ahead of them. And then once they had conquered the northernmost territories, Key'hán and Saz'nár would travel to their mother's home. There, they would make their own home - for a while at least - until the king of that forest was dead, and all his immortal children with him. Their eldest brother, Gra'dón, would become Emperor, king under the forest and not sun, as was his birth right.

There was much to look forward to. A new home, a new chance to find happiness at last, and perhaps find answers to the questions they had always asked themselves. Where was this place called Ea Nanú where their mother had once lived? Did they still have family there?

If they did, then those were the only elves they would leave alive.

2

EVEN UNTO DEATH

∾

THE VIEW from his room was glorious. He knew because his eyes were closed.

With his blindfold on, he could see the aura of pines and spruces, cedars and firs. He could see the lights inside them as they flared and dimmed, sap pulsing up and down, nourishing roots. Empowering.

And this forest was powerful.

"Open your eyes."

He didn't want to. It comforted him to just sit here at the window, watch the Evergreen Wood with his eyes closed, convince himself that he wasn't blind.

Still, opening them was the only way to cleanse them of the hedge-berry powder, of the iron dust they said Band'orán had mixed in with it.

Without immediate treatment, without Sontúr's timely intervention, Fel'annár would have been left with permanent damage, even blindness. He could still remember that purple cloud streaking towards him, engulfing him. It had settled in his eyes, as Band'orán knew it would. He had used the ancient, ignoble art of blinding powders, expressly prohibited in the Warrior Code. And yet by some miracle, even blinded, he had avoided Band'orán's blades.

Not a miracle. The Evergreen Wood had lent him its eyes, still did.

It was not sight as Fel'annár understood it. He couldn't see faces or expressions. He couldn't see clothes, gestures or the truth in a person's eyes. All that information was lost to him. He was left only with light, light from the bodies of others, light from the moon and the stars. Light from the funeral pyres that burned from afar at the Silvan encampment, and then closer, dotted around the city and before the gates. He had watched them last night after his unexpected visit to the Elders, unable to sleep for all the things they demanded of him, things he needed to achieve in just two days.

To anyone else, the prohibited Evergreen Wood sat silent and serene, majestic beauty none would suspect of a killing spree. None save for those who had seen it rip their enemies apart: Band'orán and his renegade captains. Even had it not been a prohibited place, no one would dare set foot inside the guarded gates now. They didn't need to be reminded of Or'Talán's prohibition, of Thargodén's ratification of that decree.

They were frightened – even the Silvans.

Fel'annár was only glad they had not been able to hear its triumphant bellows, feel its glee as it slaughtered Dinor and Bendir and then ultimately, Band'orán. There had been something disturbing about that. It was something he had never felt in a forest before.

But that was not all he could hear. There were undertones, a distant voice, still the forest and yet different if that were even possible. He heard its welcome, and even though it proclaimed him lord, there was a warning beneath the recognition, like wise advice one was expected to take.

Band'orán had been dead for a week and Fel'annár had missed most of that time. He had been brought here after the battle, had kept himself aloft long enough for the king and princes to leave. And then he had succumbed to exhaustion and injury, slept for longer than he ever had. His only memories of those days were of Llyniel, Sontúr and sometimes Galadan, flushing his eyes with water and then bidding him sleep. But then the forest had felt a familiar presence and Fel'annár had once more heard the song of the Nim'uán.

"Is there any improvement?" Llyniel approached him from behind. He could hear her quiet steps, feel the warmth of her body, the soft ripple of air around her.

Fel'annár half turned where he sat. "A little." He knew what she wanted, tilted his head back and allowed her to tip the now customary cold liquid into his eyes, a cloth in his hands. Llyniel and Sontúr had concocted it, changed it almost every day, added this and that as they discussed new ideas. It filled his eyes, welled and spilled out and still she poured it in. He grit his teeth against the burn, felt the water run down his face, into his hair, caught as much of it as he could from dripping onto his clothes.

When she had finished, Fel'annár held the cloth over his eyes for a while, heard her pad back to her table close to the fire. Calm and confident, understanding but not doting. He trusted her when she said he would see again – with his own eyes.

He had to.

"I must speak with Pan'assár. We have two days to make this work. Once he sees the benefits of a restructured army, once Thargodén gives me that decree from the Royal Council, I must ride back to the encampment."

"It's too soon, Fel'annár. Wait at least until you can see a little better."

"I can't, Llyniel. You heard them last night as well as I did." He didn't need to look to know that she was holding her tongue. It wouldn't last long.

"Someone else can do it. You can delegate."

"Our people won't listen to *someone else*. You know that."

A brief silence. "And if you collapse?"

"I won't collapse. I'll be careful, and I *can* see – enough to get by – and I have The Company. Sontúr and Galadan will be with me."

She would be staring hard at him, jaw clenched and eyes glittering. He knew she understood and didn't want to. Still, she said nothing more on the subject.

"Will you return to the encampment to take over from Kristain today?"

"Yes, for a while at least. Sooner or later, I must face the consequences of what I have done. I defied the Lestari, took supplies I was not authorised to take. But there's no going back. If he expels me from the Halls, then so be it. I'll have to find somewhere else to put my skills to use."

He heard the swish of her robes and then the rustle of paper. "I'll find the things on Kristain's list and then ride out around mid-morning, stay at the camp until I'm sure everything's under control. The lesser injured are being tended to by their families, but there is still a good number of warriors who need specialised treatment." She breathed noisily, was probably scratching her temple. "I want to see Handir about it. I want Nestar publicly repentant. If I am to lose my position, he will at least be openly shamed for what he has done."

"Good for you."

She squeezed his shoulder. "I have to go. I have supplies to pilfer and a prince to talk to. I won't see you until later this evening."

He reached out, fingers brushing over her retreating arm. She stopped, half-turned towards him. He leaned into her for a moment, savoured the heat of her skin close to his. Every time they parted, they both knew it may be the last, and every time he returned there was a desperate kind of joy in their reunion. It was a fact they had accepted, the day she recognised her soulmate and he his Connate.

The smell of herbs and clean linen faded, and the door shut with a click. Fel'annár turned back to the window. For a moment, neither the impending deadlines, Llyniel's predicament or the reconstruction of a broken army were enough to distract him from the lingering questions in his mind.

Idernon had given him an update at his request, and the news his friend had brought weighed heavily on his mind. Over a hundred Silvan warriors had died in the battle, and another two hundred lay wounded at the Silvan encampment – not in the Healing Halls where they belonged.

Over a hundred dead, scores of warriors who would never be able to fight again. This civil war, the charge of the Silvans, had been his first command over an army, the first time he had led warriors to their deaths.

They were calling it the Battle of Brothers.

Later, he had spoken with Gor'sadén. He had assured Fel'annár that he had acted correctly, that he had made no mistakes. He said that losing warriors was expected, that the only one guilty of their deaths was the instigator – Band'orán.

But had he really taken the right decisions? Had he led the Silvan warriors in the best possible way? Fel'annár had heard Gor'sadén's words, understood them and then willed himself to believe them. Still, the weight of uncertainty brought unwanted feelings of inadequacy, emotions he needed to bury, because they made him feel weak, incapable. Besides, there were priorities now.

He pulled his blindfold into place once more so that his eyes wouldn't move around in his head and scratch. Instantly, the lights were back, an aura around everything living, the glow of fire in the hearth and from the candles.

He stood, arms out beside him. Yes he could see living things, but he could not see furniture. He walked slowly, past the bed and to the door of the bed chamber. Beyond was the living area and soon his fingers touched the fabric of a comfortable chair he knew lay beside the unlit hearth. He sat, already tired, a light shake of muscles, heart a little too fast.

A knock at the door, many boots clicking over stone and then thudding over spun wool, one set of feet much heavier than the rest. A strong hand on his shoulder; Ramien, Wall of Stone.

"Morning."

Fel'annár waited for them to accommodate themselves around him, knew the questions upon their tongues – about the Nim'uán and his faulty eyes.

"Any news?" Idernon's cool tone, the rustle of wool and the creak of leather.

"It's not in the forest. Not too close to it. Small mercy, seeing as there are no more than five hundred warriors at barracks, none of which are Silvan."

"And where did they come from?" asked Galadan. "After the battle, there were barely a hundred loyal Alpine warriors left."

"From returning patrols in the forest, and to the south. It seems

Huren deployed more than he needed to before the battle, intentionally, no doubt."

"What I don't get is why the Silvans don't trust you when you tell them their demands have been agreed to. All they're missing is the king's seal," exclaimed Carodel, hands out to his side. "Why must we run ourselves into the ground and do it all in just two days?"

"They want promises fulfilled. Now that the battle is over, they are wary of them not being honoured, especially after Nestar's unfortunate performance. Point being, they see me as Warlord in word only, with no seat at the Inner Circle as yet, where Pan'assár is still commander general. *His* word means nothing to them. You see, the Silvans were welcomed when they were needed to fight Band'orán's forces but to them, it looks like they will be rejected now in a time of peace. They wonder whether everything will revert to the way it was."

"Not even *your* assurances mean anything to them." Idernon's voice was hard, reproval swirling under the even tone, but Sontúr's was an invitation to approach the issue in a different way.

"They want to, but I think they are looking at this from the perspective of their people, and I am sure it is a very different one." Sontúr shuffled to the edge of his seat. "It is a basic assumption one learns in statesmanship. You can't move an entire nation of people on the strength of promises made by people they do not know. They need the assurances of their elders. However much they want the return of the Warlord, there has been little time for your people to know you; to see you. Their trust is conditional on the results you garner. That is what they are waiting for. All they know for now, is that you led them to victory over Band'orán, that you are their best warrior, that you are blind and that you look like Or'Talán."

Sontúr's face would be utterly straight save for one, acutely arched eyebrow and Idernon would be grinning at his irony. Fel'annár could see them in his mind's eye, wished he could see them with his open eyes. Still, he wondered at Sontúr's use of the word *victory*. Was the loss of hundreds of warriors ever a victory? He nodded slowly, breathed deeply, fatigue and irritation surely apparent. He didn't even try to hide it, not here with The Company.

A bright blue light flitted across the darkness. He thought it was

Tensári but couldn't fathom where she'd been standing or where she was going.

"We have two days in which to work with Pan'assár, with Handir and the king. And then we ride back to the encampment and we bring our warriors back to barracks."

"You're not fit enough to do all that," said Carodel.

"Neither are *you*," countered Fel'annár. Carodel had taken a knife to the side in the final battle, and although not deep, it had bled enough to make him ill. "We'll do what we must, and we start now."

"And Sontúr, Llyniel and Galadan will pick up the pieces," droned the Alpine prince from where he sat close by.

Rustling cloth, the creak of leather, an irreverent snort and an accent Fel'annár knew well. "We're all summoned to the Circle this morning. Seems like there's going to be some announcement," said Galdith.

Galadan stood. "We have half an hour. Get dressed Fel'annár." He turned to Tensári and then Sontúr, saw his subtle nod. The prince would stay to help and Tensári would guard his door.

With The Company gone, Sontúr turned to Fel'annár with a wry smile.

"You can breathe now, you twat."

Fel'annár offered a fleeting smile then stood stiffly, Bredja's jolly old face dancing in his mind's eye. He had played down his tiredness, the constant ache in his eyes so that the others would stop insisting he rest. He couldn't, not now. Still, Sontúr was a healer, and a good one. He could hide nothing from him.

Llyniel had laid out his standard issue uniform as a lieutenant, bless her soul. His Warlord armour was being restored and cleaned and had not yet been returned to him.

The tunic he knew was blue, the brown leather cuirass attached to the war skirt and a single pauldron. Along the high collar, he felt the long, silver strip that denoted the rank of a lieutenant, the very same one that Sontúr, Galadan and Tensári wore. Everything had been cleaned and polished; he could smell the oils, feel the leather smooth and supple, the fabrics soft and fresh. Finally, he felt Sontúr encircle his waist with the warm velvet sash of the Kal'hamén'Ar, still the dark grey of a Disciple. Fel'annár tied it off to one side and then reached up and gathered the upper layers of his clean and twisted hair, tying it into a knot. He couldn't see the result, but still he smoothed it down out of habit. One hand searched over the bed for his blades. They slipped into his hands with a little help from Sontúr. A longsword and a short sword. He pushed them into the harness on his back with practised ease and then walked towards where he knew the main door was. Sontúr opened it and they stepped out into the corridor where the Company stood waiting. Tensári's brilliant blue aura was before him. He tried not to startle when he felt hands in his hair, and then a tug.

"You look like some avenging forest spirit. Better this way," she murmured.

"Thank you for that then," he ground out, and then adjusted the black cloth around his eyes. He followed behind the moving lights, aware that they walked slowly. Fel'annár was thankful for that, if frustrated. He knew his sight would return soon, Llyniel had said so. But in the meantime, he felt useless, dependent. He had never dealt well with weakness.

"What are they like? The people, I mean. Is there tension? Danger?"

"There's a silence about them. I think it's pity, shame even, for what it came to, I mean," said Idernon.

Fel'annár nodded, well understanding how it would be that way. Pride had been damaged, trust had been shattered and the task before him – before them all – loomed like a high wall with no door. Every realm needed an army and Ea Uaré was no exception. Sand Lords from the north, Deviants from the east. But now, they could add the still distant threat that perhaps a Nim'uán was lurking on their northern borders.

As Fel'annár and The Company made for the Inner Circle, servants and scribes, academics and tutors followed them with eyes that spoke of gratitude and respect – of curiosity and a hint of fear. The Silvan Warlord had faced Band'orán in the Kal'hamén'Ar and won, and then he had commanded the trees to rip him apart, limb for limb. Good that he was blindfolded then, so that he couldn't see their fear.

≈

THE CROWN PRINCE of Ea Uaré sat in the uniform of a royal general, hungry for breakfast and thoughtful of the days that had preceded this one.

Pan'assár had been busy, in fact the only time Rinon had seen him was when he had called Turion and himself to that first meeting at the Inner Circle. A damaged kingdom and a broken army, the commander general had rallied those who remained, bolstered their spirit as much as he had been able, and officially named and promoted his two closest collaborators.

One hand rose to the collar of his blue undertunic, fingers brushing over the parallel lines that marked him a general. Ea Uaré had only ever had one general – Huren. Now, it would have three.

He remembered his father's words of pride, words he had savoured.

You honour your family, son. You honour the house of Or'Talán.

Rinon had even allowed the king to see how much those words had meant to him, had enjoyed the surprise and the satisfaction on his father's face when he had.

He would be limping for days to come, or so Lestari Nestar had said. He was just thankful the arrow had not pierced anything unfixable, but in truth, Rinon had suffered more from the fatigue that had settled over him after Band'orán had been vanquished and they had returned to the palace. That had been nothing but a week ago, and yet even now he could feel an ache in his bones, an unnatural tightness to his muscles.

Rinon had fought his biggest and longest battle, had spent all his energy, not just the physical kind. The months leading up to Band'orán's strike on the throne had been intense, worrying, taxing in every way and now that it was over, it had all left him strangely empty.

A knock sounded on the outer door of his suite of rooms which stood next to the king's. Thargodén had once occupied them, as crown prince to Or'Talán. They would have been of an age, mused Rinon. It was to these very rooms where his father would come to ponder his love, and then curse his father for disallowing it. If these walls could speak, would they do so kindly of the former crown prince?

He stood, limped across the sitting area and opened the door. A guard stood there, a folded parchment in his gloved hand. Rinon nodded, took the missive and stepped back inside, closing the door behind him.

He wandered over to the windows on the far side. The view from here was almost as spectacular as it was from the king's suite, only there, it was enhanced by the full-length windows and the gardens beyond. He realised he had never appreciated it as much as he did now, even from this lesser perspective. When his father had been taken captive, Rinon had been king for weeks, enough to understand the weight of it. He never had done before – had never understood his father's position, one he would inherit should Thargodén ever leave these lands.

He sat on the window seat, lifted his wounded leg up to rest on the wooden ledge and leaned back. With the woods to his left and his room to his right, he lifted the parchment to his tired eyes.

It smelled of the sea.

Heart racing, he broke the royal seal and opened it, a nascent smile on his thin lips.

'Brother. I am coming home.'

The dawning smile widened, cracking the icy façade, warming frigid eyes, smoothing the creases between his brows. Princess Maeneth was returning to the Great Forest, after more than fifty years abroad, away from her family. Away from her twin.

The Gods, but he would be whole once more.

THARGODÉN HAD KNOWN the Master Healer all his life.

Nestar was good, had studied with Arané and Tanor, had a world-famous treatise on ligaments and had helped with more than a few knocks and scrapes he himself had suffered as a child.

But he had never liked the elf who had been honoured with the title of Lestari so many decades ago. He vaguely remembered his own negative vote on the council, back when he was still crown prince, but Band'orán and his purists had tipped the balance, and the appointment had been decreed. Treachery had already been afoot; he knew that now.

Since the Battle of Brothers, the king had worked incessantly, rebuilding the city and visiting the wounded. He had seen Nestar working in his element, knew the elf was eager to please royalty, as reticent as he was to discuss his treatments, defensive even. He was happy when asked for advice, pedantic when he gave it. And now this. When the battle was still so raw, when the Healing Halls which he directed had been full of suffering warriors and worried families, he had opened his mouth and given an order to prioritise the treatment of the Alpine warriors. Only one healer had spoken out, had dared confront the Lestari in front of his team of healers and aides.

Llyniel, Thargodén's law daughter.

But she had not told the king. The incident had come to his attention through Aradan, who had surely heard it from Miren. It was just what they hadn't needed, a needle in the eye, a slap in the face. Nestar's bigotry had complicated an already delicate situation, leaving himself and all those closest to him with the onerous task of mending it, not least of them Fel'annár.

Do you think he did it on purpose?

Handir had said that and Thargodén still remembered how that question had taken him aback. The idea lingered in his mind, wouldn't go away.

He turned away from the window, glanced at Aradan and Miren who stood before the bookshelf, close to his desk here in his quarters. They spoke quietly and Miren rubbed her hands together – not in glee but in nervous anticipation. Her eyes were wide and hopeful, while Aradan's were amused and indulgent. But Thargodén knew his joy, could see beyond that veil of neutrality he always wore when he and the king had company.

The double doors opened into the king's study and Lestari Nestar walked in. Behind him, Handir and a dishevelled Llyniel. Thargodén rather thought she had no idea what was about to happen, had obviously been dragged here unawares by her friend. Thargodén wondered if she thought she was in trouble, watched as her eyes darted from Handir to her father and then the king himself, in search of clues to reassure herself. Handir could be cruel sometimes, he mused.

Nestar stopped in the middle of the room, eyes on the king who stood before the windows. Thargodén regarded him for a moment and then walked slowly towards him, hands clasped behind his back.

Nestar shifted his weight, seemed unwilling to make eye contact with any of them.

"Lestari Nestar."

"My Liege."

"Do you know why you are here?"

"I assume it is because of my careless comment. You have my assurances of course, that it will not happen again."

"No. No it will not. I know that. But here is my problem, Nestar. It is an ethical problem, a question of morals. You are Lestari – Master Healer – elected by royal appointment to lead the Halls, to care for our people, their injures and those of our warriors." He paused, knew Nestar wanted to speak. He would allow it because he realised that he had never really conversed with the man. If he was to take his highly coveted position, he would concede that much at least.

"Sire. I have done just that. I have studied with the greatest, have written three books and have introduced pioneering techniques in the repair of ligaments. I have served you well."

"In all but one thing, Nestar. Your hatred of the Silvan race is unacceptable – here in Silvan lands – anywhere."

Nestar's mouth worked of its own accord, but no words were forthcoming for a moment. "It is not hatred, Sire. I simply prefer the company of my fellow Alpines, 'tis all."

"Tis all ... an *anecdote*, you would say. A petty issue that needs no further mention." The king stepped closer to the now indignant healer. The king had mocked him, and it did not sit well with Nestar at all.

"The Silvan people rode at the behest of the Warlord. They rode for me, so that this city would not fall into the hands of a tyrant. Do *you* think Band'orán was a tyrant, Nestar? Or do you think he was a saviour, perhaps?"

"You are not implying I had any relation with Lord Band'orán?" Nestar's indignation had turned into outright anger, but there was a hint of panic beneath it.

"And why not? You call him *lord*, you share the same hatred for the Silvan people. It would be a logical assumption to think you would have been comfortable in his presence."

"That we share one value is hardly proof that I enjoyed his presence, my king."

And there it was, that pedantic tone, as if Nestar spoke with a child with no knowledge of reasoning and logic. Thargodén pursed his lips. He had never enjoyed being undermined.

"Not proof, no. But it is the *possibility* of proof, Nestar. It is a reason for me to suspect, but come – let us not fall into a debate on faulty reasoning, Lestari. You would lose, especially if I allowed Prince Handir to speak for me." Thargodén watched, until he saw what he was looking for. Barely repressed anger. His own father had taught him that was the moment when the truth often emerged.

"Now, you have all but admitted that you are unkindly predisposed to the Silvan nature. And yet you serve in Silvan lands, are duty-bound to heal them, and this is where my confidence in you has been sorely damaged."

"I have already told you it will not happen again."

Three strides and Thargodén was standing just a little too close to Nestar. "Do not play me for a *fool*, Nestar. That you say it will not happen again does not make it *true*. You cannot effectively treat an elf you despise, for the simple reason that he has brown hair and dark eyes. You cannot maintain the same high standards of diagnosis and healing on an entire race of people you consider inferior, and my reasoning is simply this: you don't care about them. And if you don't care about them, you cannot heal them to the best of your ability. You lack the motivation; your heart is not in it."

"That is not true, sire, I ..."

"Tell me, Nestar. Are you not a learned man? A scholar? An elf who keeps abreast of current affairs in the city?" The king held out a hand to the healer. "No need to answer me. I know the answer and I must ask – I must suspect – that you knew exactly how your words would be received. I suggest you chose the moment well, and that your motivation was not to help the crown but *hinder* it. And if not, how very clumsy you were, Nestar, scholar that you are."

"My king. I am not a traitor, I can ..."

"I am relieving you of your royal appointment. Willingly or other-wise, you have complicated crucial matters of state. I do not want you caring for *my* people. Time will tell whether you planned that incident. I suggest you pray I do not find incriminating evidence against you."

Nestar's nostrils flared, lips twisted, and he turned, glared at Llyniel. "You. *You* have brought this about. You always wanted my position, thought you could get it simply because you are the Silvan's wife. Is that why you lie with him? To gain the king's favour and worm your way into *my* domain? You're not good enough, girl. You are just another ambitious Silvan peasant with dreams of greatness you will never achieve. You have not the mind for it. You are nothing but a worthless half-caste with air in her head and ..."

"Nestar." Deep, loud voice that Thargodén would never have associated with *Handir*. Nestar stood rigid before the king, perhaps only now realising how far he had gone. He turned to the second prince, the king's royal councillor.

Cool blue eyes, an air of authority about him that drew Aradan and Thargodén's keenest attention. It wasn't only Handir's *voice* that had changed.

"You are quite the storyteller, aren't you? The Silvans would call you *Nanern,* ask you for bedtime stories. Lady Llyniel did *not* pursue your position. She did not even tell you or anyone else she was *Master* Healer, and shall I tell you why, *Nanern*? It is because you, her Lestari, never asked her where she had been and what she had studied. You never asked her about her speciality, about her aspirations. You saw her auburn hair and honey eyes and you didn't *care*. You ignored her, never thought she would be an asset. She has studied with Lestari Arané, Lestari Tanor, knows more about the healing properties of tree barks than anyone known to elvendom. She has created an antidote to the bite of a Nim'uán, and she brought back the Warlord from the surety of death – ah, excuse me – you would know him as the *Silvan*.

"You disgust me, Nestar, you and all those Alpine Purists and if it were up to me, I would see you banished from these lands, so that I would never have to see your stupid face and remember just what this nation almost succumbed to."

Handir stared hard at the healer, dared him to answer.

He didn't.

Thargodén nodded at Handir, hid his utter surprise at his son's eloquent anger and turned to Llyniel.

"Lady Llyniel Ara Aradan, step forward."

Llyniel smoothed a hand down the sides of her black robes, looked about the room and then back at the king.

"I, King Thargodén Ar Or'Talán, officially appoint you Lestari of the Silvan-Alpine lands of Ea Uaré. Do you accept?"

She opened her mouth to speak, glanced at a seething Nestar to her left. Her shock turned to disdain and she turned away from the healer she had once looked up to.

"I accept, my king." She bowed, Thargodén returned it and then stepped towards Nestar.

"You are no longer Lestari. After your insults towards my law daughter, a member of my family, I will not write letters of recommendation. I will not exile you from these lands, not unless I find evidence to suggest you planned this in order to hinder the restoration. You have one day to remove your belongings from the Halls. As of tomorrow, a new Lestari will take your place. A Silvan-Alpine noble with much more than air in her head."

Nestar clenched his jaw, turned away from the king and with his wrathful gaze fixed on the door, he left.

Someone breathed out noisily, someone was running. Miren, arms out she ran to Llyniel and hugged the still stunned, newly appointed head healer of Ea Uaré. Tears streamed from Miren's eyes while Llyniel's were still wide in shock, for the insults she had received, for the highest honour the king had granted her.

Miren shook her hard then turned, ran for Handir. He braced, just before she crashed into him, hugged him until the stunned prince smiled. It was the king's turn next and by the time she had finished, there were chuckles and smiles all round.

Aradan made his way to Llyniel, a challenge in his eyes, a smile upon his lips. "Our king honours you, honours me with this appointment, and my joy at your return is complete. You are Lestari and I will proclaim it across these lands I serve." He took her shoulders. "The Gods but Aria blessed you with Alpine tenacity and Silvan strength and it sings in my blood I tell you!" Aradan sounded angry but Thargodén was smiling while Miren continued to cry.

The king walked towards Handir, eyes searching his. He had heard of his son's intervention at that last royal council in which Band'orán's treachery had been unveiled. He had heard of his skill, of how he had outwitted Or'Talán's brother. But today, he had seen a little of that skill for himself, seen how much Handir had learned during his time abroad. Pride surged through him and he reached out, placed a proud hand on his son's shoulder, nodded curtly, wicked smile on his lips.

As for Llyniel, she stood there, shock slowly wearing off and then suddenly, all the years of her absence melted away, as if they had never transpired at all. She loved her mother, adored her father, knew that they loved her, always had. She buried her head in their shoulders, didn't notice when Thargodén and Handir stepped outside the door.

FEL'ANNÁR and The Company stepped through the double doors which led to the Inner Circle, their boots echoing off the stone as they strode down the corridor.

If this Inner Circle was anything like the one in Tar'eastór on the inside, they would turn right, right, and right again until they reached the Great Hall.

Fel'annár had only ever seen the Inner Circle of Ea Uaré from the outside. All he knew was that it was circular, crafted from black stone, and that it had no windows, just like in Tar'eastór.

They had passed two guards, he had seen their aura, but even now, as Tensári led them on and he followed, he damned Band'orán to the pits of Galomú. He still remembered how he had felt the day he had stepped inside Tar'eastór's command centre for the first time. He had run his questing hands over the smooth stone, curious eyes flitting from painting to tapestry to historic weapons with stories he had grown up loving. It had reminded him of why he had become a warrior, of the choice he had made as a young boy.

It reminded him that he was blind.

He wondered if those paintings and tapestries he was surely passing

now, depicted the Battle Under the Sun, or perhaps the great colonisation – his grandfather's face everywhere. Strange, he mused. Just weeks
ago, it would have bothered him, and yet now, with the revelations they
had discovered in Or'Talán's final journal, he was curious, no longer
ashamed. He was grudgingly proud, he realised.

They turned right for the last time, and he heard guards stomp to
attention as they passed. He was only a lieutenant to look at, Warlord in
nothing but word, and he briefly wondered if some captain followed
behind him, whether those ceremonial salutes were not for him but for
someone else.

Ahead, he could see the lights of many people. They would be the
remaining captains of the Inner Circle, fifty-six or so he had been told.
The commanders and crown prince would surely be there at the fore, as
would Turion. Indeed, Idernon murmured in his ear, told him that both
Turion and Rinon bore parallel lines. They were generals, not captains.

Fel'annár was happy for his first captain in the field, the one who had
taught him so much of the enemy and warfare together with Lainon,
back when the world had still been so simple. As for Rinon, he supposed
it was fitting that a crown prince be a general, but then Pan'assár would
not have promoted him unless he genuinely had been a good captain.
But Fel'annár would reserve judgement. Rinon was volatile and that did
not speak well for his ability to command.

Fel'annár recognised Gor'sadén's aura, just where Idernon had told
him he was standing beside Pan'assár. He watched as it passed the other
lights and he remembered. The captains would be sitting or standing in
a circle, and whoever spoke would be inside it. Gods but he wanted to rip
the blindfold from his face and pry open his scratchy eyes and *see*.

But he couldn't and as he stood there waiting for the Circle to
quieten down and begin, his mind took him back to the recent battle.
Seven days ago, Pan'assár had confronted Captain Dinor here, and ultimately, General Huren. He had revealed how Or'Talán had been
purposefully left without aid – condemned to an atrocious death at the
hands of Sand Lords. Band'orán had ordered it, Huren had executed it,
and the consequences of that revelation had led to Huren, Dinor and
Bendir's disgrace, and ultimately their deaths, one at the hand of
Band'orán himself and the others, courtesy of the Evergreen Wood.

Strange that the people had always feared a battle between Alpines and Silvans and yet, it had been Alpine against Alpine in the end. The Silvans had tipped the balance in favour of those loyal to the king. If only he could see their eyes, know their thoughts, whether they were indeed loyal, whether some of them were lying to save themselves from exile or worse.

Fel'annár could imagine Gor'sadén and Pan'assár standing before the captains, their exquisite armour shining in the warm, orange candle-light. He envisioned that fine, velvety hair he himself did not possess. He could almost see their neat, elaborate braids, trailing over strong, broad shoulders, down muscled arms. Their blades would be tucked away but not out of sight, purple sashes utterly still around unmoving legs. They garnered respect, instilled authority in their powerful silence, and a wave of pride washed over him. They had been his grandfather's closest friends, closer even than brothers. They were the commanders that Fel'annár was not.

Commander General Pan'assár's voice broke through the quiet murmurs.

"Fifty-six captains are all that remain of the one hundred and one. Now, it falls to those of us still standing to complete the Circle. But we must not make the same mistakes as we have done in the past. This new Circle will be an Alpine and Silvan circle, equal in all things. We must bring our Silvan captains back, recruit more, on the basis of merit only and we must do so quickly, before a new enemy threatens our entire kingdom, no matter our race.

"You know of the Nim'uán, know that its presence has been noted far to the north, its destination still unclear. We have only so much time – the time it takes to understand its motives – to rebuild this Circle, repopulate our barracks and defend these lands. Heed me well, captains. We can do none of this if the Silvans turn their backs on us. We needed them to fight with us, against Band'orán's traitors. We will need them again, as much as they will need us. To this end, I and Lieutenant Fel'annár will work hard to bring them back. You must do no less."

It was an odd sort of silence that followed, mere seconds and yet so eloquent. If Fel'annár could see their faces, he thought that perhaps he would see expectation, anxiety for the consequences of their silence, curiosity at what Pan'assár would do now.

"Some of you will have heard of the incident at the Healing Halls yesterday. One unjust command is all it took for the Silvan warriors to turn their backs and walk away, and who can blame them? They fight for the king and this realm, only to be told they are second to any Alpine warrior, loyal or otherwise. Petty, some say, but to me, it is like spit in the face, hatred that must not be tolerated. Some of those healers obeyed discriminatory orders, only one contested them, a *civilian*. This must not happen here at the Inner Circle.

"My first order to you today, in these times of turbulent peace, is that you follow my lead and openly express your gratitude to those brave and loyal Silvan warriors. After the way some of us treated them, after the way *I* treated them, it is a miracle they answered our call for aid at all. Indeed, had it not been for Lieutenant Fel'annár, they would not have. Band'orán would be ruling these lands. I would be dead, the king and his entire family slaughtered, our own people, our families at the mercy of a cruel dictator. Remember who helped us to avoid that."

Pan'assár was moving around the circle. Fel'annár could envision him, eyes narrowed as he watched, analysing his captains, reading their thoughts on the strength of their eyes, their expressions, the set of their jaws and the tilt of their heads.

Another light approached the commander and stayed there. He wanted Idernon to tell him what was happening, but his friend remained silent beside him.

"As most of you know, Captains Rinon and Turion have been promoted to General, in recognition of their service and bravery. Today, now that they are sufficiently recovered from injury, we must acknowledge the extraordinary deeds of one small patrol of warriors. The Company saved our king from captivity, delivered him to us when no one else could, while their leader went far beyond the imperatives of the Warrior Code. He rallied the Silvan warriors to fight with us, despite their unsatisfied demands for equality. That figure is the Warlord. We welcome him today - as a *general* of Ea Uaré."

Fel'annár had heard the words but they had yet to be understood. His mind stuttered clumsily in some strange limbo in which meaning was clear and yet made no sense at all, even as barely suppressed gasps of surprise sounded around him and throughout the Great Hall. There had never been a general under the age of five hundred. No captain was recorded to be anything less than a century, and Fel'annár was fifty-three.

A general of Ea Uaré.

"Fel'annár Ar Thargodén Ar Lássira. Step into the Circle."

A soft nudge in the side, and then another, whispered congratulations and a hand pushing him discreetly in the back. Tensári's light was moving before him and he followed.

A child scribbling on parchment, tongue out to one side as he formed the letters, slowly and painstakingly. Captain Fel'annár.

His feet were moving, through the Alpine lieutenants and captains.

A boy sitting at his desk, brow furrowed, quill in hand. 'Why are there so few Silvan captains? Why are there no field Halls in the north?'

He stepped into the Circle, Pan'assár's light coming closer and closer.

A young warrior, sitting upon the ground, a journal in his hand. 'Silor is not suited to command. Why does Pan'assár allow it?'

He felt the ground beneath his boots and yet he was falling, not enough air in his lungs. He had always wanted to be a captain of the Inner Circle, but a general was beyond his wildest, most colourful of dreams.

Tensári had stopped and so did he. He watched as she stepped to one side, knew that he was now standing before Pan'assár.

"Do you accept the honour of serving your people, your king, even unto death?"

There was much more than a simple question in Pan'assár's tone. It was an invitation, a plea to accept, a request for forgiveness. Was it the trees that told him that? Or in his blindness, had he become more sensitive to the connotations of language? But doubt assailed him. He was too young, but then did he not have Gor'sadén at his side to guide him? He opened his mouth. Closed it and then answered, as was expected of him.

"I accept."

Sound from the outside world came back to him, weight returned to his body, his chest. He saluted the commander and then wondered what he should do now.

"Welcome to the Inner Circle, General Fel'annár."

Fel'annár felt fingers at his collar. They unclipped the single silver strip that Silor had once worn. And then, those fingers were back, the soft click of a pin moving into place. Fel'annár's hand reached up, brushed over it, felt the parallel lines he knew would be gold - the mark of high command. It was a small object, but why did it feel so heavy?

"General Fel'annár kept our king safe during his captivity, and he protected our youngest prince on his ill-fated journey from Tar'eastór, so that he in turn, could show us the face of the traitor. General Fel'annár led our Silvan warriors into battle against the enemy, and then faced its leader with blades in the Kal'hamén'Ar. King Vorn'asté awarded him the Blue Mountain - Tar'eastór's highest honour - for his acts of bravery against the Nim'uán. This nation must do no less and so, I hereby award you the Forest Emerald. There is no greater praise."

Pan'assár was touching his collar again and when he had finished, Fel'annár stood breathless, his mind scattered and he forced himself to feel the ground beneath him, call on all his self-control, will the ringing in his ears to cease. A soft pull on his arm and Tensári ushered him sideways until he thought he was standing just behind Pan'assár.

"Warriors Idernon, Ramien, Galdith and Carodel. Lieutenant Tensári. Lieutenant Galadan. Lord Lieutenant Sontúr of Tar'eastór. Step forwards."

They had been standing together outside the Circle save for Tensári. They had been smiling and enjoying Fel'annár's promotion and Pan'assár had secretly enjoyed their youthful ways. But their smiles promptly vanished, and they looked to Galadan and Idernon in panic. The Wise Warrior hesitated, moved only when Galadan gestured with his head, the hint of a grin beneath his stony features. The others followed his lead and soon, they stood before Pan'assár, while Tensári left Fel'annár's side to join them.

"Without The Company, we would not be standing here. They found our king, protected the Warlord so that he could bring our Silvan warriors home, from where they should never have left. For your acts of bravery, Ea Uaré thanks you with the Silver Acorn, to be worn as an Honour Stone, if you so wish."

Pan'assár handed one decoration to each of them and then saluted.

Returning it, Idernon dared to stand before Fel'annár, acorn clutched in his fist. Fel'annár watched, knew who he was, knew that he was bowing low from the way the light moved. He almost swayed sideways and then watched as one by one, The Company paid their solemn respects to him, not as their friend.

As their Warlord.

They more than anyone deserved this honour; more than him. In their diversity, they were a symbol, a reminder to others of the changing times. They were Silvan, Alpine and Ari'atór. One was a prince, another was a woman. He damned Band'orán for his ignoble ways, for blinding him and taking away this moment he so dearly wished to *see*.

The Company made to leave the Circle, but Pan'assár's voice called them back.

"Lieutenant Galadan."

The Fire Warrior started, glanced at Idernon beside him. He made hesitantly back towards Pan'assár, saluted, saw the soft smile on the commander's lips, and then heard the words meant only for him.

"I hope you will accept this now. You refused it once, and I cannot blame you for that. But in these times we now face, I would have you here, where you always belonged."

Pan'assár reached for a Golden Sun, held it in his hands and spoke, voice no longer soft but strong and proud, so that the entire Circle could hear.

"Do you, Galadan Ar Essare, accept the honour of serving in this army, as a captain, even unto death?"

Galadan's Alpine eyes searched those of Pan'assár, knew there was no longer a reason to refuse.

"I do."

Those frosty blue eyes softened, even though the voice did not. "Welcome to the Inner Circle, Captain Galadan."

The new captain straightened, words sinking in. He was a captain, but he would always remain in The Company.

"Warrior Idernon. Step forward."

Galadan watched Idernon, saw his questioning glance at Sontúr, then at Fel'annár at Pan'assár's shoulder. He stepped forward.

"Do you, Warrior Idernon Ar Denmon, accept the honour of serving in this army, as a lieutenant, even unto death?"

Idernon's eyes were wide, some intensity spilling from the depths of his soul. Galadan watched his young friend, the one he had always recognised as Fel'annár's natural second. He had told Pan'assár, asked him to watch, and watch he had.

"I do."

There was nothing in Idernon's collar to take out and so, for the first time, Pan'assár graced it with the single silver line he had taken from Fel'annár's collar. Galadan well knew how heavy it would feel sitting there, and so he promised himself that he would help Idernon reach his potential, limits Galadan had yet to see.

It was Commander Gor'sadén who spoke next.

"Lord Lieutenant Sontúr."

One eyebrow arched acutely as the prince turned to his commander general. He stepped forward.

"Do you, Lieutenant Sontúr Ar Vorn'asté Ar Lerhal, accept the honour of serving in the army of Tar'eastór, as a captain, even unto death?"

Galadan watched Sontúr, then glanced at Fel'annár. He would be damning the Gods for his blindness and who could blame him? None of them had imagined what Pan'assár had planned for them this morning.

As for Sontúr, he seemed so sure of himself, where Galadan knew he had not been just months ago when they had set out from Tar'eastór. There was no doubt in the prince's eyes at all. Where once he had asked himself what he would do, heal or fight, now, he knew that the answer was both.

"I do."

The single silver strip was gone, and a Golden Sun replaced it. Sontúr saluted, Gor'sadén bowed low.

"Let it be known that Captain Sontúr is officially assigned to Commander General Pan'assár, for so long as King Vorn'asté allows."

Pan'assár nodded at Galadan, a gesture his erstwhile lieutenant understood well. Tensári led them away, outside the Circle and Pan'assár made for the very centre.

"There will be time enough to celebrate your achievements. In two days' time, we will return here, when Silvan warriors stand amongst us once more to share that day. Whether there are two or two hundred, no one can say, but it falls to all of us, to General Fel'annár to represent us now and bring as many as he can to the place from which they should never have left. Aria lend you strength and luck for the task ahead."

Fel'annár nodded, hoped it was in the right direction. Pan'assár's words had bolstered his cause, a low burning fire that was gaining speed and heat. He felt proud of The Company, so wanted to see Galadan and Sontúr's Golden Suns, the prince's quirked brow and Idernon's stunned face. He wanted to see Turion's parallel lines and the pride in Gor'sadén's eyes, pride for his son and yet he did not deserve this promotion to general. Still, it would be helpful in the days to come, and perhaps one day in the future, he would be worthy of this honour.

Pan'assár gestured at Turion, who walked into the centre of the Circle where Pan'assár had just been standing.

"In two days' time, there will be a solemn ceremony in these very halls. It will mark the beginning of a new era, a better time in which the true meaning of service must be remembered. But our Silvan captains must be present, must be made to feel a part of this new reality. And so I say polish your metal, hone your blades. Bolster your minds and rid yourselves of the past. Serve your king, honour the Golden Suns upon your collars and never take them for granted." Turion saluted.

Fel'annár heard the thump of fists over finely crafted cuirasses and the soft murmur of the captains as their lights separated and dissipated. And then Tensári was moving and Fel'annár followed her. He felt The Company around him, their hands on his head, shoulders, back. He had always been the Warlord to them, but Pan'assár's public recognition of his status was a cause for celebration – and relief. And yet, anxiety was working its way into the back of his mind once more, telling him what still needed to be done and how little time he had to achieve it.

He reached out, to the Sentinels in Sen Garay, and then further afield to Oran'Dor, Lan Taria and Sen'oléi. He had never been further north than that, but still, he felt himself propelled, towards the borders of Calrazia.

Nothing had changed. The song of the Nim'uán was still distant.

"Here come Rinon and the commanders," whispered Idernon and Fel'annár turned to face them.

"Commanders, Warlord. The king requires your presence in his chambers for private counsel immediately."

Cold, commanding words, no congratulations.

Rinon.

3

LESTARI AND THE GENERAL

~

NESTAR, former Lestari of Ea Uaré, stood before the windows of his office
at the Halls of Healing, offices he had occupied for decades.

This was *his* domain, *his* realm. Here, he was king, ruled supreme.
How *dare* Thargodén take it from him. After so many years of service,
one simple order had been enough for the king to end his exalted career.

Anger so deep it hurt. He wanted to rage at the injustice, the outra-
geous disregard of a failed monarch who would name a *Silvan* Lestari, a
woman.

He wanted to scream, break things. The fool had asked if he had
done it on purpose. Of *course* he had! He didn't want to live in a place
where Silvans and their barbaric ways were allowed to taint the purity
and superiority of the Alpines. He would do it again, and again and
again until they were all gone, into the forest where they belonged, not
here, in *his* domain.

He turned to a knock at his door. Nestar considered ignoring it. It was
surely the half-caste, come to gloat and take possession of the Lestari's
office. The bitch would last two days. All he needed was to find a way to
...

The knock was louder, more demanding. He could feel his face red and hot, body ready to explode and he strode to the door, yanked it open. His eyes flickered wide, anger turning to embarrassment and then submission.

"Forgive me. Please, come in."

He felt like a fool, didn't want to. It was not in his best interests. He closed the door and turned to the woman who stood in the centre of the large room.

Pale skin, white hair, frosty eyes with overly large pupils made her look strange. It didn't help that the woman hardly had any eyebrows. She over-compensated for it by darkening them with some substance they said she imported from human lands. Why she saw fit to draw them in such a pronounced arch was beyond him.

Still, for all her oddities, the woman was imposing. What she lacked in personal appearance and elegance, she made up for with a sharp mind and a shrewd eye for business – and scheming.

"Lady Melu'sán." He bowed low, straightened, and then made for the wine decanter. Pouring two glasses, he approached, admired the fine scent that lingered around her, the gaudy cascades of silk and velvet that hung from her form.

"You have heard what has happened, Lady?"

"I have, Nestar. You have my condolences. Your sacrifice to the cause is noted."

Nestar had always loved her voice. So deep and rich, words enunciated so clearly and purposefully.

Nestar drank, breathed out through his nose. "What now, Lady?"

"We wait, Nestar. These are dangerous times for us all. Peace is volatile and we must choose our battles well. You fought a hard one, and although you have lost your position, you have placed the king's realm in serious jeopardy. The Silvan warriors will never return to barracks now and that is a battle won, Nestar. With so few loyalist warriors left, our incarcerated heroes will easily overcome them, and our dreams of an Alpine paradise will be at our fingertips."

Melu'sán drank slowly and deeply, eyes on Nestar as she did so.

"What would you have me do, Lady?"

"Wait for my orders. We must see what happens at the Inner Circle, now that the Silvan warriors have been *persuaded* to stay away. Once that is fact and the forest dwellers leave, then we take advantage of the king's military weakness. We must be patient, take any opportunities that arise that may prove advantageous to us."

"But what of the Royal Council. We no longer hold sway there."

"No. But what does that matter when a kingdom has no army, Nestar?"

He nodded in agreement.

"So come, my friend. Lighten that heart of yours. You will be Lestari once more. And you will have justice for the damage inflicted upon you." She carefully placed her jewelled goblet on the long, rectangular table in the centre of the room, and glided graciously towards Nestar.

"I will see you again soon. Be ready, Nestar. Once the Silvans leave their encampment we will act again."

"I am at your service, Lady."

"And you have served well, Lestari. I will make sure the others know of your selfless sacrifice to the cause."

She placed a long, pale hand on his shoulder as she passed him. Nestar turned, watched her leave, and then he turned back to his window.

He smiled. It had been worth it and soon, he would receive due recompense for his contribution. All he needed to do was stay vigilant, wait for the right moment in which the royal family would be vulnerable, because sooner or later, they would let down their guard.

And then, the purge would begin.

THARGODÉN WATCHED his Silvan son walk slowly and carefully towards the light, to the wall of windows where he himself would stand when he needed to think.

He wondered if Fel'annár could see the sun, or whether it was the trees that were beckoning to him. With one last glance around the room, Thargodén gestured to his guests to take their seats.

Ten chairs had been carefully arranged into a circle. But then Fel'annár had insisted that Idernon and Sontúr join the council. Rinon had frowned but the king had allowed it, and two more seats were added.

Thargodén knew how close they were to Fel'annár, but he also understood why he had wanted them there. One was a prince, versed in statesmanship, a healer and now a captain, and Fel'annár trusted him implicitly. The other was a lieutenant, wise and insightful, always close to Fel'annár's side. The three sat together while Tensári faded into the shadows at the back of the chamber. No one had questioned her presence, not even Rinon.

Handir sat beside Aradan, Rinon beside the king, with Pan'assár and Turion on his other side. With a glance at Panássár, Thargodén stood and opened council.

"General Fel'annár."

He looked up, as if he had been startled from his thoughts.

"It has been many years since I have set eyes on the Forest Emerald, many years since I stood before one who deserved it as much as you do." Thargodén saw his brow twitch and then smooth out, wondered what his son was thinking, yearned to ask him, but this was neither the time nor place to do so. If only he could see past the blindfold, contemplate those expressive eyes, Lássira's eyes. He promised himself he would find a moment to seek Fel'annár out later, tell him how proud he was of the things he had achieved.

"Thank you, my king. I am honoured."

Thargodén watched, heard the sparing words - expected words. They should be embracing, laughing. He should be mussing his son's hair, clapping him on the shoulder as any proud father would, as he himself had done just recently when Rinon had been named general. He banished those thoughts, forced himself to focus on the task at hand.

"I have gathered you here to discuss the Silvans and their intentions after the incident at the Halls. Once we understand their minds, we can turn our efforts to ensuring that justice is served, and that our army can begin the long and arduous road to recuperation. I want the facts; I want your thoughts and constructive suggestions as to what we must achieve, and how. This will not be quick, and I am aware that some of you are still convalescing. However, the stakes are high. The unity of our nation is at risk once more, and an enemy stirs in the north, one some of you are intimately familiar with. We are not ready to face it should it come our way. We need to act, and we must do it now.

"General Fel'annár. Please report on your – irregular – visit to the Silvan encampment."

The Warlord didn't flinch, and Thargodén credited him for that. If Fel'annár had had any doubts as to the convenience or otherwise of his nocturnal visit to the camp, they didn't show.

He stood to answer. "The Silvan Elders are angry, sire. They wonder why the king has not reached out to them, why he has not *opened the door*, as they put it, and welcomed them. They wonder why they are not a priority after what they consider was an act of loyalty and selfless service, and they ask why no signed documents have been presented to them with their just demands met." He paused here and Thargodén was grateful for it.

"There has been no time. There were and still are many wounded. Deaths to inform of, grieving families to thank and help. Basic services need restoring, supply chains reopened. There are hundreds of prisoners to deal with, traitors still to weed out ... did you tell them this, Warlord?"

Fel'annár nodded slowly. "I did. But as far as they're concerned, the Silvan people were one of those priorities. The way they see it, my king, is that they rode to your aid at my behest, when others would not, and still, they are not important enough for your immediate and undivided attention. They feel relegated to second, or perhaps third place and if that were not bad enough, Nestar showed his open and very public disregard for my Silvan fighters. It is all so familiar, too similar to the way things were before the battle, before Band'orán's death."

"They see it only from their perspective."

"I know, sire. But that is all they have, just as you see it from your perspective because it is all you have. In any case, this situation is not what they had imagined these post-battle days would be like. They had anticipated that with the return of the Warlord, an equal and just Royal Council would already be deed, signed and sealed. The Silvan Summit needs to have meant something to them and yet still they wait. They won't for much longer."

Fel'annár glanced to his left where he obviously knew Idernon sat, and then walked into the centre of the circle. Thargodén wondered how he dared to, blind that he was. He was reminded of Handir's penchant for pacing while he spoke.

"We have two days. *I* have two days, as of today, to show them my promises were founded. I must show them my status as Warlord is fact, and I must present them with the king's royal decree as to equality on the Royal Council. One of those things has been achieved this morning and I thank Commander Pan'assár for his most strategic thinking."

The king glanced at Pan'assár off to his left, wondered what he was thinking. Did Fel'annár believe that the commander general had made him general only so that he could satisfy the demands of the Silvans? He turned back to Fel'annár, thought he was looking straight at him.

"I must assume that the Royal Council will make that document available to me by tomorrow evening at the latest."

The king resisted the urge to arch his brow at the Warlord's demands, but he decided to say nothing. Rinon though, had no such inclination.

"You want it all, and you want it *now*."

Fel'annár turned to the new voice and Thargodén braced to intervene.

"The Silvans want what is theirs by right. They have waited years. I believe that is long enough, Prince Rinon."

"Perhaps. But try if you will, to see this from both sides. You missed these first days after the battle. You seem unaware of the endless work others have done. There was no avoiding this delay."

Thargodén turned back to Fel'annár, wondered what tone he would adopt after Rinon's uncharacteristically cautious reprimand.

"I know that. I am well aware of the things I have missed and shouldn't have. But the Silvan elders cannot see beyond our walls. And that's a problem that must be solved. I am sorry if my tone was out of place."

Rinon simply nodded, sat back down and Thargodén stood to speak.

"We are all anxious and tired, are we not?" He turned to his second son. "Prince Handir?" Thargodén gestured with his hand for him to stand while Fel'annár made his careful way back to his seat.

"What is left of the Royal Council is quiet and submissive. Whether they are loyal is yet to be seen. There are only ten left, six of whom are

Alpine, and four Silvans, but only one here at court. The Alpines worry that you will relieve them of their collars, and thus are unwilling to vote against you, whatever their real thoughts on the matter. For now, this works in our favour, and I have no doubt that they will vote favourably tomorrow. Once that is achieved, Councillor Aradan and I will begin the search to complete the twenty. Ten Alpines, ten Silvans, each with their apprentices.

"However," Handir held up a hand. He had answered the king's questions but there was one more important point to make. "I urge you all to be vigilant. The king knows of my suspicions that Nestar may have done what he did purposefully. If this is the case, he is not acting alone but at the behest of another. And this means there may be more. Whether they are amongst the six Alpine councillors that remain, or whether they are in some other position where damage can be done, we cannot know. We must simply be aware that there may be those still loyal to Band'orán, or to his ideas, those who would see the Restoration fail."

Thargodén nodded thoughtfully, still in doubt as to Nestar's motivations but cautious enough to heed Handir's plea for vigilance. "Then with some luck, the Council will pass the vote by tomorrow." His eyes settled back on Fel'annár. "Will that satisfy their demands, Warlord?"

"The demands of the Elders, yes. But the advent of the Nim'uán adds a third, equally important element, sire." He stood with the intention of walking into the centre, but Thargodén stopped him.

"You can remain seated, Warlord."

Fel'annár sat back down, cleared his throat. "According to Commander Pan'assár, we have but five hundred able-bodied warriors at the city barracks, and needless to say, none of them are Silvan. If we are to face an invasion, this army needs rebuilding, and we need to do it quickly. I need to find a way to bring the Silvan warriors back. I need to give them a reason to do so, beyond equality on the Council, beyond my promotion, beyond the dictates of the Silvan Elders."

"You are suggesting the Elders have no sway over their people?" asked Rinon.

"No. They do. They are respected and heeded in all things civilian. But the military has been especially undermined in these last years of Alpine Purism. Those few Silvan captains who remain, are concerned about the well-being of their fighters and they have yet to see that change has come." Fel'annár turned to where Pan'assár sat and for the second time, Thargodén wondered how he knew.

"Commander Pan'assár?" prompted the Warlord.

"My king. I concur in that, to be sufficiently defended from any foe, we should have five thousand warriors around the various barracks inside the city and on the outskirts. Even a large group of Deviants would be a challenge to us now. This must be our foremost concern. As to what the Silvan captains want, I have an idea of what you are imply-ing, General. It is my hope that with those parallel lines in your collar and the king's written decree on the return of the Warlord, that some of them at least, will return. However, I am not sure they understand the urgency of our situation."

"They do. I told them of the threat, so that they would understand the stakes. Their very civilisation may be at risk because if that Nim'uán is coming to our forest, it will be *their* villages it will raze to the ground. They know they cannot survive without unity – if they don't work together with the Alpines."

"So what are they waiting for?"

Fel'annár turned to the crown prince. "They are waiting for their *reason.*" Thargodén could see Fel'annár's patience slipping.

"They have it. Come back or face the possibility of annihilation."

Fel'annár looked to the floor and once more, Thargodén wished he could see his son's eyes. To his surprise, it was not Fel'annár who answered Rinon but Pan'assár.

"History, Prince. The Silvans have been alone in the north for many years. For as many as Band'orán was poisoning the Royal Council and the Inner Circle. You may remember how they pleaded for outposts, for more warriors. They never got those things. Annihilation has always threatened them, because our army believed they should leave their homes, come here to a stone building where they do not belong. They resisted then and they resist now.

"As the Warlord says, they want a reason to return to an army which has discriminated against them for many years. They want a reason to come back to an army that took for granted their scouting and tracking capacity, their prowess with the bow and instead, sent them for water or set them to cooking for others." Pan'assár turned to Fel'annár. "They ask themselves if they should return to that army that is still under the auspices of Commander General Pan'assár, the very commander who condoned all these dishonourable acts."

Silence fell over them, even Rinon held his peace, obviously as surprised as the king himself at Pan'assár's admission of guilt.

"They question your ongoing command, yes," continued Fel'annár. "And admittedly, this is my greatest challenge. But *I* do not question your command. I have come to respect you. I would have no other stand before our warriors in battle, as our Commander General."

Pan'assár took a step closer to the blindfolded Warlord, regarded him as if it were the first time.

"I have done dishonourable things, used unacceptable words, watched my warriors humiliate and belittle my other warriors. I hated you. That you have come to respect me is my honour. But it is the Silvan troops that must respect me, and they do not. I am the reason they will not return." Pan'assár turned to the king, strong emotions in his eyes even though his features had not softened at all. Thargodén would not accept the request he knew was coming.

"I will not take your command, Pan'assár."

The commander stared back at him, nodded awkwardly, as if he was shocked at what had almost happened.

"Then I must find a way to convince them those things will never happen again. I must undo it all, start again but I need them to give me that opportunity."

"And I would give it to you. You and I must find a way to turn this around," said Fel'annár.

"And what is your suggestion, General?" asked Aradan from beside the king.

Fel'annár's head turned to just right of where Aradan sat. He hesitated and Thargodén frowned. His son had shown no doubt so far in this meeting.

"Speak it," he urged.

"I ... I propose we change the structure of our military system. Now, we have an army with specialised contingents, each of which is split again into units and then patrols. What I am proposing is a split at the highest level. I say we create two divisions, both under Commander Pan'assár. A Mountain Division, and a Forest Division, each led by a general. Within each of these divisions, we continue with our contingents, units and patrols. In order for me to convince our Silvan warriors to return, I would command the Forest Division."

Thargodén sat back, crossed his arms, gaze drifting between Fel'annár and Pan'assár who was still standing at the centre of the circle of chairs. It was Turion who spoke next.

"Will this not invite more racial strife? Silvans on the one side, Alpines on the other?"

"That's not what I'm saying, General. *Anyone* can join any division. It's the specialised units that will appeal to each warrior, irrespective of race. Granted at first, most Silvans will want to serve in the Forest Division. But with time, Silvan archers will wish to join the infantry within the Mountain Division. Perhaps our Silvan Listeners will wish to serve as Shadows, within that same division and who is to say that Alpine trackers and those specialised in close combat will not want to join the Forest Division as rangers? In time, a balance will be found, but for now, our priority is to bring them back to barracks. This is my proposal; one I believe I can defend at the Silvan encampment tomorrow. They will listen, at least."

Pan'assár said nothing, stood silently watching the Warlord.

"Well, this is new," said the king. "An army with two Divisions. Your thoughts, Commander Pan'assár."

The king recognised the set of his commander's jaw, the crease between his brows. It was entirely Pan'assár when he was thinking, strategising, wondering as he was now, whether this idea of Fel'annár's could work. Finally, the commander general spoke and when he did, it was to the Warlord.

"They will not come for me. But they may for you."

Fel'annár nodded slowly.

～

WHILE THE DEBATE in the king's quarters continued, Llyniel cantered into the Silvan encampment together with two Alpine healers, overstuffed packs across their chests, and their horses' paniers filled to brimming. Dismounting at the stables, they handed their mounts over to a young girl and hefted their supplies over their shoulders.

They made their way to the far side of the camp where the Silvan warriors had created a makeshift Healing area. It was an expanse of tarpaulins, hastily erected pavilions with no doors to speak of. From afar, they would look like stables, until you stepped closer, heard the muffled voices. Some were angry, others placating. It was a place of suffering and mercy, a place where indignant words rippled and spread like wildfire.

Was this all they had achieved? Was this the colour of Alpine gratitude?

Her two companions left with the supplies they had brought, knew exactly where to take them while Llyniel went in search of her head healer. She found him bent over a warrior who lay on a low pallet. She watched him for a while, mind wandering to the little she knew about this singularly gruff healer.

It was Dalú who had once spoken to her of him. He himself had almost lost his leg. But sheer, Silvan obstinance served Dalú well, and after years walking, or rather limping the road to recovery, he returned to his active duties in the field.

But not so Kristain.

He had charged into battle with Deviants, out on the western borders. He had fallen from his horse. Dazed by a blow to the head, he had not been able to roll out of the way of his mount. It fell over his legs, crushing his knee.

One healer had wanted to amputate his right leg, but another had operated instead. They had saved his limb but not his vocation. His limp was too pronounced. He could no longer run, not even jog and Kristain had been forced to leave the army he had always loved so much.

Yet here he was, retrained as a healer, still a close friend of Dalú. Llyniel had chosen him as her head healer because he was good. But so too was he good at reading the minds of wounded warriors. It was a skill not often found because healers were rarely ex-combat warriors. Besides, she liked his no-nonsense approach, the way he picked them up, showed them the way forward when they couldn't see one.

She stepped into the shelter and approached the warrior-turned-healer.

"Report, Kristain?"

"There are still three serious cases. The others have recuperated well enough, should recover without much consequence in a week or so. What worries me the most is their anger, Llyniel. It's escalating, brewing, almost disproportionate. They've lost sight of the tolerant Alpines, forgotten that they exist save for these healers here."

Llyniel knew he was right. Even now she could hear the angry whispers that spoke of humiliation, of provocation.

"The king is moving, Kristain. Nestar has been expelled for what he did."

Kristain stared dumbly back at her, only for a satisfied smile to spread all over his face. "That's a bloody good start. What Alpine's taking his place?"

"Eh ... me?" She said it so quietly he had to lean into her to hear.

"What?"

Heads turned and she flapped her hands in the air for him to lower his voice, but Kristain was shaking his head, even as he raised his voice and drew the attention of patients and healers alike. To one side, Dalú watched, arms crossed over his chest.

"Justice has been done. Nestar the ungrateful has been ousted, cast from his seat of power at the Healing Halls. The king has stripped him of his robes of office and in his place, Llyniel of the Silver Wolf is our new Lestari!"

Dalú uncrossed his arms, almost flinched when the defiant cheer went up around him. Even the Alpine healers held their fists in the air and smiled.

Llyniel was mortified, glared at a grinning Kristain. She knew why he had done it, knew it was in their interests to proclaim it, now when their anger was threatening their capacity to reason.

She smiled, gestured with her hands for them to quieten, didn't miss the approving nods from the wounded, from the Silvan families and helpers that were milling about the place. She turned back to Kristain.

"If you've quite *finished*?" She stared hard at her second in command, felt her own lips twitch, knew that he had seen it. "I'll stay here until this evening, but I'll have to leave later. Things are happening fast and Fel'annár thinks he's whole and entirely hale when he's not."

"Is his sight coming back?"

"He says it's better, but whether he's saying that to brush me off, there's no telling."

"Stubborn?"

"You have no idea."

She set to work visiting each bed, greeting families and discussing treatments. She spoke to the healers who had turned their backs on Nestar to come here, assured them that their positions at the Halls were safe, that she trusted them implicitly, that she was proud of the Alpine side of herself. After hours of work, she finally allowed herself a respite.

Smoothing her unruly hair back, she started at the steaming cup someone held out to her. Beside it, a chunk of bread topped with honey. She looked up, into the uncompromising stare of Amareth. Llyniel obeyed the silent command to eat and drink, even as her eyes surveyed the area beyond the pavilions. Kristain would be back soon to take over.

"I've heard Thargodén has named you Lestari. It's a step in the right direction for our people, the first concession the king has made."

Llyniel stopped chewing, turned to the woman beside her. "It's not a concession."

Amareth stared back at her for a moment. "I don't mean to imply you don't deserve it."

"It's not that. You make it sound as if the king named me Lestari to placate the Silvan people. He didn't. He did it because I have the necessary qualifications and recommendations for such a position of responsibility. It was not a political decision, Amareth."

The woman nodded slowly. And then she smiled. "Then I'm doubly pleased. You're family, and it honours the houses of the White Oak and the Three Sisters that one of its daughters is held in such high esteem. Congratulations are in order. I just wish we were in a better position so that we could celebrate it."

"There'll be time, I'm sure. Fel'annár will make sure of that, once I have time to tell him."

"Where is he?"

"At the Inner Circle I imagine. I'll see him this evening."

Amareth nodded. "And his sight? Is there any improvement?"

"Not much, but that won't affect his work, Amareth. He'll do what he said he would."

Amareth cocked her head to one side, shrewd eyes seeming to read the feelings behind her words.

"Llyniel, about what happened last night. It was not my intention to come across the way we did. I love Fel'annár as the son I never had. I understand that he believes my motives to be political and they are, I can't deny that. But that doesn't mean I don't care. I do, more than anything, more than politics and more than the plight of my people."

"Have you ever told him that? In the way you just have to me?"

"I tried, and probably failed. I'll have to do better."

Llyniel offered her a tired smile, then smoothed her hair back from her face again. She would soon be free to head back to the city. By that time, hopefully, Nestar would have collected his things and gone. She would ask Kristain to begin the return of their wounded to the Halls, where they could receive the best treatment possible, with a roof over their heads and a modicum of privacy.

Someone was approaching the camp from the forest, just breaking through the tree line. Amareth's profile moved in the corner of her eye, and Llyniel turned, and then frowned, because Amareth seemed shocked. She watched her stand slowly, the way her palms smoothed down the front of her tunic. Llyniel followed her line of sight, towards the tree line and the three figures who emerged from the forest on horseback.

"Who's that?"

Amareth didn't answer immediately and Llyniel watched as the three elves made for the stables, slowing to a trot and then a walk. The tallest of them carried spears on his back and the warriors turned to him, saluted even though he wore civilian attire.

"Whoever it is, Fel'annár will want to meet *him*."

Amareth whirled around to face her and Llyniel started.

"Why do you say that?"

"The spears on his back. Fel'annár's obsessed with mastering them but can find no one to teach him."

Amareth stared back at Llyniel as if she had lost her mind. Llyniel didn't understand. "What is it? What's wrong?"

Amareth straightened, visibly collected herself. With one last glance at the newcomers, she spoke.

"It's time to break fifty-three years of silence, Llyniel. It's time for me to face the consequences of my promise to Lássira. They are Fel'annár's family, the family I never allowed him to meet."

Amareth's eyes were wide, shock warring with fear. Llyniel wanted to meet them, as much as she knew that this was not the time. There was business between Amareth and her family. Things they needed to fix, if such a thing were even possible.

"I wish you luck, Amareth. You deserve it."

Amareth smiled sparingly. "Congratulations, daughter."

Llyniel watched her walk slowly yet resolutely, towards the Silvan family Fel'annár had never met.

WITH FEL'ANNÁR'S plan on the figurative table, it was time to discuss the idea of two divisions, and then vote to accept or reject it. Fel'annár's heart was beating far too fast. He had blurted his life-long project to them in one, simple minute.

"I do not blame those warriors for not wishing to serve under my direct command. I must strive to change that in the coming months. This new system however, is no guarantee that they *will* return, General. I will still be there. Their Warlord will be under *my* command."

"But at least I have a chance of convincing them, Commander. They have seen us together, know that I accept your command. But I will tell them that I stand for *them*. That I will not allow the past to return. I will tell them that I will obey every command you issue, except those that are damaging, unfair, humiliating or unjust."

"And who will be the judge of that?" Rinon stood, stepped towards Pan'assár, as if he would defend him.

Fel'annár took his time answering, so that his irritation at the prince would not colour his words.

"Our conscience, Prince."

"That is hardly impartial," said Rinon, words dripping with sarcasm. "Or are you suggesting everyone's conscience is the same?"

"I am saying there is a *right* and there is a *wrong*. I am the *Silvan* Warlord, Prince. The very term is partial. It is my duty to ensure that the Silvan warriors are treated equally. However, I myself am under the command of Pan'assár, an Alpine. And yet in our beliefs, in what we know to be fair or unfair, I know that we agree. But, if it ever came to a disagreement we cannot reconcile, he has the authority to take my command."

"But he will not, will he? Because you will rally the Silvans behind you."

"They are already behind me, Prince. No need for *rallying*. Does my judgement of what is right and what is wrong worry you so much? Have you not learned in these past weeks that I am loyal to the king?"

"I will not question your loyalty, no. But these questions must be asked because rest assured others *will* ask them, and it falls to the rulers of this land to answer them."

"And I take note of your comments, Prince, valid as they are." Fel'annár nodded his head in respect, watched Rinon return it.

"In theory, Commander Pan'assár, can we agree to this new structure?" asked Thargodén. "The figure of the Commander General and his two divisions, mountain and forest. Within them, specific contingents and units yet to be defined."

"In theory, I believe it may be the *only* way – unless you relieve me of my command and name another the Silvans would serve under."

"I said no." Thargodén turned from Pan'assár, unwilling to hear any more about that suggestion. "This is what I suggest. We draw up an official document, clearly stating this new military structure. I will sign it, as will the Warlord, the Commander General, and whoever he names as General of the Mountain Division. With that, at least, the Warlord has a chance of bringing some of our Silvan warriors back."

The king walked into the centre of their circle.

"We vote. Who says aye to this new structure? Commander General Pan'assár."

"Aye."

"General Turion."

"Aye."

"General Fel'annár."

"Aye."

"General Rinon."

Pursed lips, head tipped back. "Aye."

"Then it is settled. Aradan, Handir, draw up a document which outlines this new army, have it ready for tomorrow."

"My king."

Thargodén turned to Sontúr. "Captain. Is the Warlord fit enough to ride to the encampment?"

"He is sire. So long as he heeds his healers' advice. I will make sure that he does."

The king nodded. "Then the Warlord and Prince Handir will ride to the Silvan encampment tomorrow with these written documents. Your missions are clear. We must bring the Silvan Elders back to court and begin the process of regenerating our Royal Council. And we must convince those Silvan captains to rally their warriors, bring as many as will come back to the city. It will be slow at first, I have no doubt. But once five come back, ten may follow. I just hope that the Nim'uán takes its time, and the Gods forgive me, that it sets its eyes on somewhere else. We need time, and we must start now."

Fel'annár couldn't quite believe that his plan had been deemed in any way suitable. He knew that it was, but he had somehow convinced himself that someone would object. He had been ready to counter their criticisms, had bolstered his mind for their disapproval, especially Rinon's. He watched a light approach him. Not the king, not Handir. He looked up, realised that the movement did not hurt his eyes as much as it used to.

"How long have you been planning this?"

Pan'assár, then. "Since I was twelve," he answered, somewhat defensively. "It started as a hobby. I never imagined there would ever be a use for all those journals I filled."

"Were you ever just a *boy*?" The commander's voice was low, meant only for him.

Fel'annár hesitated, not quite prepared for this unknown side to Pan'assár. "Yes, I was a boy. It was all a game back then, playing generals with Idernon and Ramien." A soft smile played on his lips, but it slipped when the enormity of the task before him finally began to sink in. "I have specifics I would discuss with you, Commander, when there's time."

Pan'assár lingered before him and then moved away. "General Turion. I would have *you* command this Mountain Division, fill the post Huren disgraced, and that I know you will honour. Do you accept, General?"

Fel'annár tried to imagine Turion's face, wondered if he had expected to be chosen over Rinon. His hesitation was testimony to his shock.

"Accept, Turion," said Rinon. "You are the best choice. As Crown Prince, I have other duties that would not be compatible. I told you once that you would be a pivotal part of his new army. Our Silvan warriors respect you, remember your work at the training barracks in the Deep Forest. They remember your love of that place, your respect for their ways."

Turion tore his eyes away from Rinon and back to Pan'assár. "I accept that honour, will not fail you or our king."

Pan'assár allowed himself a modest smile. "Good. Very good. Then let it be known that my second in command is General Turion. Should anything happen to me, he is the future of our army."

Fel'annár smiled, wished he could see Turion's face now, wished he could see Rinon's, so that he would know how the prince felt about that.

"I am pleased, Turion. You are held in the highest esteem by us all." The king's voice, and Fel'annár turned to where he thought Turion stood. He could hear the emotion in his first captain's voice when he answered.

"I will not fail you nor your family, my king."

"Well then we have a plan. Warlord. I require your detailed report tomorrow evening on your return from the encampment."

"My king, Commander." Fel'annár bowed, heard others moving around him, watched their lights and tried his hardest to understand who was who, where they were going, what they were doing.

As for him, all he wanted was to return to his quarters to rest and think. And then he would listen to the forests, both of them, make sure he had missed nothing, that the kingdom was still safe. And when

Llyniel returned, he would take comfort in her presence, alone, for the first time in what seemed like an age.

Everything else could wait for tomorrow.

NESTAR HAD INDEED GONE. He had even taken his world-famous treatise, damn him. Luckily, most of its contents was in her head. She wondered if there would be a copy at the Academics Guild. At least Arané and Tanor's books were still here. Nestar had not taken those.

The Lestari's office was large, had its own fireplace, inside which sat a frame and a large pot for boiling water. There was a floor to ceiling bookshelf that any scholar would die for, and there was wine sitting in an ornate decanter upon a side table, where sparkling glasses waited to be filled.

At the very centre of the room, a long, rectangular table stood, filled with vials and jars, dried and fresh herbs and beside them, four pestles and mortar. This was her domain now, and for the first time, a sense of trepidation rolled over her. She had the knowledge, but did she have the skill to lead such a large team of healers and apprentices?

She trailed a hand over the high shelves, tipped her head backwards and to the very ceiling, books and scrolls everywhere. She strolled over to the windows, fingertips sliding over the dusty sill. She rubbed it between her fingers, glanced at the twilight forest beyond, and then turned and walked to the hearth that was burning low. She reached for a log, placed it carefully on top of the almost spent embers, watched as small flames licked at it, became stronger.

She had been surprised to find a large bathing area, for the exclusive use of the Lestari. It was not a luxury but a necessity, and today was no exception. She would bathe, change into fresh robes, black as usual, as protocol dictated, but where before her sash had been green, now, it was the only red one in the entire realm.

Llyniel was Master Healer – of her own lands – at last.

After her bath, she would return to her quarters on the last floor of the palace. Fel'annár would be there. She would flush those beautiful eyes she had missed so much these past days. She would tell him of the day's extraordinary events, and he would do likewise.

And then, in spite of the daunting days ahead, the uncertainty and the distant threat of invasion, she would have him to herself. No Company, no Gor'sadén, just her soulmate, his Connate and a night of comfort before the coming storm.

With her plan firmly in place, Llyniel bathed and changed, took up a brush and worked it through her hair. A soft smile played on her lips, eyes on the now healthy fire that crackled in the hearth.

She jumped at the knock on the outer door. A healer come in search of advice or some such thing, she supposed. She strode to the door, opened it too fast and then startled at the sight of Fel'annár, standing there in civilian clothing, blindfold in place, hair not quite dry.

"I heard what happened. That you're Lestari."

She smiled, let out a breath and reached for his arm. With an apologetic glance at Tensári, she watched her wander away from the door and then pulled Fel'annár inside, locking the door behind them.

"There is a sofa to your left. Sit."

He found it easily enough, and Llyniel wandered over to the long table that took centre place in the room. She had all the ingredients she needed at hand, and she soon stood swirling the liquid in a glass vial. Coming up behind Fel'annár, she pulled at the ties of his blindfold, passed him a cloth and flushed his eyes, watched from above as he blinked and mopped up the excess that ran down his cheeks. His brows twitched.

"Does it still hurt?"

"No. It's not that."

"What then?" She moved to crouch in front of him.

"I can move them without pain, I can see a little, blurry and with no colour, but I can *see* ..."

Llyniel's smile was quick and wide, and she wondered if he could see that. She peered up at him. "And me? Can you see me?"

"Your hair is black and your eyes grey. Your skin is the colour of ice and your lips are like charcoal. But the Gods you are beautiful to me, Llyniel."

Liquid glistened in his still faulty eyes, while her own vision blurred.

She knew how frightened he had been, knew that he had held on to her words of encouragement bravely, still wondering if she was right. A calloused hand came up to touch her cheek, slid down the side of her neck. She turned, kissed his palm and then moved from the floor to the sofa, sitting as close as she could to him.

Fel'annár leaned back, breathed out slowly, spoke quietly. "Pan'assár made me a ... a general today."

She had been leaning into him, senses coming alive, but her gaze snapped to his, mouth unmoving at first, until it stretched into a wide smile.

"You always wanted to be a *captain*."

"So I did." He breathed in, chest inflating and then deflating with another rush of air. "A dream I will never fulfil. I never wanted all this, Llyn, and yet Aria conspires to bring everything together, too fast and too soon. Me a general, you the Lestari. The royal decree and the restructuring of our army. My visit to the camp tomorrow will be vital, crucial to the future of our lands, Llyn."

"I know. But that's tomorrow." She leaned into him, rested her cheek on his strong chest, one arm wrapping around his powerful form. "Then let's just forget it all, just for tonight. Nothing is happening outside those bolted doors, Fel'annár. Nothing can touch us here."

She took his face in her hands and kissed him, hard and desperate, hands smoothing over his temple, into his thick hair. To her, nothing was more important than this simple thing. The elf she loved, staring back at her with the same need in his eyes, a need she would satiate until night gave way to dawn, and duty must begin again.

And then she would tell him that his family from the Deep Forest had come.

4

A NEW REALITY

~

FAR TO THE north of the Great Forest Belt, just two days' trek from Abiren'á, former capital city of the Silvan people, swords, scimitars and daggers clashed and clanged and scraped together. Bows thwacked and arrows thudded into wood, armour and flesh. Warriors grunted and gasped, screamed and yelled as they fought. The elves were outnumbered but not outskilled, not here on the fringes of the Wetwood.

"Retreat, retreat south-east, area one!"

What was left of the elven patrol ran after Lieutenant Yerái, knew the Sand Lords would not resist the chase. Their thudding feet were getting closer ...

"Now!"

The elves jumped and grabbed at the overhead ropes, invisible to any ignorant of their existence, and then climbed as only Silvan elves could, or Alpines if they had been in their company for long enough.

Yerái looked down at the unwitting enemy below. They had not expected the Silvan elves to all but disappear into the air. In their moment of confusion, they had run straight into the quicksand, as Yerái knew they would. They were already half buried in the liquid ground, shocked faces looking for a way out but there was none.

One of them was already neck-deep in it, and he shouted out, to anyone who could hear him. In his panic, he was surely kicking his legs and flailing his arms under it, making his end quicker than it should have been. Slowly sinking, the others stared in horror but soon enough, their screams were strangled and suddenly gone. A quick count of the rings upon the surface of the fine sands told Yerái that one of them had escaped the pit. As his patrol climbed higher into the branches, knowing it was already too late to track him down. Even from up here, there was no sign of him.

It was dusk of the following day by the time they returned to Abiren'á, and Yerái had reached the same conclusions as he had done after the last incursion, and the one before that.

The Sand Lords were risking everything with these small yet seemingly coordinated patrols. They were never first to attack, so what were they doing?

Yerai climbed into his tree home, a humble structure close to the centre of the city. He was too tired to eat and so he washed, and then slept and when next he woke, the sun had already risen.

He stepped out of his house and stood upon his front plateau that looked down over the forest floor, far beneath him. He breathed in the smell of freshly burning resins, the tantalising aroma of his neighbours' breakfasts wafting around him from above and below.

He stepped to the very edge of the wooden platform, looked down at the softly swaying ropes that hung from it, all the way down to the ground, pulley and hooks clacking, soft and rhythmic. A friend navigated the rope and vine bridge between branches off to his left, called a greeting. They had not seen each other for weeks. Yerái had been on patrol ever since he had returned from his mission for the king. He was waiting for orders; they all were.

And still, none had come.

They said there was strife at the king's court, a rebellion at the Inner Circle. Their Silvan Council of Elders had issued an ultimatum, demanded the return of the Warlord and equality on the Royal Council. Yerái remembered the Night of a Thousand Drums, had stood here, listening to the mighty war drums of the north which had joined that extraordinary symphony that had sounded throughout the entire forest.

And then nothing.

Had it come to battle? Or had Thargodén and the Inner Circle agreed to the return of the Warlord? Yerái was a Listener, but the trees said nothing about that, or if they did, he did not have the power to perceive it.

On his return from Tar'eastór, he had come home, sought out Bulan and told him what he had seen, *who* he had seen. He well knew of the family ties between his friend and the Warlord, knew of the estrangement between the captain and his sister, she who had refused to bring the boy here as a child. It hadn't taken the former captain long to pack his things and make for the city in search of his nephew. Yerái had briefly considered joining him. But for whatever reason, he thought he would be more useful here. Warriors were scarce these days, and the remaining lieutenants were organising patrols on their own because there was no news.

There were no orders.

He had listened every day, still did, in the hopes that he could understand what had happened. There were not many Listeners. Yerái himself had only ever met two. A woman in Ea Nanú could sense danger well before it materialised, just like he himself could. Only Yerái could also tell the nature of it. Marauding Sand Lords, a pack of Deviants or some impending natural accident.

But there was something else. He had known who the Warlord was the day they had met, quite by chance on the road to Tar'eastór. He had felt the power of him, *knew* he was a Listener, long before he met the group.

Yerái tilted his head back as far as it would go in order to see the topmost branches, and the buildings nestled inside them. These constructions were made to accommodate dozens of people, so large they cast shadows on the ground below. The view from here was breathtaking, but he knew that it was even more stunning the further up you were. He huffed. Yerai would never be able to afford accommodation up there.

A small, dark face looked down at him, peering through the leaves, bright blue eyes twinkling in curiosity. The child giggled, an invitation to play. Yerái smiled widely, adopted a ready hand-to-hand stance and watched as the child deftly thudded onto the platform, not half his own height.

She was ready and Yerái went through the motions of the basic stances he knew the child would already have mastered. She smiled and laughed as they battled and Yerái returned it, indulged her because in a scant few years, that playful smile would be gone and, in its place, concentration, dedication. Faith and experience in dealing death. It would no longer be play to her but divine duty.

She was Ari'atór.

A distant beat of drums sounded around them, and the child turned towards it, slanted eyes glittering with too much intensity for one so young. She was gone, away to training and Yerái's smile faded.

He turned west, to where the mountains were visible behind the towering trees. This rocky formation was one of the reasons why this city had never been taken. It was a bastion in more than one sense of the word. Here, the Silvans had never been invaded. It was here that people like Captain Bulan had taken refuge when Pan'assár had refused to take action, allowed the Alpine Purists to debase and insult their Silvan brethren.

And then his questions were back. What were the Sand Lords doing? Why were their patrols so small, unwilling to engage in battle unless confronted with no other option? Why were they increasing in frequency?

Words danced in his mind and Yerái was unsure as to whether they were his own, or if they came from the trees.

Maps.

They were mapping the area ... for what? But the trees said no more. And yet there was something he was missing, a sentiment which lay beneath the cryptic messages from the trees, some worry Yerái had yet to identify.

A deep breath, a suspicion he cast into the forests, upwards and away, to no one in particular; to anyone who could hear.

Why would a Sand Lord make a map?

~

THARGODÉN STOOD IN HIS CHAMBERS, at his favourite spot by the windows, but his eyes were not on the Evergreen Wood. They were on Rinon, watching as he spoke with Handir about the morning's Royal Council meeting – or rather what was left of it. Eight pasty-faced councillors who had not dared open their mouths while Handir and Aradan spoke. Thargodén himself had addressed them, explained the workings of the new council. Handir had indeed been right. They had listened, and then approved. No discussion, no interventions, no interruption at all.

And then Aradan had told him that the Warlord had apparently regained his sight. Miren had seen him walking across the courtyard with Llyniel, sure-footed and with no blindfold. He made a mental note to himself to visit his son later to congratulate him on his promotion, and for regaining his sight – if the rumour was true. He should have done it yesterday, but time had not permitted, and then exhaustion had made him forget.

But the truth was, that circumstances conspired against them. When he was free, Fel'annár was away. He snapped himself out of his musings and turned to his second son, held the two scrolls out to him.

"Here. By sending you, I want them to understand the importance I place on these decrees. I would go myself, save that Pan'assár is adamant I take no risks until we are sure that Band'orán's legacy can no longer harm this family. Still, I would take private counsel with the Elders tomorrow. Tell them the door will be open for them; no need to knock. And take this for Lady Amareth. I would have her on the Royal Council." Handir took the scrolls and the folded parchment, watched his father turn to Rinon, as if he expected him to object.

He didn't, and Thargodén continued. "The Inner Circle gathers tomorrow, and the Royal Council begins its search to complete the twenty. Fel'annár rides to bring our Silvan warriors back to the ranks while Handir here will strive to guide the Silvan Elders through the door I will hold open for them. Everything is in motion, princes. There can be no rest until we have rebuilt our institutions. Especially not now that that – thing – is out there somewhere. We can only pray it does not set its eyes on our forest before we can sufficiently populate our army."

"Could they not have chosen a more appropriate name for the thing? *Beautiful Monster* is simply ridiculous," said Rinon.

"It is what the trees call it," said Handir, as if it were the most obvious thing under the sun.

Just days ago, Rinon would have scoffed at such a claim. But after the battle, after what they had seen inside the Evergreen Wood, Thargodén could see his hesitation. He changed the subject, to the one he knew was foremost in Rinon's mind.

"Maeneth returns."

Rinon smiled at last, the cutting edges of his features softening. Thargodén couldn't remember the last time he had seen Rinon like this. He was suddenly reminded of Canusahéi.

"Father. I would ride out to meet her. Escort her into the city with full honours."

"And when will that be?"

"Four, perhaps five days."

"All right. But take The Company with you."

"Not with *him*."

It had been too good to be true, mused Thargodén. Rinon's good mood was souring with the mere thought of Fel'annár.

"With *him* – if he can be spared. It is too early to place my trust in any others. With Nestar's actions under scrutiny, who is to say there are not more of Band'orán's followers striving to take advantage of our weakened state? Call me over-cautious if you will, but this is my condition, Prince."

Rinon's jaw pulsed but he held his tongue, if only barely. Surprisingly to the king, it was *Handir's* temper that flared.

"What is wrong with you, brother? Have you no sense of gratitude? Can you not put this antagonism behind you?"

"He is a warrior of this realm, a good one. I know what happened at Analei and I know what happened at Horizon Falls. I respect him for his skill and his loyalty. But I do not have to *like* him, Handir."

"Then you will respect *my* wishes and be civil to him, if nothing else. He is my brother."

"I will not disrespect him. And he is your *half*-brother."

"No." Handir stepped closer to Rinon, too close for the crown prince's comfort. "Anyone who saves my life, that puts his own at risk for me is a brother, *full*-blooded and loved." Handir turned to his father, and for a second time in just as many days, Thargodén saw this new side to his son. He was bolder, braver, more assertive. Lord Damiel had taught him well. As for Rinon, he wondered if Maeneth would take kindly to Fel'annár, and if she did, would she in turn, convince Rinon to give their Silvan brother a chance?

Rinon said nothing, and Handir took his leave. "I have much to prepare for my visit to the camp. I will see you both later." He bowed to his father, to Rinon and then left. The crown prince made to follow, but Thargodén was speaking.

"He saved *my* life too, Rinon. Yet more than this, he saved this city from ruin. He deserves much more than your disdain."

Rinon stared back at him, almost apologetic; almost repentant. "I know. But he reminds me of mother." He bowed slowly and then left.

Thargodén breathed deeply, turned back to the Evergreen Wood. He knew why Rinon acted the way he did with Fel'annár, despite the fact that they hardly knew each other. He remembered seeing them fighting in close proximity on the battlefield, knew they had spoken only briefly. Still, when Rinon looked at Fel'annár, he remembered his mother's plight and the anger would return. Even after everything that had happened, everything Fel'annár had done to show his loyalty, Rinon was still not able to disassociate him with the pain of those traumatic memories from his youth.

Of the few things Thargodén remembered of his former life of misery and aimless wandering, he did remember being hard-pressed to look at his own daughter. She reminded him of Canusahéi, of her departure and their broken bond. He had felt guilty then, but not anymore. He had put all that behind him. He had not been responsible, would not take the blame that was only Band'orán's, and perhaps Or'Talán's for not telling him of his plan to unite him with Lássira.

And then there was his father's last diary. He would ask Pan'assár for it later, so that he could read it and perhaps, fit together the last pieces of that puzzle. Or'Talán had not forsaken him, he knew that now, but why had he never told him that?

It suddenly occurred to him that there was one elf who may have answers to that puzzle.

Draugolé, ex-Royal Councillor. Disgraced follower of Band'orán, one of the most able minds that Thargodén knew.

And the most dangerous.

~

ERTHORON ADJUSTED HIS POSTURE, sitting under a mighty eucalyptus tree. It lent him some shade from the early morning sun. Beside him, Lorthil of Sen'oléi, a wooden board on his lap and over it, papers. Close by, an ink pot and in his hand, a quill.

"Do you believe Fel'annár will come today?" asked Lorthil.

"He has to. We've been demanding on him timewise, but we had to be. Our people are preparing to leave, even the warriors. They're restless, looking for direction, but we can't give it to them unless we have the undisputable evidence that our demands have been met. And every day that passes, they lose hope, while we lose their confidence. Soon, they will simply turn away, listen to us no longer."

Lorthil nodded. "Still, in hindsight, it was callous of us. Miren said he was blinded in the battle. Did you believe him when he said he could see?"

"No. We both saw how he came back from the forest. You know sometimes the battle seems like an age ago, but it's only eight days, Lorthil. Llyniel says he will regain his sight in time, but time is what we don't have."

"And that creature he mentioned..."

"What's one more threat to a people who have lived with them for decades? Surely it can't be as bad as the cruelty of Sand Lords we've had to deal with for so long." Erthoron paused. "I don't think this new threat is enough for our warriors to return. And in any case, it's not the Silvan Council of Elders that'll persuade our warriors to come back. It's the veteran captains, and only the Warlord can change *their* minds. But to do that, he needs time. He needs to journey into the villages, speak with them, allow them to know him and follow him if they will."

"That'll take weeks."

"Yes. Too many weeks. Our people will be long gone from this encampment by then."

They both worked quietly for a while before Erthoron broke the silence.

"Amareth was disappointed in us for treating Fel'annár the way we did."

"We deserved it, I suppose. It was all too easy to see him as the enemy. I know that he's not, but he doesn't seem to be protesting against Pan'assár's ongoing command of the army. It does him no favours."

Erthoron sighed. "And what if he's right not to? What if Pan'assár *has* changed? He was certainly instrumental in Band'orán's downfall, and he doesn't argue the return of the Warlord."

Lorthil stared hard at him before looking away and shrugging. "That would surprise us all then, wouldn't it?"

Erthoron supposed that it would, although especially their captains. But Amareth wouldn't forgive them any time soon, and he told Lorthil as much. The leader of Sen'oléi stared at his old friend, took his time before he asked his question.

"How long have you loved her, Erthoron?"

The Silvan leader started, turned to Lorthil and his knowing eyes.

"Since I saw her laughing with Berona over a loaf of bread that had slid from her basket. A pup had snatched it up and made away with it, only to trip and roll head over heels. She was fifty and I was ... well, older." He smiled fondly at the memory.

"I've never seen her laugh, not really. She seems cool and unmovable at times."

Erthoron was shaking his head. "That's her defence, Lorthil. She wasn't like that before. She was young, carefree, fun and mischievous. So very bright, too. But her promise to Lássira, the decisions she believed were right – they took a toll. She lost her youth, lost her family in a way. It almost became an obsession to her."

"And what now that Bulan has come?"

Erthoron nodded slowly. Lorthil was right. Amareth had not seen her mother or brother for fifty-three years. She had never met her niece. Yesterday, he had watched as she made towards them no sooner they had arrived at the stables. They had spoken for scant minutes, and then she had turned, walked away from them, face pale and subdued.

Later, he had asked her if she would return to them, try again. He remembered those heavy eyes, the slight shake of her head. Whatever had happened in those five minutes had not surprised her, had hurt her even though she had been expecting it.

Erthoron understood Bulan, damned him all the same for the suffering he caused Amareth. She'd had enough of that, deserved better, much better.

"It'll take time to mend that rift, Lorthil, if it's even possible. I wonder though, why he's come now. Is it for the warriors? Or perhaps he's come in search of Amareth, to mend what she broke all those years ago."

"No."

Erthoron and Lorthil turned where they sat, watched Narosén walk towards them, pass them and peer into the distance, as if there was something there that they couldn't see.

"Bulan has come for Fel'annár. He has come to meet the Ber'anor, his nephew."

~

MID-MORNING, and the Silvan Warlord walked across the busy courtyard, his hand-crafted armour a thing of beauty that drew the eye.

An emerald winked in the late summer sun, almost as bright as his own eyes that were no longer covered with a blindfold. With his step sure and confident, it was clear to all that he had, indeed, regained his sight, if not his ability to see colour.

Around him, The Company wore their usual uniforms, but after their promotions, Galadan, Idernon and Fel'annár would need a trip to the tailors. Still, the Silver Acorn in their foremost braids was a sign that they were no ordinary warriors, proof that Pan'assár had publicly recognised their deeds and lifted the ban on Honour Stones.

Stable hands led their mounts out into the open, and moments later, all save for Fel'annár sat in the saddle. They watched as Prince Handir walked towards them, two guards at his back.

Fel'annár stepped forward. "Good morning, Prince."

Handir was looking closely at his brother, eyes moving from one side of Fel'annár's face to the other. "It is true then. You can see?"

Fel'annár smiled, in spite of their impending visit, the importance of it.

"I can. Just don't ask me the colour of your cloak."

"Will the colour come back?"

"Llyniel believes that it will. Still, we'll have to see. But for now, this is more than enough, brother."

Handir nodded. "Are you well enough for this trip?"

"No." Fel'annár huffed and smiled at the same time. "But I have an agreement with Sontúr. I can ride, walk and talk, nothing more. That's all I need."

Handir smiled at him, clapped his brother's shoulder and shook it. Slinging his satchel over his chest, he mounted his horse carefully, waited for it to settle. By the time he was comfortable, Fel'annár was on his own horse, looking at him with a grin. Handir returned it ruefully. He had never been good with horses, even though his skill had improved since his journey to Tar'eastór and back.

Fel'annár raised his hand and together, The Company and Handir set off towards the gates.

"On the road again, eh Prince?" asked Fel'annár as they rode towards the city gates.

"I may even come to like it one day!" A soft breeze played with his hair and a ray of sunlight caught the unassuming silver crown he wore.

"Llyniel was at the encampment yesterday. She told me visitors arrived."

Handir glanced sideways at Fel'annár. "Warriors?"

"No. My mother's family. Her brother, her mother and a cousin."

Handir was surprised because he suddenly realised he knew so little of Fel'annár's family, except for Amareth, and their relationship was not close from what he had seen. "And how do you feel about that?"

"Worried for Amareth, I suppose. She hasn't seen her mother and brother for over fifty years."

Handir turned back to the fore, unsurprised that Fel'annár had not told him how *he* felt. "Did Llyniel meet them?"

"No. She was at the healing tents but apparently Amareth did go to them. Llyniel thinks they argued."

"About you? About why she never allowed you to meet them?"

"I don't know. Perhaps."

Handir knew he wouldn't get much more out of Fel'annár. Family was a difficult concept for him, one he wished his brother could overcome. "Whatever happens, Fel'annár, you must try to enjoy this meeting. Remember that the distance between them is not your fault."

All Handir got from Fel'annár was a thoughtful nod. Time to change the subject.

"Now that we carry the signed documents, Erthoron has no more arguments against returning to court. But the question is whether he and the others will be able to rally our warriors, persuade *them* to return."

"Lord Erthoron is an efficient leader, but he's not Dalú, and *he* is clearly opposed to serving under Pan'assár."

"Do you think our father should have replaced him? With Rinon or Turion?"

"No. Pan'assár is the best Commander General we have."

"Well, you will have to find a very convincing way of saying that to those warriors."

"I know. Pan'assár has been their enemy for so long, Handir. Our commander knows this, has set out to show them he has changed but they have to see that for themselves. And the only way to achieve that, is to return to barracks and give him that chance."

"And you will defend his command?"

"Yes. He stays or I relinquish mine."

Handir stared at his brother's profile, understood that this was Fel'annár's final gambit. If they resisted, he would tell them he would no longer be Warlord.

Interesting.

As they passed through the main gates, Fel'annár nudged his horse into a canter and for a while, they simply rode, enjoying the warming sun and the breeze on their faces.

The Silvan encampment was closer now, enough to see that it had shrunk on one side and grown on the other, where the wounded had been given shelter. The exodus back into the forest had already begun,

realised Handir. This really was their last chance at peace and coopera-
tion. If no agreements were reached with the troops, the damage would
be deeper even than when Band'orán had been alive.

Two mounted warriors were approaching at a canter and Fel'annár
raised his hand for The Company and Handir to stop.

Slowing to a walk, they came to a stop before the guards and Handir
observed them, followed their wandering gazes and their tight grip on
the reins.

"Welcome, Warlord."

Handir could see their surprise. They had thought the Warlord
blind, but it was plain now that he was not. His brother stared back at
them in the way he often did when he slipped into the role of commander. He was cool and strong, calm and yet imposing. They said Or'Talán
had been like that, and Fel'annár had certainly inherited that ability; he
was too young to have learned it from experience.

"The Elders await. We have been expecting you."

"Then lead the way, Lieutenant."

With a wide-eyed nod, the two guards wheeled their horses around
and trotted back to camp, the Warlord, a prince and The Company
behind them.

So FAR, so good, mused Fel'annár.

True, the guards had not greeted Handir as they should have, but
neither had they been rude.

At the stables, they dismounted and Fel'annár stood still, allowed the
gathering crowds a closer look. Those who had not seen Fel'annár
before marvelled at his resemblance to Or'Talán, whose name was still
respected. Others were silently angry, quietly curious as they stared at
the second prince of Ea Uaré.

They made towards the command tent, and the growing crowds
followed. The Company gathered closer around Handir, eyes alert for
the slightest hint of danger. But as the Silvan people began to notice the
Silver Acorns, worn as Honour Stones, the parallel lines in the Warlord's

collar and the Forest Emerald next to it, their hard stares slowly crumbled into frowns, raised eyebrows and rippled murmurs.

At their destination, the Council of Elders stood outside the tent, and with them, Captain Dalú, cool regard changing into dazed surprise as Fel'annár drew closer. They crossed gazes, a challenge in one, stubborn resistance in the other. Fel'annár was not wrong in his assumptions. Dalú was the one he had to convince, not the Silvan Elders. He would leave them to Handir and his scrolls and speak with Dalú as soon as protocol permitted.

Amareth was staring at Fel'annár too, surely for the same reasons as Dalú, but there was something else. There was an urgency about her, something she would warn him of.

"Welcome, Warlord. We have been waiting for your return." Erthoron and the others bowed and Fel'annár, Handir and The Company returned it.

"We're glad to return. We've escorted Prince Handir Ar Thargodén. He brings news from the king while I bring tidings from the Inner Circle."

"Then enter, take some refreshment. There is much to speak of," said Erthoron. Dalú passed him, held the tent flap open for the Elders and their visitors, and then entered, settling towards the back of the tent.

The Company positioned itself between Handir's back and the entrance, while Tensári lingered a distance behind Fel'annár. Silence soon settled over the room.

It was Amareth who spoke first.

"Your sight has returned, Lord?"

"It has – almost completely." Fel'annár looked at Erthoron, was glad that he didn't turn away.

"That is a relief," she breathed.

Fel'annár turned back to her. "That is an *understatement*, Lady."

The others chuckled and the tension relaxed a little, a moment Handir chose to begin his work.

"Lord Erthoron, venerable Council of Elders. I bring tidings from King Thargodén Ar Or'Talán, and his grateful thanks for your aid in the battle against our common enemy, one we now call the Battle of Brothers.

Those traitors who did not die have been detained and await trial in our dungeons, and the Restoration has begun in earnest. Legislation has been passed, is being implemented as we speak and to this end, I bring news."

Erthoron nodded, gestured to the long table and waited for everyone to be seated. Handir placed the two scrolls on the table where he knew the Silvan leader would sit. He himself occupied the chair on the other side of the table.

Neither Dalú nor Tensári sat, and when the table had settled, Handir leaned back, laced his fingers together and spoke.

"I bring you two missives. One is signed and sealed by the Royal Council and the king. In it, a new law is passed, one which states that our council must comprise of equal numbers of Alpine and Silvan councillors." Handir gestured to the scroll, watched as Erthoron took it, cracked the seal and read. He then passed it to Lorthil on his right.

"There are particulars to discuss, Lord Erthoron, but no conditions. The second missive is a royal decree, signed by Commander General Pan'assár and King Thargodén. General Fel'annár is the Silvan Warlord, in word and deed." Handir gestured to the second scroll and waited for Erthoron to read it.

"The Warlord is recognised, our army divided into two. A mountain and forest division, one commanded by General Turion, and the other by General Fel'annár. Commander General Pan'assár remains in his current role."

Handir held Erthoron's gaze, while Fel'annár glanced at Dalú, but turned back to the table when Erthoron spoke.

"Then although Fel'annár is Warlord, he must continue to take orders from Pan'assár?"

Erthoron's lack of protocol was not lost on any of them and Handir glanced sideways at Fel'annár, silent invitation for him to speak, and Fel'annár did.

"I take orders from *Commander* Pan'assár, Lord Erthoron, unless they are in some way detrimental to my people and then I will question them."

"And if he doesn't yield ... will you?"

Fel'annár leaned forward, curbed his anger at Erthoron. Even now when he had all he wanted, signed and sealed in only two days, just as he had promised, it was not enough.

"I am no puppet to be played by the Alpines, Lord Erthoron. But neither will I be played by the Silvans. You have what you wanted, what's fair. All of your demands have been met. Now, it's time to uphold your end of the bargain and leave the rest to *me*. I will speak to our warriors, explain this new army and I will tell them why Commander Pan'assár should remain. His presence or otherwise is a *military* affair, Lord." Fel'annár couldn't help one final glance at the still silent Dalú, standing close to the entrance. He needed to speak with him, allow him to speak his mind because if he didn't, he would never accept Pan'assár's command. He would never come back to barracks and if Dalú didn't return, no one would.

He was thankful that Handir pushed forwards.

"The Warlord is right. These are early days, but you have our promises that equality will be restored. It is time to come together, build a new Royal Council, a new army and prepare for the possibility of a new threat. Aria forbid this Nim'uán is coming to Ea Uaré but if it is, we must be prepared."

Fel'annár's heart sank when Dalú stepped forward and spoke for the first time.

"We've faced threats before, Prince, for as long as we've been arguing that we needed outposts, more warriors in the forest. The Silvan people have lived with the threat of battle for decades. This is nothing new to us. We've been alone in the defence of these lands for so long, now is no different." Dalú stared at Handir, and Fel'annár thought he hadn't finished. But Handir gave him no opportunity.

"That was Band'orán's doing, his and that treacherous Council he poisoned. But he is dead, Captain. There is no need for you to face this new enemy alone. Why would you, when help is freely offered?"

No one spoke for a while, each of them considering the prince's words. It was Amareth who eventually spoke.

"Prince Handir is right. Trust and faith are our best choice, given the circumstances. But I would hear the particulars, Prince. This monster that comes, how likely is it to invade our forest?"

"Lord Fel'annár will explain the details to your military leaders while

I can provide the particulars on the restructuring of our political system, if that is acceptable?"

Erthoron moved away from the table, gestured to the central firepit, around which large cushions lay on the ground. Fel'annár watched Handir rise, follow the leader and then sink down into one of them, unsure as to how he should arrange his legs. Fel'annár repressed a grin and then turned to the veteran Silvan.

"Captain Dalú?"

"Of course. This way, Warlord."

Fel'annár clapped Galadan on the shoulder, eyes gesturing towards the prince.

"We have him," he murmured.

Amareth stepped forward, but Fel'annár was already following Dalú from the tent, Tensári behind him. There was no time to warn him. All she could do was pray that Llyniel had told him who had come. Later, Fel'annár would surely ask her why she hadn't said anything, and she would tell him that she hadn't known. He wouldn't believe her, why would he? She had hidden him from his family for decades. She closed her eyes, briefly caught Erthoron's gaze from where he sat before Prince Handir and then joined them, resigned to Fel'annár's impending anger.

She had tried so hard to make him see that she loved him, that he was not merely a political tool. Yet with each passing day, she thought she was losing him just a little more.

5

SILVAN FIGHTERS

⌒

OUTSIDE THE COMMAND tent at the centre of the Silvan encampment, the people had not moved at all. But when Dalú and the Warlord emerged together with the Ari lieutenant and a Silvan warrior many knew were Tensári and Idernon, the whispers and murmurs began again.

They wondered if today would be remembered as the end of the Night of a Thousand Drums, if it would be marked in the Silvan Chronicles as the day equality returned to the Silvan people.

The prince was still inside with the Elders and now, they said Fel'annár would negotiate a return to barracks with their veterans. They were not wrong, and some followed Dalú and his guests to a nearby tent, while others stayed in the hope of news from the Elders.

At their new destination, Dalú held the flap to one side, waited for Fel'annár, Idernon and Tensári to enter, and then followed.

Standing beside a map-strewn table, were Lieutenants Salo and Henú, together with two captains Fel'annár did not recognise.

Fel'annár nodded and smiled at the two young lieutenants who had proved themselves in battle against Band'orán's renegade Kah Warriors.

He liked them, thought that any resistance to Pan'assár's ongoing command would not come from them but from the veterans.

"Will you introduce us, Captain Dalú?"

"Of course. This here is Captain Amon, just recently returned from Oran'Dor where he was stationed unnecessarily by General Huren."

Fel'annár nodded, watched the Silvan captain salute him.

"This is Captain Benat of the Grey Bear. Likewise, needlessly stationed to the north-east."

"Captain."

"Warlord."

Wary, they were as shocked at his appearance as they were unsure of him. They didn't know him save for the hearsay that would surely have reached them. But Fel'annár knew their names, legendary captains who had been loyal to Or'Talán, two of the few Silvans who still held their chairs at the Inner Circle.

Fel'annár introduced his two companions and then turned back to Dalú, ready to begin his explanations, but he was interrupted by shouted greetings from outside. He frowned, turned to the entrance.

"Excuse me," said Dalú with a nod. He left the tent but was soon back.

He was not alone.

Beside Dalú, a taller warrior stood in the uniform of a captain and yet no symbols rested on *his* high collar. Fel'annár studied the features, the brown hair and the bright, almost amber eyes. The structure of his face, the slant of his eyelids and the cut of his jaw, so similar to Amareth. And then his eyes strayed to the two spears that jutted far out over his left shoulder. This was surely Bulan, his mother's brother.

His uncle.

Fel'annár took a tentative step forward and Dalú, Amon and Benat watched in silence. They knew it was the first time that uncle and nephew would meet.

"Captain Bulan," said Fel'annár, noting the momentary crease of his uncle's brow, his widening eyes and open mouth. He would be thinking of his resemblance to Or'Talán, perhaps wondering how he knew who he was.

"Your spears." Fel'annár gestured to the weapons on his back, answering his uncle's unspoken question, the one that seemed to have stuck at the back of his tongue.

"*She* has told you of them?" Fel'annár hadn't expected that strong, northern accent.

"If *she* is Amareth, then yes. Well met, Bulan."

The captain's scrutiny was plain and Fel'annár allowed it. He reminded himself that this elf was the only one who had fought for him. He had begged Amareth to allow them contact and she had refused. Bulan had wanted to know his nephew and Fel'annár felt – *privileged*. Yet the way he had referred to Amareth brought mixed emotions. He wanted to ask, talk, listen, know this elf but there was no time, not here, not now.

"I would speak with you later."

Bulan nodded. "As would I. I have questions."

"Yes. Questions," mirrored Fel'annár, ripped his eyes away from his uncle, reminded himself of what he had come here to achieve. "Captain Dalú. Four captains are all we have?"

"Yes. Although technically, Bulan here is no longer a captain. Yet even if he were, we have no intention of serving under Pan'assár, Warlord."

"*Commander* Pan'assár, Captain."

Dalú nodded curtly but didn't look sorry, and neither did he rectify.

"How many lieutenants?"

"Thirty-two. Salo and Henú you already know."

"Warriors?"

"Close to two hundred here at the encampment, more still in the forest."

"Four captains, thirty-two lieutenants ... how many are eligible for a higher command?"

Salo and Henú shared hopeful glances.

"Difficult to say, I ..."

"I want a list of all lieutenants, all warriors who show the promise of command. How long, Captain Dalú?"

"A moment ... two, three days."

"I want a list of women who wish to serve, and I want the names of all those who are known Listeners. I want to know which of our warriors have specific skills and talents. Masters of the bow or blade, hand-to-hand, trackers, whatever. Do we have warriors skilled in woodwork, metallurgy?"

"Lord ... that is a long list of ... *lists*."

Fel'annár's lips twitched, watched as Dalú raked a hand through his hair and then Bulan as he stared unabashedly. This technique he had seen Handir use was effective. He pushed on.

"What are they for?" asked former captain Bulan.

"I told you things would change, captains. I am preparing the creation of a new army with *two* divisions. Mountain and Forest. The Forest Division will be commanded by me."

The captains looked interested, but Dalú stepped towards him, barely repressed anger on his face. He had clearly wanted to speak of it before in the command tent, and now that he could, he gave free rein to his opposition.

"And Pan'assár is still in command. Not much of a *change*, Warlord. Don't get too excited, captains." He jumped when Fel'annár all but cut him off.

"*Stop* this, Dalú. It's not helping. Your prejudice is not the way forward. I'm asking you to trust me to make this happen. If it doesn't then I know you'll tell me that you *told* me so, but until then, as a captain under your Warlord, you are beholden to at least *try*. Like you, many of our warriors will feel the same, and if we cannot change that mindset then we're doomed even before we begin. It has to stop. We must stop it, before it's too late and we're overrun by the enemy."

"What enemy?" asked Bulan, but he was ignored.

"I won't accept submission in exchange for defence, Warlord."

"Do I look like *I* will accept it? For the sake of Aria step out of this circle of hatred. If Pan'assár has done it, then so can *you*."

Dalú's nostrils flared, but he held his tongue and Fel'annár's eyes travelled from Amon to Benat, to Salo and then Henú. They said nothing and he chanced another glance at Bulan, wondered what *he* was thinking, whether he agreed with Dalú. But his expression was guarded and Fel'annár wondered how old he was. He was suddenly reminded of Galadan.

"You were wrong back there, Dalú. This threat is not the same as what our people have suffered these past years. You've faced marauding

Sand Lords and Deviant packs, but you haven't faced a Nim'uán, Captain. I have, in Tar'eastór. It almost killed me, would have if it hadn't been for the Lestari. It took an army of thousands and an entire forest to defeat it. Believe me, if it's coming to my forest, in our current state, we will be overrun. We will be slaughtered, Silvan, Alpine and Ari alike."

The captains looked concerned, Bulan included, but Dalú pushed on.

"And the same Commander General who turned his back on us is suddenly repentant? It's all talk, Warlord. He does it to cling to the power his position brings. He does it to keep his dignity. He couldn't give a flying shite for my warriors."

"Aria but you're a stubborn fool, Dalú." Fel'annár breathed deeply, turned away for a moment to gather his thoughts. Facing them once more, he willed Handir's face into his mind, remembered how he handled situations such as these.

"The Silvan people have spent a life-time raising me as their Warlord, unbeknownst to me. Tell me, what was that for, Dalú?" He spoke to the veteran, but his eyes had not left Bulan. "Let me tell you that was not easy – for anyone – but if you won't listen to me then it will have all been for nothing. It's time for you to trust me, to follow me and I will lead us to equality in this army. Band'orán is dead, the trees killed him. The future has changed and so must you. All of you."

Fel'annár's gaze travelled from Dalú to Idernon, and then Amon and Benat. Finally, they landed on Bulan. Wide, intense eyes, his uncle's shuttered expression was suddenly open, and in its place, was what looked to Fel'annár like fascination, and a hint of confusion.

Fel'annár turned back to Dalú, stepped closer. "I need to trust every single leader in this new army. Every single captain that sits at the Inner Circle, their Silvan houses embossed on their chairs, must have this one thing clear in their minds: we serve the people of this land, not the Silvans of this land. And if that is not clear in your mind, then none of you will ever sit on that chair. So, tell me, captains. What will you do?"

Dalú breathed noisily, looked to the ground and then back at the Warlord. "I understand your words, merit them. But you more than most, know how much recent times have impacted on our fighters, how much suffering Pan'assár has caused." Now that his anger had abated,

Dalú's eyes were no longer frigid but full of feeling and emotion. It was almost as if he were pleading with Fel'annár to understand. He was a father to his warriors, a Captain with a capital C.

"Those are the words of a Silvan, yes. They are the words of one who has suffered that injustice, the same injustice I have suffered. I am *The Silvan*, remember? You *are* right. But Dalú ... you're a *captain*, and a captain leads warriors in more than just combat. Do you think we have time to come to terms with the injustice? Do you think we must wait for them to bow and beg pardon for it? Or should we strive to understand, command with our example, show them in the best and most visible way we can, that they were wrong?" Fel'annár walked away from Dalú, stopped before Amon and Benat.

"As we are, we are vulnerable to the enemy; to Sand Lords and Deviants, to even worse things like the Nim'uán. We need unity and the only way to achieve that is to bring Silvan and Alpine warriors together. *We* are the commanders. It falls to *us* to show our fighters that this is what they should do. The Warrior Code is the only thing that should guide us. Leave the politics to princes and kings, Dalú. You and I will keep our people safe, and we will do everything and anything to achieve that, on equal terms at last."

Fel'annár could almost see their minds turning around and around. After a while, Dalú spoke, quietly, the indignant fire behind his words lessened but not gone.

"This new division, units and contingents?

"I want archers with long and short bows and mounted snipers. I want Rangers with contingents of Listeners, trackers and specialists in close combat. The details are still to be discussed between us and then presented to the Commander General. This division would be under my command, and within that command, my unit captains. Dalú ... we can have those outposts, where we know they should be. We can erect field halls so that we don't have to carry our injured for days. We can have engineers inside the forest, so that they can rebuild what's destroyed and not have to wait months. We can have all this, Dalú. All we must do is instil in our warriors the need to work *with* the Alpines, not against them. There will be no returning to the past, not while I am Warlord. You have my promise. I am accountable to you in this."

Silence enveloped the captains, each thinking, weighing the odds, their anger warring with reason, and in some cases, the glimmer of hope.

"The captains and I will speak," said Dalú. "What you ask is no easy task, Warlord. Pan'assár's continued command of this army is, perhaps, the only reason I cannot give you an answer now, and even if I accept, I will not order my warriors to do the same."

Fel'annár watched Dalú, allowed his eyes to drift sideways to the others, to Bulan.

"I never said it would be easy. It won't. Even should you return to barracks, avoiding conflict amongst the troop will be the hardest part, not whether Pan'assár will accede to this or to that. Heed me on this. Prejudice runs deep and, strangely, it lives on both sides of the wall. It must be managed, captains, and it falls to us to make them understand what is at stake. United in equality against our enemy or divided and vanquished."

"Is the king aware of the obstacle that Pan'assár is to our return? Are you sure he will not reconsider?"

"The king will not reconsider, Dalú, because I will never ask him to. If our warriors refuse to accept Pan'assár's command, then I will relinquish mine. You can choose another as your Warlord."

Dalú was shocked, stepped backwards, while the other captains turned disbelieving eyes on Fel'annár.

"You can't do that. The warriors look to you for command," said Dalú.

"Only a handful know me. These two hundred that are left. The bulk of our fighters never came."

"No. But they know of you. Your very existence brings hope to them."

"Then that is something you must consider as you speak, captains. Those are the stakes, and should you agree to return, then it will be my responsibility to prove to you that Pan'assár will not be a hindrance to this army. I won't allow him to treat anyone unjustly, Dalú but I can't prove that to you. What I can do is show you, in the field, but for that to happen, you must give me the opportunity. And so, I ask for your faith, your belief that I can make this work."

Fel'annár knew he wasn't going to get an immediate answer, Dalú had already told him that. There was only one thing left for him to say.

"Come into the city tomorrow. Meet me at the gates at sundown, and then come with me to the Inner Circle where Pan'assár will speak. Listen to him with all these reasons in mind and then come back, Dalú. Bring our captains and our lieutenants. Bring our warriors back to barracks so that we can start anew, so that we can make this army what *we* want it to be, not a self-serving institution where command is nothing but a reason to boast power and renown. It must be a protecting sword before a frightened child. It must be a warning hand against any who would dare harm our people, a blanket on a cold night. That is our job, the oath we took, one we can finally carry out with dignity. All you need to do is trust me."

The silence was back.

"I make no promises, Warlord. Except for one. We will speak today, decide what we must do, with the welfare of our people as our driving force."

Fel'annár nodded, stopped himself from speaking again because silence need not be filled with useless repetition but used to drive home one's reasoning. Handir had once told him that, and Fel'annár had seen him do it.

"Do so, Captain. By the grace of Aria, tomorrow, the Inner Circle will see the return of our Silvan fighters. As for my promise to you, it is this: I'll make them proud to serve in this new army. However few may come, others will join them, a day later, a week later, months even. All I need is a sign that the warriors of Ea Uaré are with their Warlord, not against him because that is what it comes down to in the end, Captain."

They shared glances, cautious optimism from some, veiled scepticism from others. Fel'annár had done all he could for now. He turned to Idernon, nodded, saw his friend's approval, felt Tensári's presence behind him.

"I would walk around the camp while our prince finishes his talks with the Elders. Will you accompany me, Captain Bulan?"

Bulan snapped out of his musings, nodded more to himself than his nephew and then walked towards him.

"I'm no longer a captain, Warlord, but yes, I will accompany you." Bulan's tone did not reflect the trepidation in his mind. He had come here to meet Fel'annár and instead he had met the Silvan Warlord. Now, he had the chance to speak with his nephew at last, but try as he might,

Bulan could not order his thoughts. There were too many questions, too many years between them. He was too shocked at Fel'annár's similarity to the great king, his features enhanced by the legacy of Lássira. He was too taken aback by the mastery of his speech and clarity of purpose.

Warlord, captains and lieutenants left the tent. Outside, Dalú, Benat and Amon saluted and then watched as Fel'annár and Bulan left with Idernon and Tensári a short distance behind.

For a while there was nothing but contemplative silence. How does one ford the bridge between Warlord and nephew, wondered Bulan. He didn't know, and they soon came to the pavilion where the injured Silvan warriors were being tended to. They ducked inside and Bulan allowed his eyes to adjust to the gloom. Raised pallets lay on both sides of the rectangular structure, and down the middle, there were tables laden with mortars, jars, liquids and cloths. There was a fire over which various healers sat hunched in a close circle. Some were mixing oils and creams, others winding clean bandages while some rested after a long night. Their heads turned to watch the four warriors from afar.

Fel'annár turned to the first bed, looked down upon a half-dazed warrior. At the headboard, sat another warrior, eyes cool and steady. Fel'annár crouched down, forearms resting on his knees while Bulan stood behind him.

"How bad is it?" murmured his nephew.

"He'll make it. Although in what state we don't know."

"You're a friend?"

"His brother."

Bulan could hear the hostility in his tone, wondered how Fel'annár would react to it – whether he would understand.

"Did you fight too?"

"Yes. I fought because *you* asked it of me."

Fel'annár stared back at the warrior, and when he spoke, his tone was steady and reassuring.

"We won." Fel'annár didn't look away and neither did the warrior.

"Did we?"

Fel'annár smiled and Bulan thought that he understood. All this warrior needed was to know that it had been worth it. That something good had come of their sacrifice.

"Yes. Yes we did. We have changed things, warrior. You will see that soon, see what you fought for." Fel'annár nodded, didn't wait for the warrior to answer him and Bulan thought him wise not to. Fel'annár then went on to stop and talk briefly with the other bed-ridden warriors. He asked them questions, they answered and with every visit, their tone seemed lighter, more enthusiastic. From afar, the healers continued to watch in silence, and from beside Fel'annár, Bulan stared at the fifty-three-year-old. He should have been out with the novices, talking about weapons, about patrols, about the enemy and about warm nights in the forest. Whatever he had expected to find on this journey, it was not this. The boy was of an age with Vasanth, but he could not reconcile that with the elf he followed from bed to bed. Here was a Warlord, a leader, natural commander with the honed body of one far more experienced in the martial arts, he knew from the way he walked, the way he held himself, and grey sash around his waist that marked him as a Kah Warrior.

But it was the parallel lines of a general and the green wink of the Forest Emerald that especially drew his attention. For any Silvan warrior, becoming a general in this army was an unreachable dream. Yet Fel'annár had said that he would give it all up, in defence of Pan'assár, the very reason Bulan had left the army, turned his back on his dream. Was it possible that the Alpine commander general had indeed changed, for reasons he had yet to understand?

With their visit over, they ducked out of the pavilion and Bulan turned to Fel'annár.

"Will you accompany me and meet your grandmother, your cousin?"

Fel'annár peered into the distance, at the largest tent where Handir would be debating with the Elders. He couldn't see much but he reckoned there would be more movement and noise had the prince already finished. He turned to Bulan, still not quite accustomed to looking at a male face which resembled his mother's – the Silvan side of himself. He nodded, tried to hide the apprehension he felt. His mother's mother stood somewhere close by.

"I don't have much time, Bulan. But we can at least meet."

Bulan gestured for Fel'annár to follow, eyes falling on Tensári, not for the first time. Together, the four made through the sea of tents until they were almost at the perimeter. Bulan ducked inside a tent and Fel'annár and Tensári followed, leaving Idernon outside to guard them.

There, at the very centre of the room, a short woman stood and behind her, a young warrior.

"Fel'annár, this is Alei, your grandmother."

Those words sounded so foreign, so unlikely. He didn't know her and yet he did. Gods but her eyes – *his eyes* – they were Bulan's too only his uncle's were amber like Amareth's. Alei's eyes were a vibrant green he had only ever seen in a mirror, and in his dreams. He was fascinated, couldn't look away, started when she moved towards him. Perhaps she had understood that his feet would not move. It was hard enough getting one word out of his mouth.

"Aba."

He watched her slow smile and her hands as they came up and took his head between them. She couldn't reach his forehead, but he bent forwards, leaned into her kiss on his brow, closed his eyes for a moment.

He saw his mother, smiling down at him as a babe.

When he opened them once more, she was staring back at him, as if she could see what he could in his mind. But her brow creased, and her hands dropped away from his face. She stepped backwards, glanced at her son who was watching carefully.

The young warrior stepped forward. Fel'annár could see her resemblance to her father, but her hair was a striking blue-black. Strong features, forbidding eyes for one so young and then he wondered just how young she was.

"This is my only child, Vasanth."

She stepped forward, choosing to salute him rather than greet him as family, eyes roving over his symbols of office. He could see her dreams in her eyes, glowing like fire. He had looked like that once, before recruit training when all he had wanted was to be a captain.

He returned her salute. "Vasanth. You are a warrior?"

"I will be. If you will allow it." It wasn't a question. It was a challenge, one Fel'annár had already decided upon.

"You are allowed, Vasanth. After tomorrow, I will call on all those who wish to join our new army, male and female."

The fire in her eyes flared, as surely as her nostrils but she didn't smile. Instead, she nodded, stepped sideways and Fel'annár turned back to Alei and then Bulan.

"I have to go. I have temporary rooms on the last floor of the palace. You are welcome there any time. I would have you meet my bonded, Llyniel."

Alei's eyes strayed to Fel'annár's bonding braid. She smiled.

"Will you heed my call and come to the Inner Circle tomorrow?"

"I don't know. Dalú and I must discuss it. As for myself, I will not go against the wishes of our warriors, but I will encourage them to try. However, I admit that I can't understand why you think Pan'assár deserves a chance to right the wrongs he has committed against our fighters. I left all this behind, Fel'annár, because of him, because of how he treated my warriors."

"But you've been away, Bulan. Pan'assár *does* deserve it. I've fought at his side, saved him as he's saved me. I know the reasons for his fall, and I've seen how he's picked himself up, how he's sworn to prove himself, to not stop until those very Silvan warriors he once debased, salute him, not for protocol but for respect."

"We shall see, then. But I'm not sure there is thread enough to mend the tear."

"I suppose we must pull from both sides then. But Pan'assár should not be your primary concern, Bulan. The protection of our Silvan lands is what is at stake here. The Nim'uán is coming, sooner or later, to Ea Uaré or Tar'eastór, perhaps even Araria. The safety of our people must take precedence over history, even over pride, Bulan."

The veteran warrior stared back at his nephew, his struggle all too clear to Fel'annár.

"I'm glad you've come, Bulan." He wanted to say more but he had to stop. Gods but he *was* glad. What he would have given to have found them before, when he had been a lad who dreamt of having a family like everyone else.

But he hadn't. He shook himself back into the present and the task at hand.

"I pray I will see you tomorrow, Bulan. Alei, Vasanth. We'll speak soon."

Alei cocked her head to one side and Fel'annár rather thought she was listening to something. Was she a Listener? he wondered, but no – he would surely have known.

He bowed to them and then left, Tensári behind.

Bulan turned to his mother, but her eyes were still on the door.

"Zéndar stirs in my mind."

Bulan had never understood how his mother could feel his father so acutely. She was not Ari'atór; Zéndar was her bonded, not her Connate. And yet he would never think to gainsay her.

"How so?"

Alei's eyes focussed on nothing but they were not dull. They were alive with some new light. "There is a power in him. It speaks to Zéndar."

"I don't understand."

"No. And neither do I." Alei's words were nothing but a whisper, but they echoed in Bulan's mind and would not stop until he met his nephew once more. Never in a thousand ages had Bulan imagined Fel'annár like this. The face of Or'Talán, the eyes of Lássira. The heart of a warrior and the right of a prince in the eyes of the Silvans. But Alei was right, there was something in his gaze.

It was something far older than *he* was.

FEL'ANNÁR, Idernon and Tensári made for the command tent where Handir and the rest of The Company stood outside in the presence of the Elders.

"Ready, Prince?"

"Ready, Warlord." Handir's eyes strayed to the crowds behind and then back to his brother. He had questions, Fel'annár knew that look, but it was neither the time nor place to ask them. He bid the Silvan Elders farewell while Fel'annár made for Amareth.

"I'm sorry child." It was almost a whisper. "There was no time to warn you." Her eyes told him she thought he would not believe her, but he did.

"It's alright. Llyniel had already told me. Have you spoken?"

"Not so much with my brother, but a little with my mother and my niece. But tell me, how did it go? Were they kind to you?"

Fel'annár couldn't help the smile that escaped him. "Yes, they were more than kind. Amareth ... I would stay longer, but I can't. Tomorrow is the Inner Circle ceremony and I believe you and the Elders are invited to a private council with the king."

"We are."

"Will you come?"

"Yes, the Elders at least, will come. It's decided. But whether our warriors accompany us remains to be seen. We know they'll not heed us, not in this. We've no sway over them but Dalú does; you do."

"And Bulan, from what I can see. He's well-respected."

"Yes, by the older warriors, those who still remember when he sat on his chair at the Inner Circle."

"The days ahead won't be easy for you, will they?"

She smiled, shook her head. "No. But the distance had to end, eventually. We must talk, understand one another if we can."

Fel'annár nodded. "Come to my quarters at the palace before your council with the king, tell me if you've made progress."

Her hand brushed down the side of his arm, aware that the others were waiting for him, and that Bulan was watching keenly.

Saz'nár finished buckling on his ornate vambraces. Reaching for his cloak, he tied it around his neck, pulled up his hood and slipped his sword into its harness at his hip. A curved dagger sat at his waist, one he never used. It was a symbol of that which was pure in his blood. A symbol passed down to him by his mother. She had given him eternity, but his father had given him royalty. He had given him *strength*.

One hand rose to his chest. Below the simple tunic, his most prized possession lay. He reached into a breast pocket and retrieved it, just as he did every morning before he faced the troop beyond the tent he shared with Key'hán.

He smiled down at it. Bright blue eyes softening with fond memories of a woman he remembered little of. All he knew was that he loved her, wished she had stayed with them. She had feared the consequences of her actions, thought her sons would rot away until life was no longer sustainable. And so, she had taken her own.

She hadn't known that her children were Nim'uán, not Deviant.

A familiar wave of pity, the rising tide of frustration, and then anger. He put the sketch away, in the safest place he knew, in a place no one ever visited, no one except his brothers and the memory of his tragic mother. Close to his heart.

He stepped out into the brilliant morning sun. It was still chilly, but in an hour, it would be unbearably hot. A group of Sand Lords approached, bowed low. Their shifty eyes told Saz'nár that something had happened.

"General. We have important news from the borders of Ea Uaré." The captain's voice was deep, whispery with overuse.

"Speak," came the deep, velvety smooth voice of the Nim'uán general. The contrast was a powerful one, as evident as the differences in their physique, not that Sand Lords ever showed much of themselves.

"A messenger from Port Helia. One of our lizards escaped its confines some weeks back at the cliffs. It managed to swim out a fair distance, enough for a group of locals to spot it."

"Are they dead?"

"No, sir. They saw it from afar. It was in the water. We believe they may have mistaken it for a Rainbow Jumper."

"*May* ... our warriors did not intercept these witnesses?"

"No sir. Our messenger can offer more information. He is resting after his long journey."

"Bring him."

"Sir." The Sand Lord bowed, shared a glance with his fellow warrior, duty and fear warring with empathy for their unwitting companion.

Moments later, the messenger stood respectfully before the Nim'uán, just as his twin brother came to stand at his side. Key'hán was imposing, but not as much as his brother in the south. Gra'dón struck terror in all who set eyes upon him.

"Why?" asked Saz'nár.

"Sir?"

"Why did my brother send *you* to tell me this?"

The messenger paled, and then bowed low, exposing the crown of his head for much longer than was necessary. "I was in charge of the operation, General. I feel sure that they ..."

"Why did you not kill them?"

"They were far away. Had we hunted them, the risk of exposure seemed greater than the possibility that those locals knew what they had seen."

"It was a bad decision."

The messenger opened his mouth to speak but couldn't. Saz'nár was no longer before him but the booted feet of his friend Malark. He didn't understand. His last vision of this world was a cloth someone placed over his head, his lips working but not producing the last words in his head.

Where am I?

Malark stood, turned to the general, could not meet his eyes. "Stake it up for the scavengers, as a reminder to our warriors. Failure is not acceptable in this army."

"General." Malark saluted and then grabbed the severed head and left to do his bidding, the cloth he had placed over it falling away.

Saz'nár cast his eyes over the silent sea of troops. Soon, they would continue their march southwards. Just a few days more and then they would veer west so that the Ararian border guard would not see them. The first trees would come soon after and then stealth would no longer be possible. All they needed was a few more days and after that, it didn't matter how fast the elves could give the warning. The Nim'uán twins and their invading army of Sand Lords would occupy the forest before any elven army could stand against them. And then the Deviants would come.

Abiren'á, the Silvan capital of old, before the colonisation. They called it a blessed place outside Araria because one in every ten children born there was Ari.

Ari'atór, Spirit Warrior, Spirit Herder. Bane of his existence, Saz'nár would smash them all to pieces. Ruin their bodies and their families, crush them into the ground and watch their suffering. And then, when Abiren'á was theirs and water could be channelled northwards to his allies, they would march upon the king's city of stone.

And then Gra'dón would come.

The forest would be theirs, a home at last, and from their stronghold in Abiren'á, a new road would begin. Not long, not short, but a warring road, to Araria and beyond, a destination that should never have been denied his family.

Valley and the Source would be open to the Nim'uán at last.

6

A DANGEROUS MIND

~

WHILE FEL'ANNÁR and Handir were at the Silvan encampment, Thargodén swapped his robes of office for a calf-length tunic and breeches. With his crown on his head, intricate braids of office, rank and status along the back and sides, he strode down the great stairway, to the third level below ground where the dungeons lay.

They were full.

At the bottom of the stairs, the duty officer snapped to attention. "My King."

"Lieutenant. I am here to see Draugolé."

The warrior shared an alarmed look with the two guards behind Thargodén. He was considered one of the most dangerous prisoners, not for his skill at arms but for his acute intelligence, his ability to manipulate others.

"You will allow us to escort you of course."

"No. Thank you. My guards will be outside. I will leave the door open."

"Sire, I do not think it wise."

"Indulge me."

"Of course, my King." The duty guard bowed, unhooked a large set of keys from his belt and made down the central aisle. On either side, thick iron doors with nothing but a small, barred window, through which he could see some of the prisoners. He vaguely recognised some of them, even their voices as they called out to him, pleaded for mercy, claimed innocence.

But Thargodén was unmoved.

At the end of the aisle, they turned right and at the very end of that aisle was Draugolé's cell, out of earshot and sight, isolated from the rest of the prisoners in case he should mastermind some plan and escape from where no one had before.

The heavy bolt slid sideways, and the door groaned inwards. The king's two guards remained outside the open door, shared a look of trepidation as their hands came up to rest on the hilts of their swords.

It was dark save for a single candle, perched on a desk at which an elf sat, bent over a book. Thargodén stepped closer, the clack of his boots echoing off the damp walls.

Draugolé.

Gone were his robes of office, the opulent brocades and silks and the bejewelled collar of a Royal Councillor. It made the elf look smaller, almost gaunt.

"Why have you come?" It was nothing but a murmur, voice soft and beguiling.

"Perhaps I shouldn't have. They say you are a dangerous elf."

"I am ... not in my element. Here in the silence, I am harmless, Thargodén."

There were no windows in this place of punishment and so Thargodén sat upon a stone ledge along the back of the cell and Draugolé watched him from where he continued to sit at his desk.

"What are you reading?"

"Cor'hidén. His treatise on advanced rhetoric and semiotics. And you, Thargodén? What are you reading these days?"

There was irony in the question, enough to banish the feelings of pity that had assailed him just moments before. "My father's journal. Or'Talán's final account of his life, up until his death at the Battle Under the Sun."

Draugolé closed his book, slid sideways on his simple wooden chair so that he faced the king. "I see. You must be pleased to learn that he wanted to help you."

"You knew that?"

"I should. I have read it."

Thargodén stood slowly, mind scrambling to keep up with what Draugolé had said. "You knew Band'orán conspired to kill my father and still, you followed him. Have you no scruples?"

Draugolé smiled humourlessly. "Very few. Sulén had that journal for many years, said it was his guarantee against Band'orán, should he ever turn against him. Sulén was always a fool. Is he here, in the dungeons?"

"He's dead. He was killed by Deviants and then mutilated along with his gutless son, Silor. Their heads were decorating the path to the Glistening Falls."

A slight pause. "Ah. Well, that's one problem less for you then, isn't it?"

"True, but *your* problem remains, Draugolé. You know the penalty for high treason."

"I do. And I know that it is in your hands to grant exile or death, as you see fit."

"That is right. Dinor and Bendir were executed by the forest. Not the cleanest of deaths and yet that would be a fitting end for you. Still, I suppose your willingness to help me in my investigations may prove pivotal in the decision I must one day make."

Draugolé stared back at him from his seat at his desk, back hunched over, long black cloak hanging about him. It made him look like a bat, thought Thargodén.

"If I can be of help."

"You can, if you so choose. Of course, I understand you may still be loyal to Band'orán."

"I am loyal to no one except myself, Thargodén. Band'orán was ill, poisoned by circumstance and time, by the love of a woman he could never have and the disproportionate fame of his brother."

"You followed him."

"I followed fame and wealth. I followed the promise of power. Band'orán would have been a good king, but he would not have been able to rule without me at his side. He knew that. Speak to Barathon. He followed his father for who he was, not me. He will tell you of the unpredictable nature of his father."

"Barathon is dead. He was strangled by his own father."

Draugolé stood, too fast for it to be a casual move. He was disturbed, for the first time since Thargodén had come into the cell. That smooth, expressionless façade had utterly cracked, and a hint of horror pulled at Draugolé's eyes and lips. The king was fascinated, moved closer to him.

"You liked the boy."

Draugolé clenched his jaw. "I *pitied* him. Always grovelling, seeking his father's attention, putting his foot in it and looking to me to get him out of the hole he invariably found himself in."

"You do not fool me. I can see that you liked him. Did you protect him from his father then?"

Draugolé turned away. "I tried. But my desire for power was stronger than the fondness I felt for him. My only regret is perhaps telling Band'orán of his son's misgivings. Barathon knew his father was going to kill you. He came to me to ask my advice, about what he should do. I told Band'orán."

"And Band'orán strangled him for it. Do you feel guilty?"

Draugolé didn't answer and he shuffled over to the far wall, his back to the king. After a while he spoke.

"He was just one more victim of your uncle's scheming."

"Who else fell before him?"

Silence.

"Draugolé?"

"You know who."

Thargodén steeled himself, stood tall. He wouldn't falter.

"Say it."

"Lássira Ara Zéndar of Abiren'á." Draugolé turned back to Thargodén, waiting for the inevitable question.

"Did he kill her himself?"

"No, no. All I know is that he used his contacts in Tar'eastór, hired the best his money could buy. The assassin was to kill her and the child. We later realised only half of the deed had been carried out. Of course by then, it was too late."

"Is there anyone left who may know the identity of the assassin?"

"Hard to say. Here, no. In Tar'eastór, perhaps one of Sulén's collaborators would have contracted the assassin. You would be better off asking them."

"How do I know you are speaking the truth?"

"You do not."

Thargodén nodded slowly, made towards Draugolé so that he could see his eyes.

"As you have read the journal, you know that my father planned to reveal his brother's treachery, was waiting only for the right moment in which to do so. But then the Battle Under the Sun was looming and he went away to war. What do you know of that?"

Draugolé held the king's gaze with surprising ease. "I know everything. And if I were to guess, I would say that you want to know *why* ... why he did not tell you that his prohibition of your love for the Silvan woman was a simple ruse. You want to know why he left you thinking he was cruel. You want to know that he *loved* you, that he did not betray you."

Thargodén stared back at Draugolé, a warning in his glittering eyes. The ex-councillor smiled softly. "Is that not what we all want? To know that we are loved? That we are valued? Band'orán wanted that, went mad for it. Barathon wanted it, was murdered for it. And then you ..." Draugolé shuffled closer to the king, cocked his head to one side, unbraided hair sliding forwards over his shoulder, like a spreading oil stain.

"He wrote a letter, gave it to Lord Ileian in confidence. He told him that should he die in battle, that he was to give it to his son."

"Lord Ileian?" Thargodén was wracking his mind, remembering that fatidic day in which his father's Royal Councillor had told him Or'Talán was dead. There had been no mention of a letter. "He was corrupt?"

"He was of like mind with Band'orán and myself. He was my predecessor at your uncle's side."

Thargodén looked away, mind working but Draugolé was one step in front of him.

"Just as Sulén inherited Or'Talán's journal from Ileian, it is entirely possible that the letter also passed to his son. Of course, Sulén may have burned it, but my guess is that he would keep it, as leverage should he need something from Band'orán or someone else."

"It would make sense," murmured the king.

"Yes, it would. Perhaps it is sitting in some dusty old chest, hidden away like ancient treasure." Draugolé made his way back to his small desk and the fluttering candle.

"Have you read that too? The letter?" Thargodén could feel his indignant anger rising. Outrage at the violation, of such a crude invasion of his privacy, and once more he could hear that subtle undertone of irony, one Thargodén knew Draugolé used purposefully.

Draugolé shook his head. "Now that you have the information you wanted, do with me what you will." He sat in his chair once more, stared at the closed book before him. It didn't last long. He turned to the king, just in time to see his final stride towards him. A fist bunched at his collar, strong arm pulling him up and then pushing him back.

"You try my patience, traitor. Even here, with the prospect of shameful death over your head, you speak to me in riddles and half-truths. You laugh at a son who loved his father and was loved back. Tell me, do you know what it is to love? Is there anyone in this world that could possibly love one such as you?"

The king glared into Draugolé's wide eyes. He shoved him back against the wall, enjoyed the jolt, the thud of his head against stone. He turned away, took a deep breath and willed his ire to settle.

On the other side of the cell, he turned, observed Draugolé from afar. That neutral veil of intelligence, of untouchability had gone and, in its place, poorly veiled anger.

"I will find out what happened with that letter. And should I discover that you have lied to me or, that you have withheld the truth, your sentence will be death, Draugolé. I will hang you before the entire city, shame your name to the four corners of Bel'arán. You will never find yourself on the other side."

And Thargodén would. Draugolé possessed a dangerous mind, Thargodén knew that, just as he knew that given the chance, he would mastermind his way out of here. It was why they had housed him far away from the other prisoners. He had spent years on the edge with

Band'orán, had risked it all for the wealth he had accumulated. He was not fooled by Draugolé's calm and controlled demeanour.

"I will return, Draugolé. There are things you may still help me with, and of course you may change your mind. Or perhaps you will remember things that you have forgotten. And, I have a pending conversation with Poronir. Your *beloved* may remember those things that seem to elude you now. I wonder what she will say to save herself from exile."

Draugolé stared back at the king, willing his face to remain straight and his eyes to not look away. But Thargodén's stare was long and searching and he felt his eyelids flicker, knew the king would interpret it for what it was.

Apprehension.

"I will be back, Draugolé."

The king's words echoed off the humid stone walls, and then the click of his boots, his sure step and then the groan and bang of his cell door as it was closed once more, freedom just beyond.

He walked back to his desk, his right hand coming up to smooth over the carvings that decorated the wooden surface.

He hadn't lied to the king, but neither had he used his final bargaining piece. There was still hope for the future he and Band'orán had envisioned for themselves. He still had allies, but time was running out. In these times of volatile peace, Draugolé must act fast or see everything he had fought for crumble around him.

His cunning mind ground to a halt, just for a moment and Barathon's face was before him, half smile half frown, never really understanding but always trying. All the boy had wanted was the love of a father he had venerated, love he had never received and so he had turned to Draugolé, trusted him. But Draugolé had betrayed that trust. Barathon had surely known in those last moments, before his own father had killed him. Barathon would have known, would have been shocked, hurt that the one he had looked to as an older brother had forsaken him.

Words tumbled from Draugolé's mouth unchecked.

"I am sorry, Barathon."

〜

No sooner had Fel'annár arrived back in the city than he made for Pan'assár's quarters where he knew Gor'sadén would be. He had promised to brief them on his trip to the Silvans. He could just imagine Llyniel's protests that he should rest, but it was vital that Pan'assár be briefed on just what was going on at the encampment.

It hadn't taken him long to summarise, but he had yet to offer his conclusions. The commanders watched him carefully, no doubt searching for signs that the trip had been a success, that they could at least be assured of a number of Silvan warriors returning to barracks.

But Fel'annár would not be able to assure them of anything.

"You are quiet." Pan'assár was staring at him.

"I'm thinking."

"You are thinking I am an obstacle, aren't you?"

"No." He turned to face the commander. "You are not an obstacle – as you are – as I know you now. But *they* have had neither time nor opportunity to see that. They remember the old days and I ask you, Commander, to understand that."

"They do not want to come, do they?"

"No. But the promise of a new division, a new strategy in the forest. The existence of outposts and specialised units and contingents, the king's express recognition of the Warlord. These things may yet change their minds. They wish to look forwards but are wary of the past."

"Pan'assár is not the past." Gor'sadén was angry and Fel'annár held up his hand.

"I didn't mean it in that way. I mean, that they are wary of Pan'assár's continued command because they know him as he *was*. They need time to see you as you are now, as they say you were before the Battle Under the Sun."

Pan'assár started. "They say that?" The question seemed light, almost unconcerned, but both Gor'sadén and Fel'annár knew that was not the case.

"They do. And they wonder what happened, that you changed so much, especially the more veteran warriors."

"Dalú, for example?"

"Dalú. And ... Bulan." Fel'annár watched Pan'assár closely, saw his hesitation.

"Bulan is here?"

"He arrived yesterday. I believe you know him."

Pan'assár nodded slowly. "We were acquaintances. A long time ago."

"What happened?" He knew it was a risk, that at the very least, Pan'assár would ignore him. He didn't.

"I lashed out at his people. He could not condone that, and he was right not to. He returned his Golden Sun; told me he would never wear it again."

"But he's come, Pan'assár. For whatever reasons, he's here, and he actively participated in our discussion. If Bulan agrees to come tomorrow, we have a chance of at least some warriors following him. They remember him, look up to him, I saw that."

Pan'assár drifted thoughtfully over to his sideboard and poured three glasses of his prized brandy. He passed one to Gor'sadén and another to Fel'annár.

"You have done well. However many come tomorrow, I will celebrate it. But if none come, I must step down. I will hand my command over to General Turion."

"It won't come to that, Pan'assár." Fel'annár had said it with such conviction he surprised even himself. Pan'assár and Gor'sadén were staring at him and he wondered what they were thinking. He drank, startled at the fiery liquid in his mouth – no alternative but to swallow it now. He grimaced and then cleared his throat.

Gor'sadén suppressed a grin, turned to Pan'assár when he spoke.

"You need a trip to the tailor, get you measured and fitted for your new uniform. Those parallel lines deserve a fitting background."

"You don't like my Warlord armour?" Fel'annár looked hurt and again, Gor'sadén wanted to laugh.

"It is magnificent. But I believe that armour was made for special occasions, not for everyday use."

Fel'annár seemed relieved. "Speaking of uniforms, in my proposals for the Forest Division, I have requested a change of colour for tunics and cloaks."

"It makes sense, so long as it is the only difference."

Fel'annár smiled, slowly began to relax, to understand that he had done everything he could, and whether that was enough was no longer in his hands but in the hands of the Silvan captains and the Elders. There would be time enough to fret over it tomorrow, but for today, he would indulge Llyniel, he would rest and distract himself as best he could from the worry and anxiety that hung over him, would continue to do so until the Inner Circle ceremony was done.

Gor'sadén held his glass up. "To the return of the Silvan warriors, and Pan'assár's ongoing command of this new army."

The clink of three glasses coming together, and then silence as they drank, hot, spicy vapours warming their throats and chests. Fel'annár had taken a smaller sip this time.

"You know, you could have warned me of my promotion, Pan'assár. My uniform would have been ready for tomorrow."

"And it would have been the wrong colour, it seems. Besides, where would the fun have been in warning you? Old commander generals deserve a moment of indulgence."

Fel'annár huffed through his incredulous smile, glanced at Gor'sadén, wondering if he was just as shocked at Pan'assár's behaviour. He wasn't.

"I would have given anything to see your face behind that blindfold when I named you general."

"Like Warrior Ramien in a sausage kitchen?" suggested Gor'sadén.

Pan'assár drank once more, and Fel'annár stared back at him in shock. He simply couldn't reconcile the playful banter with either of the commanders. He turned back to Gor'sadén, started when he spoke.

"Like Prince Sontúr before the honey cake god?"

Fel'annár chuckled, part disbelief part mirth but Pan'assár was speaking again.

"Or better, Prince Handir when the trees flung him through the forest backwards. That hair," he tutted.

Fel'annár barked out and then wheezed and Gor'sadén just managed to take Fel'annár's glass off him before he spilt it all over himself. His own shoulders shook with mirth while Pan'assár laughed for the first time in what seemed like an age.

A knock at the door and Pan'assár left them to open it, still laughing. There in the doorway was the king. His eyes drifted past Pan'assár and to the laughing elves behind him. He hesitated, murmured to the commander. "I just came to congratulate Fel'annár on regaining his sight. Llyniel told me he would be here briefing you."

"I'll get him," said Pan'assár.

"No. No leave him be. It can wait." Thargodén nodded, turned, and made down the corridor, bound for the stairs and back to his quarters on the floor above. As he did so, he damned his pride, knew he should have stayed, should have explained or simply waited but what would Fel'annár have said? He would have asked him to join them, and Thargodén couldn't do that. He had seen them laughing together, had seen the pride in Gor'sadén's eyes and the wish to please in those of his son.

Fel'annár already had a father. He didn't need another one.

Before he could reach the stairs, a voice called from behind.

"My King!"

His step faltered but he did not stop. He just needed to get to the stairs, almost there.

"Father!"

Thargodén froze, turned slowly, watched as his son approached carefully, as if he stalked a deer. He searched his son's eyes, saw the curiosity.

"I just thought I would visit – to congratulate you. Your sight has returned, and I never got the chance to speak with you in private after your promotion."

Fel'annár smiled hesitantly, looked as if he did not entirely understand. A wave of sadness hit Thargodén so violently he almost swayed where he stood. The boy struggled to understand Thargodén's pride in him. He had not expected it, and now that he had it, he did not quite know what to do. He desperately wanted his son to understand – that he cared – that he always would have, had he known he was here, in Bel'arán.

"You are our youngest general, our brightest promise. I am proud of you." His voice had only slightly wavered, enough that Fel'annár took a step forward, for pity, Thargodén was sure. He smiled, could see that his son was lost for words, or perhaps he was thinking. He didn't expect Fel'annár's question, softly spoken, curiosity and fascination in his strange eyes.

"I make you sad, don't I? You see my mother when you look at me."

"Oh yes, I see her, and her absence is like an incandescent blade in the gut, impossible to remove. And then I remind myself that you are not her. But then I see my father and I am reminded of the questions I would still ask him."

Fel'annár didn't know what the king was referring to, wondered at his humourless smile.

"And then I remind myself that you are not him either. You are Fel'annár. You are my legitimate son, a prince to my eyes. You make me sad and you bring me joy, you remind me of things that until recently were cause for grief. Now though, with what I know, that grief has turned into fond memory. They are not lost to me. I will see them again and so now, I must learn to see you and rejoice – for what the future may hold." He smiled at his wide-eyed son, saw Gor'sadén standing outside the door, watching from afar. "Go, to the one you call father. I will see you tomorrow."

The king turned, walked away, up the stairs and to the very top of the palace and Fel'annár stared at his back. He wanted to comfort him. Tell him that he too was his father, that perhaps one day, they would embrace as father and son, not because it was expected of them, but because they wanted to.

Because *he* wanted to.

But his feet would not move.

Thargodén had gone and in the wake of everything that had happened that day, a wave of physical and emotional exhaustion swept over him.

A hand came to rest on his shoulder. He knew who it was, wondered how much he had heard. He was grateful that Gor'sadén said nothing.

"Come. Time for you to go home. It's been a long day and you do not fool me with your futile attempts at hiding your fatigue."

"I thought I'd done a passing job," mumbled Fel'annár.

"For any other, perhaps. But not me." Gor'sadén gestured with his head for Fel'annár to follow him and together, they made for the floor above where Llyniel would surely be waiting.

"I met my uncle today. My mother's brother."

"Oh?"

"Bulan. Former captain of the Inner Circle. He's a Spear Master."

"What? Did you know? Why didn't you say something before?"

"Because I didn't think he'd come. Amareth kept me from him and my grandmother all my life. She said it was too dangerous to involve them in my upbringing. They haven't spoken since I was born."

"Why didn't you expect him to come?"

"Because he's angry with his sister. Because they no longer act like a family." He huffed but it was humourless. "And what would I know?"

"He wanted to meet you. I wager it has nothing to do with his problems with your aunt."

"He did say that."

"And you don't believe it?"

Fel'annár didn't answer for a while but when he did, it was soft, a lost voice in a sea of emotion. "I want to."

Gor'sadén stared at his profile. "Just like you can't believe Thargodén came here looking for you, because he is proud of you. Just like Amareth when she said she did what she did for you. Do you *want* to believe them too?"

Again, Fel'annár didn't answer, but Gor'sadén was not surrendering in his mission to make him see that there was a pattern.

"You wanted to be a Kah Warrior. You wanted to know who your mother was, who your father was, and you have achieved these things. But what you always wanted the most is what scares you halfway to Valley.

"Family.

"Don't run from your dreams, Fel'annár. Embrace them even though they petrify you. You call Handir your brother now, against all the odds and now you must believe that Thargodén wants to be a real father to *you*. That Amareth loves *you*. You must believe that Bulan came for *you*."

"How can I be sure?"

"You can't. Time will tell, but meanwhile, don't shut the door son. Don't shut the door."

Fel'annár's step faltered and then he nodded thoughtfully. "I must try harder then."

"Indeed. And you have the perfect excuse. You must see if this Bulan will agree to train you with the spears."

Gor'sadén saw a passing glimmer of fear in his son's eyes, some deep-rooted concern that perhaps Bulan wouldn't want to train him. Perhaps he thought his uncle would reject him in some way, for being responsible for the schism of his family, albeit unwittingly.

"I'll think about it." It was a muttered declaration of intent, almost to himself, and Gor'sadén thought it unwise to press the issue any further than he already had.

"Then go and rest. There is much to be done tomorrow. Much to achieve. If the Silvans come, it will be the dawn of a new era, Fel'annár, one in which you will shine as brightly as Or'Talán ever did. This too you must believe."

Those green eyes were back on him, surprised for the second time that afternoon.

"Thank you." With those simple words, Fel'annár left and Gor'sadén watched him for a while. Strange that Fel'annár was an elf of faith. An Ari'atór, confident in his skills, in his ability to lead. He would soon be a Kah Master, was already a Warlord to his people. Now, all he needed to do was believe that he – Fel'annár – was worthy of his family's love.

AMARETH KNELT before the fire inside her tent. She had invited her mother, her brother and niece but they hadn't come.

But what had she expected? She glanced at the cold food upon the low table by the fire, the unstained glasses and the full jug of wine.

She had expected curiosity at least, she supposed. Questions and animosity too. But this quiet disregard?

The first time they had spoken, just after they had arrived, they told her they had come for Fel'annár, that she could no longer stop them from meeting him. They were defensive, thought she would be against the idea when the truth was quite the opposite. She had wanted to explain, spew the entire story so that they would understand. But all she saw in their eyes was condemnation.

She had never felt hated before.

She poked at the fire, and then startled at the rustle of oiled cloth, the soft breeze as someone entered. She turned to the entrance, saw Bulan standing there. She held his gaze for a moment, tried and failed to read his mood.

"Come sit," she invited, poking again at the incandescent wood. She felt his presence at her side, briefly wondered why Alei had not come. "Any progress on what you'll do tomorrow?"

"I've said my piece, as have others. It's time to think, contemplate what's best for us all. By morning we'll know whether we return and try again or walk away and create our own army."

"If you do that, Fel'annár will walk away from us."

"Yes, I believe he will." He breathed in through the nose, out through the mouth. He seemed unwilling to comment any further and she supposed that was because he had been listening to the other captains all afternoon. Besides, he surely hadn't come here to speak about the army. Still, she didn't expect his question.

"How did she die?"

Straight to the point, as it had always been with her brother. She searched for the right words, comforting words but she found none. "She was stabbed."

Silence save for the crackle of the fire, the rustle of oiled cloth in the gentle breeze. And then another question.

"Did she suffer?"

"I don't know, Bulan. She was dead when I found her."

"Did you see him? See his face?"

Amareth turned to her brother, saw the grief in his eyes, the intensity of it. He had always been close to Lássira. He needed the closure that Amareth had never granted him. She was sorry for that.

"I saw him from a distance, through the trees as he ran with a bundle in his arms. I thought nothing of it save that he was a fast runner."

"Was he Alpine?"

"No."

"*Silvan*?" Incredulity, a creased brow. Bulan searched for the truth in her eyes. Could she lie to him?

"No."

He blinked, confused. "Tell me."

"His hood flew off as he ran. He pulled it back up, but I had already seen enough. He was *Ari'atór*, Bulan. I saw his hair, the colour of his skin. I didn't realise at first, until I saw Lássira, lying still on the ground, and Fel'annár was nowhere to be seen."

Bulan scrambled to his feet, eyes wide, head shaking from side to side. "That's not possible."

It was nothing but a hoarse whisper, incredulous eyes searching Amareth's, for any sign that he had misunderstood.

"Why ... why didn't he kill the boy?"

It was a good question, one Amareth had asked herself a thousand times. She knew that Ari'atór do not kill children – unless they are Incipient or Deviant. It is the worst kind of crime for a Spirit Warrior to commit, a guarantee of death and oblivion. The assassin had killed the mother but had fled with the child.

"I can only assume that the assassin faltered, that he couldn't bring himself to kill a babe and so thought to abandon him in the Deep Forest. It would be a surety of death for any other new-born."

"But?"

"I ... we thought him dead. Erthoron, Golloron and I searched for days, found nothing. We lost hope, mourned his death. We thought he had been taken by scavengers, or perhaps thrown into the Calro and drowned, washed away ... but then we found him, high in a tree, lying upon a nest of twigs and leaves, healthy and happy ... as if he had been waiting for us."

"That's ... that's not possible. How did he get up there? What did he feed on? He was new-born."

"I know, brother. These were the questions we asked ourselves time and again – still do. But we never found our answers. Now though, knowing what we do, of the skill he possesses, we think he may have ... *been cared for* ... by the trees."

Bulan stared incredulously at his sister, head moving from side to side. "Someone was there. There must have been someone who cared for him, made sure you found him."

"If there was, we never found them."

Bulan ran a hand through his hair, confusion battling with denial.

"Why didn't you tell me?"

"I couldn't risk a letter. To speak of such a heinous crime in the very heartland of the Ari'atór."

"Why didn't you come then?"

"To take Fel'annár there, when I had no way of knowing why the

Ari'atór wanted him dead? No, and besides, what would you have done? Would your revenge have served any purpose other than to ostracise you in your own land? In this at least, you know I was right."

"You're always right, aren't you?" Bulan turned away from her, cape flying around his legs as he walked to the back of the tent, as far away as he could be from her. "There's always a justification for your actions, isn't there?"

Anger was taking over her capacity to remain calm. She had contained it for so many years while she had purposely kept family away from her charge. She had done what she had for all the right reasons, but however much she tried to explain, all she ever received, from Fel'annár and now from Bulan, was criticism.

Amareth forced herself not to flinch as Bulan began to pace. "Did you think of your family at all? Or was it always the plight of the Silvan people, politics, machinations, creating for yourself a puppet Warlord you tried to mould into the saviour of our people. Tell me, does he thank you for that?"

Amareth was on her feet, face hot, her own righteous anger pouring into her words.

"Everything I did was for him. My life has meant nothing these past decades. No family, no love, no life, Bulan. I love him, and he doesn't believe that. He doesn't thank me for what I've done and that's my punishment for keeping him from his family. It's my punishment for protecting him!"

"You, all by yourself, assumed that we would take him to Abiren'á, but by the great Gods, Amareth, did it never occur to you to tell us of the Ari assassin? We could have moved here to Lan Taria. I could have protected him. I am a trained warrior. I could have taken him into the deepest parts of the wood, I could have taken him to other lands, far from here and Band'orán's scheming. I would have brought him up as my son, given him the father he has never had. I had just as much right to do that as you did to keep him locked away in Lan Taria."

Eyes swimming, lips trembling, she blinked furiously.

"Bulan ..."

He wasn't moved, or if he was, his anger was still greater than his pity.

"You confided in Erthoron and Golloron to help you when it should have been his family. You trusted them more than you trusted us, and you reared an orphan." Bulan shook his head. "He could have had a *family*, Amareth."

Both stood face to face, silent and observant, until Amareth spoke and it was soft, sincere apology.

"I am sorry, brother. Larissa entrusted me with Fel'annár's safety. I was ... scared. The Ari'atór killed her, and I was sure that Band'orán must have ordered it. I only did what I felt was best to keep Fel'annár safe. In hindsight, I could have done things differently. But I can't change what I did."

Bulan breathed out, slid a hand down his face and then sat heavily at the fire. Amareth knelt beside him, watched the dancing flames, wondered if they were mocking her now.

"Does Fel'annár know an Ari'atór killed his mother? Wanted to kill him?"

"No. He has other things on his mind now. But I will tell him. I made a promise to him, Bulan. I'll keep it but only when the time is right and we are at peace. Then I'll tell him what he needs to know."

"It's his right."

"And if he ever asks, I'll tell him. There are reasons, Bulan. Things that are not for me to say. I know you will seek him out but think twice before you reveal this. See what he is up against, what he must achieve in such a short time. A distraction such as this would only serve your own devices, not his."

"You underestimate him. You all do. You see him as the child you raised while I see him as a Warlord."

Amareth was unsure about how she was supposed to see him in any other light. He *was* the child she had reared. He was *her* child. But she had been wrong, she knew that now.

"Will you at least tell me what he *does* know?"

"That she was killed. He understands it was at Band'orán's behest. I told him I kept him from his family to protect him. He understands."

"So everything is right between you?"

"No. Not yet. I ... I made a mistake, Bulan. The day he left for recruit training. I should have told him who he was. I should have told him about his father. He was leaving, my purpose almost done. I couldn't stand the idea of bearing his hatred and so I did the cruellest thing I've ever done. I left him to find out from others."

"Dear Gods."

"I've been strong all these years, Bulan and yet in that one moment, I was a coward. I thought he would leave Lan Taria hating me. I thought he would insist on finding his father, knowing about his mother; it was all he ever wanted." She stood, walked to the back of the tent. "Day after day, his questions cut into my very heart, but how could I tell him he was the king's son? How could I tell him that he was the very image of Or'Talán? That should his presence be known, he would be murdered, as surely as his mother had been. How do you tell a child these things?"

"You don't," murmured Bulan. "But he was no child when he left for recruit training. He could so easily have walked into Band'orán's treacherous arms, and then all those years you spent protecting him would have been for nothing."

Amareth flinched, turned back to the fire. Her brother was right in that too. Still, she couldn't tell him the rest, couldn't tell him that Fel'annár was Ari'atór, that he was Ber'anor. That was not for her to say but she knew Fel'annár would tell him eventually.

"You will like him, brother. He has Lássira's boldness and her eyes. He has her wisdom and his grandfathers' skill at arms and command – both of them. He has the face of an Alpine. The heart of a Silvan." She held her brother's gaze, a plea in her own, for forgiveness or understanding at least. "I never meant to hurt you, brother. I never meant to exclude you or mother from his life, but I felt that I had to. It was the hardest thing I've ever done, but I made a promise to our sister, that if anything should happen to her, I would look after her child. I promised to protect him until the day came when he could protect himself. I did that, sacrificed everything to honour that oath. My mistakes have cost me dearly, and the price is the distance between me and him, a distance that may never be forded. I lost my own family; you, mother ..."

Bulan heaved a deep breath, met her imploring eyes.

"You didn't lose us. You hurt us deeply. Wounds like that take time to heal, Amareth. The story you've shared with me gives some insight at least as to what you were facing. Mother didn't come so that I could speak with you freely but she too, should know, Amareth."

She nodded and for a while they simply sat, shoulder to shoulder. Amareth had given Bulan much to think about, had revealed as much as was hers to reveal. The rest of it would remain in her heart, the wound open, the pain dulled. Gods but she remembered her brother so well, the halcyon days they shared in the forest. She had loved him so much – still did.

"What's he like under that uniform?"

Amareth smiled, but it faltered when they heard shouts in the distance. A sudden flurry of bird call and Bulan strode to the entrance, walked through the flap and turned to the still distant noises.

He strained his eyes towards the tree line.

Nothing.

But then he saw movement in the dim light. It would soon be dark, but something was approaching. Not the enemy for the birdcall was friendly.

Allies approach.

He walked slowly, warily and all the while he tried to see beyond the silver and brown trunks of the sheltering trees.

His eyes widened, heart racing as he realised what it was that came from the forest.

Warriors, line after line of them, some in civilian attire, others in the uniforms that were tattered and faded from use. Bulan shook his head, unable to comprehend what his eyes were seeing. There were so many of them.

But then he remembered seeing the queues at the anvils on his journey from Abiren'á. Were these the ones who had seen him passing through? Had they followed him?

He heard feet, running towards him from behind, a flurry of robes and hair and Captain Amon all but skidded to a halt beside him.

"Holy mother ..."

"Amon. Go. Tell Dalú." He turned to the captain, eyes wide.

"Tell him the *forest* has come."

7

STAND A WARRIOR

~

THE INNER CIRCLE was bustling with activity, despite the fact that half of its captains were missing. Lieutenants, aides and other warriors carried out the preparations for the evening's protocols, lending the final touches to the Great Hall, all of them wondering if it served any purpose.

The standards had been beaten clean, sconces polished, candles placed in every holder. The table upon which the Warrior Code would sit on display had been especially cared for. The book itself would not be placed there and opened until this evening, by Pan'assár himself.

The Commander General of Ea Uaré turned from the window that overlooked the inner courtyard. Turion stood watching him while Rinon dragged his fingers over a line of books on Pan'assár's shelves. In their new uniforms and symbols, they reminded Pan'assár of his times in Tar'eastór, the Glory Days when everything had been right and Or'Talán was still alive.

Pan'assár turned to his two generals.

"Time to face the future, at last. Today we must hold to hope that we will see our Alpine and Silvan warriors come together once more. I will not say it will be easy. It will not. It will be tense, uncomfortable, volatile. I just hope each side will make the effort and avoid conflict."

"If any Silvans come," murmured Rinon, eyes still on Pan'assár's bookshelf.

"Indeed. That is the question. We must be mindful of Prince Handir's suspicions. This event lends itself to sabotage, generals. Remain watchful, especially of our royal family."

"Are we not past that point, Pan'assár?" asked Turion. "There is no army to speak of, no purists left on the Royal Council."

"No. But still, we have seen how little it takes to jeopardise peace. I am not saying it is likely, just that we should be vigilant."

Turion nodded while Rinon pursed his lips.

"Still, whether the Silvans return or not, the Restoration is a fact. This army will evolve, with or without me as its commander. But if they do return, then I pray that pride does not get in the way of atonement. We must foment humility in our warriors, generals. It is *key*. That is written in the Warrior Code, something I forgot for many years. I will not do so again. If *I* can ask for forgiveness, then so can my captains."

Turion nodded, glanced sideways at Rinon.

"Perhaps you will tell us, one day, what brought this about, Pan'assár. I am glad of this change, but I confess my curiosity." Rinon cocked his head to one side, an invitation to speak, but Pan'assár said nothing and Rinon made for the sitting area, seemingly unsurprised.

Pan'assár was not ready to discuss that, was glad that the prince did not insist. He wandered back to his table and then sat down. Before him, a cushion, and upon it, a line of decorations. Silver stars and acorns for acts of extreme bravery. Golden Suns for new captains, some of which he could only pray would be Silvan, perhaps not today, but soon.

He closed his eyes, refused to consider the possibility that it was simply too late, that no one would come.

And if they didn't, then Pan'assár would pass the heavy burden of duty to Turion, despite the king's wishes; despite Fel'annár's public endorsement of his continued command.

~

FEL'ANNÁR HAD ASKED Dalú and Bulan to come to the city with whoever would follow. His stomach flipped at the thought that they may not, that he would be left standing at the gates, waiting in vain like a fool.

Pan'assár and Gor'sadén were at the Inner Circle, overseeing the final touches of the evening's event together with Rinon and Turion, but Fel'annár had stayed in his quarters, sitting in his study and working on the rationale he was preparing for Pan'assár. He had laid out the entire structure of his future Forest Division. Rangers, close combat experts, Listeners, engineers, the return of female warriors to their ranks. It was all there, on paper; forty years of thoughts and notes from eight field journals he had been keeping since childhood.

Just a year ago, it had been nothing but a hobby, although Idernon once called it an obsession. Fel'annár would scribble ideas that came to him after he'd read a book or discussed something with the weapons master. He would observe lieutenants, the way they gave orders. He watched warriors, the problems they encountered and how they were solved. He saw the hardships, wondered how they could be eased, had even once emptied the standard kit bag of a warrior and noted down its contents.

But not once had Fel'annár thought that those impressions would one day form the basis of a rationale for the restructuring of an army. Never had he imagined his vision could one day become a reality.

One hand reached out to brush over his latest journal, the only one in his possession. There were seven more back in Lan Taria, but their contents were in his head for the most part.

He still remembered the oldest of them. It was hand painted in gaudy colours, reminding him of how young he had been when he had started it. As the years progressed, the covers became simpler, less exciting on the outside but more coherent, more innovative on the inside. He smiled softly, allowed himself a moment of rueful indulgence, dared imagine the possibility that it had served some purpose beyond his own education.

But reality slammed into him, and his fertile imagination conjured the image of a lonely Warlord atop the balustrades, looking out over the barren plains of Ea Uaré. No Silvan encampment.

No warriors.

He rubbed a hand down his face, willed himself to stop fretting.

If Dalú came today, Fel'annár could begin the task of investing Silvan captains, assigning them to the new contingents and units, *if* Pan'assár agreed to them.

If, if, *if!* Frustration was getting the better of him. He was nervous. So much hinged on today, on Dalú and Bulan's presence at the gates, no matter nothing but a handful of warriors followed. He told himself that in time, he could make this work, go out into the villages so that the warriors could meet him, see for themselves that he stood for them, as much as he did for the forest.

So long as Bulan and Dalú were with him, he could show them all that Pan'assár *had* changed.

The Company, save for Tensári, had stayed away. She was milling around outside, on the balcony, behind his door and even at the end of the corridor. He had begged her to leave, promised he would not leave his rooms, but she had told him that the city was tense, that the people were well aware of the importance of the day and its implications. There was fear, just as there had been before the Battle of Brothers, yet so too was there hope, that lessons had been learned, and mistakes would not be repeated.

Still, Tensári had refused to leave, promptly reminding Fel'annár of Handir's suspicions as to Nestar's actions and whether they had been purposeful. Who was to say there were not others, out to hinder the Restoration and keep Band'orán's flame alive? Fel'annár had not been able to answer that and so, the hours had passed.

He breathed out, rubbed his tired eyes, eyes that still saw no colour. Dropping his quill, he stood, rolled his shoulders and looked out of his window.

Time to prepare.

He bathed, had tried to relax in the warm water, but not even that was enough to calm his mind and so he washed, dried off and stood now in nothing but his black leggings. He padded to the window of his bed chamber, stared out over the forest.

Tilting his head back, he allowed his colourless gaze to focus inwards, to the forest beyond the gates, the familiar path of Sentinels in his head. He followed one and then the other, all the way to the

Xeric Wood. In his mind they were brown and green, not black and white.

Nothing. The Nim'uán was not there.

The door clicked open and his eyes focussed on the black-and-white world outside his mind.

"What is it?" asked Llyniel.

He turned to her. "Nothing. Just listening," he murmured.

"I've seen the Elders arrive. They'll be escorted here until the king calls for them."

He wandered over to her, saw her eyes travel over his hair, his chest and downwards. He didn't stop but gently pushed her backwards until there was nowhere else to go. Flat against the wall, she smiled up at him as his hand smoothed down one side of her face.

"I wish they would go somewhere else," he murmured into her ear, breath as hot as his skin.

"So do I." She kissed him softly, stroked his face. "It'll be a long evening."

"There'll be time for us."

"Always." She snuggled into him, wanted him as much as he needed her. "I know what this means to you, Fel'annár. It's about more than the new army, whether it'll be deemed valid and put into motion. This is about you, too. It's almost as if you've been preparing for this moment all your life."

He looked down at her, wondered why he was so shocked at her insightful words. She was right. These next few days would be the last in a project that had taken him forty years to complete, a project that would see the light and be judged by the greatest military strategist known to elvendom.

But before that could happen, the warriors needed to return.

"Let me see to your eyes before the Elders arrive."

Fel'annár pulled away, allowed her to flush them and then wandered over to his wardrobe. He would use his Warlord armour, and in the high collar of the new green undertunic that denoted the Forest Division, he would wear the Blue Mountain, the decoration King Vorn'asté had granted him. On the other side of the collar, the sparkling Forest Emerald and just behind, the parallel lines of a general.

Over his chest, the intricate cuirass, at the centre of which sat the White Oak, exquisitely carved, overlaid by the thinnest layers of brass that swirled around the symbol and outwards.

Over the material of his right bicep, he would wear his Master Bands. One for the bow, another for blades and around his waist, the symbol of the Kah Warrior, grey velvet over the reinforced brown leather of his war skirt.

His hair would tell the story of his heritage. Silvan, Alpine and Ari but not Ber'anor, not yet. Handir didn't know, and besides, he wanted to know if the Silvan warriors would follow *him* as their military leader, not because Aria demanded it of them. He would use that later, if it was ever necessary at all. The Heliaré and Alféna's honour stone would complete the symbols.

Once he was finished, he stood before the mirror. In it, he saw a child, white linen shirt crumpled and full of twigs, but he smiled, waved, and then ran away, perhaps to play. And then the decorated Warlord was back, staring at him. In those bright green eyes, Fel'annár saw strength, and he saw vulnerability. He saw confidence and he saw doubt.

Could he overcome the voice in his head that said he was too young for such a position? That he was too untried to lead an entire division as its general?

Green eyes held his gaze, told him today was the day he must accept the challenge, to whatever end. He had come this far ...

"I need to start getting ready," said Llyniel. "I would at least be dressed for when your aunt arrives."

Fel'annár turned to her, grinned at her from across the room. "That would be wise." He watched as she walked towards him, placed a hand over his heart.

"When the Inner Circle is finished, we'll all be waiting in the king's quarters. I pray your news is good but if it isn't, it's not the end, Fel'annár. There'll be more opportunities to rebuild this army, you'll see."

Fel'annár stared back at her, saw the conviction in her eyes, knew that in his, all she would see was doubt.

∼

LLYNIEL'S DRESS WAS SILVAN, made by Pobdil of Sen'uár and Oran'Dor. It was daring, absurdly elegant and entirely the colours of the forest.

The fabric was the same green as Fel'annár's eyes, the form fitting, trailing down past her feet, pooling behind her. It made her look taller. The neckline was low, but she did not wear jewellery around her neck. Instead, she wore a Tona Lia, traditional forest head dress. Expertly woven vines formed a V at the centre of her forehead and then fanned backwards, past temples, over ears and then tied at the back. From it, dried, powdery blue flowers spilled down the back of her loose, wavy auburn hair, reaching to the small of her bare back.

What the hell, she thought, as Nuthead Rinon would say. She didn't often wear dresses; they weren't practical for a healer, not for anyone really. But if you're going to wear one, make it count. She grinned to herself, saw Fel'annár's fiery eyes when he had first seen her in it. Her mother would be shocked.

She liked it.

A knock at the door and Llyniel walked across the front room, pulled it open. There, the entire Council of Elders stood in their blues, greens and browns. The odd sparkle of precious metal, the abundance of vines and flowers instead of the jewels the Alpine nobles favoured.

"Welcome, Lady, Lords. Please come in." Llyniel led them in, made her way to the hearth where Fel'annár was already standing, and then pulled on the cord that ran from the ceiling and down the chimney breast, bare back on display.

The tension in the air could be eaten with a spoon. It was the first time they were seeing the Warlord and his Connate together in a formal setting, as lord and lady, but eventually, Erthoron and the Elders bowed.

"We have time for some light refreshments before we are due in the king's presence. I have prepared rooms for the evening, should any of you wish to stay."

"Our thanks, Lady Llyniel." Amareth's eyes were everywhere. On Fel'annár, on her, on the Tona Lia in her hair and the symbols in Fel'annár's collar. Llyniel could see the conflicting emotions in her eyes, could guess at the nature of them.

Erthoron cleared his throat. "Well then, perhaps we can dispense with the formalities here at least? There will be enough of those tonight."

"Of course," said Fel'annár. He wandered over to a side cabinet and poured wine into polished glasses that stood waiting. Llyniel helped him to pass them around. It was Erthoron who first raised his glass and his voice.

"To better days. A brighter future."

"Aye!" they toasted and then drank.

"Any news from our captains, Erthoron?" asked Fel'annár, eyes on his wine, breath stuck in his throat.

"Dalú has said nothing. Whether that is because they are not coming is hard to say. It's been made clear that their return is a military affair. It is possible that they were still undecided when we left. We shall have to wait and see."

Fel'annár said nothing, took a deep breath and drank. Placing his goblet on the mantel, he turned back to the Elders.

"Then it's time to see how many have heeded the call. I will see you all later, at the king's reception." He made to leave, but Amareth's voice stopped him and he turned back.

"I'm proud of you, my son." She stood there, watching the impact of her words, the flicker of surprise Fel'annár had not been able to hide. "Whatever the Commander General has in store for the Inner Circle tonight, I know you will shine for your people."

Fel'annár bowed, his smile genuine, not sad as it often was when he looked at her. His eyes drifted to Llyniel, lingered there for a while, before he turned and left.

She watched his retreating form for a moment, heard the click of the door and the clink of a glass, a soft rush of breath.

"They have to come," said Erthoron.

"Bulan came for Fel'annár. Now is his time to prove that. He won't fail us, Erthoron." Amareth stared at the Silvan leader, while Llyniel watched her closely, saw the conviction in her eyes, wanted to share it. She herself had told Fel'annár that even if they didn't come today, there would be more opportunities. And it was surely the most likely scenario. Fel'annár had done great things in his short years, things he never seemed to credit himself for. But it would surely take more than one simple plea for their warriors to return.

She turned, almost flinching when she caught sight of the Ari'atór Narosén staring back at her. She watched his slow smile, some truth in his eyes that she had yet to understand.

"WELL? HOW DO I LOOK?" asked Carodel. Galdith turned and nodded.

"You look smart, brother. And me?"

Carodel wandered over to him, peered at his hair and then the collar of his new green undertunic. Reaching up, he straightened the Silver Mountain that sat proudly on all their collars, and then tugged on the Silver Acorn at the end of his foremost braid. "This new colour for the Forest Division suits you well."

Galadan watched him, lips twitching at the Bard Warrior's antics. He turned to Tensári.

"You look magnificent, Ber'ator." Galadan swore her blue eyes shone brighter of late, her Guiding Light a play of colour that garnered attention but did not startle. Hers was the ceremonial uniform of Tar'eastór, blue tunic and black leather with silver inlay. He himself had worn that uniform for centuries, the very same one Sontúr now wore. He too was a captain, but the symbol of his father's royal house was emblazoned upon the precious metal of his breastplate and a finely wrought crown sat over his grey locks.

Idernon stood before them, his back to the door of the quarters Handir had given them, on the floor just below Fel'annár.

"We wear different uniforms, different braids, different symbols of office in our collars, in our hair, but all of us wear Honour Stones. And this is what tonight is about. Unity, diversity. We seven are one, despite those differences – because of them perhaps. Now, it falls to us to show our warriors what Fel'annár and Pan'assár have set out to do. Unity is possible; we are proof of it.

"Since that first gathering of the Circle, when our commander general bestowed upon us the Silver Acorn, The Company is known to all. They speak of us, know our names and what we've done. It falls to us to set an example, to lead the way."

His bright eyes raked over each one of them and Galadan watched him. They all felt proud of the singular status they had achieved, and he wondered if Fel'annár would allow himself a similar indulgence. It was time to find out, join their young leader and walk to the gates, to whatever awaited them. It was time to see for themselves, the fruits of Fel'annár's endeavours.

Galadan hadn't been wrong about Idernon. He was a leader indeed, a newly promoted lieutenant who would one day take up his own seat at the Inner Circle. He smiled again, and then turned at the knock on their door.

It was time.

THE COURTYARD WAS STRANGELY EMPTY, and the crunch of grit under their boots seemed overly loud as Fel'annár and The Company made their way to the gates.

Even the rebuilding had stopped, half-finished buildings abandoned. There were no merchants carrying their wares, no clerks scurrying here and there, no horses – nothing, at least not in this part of the city.

Fel'annár wondered if they were frightened of what might happen between the warriors. Perhaps they thought they would fight, and who could blame them?

They slowed their pace, and the nearer they came to the closed gates, the more Fel'annár's heart sank. Nothing. Not a single sound that told him warriors stood behind it.

He heaved a great sigh, looked at the stone beneath his boots. Reality was sinking in. His worst fears had come to pass. It had all been for nothing. In the end, Pan'assár's continuation as commander general was more important to the Silvan warriors than Fel'annár's reasoning, his call to return, his promises of change.

And then he felt Idernon's hand on his bicep. Too tight.

"The guards."

"What of them?"

"They are not standing straight. They are leaning over the side ..."

Fel'annár scowled at him, didn't understand, and then he started when what seemed like the loudest, most unexpected thump all but sent him shooting into the air.

Breath froze in his chest, eyes moving from one side of the gates to the other.

A deep groan, the clank of chains and the grinding of heavy wheels. With a clatter and rattle, the gates began to move inwards.

Fel'annár steadied himself as best he could, braced for whatever was on the other side, mind paralysed, unable to enumerate the possibilities.

And then another thump, like a boulder falling onto forest moss. And then another, ground trembling beneath his feet, chest vibrating with every beat.

The Silvan war drums, drums he had only ever heard at festivals and celebrations but never like this. Never so many of them.

The gates opened wider, and Fel'annár's admission of defeat was utterly forgotten.

Captain Bulan sat upon his charger, spears jutting to the heavens and beside him, Captains Dalú, Amon and Benat.

"Merciful Gods!" whispered Galdith behind him, but Fel'annár couldn't move, couldn't speak, brain still not quite interpreting what he was seeing.

The gates banged open, and behind the four, mounted captains, a Silvan army of thousands stood, utterly silent in their perfect ranks. Line after line of them but where had they come from?

A practiced yell, a voice broken from overuse, raw yet uplifting, an order impossible to defy. The drums picked up their beat, a marching beat and the intimidating thud of thousands of boots made Fel'annár's blood sing. Gods but the sight of them, the pride in his chest, the heat in his eyes and the prickle at the back of his throat. He wanted to sink to the ground, cover his eyes and cry in utter relief, thanks, *exhaustion*.

They were so close now that Fel'annár could see their Honour Stones, the colours of their eyes and the emotions behind them.

Why had the trees not warned him they were behind the gates?

He listened, heard their playful whispers, couldn't remember a time when they had purposefully misled him.

Another cried order and the ranks stomped to attention while the four captains dismounted, watching the clearly flummoxed Warlord and his closest warriors, standing in the new greens of the Forest Division.

Later, Fel'annár would wonder how his stupid words had even made it through his numb lips.

"You've come."

Dalú stepped forward. "A conditional return, Warlord. If the Commander General of Ea Uaré honours his promises, we will stay. If he doesn't, we leave, never to return."

Dalú stared back at him, waiting for an answer, honour stones gleaming in the failing light. From the neck down they were the king's fighters, but from their high collars and upwards, they were Silvan warriors, awash in a sea of colour. All that culture had been suppressed for many years, but it had bloomed today – the defiant return of the Silvan warriors.

A surge of pride washed over Fel'annár. To be a part of this extraordinary culture, to watch its resurgence. Fel'annár had only ever read of their past glory, but Dalú, Bulan, Amon and Benat had surely lived it, had missed every day of it.

His gaze moved to the ranks behind the captains, wanted to salute and thank every one of them, show his gratitude and his relief, tell them that he understood why this decision had been so hard to make. He needed to show them what this meant to him, show them that he wouldn't disappoint them.

He searched for anything he could use to make himself visible. It was Bulan who approached, held out the reins of his horse. Fel'annár took them, mounted and guided the horse to the front lines.

He took a moment to marvel at the straight lines, perfect symmetry. Eyes to the fore, faces blank and foreboding. What were they thinking, he wondered?

"You step upon this ground once more, no longer in battle but in peace. From tonight, the Warrior Code will once more occupy its rightful place at an Inner Circle that was corrupted, by an enemy that is no longer present."

He had raised his voice as much as he could, but there was no way those further away could hear his words – at least not from his own lips.

He wondered how the veteran captains made their orders heard in a full-scale battle, a war even. He had only ever seen Dalú at the Battle of Brothers. He had somehow heard everything he had said. No wonder his voice was scratchy and hoarse.

"This is no longer about Alpine and Silvan. It's about loyalty and treachery. It's not about race; it's about duty. He who spites us, goes against the Warrior Code, and such breaches will no longer be ignored. Not by me. Not by Commander Pan'assár. Not by any captain who sits at the Inner Circle."

Fel'annár nudged his horse forwards, until he was as close to the troops as safety dictated.

"I call upon your temperance. I call upon your nobility and your sense of honour. We will not fight our fellow warriors. We will not raise our voices or dredge up past grievances. We will not rise to bait but step back and report. This is my first order to you in times of peace: open the book of the Warrior Code in your hearts. Stand tall, stand proud. Stand Silvan but above all, stand a *warrior!*"

"*Aye!*" they thundered, even the captains, even Bulan who finally found the wherewithal to break his stunned silence for the first time. He had not missed the braid in Fel'annár's hair, the one that marked him as Ari'atór. Amareth must have known, and still she had not told him. But that was not the only reason for his shock. Fel'annár was the king's son, a prince in bearing, a commander in word. Only now was Bulan beginning to understand his nephew's innate ability to lead, even at the tender age of fifty-three. He'd seen a modicum of it at the encampment, but the elf who now stood before thousands of fierce Silvan warriors, was a commander in deed.

From the other side of the courtyard, at the entrance to the Inner Circle, Gor'sadén and Pan'assár stared at the army of Silvan warriors who had heeded Fel'annár's call. Gor'sadén clapped Pan'assár upon the shoulder, and then squeezed when he felt the tension there. He turned to the noble profile, smiled at the wide eyes and open mouth. Pan'assár hardly ever allowed himself such an open expression of his feelings. He could only guess that the relief had utterly overwhelmed him.

Gor'sadén's smile faded, understood the stress and the strain it had cost Pan'assár to come as far as he had without relinquishing his command. Had he done that, he would have failed in his promise to protect the line of Or'Talán, but Fel'annár had devised a plan to restructure the army. It had worked.

"He does you proud," muttered Pan'assár.

Gor'sadén ripped his eyes away from his distant son, stared at Pan'assár.

"Yes. Yes, he does."

8

WARRIOR CODE

~

THE GREAT HALL inside the Inner Circle building housed one hundred and one ornate chairs, placed in an almost perfect circle. Each chair bore the arms of he or she who would occupy it, not that there had ever been any female captains in Ea Uaré.

Half of the chairs were covered in green cloths, and upon some of them, a single flower. Before the remaining seats, Alpine captains stood in full military regalia and amongst them, Sar'pén and Eramor. Blue, black and silver contrasted starkly with predominantly blond braided hair and blue or grey eyes that shone in the bright light of the many candles and torches that illuminated this windowless place.

Apprehension. Caution. Curiosity.

Inside the Circle, at the very centre of it, a small table stood, and upon it, a closed book – the Warrior Code. Beside it, a single, unlit candle.

Outside this circle of half-occupied chairs, there was standing room for hundreds of people, not that it would be anywhere near full today.

Or so Pan'assár had thought.

The revelation of what lay behind the gates had threatened to send him to his knees in shock and blessed relief. There was no way he could have counted them, but from where he had been standing, he reckoned there were surely a good few hundred, many more than his wildest guesses these past few days. But he was no fool. He knew they hadn't come for him.

Pan'assár made his way through the Alpine lieutenants and warriors, five hundred of the thousands they had once boasted. There were over two hundred Alpines sitting in the dungeons, awaiting trial for their mutiny, for daring to learn the Kah from one who was not a Master – for shaming the revered art of Kal'hamén'Ar.

At the head of the Circle, the commander general's chair was slightly larger than the rest. He stood in front of it, waited for the others to take their places, knowing that Gor'sadén stood just behind him.

On his right, Turion, his second in command, and next to him, Rinon. His left was reserved for the Silvan Warlord, but Fel'annár was still outside and Pan'assár had not missed Rinon's frown, unaware as he was as to the reason for his half-brother's absence.

As they waited, Pan'assár's eyes wandered over the finely decked hall. Ea Uaré had not seen such pomp for many decades. Sigils hung from the high ceilings, clean and fresh, no longer dust-clogged things from the past but a living, hopeful present. The colours of the noble Alpine houses swayed majestically over their sons, like proud parents watching from the skies. Soon, there would be Silvan symbols there: White Oak, Silver Wolf, Fire Fox and Grey Bear - perhaps even Three Sisters.

Emotion. Feelings Pan'assár had not allowed himself to acknowledge for so long were pushing to the fore. This night and all the effort it had taken them ... it *had* been worth it. A Silvan leap of faith in the Warlord, that this new army might work. Gods but if the boy were standing before him now, he would hug him, shake his strong shoulders and shout to the heavens that he had *done* it. Somehow, some way, in spite of himself and his ongoing command.

Drums.

They could hear drums and the hall fell silent. It was a marching beat, steady and stubborn, louder and louder until it stopped, just beyond the open doors. The warriors looked at each other and then towards the doors, eyes wide in surprise and confusion.

Fel'annár and The Company walked through the double doors, past the onlooking Alpines, didn't stop until they were just outside the circle. Fel'annár stepped into the circle and took his place on Pan'assár's left. Turning to the commander, they exchanged gazes. There were questions in Pan'assár's eyes, some unknown emotion in Fel'annár's and then he turned back to the doors, and to whatever stood on the other side.

Near silence descended on the hall, all heads turned to the doors where Bulan, Dalú, Amon and Benat now stood, like a tapestry from the past, one more reminder of what Pan'assár had destroyed. Three of them had never relinquished their chairs, still bore their Golden Suns but the fourth had no adornments in his collar.

Bulan looked at the Warlord, waited for his nod and then raised his arm in the air.

Pan'assár held his breath, tried to remain calm but couldn't quite managed it. But it didn't matter because no one was looking at him. They were watching the hundreds of Silvan warriors who were now swarming the room and still, there were more outside.

The doors would remain open, because there was no room to close them.

Pan'assár's breath hitched in his throat, emotions threatening to overwhelm him. How he had dreaded this moment. He had managed to convince himself that hardly any would come, that he would be forced to relinquish his command, in spite of the king's refusal to take it. He would fail in his oath to Or'Talán to protect his line. When he had given it, it had been unconditional, intemporal, a promise made unto death.

It would have been the end of him, the end of his life on Bel'arán.

Next to the commander, General Rinon was nodding his head at something Turion was murmuring as he pointed to this or that warrior or lieutenant amongst the crowds. It was nothing short of a miracle they said, and their eyes drifted to the Warlord who looked on in satisfaction and wonder.

With a nod at Bulan, Dalú, Amon and Benat stepped into the circle and occupied their chairs for the first time in many months.

The crack of a wooden staff on the stone floors and the Ceremony Master raised it high over his head, his powerful voice rising above the growing voices.

"The Inner Circle turns."

Pan'assár stepped into the Circle, his face as straight and controlled as he could make it. Perfect to those that didn't know him well, but the generals close by could see the turmoil of emotions beneath those icy eyes, beneath the hard lines of his features.

And then he caught sight of Bulan as he came to stand with The Company. He hesitated, forced his gaze away from those wary Silvan eyes.

"Tonight, we gather together – Silvan, Alpine and Ari - for the first time since the enemy was vanquished, for the first time since the death of Band'orán and his doctrines, his treachery and that of Huren, Dinor and Bendir. Welcome, warriors of the forest.

"Tonight, we take our first steps upon the road towards a new future. It is the Restoration, the king's promise of peace and unity. We will never forget what happened here, in these hallowed halls, will never make those same mistakes again, as Aria is my witness. *I* – will never make those mistakes again. I am sorry for the injustices of the past. Sorry for the complacency and disdain and I now strive to regain your respect. This will be my objective now, my driving force, the reason I continue to command this army. I will not fail you."

He had said it. His voice had not faltered, and his eyes had not welled. But once more, they were drawn to Bulan, found him staring back at him. He wrenched his eyes away one more time.

"Soon, these hallowed chairs will all be occupied by Silvan and Alpine captains alike and in equal measure. Our only consideration for their promotions will be their ability to command. Social status, race or family affiliation will not influence our decisions. Once the Circle is complete, a new army will emerge, one General Fel'annár has put to me and that I have accepted.

"One army, one commander general. Two divisions, two commanders. General Turion for the Mountain Division and General Fel'annár for the Forest Division. They are not exclusive, warriors. They are open to any and all, in accordance with where you wish to serve and in what capacity.

"It will not be a quick transition, but work has already begun to make this a reality. And yet time is not on our side.

"Some of you already know of the still distant threat of the Nim'uán. Those of you who have joined us in the past few days will soon hear of it from your commanding officers. This beast may be coming for our forest, or perhaps it is returning to Tar'eastór to finish what it began. It may also be heading for Araria and the Last Markers. We do not know.

"But we must be ready, to defend these lands or those of our allies."

The commander walked slowly around the Circle, eyes resting on every captain as he spoke.

"It is time to correct our errors, and to this end, I have gathered us all here to witness this new beginning – the Restoration – a return to our own days of glory in which Silvan and Alpine warriors were brothers and *will* be once more." His eyes drifted past Amon, Eramor and then Sar'pén.

Pan'assár turned to the side and nodded at a warrior who then made for the small table at the very centre. He lit the candle which sat beside the still closed Warrior Code and then stepped away, making room for the commander. Pan'assár reached out and opened the hard cover to the first page. And then he read in his finest voice of command.

"The warrior is the servant, the protector of peace. With his arms he guards it fiercely, shields others from harm. And so he is love, in its purest, most valiant form."

"These are the opening words, wise words we must all rekindle in our hearts. This is our law once more and I its staunch defender. In this our code, there is no mention of race, no mention of higher or lesser warriors. There is no mention of the boons owed a warrior, no rights save for the recognition and thanks of those we seek to defend – our king and our people. He or she who upholds this simple principle, is welcome to serve in this the Inner Circle which I command once more. And as its commander, I will no longer tolerate injustice, wherever it comes from. You have my solemn oath."

A moment of thought in which the room seemed to fade away and Pan'assár saw himself kneeling before Or'Talán, pledging his oath of fealty. He glanced upwards, to the heavy drape upon which an acorn and emerald slowly swayed to and fro, and then he sought out Fel'annár, green eyes staring back at him. Yes, the Warlord understood his mind, but his expression was neither indulgent nor conciliatory. What he saw there was expectation, a demand to fulfil his promises, the surety of his wrath should he fail. Pan'assár understood that sentiment. Fel'annár had put his own status in question, had told these warriors that he, Pan'assár, had changed. The Warlord had made promises to them, risked his honour for this one, last chance Pan'assár had, to right the wrongs he had committed after Or'Talán died.

Pan'assár wouldn't fail these warriors. He wouldn't fail Fel'annár Aren Or'Talán.

"May the Restoration begin!" Pan'assár gestured to Fel'annár, who then turned to a warrior beside him, a large cushion in his hands. Upon it, three Golden Suns, one of which had once sat in Bulan's collar.

He stepped into the Circle, the warrior at his side.

"Lieutenants Salo and Henú. If you wish to serve as captains in this army, step into the Circle."

All heads turned to the two lieutenants who stood as stiff as iron posts in winter frost. They eventually found the wherewithal to take a step, the hands of their fellow warriors moving them along, patting them on the backs and cheering as they stepped into the Circle for the first time.

Fel'annár watched them salute him with dazed eyes, and with a smile of his own, he removed their single silver lines, replaced them with a Golden Sun. And then, he gave them their first salute as captains. He gestured to the seats they should occupy, and Dalú corrected Salo when he made for the wrong one.

Fel'annár's eyes landed heavily on his uncle, but for all that he tried, he couldn't read his mind, his intentions. "Bulan. If you wish to serve once more in this army, step into the Circle."

There. He'd said it. He waited, watched, saw Bulan's hesitation, willed him to move but he just stood there, the warriors around him staring. There was nothing more Fel'annár could do. It was not for him to convince Bulan before the Circle. Besides, he had already spoken enough. Bulan would either come forward or stand there and make a fool of him.

But he didn't. Placing one foot before the other, Bulan walked slowly into the Circle where once he had sat and served, in a time when the great king still ruled and Pan'assár had been noble. Fel'annár followed his line of sight, to the chair Bulan had once held, the only one that bore the symbol of the Three Sisters. The ex-captain looked at Pan'assár, a message clear in his eyes. Fel'annár could see how much it had cost him to leave, how much it cost him to return. Bulan stopped before the Warlord.

There was nothing in Bulan's collar to take out and so Fel'annár placed the Golden Sun there, smoothed his fingers over it and then saluted. Bulan returned it, and the ruckus that followed was like nothing Fel'annár had ever heard.

There was no silencing them. They cheered and clapped as Bulan slowly sat in his chair, the only one to bear the sigil of the Three Sisters. Yes, Fel'annár had asked the captains to return and they had. But the warriors were here for Bulan. They followed their greatest of captains, and Fel'annár wondered if they would ever follow him in that way.

Pan'assár came to stand beside Fel'annár and then turned to the crowds. "As of today, a new army will rise. The Warrior Code stands open once more, marks this day of glory, a day to be registered in the Silvan Chronicles of Ea Uaré, in the Alpine Chronicles of Tar'eastór and the Book of Initiates of Araria. From this day forth, in service to king and land and *all* her peoples, we stand to defend!"

The thud of the Ceremony Master's staff signified the end of the proceedings and for a while, they simply stood or sat in silence, contemplated the strange sight of Silvan captains sitting in the Circle, their Warlord of old standing at the head of it.

Someone spoke, and then another, and the shock of all the things Pan'assár and Fel'annár had said and done began to wear off. The noise rose until it was almost unbearable.

The ceremony was over, Pan'assár's role in it done and only now did he seem to truly realise the impact of what had happened. He stepped away from the crowds, stood on the side-lines and watched the captains and the lieutenants as they approached each other. Alpines nodded and smiled at the returned Silvans, for the most part at least.

"It is hard to put into words, isn't it?" asked Gor'sadén from beside him.

Indeed, Pan'assár said nothing and his eyes strayed to Fel'annár, Tensári and The Company close around him. They did well to be wary, thought the commander. The danger to him seemed to be over, but there was no point in taking risks in such a crowded place, with their new-found concord so fresh and raw. He watched Tensári as she watched everyone with her shiny blue eyes, and then he saw Galadan nod at Fel'annár and start towards him.

"Commanders," greeted Galadan with a salute.

"Captain," said Pan'assár with a smile, watching as Galadan took up a place on his right, as he had done so many times in the past when they had been in the field, before Galadan had joined The Company.

"Who would have thought," murmured Galadan, so softly Gor'sadén had to lean sideways to hear him. "Who would have thought we would live a day such as this? I still remember when we were all brothers. Back then, we would never have dreamed any of this would be necessary. How much damage one elf can do, given sufficient time and the power to persuade."

"Wise words," said Pan'assár as he continued to watch the hall. "Idernon's presence is rubbing off on you."

"A welcome thing. It will take years to eradicate Band'orán's lies completely. Still, I know Fel'annár is just as shocked as the rest of us with this response."

Pan'assár knew the loyalty of the Silvan warriors to Fel'annár – the ones who knew him, those who came from the encampment. But many of these warriors seemed to have come from the forest from what he had seen and heard. His gaze drifted to Bulan, remembered him well. He turned back to Galadan.

"The Spear Master will be a great asset to this army. I remember how he was respected. When he relinquished his command to me, I did nothing. I held my hand out to him, accepted his Golden Sun and watched him walk away. That was the beginning of the end for me."

"And so he returns and it is a new beginning," said Galadan, determination lending his features a hard edge.

Pan'assár looked back at him, thanked the Gods for this irreplaceable captain who had always understood him, even during the worst moments of his life.

"So it is, Galadan. So it is." Pan'assár's eyes were back on the crowds. "They all deserve to enjoy this moment."

Galadan turned to him, studied the familiar face, the one he had always respected, even in the face of bigotry.

"So do you, Commander. So do *you*."

He saluted, nodded at Gor'sadén and then returned to The Company.

"What an extraordinary elf," said Gor'sadén. "He's as old as we are, has his own wisdom he imparts sparingly. An elf of few words and great deeds."

"Fel'annár is lucky to have him. Still, I would borrow him occasionally, for old times' sake."

"Well then. Tomorrow, the work begins in earnest. New contingents and units, captains to invest – the usual," said Gor'sadén with a smile.

"Silvan warriors to welcome back, create new barracks for any females who wish to join. And recruitment – for apprenticeship in the Kal'hamén'Ar."

"That is a very long list, Pan. Still, I am here for a while at least."

Pan'assár allowed himself a smile, reckoned he deserved it, and for the first time, his eyes landed squarely on his friend. "Yes, yes you are here. And the Gods know I will need you. I am the stumbling block in this structure. My presence is, perhaps, the only thing that can hinder our progress now."

"You have me, you have Fel'annár's unconditional support. He told the Silvans that if they did not return because of you, then he would relinquish his position as Warlord."

Pan'assár stared at Gor'sadén, processed the words.

"*He* told you that?"

"No. Handir mentioned it."

Pan'assár looked away slowly, eyes finding Fel'annár once more. Gods but it could have been Or'Talán standing there. His grandson was entirely his own person, similar yet different in none of the ways that mattered. He had hated Fel'annár once and yet now, he was coming to love him.

He made a promise then, as steadfast as the promise he had once made to Or'Talán. He would show the Silvans that the Warlord had not spoken in vain. He would protect him as he had the king and his children.

And he always would.

COMMANDER HOBIN NARROWED his bright blue eyes, a tattered parchment in his hands. He had read dozens of these, reports from the past in which a half elf had been involved in an encroachment at the Last Markers. Elven families who had adopted a half elf, or human families with mixed species children. Those who had been caught in time had been turned away, while those who had passed the Last Markers had been killed. But there was always the chance that they would try again. The Shirán knew where most of them were, had tracked their movements for years.

But this was new.

A mother of four half-elven children who had not been tracked. Hobin's eyes raked over the careful script of the commanding officer's report from many decades ago, over the date and the description of his encounter with the small group.

Strange tongue.

He scowled, sat and bent over the script. The woman had had an accent the Ari'atór had not been able to identify, and the children clicked and trilled like birds or perhaps insects.

A wave of burning needles swept over his skin. Sand Lord? Had the mortal father been a Sand Lord?

Further down the scroll, almost to the end.

Auburn coloured hair, light green eyes. Probably of Silvan origin.

They had been turned away, but the warrior had alerted the night patrol. She was likely to try again, he said.

On the very last line was a name: Ankelar of Ea Nanú.

He let the parchment fall from his hands and onto the table. He stood, one hand resting on his hip, the other over his mouth. He needed to think. He walked to the shelves of books which lined the walls of his private office, slightly favouring his left leg.

Hobin didn't know if she had willingly walked into a relationship with a Sand Lord. Perhaps she had been forced during a raid, abducted even. But he had her name and her origin and that was enough to trace her line, document it and investigate it. If any Nim'uán were still alive, perhaps she or a member of her family would know where they were.

He shook his head, trying and failing to imagine the heartache of never passing into the next life. Never seeing your departed family again because should she cross, she would never see her children again.

Half elves were not allowed to cross the Veil. It was prohibited because it was said that on the other side, they would no longer be human and yet neither would they be Deviant. They said Deviants didn't exist on the other side of Valley. Hobin had always wondered how anyone could know that. As far as he was aware, it wasn't possible to go there and then return here.

It was one of the great questions that occupied the minds of the Spirit Herders, the reason for the very existence of the Shirán. That closed circle of singular Ari'atór had their own agenda, one they shared with no one.

Still, the onus was on him to inform them and they, in turn, would send news of any trace they could find of what may be left of this Silvan woman's family.

Ankelar of Ea Nanú. What happened to you, sister?

MAENETH LOVED THE SEA.

Under a blue summer sun, a slate winter sky or the deep dark of a star-strewn night, there was nothing like the comforting feel of water below her. She would allow it to take her, and as it did, she indulged in a moment of reflexion.

Tonight was one of those cloudless, moonless nights. It was cold, and the stars always seemed to like that for they dressed in their finest and most colourful on nights like these. There was red and blue, yellow and white, even green. She had always wondered why that would be. And then she tried to imagine being on one of those colourful balls, looking at this world she lived in. What did it look like from the other side? What colour was Bel'arán?

Why?

Saltwater slid over wood, hissed as the bow cut through it. She licked her lips, tasted the salty brine and then looked over the side of the railing she held on to with one hand. Rainbow jumpers slumbered beneath those inky depths, waiting for the dawn of a new day so that they could play their games, boast their colourful fins and steal the breath of any lucky enough to watch their galivanting.

Winches creaked and clicked behind her, sails billowing softly above her. She looked up, past the high masts that jutted skywards, reaching for the stars, as if they pointed at them, bid her look at the majesty of nature she had always wanted to understand.

Strange night, as if she hung between two realities, like an interlude, a rare moment of inflection in which she was nowhere in particular, oddly detached and yet strangely comforted by the sheltering sky above her, the undulating currents beneath her.

How beautiful the world was when one was free to see it like this, with time to observe and reflect. No baggage from the past, no worldly wisdom born of experience. Just eyes curious enough to look, bold enough to ask. Brave enough to understand the truth.

She would soon be home.

Ea Uaré, forest cradle, it hummed in her blood, its tune still distant and diluted.

Four days away. Four days closer to an estranged father, a brother she had missed, and a twin that she loved more than anything.

Rinon.

WHO WILL FOLLOW ME?

~

RINON STRODE DOWN THE CORRIDOR, bound for the king's chambers where both his and Fel'annár's families waited for news from the Inner Circle.

Fel'annár was glad that Rinon had chosen to lead the way rather than walking at his and Tensári's side. It would have been awkward, especially because he was sure that neither of them had any inclination to speak to each other.

They came to the king's doors and his guards, who stomped to attention and opened them. The prince was inside before Fel'annár reached the threshold. He glanced over his shoulder, saw Tensári take up her spot in the corridor and then turned back to the open room, contemplating the scene before him.

Rinon was with the king and his guests, surely informing him of what had happened at the Inner Circle. It was a while before Llyniel noticed him standing there. She glided over to him, beautiful in her Silvan dress and Tona Lia. It was her face though, that finally drove home just what he had achieved, what they had all achieved. Her hand rose to his face, smoothed down a cheek and he mimicked her gesture, smiled down at her with the same devotion in his eyes, an overwhelming urge to pull her close.

Who exactly had initiated their embrace, neither could say, but Fel'annár relished it, simply stood there in her arms upon the threshold of the king's chambers, neither inside nor out.

Miren smiled at them, while Handir watched from the king's side and Rinon made for the drinks cabinet. Amareth approached them, waited for the two to step away from each other.

"We saw them, Fel'annár," said Amareth. "We saw rank after rank of warriors and our four captains before them, even Bulan. We heard the war drums, felt their beat in our souls."

Fel'annár nodded at her, saw Lorthil, Erthoron and Narosén behind her. He wanted to say something, but no words would come. Reality was settling in his mind, and the enormity of the project, the burden that now sat upon his shoulders was almost overwhelming. Llyniel frowned at his silence, while Amareth cocked her head to one side.

"Let Bulan help you, Fel'annár. Our warriors respect him, at least as much as they do Dalú."

"I know." He could only smile at her tone. She thought he would reject Bulan for some reason, didn't understand that of them all, his uncle was the one he felt most comfortable with. Strange, because he had only just met him, had hardly exchanged words with him at all.

Handir joined them, held out a glass to Fel'annár and Llyniel and on his face a smile and the promise of conversation once the formalities had been dispensed with. But for now, it was the king who spoke.

"Two of my three sons are generals, instigators of a new era. My other son started it, a royal councillor, mastermind of our new political system and my law daughter is the first female, half-Silvan Lestari. To my children and their accomplishments, and to the new world they will create." He held his glass high, watched as every arm rose to join it. They drank.

"I bid you all dispense with formalities. Leave the lords, ladies, princes and sires for the court. Tonight, we are family, and soon, that family will be complete. Princess Maeneth returns from Dan'sú."

Rinon's smile was wide, made him look utterly different, more like his father, *their* father, Fel'annár corrected himself.

"That's wonderful! It's been over fifty years since I saw her. I wonder how things have been." Miren was rubbing her hands with glee.

"They've been good," said Llyniel. "I haven't seen her since I left Pelagia for Tar'eastór, but she's been happy. The two kings have been most gracious with her. We'll soon be toasting her deeds too. She has made quite a name for herself."

"As what?" asked Thargodén.

Llyniel smiled, a hint of sadness in it. As her father, he should not have had to ask that question. "It's hard to describe. She is an agriculturist, a forester, a fish farmer and an economist. A land reformer and a merchant – all rolled into one." She shrugged and then drank.

Rinon was beaming, but the king's eyebrows were almost at his hairline. He, like most of the others, thought Maeneth was a botanist.

"She grows things in unlikely places, changes those places and renourishes the ground. She improves the yield of vegetable produce, teaches others how to do it so that they can be self-sufficient."

The concept was foreign to everyone except to Rinon, who had always kept regular correspondence with his twin. They had imagined her as an academic, sitting in the guild and studying plant structures.

"Has she found love?" Miren's eyes were intense, comically curious and Llyniel grinned. "Not love, no, to the great ruin of many an attentive courtier. She's too intelligent for most of them. They want to talk about quiet walks, parties and holding hands while she wants answers to the mysteries of life, spends half her time with her hands and feet in mud." She chuckled and shrugged her shoulders. "She'll be in fine company with Idernon and Sontúr."

Rinon's lips curled upwards and back. "Who is Idernon?" It was almost a growl and Fel'annár didn't need to turn to him to understand the look on his face.

"Idernon the Wise is my brother in The Company. You seem to have forgotten that you met him, Prince."

Rinon stared back at him. "So I did. He *defied* me."

Fel'annár smiled, not kindly. "So he did."

Icy blue eyes flickered, but Fel'annár wisely said nothing and Miren skilfully changed the subject.

"And now that you are bonded in the eyes of the Silvans, when will you marry – in the way of the Alpines?"

Llyniel frowned at her incorrigible mother. "There are priorities, and I know Fel'annár will be away for most of the time these coming weeks. But when circumstance permits, perhaps you and Amareth will organise it for us?"

Miren's eyes widened, almost as wide as her mouth. "Of course! Oh, and what a wonder it will be. A celebration, Thargodén, in the great Banqueting Hall if you please. It would be the perfect excuse to bring our people together, wouldn't you agree, Aradan?"

"There is political merit to the idea. We all need a reason to celebrate, one that will be inclusive of both cultures. What would you say to that idea, Amareth?"

"I believe it would do much to bring our people together. I second it although I wouldn't be much good with the finer points, Miren. I'd leave that part to you."

"Is it not too early, Aradan?" drawled Rinon. "After everything that has happened. Gods but we were killing each other not a week past, the pyres still burn, and we would celebrate a *wedding*?"

"Rinon. That is precisely why we *should* consider this," explained Aradan, and Amareth nodded.

"And perhaps you are both right," said Handir. "There are priorities, and giving the people time to return to whatever normalcy they can, may work in our favour. There is no reason to force the issue, is there?"

"Well said." Thargodén raised his goblet and drank once more. "Come and sit. The evening is beautiful."

Fel'annár glanced at Amareth, willing her not to enter into the political discussion. He was tired of it, just wanted to relax, as much as he could in the presence of his father and elder brother, after what had happened at the Inner Circle.

They followed after their father. Rinon shot Handir a cutting glance, one that was returned with cool regard. Fel'annár could almost feel the tension between them, as surely as he felt Rinon's aversion. But he was distracted by the landscape that loomed before him as they stepped outside and towards the finely decked table.

The king's gardens, which spread out over the Great Plateau, was a stunning piece of natural architecture. It stretched forwards and outwards, giving the impression that you were standing upon the helm of a mighty ship, floating not upon the salty waters but above the very boughs of an ancient forest with arcane secrets not even Fel'annár was privy to. He wanted to run to the very end of it, open his arms and soar on hot currents.

They make maps.

He frowned, indulgent thoughts cut short by the intruding words. It had come from the forest, almost flippant. But who was *they*? *Who* made maps?

Step into the Evergreen Wood, Lord.

He sat straighter, head cocked slightly to one side. And then he jumped at Miren's sudden laughter, turned back to the table and focussed on the people around him.

He, Llyniel, Miren and Rinon sat on one side of it and opposite, were Handir, Amareth, Lorthil and Narosén. At one end was Aradan and at the other, the king presided.

Servants moved around them, and when they had finished setting down the dishes and wines, the king nodded his thanks. For a while, they ate as Rinon and Fel'annár related the events of the Inner Circle, and by the time dinner had come to an end, Erthoron gestured to Lorthil and Narosén. They stood, turned to the king.

"We will take our leave, my king. Know that we will be on the Royal Council, for whenever you call. We look forward to this new era, Thargodén. It has cost us all so much, but in the end, common sense has prevailed. It will be a slow but welcome return to normalcy, to the way things were under your great father's rule."

Thargodén stood, nodded his thanks. "And I look forward to that normalcy, Erthoron. It is time to push forward, time for progress. I look forward to your contributions on the Council."

With a bow, Erthoron glanced sideways at Amareth, smiled, and then left with Lorthil and Narosén, leaving her alone with her family.

Thargodén sat, leaned forward, forearms resting on the edge of the table.

"Well then, here we are, celebrating at last. You are my family, complete save for Maeneth, Canusahéi and Lássira. This day merits nothing less and I would mark it with a revelation, one which until now, I was never at liberty to discuss."

Aradan leaned forward, the two princes froze and Fel'annár watched the king closely.

"There are some of you here that do not know about the extraordinary events that led up to the battle and the enemy's demise. And I know it is something you have questions about."

The king reached into his ample robes and placed a small, leather journal upon the table, one Fel'annár immediately recognised. Thargodén opened it, rough cut emerald sliding around his finger. He flipped to a page and pressed the journal open. There, upon the weathered parchment, was the sketch Or'Talán had made of Lássira, her Bonding Braid prominent in the foreground. Handir and Fel'annár had already seen it, but the others around the table had not. The implications of Lássira's braid were clear.

"I wanted you to be the first to know, before you find out from someone else. Despite gossip and hearsay, Fel'annár is not an illegitimate child."

"Our *queen*," stated Amareth.

"She was not *our* queen." Rinon stared at her from across the table and Amareth glared back at him, seemingly unimpressed with his cutting blue eyes.

"She was a queen under *Silvan* law, my son. Still is. Fel'annár is not illegitimate to them. He is the firstborn son of the Silvan queen. Lássira and I were bonded but I never spoke of it because as you all know, she was forbidden to me. I could not disrespect my father's wishes, not publicly."

"There can only be one queen."

"It is not my fault that there were *two*, Rinon. Amareth knew, Or'Talán knew and so did the enemy."

Rinon's wide eyes rested on his father, willing him to continue.

"I mention this because I have come to understand that my father's intention was to help me – help us – so that we could be together without incurring Band'orán's ire. It is all here, in this last diary before his death. Now that I have read it, now that I know he never betrayed me, that he had welcomed Lássira as my queen, only one mystery remains. It is this mystery that I must solve, and when I do, I will weave my own Bonding Braid in my hair."

Rinon leaned forward, about to speak but Thargodén continued before his son could protest.

"It does not affect my marriage to Canusahéi. By marrying her, any previous bonds would be considered null according to Alpine law. But not to the Silvans. To them, that bond cannot be broken unless it is by those who undertook it." He breathed deeply, glanced to his right and the shadowed forest.

"You are my family. You need to know, and I ask that you respect my bond with Lássira, as much as you respect my marriage to Canusahéi."

"Is that why you were so quick to accept *him*? Because you felt guilty?"

"Rinon," warned Handir, and Thargodén held up his hand for silence, chanced a glance at Amareth's forbidding face, Fel'annár's glittering eyes.

"I was quick to accept him because he is my *son*."

With a noisy breath, the crown prince poured himself another glass of wine. "You should have told us."

"And what would have been the point, Rinon?" asked Aradan from the other side of the table. "It would have angered you, even more than it already has. There were other, more urgent issues to attend to."

Rinon said nothing to that and a contemplative silence fell over the small company.

"Now. Peace is fragile at best. As Rinon has said, it has been mere days since Fel'annár and I nearly died at Analei. But The Company found us and we have our lives. Everything else matters little. Our arguments, our disagreements on such matters as to whether I was bonded or not, whether Fel'annár is illegitimate or not – they mean little when you consider the love I will always feel for Lássira, for my son. I am not asking you to agree with me, I am not even asking you to like it. But I am asking you to show our people that we are united as a family. They need a strong king, a strong crown prince. They need to understand that there are Silvan members of this royal family, and that we are all the stronger for it."

Aradan nodded and Miren smiled while Handir's eyes seemed lost to some memory he gave voice to. "So much has happened in so little time. The revelation of Or'Talán's diary, of his thoughts and worries. The battles and the treachery of Band'orán exposed in its pages. For some of us, these past weeks have been the greatest challenge of our lives."

Fel'annár smiled softly, not in joy but remembrance. "And not all of us returned. Our brother Lainon was lost in the mountains."

"And Fel'annár faced a truth he had never expected to hear, the identity of his family." Handir turned from his half-brother to the king. "When I think of it now, our interaction at first was a study in grief, in pride, anger and confusion. But we worked it out, because there was a plan, a plan that was bigger than the pain that divided us. It was a plan I, Lainon, Turion and Aradan here traced. Today, that plan is complete, played out in the best possible way that it could have."

Thargodén, Rinon, Aradan, Miren and Amareth sat riveted, heads moving from Handir to Fel'annár. As for Llyniel, she smiled. She had been there, on that adventure of a lifetime and survived. Fel'annár took over from Handir.

"Only this time there are no raging rivers to sweep us away."

"And no Hounds to rip us to pieces," said Handir.

"No crumbling cliffs to fall off." Fel'annár's gaze was challenging.

"No gummy, drunken townsfolk barrelling into us."

Fel'annár grinned. "No pirates to punch and break your knuckle."

"No mercenaries to run from." Handir leaned forward, Fel'annár followed.

"No Shadows to fear."

"No *Band'orán*." Handir leaned back in his chair, triumphant.

"We did it, didn't we?" said Fel'annár, turned to Llyniel as he said it and then back to the prince.

"We did. And we can do *this*. I do not say it will be easy, rebuilding trust, but you and I together ..."

Fel'annár's eyes filled at Handir's words, and Lainon stirred in his mind. He rather thought his first Ber'ator would be proud.

Handir held up his glass, Fel'annár and Llyniel met it. They toasted and they drank, under the watchful stares of the others. The king smiled, wondering perhaps, if he would ever hear those tales from their journey home. He caught Aradan's gaze and then Amareth's and then watched

Rinon as he watched them. The anger had gone and in its place was caution and carefully concealed curiosity.

From the moment Handir and Fel'annár had broken the awkwardness, Fel'annár had pushed his feelings of trepidation away and began to enjoy himself.

They had risen from the table, scattered into the gardens beyond as they drank from the king's coveted collection of fine wines.

Miren was already planning her daughter's Alpine wedding and Llyniel was indulgent with her for the most part. But it had eventually become too much, and she had broken away to speak with Handir. And so, Fel'annár wandered off into the gardens, to the very edge of the plateau and stood high above the splendour of the Evergreen Wood, seeing it from the heights for the first time.

The Evergreen Wood awaits.

Thargodén saw him from afar, nodded at Amareth and ventured into the gardens. Her anxious stare followed him for a while, and then she forced herself to turn away. Before long, the king stood silently beside Fel'annár.

"What is it that you see?"

Fel'annár was silent for a while and Thargodén knew he was considering his answer.

"Beauty, strength, a mystery I have yet to solve."

His son's voice was far away, almost whimsical. They had yet to address this affinity they both shared with the forest, but Fel'annár's strange gift was far beyond what Thargodén had ever been able to do.

"How does it work, this skill of yours?"

"That's a good question. Perhaps it's best to consider it an energy which is malleable. It can be initiated on one side, felt on the other, acted upon. The question rather, is where that energy comes from. I have the ability to stir it, with the trees as a catalyst but so do they, and in turn they use me as the instigator. I can build on that energy through the Dohai, call on it in battle, either to enhance my own fighting or to enlist the help of the trees."

"No simple Listener then."

"No. I am that, but I believe these are two separate skills, that work together to make an entirely different ability."

"And what of Aria's hand in this?"

Fel'annár turned to his father for the first time, studied him for a moment.

Thargodén smiled. "There is a lot of your mother in you. That thoughtful expression on your face, the fleeting pout when she was considering something. She would be proud of her Ari son."

Fel'annár said nothing. He already suspected his father knew from the conversation he had overheard after their rescue from Analei.

"I deduced that much – and more. It was Tensári's eyes that told me the whole truth."

Fel'annár just stood there, waiting for him to say it and Thargodén did, quietly.

"She is Ber'ator, I heard Gor'sadén say it. The rest was easy to guess. Was Band'orán your purpose?"

"No."

Thargodén hadn't expected that, remained silent in the hopes that his son would clarify.

"It was a necessary requisite, a part of the whole. I am to unite these lands. Bring Silvans and Alpines together, to achieve an ultimate goal I have yet to understand."

"Is the purpose not simply that? To unify the land?"

"No. Aria is Guardian. The duty she sets her servants is always to protect, to defend. Unity is a wonderful thing, but that is not her primary concern."

"You think there is some threat she seeks to defend us from?"

"I do. I know that it comes – the Nim'uán – and the question is, will we be ready to confront it? Will our army and our people be ready in time for us to defend ourselves from invasion? If we're not, then between Ea Uaré and Araria there is but a mountain range."

"She seeks to defend the Source itself?"

"I believe that may be the case. Thargodén ..."

"You find it hard to call me by my name ..."

"I do. I'm just not ... not used to this, to having a father with a name."

Thargodén stared at the extraordinary profile, the face that reminded him of his own father and the puzzle he had still to solve about Lássira and her assassin, about why he never received Or'Talán's letter.

"I haven't told Handir yet. He knows I am Ari but not the rest and I am sorry for the way he found out about that. I will not have him think he is unimportant to me that I can't confide in him. Let me tell him."

"I will not tell anyone, Fel'annár. That is for you to reveal, if and when you so desire. But be warned. Handir is far more observant than any of us. He may already know."

The idea was unwelcome, and yet if Handir did know, he wasn't angry. His gaze drifted over the treetops and for a moment, his eyes flared and then dimmed. Thargodén watched in fascination.

"It is a wary welcome they give me, like a mother with open arms and a foot jamming her door closed. I am welcome to explore up to the lake beyond this first area before us. See it there?" Fel'annár pointed into the distance.

"I cannot see it at night, but I know where you mean."

"Beyond that point, my presence will not be tolerated. And I wonder. Did you know that this forest is not quite – friendly?" Fel'annár turned to him, waited for an answer to a question that had surprised the king into silence.

"No. My ability to listen is weak at best, Fel'annár. I sometimes feel their joy or their sadness, but nothing more than that. What exactly do you mean?"

"It's almost as if it's … defensive. For some reason, it sees me as a threat and yet doesn't want to. It doesn't make sense, not yet at least."

"But it wishes us no harm, surely?"

"No. It's not that. But what we saw that day, how it destroyed our enemy. Although I have seen that before, I'd never felt the glee of death in a forest. And that unnerves me."

Thargodén stared at Fel'annár's profile, more shocked than he would admit to anyone else. This had always been his favourite place to be. He had felt nothing but peace and calm. But to think this forest had enjoyed the killing …

"Then we must pray it remains on our side."

"It helped us once. It'll do so again if the need arises. But there is a mystery to this place, one not even I am invited to know."

"Will you tell me if you discover it?"

Fel'annár turned to him. "If it is not a secret, yes." Fel'annár turned back to the forest, and Thargodén saw his hesitation.

"Would you allow me to enter? I know it is forbidden, open only to the Silvan foresters but they don't go there either, at least not that I know of. The trees call me lord, bid me enter, and I wonder if that is enough for you to make an exception?"

Thargodén considered it. Or'Talán had indeed forbidden entrance to that place and for the first time he questioned the reasons he had been given at the time. His father had said it had been a concession to the Silvan people, a stretch of the kingdom that would always be entirely theirs, despite the Alpine king who ruled over them.

"I will allow it, so long as you do not go beyond that place you speak of. If you can promise me that, if you can later tell me of what you see, then you have my blessing."

Fel'annár's smile was quick and wide. "Thank you then, Thargodén."

His name on his son's lips sounded better now. But there was one other name he wished he would use, one more time. Fel'annár had said it in the flood pit when his death seemed a surety and he had said it again just recently, when Thargodén had interrupted his moment of respite with the commanders.

Father.

He was startled from his thoughts with Fel'annár's next words.

"It has been a good evening."

Thargodén smiled, tentative at first and then wider.

"Yes, yes it has."

HEAVY IRON KEYS rattled outside his door.

He sat up, swung his legs over the bench, thin blanket slipping away.

He peered into the pitch black, saw a slit of light under his door. This was, perhaps, the worst thing about captivity.

The darkness.

He sat, watched and waited as the orange slit became a bright light. Bright, at least, to one who had sat in the dark for so many days.

One elf. One candle. He craved it, wanted to reach out and touch it, no matter it burned.

"I bring news."

He sat straighter, steeled his nerve. "Speak it."

Silence. Not good news then.

"The Silvans have returned. Over two thousand of them."

A drop of water, its sound overly loud in this tomb-like silence. It was not what he had wanted to hear.

"Then the Lestari's sacrifice has been in vain. It seems provocation is no longer effective. We must move on, cut the limbs from the body, so that the head can no longer rule over it."

"What would you have us do?"

"Lie in wait. Watch. Take advantage of the opportunities that arise. Be subtle, be patient. Lead them into danger."

The click of a boot over stone, a pale hand rose, snuffed out the candle.

Silence. Another drop of water, something scurrying over the stone floor.

An exhale of breath.

"I have to go."

"I pray you will have better news, next time."

He received no answer, listened to the boots that shuffled towards the door, slow and careful lest he fall and make too much noise.

The slit of orange light was back, just for a moment and then it faded, into darkness once more.

10

THE FOREST DIVISION

∼

WHAT A GLORIOUS EVENING it had been.

The Inner Circle and the unexpected return of so many Silvan warriors, and then his first dinner with his Alpine family. It had gone well, despite the underlying tension with Rinon.

Fel'annár and Llyniel had retired to their quarters, and now, the victim of their own, private celebration lay in ruins on the floor.

Llyniel's Pobdil dress.

It had not survived the night and Fel'annár wondered if it was completely beyond repair. There was no remorse though. It had been worth it, and his smile became a grin as he watched his wife sleep soundly next to him, bare shoulders peeking out from under the coverlet. He longed to join her in slumber, tired and relieved as he was.

But when he did, finally sleep, he dreamt of Aria. She stood at the gates to the Evergreen Wood, arms out, gesturing for him to follow.

He had told the king that his purpose as Ber'anor was to unite these lands, to bring Silvans and Alpines together, achieve an ultimate goal that he had yet to understand. But with each passing day packed with urgent tasks, all geared towards preparing their army to face the possibility of invasion, he had not had time to ponder the deeper questions that still haunted him. He wanted – needed – to know. What was it all for? What was his ultimate purpose?

What did Aria truly want of him?

All nations had conflicts, enemies to vanquish, people to protect. Why was Aria's intervention necessary in this case?

If the Nim'uán was headed to northern Tar'eastór, then it was either seeking to do what its brother failed to and take the Alpine citadel, or it was making for Araria. But Hobin's army was reportedly larger even than Vorn'asté's. It would take many thousands to overrun the Supreme Commander's forces and even then, there was no guarantee that they would even find the Source. It seemed almost self-destructive.

But the alternative was even more puzzling. Should the Nim'uán turn southwards and make for the forest, what was here that merited Aria's divine intervention?

The only unchartered territory was the Evergreen Wood, a place Or'Talán had declared off bounds. What lay in that place that the great king knew of, and had wished to keep secret?

He needed to know what it was, whether it was related to his purpose, before the enemy set foot inside the forest. If he was to protect something or someone related to that place, he needed to know what it was – now – before it was too late.

He turned in his bed, agitated yet tired but his resolve was bolstered. With Thargodén's permission in his pocket, he would step into the Evergreen Wood, and if his answers *did* lie there, then he would find them.

Llyniel stirred at his side, turned over to face him. With one arm propping up her head, the other trailed down his chest. "Isn't it a little early for pondering the conundrums of life?"

He turned, smiled at her beautiful face, her messy hair. "I am thinking about my purpose, its relation to the Evergreen Wood."

Her hand stopped its lazy wandering, shrewd Silvan eyes on him. "Why would there be a relation?"

"I don't know. But I need to find out. I need to go there, see what it is Aria wishes me to see."

"She calls you, inside that place?"

"Yes. But it's almost as if there were two entities. While Aria bids me enter, the forest gives a tentative welcome. It warns me not to pass the lake."

"And you are going inside, aren't you?"

"I asked the king's permission. He granted it."

"Did you forget to tell him that forest is hostile?"

"It's not to me, Llyn. So long as I don't pass the lake. I'll push back only as far as I can. I've no desire to be skewered on a branch or strangled by a vine."

Her eyes watched him closely. She knew him better than anyone, knew there was more.

"You know, this may not be the time, Fel'annár. This new army, this volatile peace we live in. It's you who holds the army together. Bulan came for you, the warriors came for him and you."

"I'll only be two, perhaps three days."

She narrowed her eyes. "There's more, isn't there? Otherwise, why the rush?"

He turned to her, considered how much he should tell her. "I told you I feel there is a connection between the forest and my purpose. If the Nim'uán is coming to Ea Uaré, that means I will march to war. Something tells me I must know, one way or the other, before that happens."

"You're acting on an intuition."

He searched her eyes for any traces of anger, found none.

"Yes. And it's something I must do alone. I need to think, to empty my mind, forget the army, the Kah, the threat of more traitors, my family ..."

"I understand, Fel'annár. I do – I'm not happy that you're going alone. But far be it from me to question you on this. You know my misgivings where Aria is concerned. But you, you're Ari'atór – Ber'anor. I just hope you come back to me, in one piece, on your own two feet."

He turned to her, pulled her to him and kissed her, hands roving, legs entwining.

It would be a late start for the General and the Lestari.

THARGODÉN WAS HAPPIER than he had been for many years. Maeneth was coming home, his army was slowly coming together, he had told his children of his bond with Lássira, and he had spoken at length with Fel'annár.

A soft smile pulled at his lips and he placed his quill in the ink well which sat on his desk, turned to the window and the warm morning sun.

There were surely hard times ahead of him, but he thought that the hardest ones were finally behind him. Everything was coming together, except for one thing.

Or'Talán.

His father had marched to war, knowing full well that he might never come back. And so the king had written a letter for his son, to be opened only if he fell in battle.

But Thargodén had never received it.

Draugolé had revealed this and more. He said Ileian, his father's Royal Councillor, had been disloyal, had surely kept the letter, or perhaps handed it down to his son Sulén, along with the king's journal.

But had Band'orán's right hand been telling him the truth?

If he had, then Thargodén needed to know the contents of that letter. He needed the closure, to read that final goodbye from a father he had loved and looked up to for so many years.

But how to achieve such a thing? It could be here, in Tar'eastór, anywhere on Bel'arán after so many years. It could also have been destroyed but he doubted that. It was worth too much to the right buyer.

And then a thought struck him, and a singular face came to his mind's eye.

Lerita.

She had known Or'Talán as well as anyone could. She had been his right hand in many things. While Lord Ileian had been his father's royal councillor, Lerita had been his confidant, his eyes in the military beyond those of Pan'assár, beyond what any normal elf saw.

Because Lerita, Or'Talán had once said, was no ordinary elf.

How had he not made the connection? Surely she would know about those days, about Or'Talán's troubles with his brother, about the letter he had written and where it might be – if it even existed.

He turned from the window and the Evergreen Wood, collected his long cloak and left together with the two guards at his door, bound for the Academic Guild.

Nothing could stop him now. He had told his children of his unbroken bond with Lássira, but he could not proclaim it to the world until the last piece of this life-long puzzle had slipped into place. He needed to know his father's mind before he could right a wrong that had been committed fifty-three years ago, against him, against the entire Silvan people.

The king and his two guards crossed the courtyard and ventured into the outskirts of the city proper, where the guilds dominated over the other, smaller and less ornate buildings.

If one continued across this square, along the main road, the city became more and more populated, the buildings smaller and the noise louder.

The market square came next, and then the artisan's quarters and beyond, all manner of places, some of them not quite safe.

Here though, the damage the recent battle had wrought was evident. Behind the everyday sounds of horse's hooves clip-clopping over stone, carpenters sawed through wood and masons chipped away at stone.

To his right, what had once been the community hall was a complete ruin. Fighting between the loyalists and the rebel Kah warriors had been fierce here, and what remained of this building would need to be pulled down and then rebuilt.

At the centre of the square, the fountains were still not working, and the trampled gardens looked wan and sorry. It would take months, if not years to return this part of the city to its past splendour.

The Merchant Guild, the Academic Guild and the Artisan Guild stood together with a public library and a place for quiet contemplation, where candles always flickered, and statues of Aria, Duria and Galomú stood in shaded corners, perched upon high cornices, looking down on the immortals some said they watched over. Thargodén believed in Aria at least and from time to time he had come here, cloaked and alone, sometimes in search of forgiveness, other times in search of hope.

He stepped inside the Academic Guild, stopped on the threshold and took a moment to look around him. As a child, he had always loved this place because it was mysterious and imposing, darker than the other buildings, but not for lack of candles. There were plenty of those. Rather, it was the book-loaded shelves that seemed to suck the light away.

There were books and scrolls everywhere. They lined the stone walls from floor to ceiling. Dark leather studded with muted colours of red and blue, green and then gold and silver filigree. They sometimes reflected the flicker of wall sconces, like a cheeky invitation to come and open their covers, look inside the pages and dare discover the mysteries of life and death, of Valley and the nature of the Source.

There were books here that Thargodén reckoned some would kill for.

It was what the academics did here, in part at least. Their endeavour was to care for the books, write and read them, understand the enigmas of the world. Who are we? Where are we? What lies beyond the Source?

His eyes wandered to the railings that surrounded the first floor and then travelled upwards to the second, the third and the last floor where he knew the Guild Master reigned supreme.

But Lerita was not in her quarters. She was on the ground floor, speaking to two preceptors in their blue robes and with them, an apprentice dressed in white. But the guild master always wore a deep purple robe and upon her head, the customary black turban that tied at the back, and then trailed down to her waist.

As a child, Thargodén had always wondered if they wore these head-dresses so that their massive brains would not flop out of their ears. He resisted the urge to smile at the memory and watched as Lerita dismissed the preceptors and turned to Thargodén, bowed low and then stared back at him. No emotion, no flicker of curiosity at all. It was a singular ability she possessed, one Or'Talán had commented on many times.

Thargodén had called on her just recently to decipher the contents of Vorn'asté's singular missive. She had done that, wondrous mind seeing through the images and the abstract words. She had solved the mystery in hours, a feat that would have taken any normal immortal days, if ever.

"Lerita."

"My king."

"Can we talk?"

"Of course. Come, tell me of the Inner Circle and the Restoration. I hear young Fel'annár has brought our fighters back to the ranks."

Thargodén smiled as they began to climb the stairs. They passed white-clad apprentices hanging from long ladders, replacing books and retrieving others that had been requested by the preceptors. They bowed as the two passed them.

"He has. If that Nim'uán is coming here, we will be half prepared at least. Our army will be entirely restructured – but I'm sure you already know all about that." The king half turned to her as they continued to climb, marvelled once more at the utter lack of emotion she showed.

"We know, yes. Of the army, of the new council. You are doing a fine job, Thargodén. All that is left to address now, is the blight that Band'orán left in his wake. There are those who still live amongst us, and who poison the minds of others, wishing to continue with his unnatural doctrine of supremacy and domination."

"Give me names and I will arrest them."

"No. Not yet. You'll find no proof. Wait until the time is right, Thargodén."

The king frowned, turned to her profile, wondering how she would know when that time came. But then he reminded himself of what Lerita had been to this kingdom when Or'Talán had lived. She had been a daily figure at the palace, so often at his father's side. She had always given Thargodén the chills, couldn't remember a time when she had smiled. But he did remember the gleam in her eyes when she walked at the great king's side.

Once he had considered the possibility that they had been lovers. Or'Talán's queen had taken the Long Road when Thargodén had come of age and his mother and father had broken their bond. Many years of passionate love had slowly turned into friendship and both had decided to part ways. It had been civil and kind, and Thargodén had been old enough to understand. But even to this day, his suspicions about his father and Lerita endured.

The double doors creaked open and Thargodén turned to his guards, nodded, and then closed them.

"Wine?"

"Yes." He sauntered over to the hearth, admired the painting of the Evergreen Wood that hung there. He had never seen this one before.

"Here."

Thargodén turned, took the wine Lerita offered him.

"Now then. Tell me what brings you here."

Thargodén nodded slowly, sipped his wine. It was rich and spicy; must have cost her a fortune and he drank again.

"My father's journal." He watched her closely, saw nothing that could be called a reaction and so he continued.

"Pan'assár found it on Sulén's dead body."

"Ar Ileian is dead, then?"

"Ambushed by Deviants close to the Glistening Falls. They cut off his head and staked it up with the rest of his travelling companions, Ras'dan included."

There. Thargodén was sure he had seen a flicker of curiosity.

"As you can imagine, Pan'assár laboured over whether he should read it or not, but eventually he did. In it, certain – facts – came to light."

"Regarding Band'orán?"

"Amongst other things, yes. And I wonder, Lerita. How much of what he says did you already know ..."

She stared back at him. He couldn't be sure if it was suspicion he could see behind her immaculately concealed emotions. But something had changed.

"Or'Talán was a brother to me. You know that. Admittedly, he did make certain confessions to me, things I would never dream of revealing – to anyone."

"Not even if I was meant to know those things?"

"What are you talking about?" There was a hint of irritation behind her question. Her cool calm was cracking, slowly and subtly.

"I am talking about the reason why he never told me he approved of my love for Lássira. The reason why he never told me before he marched to battle."

"Your father loved you more than anyone. He would not have hurt you intentionally."

"Leave the ciphers for your books and your research, Lerita. With me you speak plainly or not at all."

She held out a calming hand. "I know that he wrote a letter, that he gave it to Ileian for safe keeping, in case he fell in battle. With Ileian dead, I suppose we will never know what came of it."

So Draugolé had been telling the truth. Thargodén pressed on.

"Who else was close to Ileian? Someone who might have inherited it."

"It may no longer exist, Thargodén. In fact, it is most likely the case."

"Come Lerita. Let us not play children's games. Sulén kept my father's journal as leverage, should anyone dare threaten him. That letter would have been a valuable thing indeed in the wrong hands, something that could be used against me, as king. No, no one destroyed it, not purposefully.

"I want your undivided attention, Lerita. I want you to deploy all your assets. You know where to look, how to look and you have the contacts you need to see it done discreetly. I want your reports, I want to know what you are doing, your thoughts, your ideas, anything that may uncover the whereabouts of that letter."

Thargodén turned away. He needed to compose himself. With his back to the room and Lerita, he was once more before the painting of the Evergreen Wood.

His eyes travelled over the trees, around the idyllic glades and the cascading water. It was such an unusual painting. So much colour. He had never seen a style like this one. Expressionist he supposed, and yet so very real.

Lerita watched from behind and then glided over to his side. "I found this painting some months ago, in the depths of the guild where old furniture and cloth is stored – or rather hoarded for reasons I cannot fathom." She glanced sideways at the king and then back at the painting.

"Fel'annár is taking a short trip there." His eyes swivelled sideways to the guild master.

Lerita stood just a little straighter, eyes a tad wider, nostrils slightly flared, but it wasn't anger that Thargodén could see there. It was veiled alarm. He was intrigued and he turned expectantly to her.

"Or'Talán forbade it. He has no right."

"He asked me, and I conceded."

"You shouldn't have."

"Why not? He is a Listener. The trees call him lord. They fight at his behest. Tell me, Lerita. Why should he not go into the Evergreen Wood?"

"Or'Talán had his reasons. He prohibited it and it is our duty to see his wishes fulfilled."

"Is it? I am starting to believe you know more than you say. In fact, I am sure of it. Do you know the reasons why he closed that place to any save the foresters?"

"I do not have an answer for everything, Thargodén."

Rhetoric. He knew enough about that to know she was unwilling to admit to it. If she was under oath, from Or'Talán himself, then Thargodén knew she would never tell him. Still, that would not stop him from trying to find out. As king, was it not his duty to know the real reasons why the Evergreen Wood was off bounds?

He turned back to the painting, squinted at something between the trees. And then his eyes drifted downwards and to the right. There, a signature, one he recognised beyond the slightest shadow of doubt.

OT - Or'Talán.

~

FEL'ANNÁR RUMMAGED IN HIS POCKET, retrieved the key Pan'assár had given him yesterday, tossed it once in his hand as they ducked inside the Inner Circle. He was almost blinded for a moment, until his eyes adapted to the dim light. Even so, it wasn't hard to see that it was busier than he had ever seen it.

Alpine captains, Alpine lieutenants rushing here and there. Pan'assár had them all busy with the new army and its ramifications. New offices, new orders, new registers, uniforms, briefings, the list went on.

They came to a courtyard, the only place where natural light entered the building. At the centre, a three-tiered fountain gurgled, and water splashed over the sides and into a pool at the base. There were holly, cinnamon and staghorn ferns growing around it, and then vines winding up the columns of the building itself, in search of light high above.

Around the courtyard, door after door, the name of a captain or general on only half of them.

General Fel'annár.

They had arrived and he pushed the key into the lock. He hesitated, turned thoughtfully to Idernon and The Company.

"Give me a minute, will you?"

Idernon nodded, turned to the rest, gestured for them to wait.

Fel'annár took one handle in each hand and pushed down and then forwards. The double doors opened, and he stepped over the threshold of his first office at the Inner Circle.

Someone had already been here, was still here, standing beside the hearth – watching him.

At the far end of the room was a desk, empty save for a candle, an ink well and a long quill. He dragged his fingertips over the smooth surface and then faced the floor to ceiling bookshelf behind. It was full of leather-bound tomes. He peered at the spines, names registering in his mind. Many of these books had been forbidden to him as a child, in case Or'Talán appeared on one of the pages and Fel'annár find out the secret of the Silvans.

Gods but he had had a vivid imagination as a child, and yet he had never imagined this. Parallel lines in his collar, standing in his own office, in command of an entire division. His stomach fluttered at the thought, the weight of duty, the expectations were all real now. He had promised them change and it was time to show them it had not been in vain.

From beside the unlit hearth, Gor'sadén watched him silently.

"I still remember the day I got my own office, when I was promoted to captain. I had been so determined to achieve command, so driven and confident and yet the first time I stood in that room, I felt small and lost. I suddenly needed help but would only admit that to Pan'assár and Or'Talán. As luck would have it, we were promoted at the same time and together, we worked out what to do, how to do it. You have me, and Pan'assár. Turion too. Your only enemy is yourself. Don't hesitate to ask, Fel'annár. No one will think any less of you for not knowing what to do or how to do it."

He knew Gor'sadén was right, but he had learned not to expose himself to the judgement of others from an early age. He had learned it was better to just get on with things and hope for the best. Needing help was tantamount to weakness in Fel'annár's eyes and Idernon had told him he was wrong many times. But breaking that trait was a slow process, one that would have been even slower had he not met Gor'sadén.

"I will hesitate. You know me. But I'll ask *you*."

His Master simply nodded. "And will you ask Pan'assár? When I am gone?"

Fel'annár turned back to him, a little too quickly, and then calmed himself. "Hopefully, that will not be soon."

"But it *will* happen, you know this."

"Then I'll think about it when the time comes. But in answer to your question, yes, I will ask Pan'assár."

Gor'sadén watched him, how Fel'annár avoided his gaze as he continued to admire his office.

"What bothers you?"

A moment of silence as Fel'annár's eyes continued their journey around the well-appointed room.

"There's a lot to be distracted by. This new army, the return of the Kah, the promotions, my Silvan and Alpine families. It sometimes feels like I'm forgetting the Nim'uán. I listen all the time, know that it's there somewhere, that if it does enter the woods, there'll be no time to lose because that is the limit of my senses. Past the trees I can't hear."

"Everything we have done these past two days was necessary, Fel'annár. We cannot fight without a united army, and we cannot ride without knowing it is coming to us and not on a path somewhere else."

"But we can fortify the northern territories."

"With what troops? They must gather and be organised. We must ensure provisions: arms, food, medical supplies, commanders ..."

"What worries me, Gor'sadén – what *terrifies* me – is that by the time I sense it coming, it will already be inside our lands. It will be a matter of how far into the Deep Forest it will reach before we can intercept it."

"And if we leave now, without the troops, the supplies, the organisation ... that thing will run us over and march on the city itself, leaving us with even fewer troops than we have now."

Fel'annár stared back at him for a moment. He was right. But the frustration was bothering him. That first alarm from the trees had been so strong, so sure. And then there had been nothing at all. Had it turned east, perhaps? Was it marching on northern Tar'eastór? On Araria?

"You are already working as fast as you can. But remember your objective, Fel'annár. The people must be defended, and if that must come with losing territory, if they must all come here to the city, then that is the price. Trees will be lost; you cannot avoid that. But you can avoid the loss of elven lives."

"We'll have to drag them away from their homes, Gor'sadén. You've yet to see our villages: Ea Nanú, Lan Taria, Sen'oléi, Abiren'á, our cities in the trees." He huffed. "*I* have never seen most of them save in books. But to lose all that, know that it burns in the wake of the enemy is ... inconceivable."

"Do not get ahead of yourself, Fel'annár. While you are right, the very thought is enough to colour your decisions. Stay focussed, in spite of the distraction. Keep your mind on the safety of your people because that uniform is your witness. Save your people, Fel'annár, and then save your forest, if you can. Trees can be replanted, but people cannot be replaced."

Those were the decisions Fel'annár feared the most. The ones where he would have to choose between two terrible things. He nodded, more to himself than Gor'sadén and then strode to the door. Opening it, he stepped to one side, crossed his arms and drifted over to his Master as The Company wandered inside.

"Fancy," murmured Ramien from behind Idernon.

"Look at all these *books.*" Idernon strode, almost lunged past Fel'annár and to the bookshelves behind his desk. He pulled one out with two fingers, inspected the front cover and then pushed it back.

"All for you to read, in good time," murmured Fel'annár, making his way to them, gesturing to Idernon that he should follow. "Our Forest Division is a reality. I will brief you all fully later this evening. For now, know that The Company is officially a unit, within the contingent of Rangers."

"You did it." Idernon smiled, shook his head. "Do you remember? We must have been eleven or so. You were a captain and you assigned me as head ranger, Ramien was jealous and ..."

"Shut up, Idernon," said the Wall of Stone and the rest chuckled.

"Funny you should remember that." Fel'annár approached his friend until he was standing before him. Gor'sadén watched from where he now sat in a stuffed armchair beside the hearth.

"I want you to represent me while I am away."

"What, where are you going?" asked Galdith.

"Into the Evergreen Wood. No more than two or three days. It's why I need you all to be present today with the captains, so that you can continue the work while I'm gone."

"You're not going alone?" asked Ramien, obviously suspecting that he was. Gor'sadén repressed a smile as he watched the predictable scene play out.

"I am. No one else will be allowed. And besides, I want that time to myself, to think – in silence."

"The wood will allow me inside, Fel'annár." Tensári stepped forward, arms crossed, stern eyes.

"It won't. But you're welcome to try."

And well he knew that she would.

He reached for a chair, placed it in front of his desk and then made for another. Carodel helped him until there were six of them placed in a neat line.

"How necessary is this trip of yours, Fel'annár?" asked Galadan. "In these times of volatile peace between our warriors, your presence here seems essential."

"I understand that. I've debated it myself many times. But I always come back to the same conclusion. There's something there that I need to know about. Something that both calls me and bars my way. I believe it's related to my purpose. I believe the root of Aria's concern lies there. Call it intuition if you will, but I've never turned my back on it where the forest is concerned. You can keep our work going while I'm away, and I won't linger. Two days, three at most."

"If you do, we'll go in there and drag you out, killer trees or no," said Ramien.

"Well, it won't be me to keep you from that duty, to yourself as much as to the forests," said Idernon. "So long as you're sure you'll be safe."

Fel'annár stared back at his friend, desperately searching for a way not to lie to him.

A knock on the door and Tensári rose to answer it.

"That will be the captains. Listen closely, Idernon, Galadan, Sontúr. It falls to you to continue my work while I'm away."

Six Silvan captains entered the room. The Company saluted and then sat at the hearth, while Gor'sadén took his leave.

"Take a seat, captains," said Fel'annár from where he now sat behind his desk.

"Warlord." They saluted and then sat, eyes wandering around the room.

Fel'annár watched them, waited for them to finish their inspection. "The Forest Division is a reality, and you are my foremost commanders. For now, we will start with two contingents. Rangers and Logistics. This will allow us to effectively deploy our warriors where they need to be – no political interference – and it will allow us to procure and transport what they need in order to carry out their duty."

He paused, sat forward in his chair, placed his forearms flat over the desk.

"Dalú, I want you to take charge of logistics while Bulan takes the rangers. As contingent captains, you will need to create those units you see fit, give them each a commanding officer and clearly outline their functions. I require a report to this end so that I, in turn, can ascertain what equipment must be transferred or fabricated, and by whom. I also want a system of recruitment, regulations that must be approved and registered, and I want a special emphasis on the inclusion of females into the Forest Division. Where will you be based? Do we need new buildings to accommodate these contingents? I must know all this – in four days."

Dalu's brows rose almost to his hairline while Bulan sat motionless, mind racing far ahead of his mouth. Amon and Benat fidgeted in their chairs, trying and failing to remain aloof while Salo and Henú shared an excited glance with each other.

"I venture I could get out an overview to you in that time," said Bulan.

"It will do. Dalú?"

He nodded slowly. "Some groundwork has already been done."

Fel'annár turned to Amon and Benat. "While Bulan and Dalú give structure to their contingents, I need you two to guide Salo and Henú and begin the recruitment process. Find recruits, tell our women why they must fight in this army. I also want you to oversee our warriors at barracks, ensure they have all they need, that there is no conflict. I would also create a list of veteran warriors who were wounded and no longer serve in the army. I want to know what they are doing, why they left and whether they wish to return. When we have our plan, we can begin on training regimes, request funds for buildings and supplies."

It felt as if he had been speaking for hours and he wondered if he had overwhelmed them with the sheer amount of work he was asking them to do.

"Dalú, do you have those lists I asked you for?"

"Here." He placed a large scroll on Fel'annár's table. "I'll need to update them in a few days as more of our warriors return from the more remote regions of the forest. I gave priority to the lists of warriors capable of a promotion. I am still working on the others."

"Can you do it in four days?" asked Fel'annár, eyes fixed on Dalú as he considered his words.

"I can do it, but you'll have a pile of reports on your table that will take you a week to read. Aria preserve the unlucky sods you'll be setting to work."

Amon snorted irreverently and Benat laughed incredulously.

Fel'annár didn't look at The Company who were surely listening. They were the *unlucky sods*, but he'd face that later, once he was back from the Evergreen Wood.

"There is something I must see to in the next few days, but as soon as I'm back, we'll meet again. You'll tell me what you need, and we must make captains of those lieutenants who are skilled enough. Captains Galadan and Sontúr will be here in my absence."

Bulan nodded and then stood. "Our tasks are clear, Warlord, and our own offices await. No sooner we're settled, we'll get to it but tell me, where are you going?"

Fel'annár smiled, as confidently as he could manage. "Into the forest for a while. I would listen, make sure we are still safe, that the enemy has drawn no closer."

Bulan stared back at him, but if he suspected Fel'annár had not been entirely truthful, he didn't say. "Safe journey then."

"Bulan, I was wondering. I would speak to you about the possibility of training ... with the spears. Will you come to the Evergreen Wood at the eighth hour tomorrow?"

Bulan's eyebrows rose. "We can certainly speak about it yes."

Fel'annár smiled, nodded his thanks. There was no guarantee that Bulan would accept, but Fel'annár would do his best to persuade him.

"At eight tomorrow then." Bulan saluted one more time and made to leave together with the other captains. He hesitated, turned back to the Warlord.

"You truly believe we can do all this, without Pan'assár's intervention?"

"I do. Together, we will make this new division a thing of legend."

Bulan stared at him, his desire to speak privately with his nephew even stronger than it already had been, than it always had been.

"It already is, Fel'annár. It already is."

11

I AM HARVEST

THE FOLLOWING DAY, just after dawn, Gor'sadén sat upon a boulder, legs crossed, eyes narrowed as he called out his instructions, observed his Disciple's performance. The precision of his movements, the ripple of the right muscles, speed measured and powerful, projection infusing strength into the ancient forms, making them all but unanswerable – except by a Kah Warrior.

There was nowhere to train in private at the Inner Circle and Fel'annár had suggested they come here. They had stopped just past the gates and he had placed his hand upon the bark of the nearest tree. It was a while before he turned to Gor'sadén and gestured for him to follow. He had, eyes darting from one tree to the other, hand never far from the dagger under his sash.

Gor'sadén clearly remembered standing here with others as they desperately tried and failed to help Fel'annár while he battled with Band'orán. These trees had barred their way back then, but now, they allowed Gor'sadén to pass at Fel'annár's behest, although reluctantly, or so it seemed to him.

They closed in on him, made him nervous. But he was not easily distracted, and he continued to watch as Fel'annár performed the Kal'hamén'Ar movements, slower, better – almost a Master himself.

His Disciple's arms and hands moved through air, feet stepping this way and that, smooth as boots sliding over ice. Fel'annár was listening to Gor'sadén's voice, checking his posture, adjusting the movements accordingly.

"Hen – arai – Enha'rei."

Execute. Begin. Execute.

Fel'annár had been visibly tired after his visit to the encampment, yet this morning, as he performed the Dohai for the first time since the Battle of Brothers, it seemed that the forest was feeding him strength.

"Hen – arai – Enha'rei – Sedún!"

Faster, unknown element.

Fel'annár's blades glinted in the early morning sun. One, two, three, strike, turn and parry. Power surged through Fel'annár's veins, infusing his body, so sudden it took his breath. He struggled to keep up, tried to quell the rising energy in his chest and still, Gor'sadén did not stop.

"Hen – arai – Enha'rei – Sedún!"

One, two, three, strike, duck and turn to a new enemy. Another wave, his muscles trembled under the onslaught. He thought he could run a league, jump through the canopy of trees to the very horizon and embrace the sun.

"Stop."

Fel'annár remained in his crouched position. A deep breath, a gasped exhale and he stood slowly, turned to Gor'sadén. Bowing, he approached his Master, placed his two swords upon the ground. Crossing his ankles, he sat before him, visibly calming his breathing.

Gor'sadén's eyes rested on Fel'annár's trembling hand as he spoke. "Out here, in this forest, your Dohai is as strong as it has ever been. Your health has almost returned."

"I know. There's a power here that helps me heal, but I don't recognise it. All I know is that it wishes to remain hidden."

Come, Forest Lord.

"You speak of it as if it had a mind of its own."

Fel'annár stared at his Master, only now agreeing that it had been a strange thing to say. But that was what it felt like.

"I can see that power in your projection, in the way that you struggle to contain it. But what do you mean by wishing to remain hidden?"

"I don't know. I told the king, asked him if he had ever felt this."

"And?"

"He had no idea." Fel'annár leaned forward, elbows resting on his knees. "Did Or'Talán ever talk to you about this place?"

"No, and I wonder if it would not be best to leave it be, Fel'annár. If Or'Talán kept it from The Three, he had a damn good reason."

"For sure. But I can't walk away from this. They call me lord, Gor'sadén. They invite me and they push me away at the same time. They want me to go in and yet they make the boundaries clear. I've learned not to ignore these things. Besides ... I have a theory."

"What theory?"

"That there's more to my purpose than uniting these lands. I already suspected this, mentioned it to you, but the idea is growing in my mind – that this wood may have answers."

Gor'sadén looked up into the canopy that sprawled above them. Who was he to gainsay Fel'annár in the ways of the trees? No one, clearly. But it was this ambiguity that Fel'annár described that worried him.

"When are you leaving?"

"Tomorrow."

"Does Llyniel know?"

Fel'annár pursed his lips, turned to Gor'sadén. "Yes."

"And she was not happy," he guessed.

"She knows me better than anyone, Gor'sadén. She wasn't happy that I'm going alone, but she understands why I'm doing it. I promised I would return in one piece." Fel'annár smoothed a hand over his hair, then clasped them in his lap, their shake almost gone.

"If I am here, sitting with you, why would the trees deny a Ber'ator? Can you not take Tensári with you?"

"They accept your presence because you are with me and you go no further than here. But I need to go to the lake."

Gor'sadén sighed and then stood. Jumping from the boulder he had been sitting on, he turned to his Disciple, looked down at him.

"How was your dinner with the king?"

Fel'annár looked up, eyes clear and bright. "Surprisingly good. It's

Rinon I just can't get along with. He doesn't trust me, makes it clear." He stood, eyes on his shirt as he walked towards it.

"I have had few dealings with him, enough to know that he is quite the character." Gor'sadén's tone was light, almost flippant but not so his gaze which was still on Fel'annár. With the slightest movement came colour. It was like painted mist, visible only when he moved. His frown deepened.

"One way of putting it. We're prone to clashing, Gor'sadén. He goads me and I rise to it."

"You will have to work it out eventually. I pray I will be lucky enough to see that. It may prove very amusing."

Fel'annár snorted, and then stood, a flare of green and blue light shimmering around him. Gor'sadén watched in fascination as he picked up his weapons and slid them back into his harness. He knew Fel'annár could not see it, was still unable to see colour.

"Your eyes are bright."

"Glowing?"

"No, not that much. Is there some message?"

"No. Not that I'm aware of, at least nothing new. I did hear a strange echo recently, about someone making a map but I felt no danger in their tone ..." he hesitated, stood taller. He turned sideways, listening.

Angry whispers, ill intent.

"Someone's watching," he murmured. Gor'sadén cast disapproving eyes around the glade, saw nothing.

"Is there danger?"

"No. Not to us, at least." Fel'annár was walking, unconcerned with his half-naked state. Gor'sadén followed a way behind. A strangled yell, the creak of wood and the harsh rustle of branches brushing against each other.

Slower now, Fel'annár moved towards the sounds of harsh breathing and a rhythmic creak of stretching wood.

And then he saw Bulan, hanging upside down, a vine twisted around his ankle, more of them reaching towards him from the sides, as if to cocoon him. The Silvan captain raised his arms to protect himself from the attack.

Fel'annár strode forwards, suddenly angry at this forest for its strange ways, its unnecessary antagonism. Bulan was not dangerous, they knew that. He placed a hand against the trunk but there was nothing soft or reverent about his touch. Still, he could feel its rebellion. It didn't want to let go. Bulan angled himself sideways as best he could from where he dangled above the ground. It was enough to see who had come, what was happening.

Release him carefully.

Intruder.

Friend!

Silence. A root rippled under the surface below him, pushed out of the ground and rose up to Fel'annár's face, like a snake ready to bite, the smell of loamy earth around it.

You will obey.

A breeze, sudden and confined only to the space around Fel'annár. Provocation.

You will not challenge me. Aria commands it.

A creak and Bulan was lowered to the ground. Releasing its hold around his boot, the vine slowly slithered away, as if disappointed, and Bulan watched it in fascinated horror. His head whipped to his nephew who was standing over him, eyes glowing like emeralds under rippling summer water.

The breeze died, Fel'annár's locks rested over his bare shoulders, eyes no longer blazing but glowing softly, still terrifying to one who had not seen it before. Fel'annár turned from the tree to his uncle, looked down at him. He approached, held his hand out. Bulan hesitated, then took it, hoisted himself up.

"You shouldn't have entered this forest."

"You told me to meet you here at the eighth hour."

"At the gates, Bulan. I assumed you would understand."

"I didn't. I thought you must already be inside ..." he was rattled, his mind surely full of questions.

Fel'annár damned himself for not being clearer. "Come."

Fel'annár strode back to their training area together with Gor'sadén. Bulan retrieved his spears which had fallen from his harness when the trees had hoisted him aloft. He shivered at the memory, walked slowly behind the retreating Kah Warriors, pulling his clothes straight, patting down his hair and willing his erratic heart to calm itself.

Gor'sadén reached for his shirt and slipped into it, spoke to Fel'annár as if Bulan was not there.

"I want to push ahead with the Triad."

Fel'annár's head shot to his Master. "The Wheel of War?"

"Yes. In six months, I believe you will be ready to perform your first Dance. You must master the Wheel, and that is how long it will take. It is the last step upon the path to mastery, Fel'annár. While you learn the Triad, you must perfect the element of air, and your third weapon – spears – if Bulan here agrees to train you." With his weapons upon his back, Gor'sadén turned to the captain, and then back to Fel'annár. "I will tell Pan'assár you will be a while."

Fel'annár bowed low, Gor'sadén nodded, then shot Bulan a warning glance and was away, limp almost imperceptible.

Bulan watched him for a while. He felt like a fool, wondered if Fel'annár would tell him that was, indeed, what he was for entering the wood and not waiting for Fel'annár at the gates. The boy turned to him and only now did Bulan's eyes register the mangled flesh on the left side of his chest. He started when Fel'annár spoke.

"I've always been fascinated with the spear. I've read about how they're made, the importance of weight and balance, of the various alloys used with the tips and blades. I've read of the different models and their advantages in specific circumstances. I've practised with a wooden pole," he smiled, "beaten the pulp out of melons and pumpkins, much to Amareth's dismay."

Bulan snorted, couldn't help it. "Strange coincidence that you should be drawn to spears. Both your grandfathers were. I've spent decades training recruits in the forest and not one of them ever wished to touch a spear."

"*Both* grandfathers? Zéndar used spears?"

"Oh yes. He was good. Better than me. For such a weapon to perform more effectively than say twin swords, its wielder must be exceptionally skilled. A standard spearman is at a disadvantage if he cannot perform the aerial pivots. And that takes time. Mastery comes with years of dedication. I believe this is why the art is dwindling. Many of our younger recruits are too impatient."

"My Kah element is air."

"That sounds like an advantage." Bulan stepped closer, wondered if Fel'annár would address what just happened, tell him of the power he had seen in his eyes and the moving tree.

"The training pits have not seen spears since Or'Talán died. I remained in the army for some years, practicing on my own. But then I left."

Fel'annár nodded. "Why did you leave?"

"Pan'assár."

Fel'annár remained silent, thinking perhaps Bulan would offer more information. But he didn't. There really was nothing else to say. It was as simple as his words had been. He reached behind him, drew both spears from the harness on his back and rested one tip on the ground before him.

"I am surprised at your interest in the spears – pleasantly so – and because it's such a rare thing, it makes it all the more important to me that you learn it well. I won't allow you to become a Master easily. This art is all but extinct. I can take it to the grave or pass on my knowledge to you. But I won't do that lightly. Here." He held out one of the spears and Fel'annár took it reverently, smoothed a hand down the long shaft and to the tip well past his head. It was much bigger than those used for arrowheads. At the other end, a short, double-edged blade. His eyes registered the smooth wood and petal-thin metal overlay, and then the flowing script down one side. Ararian script he had never had to learn.

"What does this say?"

"I am Harvest, servant of Aria."

Fel'annár stared at Bulan in confusion.

"This was my father's weapon, given to him by the Ari'atór of Araria, in recognition of his purpose."

"I can't wield this. It deserves a Master ..."

"We begin."

Bulan ignored his objections, raised his own spear in both hands, only to let his right hand fall away. He tucked the shaft under his left arm, arrowhead pointing somewhere over Fel'annár's head. His nephew copied the movement slowly.

Bulan reached for the shaft with his free hand and pulled forward, as if he were unsheathing a sword. Soon, both his hands were clasping the spear, equidistant, not too tight. Fel'annár mimicked him.

The next few movements were stances too, meant only to familiarise the student with the weight and dimensions of the weapon, but Bulan watched Fel'annár carefully. The precision of his movements, the play of his feet and the concentration on his face.

With the stances completed, Bulan showed his pupil an attack and defence move. Bulan attacked, Fel'annár defended. Fel'annár attacked, Bulan defended.

"Strike harder. You won't break it."

The clack of wood on wood grew louder as the two circled each other, and then stopped. The next move was more complex, a double sequence Bulan incorporated to the first. Ten minutes later, Bulan called a stop.

"At rest, you hold the spear like this." Taking it in one hand, he turned the arrowhead to the ground, so that the shaft lay over the back side of his arm, the blade tip sitting far over his right shoulder.

Fel'annár copied the move then looked back to his uncle.

"I can see why the commander has taken you as a Kah Disciple. You're strong and precise, and once you overcome your worry that you may break Zéndar's spear, you'll be formidable with it. I accept the challenge, will expect you to train every morning with me, no excuses save where your duty may lead."

"At the Inner Circle?" Fel'annár cocked an eyebrow, subtle grin pulling at one side of his mouth.

"At the Inner Circle. This place is unwelcoming, even to a Silvan." Bulan cast his eyes about the glade, as if he expected another root to jump out at him.

"It harbours secrets, Bulan. Even from me."

Bulan studied his nephew, recalled the terrible sight of him just minutes ago, wondered if he had imagined it all but he knew he hadn't. "What are you, son?"

"They call me lord, the trees I mean. I can understand them, they understand me. They respond to me, sometimes physically, if I call on them."

"Is that what happened with Band'orán? You ordered them to rip him apart?"

"No." The word was loud and fast and Bulan swayed backwards. "I had to hold them back from massacring him from the very start, but in the end, I couldn't avoid it."

"I confess, I find the concept of killer trees hard to reconcile."

"As do I. I've never come across such a thing. This forest is not the Great Forest Belt, Bulan. This forest is strange, different. I've always wondered if Or'Talán knew that, if perhaps he closed it for a reason he never disclosed."

"We'll never know."

Fel'annár smiled, wondered if he might, after his trip to the lake.

"You knew Or'Talán, didn't you?"

"Not well. But yes. I met him. I followed him. You are his spitting image save for the texture of your hair and your mother's eyes."

"I know." Fel'annár huffed at the understatement. "What was he like?"

Bulan pursed his lips, sat on the boulder Gor'sadén had used earlier.

"Or'Talán was a great king, in that our people do not exaggerate. He was his own commander general, the backbone of that army, Fel'annár. We worked together and in peace. There was no Silvan-Alpine nonsense back then. Just loyalty and hard work that was always recognised."

"And then Or'Talán forbade my parents' love."

"Yes. And the Gods but I can never forgive him for that. I will never understand it."

Fel'annár turned to his uncle, took a step closer to him.

"You will, Bulan. You have only just arrived after years away from this place. You don't know of Or'Talán's journal, what we found there."

"What? What did you find?" Bulan sat taller on the boulder, ready to spring to his feet.

"It was a ruse. Band'orán threatened to kill Lássira, her entire family if his brother did not forbid their union. Or'Talán realised then that not all was right with his brother. He told him he would accede, to protect her. In his journal, he explains that he was simply biding his time, searching for a way to incriminate his brother but he needed to do it carefully. Even then, Band'orán had a following, people in high places, hungry for coin and renown."

Bulan rose slowly to his feet, jumped off the boulder. "Continue."

"Or'Talán was called away urgently, before he had time to return to the city. He marched to the northern borders and was killed, a death that was skilfully orchestrated by Band'orán and Huren. The missing piece to the puzzle, Bulan, is why Or'Talán never told his son of his plan. Why he left Thargodén to think he had betrayed him, that he didn't care that his son had bonded with Lássira."

Bulan ran a hand down his face, pulled at his chin. "Holy Gods."

"When Or'Talán was killed, that was when Pan'assár began to change."

"Yes. And how he changed, Fel'annár. When I could no longer take his disdain. I left and Dalú stayed but he kept as far away as he could from Pan'assár. He had betrayed us, turned his back on the people he had sworn to protect. He broke the Warrior Code in as many ways as it can be broken."

"But he's come back, Bulan."

"Has he? You'll forgive my scepticism. Or'Talán's death was a tragedy but it should not have triggered such an adverse reaction from a commander general."

"You don't know the circumstances of it."

"I heard of it, Fel'annár."

"But you didn't see it. Admittedly, I don't know the details. Only Gor'sadén does. I suffered his disdain too, Bulan. He all but killed me when he conceded to test me for the Kal'hamén'Ar. But he seems to have come to terms with what happened, has come to understand why he reacted the way he did. I've come to respect him, like him even and I can see his need for atonement. You saw it yourself last night."

"He said what the Silvans needed to hear."

"No. He spoke from the heart, Bulan. Give him a chance to show you."

Bulan didn't answer. Instead, he turned, wandered away, not too close to the trees. "Tell me of Amareth. How are things between you?"

"Better, now that we've spoken at last. She told me as much as she knew of my mother, of what happened. She told me about you, about Zéndar."

"A bit late, don't you think?"

"Yes. Our relationship was always strained. Even when I left for recruit training – even then – she said nothing and look at my face, Bulan. What did she think would happen?" He breathed deeply, told himself he was past all that. "Still, she admits that she was wrong in that, at least. As for me, I must find a way to understand that she did it all for *me*, not for our people. I need to convince myself that it was not all about politics but about love. She says that it was, but I can't seem to bring myself to believe it."

Bulan nodded. "We wrote to her. Your birthdays, your special days. We wrote and we asked how you were. She told us of your antics, of your achievements, of your obsession with weapons and with being a captain." Bulan smiled and Fel'annár watched. Amareth had told him of these letters, of the interest Bulan had always shown in his childhood.

"I was, still am angry with my sister for keeping you from us, even more so now that I know you are Ari'atór. Tell me, did she know?"

"She said she suspected."

"I used to think there would have been no safer place for you than in Abiren'á ..."

"Used to?"

Bulan suddenly remembered that Amareth had not told him that Lássira's assassin had been Ari'atór. "I still do."

Fel'annár pursed his lips, regarded his uncle for a moment. "Perhaps. Still, I would make amends with her. She's sacrificed much for me, be it for politics or love or whatever."

Bulan's eyes were on Fel'annár's braids and his still gently glowing eyes.

"You are the first pale Ari'atór to exist, as far as we know. I wonder why that has happened." When Alei had first met Fel'annár, she had spoken strange words and then refused to explain herself any further. She had said there was something in his eyes that was far older than the boy himself. He was beginning to understand what his mother had meant.

A deep breath and Fel'annár broke their mutual gaze. He tipped his head to the ground, as if he was considering something. When he looked up again, the strange glow had gone and there was nothing but the clear green gaze of Lássira's son.

"It was Supreme Commander Hobin who told me what I am, answered the mysteries of my youth. He told me of his own realisation, of how Aria showed him his path, so similar to the way she showed me. It was he who first told me of you, of my grandfather. He told me he carries Zéndar's Guiding Light."

Bulan's eyes widened, a cold yet burning wave travelling the length of his body.

"It's not possible ..."

"Aria came to me in the trees, looked down on me as a babe and later, as a young warrior, showed me an acorn and an emerald. For Hobin she sat on the mountainside of the Motherland."

Bulan felt his eyes fill with hot tears, not of pain but shock. He was shaking his head, brow deeply furrowed and yet there was nothing but truth in his nephew's eyes.

"You are Ber'anor ..."

"It's not widely known. Llyniel knows, The Company, the king and Gor'sadén.

"You are close to him," muttered Bulan, forcing himself out of his shock, eyes meeting those of Fel'annár once more.

"He was the father I never had, still is. I've made some progress with the king, but it'll take time to build a relationship with him."

"Do you want to?"

"I didn't at first, told myself it was all so forced, so unnatural. But someone opened my eyes to the paradox of my words, said that staying away from my natural father was even stranger."

"I suppose they were right. You didn't have the pleasure of growing with a father as a child. I, on the other hand, was the luckiest child of all."

"You loved your father very much."

Bulan met Fel'annár's eyes. "My father was my world. He was the elf I looked to for example, the one I would ask when things didn't make sense. He was noble and brave – the best warrior I have ever seen. It's why I wanted you to live with us, Fel'annár. I wanted you to have a father too. I would have taken you in as the family you are. I would have been that father for you."

His words had taken Fel'annár by surprise. He could see it in the way his nephew stood, in the way his eyes would not stay still and the confusion on his face. And then the rather severe young Warlord he had only just met, changed before his very eyes. The fierce mage he had seen command the tree was replaced by an exuberant young elf, the fires of determination in his eyes, lips stretched, eyes wide and eager. For a moment, Bulan thought he would run forwards and hug him, but he didn't. He watched as the Warlord slowly regained control of himself, damning Amareth for the unwitting damage she had done.

"It seems we both have obstacles to climb. You with Amareth and Pan'assár. Me with Amareth and Thargodén – and Rinon."

"Thargodén is a good elf, Fel'annár. He would never have forsaken you, had he known what he does now, believe me."

The Gods but Lássira was standing before him. Her legendary eyes were alive and Bulan suddenly knew what he needed to do. He stood, jumped from the boulder and reached for the black spear Fel'annár had used.

"Harvest needs a new Master. It's fitting that he passes from Ber'ator to Ber'anor. Zéndar would want you to have this. Harness him, and when you are skilled enough, carry him proudly into battle."

Fel'annár was shaking his head, even as he allowed his hands to smooth over the script.

'I am Harvest.'

This spear was the first weapon he would inherit, a concept Bulan wagered was odd, foreign to a lad who had believed there were no other warriors in his family.

Now, Bulan's resolve to know his nephew, to train him, was stronger than it ever had been. He had come here with scepticism in his heart, despite Vasanth's blind faith in Fel'annár. But those doubts had vanished and, in their place, a growing sense of excitement. He would teach a Ber'anor the art of spears.

"I will make Zéndar proud, with your help Bulan. You bless me with this gift, more than you could ever know." He bowed, turned away a little too quickly and reached for his shirt. Bulan saw his youth again, perhaps his only vulnerable spot. He reached for his own shirt, strapped on his harness and sheathed his remaining spear. He turned to Fel'annár, Harvest in his hand. A strange sense of purpose washed over him. It felt so right to see the Silvan Warlord carry such a weapon, as right as it felt that this extraordinary child was his nephew.

12

INTO THE EVERGREEN WOOD

~

THE FOLLOWING DAY, Gor'sadén and The Company stood at the gates, watching as Fel'annár slowly disappeared into the Evergreen wood, a cloth bag slung over his shoulder.

Idernon gestured with his head for them to leave but Tensári just stood there watching, clothes askew, hair a mess. No one dared look at her. She was angry, seething because she had tried to follow Fel'annár and been held back by the angry trees.

"You go, brothers. I would stay here for a while." She ground the words out, eyes still on the spot where Fel'annár had disappeared.

"There's nothing more you can do, Tensári," said Galdith. "If the trees won't let you pass, then surely it's Aria's will."

"I remain here." Rebellious blue eyes turned on him, brooked no arguments and the Fierce Warrior conceded. He spared Gor'sadén a glance, saw his concern and then his determination as he turned to address them.

"To the Inner Circle then. The Company here has work, and I promised Pan'assár to draw up the schedule for the Kah trials. Fel'annár is in his element in there. Nothing will happen to him in such company he shares now."

Tensári wanted to believe him, but they all remembered Fel'annár's words, his confusion at the hostility he had felt from these trees. The Ber'anor was not impervious to them, not if he defied their will.

~

Lerita walked towards her visitor, thought she vaguely remembered him from some past decade but couldn't quite place when or where that had been.

Anyone else would be standing close to the door, one hand ready to open it and the other on a dagger. But not the guild master. She had seen plenty like this one, all rough and half mangled. Scars that would take years to fade, if they ever did, and not only of the flesh, she wagered.

She knew he had seen things very few in this world could boast, done things that even fewer would have. None of that would surprise her. She had been doing this since Or'Talán had become king, had been appointed by him to do those things that no one else would, or could.

Lerita of Dan'bar had a keen mind, like Handir and Damiel, like Cor'hidén and Calro. But there were things that separated her from those illustrious men of state and philosophers. She was a master of cyphers. An expert on elven nature. She was a historian of political intrigue and a reader of metaphysics. These things gave her many different perspectives from which to observe things and people.

And observe she had.

"You come highly recommended."

"Goes with the price."

"And your loyalty to the task you are appointed?"

"Depends on the loyalty of she who appoints it."

She cocked her head to one side, eyes running over the silvery scar that ran from forehead to chin, straight over one eye, pulling it down. There were other scars too, more recent.

"Can you see through both eyes?"

"Well enough."

"Then look closely, Shadow. My loyalty is to the king, not you."

"I didn't *expect* your loyalty, Lerita. But I'll no longer serve with traitors, even for the highest price. Did that once and regretted it. Only job I never carried out."

"You must tell me that story one day ... your name?"

"Macurian."

"Well then, Macurian. I have a job for you."

FEL'ANNÁR WEAVED his way through the forest, past where he had fought with Band'orán, further than he had ever gone and although he walked unhindered, he felt some invisible force pulling him back. It was like swimming in a reed-ridden lagoon.

He knew how far he would be allowed to venture, he could hear it in his mind, upon the wind, like a distant and foreboding chant. He would make for that place, set up camp and simply listen, enjoy the time alone and perhaps understand why it was that this beautiful place was not to be shared.

Adjusting his cloth bag across his chest, he walked steadily, enjoyed the warm sun, the dappled light and the sight of the magnificent conifers, yew, spruce and cedar, towering upwards, over him, looking down on him. Deep greens, pale greens, wispy and inviting. The smells too, were musky and woody, undertones of sweet honey and resins, of dry bark and soaking moss. The earthiness of loam and the bitter, salty edge of wet rock. He wanted to roll in it all, swim in it, wrap himself in its blanket and sleep long, dream sweet.

Was Abiren'á like that? he wondered. He had never been allowed to travel as a child, had never understood why. All he could do was listen to the tales of wonder from other children, and then cry in frustration, at how unfair his life was. But with Bulan's coming, he thought he might go there one day with his uncle, see those marvels of nature for himself. See the Three Sisters at last.

At midday, he sat upon a rocky outcrop that looked out over a flower-dotted meadow. Purples, yellows, creamy whites and the odd splash of red upon a canvas of every shade of green. He wished he could fly over it, wings brushing over the papery petals. It was a beautiful place, more striking the further he travelled, so very different to any other forest he had travelled through.

It was then that he realised he could see it all. He could see colour, far more vividly than he ever had.

He pulled out a cloth stuffed with food which he had placed carefully at the top of his pack. Placing it on the ground he opened the four corners and smiled down at it. Creamy cheese and bread, a tart apple and a pastry. He made light work of it, brushed the crumbs from his front and reached for his canteen. He startled, hand frozen in the air.

Beside the receptacle, a creature sat serenely, looking up at him expectantly. He stared at it, fascinated because it simply sat there, unafraid of what he might do to it. It looked like a squirrel but it had no fur, only the thick grey hide of a lizard. The face was that of a friendly rodent but there were spikes around its neck and the claws on its hands and legs were long and curved, designed for ripping, or perhaps climbing bark. It stared at him with eyes as blue as a clear summer sky.

All that occurred to Fel'annár was to turn his hand over, open his palm, show he was a friend. He forced himself to stay calm when he felt its weight, the strange texture of its hide. It sat up on two legs, eyes steady on him, and then it let out a long string of screeches and squawks, a squirrel in the hide of a lizard.

Eyes wide, face as far away from it as he could manage, he watched as it scurried away into the brush. He calmed his breathing, wracked his brains for what the creature might be. A new animal, he mused, or one he was simply ignorant of. Fishing inside his bag, he pulled out his journal, opened the next blank page and drew it with his charcoal. A note in the margin, arrow pointing to its eyes.

Blue.

Title at the top of the page.

Squiliz.

He huffed in disbelief at the drawing before him, the stupid name that had occurred to him. He closed the journal and packed his things. He had a way to go before he reached the lake, his final destination for the day.

With the sun now descending from its highest point, Fel'annár continued his journey through a landscape like nothing he had ever seen. It was paradise to a Silvan elf with its towering trees and gigantic rocks, deep lush-green valleys and water, so much water. But there was something about the colours. So vivid, enhanced by some element he could not see. Blues deep and warm, shocking, gaudy reds, honey-sweet pinks and vibrant, crisp greens. Gods but if before he had not been able to see colour, now, he could see it better than he ever had. He wondered if that was just another anomaly of his damaged sight, or whether this was real. Of course, that might have been why the Squiliz seemed to have blue eyes. Perhaps his eyesight was tricking him. For the first time on his journey, he wished for company, so that he could ask them what *they* saw.

The idea that his eyes were tricking him took hold in his mind as he descended a rocky incline. With the lake well in sight now, his pace increased. But that resistance was back. It was like walking through mud, he thought. Like wading through the waterlogged sands they said existed in the Wetwood. It was tiring but soon, he could smell the water, feel it in the heaviness of his breath.

He walked a little further, until the trees began to thin in the distance, the glitter of blue water sparkling beyond the trunks.

He had arrived, just as the sun touched the western horizon, to the right of the lake which sat due south. In the rapidly failing light, the waters stirred and Fel'annár walked cautiously towards the shore, not too close. Water gently lapped at the soil, washing it away. The smell of wet rock, the soft breeze and the foreign aromas it brought with it. It seemed to Fel'annár that he had stepped into another world, where things did not quite work in the same way.

He peered at the surface of the water, a circle of ripples working outwards where something had stirred beneath. He considered fishing for his supper, but the circle of ripples became a bulge of surging water. He stepped backwards, felt it before he saw it. From the silvery depths, an animal rose. It was the size of Ramien, he thought, but it wasn't a fish – was it? There were no scales, just smooth, grey skin and the face of – the face of a *bird*? He wasn't sure, felt utterly confused. It had a beak, no gills. It rose from the water, but how much of its body was above the surface was a mystery. Opening its beak-like mouth it squawked like a hunting bird, and then clicked like a beetle. He took another step back, his bright green eyes wide, fixed on the blue eyes that stared back at him steadily. There was intelligence behind that gaze, just as there had been in eyes of the Squiliz.

What was this place? Was it some sort of nature reserve for these blue-eyed creatures? But then why would Aria want him here?

Or'Talán's prohibition had never made much sense to Fel'annár, and only now did he realise that his grandfather had lied about his reasons. Had he done it to protect this place and its inhabitants?

The fish that was a bird sunk beneath the water, now a dark grey in the waning light. The moon was still low in the sky but later, it would bring this lake alive in silvers and blues. So many things to see and feel. Fel'annár surely wouldn't sleep this night.

He ate frugally, mind too distracted to bother with anything other than nuts and dried fruit. The moon and its reflection upon the water lent him just enough light to draw the new creature that had stood before him and squawked. He scribbled a word at the top of the page.

Fibird.

And then an arrow pointing at the creature's eyes.

Blue.

He sat back, journal open at his side. The trunk of a tree at his back and one knee bent, he allowed his eyes to wander as far as his mind. Were these animals described somewhere? Would Idernon know of them? Did they have names and descriptions?

His eyes landed on the lake that glittered and undulated soothingly, its voice like a whispered sleepsong. Beyond the far shore was forbidden territory and yet how he knew that he couldn't say. If he could find a Sentinel, maybe he would have his answer. But he felt none, and now that he thought about it, he had not heard the trees at all after their initial welcome.

Against the odds, despite his enthusiasm to ponder this strange new world beneath a waxing moon, Fel'annár closed his eyes and slept.

~

BER'ANOR.

He jolted, eyes flew open, looked around him. Someone had spoken in his ear, so close he could have touched them. But there was no one there. Cold needles, confusion. It hadn't sounded like the voice of the forest.

Follow.

Terror held him in place and yet his body moved. He stood and he walked but he hadn't wanted to. Had he been possessed?

The forest stretched on around him, endless horizon. His feet walked untrodden paths – prohibited wood, beautiful forest not meant for elves. So why was he being lured inside? What was this force that both wanted him to continue yet cautioned him to stop?

The trees looked down on him, as if wondering, waiting for him to take one step too many. Would they do to him what they had to Band'orán?

The echo of voices, delicate giggles and the low murmurs of caution. They were like memories from the past, from some distant place that was not here and yet close, invisible.

He needed to stop, tried to dig his heels in but his body would not obey his mind.

Follow the path, Ber'anor.

He wanted to scream at himself because his feet were still moving. What was *wrong* with him?

His eyes turned upwards, to the sprawling canopy that fanned wide, jutted high as they reached for the last vestiges of light and the voices were louder. Harsh whispers, sharp words indignant of his refusal to stop.

And then the sound of something scurrying through the trees above him, around him. There, a flash of blue and the Squiliz hung from a high branch. But this time, it wasn't the high-pitched squeaks it had produced before. It was a voice, the voice of a child.

Beware the Last Markers.

The words rang in his ears, a cold wave of shock rolling through him. He begged, pleaded with himself to stop because if this was Araria – if this was where the Last Markers stood, would he be dragged to the very Source itself?

But he couldn't stop. His feet continued on a journey only they seemed to understand, one boot in front of the other, again and again.

Panic was welling in his chest, even as his mind scrambled to understand.

He was awake, he knew he was. This was too real, he could touch, smell, see anything he wanted to. It was only his feet that would not obey him. So why was he in Araria? It wasn't possible. This was the Evergreen Wood, just a day of travel away from Ea Uaré.

Was there more than one Source?

A flash of golden hide in the corner of his eye. A blue-eyed puma sat on a rock upon the wayside and Fel'annár watched it, closer and closer. He wanted to flee, run, into the trees and to safety but the predator did not move. It stared back at him, opened its jowls and roared at him. But it was no unintelligible warning. There were words, the deep voice of an old sage.

Beware the Last Markers.

His breath hitched, he screamed at himself. He needed to stop. He had no intention of passing any Last Markers, because what if he couldn't stop? What if he walked straight through the Veil? Into the Source? He was Ari'atór. For the love of Gods, unlike other elves, he would die. He wasn't allowed to take the Long Road and besides, there was still too much to do. He had not yet fulfilled his purpose, had he?

He called out to the trees as he passed.

Help me. Stop me.

But they didn't answer, and his feet continued of their own accord.

The squawk of a hunting bird above him and he looked up, even as he continued walking. There, its silhouette visible before the deep blue sky. It squawked again, sound echoing off rock somewhere in front of him.

And still he walked.

Aria help me. Stop ...

The trees were thinning, a glade up ahead. He was walking into danger, no control over his body. He asked himself again.

Was this a dream?

But he could feel the forest floor beneath his boots, feel some invisible force pushing him backwards and another pulling him forwards. He was caught in a tide, a dialogue of nature in which two powers waged with each other. At least that was how it felt to him.

And then the trees were gone, and frigid needles pricked over his skin, painful and shocking. He screamed at himself to stop, could feel his pace slowing over the rocky path, even as the stone statues came closer and closer.

One more step, and then another. And then finally, he stopped.

Before him, a semi-circle of life-sized statues, carved from black stone. They each held a hand out before them, a command to stop.

Last Markers.

It wasn't possible. This was the Evergreen Wood. This was not Araria. He *was* dreaming, he was sure of it now. Still, there was knowledge to be had from dreams. He knew that too.

His new-found surety lent him a boldness he would not, otherwise, have felt and he allowed his eyes to focus on the rock face a distance behind the statues. It was smooth and vertical, and at the very base, a large black hole.

It was a cave.

Was this an alternative route to the Source? Or was this an entirely different Source?

His gaze focussed on the objects in the foreground, on the statues and specifically, to the one closest to him, at the very centre of the semi-circle. He stepped closer, his feet obeying him at last.

He stared and stared and then tried and failed to understand what he was seeing. Finally though, there was no denying it.

It was a statue of himself, caught in a perennial breeze, and upon his back, a long and short sword. He was fascinated, forgot for a moment that he was stuck in a hyper-realistic dream he could not quite control. If he had ever had the slightest of doubts about Aria's message to him, about Hobin's explanations of it, now they were gone. He was Ari'atór, one of the Last Markers of Araria, or the Evergreen Wood or ... wherever he was.

Was this the future then? Was this what Aria wanted him to see? That he was going to die as a consequence of fulfilling his purpose? Was the Nim'uán bound for the forest? Would there be a battle, one in which he would die? Or would it happen somewhere else? Some other time? Ever since he had discovered he was Ari'atór, he had always known that death was his only release from this life, but was this a warning that it was coming? So that he could prepare? Only dead Ari'atór were carved into Last Markers.

His heart plummeted. It seemed so very cruel. He would have to say goodbye, to Llyniel and Gor'sadén. To Handir and The Company. He would lose the family he had only just begun to know. He needed to prepare them for his departure – prepare himself, for whenever it would happen.

He stepped closer, cocked his head to one side. All he could hear now was his own breathing, harsh, heavy but still slow, mind distracted with the implications of Aria's message.

His eyes were drawn to the figure beside the one of himself. Forbidding expression, angular features so similar to those he had seen only recently.

Bulan. And yet not Bulan.

The Gods but was this *Zéndar*? Were these two statues grandfather and grandson?

Eyes roamed over the hair, the slant of the warrior's eyes. Flared nostrils and slightly open mouth. Angry, forbidding.

He followed the chin downwards, to the exquisitely carved armour, the cloak that seemed caught in some whirlwind and upon his back ...

The needles were back, digging into his skin. His harsh breaths came faster now, louder than they had been. His right hand rose, reached out, stretched forwards, fingertips almost touching the long shaft that protruded from the harness that surely lay on the statue's back, where Fel'annár couldn't see.

His eyes came to rest on the etchings that led up to the double-edged blade which sat at the end of the spear, high over the statue's shoulder.

Stop.

His hand flexed, middle finger brushed over cold stone behind Zéndar's head as he read.

'I am Harvest.'

The ground lurched violently beneath him. He held out his arms, almost fell. A roar and then the earth was trembling, the trees screaming at him to run but he couldn't. He was stuck to the ground that shook and everything was moving. And then he heard a mighty crack, rock falling, thudding onto the ground, something crashing through it.

He shouldn't have reached behind the Marker, touched the spear ...

Rock exploded behind the statues, sent debris flying everywhere. He ducked, protected his head, felt stones pelt his forearms, thud against his head.

And then the world was nothing but ringing silence save for the pitter-patter of the finer rocks and dust as it settled over the ground. Slowly, he removed his arms from his head and stood.

There, amidst a cloud of swirling green mist, stood a giant beast, as tall as the mountainside itself. Its armoured head stared down at him with blazing blue eyes, its wings folded at its scaly sides.

Eyes impossibly wide, shock rendered him utterly still, even his heart. He couldn't breathe and still his eyes roved over the two-legged creature, the centremost fold of its wings almost like forelegs.

This is a dream, a dreadful nightmare ...

With a mighty bang, one wing dug into the ground and then the other. More rock and dust fell. He could feel heat, simmering in the air around him. He struggled for breath and then it froze in his chest as the two wings flexed and the creature seemed to prepare for flight. Its mouth opened, the air so hot it distorted Fel'annár's vision. It was going to burn him, he realised. It was going to reduce him to nothing but bones in an instant.

It's a dream. It's just a *dream* ...

The squawk of a hunting bird and the beast paused, closed its mouth as if listening. It was like rope snapping, like the ground giving way beneath his feet and he moved, staggered backwards and almost fell. Another fumbling step backwards, panic taking control. He daren't turn his back on the thing.

Another step backwards and he fell hard, scrambled with his feet to get out of the way.

Run.

The beast opened his jaws wide, pulled its head back and Fel'annár was on his feet. He turned, ran, sprinted blindly into the dark forest, tentacles of green mist chasing after him. Branches whipped at his face, caught in his clothes and then he heard the squawk of the bird once more. He dare not look up but he followed that sound from above and before him while the trees remained silent as they thrashed around him, hindering his crazed escape from the Last Markers. From the statue of Zéndar and himself ...

He didn't know how long he had been running, but his legs were failing him, breath unable to fuel his body any longer and he crashed to the ground with a gasp, forehead thudding into a moss-covered rock, harsh breath sending leaves and twigs flying around him. He squeezed his eyes closed, dared open them again. The green tentacles were before him, around him, enveloping him in an unescapable cocoon. It was pressing in on him, curling around his neck. He couldn't breathe.

He should never have come here. He should have listened ...

Can you die in a dream?

Black spots danced before his eyes. The world was fading away. He *was* dying and his last memory of this world was the screech of a hawk and the wild thrashing of wings.

TENSÁRI SAT ON THE GROUND, knees bent almost to her chest, back against the gates and not the more comfortable tree just next to it. The perimeter guards had brought her food earlier that evening, knowing that she would not leave while the Warlord was in the Evergreen Wood.

It was the second meal she had eaten here. Yesterday, Fel'annár had disappeared from her sight, into the unknown and without her. She had made to follow but had been stopped by a tree root. And once The Company had left, she had tried – and failed again.

The feel of the live root against her skin had made her gasp, like an unexpected dousing in cold water. And so, she had stood there watching as the Ber'anor became smaller and smaller, until she could no longer see him. She had sensed him for a while longer, but after half a day of deep concentration, she had lost even that.

Anxiety gnawed at her gut. She was failing in her duty as Ber'ator. She had allowed him to go alone. No, not allowed; she had fought to accompany him, reasoned with him in as many ways as she could. Even Idernon had failed to convince Fel'annár and she had been forced to disobey him. Only then had she realised it wasn't a simple command from one who wished to journey alone. She had been forbidden – by the forest itself. Tensári was strong, but she could not fight an army of trees. And Aria knew that she had tried.

She had awoken in the middle of the night, eyes burning so bright their blue light illuminated the space around her, enough to show her the wall of vines that stood before her, barring her passage into the wood. The Ber'anor was in danger, Aria was calling her inside but there was no way she could get past the forest. Some new knowledge slammed into her. This impenetrable barrier was not Aria's doing.

All she could do was pray that somehow, the trees would keep him safe where she had failed, and as the night progressed and she felt no disconnection, she thought that perhaps her plea had been heard.

Fel'annár awoke at dawn.

The embers of a small fire glowing beside him. He was back at his camp by the lake, nowhere near those Last Markers. It *had been* a dream. And yet it had all been so real.

He sat up, slowly stretched his legs out before him as a hand reached up to smooth down his hair. It was full of sticks and leaves, his braids undone, half yanked out.

He frowned.

Eyes registered a softly trembling hand, cuts criss-crossing it. Higher up his bare forearm, lacerations decorated it, as if he had been dragged through the forest by the hair. And yet it had been a dream, he was sure of it.

He had to be.

He collected his feet, moved into a kneeling position. His pack lay beside him and he reached for it, opened the buckle and pulled out his journal, lay it carefully to one side and then brought his shaking hands together, willed them to still.

It had been the most intense dream he had ever had, the most vivid and real. He had been utterly terrified, panicked as he never had been before.

But what was Aria trying to tell him? What was her message this time?

As his mind calmed a little and his heartbeat lowered, he began to think and to reason.

He had been led to that place by Aria. She had wanted him to see the Last Markers and amongst them, himself and Zéndar.

But why?

If Aria was showing him the future, then it made sense. By seeing himself as a Last Marker, standing next to Zéndar, she showed him his destiny, one he had always acknowledged but never really felt.

His death.

But then why had she led him there, knowing there was danger? Fel'annár had not yet fulfilled his purpose to unite the forest and stop the Nim'uán. That beast had wanted to kill him, almost had. All he had done was touch the spear upon his grandfather's shoulder. *Behind* his head.

I am Harvest.

He *had* passed the Last Markers, if only with his hand behind the statue's head. The coming of that beast was Aria's warning to him, either that or perhaps she had no control over it. Had it been Galomú? he wondered, God of righteous vengeance?

For now, all he had was the certainty that in fulfilling his duty to Aria, he would die, sooner or later. It was time to face the evidence – himself as a Last Marker. His life may be too short to dwell on past grievances. None of them mattered in comparison to death. Amareth, his real father and his siblings – Llyniel who had always understood the consequences of loving him. It was time to embrace his life. As he understood it, it was his duty to vanquish the Nim'uán, make the forest safe and united. And if he was to die in that process, then he would make sure that the forest and its people would endure once he had gone.

A deep, painful weight was upon him, but he couldn't think too much about how he would prepare for all of this. It would hinder his mission. He had to bolster his mind as he had done so many times in the past and this time would be his biggest challenge.

He stood slowly. He needed to calm himself, weave the Dohai. He needed to drink and eat, bathe his wounds in the nearby lake. Only then would he sit and draw everything he had seen, describe everything he had felt and the conclusions he had drawn from this terrible night of revelation.

But one thing was certain. He would go no further.

He gathered his humble camp and made for high ground. Up he travelled, over rock, under tall pines until the splendour of the Evergreen Wood loomed from the rocky lip he stood upon, a carpet of green sprawled away towards the distant mountains, the mystic lake at a half-way point, and beyond, the mysteries of the Evergreen Wood that would remain.

Welcome.

He started. A friendly voice at last.

Dropping his pack, he breathed in, watched the trees around him. Did they know what had happened? Did they have answers but wouldn't say?

He smiled. This was a good place to summon the day with the Dohai. He was back in friendly territory, safe, he thought, despite the secrets the forest held from him. He closed his eyes, breathed deeply and began the morning ritual of a Kah Warrior.

A gasp escaped him, a rush of raw power seemed to hold him aloft and for a moment he wondered if he should stop, whether it was too much for him.

Control, he bid himself. *Control it.* He had just recently during his training with Gor'sadén. But this power was new, stronger than anything he had ever felt, save for just before the Battle of Tar'eastór, and then again when he had stood before Band'orán.

The song became more complex, a second and third harmonising melody. He felt uplifted. No dissonance. No resistance. No forbidding voice, no terrible destiny and for a moment, the harrowing memories, the uncertainties of yesterday dissipated and he was at peace.

An arm floated through the space over his head, hand flat and graceful while another mimicked, just behind and then swirled side-ways. Traces of blue followed him, but his eyes remained straight out before him, fixed on the heart of the secret forest of Ea Uaré, on the distant rock face, mind now schooled so that he wouldn't think of what had crashed out of that place in his dream.

He stepped sideways, one foot hovering above the ground, steady, unwavering. He stepped forward, heel first then toes, his other foot lifting, slowly, and then crossing behind and green lights swirled around him, no longer choking him but quiet and peaceful. There was no wrath, just wistful beauty, a playful power that moved with him and filled him with a peace he had never felt before, save for that dawn when he had come back to life.

He could not feel the Nim'uán. But he could feel Aria. She moved around him, through him, filled him to the brim and when the sun sailed free at last over the tree-filled horizon, colour exploded before him. Every shade of green and brown, blue, purple and orange.

Peace, Ber'anor.

A deep rumbling from some distant land, as if the entire continent groaned beneath them but it didn't frighten him. He told himself it wasn't the beast, that there was no danger.

Strange because it felt like an awakening – a communion, even now when he knew that death was near. He smiled as he danced and danced until green, purple and blue merged to create an almost blinding white and he wondered which way was up, whether his feet were still upon the ground or if he hovered above it. Whatever this power was, he had let it in and he wondered whether it would ever leave him.

He looked down at his hands that no longer shook, light concentrating in his palm, like a translucent sphere, a swarm of fireflies in the night. It felt hot, almost tangible.

He tipped his palm down, watched the shimmering ball of light slide off his hand and fade away.

ON THE EVENING of the second day, Tensári saw Fel'annár. There was no missing his eyes in the woods at night, not when he was listening.

She stood, brushed crumbs from her front, strained her eyes to see why he would be listening. He wasn't running, didn't seem to be in danger.

She took a step forward, not quite inside the gate. Closer now and Fel'annár's clothes were loose, sleeves rolled up, hair half up half down.

It was his face though, the set of it. He seemed absent and something flared in her chest.

She heard the distant cry of a hawk, watched Fel'annár turn, searching for the creature. A shiver washed over her. She calmed herself, called out to him.

"Fel'annár."

He startled, as if he hadn't known where he was. His eyes dimmed as he came closer to the gates.

"Are you all right?"

He stared at her, as if he had not understood the question.

"Yes."

"Are you sure?" Her eyes were on his messy hair, his ripped clothing and the scratches on his face, up his arms.

"Yes. Just tired." He frowned, peered at her, and Tensári frowned.

"What is it?"

Fel'annár cocked his head to one side, a twig falling from his hair. "Your eyes ..."

She held a hand over them, saw a blue tinge there. She shook her head. "Nothing's wrong. I was just worried about you."

He repressed a shiver. For a moment she was one of those blue-eyed animals, but he reminded himself that she wasn't. She was Ari'atór, carried a Guiding Light. He nodded, fell into step with her as she made for the palace. "I don't want to talk now."

She glanced sideways at him, registered the distant gaze, the confusion and the ... fear?

"I know." She said nothing more and when they had climbed to the highest floor of the palace and Fel'annár's door was before them, she bowed, knew he would return it, and then she left, bound for the quarters she shared with The Company.

She would say nothing, answer no questions. She would make light of what she had seen but one thing was for certain. Something had changed, something she did not quite know how to put into words. Despite his dishevelled state and his confused eyes, there was a newfound strength in him, something she herself had felt, like an invisible force, pushing outwards. Whatever it was it had affected her in some way, made Lainon's Guiding Light stronger, made Fel'annár ... sadder.

She greeted her love, Connate always in her mind, and then went in search of rest.

Fel'annár closed the door quietly. Llyniel would be asleep, at least he hoped that she was.

He walked towards the sideboard, poured a generous glass of wine and then sat in his favourite chair before the still flickering hearth.

The memory of the winged beast lurked in the depths of his mind where he had tried and failed to banish it. But he needed to see past the horror of his dream and contemplate the Last Markers and what they meant. Could Aria not have found an easier dream for him to interpret?

He was reminded of his own life, full of recurring dreams. It had taken fifty years of them until he had finally understood, and even then, Hobin had had to provide him with the last pieces of the puzzle. Perhaps this was no different, Aria's way of revealing the truth slowly, so that it would not shock him.

He drank, felt the spicy vapours infuse his chest. He felt warm and he felt safe, comfortable in his conclusions that these dreams would continue, that they would slowly reveal whatever it was that Aria wanted him to know. If he was right, that his dream was a slow induction to the truth that was his impending death, then it made his own remaining tasks all the more urgent.

The click of a door, bare feet padding over carpet and Llyniel was crouching at his side. Her honey-coloured eyes watched him, appraising healer, concerned lover. He looked down on her, tried to reassure her with his soft smile but it didn't work.

She stood, held a hand down to him. Placing his glass on the table before him, he took it, stood, and then allowed her desperate embrace. He slowly returned it, and then followed her into the bathing chamber.

He didn't mind her help as he undressed, as she sat on the edge of the pool that occupied the centre of the room, and methodically pulled out the debris in his hair, loosened his braids and cleaned his scratches.

He knew that look. It said peace, I'm here to help. And help she did for she remained silent, asked nothing and when he was finished, wrapped in towels and then dry and in their bed, still, she said nothing, and yet everything he needed to know.

A hand stroked up and down his forearm. Perhaps she could sense his fear, feel his tense muscles, see the questions in his overly bright eyes. But only one question passed her lips.

"Did you find your answers?"

He wouldn't lie, not to her. But neither would he stoke the fires of her curiosity.

"No. But Or'Talán was right to close that place. It's not safe."

She said no more and Fel'annár prayed that he would not dream. That he would never again feel the terror of that guardian beast, its unequivocal warning to never go beyond the Last Markers.

Fel'annár hadn't found his answers. Wasn't sure if he understood what Aria had wanted him to see.

Instead, he had even more questions that would plague him in the days and weeks to follow.

13
SHIRÁN

~

TUBULAR BELLS CHIMED over the desert city of Araria at dawn, city of the Ari'atór, the last stop before the desert became the Confused Lands and then beyond, Valley. Somewhere inside that paradise, was The Source.

It was Hobin's job to defend it, and for that purpose, he boasted the largest army known to elvendom. Last he counted, there were over twelve thousand Ari'atór and most of them came from Abiren'á.

But not all of them.

There were rare cases of Ari children born outside Silvan lands, but truth be told, Hobin could count them on one hand. One such case was Ket'subá, head of the order of the Shirán.

He had been born in the southern reaches of Tar'eastór, had caused quite a stir amongst the native Alpines, or so it was written. The young boy showed a talent for learning, even before he could read and write. By the time he had joined his brethren in Araria, he was the youngest sage they had knowledge of. When the former head of the Shirán died, Ket'-subá was his natural successor.

The elf stood before him now, looking straight past him. It made Hobin want to turn and see what he was looking at. But as far as he knew, only his wall of book-piled shelves was there, in a far corner of his cathedral home.

It was time for the morning council, time for Hobin to see how much – or how little – Ket'subá would reveal to him today.

"Stand easy, General."

He could have been talking to the stone statue of Aria just behind him for the lack of response. Still, he was accustomed to that and so he sat, gestured to his visitor to follow suit.

"What do you have for me this morning?"

He would get the same response as he almost always did. Some new investigation they were setting off on. A journey of discovery into the Icelands. An updated map of Valley and the lands beyond.

"There has been a disturbance."

Hobin looked up from the scroll before him. "A disturbance? Where?"

"In Ea Uaré. We are unsure what it may be, but after your report on the new Ber'anor, we wondered if it is something related to the political strife in those lands."

Hobin nodded slowly. "What is the nature of this – disturbance?"

"Something in the fabric of the world. Some vibration in the song, a distortion that seems to have righted itself."

"But the question is, what caused this – distortion?"

"That is correct, Commander."

Hobin was waiting for Ket'subá to continue, but he didn't. "Well? You have a plan?"

"Of course. The Shirán need to know what has transpired, whether Thargodén remains king, if the Ber'anor is safe."

Hobin was good at acquiring knowledge by observation, but Ket'subá was even better at hiding it. Pity that Hobin did not have the power to order him to speak. The Shirán had always been an independent order, with its own leader. Their only commitment was to keep each other informed. It worked for the most part, even though Hobin knew that they kept things from him, that he was privy to very little of what the Shirán really did.

They were feared, even by the Ari'atór.

"And what do you know of the Ber'anor, Ket'subá?"

"What you have said, that his purpose is to unite the forest people."

Hobin's eyes narrowed as he studied the peculiar Ari, long hair and blue eyes far brighter than most Ari'atór, like ice after rain. "And what else?"

There, a flicker of the eye, veiled surprise and then anger because Ket'subá had not been able to hide it.

"We don't know."

Hobin nodded his head. "Then you suspect there is more?" They had to, because Hobin certainly did.

"There may be, and if that is the case, he must be kept safe. We must learn from the errors of the past."

It was Hobin's turn to unwittingly show his surprise, but there was no time to press the subject because the Shirán was standing.

"Commander Hobin. Should you receive news from the Ber'anor, I would be grateful if you would pass it on."

"Of course. And if the Shirán learn anything more of this disturbance, I would have you inform me."

Ket'subá bowed reverently, and then took his leave, and Hobin's eyes followed him down the aisle until he disappeared into the morning light that flooded the main doors into the cathedral.

Hobin stood, walked to a stained-glass window, wished he could see through it, out onto the distant sands.

Fel'annár. The youngest Ber'anor he had ever guided, not that he had needed much. A gentle push in the right direction and the boy had understood what he was, that he had been chosen for a task.

But what was that task beyond reuniting the land? And what was this disturbance the Shirán had felt? Whatever the answer to that question was, one thing was certain. Ket'subá would not willingly tell him.

THE MORNING after his return from the Evergreen wood, Fel'annár stood in nothing but loose black trousers, Dohai buzzing in his chest. Before him, the two legendary commanders of The Three, similarly clad but each with a longsword in their hands.

They knew he had returned last night. Pan'assár had spotted Tensári making for her bed, after more than two days of refusing to leave the gates. But this morning was the first time they were seeing him after his solitary escapade into the Evergreen wood.

Just like Llyniel, they said nothing because there was something in Fel'annár's eyes that told them now was not the time for questions.

"The Triad. Wheel of War, used in the Dance or on the battlefield, where the odds are dire, and the enemy moves in from all sides." Gor'sadén was walking around Fel'annár as he spoke, Pan'assár a way off to the side. "It is a circular formation, in which each Blade Master executes the same move a heartbeat after the last. Most of the movements you already know, but you have never performed them in such close proximity to another Kah Master. The trick is not to decapitate the dancers but the enemy." He came to a standstill before Fel'annár, eyes glancing over the cuts and bruises on his face and along his forearms.

"The circle is three strides wide. If the movements are executed correctly, your blade will not reach those who fight with you. In extreme circumstances, the circle can be reformed by walking backwards until you meet back-to-back, and then striding outwards – one, two, three – begin again."

Fel'annár nodded at Gor'sadén, then turned to Pan'assár as he continued with the lesson.

"With skill comes confidence. With confidence, skill is heightened. You have seen this with the Duad but the Triad will take time, even with a strong Dohai and your enhanced projection."

Fel'annár nodded again.

"Questions," prompted Gor'sadén.

"The rhythm. In battle, how do you know it remains harmonious with the others?"

"You hear the blades, sense them, feel their proximity. Some Masters used sounds the others would repeat, like a chant as they danced, but Gor'sadén and I never ascribed to that method."

"It sounds difficult to keep your senses on such a high level in the heat of battle."

"And that is why the discipline of the morning ritual is so important. You must hear your movements through air, feel those of others, sense their direction."

Fel'annár nodded, turned to Gor'sadén when he spoke.

"You have done it before. When you fought Band'orán blind."

So he had. He remembered his first, floundering dodges, and then how his senses had heightened, and the trees had lent him their peculiar vision.

"Ideally, to guide you in your first steps with the Wheel, we would have a percussionist here to help dominate the technique. But there are no other Kah warriors to do this for us. Eramor claims he can do it, but he is not Kah."

"I think he wants to be, if you would agree to give him a trial?" Fel'annár looked from Pan'assár to Gor'sadén, who was already looking at his friend.

"It has been discussed," said Pan'assár. "Those illicit Kah were a stain on the ancient art. I would cleanse it, show our warriors what the Kal'hamén'Ar is truly about. I announced the trials yesterday. They will take place tomorrow at a closed training pit within the Inner Circle. Gor'sadén and I would have you there."

"I wouldn't miss it! Eramor will be there for sure, and perhaps Benat, but I wonder how many other Silvans will step forward." He was speaking to himself, lost in thought and Pan'assár interrupted him.

"And you must get to the healers, Fel'annár. I want their certification that you are fit to return to active duty. I know that you are, but it is a formality I would have you heed."

He would do that after his training with Bulan, and then study Dalú's list of Silvan lieutenants eligible for a higher command. They needed captains at the Inner Circle and there was no better way for Fel'annár to take his mind off the Evergreen Wood. There would be no time to dwell on the possibility of his own, impending death ... he stopped himself. His concentration was slipping and when Gor'sadén started again with the training, Fel'annár threw himself into it.

An hour later, breathless and exhilarated, Fel'annár turned to the sun, now well above the horizon. Activity at the palace was audible from where they stood, and his belly grumbled at the lack of food. He hadn't eaten last night, and breakfast was now his priority.

With a respectful bow, the three Kah Warriors parted ways, the rhythm of the Triad still thumping in Fel'annár's mind, the voice of the forest, deep and hollow, its welcome – its warning just beneath. He sensed Tensári's presence behind him, slowed his pace until she was at his side.

He could feel her eyes on him as they made for his living quarters, but he thanked the powers she remained silent. With Llyniel already gone to the Halls, he dressed in his new uniform which had arrived while he had been away. Llyniel had laid it out for him before she left, knowing that he would not have noticed it otherwise. It fit perfectly, was much more comfortable than it looked, and with his fully recovered sight, he could see the new green of his tunic and cloak. It was just what he had wanted for his Forest Division. Soon, all his warriors would wear these colours, proudly he hoped.

As they walked to the city barracks, Fel'annár briefed Tensári on the days' agenda, and by the time he had finished, they had arrived at the noisy mess room where The Company stood waiting for them. He'd given her no time to ask questions he had no answers to.

Idernon stared hard at him, eyes flitting to Tensári behind him while Sontúr's healer eyes were examining him where he stood. Galadan clapped a hand on the Wise Warrior's shoulders and together, they made for the mess hall.

The noise inside was deafening, and that was an encouraging sign, because just days ago, there had been nothing but resounding silence. The warriors sat at long, wooden tables, talking and laughing, eating together for the most part, but when the first warriors spotted the Warlord, they stood, waited for the others to do likewise and then saluted. Fel'annár and The Company returned it and then made for the end of one table with space for them all.

As they settled, Fel'annár's eyes wandered to a group of Alpine warriors who sat apart from the rest. He knew that look, the condescension, heads too high, eyes looking down on the world.

Purists.

He committed their faces to memory, would speak to Pan'assár about them. But then he spotted another group, far on the other side of the hall. Silvan lords, he knew from the patterns of their braids. It was a reminder of how fragile this new army was, would continue to be, until change became visible in the field and they were forced to work together.

They needed time ...

"They attacked you, didn't they?"

Fel'annár started, turned to Idernon. "No." It was the truth, the only thing he was willing to say for now.

He saw Idernon's surprise, how it turned to scepticism, and then irritation when the servants came with hot food. Many hands reached for the platters, spooning a bit of everything onto their plates. He had answered Idernon's question with one, simple word, and the pressure for Fel'annár to speak was almost unbearable. He knew he would have to say something, eventually.

"So what happened in my absence? Those lists, has there been any progress?"

Idernon frowned, pursed his lips and then turned to Galadan beside him.

"We've done as much as we can, I think. Dalú has been busy. He should have those reports for you tomorrow. We have heard plenty of lieutenants talking about the selection process. They seem eager for it to start. We have also seen the training pits getting busier and busier. Commander Pan'assár has announced the Kah trials, as I am sure you already know, and some even speak about the spears."

Sontúr nodded at Galadan, took over the report. "Prince Handir and Lord Aradan have been interviewing Silvan diplomats and philosophers. It seems Miren procured information from Lord Lorthil and Narosén. I know that Lord Erthoron and Lady Amareth were present."

Fel'annár nodded again, looked down at his food as he ate, desperately searching for more questions to fill the silence. But he was too slow.

"Sooner or later, you will have to speak about what happened in that wood." Sontúr had said it without looking at him, as if he were talking about the weather.

Fel'annár looked up and around him. Idernon, Ramien, Carodel and Galdith, Galadan and Tensári, eating and watching.

He sighed, put his fork down and leaned back.

"Listen. I'll speak of it when the time's right. You all know me well enough to realise that when there's something I don't understand, I can't talk about it."

"You mean you *won't*." Carodel stared back at him with glittering eyes.

He returned it, eyes challenging. "Yes, that's exactly what I mean. For now, we stay away from that place. It's dangerous, even for me."

~

THE TRAINING PITS were all but full.

Coincidence or otherwise, the very central pit was empty, and it was big enough for spears, open enough for the fighters inside the stone circle to be seen by all.

The many other pits inside the massive hall were occupied by two and sometimes three warriors. Two sparring, one watching – a Master correcting technique, drilling stances. But from time to time their eyes would stray to the Warlord and the veteran Silvan captain, preparing to train with a weapon many thought impractical. The Company had settled upon the low benches that surrounded the pit, out of the way and silent lest Bulan send them packing.

Fel'annár's grey sash sat over his black breeches, a reminder of what the other warriors might achieve now that they would be given the chance. An apprenticeship in the Kah. It was why many of them were here, why most of their Blades Masters and close combat experts were present. They were preparing for the test tomorrow.

"Power training. Twelve stances alone, half speed."

Fel'annár picked up Harvest, the double-edged blade facing backwards, the arrow tip forwards. One by one, he worked through the stances slowly, unaware of the lull of voices and clashing blades around him. He thrust the spear tip forwards and then backwards, over his head and then whirled around, spear paddling to one side and then the other. Finished, he stood stock still before Bulan.

"Good. Now at full speed. Freeze when I tell you, listen and adjust."

He performed the same moves, faster, until Bulan bid him stop.

"Hold your position. No shakes, no swaying, hold still." The Spear

Master circled the apprentice, critical eye observing, approving. He nodded. "Continue."

After this round, Fel'annár could feel the ache of muscles he did not often use and when he had finished his series, Bulan performed the stances with him.

And then their sparring began, and the hall fell mostly silent save for Bulan's shouted instructions, the clack of wood against wood, sometimes fast, sometimes slow. On occasion, Bulan's spear came too close to Fel'annár's face, the blade tip almost slicing into flesh. The warriors gasped and hissed but no blood was drawn and by the time they had finished, Fel'annár lay sprawled on the floor, the tip of Bulan's spear hovering over the hollow of his throat.

Bulan pulled it back, waited for him to rise.

"You must practice the cross over, side twist and paddle attack. I want it faster, harder, more precise."

Fel'annár nodded, Bulan returned it, watched his nephew shrug into his shirt as the noise in the hall swelled until it was louder than it had been before they had started. He resisted the urge to smile in satisfaction. His nephew was a natural warrior, and he would know because he had spent the last decades training young recruits in the basic skills. But he had missed this: training an apprentice for mastery, observing the evidence of his efforts, seeing the skill slowly unfold.

Fel'annár had not lied when he said he had studied the spear, read everything he had found on the art. The truth was, that Bulan was enjoying himself as he had not done for too long. He turned back to his nephew, afforded him a smile and a pat on the back.

"You will do your grandfather's spear justice, I think. A few more weeks and you will be proficient enough to carry it into battle."

"And for mastery?"

Bulan thought for a moment, took a hand to his chin and rubbed. "At our current rate, no interruptions, two, maybe three months."

Fel'annár had obviously not expected that and Bulan afforded him a smile.

"You had a head start. Your training in the Kal'hamén'Ar has honed your ability to concentrate, to learn fast. Your element is air, your aerial work is excellent, and this is precisely where many others take much longer to master this weapon. What you must still develop is the synchrony of limb and spear, the flow of movement, that and the array of moves that only time and experience can teach. Perhaps it is not only the Kal'hamén'Ar that is returning, Fel'annár. I wonder if our sessions will not encourage others to take it up."

"And will you teach them?"

Bulan looked around the hall, to the warriors who had resumed their training. He had seen their admiring gazes, the spark of respect as he had sparred with Fel'annár.

"Yes, I will teach them."

It was Fel'annár's turn to smile. Bulan was a good teacher and the thought suddenly occurred to him, that he was surely an excellent father to Vasanth, would have been to him, had Amareth allowed it. He bowed reverently, as he always did to his weapons Masters.

"General Fel'annár!"

He turned, saw Benat in the distance together with Eramor, waving at him to wait for them. They jogged through the pits, sketched a hasty bow at Rinon who was sparring with Sar'pén close by.

"Captain Benat, Eramor. You are preparing for the trials?" asked Fel'annár.

"Aye. We wondered if, well, if you wouldn't mind helping with a few tips. You are the only Kah Disciple there is, and you mentioned it in passing ..."

"Of course. I'm due at the Halls for a revision but I can be back in say half an hour?" For Fel'annár, anything that needed his attention today was a welcome distraction. Eramor seemed more relieved than content, while Benat looked smug and Fel'annár wondered if Eramor had thought he would refuse or be too busy to be bothered with would-be Kah Warriors.

Fel'annár turned to leave with The Company, but he stopped abruptly, voices exploding in his head.

Alert.

Bulan's eyes widened and he stepped back involuntarily, Fel'annár's green eyes shining too bright to be natural. The entire hall fell silent.

"What is it?" Tensári's voice from beside him.

Bulan stepped forward, eyes moving from his nephew to the Ari'atór beside him. "Tell me it's not the Nim'uán?"

Fel'annár could feel people pressing in around him, wanted them to move away because of late, the power of his messages felt enhanced, stronger, just like his projection in the Dohai.

"Not the Nim'uán."

"Then what? What's happening?" Rinon's demanding voice as he approached, Sar'pén at his shoulder. "What is ..."

"Deviants, to the south-east. They're too close to the city."

"How close, Fel'annár?" Rinon's voice, no longer imperious but alarmed.

"Descending the mountains, approaching the woods before the estuary road."

"Isn't that Princess Maeneth's route?" asked Eramor.

His only answer was Rinon's sudden flight, yelled order fading as he ran for the doors.

"Sar'pén. Ready the patrol!"

Fel'annár blinked, blinked again and then looked at Tensári and The Company. As one, they ran after the sprinting prince, leaving behind them two dumbfounded Silvans and one Alpine captain.

"Where's Pan'assár?" yelled Fel'annár, to no one in particular.

Rinon was too far ahead of them to answer, but Galadan did.

"He's briefing the king."

They sprinted over the courtyard, Fel'annár's flimsy black shirt flapping around him. People dived out of their path but one was too slow and Galdith smacked into him. He steadied the man, yelled an apology and dashed after Galadan.

Through the double doors, guards suddenly on alert and The Company took the stairs two at a time, or in Ramien's case three. They could see Rinon's boots high above them. He was indeed making for the last floor, to the king's quarters.

By the time they arrived at the open doors, Rinon was already talking to the king, who stood in the presence of Pan'assár, Gor'sadén and Turion, while Aradan watched from a little further away.

They were listening intently to Rinon's rushed, breathless report, while Aradan was staring wide-eyed at Fel'annár. Of them all, he had never seen his law-son's eyes like this.

"How large is this group?" asked Turion.

Rinon turned to Fel'annár expectantly.

"Fifty, maybe sixty. But there are conflicting numbers. There may be various groups, the warning comes from different places but all within the same vicinity." Even as he explained the message, he was listening, gaze off to one side, eyes shimmering and glistening.

"Send me out with a patrol, Commander. If we're lucky and there's just one group, fifty or sixty is not too large a group."

"And if there are more?" asked Fel'annár.

Rinon turned back to him, seemed annoyed at the interruption.

"With our fifty and Maeneth's escort, it should be enough. We're wasting *time* ..."

"Fel'annár?" prompted Pan'assár.

"Their message is jumbled. They are closer to the sea than the forest."

Pan'assár surely remembered this from their return journey from Tar'eastór and he turned away from Rinon for a moment.

"Commander," insisted the prince.

"Patience, General."

Rinon seemed to be stuck to the floor by some powerful resin, for he obviously wanted to move, but was beholden to wait for Pan'assár to make his decision.

"Alright. We send sixty."

Rinon nodded in satisfaction. "I will lead it. We can leave in an hour." Rinon's mutinous eyes bored into Pan'assár, daring him to disapprove.

He didn't and Rinon seemed utterly relieved. But his expression dropped with Thargodén's next words.

"I want Fel'annár and The Company to go with you."

"Did you get your combat clearance, General?" asked Pan'assár.

"There was no time, Commander."

Pan'assár glanced at the king and then turned to Sontúr. "Your opinion, as a healer, Captain?"

"He's fit enough, Commander."

Rinon pursed his lips, looked disappointed and he turned to Fel'annár and The Company. "You will be under *my* orders."

"The Company is under *my* command, General. You know this." Fel'annár's eyes were suddenly focussed and sharp, the green mist gone.

"And my patrol is under my command. Shall we have *two* commanders, then?"

"That is not wise," said Fel'annár.

"Then you will defer to me, as your crown prince."

Fel'annár's face turned to stone. Still, he knew Rinon was right. There could be only one commander.

Pan'assár stood before Rinon, just a little taller than he was. "Thirty minutes at the main gate then. General Rinon, you are in charge. General Fel'annár, you will provide the backup that your commander requires."

Fel'annár saluted. Facing the king, he bowed and then left the room, bound for his rooms to prepare his equipment, The Company just behind.

The king turned to his eldest son.

"Rinon."

"Father."

"Don't antagonize him."

"So long as he does not provoke."

Pan'assár turned to Rinon. "You must set an example to our Alpine warriors. You are in command, but he is your equal out in the field. Heed his advice with respect to the enemy's movements."

"If it makes sense ..."

"No. Whether it makes sense or not. Trust his intuition where the forest is concerned, General."

Rinon stared back at Pan'assár, saluted, and left the room. The commander watched him leave, heard the king's soft murmur from beside him.

"The Gods protect them from the Deviants – and each other."

14

MAENETH

~

FEL'ANNÁR STRODE down the corridor to his rooms to change and collect his gear. He prayed that Llyniel was there, otherwise there would be no time to say goodbye. He repressed a chill because he knew that one day soon, it would be forever in this life.

He found her preparing to leave for the Halls.

"What now?" She threw the cloth in her hand on the table, watched as he carefully placed the black and golden spear in one corner of the room. She closed the gap between them, anger warring with concern and disbelief.

"Deviants on course to intercept Maeneth. We ride out to provide back up."

Llyniel's eyes widened, and then she dragged one hand down her face. "Can nothing just go right anymore?" She watched as Fel'annár walked past her and into the kitchen area. A golden loaf of warm bread stood there, and he pulled a chunk off with his hands. Stuffing it into his mouth, his eyes searched for something to accompany it. Llyniel lifted the lid off a clay plate and pulled away a leg of the cold chicken that lay beneath. "Here, eat. I'll gather your things."

Fel'annár pushed the food into his mouth, knowing it would be a few days before he would taste anything as good as this. Washing the grease from his hands, he joined Llyniel in their bedchamber and together, they gathered the things he would need for a few days in the field. Tightening the buckles of his cuirass, vambraces and pauldron, he clipped his cloak to one side and then glimpsed at Zéndar's spear sitting in the corner.

His fingertips tingled, remembered that moment of temptation when he had reached out to smooth over the etchings of the Last Marker, had past Zéndar's head with just one hand ...

I am Harvest.

He turned away from it, repressed a chill, found Llyniel standing close, staring up at him.

"Your eyes have changed."

Fel'annár had totally forgotten to tell her he could see colour once more – so much of it. "They have. I forgot to tell you. It came back to me in the Evergreen Wood."

She smiled. "Well then. Here we are again." She lifted a hand, commanded his attention with it. She smoothed it down the side of his face, thumb tracing over the corner of his mouth, ghosting over a shallow scratch. "You ride with The Company?"

"Yes. We have the numbers, Llyn. Recent reports show a small Deviant colony along the eastern foothills. It's surely them. It's not a dangerous mission, just back up, should it be needed." Even as he said it, he remembered the warring voices, different numbers, different places. But what was the point in worrying her when he himself didn't know what to expect?

"Where you are concerned, I've learned to expect the strangest of outcomes."

"Is that good?" he asked, leaning in closer.

"It's very good. Never a dull day." She smiled, kissed his lips, made light of the situation.

"I didn't see you at the Halls. You don't have your certification."

"There was no time. Sontúr assured the commander I am fit enough."

"But you don't have *my* permission, Fel'annár."

"I'm all right, you know I am."

"I do, but not because you say it." One hand ran down his arm, from shoulder to hand, a hand that would soon deal death to the enemy. Strange that he and she should use their hands for such opposite tasks.

"I'll write that certificate for you, make sure Pan'assár gets it."

Fel'annár smiled at her. "Two days, maybe three."

She smiled, nodded, watched him leave, then the door as it closed behind him and when she was alone again, her smile vanished and, in its place, anger. Anger at Aria – if she even existed. Cruel Goddess, selfish deity. Can you not leave him alone for just a day?

Will you ever release him from your service?

AT THE GATES, The Company sat in the saddle, waiting for the last of Rinon's sixty-strong patrol to gather.

Idernon's eyes briefly crossed with Galadan's before he turned to his friend beside him. "Fel'annár. Don't let Rinon provoke you."

"I won't. Not while I am on duty at least."

"If he provokes, remain silent," said Galadan. "If he taunts, turn away. If he commands, obey."

"Whatever he does or says?"

"As you would any other commander."

Fel'annár stared back at Galadan, knew he was right. He breathed deeply, watching as the royal general approached with his warriors in tow. Stopping before him, Rinon spoke loud enough for everyone to hear.

"We ride towards the Calro Delta, our mission, to provide safety for Princess Maeneth's incoming escort. The Warlord reports a group of Deviants, approaching from the eastern slopes. We know this group; you have been mapping their movement for months. Our job is to protect our princess and bring her safely home, avoid conflict if we can, until she is safely behind these gates. Ea Uaré is grateful for your service!"

With that, Rinon led them out and Idernon clapped Fel'annár on the shoulder. "Well then. We ride to meet your *sister*."

Fel'annár turned to him, smiled in spite of this strange, new reality he found himself in. With all that had happened it had not occurred to him at all. Maeneth, Llyniel's greatest friend, Rinon's twin.

"And then you can tell us all about your trip into the Evergreen Wood," said Idernon, eyes still to the fore.

Fel'annár stared at his profile, knew that it had all been too good to be true. Sooner or later, he would have to tell them what had happened.

But he couldn't tell them what he thought it might mean.

Mid-afternoon, and Rinon ordered a short break, enough for water and for the horses to catch their breath. They stopped under the canopy, still dense here but it would soon thin out, just as Fel'annár's capacity to listen would be diluted.

This part of the river was narrow enough to ford in six strides. Some filled pails of water, others munched on nuts and dried fruit while the horses drank.

Fel'annár stood upon the banks of the river, the terrain familiar. They had passed this way just recently on their return from Tar'eastór. Reaching out, he listened, not to the distant forest and the northern Xeric Wood but to the surrounding lands here in the south. There was nothing amiss that he could tell, save for the same message he had heard before. Deviants hiding in the mountains to the east.

The Company were close by, watching him, he knew, but another, less harmonious presence was approaching. He half turned to Rinon and two others. Only one he recognised as Captain Sar'pén.

"Anything?" asked Rinon.

"Nothing. All seems quiet."

"Are you sure the danger is still there?"

"Yes. But the reports are ambiguous. The group I sense on the eastern foothills is of an unknown number. And distant whispers say they are further south, closer to the princess' patrol."

Rinon stared at Fel'annár for a while, until he turned to the unknown warrior and Sar'pén. "Send out scouts to the eastern slopes. We need numbers."

"General." One left to do the prince's bidding but Sar'pén stayed at Rinon's side.

"Keep me informed."

Fel'annár nodded, and then watched Rinon and his captain stride away. The crown prince was like a magnet, he thought. Forceful and so very intense, like a storm in a box. But so too was he unnecessarily curt. He would keep Galadan's words of advice present in his mind, remind himself that Rinon was his superior on this mission, that he owed him discipline and obedience, and far be it from him to wilfully disappoint.

That evening, Handir and Llyniel sat on the floor in the king's quarters, lounging on a pile of cushions before the fire. Just minutes ago, they had been in Llyniel's quarters, listening to Miren and Amareth discussing a wedding. Handir had found it all rather funny, but Llyniel had cast him an exasperated look, or rather a cry for help. He had heeded it and together, they had come here with the excuse of some favour he needed from the Lestari.

The king and Aradan sat in the garden, the sky darkening around them as they waited for the evening meal to be brought to them.

"I wonder how things are with those two, whether the forest burns in the wake of their passing," murmured Handir, but one eyebrow sat high on his forehead and Llyniel pursed her lips.

"Rinon just won't let it go, will he. He can't understand that his father loved Lássira, that Fel'annár has nothing to do with your mother leaving. He's like a child with a tantrum," she waved her hand in the air and Handir watched her carefully. The relationship between her and Rinon had always been strained.

"When it comes to families, Llyn, we are all children, don't you think? I needn't remind you of your ten-year separation from your parents. Rinon may be stubborn but you ..."

"It's not a question of stubbornness. I lost faith in my parents, and in hindsight, it was me who failed to understand."

"And that is what Rinon does not have. *Hindsight*. To Rinon, Fel'annár is not an elf but a symbol of his own misfortune, of his mother's suffering, and that of his siblings. I cannot blame him for that. I did the same when I first met Fel'annár, just as he did with me. It is a bridge that must be forded by very different people."

"Let's hope they are not carried away in the swell."

Servants were at the door, trays of food in hand and soon, the king, Handir and his extended family gathered around the table. The evening was calm, but the king's forehead was not smooth. Once the household staff had gone, he leaned forwards, elbows on the edge of the table.

"Their first night on the road."

"Did you do it on purpose?" asked Handir. The king looked up, clearly not having expected the question.

"No. Peace between our people is still fragile. I trust The Company to keep my children safe."

"Rinon can take care of himself," ventured Llyniel.

"He's not invincible, none of us are, and he will be distracted by the presence of his twin. He needs someone to watch his back."

"You have thrown them into a pot of hot oil."

"Then let's see if they melt," said the king pointedly.

"They may *curdle* ..." said Llyniel and Aradan stared back at his daughter.

"But they can't ignore each other," said Handir.

"No, no they can't. I just hope Llyniel here is not needed to pick up the pieces, or whatever is left," droned Aradan.

But she knew that was likely. Still, as luck would have it, the unexpected danger to Maeneth's caravan had deflected their questions about Fel'annár's incursion into the Evergreen Wood. She knew it wouldn't last, that Handir at least, would ask her – tomorrow – perhaps. But for now, she was just grateful for their distraction, for what would she say? That he had come back dishevelled, shaken and introspective? That she didn't know why, but that she suspected something significant had happened?

The truth of the matter was that Fel'annár himself had changed. He felt different, something in the fibre of him, that material she could not touch but only ever sense. Yes, something had happened, something important, something that he couldn't bring himself to speak of.

Even to her.

~

To the south of the capital city, the weather was fine, and the camp was quiet. The sixty-strong patrol sat talking quietly, their conversations muted and expectant. Rinon watched Fel'annár from afar, seeing him for the first time as a warrior in the field. Yes, he had seen him fight during the battle, seen him lead hundreds of Silvans and do it well. But he hadn't seen this; the expression in the eyes of others, the conviction of his command, the confidence they exuded in his presence. There was no strife here between Silvans and Alpines, only the tension between two half-brothers who clearly disliked each other.

He wondered at the scratches and bruises, how he had acquired them. He thought it may be the Kal'hamén'Ar training. They said it was hard and not for the first time, he asked himself if he would try for an apprenticeship. But again, he knew that he wouldn't. There was a philo-sophical side to the teachings that did not appeal to him, partly because he didn't believe in them. He would feel stupid dancing before the sun, praising Aria and somersaulting through the forest. He smirked at the vision of himself flip-flopping around a battlefield, cloak tangling around his feet.

"What are you smiling at?"

Rinon turned to Sar'pén and then turned back to the forest. "Nothing in particular."

"Thinking of your sister?"

"Always. And you, brother? Are you thinking of Maeneth? Don't deny it, I know you fancy her."

Sar'pén cleared his throat. "Childhood fantasies, Rinon. I would not dream of approaching your sister and facing your wrath." The captain sighed, cast his eyes upwards to the stars. "I just hope the Silvan is right. His reports are vague at best."

"I know what you mean. But Pan'assár was clear I should heed him where the trees are concerned. And watch your language, Sar'pén. Call him general or Warlord, but not *the Silvan*."

"I didn't think it would bother you. You're not exactly *close*." Sar'pén snorted. "Besides, is the commander general saying that the Warlord is never wrong? Are we to have blind faith in everything he says? Put our princess and warriors at risk with one simple word he utters?"

Rinon clenched his jaw. Sar'pén gave words to his own thoughts, but he wouldn't defy his commander general. He had promised to listen to Fel'annár, and he would. But he was his own commander. The decisions were ultimately his to make.

"Once the scouts are back with numbers, we can decide whether to engage or guide the Pelagian patrol westwards, onto the safer road."

Sar'pén regarded his prince, nodded slowly. "If it's a small group, you could leave them to the Warlord while we lead the princess' patrol away to safety."

Rinon turned to him. "That is possible."

"You would see Maeneth sooner," smiled Sar'pén, "and save her from the spectacle of battle. I know she can defend herself, but she hasn't had to yet. We don't want to take the risk of her having to wield her rusty blade."

The very mention conjured the image of a desperate battle, at the centre of which stood Maeneth, waving her sword around her, surrounded by Deviants, closing the circle ...

"When are the scouts due back?"

"Later tonight or tomorrow at dawn."

The prince clapped his friend on the shoulder and wandered away, but he remained restless for the rest of the night. At dawn, he ordered the camp packed away and the warriors ready to ride in ten minutes.

That done, he walked to where Fel'annár stood talking with Idernon and Sontúr. They turned and saluted. Rinon returned it, nodded at Sontúr and turned to the Warlord.

"Well?"

Fel'annár scowled, failed to see why Rinon needed to be so rude. Still, Galadan's face floated before his mind's eye and he gave his report.

"You're referring to the trees?"

Rinon's jaw clenched. "What else would I be talking about, the *weather*?"

Tensári stood slowly while the rest of The Company stopped what they were doing to turn and watch. Likewise, the Alpine troop observed the moment from afar as they continued with their chores. The aversion between these two generals, between the half-brothers was a well-known fact, the outcome of which more than one warrior had bet good money on.

"The trees are quiet. Had there been news, I would have informed you."

"Make sure that you do." Rinon turned and strode away and Fel'annár's upper lip curled.

"Easy, Fel'annár." Galadan watched, shot a warning glance at Idernon.

A long, muted hiss passed the Warlord's lips as he turned, picked up his pack and slung it over his shoulders. Before long they were mounted and cantering through the forest that was slowly thinning out the closer they travelled to the Calro Delta.

Fel'annár's connection was weaker here. The sea drowned the song of the trees, mercifully muted the voice of the Evergreen Wood.

He turned in the saddle, saw Ramien fiddling with the rainbow jumper in his hair. They were on the Eastern Road, the foothills of the Median Mountains to their left. The group he had sensed was surely close now. Fel'annár strained his eyes into the distance where the delta would soon appear. He blinked, felt something pull in his mind, a string, some connection. It was warm and it was cold. It was soft and it was cutting, strong like a full moon tide in his mind. Just beneath the sentiments, a lingering sense of foreboding.

Were there two groups then? One on the slopes and another further ahead, closer to the incoming patrol? He steered his horse to the right until he was close enough to Rinon to be heard over the noise of over sixty cantering warriors.

"Princess Maeneth is close. Half a day or so, on this course."

"This course? Are you sure? And what of the enemy?"

"It draws closer. I feel them on the slopes but there may be another group, further south. In a few moments I may know more."

"The logical route to take from Port Helia is the Western route, unless you're a warrior looking for Deviants. What were they thinking? It's dangerous – they surely know that."

"When we're a little closer, I'll have more details, numbers."

"How close do you *need* to be? So close they have already attacked and put us all in danger?"

Fel'annár couldn't answer that. He didn't know. Had they been in the Deep Forest, he would already have numbers.

Rinon turned away, and Fel'annár wondered what he was thinking beneath the cool façade and the glittering eyes. But the prince gave nothing away, and he turned back to the fore, increased their speed. Whatever Rinon hid from him, one thing was certain. There was panic swimming beneath the surface. Panic for a sister Fel'annár could see meant everything to him.

This was a side to Rinon that he had never seen. His eyes strayed to the captain at the prince's side and for a moment, they crossed gazes. Did Sar'pén feel his friend's unease as acutely as he could?

They stopped at midday to rest the horses, but the troops were watching the Warlord and the prince from where they sat. It didn't take a Royal Councillor to see the sparks between them. The troops quietly discussed a colourful myriad of possible outcomes, ranging from brotherly hugs to gruesome fratricide, and with every passing minute, the wagers grew, as wildly as their murmured conjectures.

Two horses galloped into the camp. Two of Rinon's scouts had returned, their news surely dire. They dismounted even before the horses had come to a halt. The Company watched from afar together with the rest of the patrol, even as Fel'annár blinked. When next he opened his eyes, they were brighter than they had been.

"They're close."

"The enemy or the princess?" asked Tensári.

He turned to her. "Both." He made for Rinon, The Company behind. "General!" he called from afar.

Rinon turned impatiently to him, summarised the news he had just received. "The Deviants are on the foothills, but the princess' patrol took the *Western* Road, not the Eastern, Warlord."

Fel'annár frowned, opened his mouth to speak but his gaze drifted to one side, and then green light flared before his face. Rinon hesitated.

"What is it?"

"A moment," he ground out. There was something he was missing.

"Well?" Rinon was so close Fel'annár could feel his erratic breathing, see the growing panic in his glacial eyes.

"Well *what?*" Fel'annár's anger spiked. He was losing concentration. Still, he saw the exact moment that Rinon took his decision.

"As we speak, two of our scouts are redirecting the Pelagian patrol onto the Western Road. Take the patrol, General. Skirt around the Eastern road and then sweep westwards, make sure the enemy does not follow. Avoid battle if you can and join us on the last leg home."

With that, Rinon whirled around, ran towards the horses, Sar'pén at his shoulder.

"Wait, stop!" called Fel'annár.

But Rinon didn't, and soon, he was in the saddle, Sar'pén, the two scouts and his closest warriors around him. Together, they galloped away, under the baffled stares of the patrol.

Even as Fel'annár watched the prince's party leave, he could feel his eyes flaring as the information they so desperately needed began to flood his mind.

If only Rinon had waited ...

"Deviants lie on the Eastern road, and the princess *is* on that route – not the Western Road."

There were shouts of disbelief. Many had heard the scouts, heard Rinon's orders. The prince was galloping *away* from the princess, *away* from the Deviants – at least according to the Warlord. Fel'annár could see their confusion, damned Rinon for his impetuous flight.

"Ssshhhit! Idernon, Tensári, with me. Galadan, Sontúr, take the others, protect Rinon. Tell him to veer east. Princess Maeneth's patrol is walking into a Deviant horde."

Galadan nodded, Sontúr clapped Fel'annár on the shoulder and then sprinted towards their horses, Ramien, Carodel and Galdith in tow. Soon, they too were charging away from the camp.

Fel'annár jumped into the saddle, horse wheeling around in panic. He raised his voice over the remaining patrol who were already making ready to leave.

"Mount and follow me. Our scouts' report is spurious. We must engage the enemy before the Pelagian patrol encounter them." Fel'annár didn't stop to watch but wheeled around, Idernon and Tensári beside him. A glance over his shoulder and he saw the patrol moving too slowly. He thought it was suspicion and he couldn't blame them. There were conflicting orders and theirs was a volatile peace. He glanced at Idernon, gestured with his head.

Idernon guided his horse back to the patrol.

"Move your backsides! Our princess is in danger. Our duty is to protect her. Ride! Ride hard!"

He cantered back to the fore, thunder in his eyes. Fel'annár would have smiled at the sight of him, but he was too worried. He thought of Galadan and Sontúr, of Carodel, Ramien and Galdith riding after Rinon. Why had the scouts been wrong? Had they misled the prince purposefully? And if they had, what was he riding into?

SONTÚR COULD SEE RINON, Sar'pén and four others galloping in the distance, legs bouncing off the sides of their steeds, hair flying behind them, bodies bent low over their lunging horses.

"*General!*" shouted Galadan at his side. But they were surely too far away to hear, and moments later, Sontúr tried his luck.

"*Prince Rinon!*"

Nothing. They leaned further over their lurching horses, elbows and knees working frantically. And then Ramien's booming voice from just behind.

"General *Rinon!*"

Only one head turned. Sar'pén. He seemed shocked, but they didn't slow their pace.

Sontúr frowned.

An arrow flew past Galadan's head. There were archers in the trees to their left.

"General! Right, veer *right!*" Galadan's voice. But still, Rinon continued to gallop, surrounded by his warriors. One of them fell back, leaving the prince's left flank open.

Vulnerable.

"What the hell are they doing?" called Sontúr. The gap between the two groups was closing; they were almost there.

"Carodel, Galdith!" Galadan's cry and both warriors released the reins, drew their bows and sighted. Arrows flew, but more enemy bolts were flying towards Rinon.

"Rinon, down! *Down!*" screamed Galadan.

This time, Rinon did hear and he flattened himself, just in time to avoid an arrow that skittered over his armour. But more were sailing towards them. Galdith fired, Carodel followed.

"*Stay down!*" shouted Sontúr.

But no more arrows came and Ramien, Carodel and Galdith's horses were around the prince and his warriors, forcing them to stop. Confused voices, anger, agitated horses fretting and neighing. Galadan and Sontúr directed their horses towards the group while Ramien and Galdith dismounted and made for where the archers had fallen.

"What is the meaning of this?" A seething Rinon.

"You are galloping away from the Deviants *and* Princess Maeneth. She's not on the Western road, Prince."

"So says the confused Warlord. Our scouts disagree, have seen the enemy and the incoming patrol. You will be disciplined for this outrage," said Rinon.

"Blind faith, Captain Galadan. You should listen to the *facts* ..." Sar'pén promptly closed his mouth when Ramien and Galdith returned. In the Wall of Stone's hands, a dead elf in the uniform of an Ea Uaré warrior. He threw the body onto the ground before Rinon. Sontúr's eyes travelled from the dead sniper to Rinon, saw his shock. His own was just beneath his calm demeanour.

"I believe that is one of your scouts, General."

Rinon's eyes were wide, lips quivering as reality set in. He had been played, deceived. He had been led into a trap by traitors.

Sar'pén and two others surrounded the remaining scouts, faces dour and searching.

"We're loyal, captain. I swear it!"

"I do not believe you. Dismount!"

The two scouts looked frantically about them, for any opening but there was none. Sontúr, Galadan, Carodel and Galdith stared hard at them, willing them to make a run for it so that they could skewer them.

But there was no opening. They released their reins and sank to the ground.

Sar'pén dismounted, watched as the two scouts' hands were tied behind their backs, and then to the nearest tree. With their captives secured, they mounted once more and turned to Rinon when he spoke.

"You would have killed me, killed my sister and I would know why. When we return, I will have my answers, traitors!" He wheeled his horse around, caught Sar'pén's gaze.

"Maeneth."

~

"ARCHERS READY!"

The patrol thundered behind Fel'annár, Tensári and Idernon, along the eastern foothills. In the distance, a swarm of Deviants ran southwards, just out of range of their arrows.

"Hold steady! Archers pan to the fore!"

The archers on the left spread out to the front of the galloping patrol, pursuing the Deviants. They were ready to fire, just out of reach. Just a few more yards ...

"Hold! Hold fire!" yelled Fel'annár, one hand in the air. The Deviants were in range, but so were the Pelagian warriors. They were already fighting. This group they pursued was a second wave. He watched as more than a hundred Deviants slammed into the fray.

"Merciful Gods," murmured Tensári.

"Ride! Ride hard! Fight at your discretion. Protect the princess!"

The warriors behind were drawing their blades, shouting their battle cries. Whatever doubts they had had before, had gone in the wake of evidence. The Warlord had been right. For some, inexplicable reason, the scouts had been wrong. The Pelagian captain had led Maeneth along the most dangerous route home.

"Charge!"

The roar from behind was deafening and before them, Deviants and elves turned to the oncoming cavalry. Some cheered, others screamed. In seconds, Fel'annár was on the ground and fighting, Idernon and Tensári at his side – not too close as common sense dictated in the presence of a Kah Warrior.

Fel'annár slashed sideways, taking a half-rotten head off bony shoulders.

Idernon charged at a Deviant, sliced its neck open and turned to another, while Tensári tackled a Deviant that had moved too close to Fel'annár. Soon, the three found a rhythm. They fought as they slowly advanced, further towards the trees where Fel'annár suspected the princess had been taken.

Heavy dread slammed into him, heat in his eyes.

"The Deviants are closing in on the princess."

"Where is she?" shouted Tensári as she slashed through a rotten arm.

"In that copse further ahead. I have to go, Idernon. I can travel through the boughs quicker than we can fight our way through this."

"Don't."

"Keep advancing. I'll be right there," he pointed to where he knew the princess was. "Join me when you can!"

"Take me with you!"

"There's no time, Tensári. I'll be quicker alone."

She was angry, but the Deviants were pressing in around them. With a final nod at Idernon, Fel'annár ran, and then he jumped, reached for a low-hanging branch and disappeared.

With a roar, Tensári pushed forwards, Idernon beside her and slowly, step by step, they inched southwards.

Not fast enough.

15

LAST STAND

∼

Rɪɴoɴ ʀoᴅᴇ like the winter gales on Dan'bar.

The wind in his hair, tears in his eyes. Frustration, anger at the scouts, at himself, dread at what he had brought about. He should have trusted Fel'annár, not the scouts. He should have heeded Pan'assár's words, his father's warnings.

He could already hear the sounds of battle in the distance. On the *Eastern* Road, just as the Warlord had said.

They had wanted to kill their crown prince, and there were two more scouts with the Pelagian patrol. Did they intend to kill Maeneth too? Were there more traitors in his own patrol?

He forced himself to concentrate, to stop the questions and focus on the impending battle, on finding Maeneth and the treacherous scouts. He reached back, drew his sword, held it high over his head and yelled his battle cry, loud and raw and behind him, Sar'pén, his warriors and the rest of The Company.

Moments later they were on the ground, fighting many more Deviants than they had anticipated. Had Fel'annár been right in this too?

Had there been two groups and not one? His eyes desperately scanned the battlefield for any indication of where his sister might be.

An arrow thudded close by. A warrior fell to the ground with a groan, and then another. Rinon looked down at the elven arrow stuck in his chest.

Another traitor, shooting from the trees.

A Deviant stepped too close and Rinon sliced its hand off and then stabbed another in the chest. Galdith drew another arrow, fired, and then Carodel followed. Sontúr's anxiety was growing. Someone needed to take down those snipers.

"Galdith!!" Sontúr's powerful voice rose over the din of battle and the Fierce Warrior whirled around, followed the direction Sontúr was pointing to. There, all but hidden in the boughs, was an elf, bow sighting Rinon. Taking aim, Galdith loosed the bolt, and then stared in horror as the traitor's arrow was loosed and sailed straight for Rinon. But then a body slammed into the prince and the two were on the ground.

"Sontúr!" screamed Galadan and Galdith at the same time. Gods but it was *Sontúr* who lay on top of the prince, an arrow protruding from his shoulder. Galdith couldn't let up. He had killed one archer but there was another, hidden between the shrubs at the base of the slopes. He looked to where Galadan was pulling a weakly protesting Alpine prince from atop another, and then turned back to the trees, eyes desperately searching.

There, a flash of teal cloth. Galdith had always had good eyesight. He aimed, lip curled, eyes sentencing.

He released, saw the figure fall, spat to one side in disgust.

He turned to where Rinon was rising, dazed and unsure as to what had happened. But Galadan was pushing Sontúr down onto the ground. Galdith, Ramien and Carodel formed a protective circle around them.

Rinon stood, shook his head, took up his discarded sword and glanced down at Sontúr, prince of Tar'eastór.

"Get him to safety." He turned, nodded at Galdith and threw himself into the fight and Galadan watched him move away. "Ramien, Carodel, Galdith. Go after him. There may be more traitors. I'll stay with Sontúr. It's safe here for now."

Galdith looked around, realised Galadan was right. The majority of the Deviants had moved further south, pursuing the elves he could only assume were falling back to protect the princess.

With a final nod, the three sprinted away and were soon fighting at Rinon's back.

With every Deviant they killed, they stepped closer and closer southwards, until Rinon caught sight of a familiar face.

"Lieutenant Idernon!"

Idernon stopped, turned to the yell and then spotted Rinon, and behind him, Galdith, Carodel and Ramien. He turned to Tensári, knew she wouldn't stop and so he gestured for her to continue while he waited for his prince.

She was away in a flash of black and silver, and Idernon turned to the crown prince, not before sighting an oncoming Deviant and killing it.

"Where's the princess? Where's Fel'annár?" asked Rinon.

"In the trees, moving to that copse up ahead. He said the Deviants know where she is and are closing in. He went alone, said he can move quicker in the trees than we can on the ground."

It was all Rinon needed to know, and he charged after the retreating form of Tensári, now in the distance.

He slashed, parried and stabbed. He jumped over bodies, ducked incoming scimitars, felt the presence of The Company at his back.

The Gods but he needed to find Maeneth, before the Deviants did, before any more traitors could get to her.

Rinon never thought he would pray for Fel'annár and yet here he was, doing just that as he continued to fight, frustration warring with panic as he slowly inched forwards. He prayed Fel'annár would find her, protect her from the enemy. Because if he didn't – if Maeneth died – then Rinon would surely follow her on the Short Road.

HE WAS CLOSE.

Fel'annár could feel that strange connection, hiding in the trees. It had to be Maeneth, in the company of two others.

He jumped, latched onto a branch that had already been moving towards him. It hurtled him through the air, but another branch was beneath him, carried him to the next.

Almost there.

He looked down, saw elves and Deviants fighting. This was the rear of the battle, the Deviants only recently arrived, or so it seemed, because there were hardly any warriors to meet them.

With Maeneth's tree firmly in his mind, he jumped to the forest floor and ran, as close to it as he could without singling it out. He touched a nearby tree.

Protect the princess.

A rustle of branches, like a sudden intake of breath and Fel'annár turned his back to the tree, eyes to the fore and the oncoming Deviants.

Three before him, another two, one on each side and behind them, more came. He drew his long and short swords, took up the ready stance, grey sash playing around his knees. He moved his foremost blade until it lay flat across his face.

The Deviants hesitated, watched the strange movement and the utterly still warrior. The foremost Deviant, a burly man with a chest like a barrel of wine, held out his massive scimitar, purple lips curling into the mockery of a smile. He moved the scimitar sideways until it sat across his rotting face and waited. Behind him, the other Deviants wailed.

Were they laughing at him?

No time even to frown and the towering Deviant launched himself towards Fel'annár. The Warlord stepped aside, watched him stagger away, off balance, but another two were coming for him. He ducked under one blade, sliced over the Deviants back and turned into the second, thrust his sword through its chest.

He had hardly moved, but as another wave of Deviants came at him, he jumped, somersaulted over one, stabbed backwards with both blades and pulled back.

Turning, he blocked a downward arcing blade, moved into his opponent, caught his arm in a vice and twisted. He pulled the Deviant over his shoulder, whirled away, swivelled his swords before him as he gathered his breath.

He was surrounded, the Deviants pressing in closer. He called on the Dohai, calmed his breathing and remembered his Master's words.

You must hear your movements through air, feel those of others, sense their direction.

He closed his mind to the oncoming Deviants, to the fact that he was surrounded and outnumbered. He banished all thoughts of his impending death and instead, heard the wind, the movement of material through air. As he pulled both his blades up, he saw green lights following them.

A deep breath, and he opened his glowing eyes.

Fel'annár charged at the closest Deviant, killed it, turned to another, and then another. He cut a throat, felt blood splatter over his face, turned to the next one, killed it and staggered sideways. He ducked, holding himself aloft with one hand, he used his inertia to kick a Deviant in the side of the head. It fell away and he stood, blades back in a ready stance, blue and purple streaks settling more slowly.

Dodging an incoming blow, Fel'annár stabbed sideways at one as he kicked out at another. He pulled one Deviant towards him, turned and pushed him onto the blade of another and then launched himself into the air, turning and landing behind his next target. It turned, surprised face screwing into a grimace as a blade slid through its guts.

His body worked, fluid limbs a blur as he jumped, twisted, parried and thrust and the bodies around him fell, one after the other. He didn't know how many already littered the floor around him. All he knew was that they kept coming, and he kept killing.

Exhaustion was taking its toll, but he heard the voices in the background, above the wailing and grunting, calling his name repeatedly. Tensári and... Rinon?

The elven warriors must have finally broken through the Deviant line ...

Something smacked into the side of his head. Before he knew it, he was falling, long sword flying out of his bloody hand.

Fel'annár stood on shaky feet, chest heaving, arms like lead. He held out his short sword, launched himself at a Deviant, killed it and then ducked under a sword, kicked upwards, foot smashing into a putrid face. He whirled around, punched another, slashed over a wrist.

Just as straightened himself, the world lurched sideways and the last standing Deviant blurred in and out of focus.

He was going to die.

Knees buckling, he fell to one knee. He looked up, saw the curved blade rise over his head, held a hand out, shielded his eyes from the glaring sun. He'd been right all along. He *was* going to die ...

But the blade didn't move and instead, the Deviant froze, and then fell sideways, crashing into the ground beside him.

His sluggish eyes saw an arrow through its chest. His eyes focussed, saw Tensári, bow still held high, arm still straight and true.

Fel'annár fell to his hands and knees, chest heaving in exertion. He gasped and laughed at the same time and then turned to sit. Beyond Rinon and The Company, their warriors killed the last of the Deviants. He turned to the trees behind, no longer swaying but calm and still.

Rinon had seen this strange dance before, in the Evergreen Wood after the Battle of Brothers.

One elf climbed down from the tree just behind Fel'annár. A grey-haired warrior, bloodied but alive, sword still in his hand. Rinon sought his eyes, so that he could read the truth. Was this elf loyal? Had he protected the princess, or had he killed her? He stepped forward, dread weighing him down.

Whether the warrior understood him, Rinon couldn't say, but he stepped aside, waited for another two to climb down. Another warrior and a shorter figure in a black cloak.

A strong, pale hand rose, pushed back the hood to reveal silvery-blonde hair and frosty blue eyes.

Maeneth was standing before him, wide-eyed and shaken but alive.

He ran to her, crashed into her but he couldn't speak, couldn't even say her name. She was the better part of him. She washed away his flaws, doused the anger in his veins, opened his heart to others so that he could feel their joy, their pain – not just his own. To Rinon, she was his key to the outside world.

His arms tightened. He could smell her hair, recognised the sea in it, but salt would soon be replaced with sap, with forest loam and Alpine stone. He would not be parted from her again, he swore.

"I will not leave you again, Rinon."

He closed his eyes, rested his weary head on hers. He had endangered her life with his rash flight, his disregard for the Warlord's warnings. Pan'assár had warned him to heed Fel'annár, whether or not it made sense. Rinon had disobeyed him because of his irrational hatred.

His arms slackened and he held her at arm's length. But not even his growing feelings of guilt could wash away the bliss he felt at the sight of her and his smile did not waver. She mirrored it, held his face between her hands, eyes dancing from one side of his face to the other, as if she did not know where to look.

They stepped apart and Rinon cocked his head for her to follow. Together, they made for where The Company crouched around a still sitting Warlord.

They looked up at the royal twins, eyes moving between Maeneth and Rinon, but the prince's gaze was fixed on Fel'annár. He held out one hand and Fel'annár looked at it. What was he thinking? wondered Rinon. Would he turn away and shame him for not listening? Would he accept it? Accept Rinon's apology?

Fel'annár held out his own, shaking hand and Rinon clasped it tight and then pulled him to his feet. He steadied his half-brother as he stumbled sideways. That was the first time their eyes met in something other than irritation, anger and dislike. Rinon would seek him out later, but for now, there were priorities, and Fel'annár was in no state to command the troops.

"Lieutenant Idernon. I trust no one save The Company to keep my sister safe. Will you do this for me?"

Idernon stared back at him. It reminded Rinon of the first time they had met, when Idernon had defied his orders. But he didn't this time. Instead, he bowed, then saluted, turned to a bloodied Warlord and his closest.

"You heard the general. We make for Captain Galadan's position. General Rinon. We will set up camp a distance away from the rest of our warriors. I assume we will camp here for the night?"

"We will not. We have two hours to secure the camp, see to the wounded and dead. After, we ride towards the Western Road. There are captives to interrogate, and I would get us as far away as I can from the foothills. You are all exempt from duty until our departure. I will have someone provide you with what you need."

Idernon nodded, turned to Galdith when he spoke.

"And what of you, General. You saw the colour of those arrows aimed at you, the one that struck Captain Sontúr. There may be more traitors in our midst, even as we stand here."

"Yes, traitors," spat one of the two grey-haired warriors. They wore the dark greys and light greens of the Pelagian guard. Only now did Rinon notice the golden sun in his collar, the single line in the other's.

"Your scouts told us there was danger on the Western Road. They led us to the Eastern Road, and although it seemed strange to us, it did not occur to us that they were lying. And where there are four ..."

"There may be more, General," said the second Pelagian. "You need protection, my Lord."

"I have Captain Sar'pén to watch my back, Lieutenant."

"But he's not here yet," said Idernon. "The king sent us to protect both you and the princess. We can't leave you unprotected."

"If I may," injected Maeneth, "This is Captain Airen and Lieutenant Enar from Pelegia. They protected me through this entire battle. I would trust them to guard you, brother, together with Sar'pén."

Rinon looked at the two grey-haired Pelegian officers, and nodded. "The Crown thanks both of you for your service. Follow me while the Company takes over the care of my sister."

"Her protection is our pride and pleasure. Princess Maeneth is beloved of the Pelagian people."

Rinon couldn't help the smile that spread over his bruised face. He nodded, turned to The Company.

"Go, see to your Warlord and Prince Sontúr. I trust you all with my sister's life. I will find you later."

Idernon shared a glance with Galdith, wished Rinon had trusted Fel'annár *before* the battle. They took each of Fel'annár's arms while Carodel ushered the princess into the centre of the group. Together, they walked slowly away, leaving behind them a mountain of dead Deviants and an utterly changed Crown Prince.

As Rinon strode back into where the thick of fighting had taken place, Captain Airen drew flush with him.

"The trees around us were moving while ours stood still. He killed more than forty Deviants, drew colour from the air as he fought. He did all that alone, General. I don't understand ..."

Rinon turned to Airen. "Neither do I, Captain. Neither do I."

GALDITH LED the way to where they had left Galadan with Sontúr. Logically, they were no longer there. It was Fel'annár's slurred words that guided them away from the battlefield and further into the trees, where they found the healer captain sitting beside Sontúr. The prince was leaning back against a tree, a small fire crackling before him.

Galadan stood, while Sontúr opened his eyes and stared at Fel'annár. And then his eyes drifted further behind, to the silvery-blonde-haired woman he knew had to be his friend's half-sister.

He made to stand but Galadan glared down at him. "Don't."

Idernon and Ramien lowered Fel'annár to the ground beside Sontúr and then formed a circle around the fire. Maeneth knelt in their midst, eyes flitting from Fel'annár to the grey-haired warrior whose arm sat in a high sling.

"What happened?" asked Sontúr as his good hand reached out to examine Fel'annár's head.

"This mad Ari'atór killed a horde of Deviants all by himself," said Carodel, finger jabbing at the bloodied Fel'annár.

"So selfish," murmured Sontúr, pulling down Fel'annár's bottom eyelid and peering into his eye, slightly darker than it should have been.

Maeneth stared at him. She had sat in a tree, watched the forest thrash around her, eyes pinned on the only thing between her and two-score Deviants – her own half-brother. She had thought he would die before her eyes, heart hammering in her chest as she watched unnatural lights streak around him. She had heard the stifled gasps from her guards, covered her own mouth so that she wouldn't give their position away. She was shocked to the core at what she had seen and yet – she wanted to laugh at the ironic words, the acutely-arched brow as the injured Pelagian warrior had said them.

She stood, made for Fel'annár's side and knelt beside him. "Let me help. I have rudimentary knowledge of battle injuries."

Galadan and Sontúr watched as she peered at Fel'annár's head.

"Carodel, we need more water, and bandages."

"I'll see what I can do, Galadan." The Bard Warrior made to stand, but three Alpine warriors were approaching. Galdith, Idernon and Ramien were on their feet, swords drawn and the guards startled.

"General Rinon sent us. We bring water and supplies."

"Leave them here," ordered Idernon.

The guards' eyes strayed to the small camp beyond and then back to the lieutenant before them.

"Of course."

They left two buckets of water, one empty bucket and a cloth bag on the ground and left. Idernon didn't turn his back until they were gone.

He turned where he stood. "Fel'annár. Are you well enough to sense danger?"

"Yes. We're safe." A soft yet hoarse voice.

Idernon nodded, helped Galdith to carry the supplies to the fire. Maeneth reached for the bag and rummaged through its contents. The entire Company watched her, but whether she realised, no one could say. She stood, poured some of the water into the empty bucket and then reached for a cloth. Dipping it in the water, she began to wash Fel'annár's face.

Galadan watched her as he brewed a pain-relieving tea for his patients, as did Sontúr.

"He has a mild concussion."

"Yes, I know."

"Where did you learn?"

"As a novice warrior, and at my friend's side. She is head healer."

Rinon had mentioned Fel'annár's resemblance to Or'Talán in passing, but it had been the stories from the Motherland that had reached Pelagia, that had prepared her for this moment. As Fel'annár's bruised face emerged from the grime, she realised they had not been wrong. This was no mere resemblance but a spitting image save for the texture of his hair and the colour of his eyes.

And then the Silvan's words from before came back to her.

This mad Ari'atór ...

"Why do they call you Ari'atór?" She dabbed at the cut on Fel'annár's head. It had stopped bleeding, but the swelling was rising, as fast as the skin around it was darkening.

"Because that's what I am," he said slowly, softly.

Only now did Carodel seem to realise what he had said. He looked up into the canopy above them, but Maeneth's hand froze for the second time, eyes only now straying to the braids in his hair. What else had Rinon failed to tell her? She should have been angry with him, but she remembered his desperate eyes, the way he had clutched her to him after the fight. She was too relieved he was alive, too elated to see him again.

She wrapped a bandage around Fel'annár's head, tucked the end underneath and leaned back.

"Where are your other injuries?"

"There is nothing important."

She stared at him, not really believing him but he seemed well enough save for the slurred speech and the soft shake of his hands.

She turned to the Pelagian warrior, didn't remember having seen him in her patrol.

"Is it bad?"

"He won't die," said Galadan. "But this shoulder needs attention. The arrow tip has done some damage here," he pointed. Sontúr waved his other hand in the air.

"It will mend."

"Of course," said Galadan, knowing Sontúr was more worried than he let on. None of them had missed the grimace of pain as he had tried to reassure them – and failed.

RINON ACCEPTED a strip of cloth from a warrior as he passed together with Airen and Enar, but he didn't stop.

He pressed it to his bleeding lip and cast his gaze over camp. Everything was under control, and Maeneth was safe with The Company.

They passed a group of warriors who stood talking. One turned and then the others followed suit, guilty eyes and a respectful bow. Rinon knew they had been talking about him, nodded at them with forbidding eyes. He had told the patrol that Maeneth was on the Western road. He had been wrong. The *scouts* had been wrong.

Rinon heard Sar'pén before he saw him. He was shouting orders, warriors were running here and there, collecting bodies, organising the injured. He spotted Rinon, beckoned to him, eyes lingering on the Pelagian guards at his side.

"Captain."

"General. I am sending scouts to ..."

"No."

Sar'pén frowned. "We need to know if there are any more Deviants."

"We can't trust the information we will receive. Clean up and muster the troop in two hours. We ride towards the Western road and camp there. I will not have those captive traitors prey to the predators. I have questions, and they will answer them."

Sar'pén stared at his friend, eyes drifting to the Pelagians once more.

"Very well. And you are?"

"Captain Airen of Pelagia. This is my lieutenant, Enar."

Sar'pén nodded. "I would appreciate some help with the clean-up."

"We stay with the general, Captain."

Rinon saw the flicker in his friend's eye, the set of his jaw. Perhaps he thought the Pelagians were not to be trusted. After all, he had not witnessed Fel'annár's stand, had not seen how they had protected Maeneth.

He was grateful that Sar'pén was suspicious.

"Do you not have your own patrol to see to?"

Airen stepped towards Sar'pén, searched his eyes and when he answered, it was not kindly.

"My patrol has been all but annihilated, Captain."

GOR'SADÉN HAD FELT no pity when he had bested his latest opponent almost before they had begun. The red-faced captain had stuttered something about trying again in the future, bowed and left. Another had taken his place and had been bested in three moves.

Not fit enough. Not good enough.

The training pits were full, but only one area was in use, at the very centre, where Fel'annár and Bulan had trained for the first time with spears just recently.

They had had no option but to open the doors of the Inner Circle to the crowds that had gathered outside. Not only captains stood around them now, but lieutenants, warriors and even novices and recruits. They had eventually closed the doors, to the disappointment of hundreds.

Pan'assár had faced them, warned them that they would be allowed to watch under the strict agreement that they were not to make a sound. No cheering, no jeering, no encouragement. They would not be performing Kah movements today, but concentration must be at its highest. Both commanders knew how important an apprenticeship in the Kal'hamén'Ar was to these candidates.

Silence reigned save for the clash of swords as Pan'assár confronted the Alpine captain Eramor. They had been duelling for more than a minute and Gor'sadén watched with keen interest.

He could see why Pan'assár had allowed it to continue, even though he could have embarrassed the elf almost before it had begun. Eramor was skilled with his blade, showed promise except that his body was not honed enough to be any quicker than he was. He would need to work on that, but he was certainly one of the more skilled candidates.

Eramor fell, blocked Pan'assár's downwards stroke only barely, earning himself a cut on the cheek – another one – but he picked himself up, danced out of the way of a sideways slash. It was a walk in the park for his brother but Eramor was confronting the adversary of his life.

Pan'assár shouted the order to stop, just as Eramor was hurtling towards him in a last-ditched attempt to create a semblance of danger. The commander side-stepped, watched coolly as Eramor crashed to the ground, face-down. Gor'sadén wondered if he had done it on purpose, indeed it wouldn't have surprised him. His friend had a penchant for dark humour at times.

The captain slowly moved into a kneeling position and Pan'assár looked down on him, just as Gor'sadén did as he approached. He shared a glance with his friend, understood the unspoken question and nodded.

Eramor looked up at him. There was no anger there, just embarrassment and something else. It was a plea to give him another chance, to look beyond his clumsy attempts to show his commander he was worthy of a grey sash.

Eramor had performed the trial far worse than Fel'annár had, but then Gor'sadén knew that they couldn't use him as their measure. All it meant was that these new apprentices would take longer to achieve mastery.

"All stand!"

The thirty aspiring lieutenants and captains formed a line and the two commanders made for one side of it.

They slowly moved from warrior to warrior. Most of them received a hand on the shoulder, a shake of the head and an invitation to try again the following year. By the time they reached the end of the line, only ten were left.

A warrior approached with grey sashes neatly arranged over his arm, and one by one, Pan'assár and Gor'sadén tied them around the waists of the ten, successful candidates. Tomorrow, they would be briefed and instructed on how to tie the Heliaré, amongst other things.

Gor'sadén stood before Eramor, studied his face for a moment. Of them all, with the exception of Benat at his side, he was the most promising. His wide eyes were full of emotion as Gor'sadén tied his sash and then stepped back.

"Welcome to the order of the Kah, Captain Eramor."

The captain's eyes brimmed but he didn't care. He had obviously wanted this, just as much as Fel'annár had.

Stepping away, the new Kah Disciples were dismissed and the silence that had prevailed throughout the entire session crumbled. Shouts of joy, cheers of glee at the spectacle they had all witnessed. Especially Eramor and Benat, the two captains that seemed to share a special affinity. They embraced for far longer than it took the rest to disappear into the crowds.

Gor'sadén wished that Fel'annár were here to witness it, knew that he would be instrumental during the first and gruelling training sessions. Of the ten Disciples, three were Silvan.

The Kal'hamén'Ar had returned to Ea Uaré and Gor'sadén sought Pan'assár's gaze. He found him staring back at him, a new light in his eyes. It was the light of determination, of a purpose regained, of an objective yet to achieve. This army was coming together, moving forward. All that was left for Pan'assár to achieve was to regain the respect of the Silvan troops he had once boasted.

16

ROYAL CHILDREN

~

MOST OF THEIR horses had been collected from where they had scattered. With twenty-seven dead from Rinon's patrol, and more than thirty from Captain Airen's unit, there was no shortage of them. The general had ordered harnesses be made for the injured. They would be tied between horses, making the journey home both quicker and more comfortable for those who could not ride.

Rinon had organised the patrol into two groups. He himself would lead the first of them, get to the captive scouts before nightfall. A reluctant Sar'pén would lead the injured at a slower pace. His friend had wanted Airen to lead it, so that he could stay at Rinon's side, but thanks to The Company, Sar'pén's protection was not necessary. The prince was glad now that his father had insisted they come, that he had not heeded his baseless objections to Fel'annár's presence.

Sontúr had ridden with Galadan, while Fel'annár rode behind Tensári. As for Maeneth, she rode at the centre of The Company, at the back of the patrol. Rinon rode at the fore, Airen and Enar at his side and back, and at the centre of the column, half of the remaining able-bodied warriors.

It had taken them an hour to arrive, and while The Company whisked Maeneth away from the main camp, Rinon and Airen organised it, eyes watchful, hands hovering over the pommels of their swords. With only ten warriors, The Company and himself, Rinon had soon seen to their safety, set guards around the perimeter, and secured a source of water. But whether he could trust those guards was still to be seen.

It was time to find the traitors.

He strode towards the tree where they had trussed them up, found them looking up at him with dread in their eyes. Behind him, Airen and Enar followed.

"Cut them loose," ordered Rinon.

Lieutenant Enar unsheathed his dagger, knelt down and roughly sliced through the ropes that held them to the tree. The two scouts stood on shaky legs, rubbing their numb hands.

"You have caused the death of over sixty warriors. The sentence for your crime is death." Rinon watched, saw the fear in their eyes, enjoyed it.

"Now, I have questions. Questions I fully expect you to answer."

~

IDERNON HAD LED The Company away from the other ten warriors. It felt wrong, but there was no telling who was loyal and who was not.

The warriors seemed to understand, nodded respectfully at them, even smiled at Maeneth with sorry eyes. They were surely ashamed of the greeting their estranged princess had received from her own people.

She watched Fel'annár, still paler than any Alpine she had ever met. He moved slowly, had hardly spoken on the journey here and she'd seen those warriors closest to him exchange wary glances with one other.

The overly large warrior started a small fire, and soon, they were all seated around it, a pot of water heating over it. As the Alpine Captain they called Galadan brewed tea, she watched the camp in the near distance.

There were few Silvans, mostly Alpines and a smattering of grey heads. They sat around their own fire, shared tea and spoke quietly, and Maeneth wondered what they were saying, what they were *thinking* after the discovery of the traitors and her half-brother's extraordinary stand. He had defended her, would have died for her and yet he did not know her, did not love her as a brother the way Rinon did. Maeneth had so many questions and no opportunities to ask them.

She wanted to thank him.

She turned away from the camp, back to Fel'annár who sat back against a tree. He looked like he wanted to sleep but daren't, and all the while, the Ari'atór remained at his side.

Maeneth breathed in, the smell of loam and leaves, of resin and pine. It felt like home, evoked a thrill of memories, all of them good. She had missed this place so much. Not even this, unexpected welcome was enough to curb her excitement, her desire to be home with her family at last.

Ea Uaré was nothing like Pelagia. It was no idyllic, dream-like realm of peace and tranquility, of learning and refinement, at least not beyond the royal palace walls. This land was raw, unadulterated nature and she had missed it fiercely, almost as much as she had missed her beloved brother.

In Rinon's last letter, he had said that their father had changed. But in anything related to Fel'annár, or *The Silvan* as Rinon called him, he had been sparing and vague and Maeneth knew why. With the coming of this half-brother, Rinon's past hurts had surely been dredged up once more. It had been all too easy to sense her brother's dislike of him.

But what now? She had seen how Rinon had offered his hand down to Fel'annár after the battle, how he had pulled him up.

She leaned back against a tree where she sat, eyes straying from Carodel to Galdith, Ramien to Galadan, and then to the grey-haired warrior with his arm in a sling.

"Were you in Captain Airen's patrol?"

"I ride with The Company, Princess."

"Maeneth will do, Captain."

"Sontúr of Tar'eastór, then."

She frowned. "Sontúr Ar Vorn'asté?"

"At your service, Lady."

"I, eh, I thought you were Pelagian."

"My mother's mother. I am Alpine."

She smiled. "How is it you ride with these ..."

"The Company. That is our name."

She cocked her head to one side. "All right. The Company."

"Fel'annár and I are friends, we all are. A common goal unites us in our service, and my father has granted me some time to ride with them."

"And what is that common goal?"

"That is a long story. Fel'annár will tell you one day." Sontúr glanced at him, as did Maeneth. He seemed to be listening.

"As for me, the time away from Tar'eastór will do me some good. I seek knowledge I suppose. I am a warrior, but I am also a healer. I aim to understand how the two vocations can be merged into one."

"Is it not already decided? Royal children rarely have such a choice."

"I know. But neither you nor I are first born. Our paths are not set in stone. We are the lucky ones, I think. To choose your calling, to dare take the route of a scholar and not a warrior ... My brother Torhén is a diplomat; his path as a statesman suits him just fine but me ... well, I could never decide. It is my father's hope that I will define myself while I am abroad." Sontúr's left eyebrow rose high above his right, one corner of his mouth quirked. It looked as if the prince were imagining his father's words, showing her just what he thought about them.

"Healer or warrior," said Maeneth.

"Yes. And then Fel'annár asked why I could not do both. It had never occurred to me."

Maeneth nodded. "It is often the case that we cannot see the simplest of things sometimes. I tend to analyse the details, get caught up in them and then forget the premise. For me, the question was botany or warrior. I became a novice but eventually, I left my home and pursued an academic career abroad."

"Did you ever regret that decision? To leave your military training I mean?"

"Not regretted it, no. But I have often wondered what my life would be like as a warrior now that Band'orán is dead and his old-world beliefs begin to fade."

"That may take time."

She gestured to his arm. "How bad is it?" Her eyes travelled over the sling, the strap that held his arm against his chest.

"I have damaged a tendon. It is important I do not move it around. My hope is that Llyniel may fix it."

Maeneth straightened. "Llyniel? Ar Aradan?"

"The same. I believe you know her?"

"Of course I do. Until today, I thought she was in Tar'eastór ..."

"She travelled home with us – The Company."

"That's ..." A smile blossomed on her face, changed it from serene beauty to infectious joy and Sontúr smiled with her, couldn't help it. He decided she was nothing at all like Rinon.

He liked this daughter of Thargodén.

"What has you two smiling?" asked Idernon as he crouched next to the fire and deposited an armful of kindling.

"Llyniel is in Ea Uaré," said Maeneth.

"Indeed she is, a good friend to us all in The Company, isn't she Fel'annár?"

The Warlord turned his head slowly, nodded minutely and then turned away.

Idernon watched his stubborn friend for a while longer as he suffered in silence and denial. But Galadan knew him well enough. Even now, he was rummaging through his collection of sachets, selecting the ones he would mix into a tea to relieve the thumping headache Fel'annár denied having.

Idernon shook his head, returned to the patrol warriors. He would sit with them a while longer, listen to what they were saying about the traitors and then report back to Fel'annár, if he was in any condition to hear what he had to say.

∿

It was dark by the time Sar'pén arrived with the second group of warriors.

While the injured were taken close to the fires, Rinon greeted his friend, all too aware of how his eyes searched those around him. He trusted no one and truth be told, neither did Rinon, except for The Company. He was even uncomfortable with Airen and Enar, but Maeneth trusted them, and he trusted her more than anyone.

"The traitors refuse to speak," he said, gesturing to the fire.

Sar'pén sat, accepted a steaming mug and for a moment, he just stared into the orange flames.

"They will though. On our return, my father's shadows will be the ones to ensure they give us the information we need. Whose orders were they following?"

"I would like to witness that."

"Pan'assár may not allow it. We can only ask, I suppose." Rinon glanced up at the stars, dimmed by the presence of a full moon. "Sar'pén, can you ..."

"Go. I will take care of the camp." He turned to Rinon, smiled, and then gestured with his head in the direction where Maeneth was sitting with The Company.

Rinon clapped him on the shoulder and was away, under the watchful gaze of Airen.

He could see the small fire just beyond the next tree, made sure his steps were loud enough not to startle. Even so, he came face to face with a wall of muscle. He looked up into the face of the one he now knew was called Ramien.

The sight of him was enough to intimidate anyone, and the battle axe he held across his chest was a crystal-clear message to anyone thinking to cross him.

"General." The Wall of Stone stepped aside and Rinon walked towards the small camp, eyes resting first on Sontúr, and then on a dozing Fel'annár. Finally, he met Maeneth's gaze, smiled sparingly.

"May I join you?

"Of course, my Prince," answered Galadan.

Rinon sat beside Maeneth, shoulder brushing against hers.

"How is that shoulder, Prince?" he asked of Sontúr.

"That remains to be seen. Lestari Llyniel will have more to say about that."

Rinon frowned, pursed his lips. "You took that arrow for me. My father did well to send The Company on this mission, in spite of my own misgivings."

Silence followed Rinon's words. Unlikely as it was, it seemed the prince was apologising. Maeneth watched her brother carefully, as much as she did the reactions of the others. They were just as surprised as she was.

"You have my thanks, Sontúr. Your selfless sacrifice is duly noted. I am in your debt."

"No need, Rinon. It was my duty."

Rinon nodded, turned to Fel'annár and for a while, he simply watched. His eyes were half closed, countenance a stark white, almost as much as the bandage around his head. Still, he was aware enough to know that Rinon was staring at him.

"Concussion?"

Fel'annár nodded, said nothing, and so Rinon held his tongue. He would thank Fel'annár tomorrow, when he was well enough to accept it or reject it.

Gods but Rinon wanted to speak with Maeneth, alone so that he could ask his questions; so that she could ask her own, and he knew she had many. But there was still danger. The scouts had refused to speak and who was to say there were not more, here at the camp?

They would have to wait until they were safely home.

"If all goes well, and considering our pace will be slower with the wounded, we should be in the city the day after tomorrow," began Rinon. "The Company will travel at the centre of the column with Princess Maeneth, and Sar'pén will take the rear. I ride at the fore with Airen and Enar."

Rinon glanced at Maeneth, an apology in his eyes he knew she understood. He turned to Fel'annár once more, noted the slight crease between his brows.

Just yesterday, he would have been all too eager to leave, so that he would not have to look at Fel'annár. He was like a window into Rinon's darker past; a reminder of how everything had gone wrong in his life. And yet now, here he sat, willingly looking at his half-brother, curious for the first time about who he was, what he was like and the things he had done.

Was he angry? Indignant because Rinon had disregarded his warnings of a second group? Because he had not waited for Fel'annár to give him the details they needed? All Rinon had had to do was wait. He had been mere minutes away from avoiding all this. Instead, his irrational hatred towards *The Silvan* had made him impatient, sceptical and he had chosen the word of the scouts over that of a general.

He would have to face all that once they returned. He would write a full report for Pan'assár, leave nothing out.

And then, he would await his punishment.

He stood, bowed, and then left with a head full of questions, and a conscience not quite at peace.

~

Dawn, and Fel'annár daren't weave the Dohai.

He felt better after finally sleeping, but he had already realised that his coordination was not quite right. He had stood, had to reach out and steady himself. Still, the dizziness had quickly passed, and he had been able to drink and even eat a little, prepare his own pack, and wait for the order to mount up.

Galadan had prepared some foul-smelling concoction, under the watchful gaze of Sontúr, and Fel'annár downed it in one grimacing gulp, and then climbed carefully into the saddle.

Slowly, yesterday's events were becoming clearer to him. He knew what had happened, but not quite how. His fuddled mind had sent him round in circles, unable to concentrate on one thing at a time. He knew that feeling, and so he had stopped trying and relinquished the command of The Company to a surprised Idernon, under the approving gaze of Galadan.

And so, the hours passed, and they drew ever closer to the city.

Fel'annár had listened to his friends as they asked Maeneth questions about Pelagia, about the mighty war ships and the world-famous engineers who built them.

She was knowledgeable about sea-faring crafts, about wood and metal work, and both Idernon and Sontúr listened eagerly to her explanations and descriptions.

She spoke of the two kings' court and the music that always played there. She spoke of the Poet Guild and the Music Guild, and while Carodel was surely lost in a cloud of wild imaginations, Sontúr did nothing but stare at Maeneth.

Fel'annár wanted to join them, learn a little of this woman who was his sister. But to do that, would be to take his mind away from the forest, away from the troops and from Rinon at the fore. The traitors had tried to kill him and Maeneth, and Fel'annár realised that he cared – beyond duty and honour – even for Rinon.

And with Maeneth amongst them, there was no opportunity for The Company to ask him about his trip into the Evergreen Wood. There was an upside to everything, he thought.

By the time dusk was upon them, Fel'annár had all but regained his senses, save for a splitting headache. Even when he dismounted and gave his horse over to Ramien with a grateful nod, he did not stumble or feel dizzy.

Small mercy, he supposed, as he followed Idernon and the rest to where they would camp for the night.

As the camp was settling down for the evening, Rinon approached in the presence of Airen, Enar and Sar'pén.

"Maeneth, come take a walk?"

She smiled, nodded at Idernon and left, under the watchful eyes of The Company.

Fel'annár was glad Rinon would finally be able to greet his sister. He had seen their frustration, but circumstances had not allowed them to speak much. The warriors were wary, even of one another. They were confused too, about the conflicting orders they had received from the two generals. They didn't know who to trust, but Rinon trusted Sar'pén, and Maeneth trusted her patrol leaders.

And so, with Maeneth gone, and his concussion all but healed, it left him with no defence against The Company and their inevitable questions.

Galadan made tea with the ginger root he had found, and then Sontúr bid Galdith remove the bandage around Fel'annár's head. The bruising had blossomed into colourful shades of red, but the cut had closed.

The tea was hot and strong, warmed their chests and hands. Galdith breathed out, glanced at Fel'annár and then back at his cup.

"Do you remember? When we sat in the trees back in Tar'eastór, when Tensári was still somewhere out in the wilds. You told us what you had held back for so long, revealed to us your purpose as Ber'anor. You were to unite the people of Ea Uaré, and you asked us if we would follow you."

"I remember," said Idernon as he swirled his tea around in his cup. "The Restoration was his purpose, and it would be a dangerous one. He showed us the lights within the power that binds the world, or so they say, and we all accepted that duty – to follow him and see it done."

It had been inevitable. Fel'annár had taken as much time as he could, as much as they had allowed him, but he owed it to them to speak of what had happened in the Evergreen Wood, headache or not. They followed him, always had. They needed to know what lay ahead. It was their right.

"I told you then, that my purpose was the Restoration, the plan to bring Silvans and Alpines back together. I think I may have been wrong." He cleared his throat. He'd hardly spoken a word since yesterday.

They froze. Idernon's gaze halfway between his cup and Fel'annár, Tensári's hand over the steam of her cup, Ramien's hand in his hair.

"What?" Carodel's soft whisper.

"It's connected, was a necessary step, in the same way that bringing our army together and facing the Nim'uán – if it comes – is also a necessary step."

"You believe there is a deeper purpose then?" Sontúr sat up, repressed a wince.

"I do." He took a steadying breath and allowed his mind to go back to his first encounter with the Squiliz.

He told them of the strange landscape inside the Evergreen Wood, the overly vivid colours he had seen. He told them of the incessant call to pass the lake, despite the warnings from the trees.

He told them of his dream amidst wavering hesitation and repressed anxiety. He had seen the Last Markers and he had been one of them, standing beside his grandfather, Zéndar. And then he told them of the beast, how a bird had guided him to safety, only for those tentacles of green mist to strangle him into oblivion. He had woken up back at his last camp site, scratched and dishevelled but very much alive.

"Holy Gods," murmured Galadan.

Their minds were working, trying to understand what it was that

Aria had wanted to say to Fel'annár with such an outlandish dream. Why had she seen fit to scare him half to death like that?

"There are many interpretations to that dream, Fel'annár, other explanations as to how you acquired those scratches," said Sontúr, a warning in his eye and tone of voice. "Don't jump to conclusions."

Idernon glanced fleetingly at Sontúr, apparently understanding exactly what he had meant by that.

"Seeing yourself as a Last Marker doesn't mean you're going to die, at least not any time soon – if that's what you were thinking." Sontúr stared at Fel'annár, saw the confirmation in his eyes.

"But it's a possibility. The very fact that you see fit to caution me on that, shows that you understand that."

"As a Ber'anor, that may well happen, to any of us as sworn warriors. The question is that it doesn't have to be now, does it?" asked Galadan.

"No. But why did Aria call me to that place now? Why the monster? Why kill me in that dream?"

"It wasn't a dream."

They all turned to Tensári, faces contorted in confusion and even anger.

"What are you talking about?" asked Fel'annár, angry voice, confused eyes. There were no Last Markers in Ea Uaré. Giant winged monsters didn't exist.

"I sat at the gates to the Evergreen Wood for all the time you were inside. I strained my senses, felt you alive and well. And then Lainon awoke in my mind, in the dead of night and I knew you were in danger, *mortal* danger, Fel'annár. I tried to enter, drew my sword and slashed at the vines and the branches but they formed a wall which I could not flank.

"I stood there the entire night, willing it away but it did not and all the time, Aria called to me. If that had been a dream, sent to you by Aria, she would not have called on me to help you. I would not have felt your impending death.

"It was not Aria's will for you to experience what you did. It was *not* a dream, Fel'annár, as Lainon is my witness. He is on the other side. He felt that danger too. Whatever happened in there, it was not planned."

Fel'annár was shaking his head while the others looked from one Ari'atór to the other.

"Tensári. It *was* a dream. My feet would not obey me, and there were Last Markers in the Evergreen Wood, a giant green monster. Those things don't exist."

"I don't have answers to those mysteries, Fel'annár. All I know, is that if it *was* a dream, it was not a dream of revelation – not from Aria."

Fel'annár's skin was on fire, his eyes full and burning. It *had* been a dream, but if Aria had not sent it, then who had? Or was he trying to tell himself something? He closed his eyes, rested his aching head against the tree behind him.

"It had to be a dream," said Ramien, voice soft. "'Cos that beast he described sounds like a wyvern. And wyverns don't exist outside of storybooks, do they?" Ramien looked to Idernon, but the Wise Warrior said nothing, and neither did Fel'annár.

THE FOLLOWING day would be the last on their road home.

They had made good progress, despite the wounded who travelled at the centre of the column, and the two captive elves who sat tied to the saddle of their mounts.

After Fel'annár's account of his trip into the Evergreen Wood, Sontúr found it passing strange that their mood had lifted more than it had descended. He supposed that returning to the mysteries of the Evergreen Wood and its relation to Fel'annár's purpose, to *The Company's* purpose, took their minds off the traitors and the implication that there may be more. After all, they had already suspected that something like this could happen. It was why the king had insisted The Company ride with Rinon.

Whether or not Fel'annár's experience had been real, was in question. As for Sontúr, he knew it had to be a dream and the question was, what was Fel'annár's own mind trying to tell him about the mystery of his purpose?

They had debated those questions as much as they could, until Maeneth had returned to their camp.

With Sontúr's knowledge of the Elven psyche, he had pointed out that deep in the unexplored parts of the Evergreen Wood, there was likely to be unknown species of flowers and plants, some of which could cause negative side effects if one were to unknowingly breathe their pollen or brush accidentally against their leaves and stems.

Fel'annár had remembered this theory from something Llyniel had pointed out when she had tried to make him stay. He had wondered if those vivid colours that predominated the land had something to do with this, invisible substance that may have caused him to have such a lifelike dream.

Sontúr had gone on to point out how each of the events could be tied with recent developments in his own life, mixed perhaps with memories from childhood battles with mythical creatures.

The coming of his family, the worries and insecurities it had sparked. Bulan's coming and his gift of Zéndar's spear, Harvest. His own fear that as Ari'atór, as Ber'anor, his own death was a fact, whether it happened sooner or later. Even the winged beast. It had been Galdith to suggest that it might represent the Nim'uán, that he feared *this* time, it might succeed in killing him as it almost had the first time in Tar'eastór.

Most of the others had agreed with his reasoning, except for Tensári, and no amount of persuasion would sway her. She was adamant. Aria had called her, Lainon had called her. Fel'annár *had* been in danger.

But then Idernon pointed out that perhaps those scratches and bruises on Fel'annár's body were the product of his mad thrashing in the night. Perhaps he was walking and dreaming, in danger of falling and killing himself. She had not been able to argue the point. It was certainly more probable than the existence of Last Markers in the Evergreen Wood, than the existence of a wyvern.

But whatever conclusions Fel'annár had drawn after their debating, his mood had clearly improved. He seemed relieved, and Sontúr could hardly blame him.

Not an hour away from the city gates, the Alpine warriors began to sing. After two days of tense silence, of suspicion and wary glances, it seemed to Fel'annár that they sent a clear and unequivocal message to their prince and princess.

We are loyal.

While the captive scouts looked to the floor, the troops lifted their voices to the sky and even Rinon smiled. He turned in the saddle, made for the back of the line and beckoned to Maeneth to join him at the fore. Sontúr admired her radiant smile, watched her canter away. She would enter the city gates at her brother's side.

Still, The Company would continue to watch the warriors, even the captains. They trusted no one save themselves.

A while later, as the road grew busier, bird call joined the marching songs. Fel'annár looked up, saw Silvans high in the boughs, looking down on them. They would surely be asking why two of their warriors sat tied to the saddle. But it was not enough to curb their joy at the return of Maeneth.

Fel'annár listened to the welcome from the forest, allowed it to soothe his mind. He had journeyed with the weight of impending death on his mind, but he returned with renewed hope. Aria may not have sent him that dream. He had no reason to doubt Tensári's words and certainly didn't want to.

The mystery of his ultimate purpose was still there, would surely unravel slowly, in the same way he had come to understand that he was Ber'anor.

He turned to the call of a siskin, caught sight of three children high up in the canopy, looking down on them. He returned the call, smiled when they laughed. One of the children managed to imitate a green finch, no small task and he turned to the one amongst them who was famed for his imitations.

Carodel lifted his hands, squeezed and tugged at his own cheeks, pulled an awful face that had them all laughing, even the warriors who rode just in front of them turned to watch. But their laughter froze in their chests with the most perfect imitation of a green finch they had ever heard. The Silvans murmured in awe of Carodel's ability. But they hadn't seen the face he had had to pull to achieve it, and Fel'annár chuckled. Galdith followed and Carodel lifted his hands once more, mischievous eyes on the children in the trees. Curling his lips back, teeth on display, jaw jabbering as if he was freezing cold, Carodel became a squirrel and Idernon wheezed in uncontrollable laughter, bending over the side of his mount. Even the Alpine warriors laughed.

A fleeting moment, in which Rinon turned to the rear, caught Fel'an-nár's soft smile, returned it.

Before long, The Company's high spirits had infected them all, save for the traitors and perhaps Sar'pén. Although treachery had been unrooted, it was no shock to any of them. Handir had warned them, and logic dictated that Band'orán's movement would not magically disappear. It would take time, and circumstances such as these would still occur for a while longer.

But Princess Maeneth was returning home, and even Sontúr smiled through the ache in his shoulder, sparkling grey eyes alight in curiosity for the woman who rode beside Rinon at the front of the line. He almost jumped at Carodel's voice from beside him.

"Our winged warrior soars high upon the sweet currents of love, besotted by the beauty of our silver princess." He snorted at his own, flowery words and then chuckled and Fel'annár closed his eyes.

Poor Sontúr.

"Here we go," he murmured to Galadan at his side.

Sontúr turned to Carodel, a peeved expression. "I am not – *besotted*, you Silvan fool." But his eyes were soon back on Maeneth, the same far-away smile on his face.

"Oh, oh!!" Carodel flapped his hand in the air - "I feel a melody coming to me.... Silver Princess of my Alpine heart, I...."

"*Shhshshshshut* up!" hissed Sontúr, batting at Carodel's arm with his good hand.

Galdith and Ramien laughed and Sontúr spent the rest of their journey either glaring at The Company or watching Maeneth.

Before long, the mighty stone fortress of the capital city of Ea Uaré loomed before them. They would be home in minutes and Maeneth reached for Rinon's hand. She smiled encouragingly, he returned it, thought he could face anything now, whatever Pan'assár had in store for him for disregarding his warnings.

Nothing mattered, because the better side of himself was home.

Maeneth was home.

17

INHERITANCE

~

THE PATROL HAD BEEN SPOTTED hours ago, the healers warned to expect many injured at dusk. And by the time the light began to fail, what seemed like the entire city's population had gathered in the main courtyard to greet their only princess.

The healers stood outside their Halls of Healing, black robes, white and blue sashes of the apprentices and head healers undulating in the soft breeze. At the fore, the red sash of the Lestari and at her side, Kristain, her second in command.

The mighty gates of the fortress creaked and then groaned as they slowly opened, revealing the returning patrol. At the very fore, the royal twins.

Llyniel smiled wide, wanted to wave but thought it would be inappropriate. She stared, willed her friend to look in her direction and she did.

Joy. And then surprise, her eyes fixed on the red sash of the Lestari.

The people called to Maeneth, threw flowers and waved and Maeneth was princess once more.

Llyniel's eyes travelled further down the line, saw the blond, brown and grey hair of the combined patrols. But where were the rest of them? Where was Fel'annár and The Company?

Her eyes drifted further back, had not expected to see them riding at the rear. She frowned, turned to Kristain, but his eyes were on the two warriors who sat tied to their horses' saddles.

Captives.

But Kristain used a different word, his voice nothing but a quiet murmur.

"Traitors."

Llyniel's head whipped back to the line of blond and grey-haired warriors, to the injured who lay in harnesses between the horses. They had work, and with one last look at Fel'annár, she found him staring right back at her. Yes they'd seen battle, but at least he was riding on his own. She let out a long breath.

"Let's get to it then."

Kristain nodded, followed her to where the warriors had stopped, gesturing for her healers to follow.

As the horses were being led away, Fel'annár turned to Sontúr. "I won't see you till much later. I have a report to write and perhaps an interrogation to watch. Idernon here will keep me posted. I'll come as soon as I may."

"Go and do your general things. I will be in good hands."

"The best." Fel'annár smiled and turned away.

The crowds were still effusive in their welcome, but it was muted by the presence of two warriors, their hands tied behind their backs. Rinon gestured to The Company, and then gave them custody of the captives. Ramien placed one hand on each of their shoulders, and marched them to a side door and the stairs that led downwards to the dungeons.

It was time for Rinon to deliver Maeneth to her father and brother. And then, he would follow Fel'annár to the Inner Circle and write his report for Pan'assár.

Thargodén stood, decked a king upon the steps of the fortress palace. At his shoulder, Prince Handir and Lord Aradan together with Lady Miren. Behind them, commanders Pan'assár, Gor'sadén and General Turion.

Even now, as Rinon approached with Maeneth, he could see the

Commander General watching everything and everyone, surely building a mental picture in his mind, one Rinon did not doubt would be accurate, save for one thing.

Rinon had disregarded his warnings to heed Fel'annár.

The royal twins bowed to the king, and then the crown prince turned to Pan'assár.

"We have suffered many deaths. We carry wounded, amongst them Prince Sontúr. You will have my full report on your desk within the hour, Commander. However, we have uncovered a plot to assassinate Princess Maeneth and myself. She must be guarded at all times. It seems Prince Handir was correct in his assumptions. There are still traitors in our midst."

Pan'assár's gaze was cool, as Rinon had expected it to be, but there was a storm in Gor'sadén's eyes as they drifted from a clearly injured Sontúr, and then back to the general. Rinon endured it for as long as he could. He caught Maeneth's sorry gaze, tried to smile, and then turned away, bound for the Inner Circle and his office, one which may no longer be his come the morning.

He glanced over his shoulder, saw Maeneth enter the palace with his father and brother, a vigilant Turion behind them. He wanted to be there, knew that he couldn't. He didn't expect the voice at his side.

"My warnings to you were vague, Rinon. I was not accurate, unable to give you the details you needed."

"You told me you needed more time. I did not give it to you."

"No. But why would you suspect the scouts were leading us astray? What are scouts for if not to provide the information I could not provide you with?"

"I should have heeded Pan'assár's warning. He told me to defer to you should you receive a message from the trees. I did not. I let my aversion towards you colour my decision."

Fel'annár nodded slowly. "Still, I made no claims, voiced only my suspicions. I will be clear on that point in my report."

Rinon turned to him, looked at his brother, wondered why he even wanted to help him, after the way Rinon had treated him. "Are you well enough to be writing reports?"

"Yes."

Rinon stared at the battered and bruised Warlord, half in humour and half in relief. "However Pan'assár decides to discipline me, I will be present when those traitors are interrogated."

"And I would join you, if I may."

Rinon nodded, and then startled at the unexpected voice on his other side.

"As would I," said Sar'pén. "Those rats have been taken to the dungeons. I have informed the duty guards to allow no visitors."

Rinon turned to his friend.

"Good. But I make no promises you will be allowed to attend. For now, take our Pelagian brothers to barracks, find suitable accommodation for them and their commanders."

Sar'pén hesitated. "And who will guard *your* back, General?"

Rinon offered his friend a grim smile. "The Company, Sar'pén."

The captain turned to Fel'annár, back to Rinon and then bowed. As Sar'pén strode away, Fel'annár spoke, his tone thoughtful.

"He doesn't like me."

THE WALK from the courtyard to the last floor of the palace was excruciatingly slow for Thargodén. All he could do was show patience he did not feel, allow the people to bow and smile at his daughter.

They gave her flowers, almost made her cry. He could hear Handir talking quietly to her, Turion issuing orders to the guards as they passed.

Up the stairs, to the very end of the hallway where two ceremonial guards opened the double doors and then closed them, stomped to attention and tried not to smile. Turion was glad of it, knew these warriors well. He nodded at them and then left for the Inner Circle to arrange for heightened security for the royal family – again.

Inside, Maeneth shed her cloak and turned to her father.

"Home at last," she said, intelligent eyes lingering on Thargodén. He knew what she would be thinking, whether it was true that he had changed, that he had come back from that strange land in which he had resided for so long. Gods but he wanted to pull her into his arms, tell her he was sorry, that it was all true, he had returned. And then he would beg her not to leave, if that was what it would take.

Maeneth stepped forward, public smile gone and, in its place, curiosity; caution. She cocked her head to one side, stared up at her father's burning eyes, shining crown upon his head, the one Band'orán had tried and failed to wrest from him. Rinon had been right. This was not the father she had left fifty years ago. This was not the broken king who had retreated to some place in his mind, oblivious to everyone else – even his children. This was Thargodén, the father she remembered as a child.

How she had missed him.

She smiled, held one hand before her, and then rested it softly on the golden brocade of her father's long tunic. She stepped into his waiting arms, felt them encircle her and then pull her to him.

She stood there, like a child, in a haze of love and protection, indulgent and oblivious to anything except the surety of her father's love for her. She knew Handir was watching, that he was smiling.

Stepping away from Thargodén, she turned to her younger brother, smile wide, eyes searching, reading. He too had changed, something Rinon had not told her. Not that there had been time but still, he seemed older, wiser perhaps than he already had been. His visit to Tar'eastór had changed him, or perhaps it was Band'orán and the events surrounding his treachery. They embraced.

There were years of things she did not know, that they did not know. So many events, successes, failures and projects. It felt right to be here, right that her father be happy at last.

They hugged, held each other at arm's length for a while. "Rinon will be a while. He must present his report to Pan'assár."

"Can he not wait for it?" Handir scowled at the commander's lack of understanding.

"There has been an incident, brother. You heard what Rinon said. We have traitors in the dungeons, but there is more."

"What has happened?" Thargodén's voice was slow, cautious.

"Rinon made a mistake, one I hope Pan'assár will not punish him too harshly for."

~

LLYNIEL LEFT Kristain in charge of the healers while she made for the private room where Sontúr had been taken.

Captain Galadan and Commander Gor'sadén were already there, The Company save for Tensári and Fel'annár sitting around the room. They stood when she entered.

"Arrow?"

"Yes," said Sontúr, watching as she began to unwrap the bandages.

For a while, all Llyniel did was poke and prod, manipulate the elbow, the shoulder, and as she did, she watched Sontúr, bid him move this way or that. Galadan and Gor'sadén watched the healer and the patient for any clues as to the severity of the injury.

"The tendon is partially severed. You need restorative surgery to recover mobility, and extensive recuperation to strengthen it. There will be no fighting for a while, Sontúr."

"What?" It was a low, toneless question, and Galadan placed a comforting hand on his good shoulder, while Gor'sadén bit his tongue. Now was not the time to be asking Sontúr why he had put his own life at risk for Rinon.

"They will mend it, Prince. All you need do is rest and follow your healers' orders." Sontúr looked at his Commander General, seemed so very young and vulnerable.

"When will you carry out this procedure?"

"Tonight, Commander. There is equipment to prepare and references to check, but the sooner we do this, the better for that arm."

"Can we expect a full recovery?" asked Gor'sadén, aware that he had put the Lestari in an uncomfortable situation. When she answered, her face was as straight as a lance.

"I will do my very best."

He pursed his lips, glad that Galadan spoke to Sontúr just then.

"I'll stay until you're out, be back before you wake."

"Go and rest, brothers. There's nothing you can do sitting around here."

"Yes there is. I can stay with you."

Sontúr held Galadan's gaze, nodded slowly, and then gave himself over to the Lestari.

One hour later, still filthy from their journey, Generals Rinon and Fel'annár stood to attention before their commanding officer, eyes to the fore.

Rinon was ready for the rollicking of his life.

Pan'assár had already read their reports and had then invited Gor'sadén to read them.

He stepped toward Rinon, watched him steel his spine.

"This was one of my greatest fears. That your temperament would get the better of you, that it would interfere with your performance as a general. I told myself to have faith, to believe that you could overcome that trait of yours. That you would step up to the challenge. Instead, you have allowed your personal fears and qualms free rein, acted like a petulant child. You have let me down, disappointed me, made me look like a fool for the confidence I deposited in you. Well? What have you to say?"

"Nothing, sir. I am guilty of all that. I deserve punishment."

"You deserve *demotion!*" Pan'assár had shouted, something he rarely did.

The commander glanced at Fel'annár, registered his pale face, bruised head, evidence of his desperate fight both had reported in very different ways. Fel'annár had downplayed his part in protecting Maeneth, and he knew that Rinon's account was the more accurate. Besides, he had already heard of it from the returning warriors. It was all they spoke about, that and the plot to kill the royal twins.

"I warned you, General Rinon. I specifically told you to heed him but you ... you didn't even let him finish his sentence. You disobeyed my warnings, I specifically told you to heed him even if it didn't make sense, did – I – not?"

"You did, sir."

"You walked straight into a trap. They played you like a finely-tuned lyre." Pan'assár breathed through his anger. Credit to Rinon his eyes did not waver, even when Fel'annár spoke.

"Permission to speak, Commander General."

Pan'assár turned his glacial eyes on Fel'annár, narrowed them. "Granted."

"Sir. I was vague in my warning. I could not give General Rinon the information he needed to make an informed decision before our scouts returned. He was concerned that by the time I had the numbers and the location of the group or groups, that it would be too late for Princess Maeneth's patrol. His decision was not an easy one to take."

Pan'assár stopped before Fel'annár. "You are correct. However, he knew that he was to defer to *your* judgement when it came to messages from the forest. To him, obeying that warning was a leap of faith – one he could not bring himself to make. That was his greatest mistake, General. Had he not been warned, I would not be disciplining him now. It is not for a general to question his scouts. However, he *was* warned, and there is no excuse for ignoring it." Pan'assár turned back to Rinon.

"General. For your failure to heed your Commander General's order, I am removing your command in the field. You will remain a general but will defer to Generals Turion and Fel'annár for any decisions taken during active duty. I will not return your command until I am satisfied you can honour it. Do you understand me?"

"I do, sir."

"Good." He turned back to Fel'annár. "I will speak privately with you tomorrow, General. But know that I am grateful for your service in defence of Or'Talán's line."

Fel'annár bowed, hoped he would say no more and make Rinon feel worse than he undoubtedly already did.

"Now, these traitors. We need to find out whose orders they were carrying out. We need to know who is leading this resurgence. However, I would read Captains Sar'pén and Airen's reports first. Therefore, the scouts will be interrogated tomorrow morning at the tenth hour. I am allowing you both to witness it, in case you can uncover inconsistencies. Meanwhile, I want the entire royal family under guard, at all times. That includes you, General Fel'annár. General Turion is overseeing security but tell me. Is The Company available for this duty?"

"They are, save for Captain Sontúr, of course."

"He will be commended for his selfless act in defence of our prince's life. For now, go home and stay home. Bathe and rest. Fel'annár, make sure the Lestari sees to that," he gestured to the Warlord's head. "Stay alert and then join me tomorrow morning at the tenth hour.

"And then we will see what those traitors have to say."

"Commander. We must send out a patrol to retrieve our dead."

"I have already commanded it. I want a list of the fallen."

"I have it, Commander." Rinon held out a folded piece of paper and Pan'assár took it, opened it. After a while, he breathed deeply.

"I will speak to their families if you so wish, Prince."

"No. I will do it myself. I was their leader. I am responsible for their deaths."

"No, General. You are not. Those traitors are. You were misled."

Rinon nodded, and Fel'annár knew he was unconvinced.

OUTSIDE, the captains and warriors watched as the two generals marched away in perfect unison, Tensári behind them, eyes on everyone.

By now, Fel'annár knew the entire Inner Circle and barracks would have heard about the ill-fated patrol, about the conflicting orders issued by first Rinon and then Fel'annár. And of course, of the traitors in the dungeons.

Fel'annár let out a huff and Rinon turned to him. "That went well, didn't it?"

Fel'annár turned incredulous eyes on him. It could have been Sontúr walking beside him. "*Well?* You had your field command taken away."

"So I did. I was wrong, and it will not happen again. I will regain it."

Fel'annár stopped at the Healing Halls, briefly considered entering and retrieving The Company from where he knew they would be. But their orders were to go straight home, and he knew Tensári would not leave his side. One look at her was enough to confirm his suspicion and so together, Rinon and Fel'annár headed for their rooms.

On the topmost floor, where the brothers would part ways, Rinon stopped.

"Fel'annár." The word sounded strange on his lips, for the simple reason that he had said it with no anger, no disdain. "I must speak with the families of the dead, and then with my father, tell him what I have done but I wonder – if you would indulge a request."

"Speak it."

"Come to dinner tomorrow, just Maeneth, Handir, myself and ... our father."

His half-brother stood there, as confused as he was shocked. He opened his mouth to speak but no words came out and Rinon tried again.

"It is not for duty that I say this. Not because Maeneth is here or because I feel guilty. Decline if you will. There will be other days."

"All right."

Rinon started, observed his brother carefully. He seemed shocked that he had accepted, as if he hadn't controlled himself and had wanted to say no. He was trying, realised Rinon, as surely as he himself was. Rinon had *wanted* to invite him, because for the first time since he had met Fel'annár, he realised that he was genuinely curious. For the first time, he wanted to ask Fel'annár about Tar'eastór, about his journey home, about his escapades with Handir.

For the first time, he no longer felt guilty for wanting to know what his half-brother was like.

~

FEL'ANNÁR ALMOST FELL asleep in his bathtub.

He had opened his eyes to an upside-down Llyniel, who was peering at the bruise on his head.

"You got walloped again. I suppose I can count myself lucky your brain is still in the right place. Blurred vision?"

"Not anymore."

"Nausea?"

"No."

"Confusion? Dizziness?"

"No." Fel'annár chuckled, hauled himself out of the tub and wrapped a towel around his waist. He turned to her and opened his arms.

She didn't care that he was sopping wet, stepped into his embrace, would have stayed there all night had it not been for Sontúr.

"I don't have much time. The sooner we perform that procedure on Sontúr, the better the chances of him regaining full mobility of his arm."

"When are you going to do it?" he asked, reaching for his clothing.

"Now. Well, in an hour or so."

"What? Why? I thought you would wait until tomorrow."

"There's no point waiting. I need to check a few things in my study. I won't be back this evening, but I know The Company will stay with you."

"If you can persuade them to leave Sontúr. I would go if I could, but I've been placed under guard for now."

"Only Galadan is there. The rest are preparing for a briefing with Turion. This is about those traitors, isn't it?"

"Yes. They purposefully misled Rinon, with the intention of killing him and Maeneth. Until we can find out who they were working for, it's not safe."

"Again," said Llyniel.

"Again. You must be careful too. Trust no one, Llyniel. I'll assign a guard for ..."

"No. I can't work like that, Fel'annár."

"I won't have you walking about alone."

She wanted to protest, but the look in his eyes brooked no compromise. "I have Kristain."

"He can't be with you all the time. He's your second."

"But we're together at the Halls. All I need do is come and go from here – or, I stay in the halls."

Fel'annár took his time answering, was dressed before he did.

"Then stay there tonight. Make sure this Kristain is armed and with you at all times. This may only be necessary for a few days, until we know what we're dealing with."

She heaved a long sigh. "All right. Now let me get to my books. Our prince is waiting."

He caught her arm, pulled her to him. "I love you."

She smiled up at him, kissed his lips and squeezed his arm. "Rest for tonight. Lestari's orders. You need it."

He watched her leave, bound for the room she used as an office away from the Halls. He padded into the living area, crossed it, and then cracked open the main door. He beckoned to Tensári to enter and then made for the hearth. He threw a log onto the fire, arms heavy. He was bone weary and yet it felt wrong to sleep. Sontúr would be operated on in just a few hours, there was treachery afoot, and his sister he hardly knew was just down the corridor.

"Sit, Tensári. As soon as The Company are here, I want you to go and rest."

"No."

"That was an order."

She glared at him, crossed her legs and then turned to the fire.

How lucky he was to have this extraordinary warrior at his back. She was a friend, a sister, a loyal warrior, one who had saved his life yet again.

"Thank you. If it hadn't been for you, I would be walking the Short Road."

She said nothing, nodded and then turned back to the fire. Fel'annár knew why Lainon loved her, and the memory of his Ari brother brought with it a pang of sadness. He breathed through it, leaned back in his chair.

Tomorrow would be a long day. The interrogation and what it may uncover. Briefing the Silvan captains in the Forest Division. Sontúr and the outcome of his operation.

Dinner with the king and his Alpine siblings.

Another heavy breath. Rinon had told him he was free to refuse, and Fel'annár wondered why he had so willingly acceded. He should be with The Company, sitting at Sontúr's side, telling him it was going to be all right, that he would once more fight with The Company.

The truth was, that after everything that had happened, something seemed to have shifted. Fel'annár had been allowed a glimpse at the elf beneath the crown, beneath the suffering of Rinon's childhood. He was curious because where once he had despised Rinon, now, he thought he even liked him.

He decided that he was right to have accepted. Had Rinon not opened a door to him? Should Fel'annár reject his invitation, it would be tantamount to telling him he was not interested in bridging the gap between them.

And yet he was.

He raked a hand through his hair. There were so many distractions. He needed to be listening for the Nim'uán, needed to push ahead with the creation of the new contingents and units of his own Forest Division.

He had promised the Silvan warriors change, and now it was time to fulfil that oath. They had followed Bulan out of the forest, had heeded Fel'annár's call back to barracks. They deserved to see the fruits of that valiant decision.

But so too was he glad of all these distractions, because they took his mind off the Evergreen Wood, off his dream – if that was what it had been.

He still hadn't told Llyniel about that.

He jumped at the familiar knock on the door. Still, Tensári was taking no risks and she stood, cracked the door open. Soon, The Company were filing in and making themselves comfortable.

"How's Sontúr?"

"Worried. Galadan is trying to distract him while they wait for Llyniel. It seems this operation may take a while," said Idernon.

"Did you speak with Turion?"

"We did. Ramien and Carodel take the next watch along the royal corridor. Galdith and I will take over later," explained the Wise Warrior.

"Then go and rest, brothers. I leave tomorrow for the interrogation at ten."

The Wise Warrior nodded, eyes drifting from Fel'annár to Tensári. "Go see to yourself, Tensári. I'll wait here for a while."

"You will stay until I return?"

"I promise."

∾

As FEL'ANNÁR DOZED off before the fire in his rooms, Pan'assár sat in his office at the Inner Circle, glass of wine in one hand, eyes on the flickering flames. Beside him, Gor'sadén sat in his own armchair, fingers tapping softly on the plush tapestry.

On a low table before them, Rinon and Fel'annár's reports. Tomorrow, they would read Sar'pen's and the Pelagian captain's own account of what had happened. For now, however, the picture was clear in Pan'assár's mind. He turned to Gor'sadén, found him already looking at him.

"This was to be expected, Pan. After the Silvans' unlikely return to barracks, everything has gone far more smoothly than we had imagined it would. Something like this was a long time coming. You can't eradicate decades of hatred and discrimination in a mere two weeks."

"No. And you are right. However, now that it has happened, it still came as a surprise. I suppose I had come to hope that it was over, that all that was left to do was prove to the Silvans that I have changed – that they can trust me."

"All in good time. For now, we deal with the traitors, trust Thargodén's shadows to do their job and find out who they answer to."

Pan'assár drank, swallowed, and then put his glass on the table. Standing, he walked to his desk, opened one of the drawers and retrieved a small object. Returning to his chair, he sat, opened his hand to reveal a turquoise stone. Gor'sadén leaned towards it, thought it beautiful in its simplicity.

"I have never seen you wear jewellery," said Gor'sadén.

"I do not, and neither did Or'Talán."

"That was his?"

Pan'assár turned to him. "Yes, it was his. He carried it around in his pocket, always took it with him on patrols or diplomatic missions. He said it brought him luck. He forgot it the day we marched to war."

"May I?"

Pan'assár handed it to Gor'sadén, watched him examine it closely.

"It looks like an Honour Stone."

"It is. Given to him by a Silvan lady who should have been queen."

Gor'sadén started, turned to his friend. "What? Lássira gave this to Or'Talán?"

"She did."

"I found out from the journal that they had known each other well. But to gift him with this shows friendship."

Pan'assár looked up, seemed to be battling with something. "They were family, Gorsa. He considered her the daughter he never had. Of course, this was way back, before Band'orán's ultimatum."

Gor'sadén frowned. "I do not understand. Why did you never say? You didn't even tell me."

"I couldn't. To accept that fact, would have been to validate Fel'annár's right to the title of prince. He is half-Silvan, remember? I hated him until just recently."

"And now?"

"Now? I have done so many things wrong in my life, brother. But I will do this one right, at least. I think Orta would have wanted Fel'annár to have this – to wear it, even. His grandson killed forty Deviants in defence of a sister he does not know. His Company protected Rinon in the face of assassins. Without Fel'annár, my promise to Or'Talán's line would be over. I want him to understand how grateful I am."

Gor'sadén smiled tentatively, then wider. "It is a mighty gift, an object both his mother and grandfather touched. I wonder if even with this, he will hold his emotions at bay as he always does where family is concerned."

"It is fitting, isn't it? That Fel'annár should be the rightful heir of this simple trinket. He is Lássira's son. And he is Or'Talán's heir, one that is so much like our lost brother it sometimes unnerves me. His test for the mastery in the Kal'hamén'Ar, when it happens, will be nothing but formality."

Gor'sadén nodded, turned away. "He will be overjoyed, I think. He has inherited nothing from his family, save for Zéndar's spear."

"No. He has inherited far more than that. He and Orta are kindred spirits, Gorsa. Had our brother lived to meet him, he would tell us himself. Fel'annár inherited his grandfather's *character*. Give him time, and you will see that for yourself."

18

THE SHADOW OF DOUBT

~

IT HAD BEEN A LONG NIGHT.

Galadan had spent the time helping the healers, dozing, and then writing a report for Pan'assár from his chair at Sontúr's side. He hadn't been asked to, but Galadan was troubled.

There was something about that moment in which he, Carodel, Galdith, Ramien and Sontúr had chased after Prince Rinon, Captain Sar'pén and a handful of other warriors around him, two of which were the rebel scouts, now sitting in the dungeons awaiting interrogation.

They were heading in the wrong direction, away from the danger, or so Galadan had thought. The fact was, they were leading Rinon into a trap, to kill him.

He remembered shouting out, not being heard. It had been Ramien in the end who had finally been heard, but only Sar'pén had turned in surprise.

Had the others not heard then?

Galadan remembered how one of the warriors broke off from the left flank, leaving Rinon exposed, even before the arrows had come. It had been one of the two scouts.

But why had the others kept going? Why had *they* not drawn their bows to defend their prince? Not even Sar'pén had drawn his. Perhaps the captain thought he had a better chance of keeping the prince safe by running, leaving the snipers to The Company he knew were behind.

Perhaps.

Sontúr was still under the effects of the drugs he had been given, showed no signs of waking. His gaze drifted to the chair on the other side of the bed. Llyniel was slouching in it, hand propping up her head, pulling her face in an odd angle as she slept. Galadan resisted the urge to grin.

He stood, stretched his back and folded his report. He would make for the Inner Circle and Pan'assár's office. He would have him read this before the interrogations that would surely take place later that morning.

With one last glance at Sontúr and Llyniel, he left the room, under the watchful gaze of Kristain, sword at his belt for the first time in a decade.

The sun was still below the horizon, but the sky was already a dark blue. Still, Pan'assár was an early riser.

He passed the main doors to the palace, almost missed the figure he saw leaving the Inner Circle, step sure, some purpose lending him speed. He startled when Galadan looked up.

"Sar'pén."

"Galadan."

They passed each other without stopping, but Galadan turned back, watched for a while, wondering where the captain lived, why he was not in bed and sleeping after their eventful patrol.

Then again, the same could be said for himself.

"YOU ARE sure those two scouts perished in the battle?"

"I am, Commander. Lieutenant Enar tells me it was one of this *Company* that killed them. They were aiming for General Rinon. That is when Captain Sontúr was wounded. They say he was the best archer on the field."

"Warrior Galdith, yes. He will be commended for his skill."

Airen nodded. "I would return to Pelagia knowing the fate of those traitors. My kings will want to know."

"I will keep you informed, Captain. You have my sincere condolences for your losses. Your return to Dan'bar will not be easy."

"No. Losing warriors gets no easier with the passage of time, does it?"

Pan'assár met Airen's gaze, well knew his meaning.

"No. It does not."

A knock at the door and Gor'sadén opened it. thinking it was Sar'pén come with his own report. "Captain Galadan."

Pan'assár turned where he stood beside his desk. "Galadan. Come in. What brings you here at the crack of dawn?"

"I would have you read this, Commander."

"What is it?" asked Pan'assár, accepting the folded paper Galadan held out to him.

"My report. I know you didn't ask for one, but I felt compelled to offer my perspective."

"Oh, and why is that?"

"Please read it, Commander."

Pan'assár frowned, and then began to read, while Airen and Gor'sadén shared a puzzled glance.

The silence stretched out, three sets of eyes on Pan'assár. He had surely read the report already, and yet he didn't look up. Instead, he breathed out, asked a question, voice soft.

"What are you saying, Galadan?"

Gor'sadén and Airen turned to the captain.

"I'm saying that the warriors who led General Rinon towards the west acted in a suspicious way, even those who were not the scouts."

"Even Captain Sar'pén?"

Galadan stared back at Gor'sadén, and then looked at Pan'assár, could almost see his mind working. After a while, the commander nodded slowly.

"Airen, Gor'sadén, Galadan. Say nothing of this to anyone. Let's see what Sar'pén has to say in his report before we jump to conclusions."

"I just crossed paths with him. He was leaving the Inner Circle."

"He came to leave his own report," explained Pan'assár.

"Have you read it?"

"No. Not yet."

"Then I will leave you to read. I pray you do not find inconsistencies, Commander."

Pan'assár pursed his lips, turned away and made for his desk. "If you will excuse me, captains."

Galadan glanced at Airen and then Enar. All three saluted, and then left the commander to his inquiries.

FEL'ANNÁR AND TENSÁRI WERE READY. It was time to meet Commander General Pan'assár and General Rinon at the Inner Circle. Once the disagreeable spectacle of watching an interrogation was over, they would make for the Halls and Sontúr, find out how the operation had gone.

Just outside Fel'annár's rooms, they found Rinon walking down the corridor with Idernon and Galdith at his back.

"General," nodded Fel'annár.

"General," nodded Rinon. "Shall we?"

Together, the two brothers left, Idernon, Galdith and Tensári behind. Ramien and Carodel were sleeping after their early guard on the royal wing of the palace, and Galadan was, presumably, with Sontúr at the Halls.

But he wasn't. Instead, he stood beside Pan'assár and Gor'sadén, at the door that led downwards and to the dungeons.

They exchanged salutes, while Gor'sadén clapped Fel'annár on the shoulder. He smiled, and then turned to Pan'assár.

Traitors.

Fel'annár's gaze drifted upwards, away from his companions. He blinked.

"What is it?" asked Idernon.

"Nothing new."

"Commander, Generals!" Sar'pén ran up to them and saluted. "Forgive my tardiness. I was arranging the outgoing patrol."

Pan'assár stared at the captain, and Fel'annár was struck with the idea that something was wrong. He chanced a glance at the Wise Warrior, but his eyes were on Sar'pén.

"Well then, let's get this done, shall we?" said Pan'assár as he led the way inside and then downwards, until they were on the lowest level of the palace. The duty guard was soon before them, saluting.

"Commander, we have just changed the guard. I will retrieve the keys. Our shadows are already here." The guard turned to the cloaked elves who stood in a corner a way off. He frowned because where just moments before there had been two, now there were three. He shook his head, grabbed the keys from the small office beside the stairs, and then gestured for the warriors to follow him, Shadows just behind.

The guard placed the key in the lock, turned it and then pushed it open, stuffing the keys under his belt.

He froze.

"Holy mother ..."

Before them, the hanging bodies of the two scouts, belts around their necks, two chairs overturned beneath them.

"*Sshhit* ..." Fel'annár charged forward, The Company behind and together, they lifted the bodies, untied the belts and then laid the two bodies side by side on the ground. They stepped back, just as the three shadows brushed past them.

"Touch nothing."

Fel'annár watched them, and after mere seconds, one of them turned to Pan'assár, spoke in a voice that was almost a whisper.

"They did not take their own lives."

Fel'annár turned wide eyes from the Shadow to Pan'assár.

"Arrest Captain Sar'pén, on suspicion of high treason."

"What?" Rinon's incredulous eyes darted from Pan'assár to his friend.

"You cannot be serious?" Sar'pén opened his arms, stepped towards the commander. But two Shadows were before him.

"Commander General. What have I done to make you think I would do such a thing?"

Rinon turned from Sar'pén to Pan'assár.

"You lied in your report, Captain. Those arrows that were fired at your prince did not come from the right but from the left, the flank your warriors left open."

"That does not imply high treason, Commander."

"Not in itself, Captain. But tell me, why did you visit the outgoing duty officer here, just this morning?"

"He is a friend. I just stopped by ..."

"And soon after, these scouts were killed."

"I – no. I know it might look strange, but I had nothing to do with this treachery. Rinon ..."

The prince looked at his friend, wanted to help him but there was something about Pan'assár's words, the way he said them. That Sar'pén was a traitor was preposterous, but where was the loophole in Pan'assár's suspicions? He would find out.

"Peace, Sar'pén. We'll work this out. There has to be a mistake."

"Of course there is. Brother, I would never betray you. You *know* this." Sar'pén reached out with one hand but the Shadow pushed him backwards, disarmed him and marched him away.

Rinon watched, and then whirled around to face Pan'assár. "As your crown prince, you will give me a full explanation for your *performance*, Commander General."

Unperturbed, Pan'assár turned to the flabbergasted duty officer. "Find the outgoing duty officer, lock him up. No visitors." He turned to the two remaining Shadows. "Question every warrior on guard last night. Anything suspicious, lock them up too. Now, my Prince. If you will accompany me to the Inner Circle, you will have your explanation."

Pan'assár left, Gor'sadén at his side and behind, a fuming Rinon. Fel'annár's mind was working, remembering all the things Sar'pén had done and said. He turned to Idernon at his side, rather thought he was doing the same.

Turion was waiting for them in Pan'assár's office, his face dour, eyes wandering from Pan'assár to Rinon.

"The reports do not coincide."

"Whose reports?" asked Rinon.

"Yours and Fel'annár's do. Airen's is consistent. Sar'pén submitted his own report in the early hours of this morning, just before Galadan. I read them both and they do not coincide.

"I set a Shadow on Sar'pén."

Rinon just stood there, as if he had not quite understood. But Fel'annár had. "What exactly, is the discrepancy?"

"Galadan's report states that the arrows came from the left, not the right as Sar'pén claims. He says, and I quote 'I repositioned the guards on the left flank to fortify the right in order to protect General Rinon.' In fact, he did the opposite, left your left side unguarded, and I believe he did it purposefully."

"He may have forgotten," offered Rinon.

"Unlikely. He erred both in the direction those arrows came from and the way in which he positioned the warriors. But tell me, why did those warriors on the right not draw their bows? Why was it The Company who neutralised those snipers?"

"I ..."

"*Think*, Prince. Sar'pén admits he knew there were arrows, that in consequence, he gave an order. That order left you in danger, and your guards had no intention of stopping it. And if his tactic was to outrun the snipers by using his warriors as shields to protect you – without attempting to neutralise the threat – that was an error only a novice would make. Sar'pén has been an active captain in the field for centuries."

Rinon was thinking, eyes moving from side to side, to anything he could cling to. "Suspicious, but not conclusive, Commander."

"No, not yet. But our shadows will do their job shortly. We shall see what comes of that. If Sar'pén is innocent, he has no need to worry."

The edge of Rinon's anger had gone. Instead, the onset of dread, that his closest friend may have betrayed him.

Sar'pén had been part of the group of officers who had initially sympathised with Alpine Supremacy. But after the revelation that Band'orán had been the one to order the murder of Or'Talán, he reneged that movement, was repentant and had fought valiantly against the illicit Kah army, pledged his alliance anew to King Thargodén.

Had he done all that to avoid the same fate as Huren? As Dinor and Bendir?

Had Sar'pén played him for a fool?

He turned away, felt a hand on his shoulder and turned, to the blue eyes of Turion.

"Wait, Rinon. Wait for the truth to emerge."

"I will do more than that. I will watch his face as he answers those questions. I will listen to every word he says. If he is proved innocent, Pan'assár and I will have words."

"And if he is guilty?" asked Turion.

Rinon's eyes turned frigid. "Then I will hang him from the highest walls of the city, shame his name for eternity together with all those who dared conspire to kill my sister."

Turion stood tall, knew that Rinon's words were no idle threat.

FEL'ANNÁR HAD STEPPED OUTSIDE, and Tensári, Idernon, Galdith and Galadan followed. The treachery of the scouts during their patrol had been shocking enough, but the twist of this morning's events had left them all floundering for words.

"I never thought I'd pity Rinon," said Galdith. "Having a friend turn on you like that ..."

"He may not have," warned Idernon.

"Well, if it was a mistake, it was a damn huge one. Seeing arrows coming at you, and then deploying your warriors in the opposite direction is – incomprehensible," said Galadan.

"When you put it like that," said Idernon as he turned towards the barracks. "I'm hungry."

"I think there's been enough intrigue for one morning. Let's see if there's anything left of breakfast," said Fel'annár. "What do we know of Sontúr?" he asked as he led the way.

"Llyniel did not say much after the operation. She was tired and that Kristain took care of things after. She fell asleep in a chair and I had not the heart to waken her."

Fel'annár smiled softy as they entered the barracks and made for the end of the ample hallway, where the dining halls were. The noise was almost deafening, and Fel'annár was reminded that not everything had gone badly these last few days.

He walked into the hall, head down as he enumerated in his mind the many tasks still to perform. But something was wrong. He stopped, looked up.

The entire hall was, indeed, full of warriors. But they no longer sat at their tables, eating and talking and laughing. Instead, they stood to attention, Alpines and Silvans alike, and a familiar voice of command broke through the silence.

"Hail the Warlord!"

"Hail!"

"Hail The Company!"

"Hail!"

Fel'annár stood tall, eyes landing first on Dalú, and then Bulan. The news of what had transpired during the patrol had spread like wildfire, it seemed.

He bowed, The Company followed suit, and then the noise was back full force. The warriors approached, clapped them on the shoulder as they waded through the crowds towards Bulan's table.

Smiling ruefully at Ramien and Carodel who had arrived earlier, they sat together with Dalú, Amon and Benat. Reaching for the platters of food, they served themselves, while Bulan's eyes were on his nephew's battered head. "Are you all right?"

"He is now," answered Galdith with a grin.

"Thanks to Tensári here," said Fel'annár, pointing to her with his knife.

"The House of Three Sisters thanks you, Lieutenant."

"No need, Captain Bulan."

"I know."

She nodded at him, started on her breakfast.

"Well then? Is it true? Have they arrested Sar'pén?" asked Dalú.

"They have. The next few days are going to be interesting. If he's guilty, I wonder how many others were privy to his treachery," said Fel'annár, eyes glancing at the warriors beyond his table.

"Well, everyone's heard about it. I wager anyone in cahoots with him has already left, in case Sar'pén squeaks. I'll take a register later, make sure none of our Division have disappeared," said Bulan.

"Thank you for that. And pass the sausages."

Benat slid the plate to Bulan, who pushed it in front of Fel'annár. He stabbed one with his knife, and then Idernon, Galdith and Tensári did likewise. In seconds, there were none left.

"Did they not feed you on that damned patrol?" asked Bulan, crooked smile on his face as he raised his hands for more food to be brought.

"Fel'annár didn't eat for two days. You know how it goes with head butts," said Galdith quite matter-of-factly.

Dalú laughed irreverently, while Fel'annár squeezed the last bit of his sausage into his already stuffed mouth.

IMAGES of the past flashed through Rinon's mind.

He remembered distant shouts, couldn't quite hear what they were saying. He remembered a cry of danger, an order to get down and then the scrape and clatter of an arrow glancing over his armour.

He remembered looking to his left and finding nothing but trees and then to his right and to Sar'pén, meeting his gaze as they galloped. The only thing in his friend's hands were the reins of his horse.

He remembered two young lieutenants returning from patrol, battered and exuberant of the things they had achieved, and then drinks in city taverns, nights of revelry and indulgence.

He remembered sincere words spoken between friends, of family and hardship, aspirations and regrets.

But of all those days of brotherhood he and Sar'pén had shared, this was the last thing he would remember. The silent, broken captain who had confessed to a terrible crime, unable to withstand the intensity of his interrogation. The weight of it had sent him to the floor where he now sat, back against the stone wall, head in his hands, as if he was only beginning to understand the magnitude of what he had done. Or was he lamenting his inability to withstand the onslaught of the Shadows?

He had confessed, said no one but himself had masterminded the attack. He had known the scouts, their ideological tendencies and had used them to act in benefit of the cause. With the death of the royal twins, Alpine Purists would claim that Silvans had perpetrated the attacks on Rinon and Maeneth. That had been his plan, but The Company had foiled it when Fel'annár had ordered half of them to follow Rinon as Sar'pén led him astray. No one was to know the identity of those snipers, but they had been shot down and retrieved, their Alpine descendance clear to all.

The Shadows had left, their job impeccably done, and Rinon stood with Pan'assár on one side and Turion on the other. The prince stepped forward, towards the self-confessed traitor, and the two generals shared an apprehensive glance.

"Was it for money? For renown and position? Or was it for conviction? Tell me ... why were you going to kill me?"

Sar'pén said nothing, head still hanging in his hands. Rinon took another step forward, looked down on the disgraced captain.

"Well? Do I not deserve to know why my close friend betrayed me?" Rinon's voice was too quiet, too low. Until it split the air around them.

"Get up. Stand up and face me! Tell me why!" Rinon pulled on the back of Sar'pén's tunic, jostled him, hauled him up and then slammed him into the wall, fist in the collar of his tunic.

"Look into my eyes and tell me *why*."

Sar'pén visibly steeled himself, raised his chin and willed his eyes to meet Rinon's.

"I'll tell you *why*. I fully believed in Band'orán's cause, Rinon. It was – it is – *my* cause now. I would not have done it for money or position. Silvan natives are not the equals of us Alpines, they should be our *slaves*. At one point I thought you would join our cause; I was so glad we were close friends. But you didn't in the end, and I was *so* disappointed in you."

Rinon was rendered speechless as the disgraced captain continued, voice gaining strength, all semblance of shame falling away from him as the *real* Sar'pén emerged before his eyes.

"Lord Band'orán killed his own *son* when he endangered the cause. I could do no less, with you. And I hardened my heart against Maeneth, as much as I like her, because she is *your* main weakness. Kill her, and you would be dead too - if not by our arrows, then by heartbreak. Your father would follow, for he would not be able to withstand the loss of both of you. Then we would only have Handir left to deal with, and an accident would take care of him easily. With the resulting fracture of this preposterous Silvan-Alpine alliance, your bastard brother would be exiled, into the trees where he belongs and sooner or later, he too would be taken care of."

"I called you *brother*." Another whisper from Rinon, shaking his head in disbelief at his now unrecognisable childhood friend.

"I'm sorry. Truly. I held to hope that you would join us. It was never personal ..."

Something snapped in Rinon's mind then, and Sar'pén's painful betrayal turned to red hot ire.

"Not sorry enough." Rinon pulled him away from the wall, back-handed him and then punched him in the gut. As Sar'pén fell to his knees, Pan'assár lurched forwards but Turion's arm was across his chest.

"Killing someone is always personal, *traitor*." He reached for the golden sun in Sar'pén's collar, yanked it out and then pushed him to the floor.

"You would have killed me, killed Handir – the Gods you would have killed *Maeneth*, my entire family!"

Rinon turned his back on the prisoner for a moment, closed his eyes and willed his wrath to calm. He turned back, looked down on the wheezing and dishevelled captain.

"That you spoke those words tells me you know the penalty that awaits you. But let me tell you how – *exactly* – that will happen. I will beg my father to see you hung from the highest parapets, so that the entire city will know the name of the traitor. I and the entire Inner Circle will watch, turn our backs on you and then burn your chair, your sigil. Sar'pén – Great Child. I will make an example of you, a message to any others – those you refuse to mention. And as you hang, your feet kicking, as the air in your chest ceases and you take your final look upon this world, it is *my* eyes you will see, damning you to the deepest pits of Galomú."

Rinon turned, brushed past Pan'assár and turned to Turion. "Melt it down. It must never sit in a captain's collar again."

Turion watched him leave, turned to Pan'assár.

"This has hurt him more than he will ever recognise."

~

SAR'PÉN'S CONFESSION of guilt had spread like wildfire throughout the barracks and Inner Circle, amidst a long and gruelling day for Fel'annár and The Company.

They had met with the growing number of Silvan captains in the Forest Division. Fel'annár had briefed them on the events of the patrol, while they had briefed him on what had happened in his absence.

He had missed the Kah trials, but Dalú had proudly told him that three of the ten new disciples were Silvan.

Later, they had worked together with Dalú and Bulan in Fel'annár's office. The now famous lists that the veteran warrior had finally put together were sitting on the Warlord's desk. Fel'annár had then written his requests for new buildings and equipment and sent them by internal dispatch to Pan'assár.

Bulan then told them of the things he had heard from the warriors.

He said they spoke of the Rangers, of how the Warlord would create specialised units within the Rangers. Close-combat, archers, scouts and Listeners.

They were excited.

But more surprisingly, it seemed that Sar'pén's treachery had not separated the warriors but brought them closer together. The Silvans had seen how the Alpines spoke ill of the traitor Sar'pén, of the scouts who had tried to kill Rinon. Meanwhile, the Alpines discussed how The Company had saved the crown prince, how Fel'annár had killed a horde of forty all by himself in defence of Maeneth.

They said he had achieved this because he was almost a Kah Master. It inflamed their own desire to become weapons masters, even qualify for the next Kah Trials the following year.

This newly formed army was merging. The Forest and Mountain Divisions were separated by nothing but the colour of their tunics. Fel'annár knew there were still some who would cause problems, but with Sar'pén's incarceration and possible execution – if that was what the king granted Pan'assár – they would crawl back into the sewers. The disgraced captain would surely receive an exemplary punishment for his crimes against the crown. It would be a clear and unequivocal message to any others who thought to follow Sar'pén's example.

It seemed to Fel'annár that the only remaining obstacle was the memory of Pan'assár's bigotry.

They finally sat back in their chairs, satisfied that the Forest Division was taking shape at last. Just as they stood to leave, there was a knock on the door. Pan'assár entered, waited for the general, captains and warriors to salute.

"Do you have a moment, General?"

"Of course. Wait for me outside will you?"

Idernon nodded, waited for the others to leave and then shut the door behind him.

"It has been a long and eventful day, has it not?"

Fel'annár huffed. "One that is finally over."

"Indeed. I have sent the king our findings. It is my hope that he will pronounce the death penalty for Sar'pén. His punishment must be exemplary."

Fel'annár nodded, and then watched as Pan'assár reached into a small pouch at his belt.

"I wanted to thank you, commend you for what you did."

"I did my ..."

"No. You did more than your duty, Fel'annár. Gor'sadén and I have trained you well but from all accounts, your stand before that tree in which our princess had taken refuge was no simple act of duty. It was a sacrifice. You were willing to die. And I thank the gods that you saw fit to send a part of The Company after Rinon. Had you not, he would be dead."

Pan'assár took a heavy breath, opened his hand and held it before Fel'annár.

"Take it."

Fel'annár's eyes rested on the turquoise stone at the centre of the commander's palm. He frowned, cocked his head to one side and then glanced back at Pan'assár. The commander gestured with his head that he should take it.

He reached out, took it between two fingers and turned it about. "An honour stone."

"Yes. But this is no ordinary river stone, Fel'annár. This was once Or'Talán's. It was given to him by ... your mother."

Fel'annár's wide eyes snapped back to Pan'assár.

"You already knew that they were friends, that Or'Talán had promised her to find a way for her and Thargodén to be together. This was a token of her thanks. It was her recognition of his bravery, that he would stand against his brother for what was right. He took this everywhere, and then forgot it when we marched to the Xeric Wood. He never came back and this stone sat unclaimed, at the back of a drawer in his office – this office."

"I can't accept this, Pan'assár. It's yours by right."

"Yes. And as such, I gift it to you. My brother would want you to have this and so it is yours, to wear in your hair, or carry wherever you will."

Fel'annár brought it closer to his eyes, turned it around, marvelled at the simple beauty of it, the intense hue. The hole through the centre was just big enough for a small lock and so he reached up, took hold of a portion of hair around his temple, and slid it through the stone. He wove a short plait to keep it in place until he could find a suitable clasp and then looked back at a smiling Pan'assár, his own eyes burning and his throat tight.

"I don't know what to say, except thank you. I've never inherited anything from family, save for Zéndar's spear just recently. To know that my mother found this – that she touched this as did my grandfather – it means a lot."

"And that was my intention, Fel'annár. So that you understand the depth of my gratitude."

Fel'annár reached up, touched the stone again, perhaps to check that it had not fallen out. Pan'assár smiled at him, thought he looked so young in that moment. "Now come. I have an honour to bestow on one of your Company."

By the time they entered the Halls, Fel'annár wore a new honour stone while Galdith proudly displayed his new Master Archer band, high on his right bicep.

As their eyes adapted to the light, Galadan had told them that Sontúr was surely awake and that the Lestari would inform them of the success – or failure – to repair his shoulder.

They were soon at the door that led to Sontúr's private room. There, Fel'annár had not expected to find Gor'sadén, Handir and Maeneth, talking quietly with Llyniel's second, Healer Kristain.

They turned as The Company approached.

"Any news?" asked Fel'annár.

Kristain turned to Fel'annár, mouth open to answer, but the door opened, and a tired Llyniel stood there, drying her hands on her apron.

"The procedure went well. Sontúr's arm has been immobilised to better protect it. All in all, I would say one month before light exercise can be taken, *if* our prince behaves himself and follows my orders."

"He will regain normal use of his arm?"

Llyniel turned to Gor'sadén. "I believe he will."

"Aria be praised!" said Galdith while the others joined him with words of relief.

"Can we see him?" asked Fel'annár.

"For a short while, yes. He will be glad of it. Just be mindful that he needs to rest. Tomorrow, if all goes well, he can return to his quarters at the palace." She opened the doors wide, and The Company stepped inside.

Sontúr lay on a bed, dressed in nothing but a long, linen shirt, feet stretched out before him and his back against a mountain of pillows.

He was pale, dark circles under his eyes because whatever they had given him to render him senseless, he could surely still feel its effects. Even so, with the knowledge that he would make a full recovery, he smiled placidly at his visitors.

"Good to see you awake and on the mend, brother," said Fel'annár, smiling back as the rest of the Company arranged themselves around Sontúr's bed. Handir and Maeneth joined them, listening to their cheerful banter, both familiar with their ways after having journeyed with them.

Gor'sadén also spoke for a while to his prince before he stepped up to Llyniel and took both her hands in his. He leaned forwards, kissed her forehead.

"King Vorn'asté will hear of your skill."

She smiled up at him, watched him turn to Fel'annár and gesture to his new Honour Stone. "Wear that proudly, Warlord." With that, he left in search of Pan'assár.

Sontúr and Llyniel asked Fel'annár how he had come about it. He explained, and then Sontúr caught sight of Galdith's new arm band. He would have clapped him on the shoulder, had he been able. Instead, he nodded in satisfaction. He had been there, had seen how difficult his shot had been, how true his arrow had flown.

Handir and Maeneth came to stand before Llyniel. "Now, you get some rest," said Handir, a warning finger before her face.

Llyniel's eyes gravitated towards Fel'annár, an apology in her eyes as she spoke.

"I need to stay at the Halls tonight with the prince."

Fel'annár wanted her to, and yet he didn't. He needed to talk to her about what had happened in the Evergreen Wood. But Sontúr was their priority now, and he had a dinner appointment.

His gaze drifted from Llyniel to Kristain, saw the subtle nod, the way his hand rested on the dagger at his belt. Kristain would guard the Lestari and her patient that night.

"Until tomorrow then. You and I have much catching up to do."

Llyniel smiled at him, surely knew exactly what he had meant. She turned to Maeneth. "Come to our quarters tomorrow. Have some *real* Silvan lunch and tell me all about Pelagia."

"Oh yes please! But did you say *our* quarters?" Maeneth's eyes were back on her friend's Bonding Braid, breath stuck in her throat, half smile on her lips.

"Mine and my husband's, of course. You've met him." She turned to Fel'annár, grinned at him.

"You and ... and ... my half-brother?"

Llyniel's grin turned into a mischievous chuckle as she came to stand at Fel'annár's side. "Why didn't you tell her?"

"Because," began Fel'annár, "I got walloped in the head and later, the opportunity simply didn't arise."

Maeneth still hadn't said a word, probably couldn't, and Sontúr's eyes roved over her half-open mouth, her wide eyes that darted between Llyniel and Fel'annár.

"Well, we were always sisters in all but blood. Now, we will be that in law too. I'm sorry I'm just ... *shocked*. Pleasantly so, though."

Llyniel turned to Fel'annár, squeezed his hand.

"Handir and I need to go now, but I'll be back to visit you tomorrow, Sontúr. There is a book I would discuss with you."

The prince nodded, smiled, hoped she wouldn't notice just how much he would look forward to that.

"See you at dinner then, brother."

Handir and Maeneth left, and Llyniel turned to her husband. "Dinner?"

"With the king, at Rinon's request."

Both Llyniel's eyebrows were at her hairline, while only one of Sontúr's arched acutely.

Here, in the presence of friends, Fel'annár thought nothing of protocol and he took his wife in his arms, a surge of pride and love washing over him. He spoke softly, only for her.

"I will be with the king tonight. But tomorrow will be only for you and I. Do you promise?"

"I demand it."

He smiled over the top of her head.

19

FAMILY

~

IT WAS A RATHER solemn king who greeted Fel'annár before the royal hearth that evening.

Accepting the sweet wine his father offered him, his eyes registered the king's casual clothing, and the absence of his crown. Even his hair was loose.

Himself on the other hand, had dressed in a deep purple tunic, its stiff collar chafing at the tender skin below his chin.

"It has been a difficult day for us all, although especially for Rinon."

"I understand he was close to Sar ... to the traitor."

"He was. He never suspected anything like this could happen. He is angry, more perhaps at himself."

Fel'annár could see how that might be. He would feel stupid, gullible for not having realised. Yet Rinon did not strike Fel'annár as easy to fool. Far from it in fact.

"Are *you* all right?"

"What – oh you mean this?" he gestured to his own head. "It's as hard as cobble stone."

Thargodén drank but his eyes did not leave those of his son.

"I heard what happened, bless the day I insisted you and The Company go with Rinon."

"We did our duty."

"Yes, you did. Would have died doing it – almost did."

"I had Tensári."

"Then I thank Aria for that. But have a care, Fel'annár. We need you whole and hale."

The door clicked open, revealing Handir, similarly dressed to his father and Fel'annár realised that he had overdressed for the evening. He pulled at his high collar, missed the king's grin as he watched his brother all but throw himself into a plush chair.

"What a day," he sighed. "You know, I never liked Sar'pén, but I did not anticipate this."

"Where is your brother?"

"With Maeneth, in his rooms. They will be along in a moment."

"Well then let's see if we can lift his spirits," said the king.

True to Handir's prediction, the royal twins arrived together. Rinon made straight for the wine while Maeneth turned to Fel'annár.

"You are looking ... formal."

Fel'annár frowned but Maeneth grinned at him. "You're with your family now, brother."

He didn't know what to say, and so he said the first thing that rolled off his tongue. "I hardly know you." He regretted it immediately, but Maeneth seemed to understand his predicament.

"No, you don't. But you will. And, while you don't know me, I dare say I know you – in all the things that matter. You saved my life. I don't know how, can't explain the things that I saw up in that tree. All I know is that you are loyal, true, and that I will come to love you. All we need is time, and circumstances such as these."

He smiled down at her, curiosity leading his eyes to wander. She was dressed simply in black leggings and a loose-fitting shirt. Her silvery-blonde hair was piled on her head, but some locks had been left to frame her face on either side. Only now did he realise how pointed her ears were, just how light her blue eyes were. Yes, she was Rinon's twin, but there was a softness in her eyes that Rinon did not have. But then he turned to the crown prince and promptly corrected himself.

That cutting ice had gone. Rinon was troubled, surely didn't want to be, but there was a depth of emotion there that Fel'annár had not seen before. There was a side to Rinon that Fel'annár had yet to see, he thought. Still, he would avoid the subject of Sar'pén for now.

Rinon turned away, made for a side table on the other side of the room, mumbling words as he went.

"I'm hungry."

"Me too," said Handir, rising from his chair and following his brother. Maeneth turned to Fel'annár, offered him an encouraging smile.

"Come on." She took his arm, steered him towards the table and Thargodén watched. For the first time, all his children were together, standing around the buffet table. He approached more slowly, savoured the moment.

"So, tell us, Maeneth, what is this new science I have been hearing about?" asked Handir as he plucked a small pastry from a plate and began to eat.

Maeneth visibly ordered her thoughts. She pushed away Rinon and his predicament, their dangerous return to the city, clearly understood what Handir was trying to do. And so, she conjured her passionate love of modern agriculture. By the time she had explained the basics of it, the plates were empty and their bellies full and their hands dirty.

"You know, there's something very Silvan about what you do. The idea of preserving and enhancing the land instead of using it until it is nothing but dry, sterile soil," said Fel'annár as he dabbed his hands into a bowl with fragrant-smelling water. "This idea of rotating the crops in a staggered way allows villages to become almost self-sufficient," said Fel'annár. This was just the sort of thing that would get Thavron all worked up. He grabbed a serviette and wiped his hands.

"Entirely self-sufficient, Fel'annár, save for any anomalies in the weather. It is a simple idea, based on a love of the land, a respect your people feel particularly deeply. Personally, I can't wait to get out there and show our people how it is done, perhaps even provide them with the basics. I want to bring the village elders together, explain the process and the benefits to be had. It can even be legislated you see, so that each farmstead is beholden to the next to cooperate, so that the chain is not broken."

"The Merchant Guild will not be happy with you," said the king as he dabbed at his mouth with his own serviette.

"To hell with them. They're worse than vultures." Fel'annár's brows rose. She sounded just like Rinon.

"There are some good merchants, Mae. Not all of them are rotten," cautioned Handir.

"No. Still, they will lose their business of importing fruit and vegetables, legumes and tubers ..."

"But that will not be instantaneous," offered the king. "They will have many years ahead of them to get used to the idea. They will find other produce to import, I am sure."

Fel'annár caught Handir's gaze, gestured at a crumb that had stuck to his bottom lip. The prince swiped it away with a smile.

"Father. I have something to ask of you."

"Tell me."

She gestured to the windows, the plateau beyond that stretched out over the Evergreen Wood. On any other occasion, Fel'annár would have enjoyed looking out at it, listening to its strange murmurings, drawing strength from it. All he could do now was repress a shiver for the recent memories it evoked.

As one, the family followed her as she talked and slowly, they made their way through the doors and outside, ever closer to the edge, where stone gave way to air.

"This building. It's beautiful, the stone native to the coastal areas of the land. The gold that coats the Summer Dome is from the crystal straits and the silver inlay that decorates our columns and pillars is from the western slopes of the Median Mountains. But what is there here, that represents these forests?"

Fel'annár remembered his own reaction, back when he had looked upon the city for the first time together with Ramien and Idernon. He gave words to the memory. "It's like it doesn't belong; a thing of beauty, carved of everything that's not the forest. It feels ... artificial, out of place. Like an armed warrior at a tea party ..."

Maeneth stared at him. "Yes. That's exactly what I mean." She turned to face the building behind her, gestured at it. "All these domes and spires are a testimony to the foundation of this city and its Alpine pilgrims. I propose that we make it a symbol of our unity with the Silvan people. I would bring green into a sea of metal and stone. I wish to plant, father."

"Plant ..."

"Everywhere," she nodded.

He didn't seem to understand and so she pressed on, the light of determination almost seeming to glow in her light blue eyes.

"Let me create an artist's image. Once you can see what I see in my head, you'll want me to do this. The Silvan people will want you to do this and our Alpine folk will kneel to the majesty of nature, will bow to the strength of harmony. I will make this building a symbol of our new-found unity. It will show our people that the Alpines stand for the Silvans, and so the Silvans will stand for the Alpines."

Rinon stared at her, and Thargodén wondered what he was thinking, whether he too thought that Alpines and Silvans were closer than the Alpines were amongst themselves in recent times. He had heard what his people were saying – his *Alpine* people. They were praising Fel'annár and The Company for protecting the royal twins, condemning the purists, and speculating on who was next after Nestar and Sar'pén's fall into disgrace.

"Then prepare that illustration for me." He smiled at his daughter, but he couldn't help the direction his eyes took, because to look at her was to remember Canusahéi.

Fel'annár followed his line of sight to a small area of the gardens to one side of the building itself. It was not well-kept, seemed overgrown and unused.

"What is that place?" ventured Fel'annár.

Handir stared at him, while Maeneth, Rinon and Thargodén looked to the floor and then away.

"That was our mother's favourite spot."

Fel'annár wanted to go there, touch those bushes and shrubs. It was all shades of green, but there was not one bloom to be seen. A thought tumbled from his mouth before he could stop it.

"No flowers."

"No. Not since she left," said Rinon, and then Maeneth continued.

"She spent hours with her yellow roses. She sang to them, stroked them lovingly and when the time came, she would cut them carefully, decorate the entire palace with the most sweetly smelling roses you can ever imagine."

The king heaved a heavy breath, not quite able to meet his children's gazes.

"Perhaps we can restore it one day," said Fel'annár.

"No." Rinon had almost cut off his brother's last word. "That place remembers her, mourns her absence ... just like us."

"Rinon."

The crown prince flinched, turned to Fel'annár. Whether his eyes were too bright, he couldn't say, but Rinon seemed mesmerised for a moment.

"One day, when you trust me enough, I would restore it for you."

They stared at one another, the symbolism of his offer lost to no one. Fel'annár had not been the cause of their mother's departure, but he was a symbol of it. Who better than to give this family a place of remembrance? A place where they could simply sit and think of their mother.

"You are a stranger to me and yet, I trust you with my life, Fel'annár. It is fitting that we come to understand each other, at least. I am glad you came tonight."

Fel'annár didn't know what to say, could only nod at Rinon. He turned to Handir, who was standing close enough to Maeneth and Rinon that he could see all three of them. His brothers and sister, their father right beside them.

The mystery that had plagued his childhood was finally gone. Here was his father, not a shamed outlaw but a glorious king. Here were the siblings he had longed for as a boy. And just over the plains, his Silvan family welcomed him.

Despite the treachery still afoot. Despite his questions about the Evergreen Wood and his dream, and the threat of the Nim'uán, Fel'annár felt complete.

He just hoped that he would live long enough to enjoy his new-found family, discover what it was to feel a part of something bigger than himself.

~

WITH THE SUN still shy of the horizon, Fel'annár made his way to the Evergreen Wood in search of Gor'sadén and the Dohai. But instead of venturing past the gates as they always did, Gor'sadén gestured to the Inner Circle.

"You missed the Kah trials. We have ten new Disciples."

" I heard. Eramor?" asked Fel'annár.

"Has passed, as has Benat."

"So where are we training then?"

"Pan'assár and the others are waiting for us in the glade behind the Inner Circle. After the Dohai, I will continue with your training while Pan'assár gets the others started on the basics."

"Poor souls..." grinned Fel'annár, gaze lingering on the Healing Halls as they passed on their way to the Inner Circle. Gor'sadén followed his line of sight.

"Stay focussed, Fel'annár. The discipline of the Dohai must not be broken, except for injury. There is a lot on your mind, but I want your best effort today. You are close to mastery, to the final Dance. Every day counts now."

They remained silent for a while as they navigated the dark corridors of the Inner Circle. The quickest way to get to the glade was through the building and out the other side, and Fel'annár supposed Pan'assár would have posted guards around the perimeter to make sure they were not disturbed or watched by those who were not Kah.

They came to a door, and the guard snapped to attention, stepped aside and opened it. Tensári would go no further and soon, Master and Disciple stood before what seemed to Fel'annár like a painting from bygone days. Not that he had lived them, but he had read of them.

In the middle of the clearing, ten black-clad warriors stood weapon-less, grey sashes hanging from their waists, and before them, Pan'assár. It was time for their first taste of the Dohai and Fel'annár could see their trepidation, their anticipation. It was the only part of the Kah that was not prohibited to others, but while some of them would have seen it performed, none had been privy to the secrets behind it.

Gor'sadén and Fel'annár stood at the front of the ten, new Disciples, and beside them, Pan'assár spoke as Master and Disciple turned to the east and began to move.

He explained each move, the significance of it, the meaning and the thoughts that accompanied them. He told them of the power of nature, its consequences on the elven body and how it could be wilfully channelled. He told them of the Dohai, the energy that could be stored, and then called upon to use, so that it could be projected. It would lend them a speed and power they could not yet imagine.

Gor'sadén and Fel'annár moved away from the main group while the Kah Disciples learned the Dohai with Pan'assár, who then went on to teach them the basic stances. But one thing became clear to the commanders, and to Fel'annár. The Disciples were neither fit nor strong enough, and already, frustration was taking its toll. Fel'annár had taken it upon himself to talk to one Alpine disciple who he had heard complaining that Pan'assár's teachings were too slow, too basic. In fact, they had not learned one Kah technique in the two days since they had been invested, yet they were all Blade Masters.

Fel'annár had patiently explained to him the reason behind Pan'assár's program. He even performed the very first of the ten stances and did so at not a quarter of its usual speed. His movement was fluid, no sways or shakes, no deviation from trajectory. He then bid the warrior repeat it.

He tried but stopped when his hand could not hold the blade still enough, just seconds into the exercise.

No one laughed, no one humiliated him, and the warrior had bowed his apology, both to Fel'annár and then to Pan'assár.

Later, Fel'annár left the glade and made for the training pits inside the Inner Circle. He trained with Bulan, and after a bath and breakfast, he spent the rest of the day interviewing Silvan lieutenants with his captains. There had been both disappointment and unbridled joy. There had been cheers and almost tears, but morale was high because those who had not passed the test were invited to try again the following year.

Tomorrow, the Silvans would celebrate the end of their vigil before the city gates. After the Night of a Thousand Drums, and then the Battle of Brothers, their demands had been met, the army restructured, and the Warlord returned. It was time to go home, but first, a Silvan feast to mark the day – woodland indulgence on the eve of departure.

Fel'annár and Gor'sadén made for the palace; one was pensive and the other curious.

"You have made a fine start with your uncle."

"I like him."

"Have you made any progress with your *father*?"

Fel'annár hadn't expected that and thought that perhaps he should have. There had been little time for conversation these past few days.

"We have spoken, and even Rinon and I have agreed to try a little harder. It was him who invited me to dinner yesterday."

"Did you enjoy it?"

"Honestly, yes."

"Well, that is progress."

Fel'annár smiled as he recalled the evening. "Rinon was a whole different person. Not affectionate in any way but there was no antagonism, no sarcasm."

"No small thing. And Maeneth?"

"Not what I expected at all. She has a plan to – Silvanise – the palace. She wants to make everyone self-sufficient, has a technique she says will reduce the amount of goods our merchants import."

"Not very princess-like."

"At least not in the way *I* was taught. I expected her to have ladies in waiting, lavish jewels and pompous eyes. There was none of that, and she seems to get on well with Sontúr especially."

Gor'sadén glanced at him as they passed the threshold of the palace.

"From what you say, I suppose it is their affinity with science."

"Perhaps."

"Tomorrow will be a good excuse for you to get to know your Silvan family. Your grandmother, and that young cousin of yours."

"Alei and Vasanth, yes."

"Enjoy it, Fel'annár. The Nim'uán is far away, and the new army has already been put into motion, passed its first test. Captains are being assigned, troops are requesting to serve in the divisions of their choice, weapons are being forged and uniforms designed and tailored. Strategy is being discussed and soon, your new outposts will be populated. We are days away from making this forest safer. You have done so well for others. Now you must do well for yourself. No training tomorrow. You will need the rest."

Fel'annár grinned. "All right. Just this one day."

As they climbed the stairs, it struck Fel'annár that it would be passing strange to see the empty plains before the city. He'd become so accustomed to having the encampment so close. It was a little piece of home on the doorstep of this singularly Alpine place. In just a few days, it would all be gone, and Sen Garay would be the nearest thing to the Deep Forest, almost two days' ride away. He suddenly wanted to see that sketch that Maeneth had promised the king, wondered if it would make this place easier on the Silvans, make this place *their* home too.

"You're Silvan. There is a party on the horizon, and you are too quiet."

Fel'annár smiled. It was true, he was pensive, and the Evergreen Wood was still there in his mind, its mysteries swirling in the depths of his consciousness. He had not allowed them to surface because amongst all the possible answers to his questions, some of them were not to his liking.

"Something happened in that forest, didn't it?"

"Why do you say that?"

Fel'annár could almost see the sarcastic pull of Gor'sadén's lips, but he wasn't going to offer information he himself didn't know how to interpret.

"You were not at your best when you left on that trip of yours but now ... there is new strength in your step; I can almost feel it around you."

"It's a strange place. There's something there that eludes me. The light is different, colours more vivid. I could almost touch the Dohai. In fact I think I did. It was like a translucent ball, solid enough to hold in my hand. I've never felt such power, never seen the lights so bright. When I fought those Deviants, that power was still inside me, so strong it was almost overwhelming. Had it not been the case, I would not have been able to do what I did to protect Maeneth."

"I doubt even a seasoned Kah Master would have been able to kill so many single handed. It is almost time for you to take the final test,

Fel'annár. But come, tell me, did you find what you were looking for in that wood?"

What could he say? He didn't know. He wouldn't lie to his mentor, but he couldn't tell him that he thought he had dreamed, that he had seen himself as a Last Marker, that a massive wyvern had crashed from the very rock face and had almost burned him to a toast?

"I don't know. I wish Hobin were here."

"Why do you think he would have answers?"

Behold the Last Markers.

He supressed a wave of cold, thanked the gods they had arrived at Sontúr's quarters and Gor'sadén could not continue with his questions. Still, he knew he would have to answer them sooner or later.

Sontúr had been discharged from the Halls, allowed to return to his own quarters with strict instructions from Llyniel.

He lay on his bed, dressed much the way he had been the day before. Some colour had returned to his cheeks, thought Fel'annár as he approached the bed. He wondered if it was because he was recuperating, or whether it was due to the presence of Maeneth, who sat beside him, skimming through a book.

Fel'annár greeted The Company, but he was drawn by that curious gaze of hers. Even now, Maeneth's eyes were on the labels of Llyniel's many jars and vials, and then from time to time, she would look at Sontúr who had lain back to rest.

There was something there, something in the way she tried to hide those glances, and come to think of it, Sontúr was doing it too. The attraction was mutual.

"You're only half here, Fel'annár."

He startled, turned to Idernon, realised the others were looking at him expectantly.

"Sorry. Did I miss something?"

"Carodel here was telling us about the celebration at the Silvan encampment tomorrow. Apparently, the king has set the palace kitchens to preparing food. They are expecting thousands to make for the plains."

Fel'annár turned to Maeneth.

"The king's initiative. He spoke to Pan'assár this morning. I heard them talking about it. I do believe our Commander General made that request."

Fel'annár was not the only one surprised at that. He smiled softly. "It's *time* to celebrate, I think. After everything that's happened these past weeks, it's time to look back and see what we have achieved. Despite the battles, the treachery and the deaths, we've come a long way. Equality has been restored on the Council and in the army, our warriors are coming together and slowly, any still loyal to Band'orán are being rooted out."

He leaned against his chair at the foot of Sontúr's bed and crossed his arms. "Will you be well enough to come with us?"

"No." Llyniel's voice of authority. They turned to her, saw the finality in her eyes.

"Then The Company will stay here," said Fel'annár.

"You will *not*. You will go to that feast, eat, drink and dance and then crawl back here the next day and tell me all about it." Sontúr seemed angry and Fel'annár smiled at him, glad of this steely resolve. He was going to need it in the weeks and months of inactivity ahead.

"Well, I am sure we can have our own little celebration here at the palace. Surely there will be no objection to that?" asked Maeneth, hopeful eyes on Llyniel.

"No wine. It will make you unstable. If you fall ..."

"I know," said Sontúr, holding up his good hand in case Llyniel had thought to continue with her warnings. "At least I'm out of the Halls and in my own rooms. And I know that I will recover the use of my arm. I have reason to celebrate, even if it is just here, sitting in my pyjamas."

"You will not be in this arm brace forever and when it comes off, you will be stronger, better," said Maeneth comfortingly, reaching forward to cover his free hand with hers. "You will be a warrior once more, ride with your Company. I'll be here to celebrate with you tomorrow, and I'm sure the commanders would love to join us."

Sontúr smiled his thanks at her and Maeneth nodded encouragingly at him, her hand still over his.

Fel'annár's brows rose and Carodel pursed his lips. There *was* something between Sontúr and Maeneth, some natural affinity that was obvious to them all save perhaps for Sontúr himself. Had it not been because he was injured, could not serve with The Company or go to the festivities, their mutual attraction would have been the source of painful ribbing, but as it was, not even Carodel had broken the endearing moment with some such irreverence.

His princely friend and his royal sister fancied each other. There could be no doubt of it now.

~

THAT NIGHT, Fel'annár finally found himself alone with Llyniel.

By the time he had arrived, she had already bathed. She stood wrapped in a towel, only half dry, and Fel'annár smiled, wanted to rip it off her but thought better of his rash idea. Instead, he drew a bath for himself, stripped and then sunk beneath the warm water. When he surfaced, he found Llyniel sitting on a stool to one side.

He rubbed water from his face and leaned against the back of the tub, enjoying the warmth of the water and the nearness of his Connate.

"You've been patient with me after my trip to the Evergreen wood. You understood that something had happened, that I needed time. I would have told you earlier, but then we rode out to meet Maeneth."

"You went in search of answers to your question. You wanted to know what your ultimate purpose is. Tell me then, did you find the answer to that question?"

He turned to her. "No."

She waited for him to continue, almost jumped when he did.

"I have only one answer to a question that had not even occurred to me. That my purpose was not to unite our people or vanquish the Nim'uán. It's something that goes beyond that, something Aria has been trying to tell me in my dreams."

"The way she did when you still didn't understand that you are Ber'anor?"

"Yes. Just as cryptic. Hobin says it's so that realisation comes slowly, so that the servant can understand and assimilate the truth more easily. As for me, I'd much rather she told me outright."

"So what's this dream about?"

He must have paled because she stood, left, and when she came back, there were two glasses in her hand. She offered one to him, nursed the other in her hands.

"Go on, Fel'annár. Better out than in as we healers say."

He almost laughed at that and instead, took a sip of his wine. The water was still warm, and the wine slipped down his throat like a velvety ribbon. He closed his eyes, wondered where to start.

"I had a dream in which Aria was drawing me past the lake, where I knew I shouldn't go. I came to a rock face and before it, a semi-circle of Last Markers."

"The dream was set in Araria then?"

"No. That's the point. We were in the Evergreen Wood, I'm sure of it."

"Go on then."

"The statues ... one was Zéndar, and beside him, myself." He drank quickly, glanced at Llyniel over the brim of his glass.

She took a sip, considered his words for a moment. "All this business of Bulan coming, of hearing about Zéndar from him, the spear your uncle has gifted you with. I would say that is your desire to have met him. Your mind is telling you that although you never knew each other in life, you will stand together as Ari'atór in death."

Fel'annár froze, hand halfway to his mouth. "You think so?" He clearly remembered Sontúr had said something similar.

Llyniel must have sensed insecurity in his voice. She put her wine on a small round table beside the bath and leaned forward. "What did you think it might mean?"

He stared at her, felt stupid but he told her anyway. "I thought it was a sign of my death, the surety that I would die in the course of my duty to Aria, just as Zéndar did."

Her smile was soft and sad. "And I believe that is possible, my love. I have always known that that is possible. It comes as no shock to me."

"But if my purpose is to vanquish the Nim'uán, my death will come sooner rather than later."

"But you just said you don't know what your purpose is. What if you are simply to defend the forest? It could be years, decades, centuries before you die. Why worry about it now?"

He put his glass down, remembered all the possible interpretations The Company had offered him, but none had been as simple and straightforward as this one. But there was one thing he hadn't told her yet.

"Tensári thinks it may not have been a dream."

She frowned. "Why?"

"Because ... I was fascinated with the statue of Zéndar. I reached out, touched the spear on his back, the very one that sits in the corner of our living quarters. My finger brushed past his head and ... something happened."

She reached for her wine, drank deeply, eyes on Fel'annár.

"A beast, some winged thing shrouded in green mist crashed out of the mountain itself. I ran, followed the squawk of some bird. I nearly killed myself running away from it, but then when I thought I was safe, the green mist surrounded me. It strangled me."

"Killed you?"

"I thought it had. I woke up at my previous camp site, terrified and dishevelled, I must have thrashed around while I dreamed. Point being, Tensári says she heard the call of Aria. She said I was in danger, she knew, tried to enter the wood and was stopped."

Llyniel said nothing for a while. She stood, reached for a large towel and held it up to him. He stood, wrapped himself in it and followed her into the front room, grateful for the fire that burned in the hearth. He sat before it, stared at the flickering light for a while and then felt her sit beside him.

"That's strange, admittedly. Still, I stand by what I said. The very fact that you saw yourself as a marker means little else other than you are Ari, you will die in your duty to Aria. You already knew that."

He turned to her. "I did. But I never really felt it, felt what it would be like to say goodbye, to *you*." He couldn't help it. His eyes filled, brimmed and he needed to touch her. He reached out, smoothed down the side of her face.

She shuffled around him, pulled her towel off and knelt in front of him, back to the fire, naked body before him but her beautiful smile was all he could see.

"In Tar'eastór, there came a time when I could no longer deny that I loved you. With that understanding, I made a sacrifice, Fel'annár. I accepted that I would one day watch you die. I would take the Long

Road and then find you. You are mortal in your immortality, Fel'annár. For you, death is a certainty. Farewell is a certainty, as certain as we will be together again, across the Veil, wherever that may be."

He reached out to her, hands smoothing over her hair, down her face and arms. He leaned forwards, kissed her lips and pressed her to him, held her in his powerful embrace, heart bursting with love.

He needed to show her what she meant to him. He needed to show her how precious life was with her in it, how empty it would be until they met again, when his duty was done.

And he did, until the moon set and the sun peaked over the eastern horizon.

His duty to Aria was still uncertain. There would be more dreams, more clues to what she wanted of him but for now, all he could do was enjoy the life he was given, rejoice in the love he was offered.

CAPTAIN SOREI OF TAR'EASTÓR had placed Lieutenant Polan in charge of the one thousand strong host she commanded.

Scouts had been deployed, the guard set, and they had not seen Deviant activity for days. Even their first and only encounter had been so minor she had not even had to draw her blade, the blade none could help but stare at.

She swivelled right, a guarding stance, long, long sword out to the fore. It was perfect, she thought as her right hand reached out to smooth over the broadest section of the blade, close to the still unadorned cross guard. She would see to that later, when she was sure that this was the one, the first Synth Blade, after so many years of studying, forging and reforging.

Attack, sweep down and arc sideways, feet moving to the left, to another imaginary foe, blade once more before her. It was heavy, but not nearly as hard to wield as it looked. The blade was thicker towards the guard, thinned out towards the tip, neither sagged nor wobbled because this was her special alloy, the one she had been striving to create for over a century.

She turned full circle. Arc, feign, dance sideways and start again. It was no more difficult to heft than her standard-issue sword, but it was almost twice as big. The warrior who wielded this weapon needed endurance to last a battle, and precision the likes of which few possessed. Sorei herself was a Blade Master, but even so, she was not able to use its capabilities to the maximum. A Kah Warrior though ... Gods but she would give anything to see Gor'sadén wield it, give her his verdict. It was just as well that he was in Ea Uaré, where she was now bound, in service to King Vorn'asté.

Two more weeks and they would emerge onto the city plains, put themselves under the command of Gor'sadén himself. She just wished she knew what they were walking into.

They had set out from Tar'eastór three weeks ago when messengers from Abiren'á had brought news of the deepening strife in Ea Uaré. That had been mere days after Gor'sadén's departure. Thargodén Ar Or'Talán called for aid and Vorn'asté answered in the hopes of avoiding what seemed like inevitable civil war.

It was a five-week ride to Ea Uaré from the Motherland, three if they took the river route. But that was a danger that acting Commander General Comon was not prepared to take with such a large contingent. He himself was duty and honour-bound to stay in Tar'eastór and protect his city, and so it fell to Comon's best captain to represent the Motherland - Sorei.

And that was what she would do. If she was lucky, she would find a forge, away from prying eyes, from others who would covet the secrets of her alloy, of her technique, her Synth Blade.

But Sorei was not telling, not until she could be sure that this was the one.

A high stance, a killing stance and she attacked the stump of a dead tree that was as tall as she was. In one arcing swoop, she sliced into it. Approaching it, she anchored one foot against the bark and pulled the blade out of the wood.

The warriors watched her, saluted as she passed them, tried not to stare at the blade that had been the talk of the troop since their departure.

Where had it come from? Had she made it herself? And where could they get one?

GRA'DÓN MISSED HIS BROTHERS. They had been apart for longer than they ever had been. The months of planning and the longer months of travel. If everything went to plan, it would still be a while before they were united, but when that happened, they would be home, at last.

Even as Gra'dón travelled, the cartographers were crafting new maps, amending old ones. They documented new routes, skilfully penning them, marking where the dangers lay, how they had been avoided. There were mathematicians too. They calculated volumes and distances and watched the stars, measured their routes across the dome. All this was studied by their engineers who crafted plans for great machines, and for the irrigation systems they would need later.

The king of Calrazia had invested well in this venture, knew the benefits and advantages of victory over the Silvan lands of Ea Uaré. He and his direct bloodline would be free of the threat of the immortal princes *and* he would have his precious water. In return, King Saranuk had provided troops and academics, everything the brothers would need to invade a forest kingdom.

Gra'dón would be Emperor, ruler of his own lands, ruler of his mother's lands together with his brothers, his generals. She was dead, had taken her own life, but did he still have a family in that place they called Ea Nanú? Was there anyone else left to tell him of the lands of his forefathers? To tell him of his mother and how it had been before she had been taken?

The journey continued and far, far away, so too did that of his brothers. *They* would set everything into motion. With the might of the Sand Lords, the Northerners and the help of the itinerant Deviants, the Silvans and their trees were doomed.

Only then, would Gra'dón strike.

20

THE END OF AN ERA

TODAY MARKED the end of an era.

The Silvan encampment would see its last night immersed in song and dance, a woodland farewell to the Alpine city of stone.

It was the conclusion of months of hard negotiations, of conflict and battle, of trust and loyalties tried, of betrayal and then renewal. Its end marked the onset of the Restoration, one that had begun with the coming of Bulan, and the Warlord's call for the warriors to return to barracks.

They had regained their equality, and with the revelation of Band'orán's treason, the Alpine Purists were all but ousted. Even now, the latest of them to be discovered sat in the king's dungeons, awaiting his sentence.

It was time to go home. It was time to return to normalcy, to the days before the death of Or'Talán.

Miren stood upon the back of a cart, a woodland garland in her hand. She reached for a branch, attached one end and then jumped down and moved the cart along, repeating the process until the glade was surrounded by the pretty adornments.

By nightfall it would be glowing and beautiful, full of multi-coloured lamps that would offer just enough light, and yet not enough to see everything that went on in the dark.

As Miren continued with her work, Amareth helped with the banquet. There were many mouths to feed now, more than there ever had been at the camp. Thousands of warriors had returned, would surely converge on the plains. Their hunters had gone in search of prey which was now being prepared for the roasting pits. Even so, there would not be food for everyone, and, as was so often the case, many would make their own fires further away, bring their own wine and food. So long as they came to mark the day, it was all that really mattered.

Amareth looked over the glade, saw Miren stretching upwards to hang her lights, and then she saw the percussionists anchor their base drums, just at the edge of the trees. Soon, others would join them, smaller drums, different tensions and tones and perhaps there would be flutes, too. She had even seen a plank drum.

Her mother had joined the musicians. She had always sung well, her voice much appreciated by the Deep Silvans, the Spirit Singers who wove complex emotions into their words, as if they could read the minds of others, weave their feelings into the song. She had not allowed herself to seek them out and hear them sing, for that was a privilege she didn't deserve.

She turned back to her work. She would watch Fel'annár and his love enjoy the evening. It would be enough for Amareth.

It always had been.

Her eyes drifted to one side, to where Erthoron stood alone, casting his eyes over the plains. In just a few hours, they would be full of people and fires. Perhaps he was remembering the days of long councils and worrying news. Perhaps he was recalling the arguments and the disagreements, Angon and his brave stand, or Faron and his betrayal.

They had lived through those times together, side by side, as it had always been with her and Erthoron. But to pursue the glimmer of happiness as more than a fellow Elder was something she would not consider.

She didn't deserve to be happy.

Distant shouts, hails from afar and four carts approached. She wiped her hands on her apron, started forwards to where Erthoron stood and waited until she could hear the voices.

"Greetings from King Thargodén! We bring fare from our lord's kitchens."

Amareth and Erthoron strode forwards, Alei just behind. They watched as the newcomers jumped down and began to untie the tarpaulins that covered their cargo.

With a flourish, they pulled them away and smiled.

Amareth's eyes widened, Erthoron's jaw dropped and Alei took both hands to her cheeks.

All it took were three hesitant steps and the shock was over. They ran to the carts, eyes feasting over the crates of wine, the carefully stacked loaves of bread. Amareth saw slabs of cheese, fruit and boiled ham. Miren saw pickles and cake, pies and large jars of nuts and preserves.

But it was Erthoron who spotted the sausages. His eyes bulged, his breath hitched in his throat and Amareth smiled endearingly at the age-old Elder who now looked more like an exuberant youth.

Just like young Ramien, she mused.

DUSK, and it was time to dress for a Silvan party, time to allow themselves this one moment of indulgence after so much worry and hardship.

Fel'annár had chosen brown leather breeches and boots. A calf-length suede tunic of muted green lay over a white shirt, open at the chest. More of his hair was down today, only some of his Ari locks sat upon his crown. Poking proudly out of the very top, was a Chiboo feather Llyniel had found and saved for an occasion such as this.

Hanging from a long lock on the right side of his temple, the Heliaré rested upon his shoulder. On the other side, two honour stones. One had been given to him by Alféna of Sen'oléi after the fires that had threatened to kill her children. The other had been Or'Talán's, given to him by Pan'assár for his protection of the royal family.

But it was much more than that.

His mother had touched this, likely found it on some riverbed in the Deep Forest. He reached up, smoothed a finger over the smooth turquoise. It was the only thing he had that had been hers, and although he had always felt close to her in his dreams, this simple stone brought her into the waking world, made her seem *real*.

He left the bathing room, entered the front room where Llyniel was waiting for him.

He smiled as his eyes roved over her form.

Her dress was light and airy, made for dancing and enticing, beautiful and elegant yet practical and comfortable. There was no corset to it, nothing that would press against her skin and yet it was fitted, a slightly lighter green than Fel'annár's tunic. Her auburn hair sat loose around her, save for the Bonding Braid she had adorned with small white flowers.

He offered her his arm, and together, they left their quarters, bound for Sontúr's rooms on the floor below.

With Tensári now walking behind them, they took the stairs and were soon at the prince's door. It was an excited Carodel who let them in.

Sontúr was sitting in an armchair beside Maeneth. While he was dressed in lounging clothes, she had changed into a simple blue dress. She hadn't bothered with her braids, her silvery-blonde hair loose around her shoulders. It would have been a scandal had they been at court. But they weren't, and besides, Llyniel knew Maeneth wouldn't have cared about that. Pelagia was different, she had always said that, and Llyniel knew the truth of it.

Opposite the prince and princess, the two commanders sat in civilian attire. Strange sight, mused Fel'annár, only now realising that he had hardly ever seen them like this, relaxed and off duty.

Around them, The Company stood, looking as splendid as Fel'annár had ever seen them. Colourful tunics and hair, ribbons and beads in Carodel's hair, his lyre on his back. It had been polished, surely tuned, ready to sing songs and cast spells whenever the moment took him.

Ramien and Galdith had both chosen purple while Galadan wore deep blue, Tensári strict black. She was the only one amongst them who would carry her sword, but that did not mean the others were unarmed.

"Enjoy your party then, Prince," smiled Fel'annár, eyes sliding from Maeneth to Sontúr. He was rewarded by an acute arch of an imperious brow.

His friend was in good hands, and with a final nod at the commanders, Fel'annár, Llyniel and The Company left.

JUST FIVE MINUTES on horseback from the city and already, the plains
were dotted with small campfires and groups of Silvans, mainly warriors
recently come from the Deep Forest. Their horses grazed nearby, while
their riders sat and talked, and their fires burned brighter against the
ever-darkening sky.

They could no longer canter and so they continued at an easy trot,
pointing at this or that warrior, or returning the many salutes they
received along the way.

Here, on the outskirts of the celebration, many still hadn't met
Fel'annár, had only ever heard of The Company from others.

The closer they drew to the glade where once, a sea of white tarpaulins had stretched far and wide, the louder the hails and the more
familiar the faces. Someone called out to Carodel, who held his lyre over
his head like a trophy and the warriors cheered. It made Fel'annár smile
and he turned to Galadan, wondered if his stony face had cracked yet. It
hadn't, but there was fire in his eyes. He would be one of the few Alpines
at this celebration.

They could see the cooking pits now, smell the roasting haunches
and see the musicians, hear them as they tuned their strings. Amongst a
sea of colourful cloth, of ribbons and streamers, feathers and velvet, a
perfect circle of sitting elves, inside which there was nothing – not yet.
That was where the performers would sing and later, where all of them
would dance to the rhythm of the woodland drums, flutes and lyres.

The Company tethered their horses and soon scattered. Fel'annár
pulled Llyniel close to his side and made his lazy way towards the centre
circle, knowing that Tensári was somewhere behind them.

Erthoron and Lorthil sat together with a scattering of lords and
ladies. On the opposite side of the circle, he saw Alei, Vasanth and Bulan.

They saw others too. Dalú and Amon, Benat who wore his Kah sash
even now, in civilian clothing. The apprentice captains Salo and Henú
were there too, talking animatedly, eyes on everyone around them,

although especially on a group of girls who sat close by, laughing and chatting.

Fel'annár was enjoying himself for the first time in months. It had been a hard and trying year for him, but in many, if not all ways, this was its culmination.

He looked up, into the boughs where others sat, looking down on the party that would soon begin.

And then the first drums began a soft rhythm, and a trio of flutes accompanied. A merry tune and the voices and the laughing became louder as feet began to tap against the ground, hands against knees, palm against palm.

Llyniel and Fel'annár shared a smile and a kiss as they made for the circle. Llyniel tugged on his arm and led him towards Miren and Aradan, the only other Alpine Fel'annár had seen so far.

The people cheered at their coming, watched the Warlord and his bonded as they sat and greeted friends, acquaintances and family. From further along the circle, Erthoron too watched them, as much as he watched Amareth from afar.

Aradan and Miren watched the Warlord and their daughter approach. Strange though it seemed, they had rarely seen them together on informal occasions such as this one. Miren smiled, turned to Aradan, saw the pride in his eyes, but it was mixed with apprehension. Miren thought she knew what he was thinking.

"He loves her, Aradan."

"I know. But his duty will always come first."

"As will yours." She smiled, saw his surprise and turned back to the spectacle.

"THIS IS THE GOOD STUFF," murmured Fel'annár as he drank, eyes on the bottle.

"Hum." Llyniel drank deeply. She knew exactly what it was. "Pelagian Green. Maeneth's favourite. This must have come from the King's pantry."

"Amareth would love this. She should be here," murmured Fel'annár as he drank again. "Instead, she's over there, serving the food, keeping out of the way." He supposed she took refuge there, so that she wouldn't have to endure the uncomfortable silence of estranged family. Now that he thought about it, she was always working, always busy with something.

Despite the merrymaking and light-hearted foolery around him, he suddenly felt sad. It wasn't right and he sat up, turned to Llyniel. Wordless yet resolute, he thought she understood him, knew that she had when she smiled and gestured towards the kitchens.

He stood, made for where Amareth was handing out plates of steaming meat. She was so immersed in her work, she startled when Fel'annár appeared before her. Her straight face cracked and pulled tight as she smiled.

"You're looking handsome." And then she started, smile evaporating, eyes on the turquoise stone in his hair.

"Where did you get that?"

Fel'annár cocked his head to one side, tried to read her emotions but he wasn't sure what he was seeing. He gestured to one side, waited for another elf to take Amareth's place behind the kitchens.

"You recognise this?"

She stared back at him, seemed torn as to whether she should tell him.

"Pan'assár gave it to me. He told me Lássira gave it to Or'Talán. The commander then gave it to me, in thanks for my service."

"You wear it proudly," she said, eyes glassy.

"Of course. It's the only thing I have of my mother."

There. It was regret he could see. Sorrow, and perhaps guilt.

"When ... when it happened, after your mother was gone, I ... collected her things, packed them away in a chest and left them in the tree where she had sought refuge. She gave birth to you there, lived there for the first months of your life. I ... couldn't bring myself to retrieve them, couldn't risk you finding anything that would open your eyes to the story of your family.

"I was wrong, Fel'annár. In so many things, and my only excuse are my own, fragile emotions, my desire to protect you above all else. I know now that it was cruel of me, but can you understand that I could not see that at the time? All I could see was her death. All I could imagine was how they would come for you – kill you."

Fel'annár could see her heart in her eyes, knew that she was telling the truth. Once, he would have been sceptical, but after everything that had happened, everything she had told him, confessed to.

He was beginning to realise that Amareth was a woman traumatised by a tragic incident, one that led her to do questionable things, without realising their impact. He smiled softly, reached out to touch her cheek.

"Then when I am free to travel, I would go to that place, find that chest, retrieve my mother's things."

Amareth's bottom lip quivered, tears threatened to spill from her eyes. So much regret. So much weight she carried in her soul. He pulled her to him, embraced her, felt her rigid body relax.

He held her at arm's length, and with a cheeky grin, he gestured to her pinny. "Come join us."

"I promised I would ..."

"Amareth. Come. Sit with us. Enjoy the day. You helped to bring this about. You deserve to enjoy the fruits of your efforts these last months." He saw her eyes wander to the fires, to those who sat there. Alei and Bulan, Llyniel and then Erthoron whom she found staring back at her. She looked over her shoulder, to her fellow volunteers who were serving the people. They smiled, waved at her to go, and then nodded at the Warlord. Amareth turned back to her son, already pulling on the ties of her apron.

Fel'annár offered her his arm, she took it and then led her towards the circle. He walked slowly, almost like a parade and as they passed, he greeted those he recognised. He turned to his aunt, her hesitant hope replaced by beaming joy. This one simple gesture, this public recognition meant more to her than Fel'annár could ever know. He knew the gossip, had heard it a thousand times but today, it would end because Fel'annár suddenly realised that he finally understood her. And in that knowledge, came forgiveness.

Fel'annár made for where Erthoron sat, watched him watch Amareth, as he always did. He walked towards the Elder, watched him shuffle sideways to make room for her. Amareth sat, and Fel'annár crouched before her. "You belong here, I think." He turned to a shocked

Erthoron, smiled, nodded and then left his aunt with the promise of a dance later.

Whether it was his imagination or not, the noise seemed to pick up and Fel'annár was soon beside Llyniel once more, eating and watching the fun.

Fel'annár spotted Narosén and Lorthil close to the trees, talking quietly, faces grave. But then he grinned at the sight of Narosén's boot tapping to the rhythm of the music.

A streak of purple and a scandalous laugh, Carodel was splitting his sides at some prank, and further along, Ramien and Idernon were talking to a group of young warriors who had surrounded them. He had still to locate Galadan and Galdith and as for Tensári, she would be up in the boughs, watching from above.

It would be a long and glorious night.

Sontúr walked somewhat unsteadily to the bathing area of his quarters, wishing the various herbs, roots and tinctures they had used to fog his mind would wear off more quickly.

He looked into the mirror, reached up with one hand and tried to comb out his hair with his fingers. He wanted to braid his side locks but that was not going to happen. He looked ill, dark shadows under his eyes, complexion too pale, even for an Alpine.

Damn it.

He picked up a small vial of scent, fumbled with the cork. He eventually managed to lever it off, the damn top flying away and rolling under the basin.

Sod it.

One more look, a scowl at himself and he walked back to the living room. But his frown soon dissolved, and his foggy eyes sharpened. He didn't care that Maeneth was likely with him because she was grateful to him for saving Rinon's life. All that mattered was that she stayed.

He sat carefully in his armchair, and then nodded at Pan'assár, watched as he poured more wine into their glasses. Reaching for it with his good hand he drank, glanced sideways at the princess, watched as she sipped, her light blue eyes drifting towards him, not quite catching his glance but knowing he was watching.

Someone cleared their throat.

"Gor'sadén and I have a dinner engagement. We are loath to leave you, but I am sure Prince Sontúr is tired." Pan'assár stood, straightened his tunic. "Have a pleasant evening my Lord, Princess." He bowed, as did Gor'sadén, and then left the room, a sly smile dancing around his mouth as they made down the hallway, to nowhere in particular.

Maeneth closed the door and turned to Sontúr. She wanted to ask him if she was the only one who thought Pan'assár had left them alone on purpose. But she didn't. It was too early to tell if he returned her feelings. And yet she held to hope. She had not missed his veiled glances at her, his attempt at grooming himself for the evening.

There was only one way to be sure.

"What will Rinon be up to now?" mused Sontúr. "Will he go to the encampment?"

"No. That is a Silvan affair. Aradan is there as Miren's bonded. The king knows it is important for the forest people to speak freely, act freely, their spirits undampened by protocol. Rinon will be alone somewhere. Sar'pén's treachery weighs on his mind, as does the loss of so many of his warriors."

Sontúr breathed deeply. "He is protective of you."

"He is overprotective, has often imagined things that are not there."

"Like what?"

"For one, he thinks I am helping you because I am grateful to you for protecting him."

"And is it?"

She set her glass on the table, but her eyes did not leave Sontúr's.

"No. I am here because I enjoy your company."

He stared back at her, words stuck in his mouth. He hesitated, daren't believe that she returned his feelings.

She sat beside him. "You know how it goes. The courtiers and their flirting, the lords and ladies that dress their children like yule dolls and vie for a place at the front line when we pass. You have seen merchants laugh at your every word and you have heard countless declarations of admiration. But have you ever heard genuine interest? Have you ever been offered friendship alone, without an ulterior motive? There are few people in my life like that."

"My experience is the same. Even in the military, most of those who ever showed an interest in friendship were ultimately looking for favour or promotion. Besides my family, Lord Damiel, and Commander Gor'sadén I had no close friends, not until The Company came to Tar'eastór. For you I wager it was Llyniel."

"Yes. We grew up together, suffered much the same only I was royalty, and she was not. There are others too, in Pelagia, and humans ..."

"Bredja and Hamon. I remember them saying they knew you."

Maeneth smiled, wide, almost unable to contain the fondness in her eyes. "Ah Bredja." The smile faded and Sontúr could only guess at the sadness that had wiped away her fond memories. He had seen that same look on Llyniel's face when they had said goodbye to the mortals who had helped them.

"And what else did they say?" asked Maeneth.

He turned to face her, waited for her to look at him. "She said you were the best everlass ... and now that I know you ..." He lifted his good hand, reached out slowly, watched her eyes for any sign that she would object. But there was nothing and his fingers brushed over soft skin. He smoothed down the side of her face. "Now I know she was right," he whispered, felt his body lean forward, pulled by some invisible force and still, he watched her face as it came closer and closer.

"You know. If I were Silvan ... if you and I were at that festivity on the plains, perhaps I would give in to my impulses, do things I would not regret."

They stared at each other for a while, and then Maeneth leaned forwards. "Then we are there, standing under the painted lights, distant music, laughter, no protocol. Can you imagine that place?"

"I can."

Maeneth bridged the last inches between them and rested her lips on his. He pressed into her, heart soaring, mind bursting. Her lips moved over his, blissful friction. She tasted of mint and honey, a touch of citrus and fragrant orange blossom. It was the best drink he had ever tasted. It was sweet and it was heady. It was spicy and yet it did not burn.

Nothing made sense. Nothing mattered except that she stay.

She leaned back, only slightly, breath ghosting over his tingling lips and he couldn't help but stare at her, felt his eyes hot and his chest tight. This was something new, something he had never felt before and he dared to think she felt the same. He could see confusion in her eyes, wonder and curiosity.

He wanted more and he leaned forward, took her lips with his, hand resting on the back of her head. There was something there, just beneath the passion and the desire that was spiralling upwards, pulling him through the clouds to whatever lay beyond.

Her hand reached out and touched his cheek, explored the contours of his face, even as their lips continued their lazy discovery. It smoothed down his neck and onto his chest, leaving in its wake a blazing trail of fire and desire. It was a gentle touch from a rough hand, reminding him that she was not a princess who idled away her days but worked hard in the field to give her people a better life. She cared, just as his own mother had. A surge of exhilarating tension washed over him as she pulled him to her.

The sofa was no longer beneath him, the room melted away, just like his own reasoning mind. That intangible truth was rising upwards until it broke the waters of his consciousness. He was floating, suspended upon strange currents – warm and calm – utterly soothing.

Gods but he needed more, wanted to touch the intangible, knew the truth that brushed against his mind.

The intangible solidified and Sontúr focussed on the darker blue flecks in a sea of ice. Maeneth's eyes reflected a truth he knew lay in his own grey eyes.

So fast. So clear. No doubts.

But he wouldn't tell Maeneth. Not yet.

THE KING STOOD in his riding gear, looking out over the Evergreen Wood, contemplating the return of Maeneth, and that first dinner together with all his children, after more than fifty years.

He had told them of his unbroken bond with Lássira, but not what he intended to do once the final puzzle about his father's letter was solved - once he knew what the letter contained. Or'Talán had approved of Lássira but Thargodén wanted to know what his father was thinking. He needed to understand his reasoning before he righted a wrong committed against the Silvan people.

He smiled softly, conjured Lássira in his mind.

He would declare Lássira his queen, and Fel'annár the prince he should always have been.

For tonight, he would go in search of an old friend, one he had not seen for many years, one he had missed. He would do it quietly and anonymously, because the Silvan encampment was no place for the king tonight. It was their celebration, one he did not want to dampen with his presence.

He breathed in the Evergreen Wood, strained his eyes over the tree-tops, as far as he could, southwards, past the Turquoise Lake where Fel'annár had recently ventured.

Thargodén couldn't hear the trees like Fel'annár did. But if he could, perhaps he would hear their murmurs of caution, sense their worries about the Forest Lord and what had happened during his trip to the lake.

If the king were a Listener, he might hear their regret and just below, something else. He would hear the voice of Aria, calming them, calling for unity. The Ber'anor must understand what is at risk, what is required of him. She had failed to make him understand because one innocent act of curiosity had brought the Guardian. She would not make the same mistake again.

There was no more time.

TWO ELVES LEANT over the plank drum. With a wooden hammer in each hand, they banged the planks, each giving a different tone of percussion. It was fast and furious, sounded like ten players and not two. Their simple melody struck a chord in their Silvan and Ari hearts. Even the few Alpines there tapped their feet, bodies swaying and bobbing to the beat. With the food all but gone and the wine still flowing, the party was coming alive.

The younger ones sat in the boughs or danced in the glade where the musicians played, but the more boisterous reels had yet to be performed. Fel'annár and Llyniel stood, bowed to Erthoron and the other elders and made towards where his other family sat. Bulan was not there, but Alei held out her arms and Fel'annár knelt before her. It was only the second time he had seen his maternal grandmother. The first time she had seemed distant, lost in a pleasant sort of way, but tonight she was present and observant, green eyes looking straight through him.

"Ar Lássira."

"Aba," he smiled, the word still strange on his tongue. "Where is Vasanth?"

"Oh ..." she batted a hand in the air around her. "Messing with the youngsters, no doubt."

Fel'annár could only imagine what she meant by *messing*. It was probably what he would be doing with Llyniel later.

Alei turned to Llyniel at his side. "Ara Miren. You are Silver Wolf. A fine, strong line. I have been to Sen Garay many times in my life, before my daughter passed."

"You went to Araria ..."

"We did. Zéndar struggled with his loyalty to Or'Talán after his refusal to allow our daughter to marry the crown prince. Fateful journey for it was then that he realised his purpose as Ber'ator. And then, when my bonded passed, I and our son Bulan returned to Abiren'á."

"It must have been hard," said Llyniel.

Alei nodded. "I don't think there is a word to describe such loss, child. A chunk of your own flesh is missing. A limb, an organ, something vital see? As if you should not have survived but did. I often wander in different places and times where perhaps I may see my daughter or my bonded, and I have often wondered what I would find, should I take the Long Road."

Fel'annár watched her, trying to decide whether she was wholly sane. He almost flinched when she spoke again.

"I wish you had been old enough to remember her, know her face."

"I know her face."

Alei frowned. "A dream, perhaps ..."

"A dream, yes. She looks down on me, eyes wide with love and sadness."

Alei straightened, eyes shining as they bored into her grandson's eyes that were her daughter's. She stared for a long while, thoughts wandering to the rhythm of the drums. "I am glad you have seen her face ... that you know her love for you." She smiled wide and then her eyes seemed to lose their focus and Alei was lost once more, in one of those places were Zéndar and Lássira still lived.

Llyniel turned to Fel'annár, squeezed his hand and stood. Pulling him up, they stood together for a moment. Fel'annár kissed her, and in that kiss was a thanks, a public show of his love for her. A soft ripple of *ooos* reached their ears and they merged into the crowds of dancing elves, a soft melody meant for reflection.

Two songs later, they left the revelry, knowing that soon, few would be *walking* anywhere. Rather they would be hopping, jumping, skipping and staggering, even crawling. Fel'annár decided he didn't want to see Carodel right now.

Inside the trees, groups of elves sat about, their own small, well-controlled fires providing enough light to talk or to tell tales. Llyniel had deftly plucked a bottle of wine from the long tables and swung it about in her free arm as they walked.

"Alei is lucid at times. She's not irrational, Fel'annár. She simply lives in two worlds, only one of which is real."

"I noticed. I wonder if that's what the king was like before."

"He was. My father spoke of that many times, said it was as if Thargodén was searching distant lands, looking for what he had lost."

It was such a sad thing, mused Fel'annár, and every time the topic was raised, he would imagine himself losing Llyniel. It was the worst kind of pain and the urge to reassure himself was strong. He pulled her sideways, step faster, eyes searching while Llyniel grinned, knew exactly what he was looking for. Privacy.

But instead, they found something else. Two elves stood talking in the distance and for some reason, Fel'annár stopped, still out of sight but not entirely out of hearing.

"... you honour our family."

"I should have done it years ago."

"You couldn't. I know the weight of loss. I bear it myself but at least I have my daughter. You had nothing of her until *he* came."

Fel'annár's hand squeezed Llyniel's. He should have announced their presence, didn't want to eavesdrop on his father and his uncle. Still he was shocked that they spoke so intimately, like friends – brothers, even. He stepped out and the two elves turned to him.

"We were looking for a peaceful place to sit."

"Of course you were," said Thargodén from under his ample hood, wry smile only half obscured. He had not wanted to announce his presence tonight.

Llyniel grinned at the sarcasm but Fel'annár was too intrigued. "I'm surprised you know each other ..."

"You are surprised we are not killing each other I would imagine," added Bulan. "No. Thargodén and I have always been brothers. We shared our suffering at Or'Talán's travesty. My father took me to Araria and in truth we have not spoken for many years. But your mother binds us as family. Your father is my law-brother and he has my friendship, my loyalty as a warrior."

Fel'annár nodded slowly, still processing his uncle's words and Bulan watched him carefully.

"I must return to the city," said Thargodén. "I came only to see Bulan for a while."

Llyniel turned to Fel'annár, ready to continue with their plan to find a place to sit, but she rather thought he wanted to stay, perhaps ask his father about his relationship with Bulan. She turned to the Silvan captain.

"Do you dance the plank tap, Captain?"

Bulan raised a brow. "I do, when the moment takes me."

"Then come and show me how it's done in Abiren'á."

"I haven't danced ... in a while."

"But today is surely a day to celebrate, don't you think, Bulan? After all these years, family comes together."

"Some are missing, Llyniel."

"Not missing. They are still here, somewhere. They're not dead, Bulan. Never forget that. You'll see them again. It is the wait that is sad, not the loss."

He stared at her, surely surprised at such wisdom in one so young. He stared for a moment, couldn't help wondering how many she had ushered onto the Short Road.

"I am a healer, Bulan. I have watched many cross, eased their journey, seen the light in their eyes as they depart. It doesn't die – it travels." Her smile was still there and Bulan walked towards her, smoothed a hand down her cheek. She allowed it.

"My nephew has chosen well. I am proud to welcome you to Zéndar's line, to the house of the Three Sisters."

Llyniel's smile widened and Fel'annár thought his heart would burst.

"Then come on and show me your boasting is merited."

With a last look over his shoulder at the king, Bulan and Llyniel left, leaving Thargodén and Fel'annár alone. Uncrowned prince and cloaked king.

"I have often tried to piece together the events, always failed. Or'Talán's journal has shown me the way forward but still, that you knew Bulan, that you were friends ..."

"Lássira and I took for granted that we would be wed. That we would bond as Silvans *and* Alpines, and we were aware that we had to fulfil both rites. We fulfilled one and to the Silvans that was enough. But I was not allowed to reveal that at court. Now, we know why. Treachery ran far deeper than any of us imagined at the time. Still, at least I know that he *intended* to tell me. That is closure enough. But I am searching for that last letter we know he wrote."

"Do you think it will reveal anything else?"

"Who knows. It was a letter meant as a goodbye, in case he never returned from the battle. It will not be easy to read."

"No. And you have me intrigued. How did you find out?"

"I paid a visit to Lord Draugolé."

"Who's Draugolé?"

"Band'orán's advisor. He sits in the dungeons awaiting trail and sentence. He was deep in the traitor's confidence."

"Will you tell me if you find it? If there is something there about my mother? I still have questions about her final days, things Amareth doesn't speak of."

Thargodén stared hard at Fel'annár from under his hood, and then cast his eyes up to the canopy, aware that it would be all too easy for him to be recognised. He wasn't sure how the Silvans would react to that. He had been loved by them once, when Lássira was alive. He started when Fel'annár stepped closer.

"I'm glad we've spoken."

Thargodén tried to hide his surprise, his joy at those simple words. He dared to raise an arm, a hand that was drawn like magic to the fabric that covered his son's shoulder. Below, his own flesh and blood, warm and alive.

"I am glad you stayed to listen. More than you can know."

Fel'annár lifted his hand, and then Thargodén felt the weight of it sitting on his own hand, saw the curiosity in his son's extraordinary eyes.

"I believe I may have spoiled your plans."

Fel'annár grinned, a mischievous sparkle in his eye. But it petered out as his gaze froze, somewhere just over Thargodén's shoulder. The grin faded, thoughts of his mother gone, everything gone.

The king watched, fascinated at the play of lights in his son's eyes. Golden specks floated forwards, as if he himself were suspended in the sky, as if he had suddenly surged forwards, stars streaking past him.

Thargodén couldn't breathe, one word tumbled from his half-open mouth.

"Fel'annár?"

No answer. The king glanced over his shoulder and then back at his son. The specks of golden light had expanded and all he could see was green, brighter and brighter until he could hardly see Fel'annár's face at all. He stepped backwards, petrified.

"What? What is it?"

Fel'annár swayed, forced himself to look at his father. He grappled for words for the chaos in his mind.

"Prepare for war, my king." He had said it so softly and Thargodén stared in shock, unsure of whether he had heard correctly. He watched as Fel'annár turned and strode away, hair moving too slowly.

∾

IDERNON LAUGHED as Ramien shoved Carodel so hard he toppled from the tree stump he had taken possession of. The wine, the heady resins and the simple joy of laughing once more. But there was discord in the melody and the rhythm, something that cut through the merrymaking, something Galadan seemed to have heard. They turned to the tree line.

A sound of a hawk, unexceptional save that there was an urgency to it that struck a chord in them all. It had been Fel'annár's call.

Something was wrong.

"There," said Galadan, pointing to the trees where a faint green haze seemed to be growing. Idernon's heart sank. "Where's Fel'annár?" His question was almost wistful.

"No," whispered Galdith.

"*Company!*" yelled Idernon, loud enough to be heard over the music, urgent enough to turn heads and for conversations to stop. The music faded, confused faces looking at Idernon, watching as the warriors of The Company came together.

Amareth stood, Erthoron beside her and then Bulan was striding towards him, Llyniel just behind. But Idernon was giving no explanations, not now and he sprang forwards, towards the trees. He was jogging, running and then sprinting through the shocked dancers. They jumped out of the way of the charging warriors, pulled each other out of their path. They screamed and shouted even as they followed The Company with their eyes, watched as they skidded to a halt at the tree line.

Green mist, like fog billowing across the forest floor, the reflection of lumoss on a humid night. It was inside the trees, creeping closer. More shouts as some searched for friends and family even as they inched backwards. Something was coming, but all they could see through the fog was the silhouette of others as they ran from whatever was coming.

Frightened elves ran into the glade and then turned back to the forest, hands out, feet retreating. Drummers clutched their hammers, cups and goblets littered the floor, plates of food upturned. It was Narosén who stepped forward, black cape billowing around him, blue eyes overly bright.

"Don't fear the Warlord, lord of these forests." His powerful voice encircled them.

The silhouette inside the mist became sharper, clearer, and more figures emerged behind. It was the Warlord and his Company. They looked upon him in fascinated horror. Some of the warriors knew this light, had seen it before yet still, they had never seen this, and their shock was as fresh as it had been the first time.

Blazing eyes and undulating hair, Fel'annár's skin seemed almost translucent, as if the light came from the inside but that was surely not possible. There were scintillating lights all around him, like sparks from clashing swords.

This was surely not their Warlord, not Ar Lássira, the one they claimed as their prince. This was a forest demon, a warlock of old, come from the bowels of the earth to wreak death and destruction and yet Narosén had said he was not. The Ari'atór strode towards The Company, Erthoron at his side.

"The Nim'uán is approaching the northern lands - the Xeric Wood - its path clear. It comes for our forest." Fel'annár faltered, his next words meant only for The Company, but Narosén and Erthoron were close enough to hear. "The wood is *screaming* ..."

"The Xeric Wood is dead," said Narosén.

"It's *not*," said Fel'annár, almost angry. He heard the warriors shouting, others ordering silence so that they could hear what was being said.

"Tell everyone to leave the forest, Erthoron." Fel'annár turned to the frightened merry-makers and lifted his voice over the growing panic.

"All warriors to barracks!"

Fel'annár was moving, striding towards the horses, tunic and cape whirling around him, hair like river reeds in a lazy stream. He mounted, waited for The Company to do likewise and then together, they led their skittish horses towards Bulan and his cloaked companion, waited for them to mount.

Fel'annár caught Amareth and Llyniel's gaze, wheeled his horse around to face them.

"Don't let our people return to the woods, Amareth. Lead them to the city, provisions will be made but expect thousands from the forest. Protect them, as you did me." His eyes wandered to Llyniel, while Amareth dared to glance at Bulan. There was a plea in her eyes, one her brother answered with a slow nod.

Fel'annár kicked his horse into a gallop and the group were away, thundering over the plains, Fel'annár's light guiding them in the dark. The Company said nothing, they knew not to because Fel'annár was surely still listening even now as they made for the Inner Circle and the War Room.

They had always known this day may come, even though some had held to the hope that the Nim'uán would attack somewhere else that was not their home.

Gods but they had come so far. Hope had turned civil war into a new beginning. They should have been rejoicing, rebuilding the land and the trust between Alpines and Silvans.

Instead, Ea Uaré was preparing for war.

PART II

WAR

21

THE FIRST TEST

~

THE NIGHT SENTINELS upon the walls had seen them coming for minutes, a small group of warriors enveloped in a shroud of green mist. Some urgency was afoot, and they stood ready and expectant.

"Open the gates!"

One guard scrambled down the stairs, gave the order and soon, the doors groaned as the mechanism was set into motion. The riders galloped through, an order yelled over a retreating shoulder.

"Commanders to the War Room!"

The group continued, not to the stables but straight up to the doors of the Inner Circle. There, two guards blocked the entrance, stood ready for battle, even though they quaked in their boots, petrified at the sight of the Warlord as he dismounted and stood before them.

"Open the doors."

They stared, jumped when another voice repeated the order. It was the voice of their king and as he stepped closer, out of the green haze, they bowed low, opened the doors and Fel'annár was striding down the corridors, to the War Room and the carved map of Ea Uaré. The noise was increasing, the alarm permeating the Inner Circle, the palace itself and then the city behind. By the time they stood upon the map, candles had been lit, and a slow stream of captains entered the room in varying states of dress. Gor'sadén and Pan'assár arrived together, and the captains made way for them.

Fel'annár stepped up onto the carved map, knowing that Gor'sadén and The Company were staring at him from the side lines, and Pan'assár was walking the narrow wooden path which led north.

The king watched from the painted trees to the west, close to the city of Abiren'á.

There was a momentary distraction as Generals Turion and Rinon burst into the quietening room and made their way to the fore.

"Where is it?" Pan'assár's opening question and the room fell into silence, save for the click of boots over carved and painted wood.

Fel'annár looked down at the Court of Thargodén, followed the City Road to Sen Garay and then Oran'Dor. Northwards to Lan Taria, Sen'oléi and beyond, to Abiren'á. He swayed where he stood, closed his eyes in pain and despair.

Help us.

"Fel'annár?"

He turned, eyes still blazing as he came face to face with Thargodén, saw the poorly hidden fear in his father's eyes.

"The Nim'uán approaches from Calrazia. On its current route, it will come to the Xeric Wood. Its objective *is* Ea Uaré.

The horizon is afire.

But Fel'annár knew there was nothing but sand there. Torches. They were talking about *torches* in the night.

"It brings an army. I have no numbers but there are enough to lighten the entire horizon. The trees say it is *afire*."

The silence was broken by the sharp intakes of breath from those captains who were familiar with that area, not the least of them Bulan.

"The view from The Doorway to the Sands is nothing but a vast expanse of dark at night. For the whole horizon to lighten would take many, many thousands of lights," said Bulan.

Turion exchanged a grim glance with Rinon. They had both been to the northern borders, to the Three Sisters and climbed the shortest of them, Bulora. The Doorway to the Sands was the last and highest lookout over the sands, to the mysterious lands of Calrazia.

Fel'annár scowled, but it was barely visible behind the haze that lingered before his face. "Are there Deviants in Calrazia?" The question was almost for himself, but Pan'assár answered him.

"Not that we know of."

Fel'annár knew that, still the trees didn't seem to.

"Can you sense anything else?" Pan'assár's left boot stopped just before the last of the trees, eyes moving beyond, across the sands and the end of the map, where Elven knowledge ended. "Do they bring Gas Lizards?"

"I don't know. But there is a ... disturbance below ground. It unnerves the trees."

Gor'sadén stepped closer. "Caves? Are they tunnelling like they did in Tar'eastór?"

"No. It's not yet clear what they mean. They speak of a *ripple*."

Even Pan'assár's deep breath was audible. No one wanted to miss what the Warlord would say.

"When will we know the numbers we are dealing with?"

Fel'annár thought about what the trees had said, how they had said it. He couldn't resist a momentary glance at Rinon. "If they can see the direction in which they travel, see or feel these ripples ... days, I would say. But how far they are from the borders is not clear."

Rinon understood that look from his half-brother. The warnings he was giving now were no less vague than the ones that he had given the crown prince on their patrol to meet Maeneth. Yet the entire Inner Circle believed Fel'annár, asked questions, requested clarification. They gave the Warlord the time he needed to interpret the warnings he was receiving. They trusted Fel'annár where he had not.

He would never make that mistake again.

Pan'assár turned to the captains. "Gather in the main hall in one hour. Send runners to bring our warriors to barracks and have them prepare. Generals Rinon, Turion, Fel'annár, Commander Gor'sadén, my king. Come with me."

Pan'assár whirled away, towards his office, mind already considering the decisions that needed making. Fel'annár turned to The Company, gestured for them to follow, even though he knew they would have to wait outside. Eyes still glowing, head aching with the prolonged connection with the panicked forest, he followed the striding generals and king, and in his mind, a distant voice.

Protect the Last Markers.

He wished he understood. The trees were sure the Nim'uán and its host were headed towards the *forest* – Ea Uaré – *not* Araria.

AN HOUR LATER, the leaders emerged from Pan'assár's offices, each striding in different directions but the king, prince and Warlord stayed inside for a moment. Fel'annár watched as Thargodén placed his hands on Rinon's shoulders.

"You are destined to protect this city, my son. Here, at the gates or in Sen Garay, you are our final bastion, should our efforts in the north fail. It will mean that Fel'annár is dead. I pray that day never comes. This is not a punishment, Rinon. You are a warrior, I know. But you are also the future king of Ea Uaré. You are our *final* bastion." He leaned forward, kissed his brow and stepped back. Whether his eyes were still glowing, Fel'annár couldn't say, but they felt full and hot as he watched.

Thargodén turned to Fel'annár, held him in the same way he had Rinon.

"I will not see you again until you are safely home. And that is my only order to you, Fel'annár. You are our front line, the White Oak and Three Sisters of your line, the acorn and emerald of the line of Or'Talán. It falls to you to protect our forest and although my heart screams to keep you near, my soul flares in pride at your departure." He stepped back, looked like he would say more but instead he bowed, turned on his heel and walked away.

A deep breath, a presence at his side.

"I wish I was going with you, know that I cannot. I understand my … our father's reasons. Still, it stings, makes me want to be a simple warrior and not a crown prince, so that I could ride out and hammer the guts out of this enemy. But I can't. You must do it for me. And when you have, then come back, see what we can make of this blood we share."

Just like Thargodén had done moments before, Rinon seemed to hold back. Something was missing and Fel'annár stepped forward, dared place a hand on the prince's shoulder.

"If I fail, Rinon. If I should die and never come back ... look after my people, Prince. Look after Amareth, help Llyniel if you can."

Rinon's eyes dropped to Fel'annár's shoulder, placed his own hand there after a while.

"You have my promise, Fel'annár."

He nodded respectfully at the prince, the elf beneath all the years of hurt, the brother Fel'annár had not wanted, and yet now hoped for. He'd had his first glimpse of him after that ill-fated patrol, but today was confirmation that it had not been a passing whim. Rinon had changed towards him.

With Rinon gone, all that was left was to find Handir and Sontúr. And then he would go home, one more time, say goodbye to Llyniel ... one more time. He breathed through his emotions, watched The Company approach cautiously. They were on the cusp of war, hours away from leading their nascent, fragile army to the north and yet Idernon smiled and so did Galdith. His own, sad smile joined theirs. He was about to find out whether his interpretation of the dream was right, or whether it was Tensári who had it right. Or was it Llyniel? She had said dreams of one's own death were a sign of change. Was he changing? Not dying?

He turned to leave but caught Turion's eye from across the courtyard. He said nothing but his head was held high, steely determination in his eye. As Pan'assár's second, it was his first-time captain who would defend the city in their absence and Fel'annár thought there was no better elf for the job. He saw pride in Turion's eye, the same pride he felt for his first captain in the field. He had believed in Fel'annár, helped him through some of the worst moments of his young life together with Lainon. He smiled, nodded and then made for the palace together with The Company.

In his quarters, Fel'annár found Llyniel and Handir waiting for him. He nodded, tried not to look at Llyniel as he made for the bathing room, pulling at the ties of his cloak.

He undressed, leaned over the bowl of water upon a high pedestal.

He washed his face with the cold water, splashed it over his chest and arms and for a moment he simply stared into the disturbed water. The green haze still lingered before him, his reflection fuzzy and distorted. He had known this moment would come. He had prayed that the Nim'uán was journeying to Araria, but it wasn't. It was heading for his forest, would be inside it well before the army reached the northern borders.

Or'Talán had found himself in this very position, decades ago on the eve of his own departure to the Xeric Wood and the Battle Under the Sun. Little did he know he would never return, and that he would leave his son thinking he had betrayed him.

He reached for a towel, took a deep breath and made for the bed chamber where Llyniel and Handir stood waiting. Silently, she helped him dress, not in the heavy armour of the Warlord but in the campaign uniform of a woodland general. It was lighter, made of reinforced leather yet still ornate. It would protect him well enough in battle, but metallic armour was not an option where they were headed. It would be one more burden to carry. Where they were headed, it was stealth, camouflage and agility they would need.

Fel'annár pulled out a large pack from his wardrobe. Opening the ties, he stuffed it with the items he would need for the journey. Some would be added later when supplies were issued. Llyniel handed him two small paper sachets.

"A Nim'uán is coming. Knowing you, you will confront it. If you get bitten, you know what to do."

He slipped them into a pocket inside his bag and then searched for his journal. Smoothing one hand over the leather cover, he pushed it down one side and drew the strings tightly closed.

Handir watched from where he stood beside a window. All that was left was for Fel'annár to arm. It was time for Handir to say goodbye. He caught Llyniel's gaze and stepped up to his brother.

"The last time this happened, I was upon the balustrades of Tar'eastór, standing in armour that was too big, a useless sword in my hands. I watched you face the horde, remember thinking that I was sorry, sorry for the way I had treated you, that we had not had time to become the brothers we are. This time, you are beside me and I *can* tell you."

"We've come a long way since then," said Fel'annár.

"You came back from that, against the odds. You must come back from this too. You have left too deep a mark on us all, Fel'annár. Father, me, Maeneth, even Rinon I think. But you must come back, brother, so that we can become the family we should always have been."

Fel'annár didn't know if he could come back, and no words could convey the weight in his heart, the thanks upon his tongue and the warmth Handir's words lent him. And so, he opened his arms and embraced his brother. After a while, Handir pushed away from him, and became *Prince* Handir.

"Serve well, General. Return victorious in life. This is the will of the King – and mine."

Fel'annár bowed low, straightened, enjoyed one last smile from his brother and then watched him leave. The door clicked shut and Llyniel was before him, eyes full, hands roaming over the expanse of leather that protected the body below.

His farewell to Handir had been too quick, just like everything else in his life. No time to savour what he wanted most. Now, as he stood before his Connate, he wanted to tell her what she meant to him, tell her she was everything, but he couldn't. All he did was stare at her, at those eyes that had beguiled him the very first time he had seen her. He marched to war now, and perhaps even destruction. The forest may burn, and the trees may fall, their voices silenced yet she would remain. She was inside him and if he was to die in this war, she would still be there. She was the strength in his arm, and the weight in his heart, like an anchor to a wandering ship, bread in an empty belly, water to a parched warrior. He pulled her into his arms and kissed her, felt her tears over his fingers, his own in her hair.

"If this is the end, then I *will* see you again. I will find you."

"And if it's not the end, I'll count the days until you return. I think I'll know if you pass ..."

He pulled her to him, tucked her head under his chin, as if to banish those thoughts. "If it happens, you must live your life here, Llyniel." Even as he said it, he could feel her head shaking from side to side.

"But if you can't, then take the Long Road, my love, take the Long Road to me."

The Gods but if he ever came back, he promised – he *swore* – that he would show his family that he cared, the way he always had with Llyniel. He would say the words he had never been able to say but had always felt, to Amareth, to Bulan, his siblings. He would tell Thargodén – his father.

He pushed away from her, had to, and then gathered his two long swords and his bow. Sliding them into the harnesses on his back, his eyes settled on the spear of Zéndar, alone in one corner.

Harvest.

He hesitated, reached for it. He didn't deserve it, not yet. Still, there were weeks of travelling ahead. He would take it, even if only so that he could continue to work with it, if time and circumstance permitted.

Securing it across his back, he banished the image of black stone statues frozen in movement and turned to Llyniel, perhaps for the last time. She was upon him, her kiss hard and desperate. One last caress to her lovely face and he turned, all but fled the room.

Armed for war, he strode down the corridor, jogged down the stairs with one hand holding Harvest in place, and left the palace.

He stood upon the steps that led down to the courtyard, watching for a moment as the warriors assembled and mounted. Torches flickered in the night, not yet dawn but the city had awoken, its citizens standing, watching silently as more came with every passing minute.

"Do you remember, Fel'annár?" Sontúr emerged from the shadows where he and The Company stood waiting. It was the first time the prince had left his rooms since his surgery. "It was me who had to leave you and The Company behind on the slopes of Tar'eastór, raise the alarm so that Gor'sadén could ready our army. We barely made it then."

"But we did." He turned to Sontúr who in turn was watching the days-old army ready itself. "And now, it's us who must leave you behind. You came here for this, to ride with The Company, but fate seems adamant you should not."

"I can still help, Fel'annár. I know this enemy, have seen its strategy. Aria forbid but if you should be defeated and it comes here, I promise you, I will guard Llyniel and your family with my life. I just pray it does not come down to that."

Fel'annár's smile was half-hearted, but there was a sincere thanks in it and he placed a hand on his friend's good shoulder. "Fare well, Prince, brother. Our paths will meet again. Here or across the Veil."

"I know. Go, and kill the Nim'uán."

Fel'annár held his gaze for a while, and then turned away, heading for where their horses waited.

AT THE GATES, Pan'assár sat in the saddle, horse agitated below him. The city burned with a thousand candles, frantic warriors and frightened people standing in their night clothes, watching the warriors muster. He had served them for many years, most of them good ones, full of satisfaction and friendship. But now, he faced his greatest challenge, since the founding of Or'Talán's realm, bigger perhaps even than the Battle Under the Sun. Or'Talán had led that campaign and now, Pan'assár would return to that place and defend these Silvan lands his friend had loved so much. He would defend its people, those he had discriminated against for so long.

This would be his last step upon the road to atonement.

In his mind, he smiled. This was his way back. From where he should never have left. His eyes landed on Fel'annár and then on Gor'sadén and ultimately, on Galadan, the one who had always followed him, in spite of what Pan'assár had done.

He cast his gaze over the two-thousand-strong host. Most of them belonged to the Forest Division, not a quarter of their numbers served in the Mountain division. This would be their first test of unity.

Further away, the clatter of wheels over stone as their supply wagons rolled towards the gates. Dalú was the newly appointed commander of logistics, a contingent within the Forest Division. As such, he would take his one hundred warriors and their heavier supplies on rafts down the Calro River. They would navigate north to Lan Taria, where Dalú would regroup with the main army.

First, five hundred mounted warriors would head to that place and then stay there until the foot soldiers arrived. Once they came together, in around three weeks, they would agree on their final strategy and push north together, to Abiren'á and beyond.

In the two weeks it would take the mounted contingent to reach Lan Taria, Fel'annár would listen and learn what strategy the enemy would employ. But one thing was clear to Pan'assár. Two thousand warriors would not be enough. His only hope would be to convince those who had left the army to return, tell them of the changes they had made. They surely lingered in the villages, unsure of the rumours, or perhaps unwilling to take the risk of returning and suffering the same fate. He needed to convince them, and Fel'annár and Bulan were his greatest hope to bring them back.

He could only pray that it would be enough.

Abiren'á could not be lost. It was the ancestral stronghold of the Silvan people, a symbol of their identity, one-time capital of Ea Uaré before the coming of Or'Talán. It was a holy place, and he knew these warriors would fight to the end to save it from the sacrilege of invasion. Pan'assár, Alpine commander, would see it done.

He would never again fail them.

Sword in hand, he turned to the king who had come to stand upon the steps of the palace. Around him, the last of the line of Or'Talán and their closest. Handir, Rinon, Maeneth and Llyniel, and behind her, Aradan and Miren.

Pan'assár saluted.

As the sun began to peak over the horizon and find its way through the distant trees, the cry of a captain, echoed by another and the long column of horses, elves, and supplies ground into motion.

From the highest turrets of the fortress palace, the Bird Masters launched their finest carriers into the air, five for each destination and across their feathered chests, leather harnesses laden with urgent news.

They flew over the long column of riders, squawking their own farewell. Soon, they would part ways. One group would fly due north, to Abiren'á, while the other two would veer left to Tar'eastór and Araria.

Their message was dire.

The Nim'uán brings an army to Ea Uaré.

Help us if you can.

"COMMANDER!"

Hobin knew that tone, turned from his window that looked out over the lands beyond the mountain.

"What is it, Jendal? Is there news from the Shirán?" It was surely too early, and a sinking feeling invaded him.

"There is a distortion on the north-western horizon. It may be an army."

He stood slowly, watching Jendal's face in case he had misunderstood. But he hadn't and he was striding from his room to the command centre, Jendal explaining what they had seen, when and where their other patrols were placed and when he had finished, Hobin listened to his heart.

It was the Nim'uán, he was sure of it. But where was it headed? Araria or Ea Uaré?

If the Shirán were right, if the Silvan Ankelar was the mother of the Nim'uán, perhaps that was its destination – Ea Uaré – the forest of its forefathers. The Gods forbid but did their enemy have a heart?

He found the thought disturbing.

In the village of Sen'oléi, Lieutenant Yerái was preparing to leave with the patrol leader, Mavorn.

There were only five of them, which was not surprising, because there were less than a hundred warriors left here, in the northernmost parts of the forest. Many had migrated south, or simply left the army, disenchanted with Pan'assár's command and the treatment they received.

"Mount up!" called Lieutenant Mavorn, already in the saddle. He watched as the others climbed up but Yerái was still on the ground, staring at the floor.

"Yerái!"

No answer. Mavorn had patrolled with Yerái often enough to know that he was listening. He dismounted, strode towards his lieutenant.

"What is it?"

Yerái had never felt anything as strong as this. It was like hail pelting down on hot skin, eyes burning, head pulsing, aching. He felt weak, wanted to sit down and then he felt a hand under his forearm.

"Divine Gods, Mavorn." He was breathing too fast, mind racing but he needed to concentrate, single in on the source of his dread, the terrible anxiety that was washing over him again and again. "Something ..." He heard an echoed whisper, floating around him, tugging on his mind, willing him to understand.

The enemy comes.

"The enemy."

"What of it? Yerái!" The hand on his arm squeezed tighter. He was trying, trying to understand where, the nature of the danger.

They come from the sands.

"From the sands ... from Calrazia."

Mavorn frowned, looked at the rest of the patrol who had gathered round.

"How many, Yerái? How *many*? Are they close by?"

Lead them to safety.

"They must all leave ... leave this place."

"Sand Lords are close by?"

"No."

"By all the Gods, Yerái, answer me. Is Sen'oléi under attack?"

Yerái swayed where he stood and all of a sudden, his mind cleared and he stood straighter. "The forest ... *Ea Uaré* is under attack."

Mavorn stared back at him in growing alarm. Yerái had never been wrong and he had never doubted him. And however unlikely his words seemed, the veteran lieutenant whirled around and ran towards the Community Hall in search of the leaders who had taken over from Lorthil and Narosén.

He needed to evacuate these people, on to the main path towards Lan Taria and then Oran'Dor. And then the warriors would make for Abiren'á and beyond, to the Doorway to the Sands. Whatever Yerái had sensed, they would surely see it from there.

If it wasn't already too late.

KEY'HÁN AND SAZ'NÁR marched at the front of the line. Behind them, a mighty host of six thousand Sand Lords.

Once the Deviants joined them from the east, they would have to keep the two contingents separate. They could neither march nor train together; it would end in death. No point in defying nature, they reckoned.

But they wouldn't meet with the Deviants for a while yet.

They were still days away from the Xeric Wood, but soon, they would be entering their new home, a place with enough water to float in.

First though, they would set up their mining towers, begin the gruelling work of creating a system of pipes, channel water northwards and into the sands.

It was a job that would take years, and how it would change the face of Calrazia. Those arid lands, where their chieftains fought for water, would become green. Their whole way of life would change; politically, geographically, and even culturally. King Saranuk knew this; it was why he had agreed to help the Nim'uán in their quest to conquer the forest.

Once their engineers had begun that monumental task, Saz'nár and Key'hán would set out towards their first and most important landmark.

Abiren'á.

Behind them, the twin brothers heard the muted conversations of the warriors. Clicks and trills interspersed with other, more familiar sounds, Key'hán and his brother knew this language well. He himself had always found it harsh, not quite elven, not quite human.

Just like the Nim'uán, he supposed.

Neither of the twin brothers had missed the surreptitious glances from the warriors. They were curious but would never dare ask their questions directly. Still, Key'hán thought he knew.

The Nim'uán were taller, stronger, more skilled at arms than even the best of the Sand Lord chieftains. They were pale, beautiful to look upon, unless they opened their mouths too wide, and their incisors would give them away. And yet there was no rot on them at all.

Not human. Not elven. Not Deviant.

The king of Calrazia had once said they were unnatural, and Key'hán felt sure he would not say it again. His brother Saz'nár had held him back from killing Jezurah the Great, but there had been time enough to see the king's fear, the downward turn of his eye.

Key'hán had enjoyed that.

He glanced behind him, to the second line of warriors and then beyond, to the black-clad Northern Reapers. They were not warriors, but their help in this cause would be vital – theirs and the other part of themselves – the part that travelled *below* the sands. They too were feared because if any of the warriors stepped out of line, Key'hán would send them to the Reapers for punishment, make the others watch.

Back in Calrazia, none dared to cross the borders into the north-western territories. Those were Reaper lands, under the command of no one. No chieftain, no warlord, only the tribal rule of the strongest clan. Always at war, it was a land of turmoil and unspeakable horrors.

Reapers were coveted by the chieftains for their *special* skills. Theirs was a kind of warfare that sent many an enemy running even before they could draw their swords.

Key'hán had paid them well for what he needed them to do. Still the trees and keep the immortal mages away from the battle.

Two, maybe three days and the first group of Deviants would join them at the Xeric Wood. Key'hán had promised them a life, a purpose beyond the mindless, self-serving slaughter. They would find a way to right the wrong that nature had inflicted upon them, find a path to the Source and true immortality.

It had been enough to secure the collaboration of the Deviants. It was already too late for them, but they would fight for their descendants, for their children's right to infinity.

Steady eyes scanned his assets, the warriors and Reapers who would march upon Ea Uaré and eventually, Valley and the Veil.

And then Gra'dón would come.

Perfectly shaped lips stretched, revealing perfectly white teeth, dark hair spilling over a perfectly formed shoulder. Key'hán tipped his head to one side and pondered his next move.

Everything was going to plan. Vorn'asté's forces were being stretched in Tar'eastór, Deviants were keeping the Ari'atór of Araria busy, just as they were in the south, close to the Elvenking's palace.

Soon, they would execute the penultimate step in their plan, and the cruelty of his father's people would be one of their greatest assets.

Fear.

Sand Lords were good at that, Key'hán and his brothers knew it well.

He peered into the distance, could still see the advance group of Sand Lords and Reapers he had sent out. They were nothing but a shimmering black stain on the wavy horizon, the forest just a week away for them.

Key'hán could already imagine the lush greenness below his boots, the refreshing cold of a forest brook on his naked skin. He could even learn to swim.

All he needed to do was find the mages, perhaps even the one who had killed his brother Xar'dón. Key'hán had no way of knowing if he was there, whether he was the only one who could move the trees. But he had resolved to take no chances.

The Sand Lords had been studying this forest for years, mapping it and observing it, learning all they could from the people before they killed them. Raid by raid, they had grafted an accurate map, had observed the mechanisms, the houses, the food and animals. They had all they needed to craft a plan to disable the trees, neutralise the threat of the mages.

It was almost time. Tonight, Key'hán and Saz'nár would dine in their tent but soon, they would feast as masters of their own lands at last.

Ea Uaré, they called it, Great Forest Belt.

Time to forge a home.

Time to find their family.

22

A NEW HOME

～

HOBIN SAT IN THE SADDLE, surveying his troops. One thousand Ari'atór already mounted, armed and ready for travel, their horses laden with the supplies they would need for the journey ahead.

The ultimate destination of what they now knew was an army in the distance, was still to be defined. But whichever the case, he could not let the beast come any closer. The Xeric Wood was uncomfortably close to the eastern borders of Araria. But it was more than that. Abiren'á must not be breached, even approached. Hobin would protect that place because their children were there, future warriors of Araria. Indeed, for many of his Ari'atór, this was a return home, a stand to defend their roots, their families. Hobin couldn't allow this place to fall, because if it did, he somehow knew that the Nim'uán would make it to the very gates of Thargodén's city.

He prayed that Fel'annár had sensed the enemy, that he was already on his way. But if Ea Uaré *was* its goal, then he knew it would be too late to stop the enemy from entering the Great Forest. Speed was paramount, but once they were at the borders, Hobin would wait for a sign from

Thargodén's forces. Although they were allies, he had no intention of thwarting Pan'assár's strategy.

Hobin had left the remaining army of Araria exactly where it was, protecting The Source. All he could do was pray that Gor'sadén was still in Ea Uaré, that young Fel'annár had accepted his duty, understood his purpose and that he was strong enough to rally his people and march north, Silvans and Alpines united at last before the common enemy.

RINON RAN a hand down his face, hair dishevelled, tunic not quite straight, not that he gave a damn right now.

He stretched in his armchair, turned to Turion who sat at his desk, hunched over a pile of papers. Both of them had worked through the night.

This was Pan'assár's domain within the Inner Circle, one Turion would now inhabit while the commander was away.

It was almost as big as his own quarters at the palace, and Rinon knew the commander often slept here. And why wouldn't he? The main area was an ample office with all the books and references he could need as commander general. But behind, was a spacious bedchamber with plenty of storage for armour and weapons, and beyond, a comfortable bathing area. Rinon wagered Turion would stay here himself during the war campaign. He needed to be close to the Inner Circle now.

"I wish we knew more about what we are facing, Turion. To think we are going into this with nothing but two thousand warriors."

Turion threw his quill onto the table before him, sat back in his chair.

"It's suicide, General. Right now, our only hope is that Fel'annár can use the trees in our favour, as they say he did in Tar'eastór. Still, there has to be a way to find those warriors who left. Yes, many ascribed to Band'orán's illicit Kah army, but it doesn't make up for the numbers we once boasted. Where are they?"

"Still in the forest, or perhaps they journeyed away, to Tar'eastór or even Port Helia. I've heard there is a growing population there. If they thought they couldn't serve in the army under Pan'assár, then perhaps they have gone into shipping, or farming, or perhaps even private jobs protecting others. It might be worth journeying there, seeing if we can't bring them back somehow."

"With Fel'annár gone, I doubt they will listen. Bulan may have been able to sway them but he's gone too."

"But if they know what we are facing, surely they would rally under you, Turion. Pan'assár would be secondary to the integrity of their native forest. It is worth a try, commander." Rinon stared at Turion with conviction in his eyes. Port Helia was a four-day ride. They could be back in less than two weeks.

"Perhaps later. For now, we need to know what's happening closer to home. That Deviant attack on the royal caravan was worrying enough to warrant a search of that area. But herein lies the problem. There are only five hundred of us left here at the city. We need help, because if anyone was thinking of invading us here in the south, now is the time for them to do it. We're vulnerable and the first thing we must ensure is that our king is safe. Once that is done, I will consider sending you to Port Helia."

"And we already know that the danger may come from the inside."

Turion caught Rinon's gaze, saw the poorly hidden anxiety there. Sar'pén was awaiting his sentence, perhaps still thinking that his family connections could deliver him from what seemed inevitable.

"You know, Pan'assár would have pressed the king for his swift verdict, and I will do likewise. The sooner justice is served, the sooner any like-minded traitors will be persuaded to desist."

"I know. My father will make an example of him."

Turion's eyes searched those of his general, of his prince, for any signs that Sar'pén's fate caused him distress. He found them, and quite uncharacteristically, Rinon did not deny it.

"But make no mistake, Commander. I will stand before him and fulfil my promise – my last words to one I called friend, brother. My eyes will be the last thing he sees in this life."

Turion nodded slowly. "It will not be easy."

"No. But I will make it even harder for him." Rinon breathed noisily, stood and wandered over to Turion's desk. "You have been thrown into the deep end, haven't you?" "You were named Pan'assár's second just days ago. I hope you will trust me to help you."

And there it was, the Rinon that Turion knew, the elf that would not show his emotions because they made him feel weak. He would need his friends in the days to come, as surely as he would not stand pity – from anyone. "You have been banned from command in the field, General. Still, these are extraordinary circumstances. I have just signed a document lifting that ban as of now. I must trust you. I have no other choice. But if you fail me, General. If you disregard any of my orders ..."

"I will not, Commander. You have my word, my personal word, as Rinon, as crown prince of these lands. I will serve at your side, do your bidding, prove to you I am worthy of the uniform I still wear."

Turion smiled sparingly, nodded at him and then stood. "Let's get some breakfast. After that, we meet with the king and then later, we have a briefing here with the remaining captains. A visit to the almost empty barracks and then we must look at the novices we have available. The more advanced of them can be drafted into active duty."

"Novices?" asked Rinon. "Surely not."

"And why not? It's how I met Fel'annár. We were suffering constant raids from Sand Lords and Deviants. We had so many wounded we had no other choice. I sent him to Lainon at the Outer City Barracks." He shook his head, the face of his closest friend before him, as clear as it ever had been. "Now that I think back to those days, I fail to understand how I hadn't made that connection. I could see a similarity to Or'Talán and no mistake. But it just did not click in my mind. It was Lainon who realised."

"Was that when this plan was devised then?" Rinon had heard only the very basics of how Fel'annár had been found. He had never been interested enough to ask about it before.

"Our plan, was to protect him from those we knew would be displeased, should his presence be known. We worked things so that we could get him out of the forest, while others paved the way, made sure it was safe for him. We got him on Prince Handir's retinue to Tar'eastór while Aradan and I began the work here."

Rinon listened, found himself more than just a little curious. "You must have stories of that first patrol."

"Oh, I do. But come, we must eat, see the king and then brief our captains. Later, if there is time and we are not already asleep, I will tell you about that patrol."

~

THAT SAME AFTERNOON, with the bulk of their troops gone and the shock of last nights' events only now beginning to fade, Amareth stood in what was once the Merchant Guild. Aradan had lent it to the Silvan leaders as a temporary refuge for those who had planned to return to the Deep Forest after last night's celebration. But once the war advanced and the fighting began, there would surely be refugees to take in. That wouldn't happen for weeks yet, but Amareth reckoned there was no harm in preparing.

Her gaze drifted over the sea of makeshift beds on the ground floor.

What the Silvans had thought to take back with them was now here, freely donated to the cause. There was a blanket on every bed, and pieces of tarpaulin had been tied to furniture, sconces, anything close at hand so that each group of beds had a modicum of privacy.

Amareth dreaded to think that there may come a time when they would need the upper levels of the guild. Those from Sen'Garay and Oran'Dor would be tempted to stay in their villages, thinking that the enemy would not penetrate that far into the forest. But what of Abiren'á, Sen'oléi, Lan Taria and Ea Nanú? What if their army was pushed back and the entire forest was forced to take refuge in the city?

The opulent feasts and wild celebrations that went on in the Merchant Guild were legendary, or so she had been told. Foreign merchants, wealthy and influential, were received like kings, revered like gods for the coin in their cellars and the power they wielded in overseas courts where trade agreements were begging to be signed.

Large kitchen, large bathing rooms, everything was decked in fine metals and works of legendary art. It was such a luxurious and unlikely setting for war refugees from the Deep Forest.

Melu'sán, head of the Merchant Guild had handed over the set of heavy keys directly to Amareth, eyes full of all things derogatory. She had not wanted to give them up, had been ordered to do so by Prince Handir and in her eyes was a warning to respect it, to not dirty her palace of greedy followers who had taken far too well to Band'orán and his promises of wealth. They would follow anyone if there was gain to be had of it, and Amareth was sure that Melu'sán had seen the disgust behind her silent nod, the almost invisible curl of her top lip. She remembered their conversation well.

"You will return these halls in the same fashion you see them now."

"I'm afraid that's not possible, filthy as they are now, if you get my meaning, Lady."

The singular woman's features had hardened, nostrils flaring, eyes almost black in her ire. But she had repressed it, because Prince Handir had ordered her to hand over the keys. She would not gainsay royalty, that was not in her favour, not anymore.

It had felt good, in a guilty sort of way.

Amareth dragged her mind back to the present, turned towards the door, only to come face to face with Alei.

"Mother."

Alei nodded, looked about the transformed hall. "I can be of some use here."

They had hardly spoken since her family had come. While Alei had been distant, Bulan had been openly hostile at first and then had admittedly mellowed after they had finally spoken at length.

"I was just leaving for the kitchens."

"You have done well. Let me accompany you."

Amareth nodded, curious because she had not seen her mother this lucid since they had come to the city in search of Fel'annár.

They headed towards the palace kitchens, where Prince Handir had told Amareth to meet with the head cook. She was to tell her what she needed on a weekly basis. The king would then see those provisions delivered to the Merchant Guild. As for meat, Amareth would offer the services of the Silvan hunters if stocks were low. But that would surely not happen for a while.

"Where are the Healing Halls?"

Amareth pointed. "Two minutes away, beside the palace itself."

"They will be flooded once our people begin to arrive. Especially when the fighting starts."

"We have time. And Llyniel is Lestari. She will know what to do."

Amareth understood her mother's concern. She still remembered the Battle Under the Sun, how she and Alei had turned Abiren'á into a base camp. Healing Halls, logistics tents, accommodation, kitchens ... Alei had been instrumental then, a prominent member of society and Amareth herself had served anywhere she had been needed. But Lássira had remained in Lan Taria, just a little closer to her prince. She smiled at the memory of the good days, before the news of Or'Talán's fall.

That she and her mother could once more work together was a chance to mend the breach between them. If Alei could continue like this, lucid and very much in this world, Amareth would draw on her experience and wisdom.

"What are your thoughts on Llyniel?" asked Alei.

Amareth turned to her mother, surprised at the question. "She's bright. An excellent healer, they say. She's a close friend to Prince Handir and Princess Maeneth, although not so much with the crown prince. Personally, strange though it may seem, I have not had much contact with her. But what little we have seen of each other is enough to tell me she is a strong, intelligent woman. She will be an excellent leader."

"Is she brave?"

Amareth turned to her mother, once more surprised.

"I believe she is."

"Good. She will need her courage in the months to come."

If Fel'annár was right, they all would. Amareth had heard of the Nim'uán, heard what they said, had seen the destruction it had wrought on her nephew's body. Aria forbid he was right, that it was *not* heading to the forest. Abiren'á was the northernmost Silvan city, their bastion of old, cradle of the Three Sisters. Her native home would be destroyed, and the Gods knew how many other villages would burn in its wake.

But he wasn't wrong, hadn't been about anything the trees had told him. All she could do was serve on the Royal Council, make sure every decision made was the right one. And when she was not on the council, she would serve her people, here at the Merchant Guild together with the other Elders and her mother.

Fel'annár had charged her with the protection of their people, and she would not fail him, not anymore.

∿

FEL'ANNÁR HAD SCARED THEM. He could tell by the way some of the warriors could not quite look him in the eye.

Some of them had seen him react to the forest before. But this time, he had been closer to them, and the energy he felt - had emitted - was stronger than it had been before.

It made sense. He'd been in the Evergreen Wood, knew that something had changed, and last night was proof of it.

Pan'assár and Gor'sadén rode at the front of their mounted contingent. Behind, Fel'annár and his Company, and then Bulan, Benat and Amon led the rest of their party.

The five hundred mounted warriors would take two weeks to reach Lan Taria. Once there, they would survey the land while they waited for Eramor and the foot soldiers to join them. If all went well, the supplies from the Calro river would already be there when they arrived.

The truth was, that their entire army save for a few hundred, had marched northwards with nothing but Fel'annár's assurances that war was coming. It was blind faith to most of them, a surety to others: The Company, the commanders; even Bulan.

It was, perhaps, the only reason why he was glad of his physical transformation. It was something beyond his control, frightened others and yet it lent credence to his claims, whether or not they made sense.

The voice of the trees was incessant, as if they feared Fel'annár had not heard. They knew that he had and still, they cried out to him, told him that the horizon was black during the day, orange at night. And with every day that passed, the stain was wider, thicker.

The enemy was closer.

Soon, they would give him more details: the nature of this approaching army, its numbers and perhaps even their intent. Not for the first time, Fel'annár wondered if there were Listeners in the north, and it suddenly occurred to him that Bulan may know.

He turned in the saddle, found his uncle right behind him. There was an odd look in his eye. It wasn't fear; more apprehension, he thought.

"Bulan. Are you aware of any Listeners in or around Abiren'á?"

"I know of only two, one of which I know personally, a friend of mine in Abiren'á. But his skill is nothing like yours. I've seen him predict the enemy's position and number. I've seen him feel danger before we come across it. As for the other, she lives in Ea Nanú, but that's all I've heard."

"What's your friend's name?"

"Yerái. Lieutenant Yerái."

Fel'annár knew that name, wondered if it was the same elf they had met on the way back from Tar'eastór.

"He rides as a messenger?"

"He does. He mentioned that he'd come across you together with Pan'assár on his final leg towards Tar'eastór. He sought me out and told me of your coming."

Fel'annár stared at his uncle. "Is that why you came to the city?"

"Yes. We'd had no orders from the Inner Circle for weeks. We knew something was wrong. It made sense to make the journey there, find out what was going on and meet you."

"Once a captain, always a captain, aye?"

Bulan shrugged. "True. I once relinquished my command, but my nature is to serve. I can't change that."

"No. No you can't." Fel'annár turned back to the fore.

Yerái.

Was he still in Abiren'á? Was his skill strong enough to hear him? He resolved to send a message later, when they had made camp and he could touch the trees, because if Yerái could hear him, then he could tell them what he could see, keep them informed of what was going on even as it unfolded.

Fel'annár looked around him, at the predominantly Silvan troops from his own Forest Division. Less than a third were Alpine, under the direct command of Pan'assár.

There had hardly been time to consolidate this new army, and none for Pan'assár to prove to the Silvans that he had changed. These wood-land warriors were wary of him, watchful of the things he did and said, of how he spoke to his captains, to the Warlord, their division commander.

Fel'annár could only imagine how Pan'assár felt. Astute as he was, he would know that this was his test of fire. One slip and he could lose their respect, even their obedience.

But Silvan, Alpine or Ari'atór, there simply weren't enough of them, not if they were to face the approaching army with any chance of defeating it.

They would need to rally those who had not returned. From village to village, Fel'annár resolved to seek them out and tell them why they needed to return – accompany them north and to war. He would tell them why they should serve once more in an army commanded by Pan'assár, the very reason many of them had left.

It wasn't going to be easy.

He took a deep breath, focussed on the tree-lined path before him. They were on the outskirts of Sen Garay, closest town to the city itself.

This was Llyniel's ancestral home, ruled by the house of the Silver Wolf.

Soon, the sounds of thumping hooves and clacking tack, the snorts from the horses and the quiet murmurs of unsettled warriors would be replaced by the hustle and bustle of the townsfolk and their concerned voices. Their messengers would already have passed this way. They would already know what had happened and an important question loomed before them.

How far south would the enemy advance before they needed to evacuate into the city?

Fel'annár had no answers. All he knew was that they would most likely be in Lan Taria before the enemy breached their borders. It was from that point that they needed to be ready for war.

Fel'annár looked up to the darkening sky, an even darker shadow passing overhead as a flock of screeching chiboos passed them. It was still the summer season, too early for them to be migrating southwards, and he wondered if they sensed the oncoming enemy, whether their flight would confuse the messenger birds. He could only pray they wouldn't. Ea Uaré needed their allies in the weeks to come.

An hour later, they had reached Sen'Garay, and Fel'annár had not been wrong.

They had set up camp in a large glade just five minutes' walk away from the town centre. With Amon and Benat in charge, Fel'annár and

The Company joined Pan'assár and Bulan, and made towards the community centre in search of the Elders.

The place was in turmoil. People ran here and there, busy carrying boxes and baskets and all nature of packages that were being piled onto wagons. Supplies, they realised. On the other side of the glade, food was being prepared in large pots that sat over open fires, steaming and bubbling away, the smell of it surely reaching the camp.

The town leaders asked the predictable questions. How many were coming? What did the enemy intend? Can we defend ourselves after what has happened at the city?

How long have we got?

That night, with their bellies full and the guard set, Fel'annár sat cross-legged before a small fire, his journal open on his lap and around him, The Company minus Sontúr. On the opposite side of the fire, Gor'sadén and Pan'assár spoke quietly.

Galadan leaned over, enough to see the sketch Fel'annár had rendered. "Why does that not surprise me?"

Fel'annár said nothing, saw movement in the corner of his eye. Idernon was similarly peering at his sketch of the Nim'uán that had scarred Fel'annár for centuries to come.

It was a vicious face, screwed up into the snarl of a predator, lips curled back and up, incisors long and curved, designed for ripping and shredding, saliva tainted with some substance that inhibited the clotting of blood. Fel'annár had almost bled to death, would have had Llyniel not created the Junar potion. But it was the beast's eyes that struck Idernon and Galadan into silence. Finally wrenching his own gaze away from the sketch, he caught Idernon's gaze.

"What is it you've not told us?" asked the Wise Warrior.

A deep breath, a moment of silence. "It *feels*."

"Feels what?" asked Pan'assár. But it was not Fel'annár who answered him. It was Gor'sadén beside him.

"Sadness. Grief. Some deep-rooted yearning."

Fel'annár stared knowingly at Gor'sadén. They had never discussed it and yet it seemed both of them had seen it, close as they had been to the Nim'uán.

"It wants something. It needs ... *searches*."

"For *what*?" asked Idernon, frustration furrowing his brow.

But Fel'annár didn't know and neither did Gor'sadén. It was one more puzzle to the existence of the Nim'uán, and Fel'annár wondered, not for the first time, what Hobin may have uncovered in Araria.

No one spoke for a while and Galadan spotted a piece of dry wood on the ground. He reached for it, inspected the quality. Good enough, he thought. Reaching into a small pocket, just beneath his cuirass, he pulled out the one thing that always accompanied him, his only path back to his origins. A small knife designed for whittling and chopping.

And so, he began work on the wood. It would take some time, but the mood had taken him and, Galadan being Galadan, he wouldn't stop until he had finished it. Galdith watched him from across the fire.

"Never seen that knife before. It's tiny."

"Not killing any Sand Lords with that!" grinned Ramien.

Galadan shrugged. "It's not designed for killing."

"Well ... what *is* it for?" insisted Galdith.

"Chopping roots. It's my mother's herb knife."

She had been Master Healer of the Downlands. She had given it to him before she had taken the Long Road. Weary of the centuries she had lived in Bel'arán, she yearned for one who had fallen in battle centuries before. Galadan smiled for the years he had waited in vain for her to tell him she would follow him. But she never had until one day, when she quite unexpectedly made her choice. The last of his family had finally walked and Galadan was left alone with nothing but this one thing and a mind full of memories.

"You miss her," said Galdith, mirth gone, face staring into the flames, deep red glow over his still features.

"It's been a while."

Galdith turned to him for a moment, studied his profile, as stony as it almost always was.

"I did not ride with the colonists you know," continued Galadan. "I was content in the mountains, living with my mother."

"You never married ..."

"No. I could never make up my mind, you see. And that was a sure sign it was not to be, not in this world, at least."

"So how did you come to Ea Uaré?"

Galadan glanced at Galdith beside him for the first time, eyes drifting to the rest of The Company. They were listening, even the commanders.

"My mother finally gave up on the idea that I would accompany her on the Long Road. She left, gave me this. There was nothing in Tar'eastór for me anymore. With our commander Or'Talán and Captain Pan'assár gone, Captain Gor'sadén took over the military. It was a new start for the warriors and I continued to serve for years. And then the Battle Under the Sun was fought and lost, and the news came that Or'Talán had fallen. I left it all behind, had no ties with Tar'eastór save for my heritage and my loyalty to the king."

Galdith turned to better hear the story, while the commanders themselves leaned forward, eager for the tale of one who had lived those years from the other side.

"It was enticing, to see new lands, new cultures. I decided I would report to Captain Pan'assár, offer my services to the new king, Thargodén Ar Or'Talán. I served many years as his lieutenant. Good times."

Galadan stopped, glanced at Pan'assár and found him looking straight back at him.

"You did not find what you were looking for, did you?" asked Pan'assár.

"No. But I have now. I am glad that I left, glad that you returned."

A soft smile graced Pan'assár's face as he turned away, memories of a time before his fall threatening to blossom. He wouldn't allow it, didn't deserve it but that one smile told a thousand stories to Galadan and The Company. It was a passing glance at Pan'assár and Galadan's life as brothers, captain and second in Tar'eastór and then bitter commander and careful lieutenant later.

Fel'annár pieced it all together. He remembered Galadan from his own journey from Ea Uaré to Tar'eastór, how he had tried to defend the Silvan troop before Pan'assár, how he had disciplined Silor. And then he remembered how Galadan always seemed to understand their commander. The subtle communication between them before Pan'assár had promoted Idernon, their complicity on the battlefield. Theirs was a long and complicated history, one seldom spoken of. It was why they had all listened, eager for a snippet of Galadan's long life before The Company and although they wanted more, Galadan would not give it and Pan'assár seemed content with that.

It was time to sleep, and tomorrow at dawn, the commanders and Fel'annár would be joined by the new Kah Disciples for the Dohai. First though, Fel'annár strolled to the nearest tree and sat. With one hand on the roots below him, he opened his mind to the wind and trees.

"Can you hear me, Yerái?"

THE ALPINE-SILVAN ARMY had left two days ago and since that time, activity in the city had been frantic. Supplies, production, preparations for the thousands of civilians who may take refuge in the city – *if* their army was defeated.

Two thousand had marched north with the hope of recruiting more warriors along the way. There would be a fair number at Sen Garay, Oran'Dor, Lan Taria and Sen'oléi, if they could be persuaded to serve under Pan'assár.

Sontúr breathed deeply, yanked his wayward mind away from the marching army and back to the city, to Llyniel's quarters and the window seat he occupied. He was allowed to come here, go back to his own quarters just down the stairs. But Llyniel would allow no more than that.

It wasn't natural.

Llyniel helped him into a loose-fitting shirt. It tied at the sides rather than the front, convenient for patients such as he with one arm strapped in leathers. Over it, she draped a cloak and then stepped back and nodded.

"Good enough for now. You're not confined, Sontúr, but you can't jostle that. Stay within the palace for now. Avoid crowds. No jogging or running. You must protect that limb."

"I know. Besides, dressed like this, I'm not going much of anywhere."

"I know you know, but I'm reminding you – just in case. Now, Maeneth is coming here for lunch. I wonder if you could possibly be persuaded to stay?" She pursed her lips, gave him that bewildered Silvan look he recognised as undiluted and unashamed sarcasm.

"My agenda is tight. Still, I must make the effort, as prince of my father's lands."

Llyniel grinned at him, patted him on the good shoulder. "Tell me, how was last night's celebration?"

"It went well." Sontúr's tone was far too neutral, far too flippant, and there was nothing neutral or flippant about this prince. She turned to him, straight face, cocked brow.

"Did you *kiss* her?"

Sontúr's mouth formed a silent O. "You are a brazen ..."

"Well?" Llyniel frowned impatiently.

"She kissed *me*."

She grinned wide. "I *knew* it." She wagged her finger in front of the prince. "Now make yourself comfortable and rest while I get lunch ready.'

Sontúr smiled, eyebrow arched as he nodded at the woman Fel'annár had chosen as his Connate. No one would ever think that her bonded had just ridden away to war against a monster. She was Silvan strength, Alpine tenacity. Later, when she was alone with time enough to think, he knew that she would search for him, hang from her connection to him in her mind, pray it would not be severed.

He watched her move to the kitchen area, sat back and tried to relax, mind pondering this new reality.

He was alone in the city. The commanders, Fel'annár and The Company had gone. He had nothing to do except sit and wait for his arm to mend. He couldn't fight, couldn't really heal anyone with the use of just one arm. Still, he had promised Fel'annár he would look out for Llyniel and his family, and if the worst came to pass, if the Nim'uán defeated their forces, he would protect them with his life.

And so, instead of being the injured Captain Sontúr of The Company, he would lend his services to King Thargodén, become Prince Sontúr of Tar'eastór, statesman and seasoned councillor. That made him feel better, that and seeing Maeneth again after their first kiss.

His heart fluttered in his chest, made him feel stupid in these times of looming war, but Aria as his witness he could not help himself.

A knock at the door and he started, rose carefully from his seat, wished he could wear one of his finer tunics. He looked like a homeless beggar, hadn't even been able to braid his hair.

He watched as Maeneth hugged Llyniel at the door and then sauntered over to where he stood. He smiled at her simple breeches and shirt, loosely tied silver hair. She had been busy, he thought, curiosity leading his eye to the long scrolls she held in her hand. She smiled back at him with a hint of some mischief.

"Let's sit and eat. I'm starving!" said Llyniel as she gestured to the table.

With Llyniel at the head, Maeneth on one side, Sontúr took the other, so that he could see her while he ate.

Maeneth reached for the wine, filled their glasses and then drank from her own, looking at him from over the brim of her glass.

Sontúr glanced to his left, saw Llyniel watching them both, noted the slight quirk of her lips. And then her eyes lost focus for a moment, and Sontúr thought she was thinking of her own love. It made him feel guilty, until Maeneth lifted the lid of the clay platter on the table.

"Oh Llyn!" It was almost a squeak and Maeneth breathed in noisily, the steam hitting her in the face. "Creamy leeks and buttered trout. Too simple for the royal cooks. The fools!" shouted Maeneth as she helped herself and then slid the platter over to Sontúr. He took the serving spoon, tried to serve himself but the platter moved about under him. Llyniel reached out, held it still while he spooned food onto his plate, jaw clenched in frustration.

"Is there any news?" asked Llyniel as they ate.

"My father has driven himself to exhaustion these past few hours. When he is not with Commander Turion and Rinon at the Inner Circle, he is in the city, overseeing our production halls or with the merchants, procuring the supplies we will need for the war. And Aradan has his plate full so to speak, making sure they do not charge outrageously for it. All of us pay for these things with our taxes."

"Father is good at that," said Llyniel. "He can put even Melu'sán to shame."

"Well, that's saying something," muttered Maeneth. She shovelled a fork load of trout into her mouth, closed her eyes and hummed deeply. Sontúr suddenly couldn't remember what he was going to say and

Llyniel grinned as she ate, eyes darting from one friend to the other. Sontúr knew she was thoroughly enjoying herself.

"Even with Handir's help he is stretched to breaking. As for me, I have been away for too long. I have yet to understand how I may contribute to our efforts against the enemy. Instead, I have busied myself preparing those plans father wanted to see. If he approves and grants me the funds I have requested, I am thinking I could offer work to those Silvans at the Merchant Guild. They are excellent with plants and it will keep them busy, their minds off their recent strife and the enemy approaching their forest."

"I would attend the war council this afternoon, if the king will allow it. There is surely something I can do. I often counsel my father together with Lord Damiel when my brother Torhén is away."

Maeneth hesitated, flaky trout before her mouth. She slid it into her mouth and ate slowly. "A generous offer, Sontúr."

"Not generous, Maeneth; selfish. And I cannot sit idle any longer. If I cannot fight, I can at least contribute my knowledge and experience."

"Call it what you will," said Llyniel, chewing and swallowing. "Selfish or selfless, we must all serve, one way or another.

Sontúr smiled at his friend, turned back to his food and his careful observation of Maeneth across the table.

"Can we see those plans?"

Eyes alight, Maeneth dropped her fork and reached for one of the long scrolls. Undoing the ties, she pulled it open, arms stretched to the limits.

Sontúr almost choked. Cleared his throat and stared at the artist's impression of what she proposed to do with the royal palace.

"Holy Gods!" He chewed and swallowed the last chunk of leek and leaned forwards, peered at the work of art.

"Well. What do you think?"

"It's ... it's ..." Sontúr didn't know what to say, but Llyniel had no such problem.

"*That* is a building *I* would want to live in!"

Sontúr watched the intense yet slow smile spread across Maeneth's face. She let go of both ends of the canvas and then grabbed the other scroll and opened it.

"See. Up here, on the flat roofs, we have vegetables and legumes. Some will go directly into the inbuilt beds while others will be inside boxes built at different levels, like here." She jabbed at a part of the more technical plan she held up.

"And then here, we have the covered areas where the seedlings can be nurtured until it's time for planting. We can even have trees so long as we plant them in the right places. I mean no one wants to be flattened by a pear tree in their sleep, right?" She stopped, seeming to realise that she had been rambling, not that Sontúr cared. He wanted more, found himself as fascinated by her vision as he was by the vision of her. She noticed, winked at him saucily.

Llyniel snorted loud and long and then dissolved into a shaking laugh, holding up her hands in apology. "Oh lords! You two will be my saving grace in the months to come." Her humour slowly dissipated, and Sontúr supposed that he understood. The distraction was a balm to her anxious soul, just like Maeneth was a reason not to think of his incapacity.

But Sontúr was no fool. The following weeks would be arduous times for them all.

23

DOORWAY TO THE SANDS

~

AFTER LUNCH, Maeneth had left for her quarters. Boxes and chests had arrived from Pelagia, personal effects, equipment she would not be parted with. Once she had finished organising it all, she would meet Sontúr in the king's rooms and escort him back to his quarters.

Llyniel insisted on helping Sontúr to correctly place his crown upon his head, and then accompanied him to the king's quarters. She left him at the doors and left for the Halls while Sontúr entered. He found the king sitting in his office together with Aradan, Handir, Rinon and Turion.

Thargodén looked tired, Handir looked untidy while Rinon stared at Sontúr unashamedly. As for Aradan, he seemed frustrated, while Turion was reading papers he had brought with him from the Inner Circle.

Handir grabbed a chair and placed it beside his own. He gestured to Sontúr that he should sit. With a grateful nod, he did, and then turned to the king.

Thargodén had immediately spotted the crown upon Sontúr's head of grey locks. But the heavy leather contraption that held his arm to his body was a stark reminder of how it had happened. He glanced at Rinon, opened his mouth to enquire as to the prince's health but Sontúr was already speaking.

"As you know sire, I am unable to wield a sword at present, but I would serve in some capacity during the upcoming conflict. I am a trained statesman who has already lived through the attack of a Nim'uán. I have seen it close enough to know the enemy that comes although, admittedly, not as close as lords Fel'annár and Gor'sadén. Point being, I would offer you my counsel, if you would have me."

"King Vorn'asté is a true ally; this he has already proclaimed. But with your selfless offer our alliance is ever stronger. But tell me, are you well enough to endure the hours of sitting and debating?"

"I am, sire. Sitting and talking is not an issue, only movement. And although I cannot write at present, I can dictate to a clerk. I hope to take some of the burden off your shoulders, if you would allow."

Thargodén nodded. "I gladly accept your experience and your counsel, Prince Sontúr. The Gods know we will need all our skill and acumen in the weeks and months to come. Aye we knew of the threat, but it has come far too soon. Our army has barely had time to settle into its new divisions and contingents."

"It has been a scant few months since the Battle of Tar'eastór," began Handir. "Yet Fel'annár says the army that comes is large. It takes time to organise such numbers and then to travel the distance from Calrazia to the Xeric Wood. I must ask, since when was this planned? Was the Battle of Tar'eastór meant to be a two-pronged effort? Not on Tar'eastór but on Ea Uaré? Perhaps that army had mined the rock with the intention of attacking the eastern slopes of the forest while another army, the one that now approaches, attacked from the north."

"It is a hard relation to establish, Handir," said Rinon.

"It is but a possibility, born of the need to explain why there would be *two* armies, both lead by a Nim'uán, ready to attack within the space of months. The other possibility is that they wish to invade *both* elven realms separately. But that seems unrealistic to my mind – unless their numbers far outweigh our worst expectations."

"They may be headed for Valley," said Thargodén.

"Unlikely," said Rinon. "Fel'annár has sensed their direction. Tell me, Sontúr, how strong is Commander Hobin's army?"

"No one knows for sure. I can confidently say that it is ten thousand strong at least."

"That is a healthy number," mused Rinon.

"But consider, Prince, that Commander Hobin will never leave Valley without its army. Even as allies in dire need, he will be reticent to send more than a thousand or two."

Rinon pursed his lips. "With our two thousand and perhaps a few hundred more who join our cause along the way ..."

"Even four thousand will not be enough," surmised Aradan. "If the Nim'uán is in alliance with the Sand Lords, their numbers are impossible to calculate. Deviants are natural allies – if the Nim'uán can control them in any way. Add them to the Sand Lords and we have a serious problem. Although I find it hard to imagine an allied army with Sand Lords and Deviants."

"The Nim'uán command the Deviants," said Sontúr. "They form ranks, have a system of communication. They follow orders and are fearless in battle. The Nim'uán is their natural leader. The question being, are there Deviants in Calrazia? Or will they join its cause from the north-eastern slopes of the Median Mountains, the borders of Araria?"

"In which case, Hobin must have seen them already," said Rinon. "He is surely making preparations as we speak."

"Our birds will take a week at least to reach our allies. In another, we may have an answer," said Turion. "Two weeks and we will know the truth of it. Where, how many, perhaps even why. Hobin is already close to the area, but the Motherland will need five weeks of travel at least."

"But if Commander Hobin knows, he will warn King Vorn'asté. Some five days to warn the king, another few days to organise the contingent and five weeks of travel..." mused Rinon.

Sontúr nodded. "If it *is* the Nim'uán's intention to invade the forest, it will already be inside by the time Tar'eastór can arrive, likely even before our own army arrives. Battle without the help of the Motherland seems inevitable. Hobin is our only hope for immediate aid."

Rinon stared at Sontúr, surely knew he was right.

"If the battle takes place inside the northern forests and not the sands, it is not numbers that will count," said Thargodén. "It is survival, small-scale, close combat that will win the day. The Silvans will have the upper hand."

"And the Nim'uán will know that, sire. If it is headed say for Abiren'á, it will surely have done its groundwork. After the battle of Tar'eastór, it came to light that the attack had been planned many years before. Who is to say this is not the same?"

The king stared at the prince for a while, wondering if all those incursions by Sand Lords had had a purpose other than mindless cruelty.

"And there is also the question of whether or not the Nim'uán has brought a Gas Lizard as it did in Tar'eastór."

The rest started at the reminder of the Gas Lizard - an animal thought to be extinct – the beast which had wreaked so much havoc on the forest and then on Pan'assár himself.

"Pan'assár did ask Fel'annár, but he could not be sure," said Turion. "But he did say the trees spoke of a *ripple* in the sand, something that had unnerved them."

"Whatever it is, we must be prepared for that possibility, even as we ask ourselves what that *ripple* may be. We can only hope the Sand Lords didn't bring something new from the lands of Calrazia. It is unknown territory; who knows what manner of beasts may live there?"

Thargodén sighed, leaned back in his chair. "If there *are* Gas Lizards, if they somehow bypass our army, how can they be stopped, Prince?"

"With many deaths, either from the lash of its tail, or because our warriors are rendered senseless from its fumes. Commander Pan'assár was able to get close enough to stab it in the mouth and kill it, not before inhaling the gas and falling paralysed. If it hadn't been for Commander Gor'sadén, he would have perished. I can do some research, sire. I have some ideas I would discuss with Lestari Llyniel."

The king nodded thoughtfully. Everyone surely knew what he had meant by *bypassing the army*. It would mean they had been overrun, Fel'annár likely dead. The gods forbid that day ever came when he would lose his son before he had had the time to tell him how much he meant to him. But Thargodén was king, and kings always hoped for the best, braced for the worse.

"As of tomorrow, the Silvan Elders will be joining us. Their knowledge of the northern lands will be valuable to us. For now, we must adjourn. There are supplies to order and wagons to fill. The supply caravan leaves tomorrow for Sen'Garay and Oran'Dor. When our troops return victorious, they will need those supplies," said the king as he stood. There was one more issue to address and he couldn't help his eyes straying to his eldest son.

"Tomorrow at dusk, Sar'pén will be punished for his crimes. I have acceded to Commander Pan'assár's wishes that his execution be carried out in public. The crown prince and I must be present. Join us only if you wish."

Sontúr would be there. The captain's treachery had endangered them all, had sickened them all because his friendship with Rinon was well known. His actions were of the worst, possible nature. To betray a friend, a warrior who had fought at your side. To wish him death even as you smile and joke and call him brother. It was despicable.

As they left the king's offices, Sontúr caught a fleeting glance of Maeneth in the front room, scrolls in hand. He smiled and then turned back to the group, only to find Rinon watching him. After a moment, the crown prince's eyes drifted past him and to the open doorway where he knew Maeneth was waiting.

Rinon frowned, but Aradan's voice pulled Sontúr back into their conversation.

"I wonder how Pan'assár is faring with the Silvan troop."

"With Fel'annár's open acceptance of him, he has a chance, I think. Although opposition is inevitable," said Turion.

"Bulan's opposition is clear, aye," said Thargodén.

"And Dalú's even more," said Rinon.

An insistent knock upon the open doors and Rinon turned to meet the guard who stood there, paper in hand. Reaching out, he accepted it and then dismissed the warrior. He turned back into the room, opened the paper and read.

He looked up in confusion.

"The eastern border guard reports the presence of an Alpine unit from the Motherland. Vorn'asté sends aid but he is surely still ignorant of this latest enemy incursion. Unless ... this must be his answer to your previous call for aid." Eyes wide with dawning understanding, it was surely too good to be true.

"We met messengers on the outskirts of Tar'eastór, heading for my father's court as we were heading here. There was a private missive for Prince Handir." Sontúr looked at the prince, saw that he remembered the incident. The leader of that group had not wanted to salute Pan'assár.

"Well, it could not be more convenient, said Thargodén, standing. "How far away are they?"

"A week or so. Their commander sends these missives for you and for Commander Gor'sadén."

Thargodén reached out to the one addressed to him. Breaking the seal, he read.

THARGODÉN.

I send you one thousand warriors to help secure your lands from the enemy within. We cannot know what has transpired, but from what Prince Handir and Lord Fel'annár have said, you may have need of your allies, to fight or perhaps to rebuild.

I place these warriors under the command of Gor'sadén, to delegate at his discretion.

If the tide is dire, my friend, call on me once more.

Your friend and ally in the mountains.

Vorn'asté.

"This is an extraordinary stroke of luck. We must discuss how best to deploy them."

"One thousand!" exclaimed Rinon. "I just wished they had arrived before. They could have ridden north with our army."

"They may well cross paths, in which case I feel sure Gor'sadén will yield a good number to Pan'assár," said Turion.

Thargodén placed the open parchment on his desk, stored the closed one for when Gor'sadén returned. The emerald on his finger glinted in the late morning sun and a smile ghosted over his lips. She felt closer than she ever had during their separation. Thargodén knew why. It had started when he had finally accepted their ongoing bond *was* valid, that in time, he would proclaim it to the entire realm, not just his family.

He glanced at Sontúr, saw the pride in his eyes for his king and countrymen. "Our humble thanks, Prince. Now go and rest. I look forward to your presence on the council tomorrow."

"I will be there, sire."

With a smile and a nod, king and crown prince left, bound for the Inner Circle while Sontúr made his careful way into the living area, Handir and Aradan behind him, talking quietly.

Maeneth approached him. "Did you say something to my brother?" It was a low murmur, meant only for Sontúr. His left brow rode high on his forehead, wondering why on earth she thought he would do such a thing. He shook his head.

"I did not."

"He suspects, Sontúr. The way he looked at me when he left. He's seen something."

"My stupid smile?" he offered.

Maeneth grinned. "Possibly."

"And does it worry you?"

"No. It pleases me greatly."

Someone cleared their throat. Only now did Sontúr realise he had been standing far too close to her. He turned too fast, repressed a moan at the stab of pain in his shoulder. It was all Maeneth needed.

"Come. Time for you to sit down and rest, Prince. The Lestari awaits."

"Yes of course," he said sourly. Bowing at Handir while trying not to look at him, he turned, and allowed himself to be led away.

With the door closed, Handir turned to Aradan. "Did you see what I did?"

Aradan stared back at him, that age-old look in his eye that spoke of wisdom.

"I believe I did, prince."

DUSK WAS USUALLY a busy time in the main courtyard.

But not today.

There should have been warriors leaving the Inner Circle in search of food and rest. There should have been merchants leaving their city, bound for the outlying villages with supplies for market.

Instead, the captains of the Inner Circle stood around a raised deck. Behind them, what seemed like the entire city pressed in on them. They wanted to see the king's justice.

Here stood a traitor, they said.

But to others, it was time to retreat, time to comply until the future offered a new beginning, a new opportunity to pursue their dreams, dreams Sar'pén would now give his life for.

Here stood a martyr, they said.

The sound of a sliding bolt, the bang as it hit iron, the creak and thud of a heavy door opening. All eyes turned to the darkness beyond, watched as a figure emerged.

Sar'pén stood upon the threshold. No uniform, no cuirass or pauldrons. No symbols of office – no salutes. Instead, he wore a simple black shirt, breeches and boots. He had collected his hair into a tail, high on his head.

Rinon knew why.

He saw the guards behind him push Sar'pén forwards, saw the hesitant step of the one-time captain, the way he looked at the crowds, and then upwards to those who looked down from the balconies and windows. His family residence was on the third floor of the fortress and Rinon followed his line of sight, to the shuttered windows and closed doors. No one stood for Sar'pén and Rinon was not surprised. They would be frightened, and they were right to be.

It seemed to Rinon that the prisoner walked in a haze. He steeled himself, willed himself not to think of what Sar'pén was thinking, of how he felt. He conjured the images of galloping horses, of the arrows coming at him, and Sar'pén's bow, in his quiver and not in his hands.

He breathed, caught his father's gaze from beside him, felt Turion's eyes on him from his other side. They were worried for him, but Rinon would show them there was no need.

He forced his eyes back on the prisoner, watched him climb the four stairs that led to the top of the platform where a block of wood lay at the very centre, where Sar'pén would lie in just moments, his neck exposed to the executioner.

Turion stirred beside him, walked up the stairs and came to stand before the prisoner.

"Sar'pén, son of Dar'sán and Eluvia. You stand guilty of high treason. The punishment is death by the sword. Your belongings will be confiscated, their worth distributed to the widows of those who died as a consequence of your actions. Your body will receive no rites or honours. Your sword will be melted down, together with your Golden Sun. The king does not grant you your last words."

Sar'pén opened his mouth to speak, but Turion's hand was fast. The slap of flesh against flesh rendered him silent, and still, Rinon forced himself to watch.

He stepped forwards, until he stood at the base of the stairs, eyes level with the executioner's block.

Two guards placed their hands on Sar'pén's shoulders, pushed him down until he knelt. They forced him forwards until his head lay over the wood, eyes level with Rinon. The prince looked at him, willed Sar'pén to look at him, but his gaze was averted as his arms were pulled back and tied.

Heavy footsteps, almost time and still, Sar'pén would not look at him. *It is my eyes you will see, damning you to the deepest pits of Galomú.*

Sar'pén was scared, Rinon could see it in his dazed eyes and the tense muscles in his neck. This was cruel ... but then he remembered Fel'annár's desperate stand to protect Maeneth from the Deviants, and then the sight of her, safe behind him. Sar'pén admitted to masterminding the attack. That had been cruel too, and these, his final moments of anguish seemed fitting.

Movement, the executioner lifted his blade and steadied it above Sar'pén's neck. Rinon recognised it, saw the acorn and emerald at the hilt. Or'Talán's sigil, his own father's sword, the significance all too clear to Rinon.

Sar'pén looked at him then, his gaze steady, even in his defeat. He had believed in his cause, would have done anything to achieve it, even if it meant killing his best friend and his entire family.

Rinon could only stand there and watch, will his features to remain steady and strong, even as the blade rose high over Sar'pen's head and then slammed down onto the block, taking the traitor's head clean off his shoulders.

The people cried out, turned away but Rinon forced himself to watch, nostrils flared, eyes wide and full, all but shaking with the effort it took him.

He started at the strong hand on his shoulder, turned to Sontúr, saw understanding in his eyes, felt the encouragement in his hand, saw his determined nod, and Rinon returned it.

Sar'pén was gone, and with some luck, his death would bring years of peace at least.

THE SCRATCH of a quill over rough parchment echoed off the bare stone walls of Draugolé's cell.

He berated himself once more for trying to find a window, knew full well there were none. He would likely only ever see the sun again when it was time for his own execution.

He would avoid that if he could.

Being a martyr was well and good, except that one could not enjoy the result of one's efforts. And Draugolé fully intended to survive these dangerous times.

He tapped his fingers rhythmically over the scratched wood of his small desk. That echoed too.

'AFTER OUR BRAVE *captain's sacrifice, it is time to retreat for the foreseeable future. We must be patient; I ... must be patient.'*

DRAUGOLÉ WOULD SEND this letter to his wife Poronir, who would then send it to Lady Melu'sán. He had told one of his guards some sob story about loneliness, despair and his own regret for his questionable deeds. The fool had swallowed it whole, his heart much bigger than his brain. Draugolé would take advantage of him, for as long as he could, and should the king find out, well, what would it matter? He was already facing the death penalty.

'YOU MUST TELL THE OTHERS, *quietly and discreetly. There must be no further attempts to hinder the realm, not until Thargodén's army is on its knees and to this end, we must pray this Nim'uán is skilled enough to defeat Pan'assár and the Warlord. When it does, that is the moment we must act. Our incarcerated brethren must be enough to overwhelm Thargodén's paltry army and then fortify the city from the inside. If the Nim'uán survives the journey here, we will be waiting for it. It will never breach these walls.'*

DRAUGOLÉ SAT BACK in his uncomfortable chair.

The truth was that they had had the best opportunity ever in the Silvan-Alpine schism to seize power. But it had slipped through their fingers, and although that new concord was still tender and volatile, there was nothing like a war to bring people together.

All he could do was hope that this beast would destroy the king's army, decimate and scatter its tatty remains. And then Draugolé would have his chance, so long as Melu'sán's greed did not drive her to impatience.

'KEEP *me informed of the news from abroad and remember. I have the greatest of weapons, one that will still the king's hand should any of us fall victim. Only I wield that power over the monarch. It is a power that can be yours, too. All you need do is follow me.'*

IT WOULD REMIND Melu'sán of who was the commander of the resistance, in case she ever *forgot.* Yes, he was locked up in this dark place with no windows. But he was not helpless.

He was still dangerous.

〜

PAN'ASSÁR'S MOUNTED contingent left Sen Garay just past dawn. The foot soldiers would do so hours later, after they had sufficiently rested. From now on, the gap between those travelling on horseback, on foot and on the river would continue to grow until they reached Lan Taria.

Dalú would make it there first, and shortly after, Pan'assár. But it would be days more before the rest of the army joined them.

Fel'annár, the Commanders and the new Kah Disciples had found a place to weave the Dohai, the newcomers standing behind the Masters and Fel'annár, still learning the movements, memorising their order and meaning. Despite their dire mission, they had been exhilarated, wishing for dawn to come once more. It was all they had spoken about until the chiboos had passed overhead, their screeching and squawking making conversation impossible.

Later, on the road towards Oran'Dor, Fel'annár's eyes had grown bright, and for a moment, those who rode with him had suspected the worst – until Fel'annár smiled. It was an odd sight - glowing eyes and a smile.

Tar'eastór warriors were approaching from the east, heading for Oran'Dor, he said. They were surely seeking the main path into the city, the one they now travelled only northwards instead of south. Still, there was a chance that they would miss each other and so Pan'assár had sent out a small patrol to lead them towards their position. If those warriors were back up from Vorn'asté, they would be most welcome on the journey north.

Bird call drew Fel'annár's attention to the skies, because it wasn't a chiboo. The trees were still open enough to afford him the view of a magnificent hawk as it flew high above them. He stared up at it, straining his eyes.

Eee Eee Eaaa Eaaa

Graceful, it soared upon the currents over the treetops. The occasional flap of wings and it glided around the caravan of warriors. It was unusually bold, showing itself so clearly to such a large group of armed elves. He glanced at Idernon who rode beside him, who was chatting to Ramien, but when the bird squawked once more, the Wise Warrior looked up, shielding his eyes from the sun.

Eee Eee Eeaaa Eeaaa

The four notes were staccato, echoed louder than any bird he had ever heard save for a chiboo. It glided downwards, wings flapping forwards and two, thickly feathered legs reached out to cling to the very last shoot of an araucaria tree. Fel'annár caught a glimpse of long, powerful talons.

As the canopy thickened, Fel'annár could no longer see the bird. He wondered if it was hunting. Black squirrels abounded in the forest, would surely make a tasty meal for this hunter.

He hadn't been close enough to see its colour or markings, but it reminded him of his trip into the Evergreen Wood. It brought memories of his mad flight through the trees, the hunting bird that had guided him to safety.

He shivered, forced himself to think of something else.

When it became too dim to safely read the path ahead, they stopped and set up camp. Fel'annár gestured to Bulan from afar, inviting him to join his fire together with The Company. Pan'assár would be there but Bulan didn't know that yet. Fel'annár had few hopes of him ever speaking to the commander as anything other than a captain who was loyal to the same king. Still, he enjoyed Bulan's company, thought there was no harm in including him in their conversation, and if that gave his uncle a new perspective on Pan'assár, then it would be one step in the right direction.

When Bulan finally joined them, it was hesitantly. He glanced down at Fel'annár with a reproving scowl, sat beside him all the same.

"The main problem we face is communication," explained Pan'assár. "Has Hobin spotted the enemy? Where is he? Has he informed Tar'eastór and if so, where are they?"

"Are there messenger birds in Oran'Dor?" asked Fel'annár, looking from Pan'assár to Bulan.

"Not anymore," began the captain. "Our warriors told us they had been crated off to the city months ago, never came back."

"Band'orán no doubt," said Pan'assár. "He used them to send his messages to Tar'eastór. Those he didn't use himself were surely shot down, their missives intercepted."

Bulan nodded. "That makes sense, yes." He turned to Fel'annár as he spoke, crossing his legs before the fire.

"Those chiboos may well be interfering with the messenger birds. There is a chance the outlying villages won't know in time to evacuate the area."

Pan'assár leaned forward. "The natives will take care of warning their neighbours, Fel'annár. Once Lan Taria is informed, you can be sure they will know in Sen'oléi and Ea Nanú in three or four days, and Abiren'á in about a week, seeing as they must skirt around the Wetwood. But those in Abiren'á have the advantage of sight. The Doorway to the Sands lies on our borders and lends an unrivalled view over the desert. In the past, our warriors have spotted Sand Lords who were still two weeks away. Even if those birds don't make it, our sentinels will surely see them in time."

Fel'annár nodded, the map in his mind slowly coming together, the distances and the difficulties inherent to Ea Nanú, Lan Taria and Sen'oléi with respect to the former capital city of Ea Uaré.

"Now this incoming group that Fel'annár has sensed from Tar'eastór," continued Pan'assár. "King Vorn'asté will have sent them after King Thargodén's previous petition for help, before the Battle of Brothers. This contingent may not know of the threat in the north. They will have been on the road for three weeks by now. It is essential that we somehow gain the upper hand and understand where our allies are, where exactly the enemy is. If we don't have this information, and if our numbers do not significantly rise in the next few days, there is a chance that we may have to delay our encounter with the enemy."

"I wonder if the Nim'uán can be frightened by the trees. We could delay their attack for a few days perhaps," said Fel'annár.

"How can we frighten them with the trees?" asked Bulan. Fel'annár raised a brow at the comment and Bulan pursed his lips. Fel'annár thought he may laugh but he didn't. As for The Company, they looked at Bulan as if he had sprouted horns and bleated.

"Fel'annár has this thing he does with the trees ..." Oddly, it was Pan'assár who grinned at Carodel's comment and Bulan watched their interaction keenly.

"If you're talking about what happened in the Evergreen Wood, I doubt that would be enough to scare an army of thousands."

"You have already seen the power in Fel'annár," began Galadan.

"Imagine that energy channelled into the trees and then multiplied. He fought a battle with the forests of my home and won it. It will be enough, Captain."

Bulan stared at Galadan and then at Fel'annár, as if he were seeing him for the first time, but Fel'annár was watching the sky, a slight reflection coming from the back of his eye.

"What is it?" asked Gor'sadén.

Fel'annár wrenched his gaze away from the treetops and to his mentor. "Nothing."

Tensári frowned at him, and then started when Fel'annár rose and walked towards a nearby tree. She watched as he reached out to touch the bark. He didn't move for a very long time.

Can you hear me, Yerái? What is it you can see in the north?

Lieutenant Mavorn and his patrol had made it to the limits of the Great Forest Belt, where the Xeric wood converged with the desert sands.

They had warned the villagers, told them to make south, tell anyone they met along the way that they should abandon the north, that something was coming. But even as Mavorn had given them the order to evacuate, it sounded strange to his ears. The threat must have been great for Yerái to think they would even consider the idea of leaving their villages.

Some had looked on in scepticism while others believed what Yerái said. He was a Listener, just like Fel'annár. Still, by the time Mavorn and Yerái had left, less than half the villagers had packed their things and prepared their wagons. Even so, they had agreed to go only as far as Lan Taria for now.

That had been three days ago and now, Yerái looked up at the Three Sisters, the giant trees upon the very borders of their lands.

Yerai had wept the first time he had seen them as a child. Most elves did. Their size and beauty was overwhelming, humbling, almost beyond comprehension. He could have stood before the Sisters all day, but it was time to climb the shortest of them and make for the Doorway to the Sands.

"What do you think we will see out there?" asked the lieutenant who should have been a captain many years ago.

"I don't know, sir. All I know is that something comes, something important enough for me to hear the warnings from the trees. I hold to hope it is not an army but a large patrol. We could, perhaps, fend them off."

"Anything more than fifty is going to prove a challenge for Abiren'á, Lieutenant. In which case we may have to call on Lan Taria for back up, if there are any warriors left there."

Yerái nodded, gestured to the small platform designed for two which sat at the base of Bulora – Cloudsister – shortest of the three giants. Together, they stepped onto it and then grasped the wooden railings around three of the four sides. Two warriors began to work the mechanism and minutes later, they were replaced by a second group. Another three groups, and long minutes later, it came to a halt.

The two lieutenants stepped out onto the circular wooden platform, still surrounded by the lush canopy.

Yerái breathed deeply, and then again. It was like being on a mountaintop, and should he stay up here for any length of time, he knew he would grow dizzy and weak.

He walked away from the air lift, towards the northern edge of the platform and as he approached, the desert horizon slowly appeared before him.

Another deep breath, a hand on his shoulder and he jumped, turned to his commanding officer, and then back to the fore.

One more step, and then another. His flesh tingled, cold needles sending spikes of pain into the back of his neck, over his scalp, crawling over his skin.

During the day, desert horizons are orange, sometimes red.

But never black.

A voice from beside him, whispered in utter dismay.

"Aria protect us all."

Yerái turned to Mavorn, eyes wide, almost trembling with shock and urgency. "We have to get our people out of here now.

"The enemy will be here in two weeks."

24

THE HUNTER

~

YERÁI, Mavorn and the patrol rode as hard as they could through a forest this dense, made it back to the city of Abiren'á in a mere hour.

Horses heaving and sweating, the five warriors vaulted from their saddles amidst the pale-faced civilians who were already preparing to evacuate their children, watching them, knowing that something had happened.

Moments later, Koldur, the village Elder was before them, together with Oruná, Master Ari'atór.

"News from the city. The Warlord says the beast they call Nim'uán brings an army from the sands, that the king's army is riding here to meet it as we speak. What have you seen, Yerái?"

The Listener's eyes noted the Bird Master at Koldur's side, and then steeled himself, kept his voice as steady as he could. "The Warlord is right. We have climbed to the Doorway, have seen this army approaching from Calrazia – the desert horizon is black. Many thousands approach, Lord, a host far greater than even our entire army can stand against. They will be here in two weeks. We must all leave, flee south to the city."

Koldur looked around the glade, watched the people watching them.

"Gather round. Come closer."

Soon, they were surrounded by the people of Abiren'á and Koldur told them what Yerái had said. The first to speak was Master Oruná.

"I will take my novice and recruits today. We'll take the long way around the Wetwood on foot and make for Lan Taria. It should take us a week to arrive. We'll take horses from there. There are not enough rafts for everyone and there is no time to build more. Better the families and children take the river. My recruits are ready, Lord Koldur. They will not fail me."

Koldur stared at the Ari Master, unsure as to the ethics behind his decision. But it was not for him to decide and so he nodded. "The other children and their carers must be ready at the docks at the twelfth hour. Bring only what is necessary. There will be no room on the rafts for anything but your clothes and weapons."

There were murmurs, angry stubborn faces, shaking heads and then raised voices. Yerái didn't think they understood.

"We can't fight this army. There are too many of them. If we stay, we die. This is a certainty and our army still needs time to reach us. The enemy will be here before they can arrive."

"Then we hold them off until they come. *Bulan* will come!"

"Aye!" shouted others.

"And the Warlord!"

"Aye!"

"Listen to me," pleaded Yerái, arms out, a signal to let him speak. "Go at least to Sen'oléi, away from the main road north. It will give us a few more days but staying here is madness!"

"Leaving here is madness!" A young warrior Yerái had once met.

"Nurodi. You must. The trees will be safe enough, but our people will not. You won't be leaving, just retreating to Lan Taria until our army can get here. Then we join them, and we *fight*."

But Nurodi was shaking his head. "Our people will do what they will, but I'm staying, Lieutenant, here, where I belong. If we leave the trees, the soul is gone from this place. You know that, Yerái. Leaving will make this forest sterile! They will die!"

"They won't die, Nurodi. They will endure, for long enough for us to return."

But to a Silvan from these parts, leaving the trees was like cutting your own arm off and leaving it to bleed. You might live, but the arm is gone, and the elf is left scarred for eternity. Only those who had lived away in the city or the mountains, understood there were alternatives, that separation did not mean death for the trees, however unnatural it would always be to a Silvan.

There were murmurs of agreement, of respect for Nurodi's words. Yerái knew most of them would stay, save for those with children. But he had tried, and with that, perhaps he had swayed some of them at least. He turned to Mavorn when he spoke.

"Those who wish to leave for Sen'oléi, be ready tomorrow at dawn. I will arrange an escort. Those who wish to make for the city directly, be ready to leave at the twelfth hour at the docks."

"I'll send the messenger birds to the king, and then I'll wait for our army here," said Koldur, "where I too, belong – with my people."

"Lord. The messenger birds may not arrive. The chiboo migration is in full force," warned Yerái.

"We must risk it. We received this missive and so ours has a chance at least. Those who travel, be it by raft, on foot or on horseback; spread the word. Tell our people what comes from the sands."

Nurodi nodded in satisfaction at their leader.

"Aye! The Warlord will come," said another.

The evacuation of Abiren'á would be incomplete. Some would stay, even to their own ruin, while the families would take to the river, and the Ari'atór recruits and novice would set out on foot, to Lan Taria and beyond.

As for Yerái, he would accompany the caravan towards Sen'oléi, and then return here to Abiren'á. He would try to communicate with the Warlord but so far, he had had no success. That was surely a consequence of his own, humble skills. Yerái had sensed Fel'annár's power even before they had met on the road to Tar'eastór. That this warning had come from the city itself was a testament to how strong the voice was with him.

The Warlord was coming, and if what they said was true – if he could command the trees – there was a chance that he could somehow protect them, protect their homes in the boughs.

It was a strange thought, that perhaps it would be the very trees they did not want to abandon, that would fight for the elves in the war to come.

ORAN'DOR HAD BEEN WAITING for Thargodén's army for three days.

There was hot food ready for the warriors, and supplies for the journey north. Fire pits had already been dug and lit, and water sat in pails, ready for consumption.

The messenger birds had arrived here at least, realised Fel'annár. It gave them hope that those villages further north would already be preparing to leave, south and to safety. But as Fel'annár looked around this place, he realised he could see no laden wagons ready to depart, no packed bags or sad farewells.

The people cheered as the troops passed the main town, hungry eyes searching and finding Silvan captains amongst the commanders, and the Warlord they had all heard of. Fel'annár listened to their excited chatter. It was true, they said. The army had been reforged, the Warlord returned. But would it stand the test of war? And why was Pan'assár still its commander? Fel'annár mused that if they truly understood what the Nim'uán was, what it was capable of and how poorly prepared they were, they wouldn't be cheering but packing their bags and fleeing to the city.

With their camp set up on the outskirts of town, Pan'assár sent Bulan and Fel'annár to speak with the village leaders. The civilians were to make south to the city, and all those capable of wielding a weapon would be urged to join the campaign north. If they weren't skilled enough, then they were to report to Turion at the city for recruit or novice training. There were only five hundred warriors left at the city, barely enough to defend it. Turion would need all the help he could get.

Bulan and Fel'annár later reported to Pan'assár, telling him that many of the civilians were refusing to leave. They said that some of the villages further north would make south, especially if they had children. They would need help on the long journey to the city and so they would stay, feed and house them and then leave, should the enemy advance as far as Lan Taria.

Pan'assár wasn't surprised at that, but he *was* when a large group of young warriors approached the camp. Bulan welcomed them, asked them of their training and experience. They had little, mostly novices with a handful of newly promoted warriors who had left the army just recently.

Fel'annár had soon joined Bulan and spent time with them, explaining the changes that were coming, answering their many questions about the new army, about the Forest Division, and whether women would be allowed to fight. A small group from Ea Nanú had even asked about Angon.

Later, when it was almost fully dark, Fel'annár and Bulan made back to the centre of the camp, to where the commanders sat together with The Company.

"How many have come?"

Fel'annár sat, crossed his legs. "One hundred and forty-two, twelve of which are women. They have no formal training, but Bulan wants most of them to join us anyway. They can be tested along the way. They'll wait for the foot soldiers and join them while those with no knowledge at all will make for the city as recruits."

"One hundred and forty-two is not much, but it's far better than nothing." Pan'assár had almost murmured it, but still the others had heard well enough.

They ate well thanks to the people of Oran'Dor, and then sipped tea quietly save for the odd comment here and there. Fel'annár dug into his bag, pulled out his journal and rested it on his lap. He turned to Galadan, observed him for a moment.

"You're quiet," he murmured.

The Fire Warrior nodded. "I wonder if they will ever forgive him for his time of weakness."

Fel'annár knew what he meant. Pan'assár was leading this campaign, yet it may just as well have been Fel'annár or Bulan. They had all heard the careful insults and slights, had seen how the Alpine warriors amongst them had held their tongue and how Galadan almost hadn't.

"It will take them time, Galadan. Even Pan'assár knows that and still he strives to right his wrongs. They will see his worth, in the end."

Galadan stared back at him thoughtfully. At length, he nodded, and

The Company settled around the fire. Accepting a mug of tea from Ramien, Fel'annár drank, and then turned to Bulan as he stood and looked down on him, an Ashorn hanging from his belt.

"Time to train."

Gor'sadén narrowed his eyes, stood when Fel'annár did. Bulan looked like he might protest his presence, but the glint in the commander's eye was enough to dissuade him. Fel'annár thought it was just as well that Pan'assár had not made to follow them.

Tensári watched, took note of the Ber'anor's path, heard the heavy flutter of feathers from somewhere high above her head. Something stirred in her chest, apprehension building. Once they were out of sight, she would follow.

GOR'SADÉN LEANED AGAINST A TREE, arms crossed, one ankle resting over the other.

Before him, the circle of torches that had been staked into the ground so that the warriors could train. The troops would have their turn, followed by any others who wished for more intensive, one-on-one instruction from a Master. As for the Kah Disciples, Gor'sadén would take them further afield, and even though it was sometimes too dark to see properly, the nature of their training was far different from any other. One didn't need eyesight to practice projection or develop muscles powerful enough to perform some of the more complicated sequences.

Fel'annár stood in nothing but a loose white shirt and breeches. No boots, presumably so that Bulan could see his footwork better.

Gor'sadén watched Bulan's movements as they sparred, listened to his instructions. He watched Fel'annár too, saw the adjustments he made as he worked. An hour later, the commander caught Bulan's gaze, gestured with his head that he should return to camp, waited for the captain to acknowledge his silent command. It had been a hard day of riding, of ensuring the morale of the troops and there were plenty more ahead of them.

"Enough for today, Fel'annár. You're progressing well. Tomorrow we can move on to the more difficult moves."

Fel'annár bowed, as he was accustomed to doing with the Kah Masters. Surprised, the Silvan captain nodded, smile come and gone so fast Fel'annár wondered if he had imagined it.

He watched Bulan leave, and for a moment, a wave of peace and tranquillity washed over him. Had the trees realised he needed some silence? They had not ceased in their warnings since that first message at the city, and however much he had assured them that he understood, the voices had been incessant.

Until now.

Alone now with only Gor'sadén, and Tensári somewhere close by, Fel'annár turned to him.

"I would sit here for a while, Gor'sadén. I won't stray from the camp."

"Is there something wrong?"

"Nothing. I would just savour this place in solitude for a while."

Gor'sadén hesitated, eyes wandering to the bushes and then back to his charge. "Don't be long." He left, bound for the fire where Pan'assár and The Company still sat. Bulan though, had gone.

Fel'annár peered into the darkness before him, where the trees were thicker. He spotted a fallen log, sat on it, and then pulled his tunic on. He took a deep breath. Alone at last, blessed silence in his head. He needed to think but so too did he need to rest.

He breathed in the fresh, crisp air, closed his eyes and gathered his thoughts.

Eee Eee Eeaaa Eeaaa

What ... He looked up, searched for the creature with that distinctive call. Was it the same hunting bird he had seen that afternoon? The rustle of leaves, the distant gurgle of a small stream, the buzz of insects ... it all seemed to fade just a little as his eyes sharpened, pupils opening to allow more light in.

And then he saw it, the dark outline of a bird perched upon a low branch. He daren't move lest he frighten it away and so he sat frozen on his fallen log, eyes drinking in as much of the predator as they could before it flew away.

A flash of blue light moved over the bird and Fel'annár turned, glanced over his shoulder in search of whatever had caused the reflection. And then he damned his clumsiness, knowing that the sudden movement would have frightened the bird away. But there were no flapping wings and he turned back to the branch and the dark silhouette.

Still there.

He frowned, wondered if he could risk getting any closer to it. He stood, waited for a reaction.

Nothing.

He listened to the trees, but all they spoke of was the north. A step forward, slow and stealthy and still, the bird did not flinch. He had never seen anything like it. The thing was fearless, unconcerned that he may whip out a knife and turn it into a succulent dinner. The blue light passed over the bird once more and for a moment he saw round, blue eyes and a yellow beak, come and gone in a moment.

Blue eyes.

All the birds of prey Fel'annár had ever seen had honey-coloured eyes, russet even and sometimes yellow. But blue? He shook his head, reminded himself that he had seen this once before, just recently. Animals with blue eyes.

In the Evergreen Wood.

The bird had him perplexed, but his bafflement was rapidly turning into sinking dread. The Squiliz, the Fibird, the skulking creature in the mists of the Evergreen Wood.

Blue eyes.

He flinched when it moved, stepped back as dark wings opened like a velvet curtain, revealing black and white stripes across its chest. Fel'annár smiled, awe warring with some fear that was rising from his gut. He wanted to reach out, smooth his fingers over the downy feathers but he daren't. Instead, he held his hand out at arm's length, formed a fist. The bird studied the outstretched hand, lifted one of its talons and placed it softly on the fist. It was soon gone, and Fel'annár's hand stung from the indent of the long and lethal talons. He offered his forearm instead, forgot to breathe as he watched the bird hop onto his arm.

His smile widened, eyes wide with curiosity. He walked slowly towards the fallen log, bird of prey on his arm and then he sat stiffly. Black, white and yellow, and those extraordinary blue eyes that looked back at him unblinking. They reminded him of Tensári and Narosén.

He wanted to laugh, wanted to cry. He wanted to assure himself that this creature had not followed him from the Evergreen Wood.

But he couldn't.

"I'll call you Azure."

Eeaa

Azure flapped his wings and Fel'annár wondered if it wanted to fly off. He held his arm out once more and the bird opened its wings, a thing of majesty, Fel'annár thought as he watched the powerful animal take flight, up into the canopy and beyond, until he could no longer see it.

He returned to camp in a haze of memories, piecing together his recent experience in the Evergreen Wood. What was the mystery of these blue-eyed creatures?

He searched for Tensári, but she was nowhere to be seen and so he sat before the fire and took out his journal. He flicked through the pages until he came to the drawings he had sketched in the Evergreen Wood. One finger smoothed over the Squiliz and the Fibird, and then down to the bold arrows and the words beside them.

Blue eyes.

How could this be a coincidence?

But then he realised that *he* was the common factor here. Was that blue light a reflection of his own eyes? Was it the Guiding Light inside him that reacted to them for some reason? He would put that theory to the test the next time he saw Azure – *if* he ever came back.

He closed his journal, sat up straighter, muscles too hard and bunched up. He stretched his legs out before him, pulled his toes towards him and felt the tension behind his knees and thighs ease.

Bulan had indeed pushed on with his training. He had even incorporated two aerial moves, a side twist and a forward somersault. The sequences were in his head, replaying even as he stretched and then cast his eyes over The Company.

Tensári was still gone, and Galadan was speaking with Pan'assár. Of all the captains available to the commander, Galadan was, once more, the one he naturally turned to.

He glanced across the fire at Idernon whose head was in a book.

"Idernon. Of all the birds of prey, which has charcoal wings, black and white feathers down the front, yellow beak and talons and ... blue eyes?"

The Company and Gor'sadén turned to him, and then to Idernon for an answer. But the Wise Warrior scowled, shook his head. "None. *Blue* eyes? Are you sure?"

He was, but to say so would open up the discussion and he was not sure he wanted to speak of it yet.

"No. Must have been a trick of the light."

"Hum. With that plumage, I would say some sort of hawk, a goshawk most likely."

"If I see it again, I'll pay more attention." He leaned back against a tree, spread his blanket over his legs and settled down for the night, just as Tensári emerged from wherever she had been. She sat beside him, nodded and Fel'annár turned away, missed her lingering gaze, the strangeness in her eyes.

Taniq stood rigid at the base of a Sentinel.

Can you hear me, Yerái?

She looked down, dark green eyes shimmering, their light reflecting off the silver belt she always wore.

"Any news today, Listener?"

She turned, spotted the tanner off in the near distance. She raised a hand, smiled at him, shook her head. She watched him wave. A nice man, good, steady aura about him. She liked Casten, but he had never shown any interest in her. Whether that was for pity or fear she couldn't say. Still, given the circumstances, she was happy enough here. As happy as she could be at least.

Yerái ... she had heard of him. A Silvan warrior and Listener. Someone was trying to reach him through the trees, the message strong and crystal clear.

Not for the first time, Taniq wished *she* could speak to the trees as well as understand them, the way this new Listener did. If she could, she would ask who sent the message, and about what he wanted.

She huffed, picked up the basket she had dropped and continued on her way to the river. She would cook herself a nice fish dinner if any of the hunters would exchange one for her lovingly nurtured tomatoes.

They were the tastiest of all of Ea Nanú, were well worth a trout or two she reckoned.

But the closer she drew to the banks of the Calro, the deeper her feelings of dread.

She passed the first villagers who were straining to see through the crowds. She pushed her way through, heard the worried conversations, their voices louder and louder until she was on the banks, looking north and to the fleet of barges that sailed towards the piers.

Sand Lords.

"No ..."

A villager turned to her, studied her face for a moment. "What is it, Taniq?"

"Sand Lords. They are fleeing from Sand Lords."

"Surely not," said another. "Not this far south."

"Aye, hasn't happened for centuries," said another.

Indeed, Sand Lords had made it this far south before. It was the last day she had seen her daughter. Eyes filling, she breathed noisily through her mouth, shut out the memories that were surfacing, concentrated on the barges.

"The trees say it is so."

The villagers turned to her, nodded, and then made to help secure the crafts. There were hundreds of refugees from Abiren'á, families with children eager to rest and eat. Their sheer numbers were enough to tell them this was no incoming enemy patrol. Something transcendental was happening, and for a while, Taniq stood to one side and watched as women, men and children stepped off the rafts and began their unbelievable tale.

An army of thousands of Sand Lords was converging on the Xeric Wood. So said the Warlord and the king had sent birds. But Yerái too, had warned of their approach, had seen this host with his own eyes from the Doorway to the Sands.

Damn them for eternity, to never-ending torment in the pits of Galomú for they had taken her daughter, to a fate she was not brave enough to imagine.

Although Taniq knew that many of her friends would stay with the giant trees of Ea Nanú, she would not – could not. She would pack her things and join these refugees if there was space. She would make for the city, be useful if she could, until it was safe to return.

Sweet Ankelar. I'm sorry I could not protect you, my child.

THREE DAYS after Pan'assár's departure from Oran'Dor, Captain Sorei and one thousand black-and-silver-clad Alpine warriors were guided into their breaking camp.

Dismounting, she made her way to Gor'sadén and saluted. She glanced at Fel'annár who stood beside her commander, eyes wandering over the parallel lines in his collar, the Blade Master armband over his bicep. She had been the one to test him for it in Tar'eastór. But back then, he had only been a lieutenant, not a general. Strange though it seemed, he was her superior now and she had questions. But she also had priorities. She saluted the young general and turned back to Gor'sadén.

"Captain Sorei. Your arrival is most timely. Sand Lords are converging on the northern lands. We have mustered two thousand and there is hope of more on the way. How many have you brought?"

"A thousand, Commander. We are to serve under your command."

"We need all the help we can get, Captain. But come, we were making ready to leave and there is no time to lose. Join us on our march northwards and later, we will speak."

Sorei nodded, turned to her contingent and signalled to Pengon that they should join the five hundred mounted warriors from Ea Uaré. Fel'annár followed her line of sight and to the familiar face of the lieutenant with whom he and The Company had served in Tar'eastór. He held a hand up, a silent greeting and Pengon returned it from afar.

The two contingents together made 1,500 mounted warriors, quite a din at a steady trot, and as they roared through the forest, Sorei briefed Gor'sadén on her mission and what she knew.

"We were deployed almost three weeks ago. I assume our king does not know of this new incursion in the north, unless they sent birds?"

"They sent birds over a week ago. If the chiboo migrations have not interfered with their task, Tar'eastór will already know. As for us, we are waiting for news from the north."

"From your patrols?"

"And from the trees."

"Ah, Fel'annár." She nodded, turned to where The Company were riding further behind. There was one missing.

"Where is Lieutenant Sontúr?"

"He was injured in battle. *Captain* Sontúr took an arrow to the shoulder, but we are assured he will make a full recovery."

Sorei nodded slowly, and then turned to Pengon on her other side. Gor'sadén's eyes strayed to the peculiar long sword that was jutting out of her harness. Something about it had drawn his attention, but what was it?

It was a dour grey, no decorations at all. No jewels, no etchings, no carved silver that marked its owner or stated its name. He peered closer, wishing she would stay still so that he could inspect it, but she was soon facing the path ahead. He would ask her about it later, once they stopped for the night.

He remembered Sorei's obsession with the forges, her claim that one day, she would create the perfect blade. But Gor'sadén's own blade was made by Colanei, legendary swordsmith of Tar'eastór. There were no finer creations than his and those of Turanés Bladecrafter.

Still, he admired her tenacity, had little doubts that one day, she would create a very fine weapon.

As the light began to fail, Pan'assár gave the order to stop.

Food and a hot brew later, Gor'sadén turned to Sorei, pointed to the sword. But before he could ask her about it, she spoke.

"Commander. You remember our conversation many years ago?"

"About swords, yes. Is this the one then?"

She nodded. "I believe so. But I cannot be sure until a Kah Master has tested it. I have brought it for you to try."

Gor'sadén stared back at her. Should he encourage her too much, he may heighten her disappointment later. He did not doubt her skill as a smith, but to share in the notoriety of Turanés and Colanei was not possible. Gor'sadén and Pan'assár possessed the greatest blades ever created, gifted to them by King Vorn'asté himself. Still, he couldn't refuse her request. He would try the blade, praise it if it was good, and hope that would be enough for her.

"Have you now. Well, Fel'annár here has his spear training with Captain Bulan, and Commander Pan'assár will be with the new Kah Disciples. Once they finish, I would be glad to try it."

"New Disciples? You are bringing the Kal'hamén'Ar back?"

"We are. Slowly for now."

Sorei held his gaze, and for a moment, Gor'sadén thought she would speak. But she didn't, and he wondered if *she* would aspire to the Kal'hamén'Ar, perhaps thought that it would not be open to a woman.

He gestured for her to follow him. Fel'annár and Bulan were sparring in a nearby glade, a good number of warriors watching, and amongst them, the newly invested Kah Disciples.

The commander watched as he settled beside a tree and crossed his arms, but Sorei stood rigid, fascinated by the whirl of spears, a weapon she had not seen wielded for years.

Bulan mainly kept his feet on the ground while Fel'annár jumped and twisted, again and again until the master was satisfied that it was high enough, fast enough.

"When will he become a Kah Master?"

"In many ways, he already is. It is experience in the field that will confirm to me that he is ready for the purple sash."

"I want it, Commander. I would take the test, if you would allow."

Gor'sadén turned to her, saw that characteristic simmer of surety in her eyes, some drive he had always seen in her that lead her to perfection in everything she did.

"When all this is over and we return to the city, if you can stay, I would offer you a test. If you are capable of it, we will teach you."

Sorei was alight, the fiery determination in her eyes flaring. "And when you return to Tar'eastór?"

"When I return, I will bring it back."

The clack of wood against wood and Gor'sadén turned back to the duelling warriors. Fel'annár held Harvest before him, the tip pointing at

Bulan. The Silvan captain held his own spear to one side in surrender. Both warriors seemed surprised, moved a little too slowly. But then Bulan nodded his head, peered at his student.

"Well done."

Fel'annár smiled. "Am I ready to use Harvest on the battlefield then?"

"So long as you pick the right moment, Fel'annár. So long as you can recognise its time to fly."

Instead of celebrating Bulan's judgement, he seemed to deflate, one hand coming up to rub down his face.

Gor'sadén knew his Disciple well. He had achieved a goal and for a moment, he had allowed himself to show all the effort it had taken him. He turned back to Sorei when she came to stand before him.

"Shall we, Commander?"

He nodded, took off his cuirass and Sorei drew the strange sword, watched his eyes flicker when he realised just how long it was. She offered it to him, watched him take it, his experienced hands as he smoothed over the edges and planes of the first Synth Blade.

He had expected it to be heavier. She saw the overcompensation and then a glint of surprise. He held it out before him, observed the centre of balance, whirled it around with a flick of his wrist, cut through the air.

The conversation around them died and Gor'sadén saw Pan'assár, standing amidst the Kah Disciples, watching them. On his other side, Fel'annár together with The Company and Pengon.

Gor'sadén stepped forward, waited for his audience to settle around him and then struck a stance before Sorei. She joined him, mimicked his actions with her standard issue blade.

They ran through the basic stances and as her sword met his, he listened, felt the vibrations, watched the give, the bend. From there, they moved on to spar. There was nothing competitive about it, the movements meant to test the sword, not its wielder.

Gor'sadén stepped back. "I would test this with the Kah stances."

Sorei hesitated, glanced at Pan'assár but Gor'sadén was gesturing to Fel'annár. She wanted the commander's opinion, his approval or whatever he would say about her blade, but she also wanted to see the Kah stances.

Although it was forbidden to mimic the movements, it was only the fighting sequences that were not to be performed in public unless it was in battle or before the king's court. Still, the Kah stances were something many had never seen and she glanced at the new Disciples, wondered how far they had come in their training, whether *they* had seen them.

She listened to Gor'sadén as he explained, watched as Fel'annár nodded, eyes wide and curious, and then Master and Disciple saluted. With Fel'annár's sword in his hand, and her Synth blade in Gor'sadén's, she started when the two warriors began to weave strange patterns in the air before them. She thought it was like writing in the wind, wondered whether there was some symbolism to it.

The other warriors closed in, and Sorei had no choice but to step forward lest she lose her front-line view.

The warriors were excited. The Silvan captain who had been sparring with Fel'annár elbowed another beside him, nudging him sideways so that he could get a better view, while others stood on tiptoe, steadied themselves on the shoulders of their fellow warriors.

A shock of excited anticipation ran the length of her body. Her finest creation was in the hands of the greatest Kah Master of all time, and her eyes were no longer cool and confident. They were wide with dread, glittering with anticipation of the stances and the judgement that would come later.

Gor'sadén raised his sword over his head and angled it side-on. Fel'annár mimicked him and then one sword swooped downwards, the sound of steel rushing through air and Fel'annár danced around it, as if he followed it, seemed to know where it was headed, even with his back turned.

His own blade arced around his body and then spiralled upwards, swooping towards his opponent's face. Gor'sadén blocked it, swords crossed before them. One slid down the other, sliced low over the ground and Fel'annár jumped over it, repeated the same movement. Gor'sadén jumped and then the movements seemed to blur. There was no stop and start as was the case with sword fighting. This was the Kal'hamén'Ar, a fluid sequence of flesh and steel dancing in unlikely harmony.

Dance of Graceful Death, they called it, and for the first time, the Kah Disciples understood why, and so did Sorei.

Gor'sadén attacked from above, Fel'annár defended, blocked the blade, allowed it to scrape down the length of his own sword and then vaulted over it, landing on the other side of the commander who turned, to exactly the spot where he knew his Disciple would be. Next stance and the strokes were faster, the blocks harder until Gor'sadén called for a stop, and both Kah warriors held their blades before their faces. They bowed and Sorei exhaled, at last, exhausted even though she had not moved at all.

But Gor'sadén had not finished. He handed the blade to Fel'annár, gestured to the stump of a dead birch which sat chest high. They had done this before. It was a test of projection, to slice horizontally through a block of wood, as deeply as you could in just one strike.

One of the first principles a Kah Disciple learned was that technique with the blade was just as important as the Dohai and the projection it gave, the power it lent to the blow. A regular warrior's sword would barely cut into the surface of the hard wood, but the Kah Masters were capable of striking into the very centre. The trick was getting the blade out afterwards.

Gor'sadén had shown the Disciples just recently, and when they had tried their hands at it, the only damage they had managed to do was a superficial scratch to the bark and a red face.

They followed Fel'annár to the stump, stayed a distance away because the blade was so long. They watched as he lifted it with both hands and then they waited.

Fel'annár closed his eyes and Gor'sadén knew exactly what he was thinking.

See nothing. Think nothing. Conjure the Dohai and project it.

Fel'annár inhaled, lifted the blade higher.

"Yaséi!"

He lunged forwards and sliced into the wood from the side. The blade sunk into it.

And then out through the other side.

For a while, the wood didn't move, until the balance was tipped, and the upper half of the stump fell away with a thud.

"Holy Gods," muttered Gor'sadén.

Fel'annár stood there, shocked eyes on the blade and then his own hands.

Sorei stared in shock, and then she turned abruptly to her commander, eyes begging him to give her his verdict. He wrenched his eyes away from his stunned Disciple and turned to her, just as Pan'assár joined them.

"Colanei and Turanés are the best Sword Masters known to Elvendom. Today, their reign is over. It is the time of Sorei. It is the time of the Synth Blade."

A collective gasp rippled over the onlooking captains and lieutenants but Sorei stood rigid before him. Her eyes filled but did not overflow and she bowed her head, stayed there for a long while. Gor'sadén smiled, knew Sorei well enough to know that she was battling with her emotions, that she would say nothing for fear that her voice would waver.

"Come. To the fires. There is much to discuss."

She swayed where she stood, as if the string that held her aloft had been severed. She watched as Gor'sadén took the blade from Fel'annár's numb hands with a grin and held it out to her. She shook her head. "I made this for you. The first Synth Blade deserves to be wielded by the greatest Kah Master."

Gor'sadén stared back at her, then at the blade. "This is a mighty gift, Sorei."

"One that will bring you victory, Commander. I can make more."

"And you must, Sorei. You *must*."

She smiled, and then she frowned because Gor'sadén was staring at Fel'annár. The young general's head was tilted backwards, his eyes a little too bright, enough to send a shiver down her spine. And then he shouted a warning.

"Alert on the northern perimeter. Friends approach."

Just seconds later, a cry from the sentinels in the trees and then a wave of screeching chiboos flew over them, panicked in their search for a safe place.

"Report!" Pan'assár's powerful voice. Gor'sadén and Sorei, Bulan and the Kah Disciples, all those who had watched the birth of a legendary swordsmith gathered around Fel'annár.

"Elves approach. Civilians and ... Ari'atór."

25

ARRIVALS

～

MINUTES LATER, Fel'annár and The Company watched as three wagons emerged from the trees and around them, dozens of elves on horseback, weapons upon their backs. Within their ranks, mounted Ari'atór - most of them children.

Fel'annár was shocked. He had never seen Ari children and he glanced at Tensári who was watching the group with a soft smile on her face.

For a moment, he couldn't decide where to look. Some could only have been nine or perhaps ten while others were older, sat taller but none of them were of age.

His eyes wandered over their clothing. The older children wore black while the younger were in white and cream and upon their backs was a bow and quiver. Fel'annár didn't know how he felt about that. They were surely too young to be killing anything.

He heard cries of joy from women and children in the wagons as they caught sight of husbands, brothers and fathers amongst the warriors. There was family in this group of refugees, and the captains allowed them their moment of indulgence.

Similarly, the mounted elves shouted greetings to their warriors. Fel'annár had thought them civilians but he had been wrong. They were warriors; deserters.

"Fel'annár. Fel'annár!"

He searched the crowd of newcomers, that voice vaguely familiar. And then he caught sight of one he had not seen for a year.

"Eloran!"

The boy who was almost a man jumped, held his hands in the air and waved.

"Over here!" Fel'annár beckoned to him and then he realised Eloran was not alone. Alféna and her twins were with him.

"Fel'annár!" Eloran rushed forwards, embraced his friend, hid his face from his mother who stood just behind him. Fel'annár caught her gaze, saw her wide, warm smile, and Fel'annár returned it. He looked down at the young twins who he had saved from the fires of Sen'oléi, back when he was a novice with no ken of his powers, of his duty to Aria.

"Well bless my eyes young Fel'annár. Look at you." Alféna stepped forward as gracefully as she could with two children clinging to her legs. She looked tired.

Fel'annár clapped Eloran on the back and then held him at arm's length.

"Are you all right?" asked Fel'annár of no one in particular.

"Just tired – and hungry."

Fel'annár chuckled. "We'll remedy that in a moment." His eyes were on the Ari children, watching as they dismounted and the eldest of them spoke with the others.

"That's Isán and his brethren," said Eloran. "They've come from Abiren'á with news. That one is their leader." He pointed at an imposing Ari'atór upon a black horse, looking down on Isán and listening as he spoke to the children.

Fel'annár stood taller, half-turned to Tensári at his side and then back at Eloran and his family. He gestured to Idernon close by. "Go with my brother Idernon. Eat, drink and rest. I won't be long."

"You're going to take counsel with the leaders then?" asked Eloran.

Fel'annár turned from the Ari'atór and the commanders and

captains who were making towards them. He smiled at Eloran, remembered just why he loved this boy so much. "I am. Go and eat."

Eloran nodded enthusiastically and was soon gone with his family to the fires amidst the curious stares of The Company. They would surely want to know who these people were, hear the story of the fires and how Fel'annár had met Eloran.

Alone with Tensári now, they made their way towards the congregating leaders.

"Who is that?" asked Fel'annár as he gestured towards the Ari'atór leader.

"That is Master Oruná. He taught Lainon everything he knew."

Fel'annár turned to her, saw the soft smile on her face and then turned back to the Ari Master who stood with Isán at his side.

Bulan was smiling, Gor'sadén was curious and Pan'assár was anxious for news; they all were.

Oruná turned from the commanders and Bulan to Fel'annár and Tensári. And then quite unexpectedly, the dour-faced Ari'atór barked an order in a foreign tongue. Fel'annár didn't understand and he turned to Tensári for a translation.

She leaned in, explained quietly. "Din hayén ber Ari. Pay respect to the servants."

By the time Fel'annár had turned back to the group, they were bowing from the waist, even the children.

"They can feel Aria inside us. They recognise the light behind our eyes, the Guiding Light we carry."

Fel'annár nodded that he understood but he didn't, not really. He crossed gazes with Pan'assár, thought he looked as confused as he himself was.

THE COMMANDERS SAT WITH BULAN, Fel'annár and Tensári, and before them, Master Oruná and Novice Isán.

"Did the messenger birds arrive, Oruná?" asked Pan'assár. The Ari Master looked at him coolly, not entirely friendly. When he spoke, his voice was rich and low, both soothing and menacing, thought Fel'annár.

"Yes. But Listener Yerái had already sensed the enemy whilst on patrol in Sen'oléi. These people here in the wagons are the only ones who heeded his warnings. From there, they rode to Lan Taria while the patrol travelled to the Three Sisters and later reported a visual sighting of the enemy to Lord Koldur of Abiren'á. The children and their carers needed all the available rafts, and so I brought my recruits on foot around the Wetwood towards Lan Taria. From there, we took horses and were escorted by these elves, erstwhile warriors of your army, Commander."

Fel'annár wanted to ask about the Three Sisters – the giant Sentinels of Abiren'á – but he was too relieved that someone had finally corroborated his claims of an approaching horde. The king had moved an entire army in blind faith – in *him*. Still, at least some of the civilians and all the children had evacuated. He had questions, but Pan'assár was quicker.

"How far away was the enemy when Lieutenant Yerái saw them?"

"Two weeks at a rough guess."

Fel'annár frowned. "He must have excellent eyesight."

Oruná didn't smile, but Fel'annár thought that he wanted to. What had he said that was so funny?

"You have never been to our city, to the Doorway to the Sands. You have never seen the Three Sisters. When you do, you will understand, Ar Lássira."

If Fel'annár was surprised at Oruná's address, he had no time to show it.

"Did you leave that same day?" asked Gor'sadén.

"We did. We have been travelling for eleven days."

"Which means, the enemy will be at our borders in about three days," said Fel'annár, tone grim, face a reflection of the anguish it caused him to know the Sand Lords would already be inside the forest by the time they arrived.

No one spoke for a moment, until Tensári quite unexpectedly broke the silence.

"Have the children taken the oath, Master?"

"No. Only Isán. Only he can fight. The rest must not. They may defend, but not take an active part in conflict. It is prohibited. They need an escort southward to the city. Tell me, is Narosén there?"

Pan'assár seemed confused and Fel'annár answered for him. "He is."

Oruná turned to him, nodded slowly. "Good. Commander Pan'assár. I need your assurances. My pupils must not attack a living being, not unless they are defending themselves. There are thirty-two of them, with only myself and Isán to protect them. They are servants of Aria; they must be escorted to safety by someone of your utmost confidence."

Oruná had said it as if he expected Pan'assár to refuse his demand. But he didn't.

"How many have come from Sen'oléi?" asked the commander.

"Twenty-three. Many had already travelled south with their leaders some months ago to join the Silvan encampment. We assume they will still be outside the city."

"They have moved inside. Look for Amareth and Narosén. They will help you," replied Fel'annár.

"All right. Fifty-five civilians, most of them children. Two Ari'atór. You will need fifty more for a safe escort. There are no Sand Lords behind us, but there may be Deviants."

"If I may," said Gor'sadén. "I suggest we send Captain Sorei. She can be of great use creating her Synth blades in the city. She can take fifty of her Alpine patrol with less or no experience in the Wetwood. Turion will appreciate the extra warriors."

Pan'assár turned to the Ari'atór. "Is that acceptable, Oruná?"

"I am content."

Pan'assár turned to Gor'sadén, gestured that he should tell his captain of their decision. She wasn't going to like it. She was an excellent leader, but her skill in forging blades was unique. Creating more of them would be a great asset to Thargodén's forces. It was the best solution. Even so, he didn't envy his friend at all.

"Oruná. Eat, rest. You ride just after dawn. Captain Bulan here will see to your needs."

Fel'annár watched his uncle smile at Oruná and to his utter shock, the enigmatic Ari'atór smiled back. "Ar Zéndar is a captain once more. I am glad to see you here."

Fel'annár watched their exchange closely. They knew each other well from what he could see. Oruná turned back to Pan'assár.

"I am glad to see you too, Pan'assár. You must lead this army to victory. Save our city – our people. So many of them have stayed, in Abiren'á, in Sen'oléi, Lan Taria and Ea Nanú. They don't understand, not fully. They have faith in the coming of the Warlord. They will not leave the trees."

"I know. And that is not for me to judge, not anymore. We will save them. We will find a way, Oruná."

Blue eyes momentarily reflected a light that was not before him and Fel'annár thought he understood. But when Oruná's gaze landed on him and stayed there, he was suddenly sure. He glanced at Bulan, who nodded back at him slowly.

Fel'annár was not mistaken. Oruná carried a Guiding Light.

AT THE COMPANY'S FIRE, Carodel was murmuring something to Galdith, who was giving out plates of food to Alféna and her children. They were tired and worried, unsure of what awaited them on the path southwards. None of them had ever been this far from Sen'oléi.

They all looked up expectantly when Fel'annár and Tensári returned from the briefing. Fel'annár needed to tell them the news the Ari'atór had brought with them, but he would wait until the children slept, knew the adults would understand.

The predictable question of how Fel'annár had met this family came from Carodel. It was Alféna who answered him. She told them of how the patrol had arrived, about the Sand Lords and the fires and how they had waited for two days for Fel'annár and the children to return.

Accepting a plate from Carodel, Fel'annár ate as he listened, remembering those days of ignorance and discovery. It was in Sen'oléi where Fel'annár had learned he was a Listener, with the help of Narosén.

He glanced at Galdith as he, in turn, watched the smaller boy sitting before his mother and beside his twin sister. Fel'annár knew why. Galdith's own child would have been just a little younger than them, had he not died in the destruction of Sen'uár.

The child grabbed at the food while his sister scowled back at him, and then laid a crumpled book carefully beside her. It was ripped, the pages misaligned but he supposed she liked the drawings that were clearly precious to her. Only then did she help herself to the food, and Eloran waited patiently until his mother too, had taken her share. He reached for what was left, and Alféna smiled proudly at her eldest son. She broke her own portion in two and offered it to him. Reluctantly, the still growing boy took it hesitantly.

Galdith watched their interaction, knew the little one would still be hungry, eyes flitting from his sister to his elder brother and then mother.

He grinned, reached into his pocket and pulled out a portion of his trail mix. He held it out to the twins. They stared at him, then at the nuts and dried fruit. The little girl chewed her lips while the boy brushed crumbs from his face.

"Go on," murmured Alféna from above them, and then smiled at Galdith.

The boy reached out, took a nut ever so slowly, and then popped it into his mouth and crunched on it until there was nothing left. He turned to his twin sister, gestured with his hand. She reached out and picked a raisin.

Within seconds, the two young children were sitting on Galdith's lap, munching on nuts and watching the grownups as they talked.

Alféna watched the handsome warrior as he fed them, wondered at the grief in his eyes, whether it was the same grief that she had carried in her own for ten years. They were warriors on the road to battle, yet here they were, caring for her family, her children. She resolved then, that when they finally reached the city, she too would find a way to help others who had left their homes in the wood.

FOOD FINISHED, Fel'annár leaned back against a tree and tilted his head, listened to the tense natter of the trees. They spoke of the lights on the horizon, how they were a little bigger, and more importantly, how they approached head on.

He had reached out to Yerái once more but still, he had heard nothing. There were three reasons he could think of. The most obvious was that Yerái's skill was not deep enough to allow him to hear specific words. The second possibility was that he *could* hear but didn't know how to answer. And then perhaps he could neither hear nor answer.

"Any news?" asked Idernon.

"Nothing. Only that the lights are bigger. I just wish we knew where Hobin is, whether Tar'eastór knows." Fel'annár was listening in all directions but as yet, all he had sensed was the enemy's approach from the north.

With the fire burning low and The Company resting, save for Galdith who was talking quietly with Alféna, Fel'annár stood and walked further into the trees. There were no fallen logs here and so he sat, crossed his legs and searched the boughs for the hawk that had sat on his forearm just days ago.

Nothing.

I wish I was like you, Azure. That I could fly swiftly over the mountains and see for myself. Or perhaps fly north and see the flaming horizon the trees speak of. I covet your wings, my friend.

A rustle from the branches just above him and he looked up, into the inquisitive face of Azure who looked down on him steadily. As if he had always been there, waiting.

He placed his hand before his own eyes.

No blue reflection. The hawk's eyes *were* blue.

A smile split his face because he was inexplicably glad that the bird had returned. He offered his arm, watched Azure glide down, reach out gently with his talons. Their faces were so close that the bird could pluck out his eyes before he could blink. But Fel'annár somehow knew that he wouldn't.

"What's your secret, Azure? Why are you so far from home, following me?" He had so many questions and no one to ask.

He raised his arm and took it to his shoulder. Azure hopped onto it and did not move, even when Fel'annár stood.

Any minute now and Azure would spread his wings and fly. But he didn't, even when a branch cracked behind him.

He turned, found Tensári standing frozen still, not far away, hands out to both sides as if ready to draw her weapons. Whether it was a trick of the eye, the reflection of the moon or her own, inner light, her eyes seemed brighter than was normal.

She didn't speak, didn't move for a while. One, tentative step forward, and then another and still, Azure stood still on his shoulder. Tensári cocked her head to one side as she approached, eyes dimming and brightening in a way Fel'annár had only ever seen once. It was when he and Thargodén had been rescued in Analei. Idernon had told him Tensári had used her Guiding Light to find him.

Eeaa Eeaa

Fel'annár could feel Azure's feet shifting his weight. He wanted to fly. He offered his forearm, waited for the hawk to hop onto it and all the while, Tensári stared.

Azure opened his wings and flapped into the air, until he was away, silently into the night and Tensári turned back to Fel'annár, some emotion in her gaze he could not quite capture.

"It has *blue* eyes."

YERAI SAT IN A CAGE, legs pulled up to his chin to make way for the others.

Their Sand Lord captors had been walking for hours, had hardly taken a break, not even for water. Yerái supposed they were used to going without.

He was the only warrior here. Around him, terrified men and women sat muttering their fears while others tried and failed to calm their rising panic.

Yerai's patrol had escorted a group of citizens from Aberina to Sen'olei, had stayed there and tried their hardest to convince the villagers to leave. They had told the leaders what they had seen from the Doorway to the Sands, and while some had decided to travel at least to Lan Taria, the rest were adamant they would stay.

Mavorn had set out to return to Abiren'á, but the patrol had come under attack. It had been quick and efficient and Yerái had not had enough time to warn them of the ambush. Whether the others had escaped, he couldn't say.

He had made it out of the area, listening as he ran. The trees had warned him of danger, but Yerái had not expected it to come in the form of a hunting trap. He had put his foot in a loop of rope and then had shot upwards. He had remained dangling there for what seemed like an eternity. Dizzy, muscles aching, he had been cut down and clumsily caught by Sand Lords and then tossed into this cage.

He rubbed his left ankle, rope burns painful, muscles tight and sore. Why were the Sand Lords taking captives? They never had done before.

Night was falling. They would surely stop soon. Travelling in the dark through these parts was not the best of ideas and Yerái prayed they would not leave the cages on the ground. They were too close to the Wetwood; they would be overcome by yellow ants. They were harmless if you batted them away. But if you fell asleep, in their search for warmth and food, they could cover an elf in less than a minute. He wouldn't die of bites or poison. He would suffocate.

True to his worst fears, the cage was set down roughly beside a tree, and those inside listened to the strange noises of the Sand Lords. The only sounds familiar to them was laughter.

Fires were lit and then the strange vibrations were back. Yerái suppressed a chill because the trees seemed to recoil. There was something about those subterranean movements that was disquieting to them.

Someone whimpered and the rest drew back, pushed themselves against the bars on one side of the cage. A Sand Lord was approaching.

Unlocking the door, the black-clad warrior reached for an elf. Yerái pulled him back, used his feet to kick out at the enemy. Screams, pleas for mercy but the Sand Lord was strong and soon enough, the elf was outside. He was dragged away, screaming and yelling the entire way to the edge of camp until they could no longer see him.

They sat, didn't want to look. This was either for sport or for intelligence, but the elf they had dragged away didn't wear a uniform. Yerái did but they had not wanted him.

Sport then.

The vibration was back. The trees recoiled and Yerái resisted the urge to cover his ears. It would be pointless; he would still be a listener. He would still be able to hear their warnings, feel the anxiety.

The vibration was stronger now and then the ground lurched and they heard the sound of something exploding from the earth, rock and soil splattering to the ground. The Sand Lords cheered. Gods but what were they doing to the poor elf?

And then the screaming began, screaming and laughter. One terrified soul amidst a gathering of demonic Sand Lords. They would be torturing him, enjoying his fear, mocking it.

Those in the cage with him were moaning, covering their ears and rocking backwards and forwards while others cried as they wondered.

Would it be their turn tomorrow?

How long had it been? Seconds? Minutes? An hour? And then the screaming escalated into a single screech and then nothing but its echo. They must have killed him but then he heard what sounded like ripping and tearing, again and again, and yet the Sand Lords were silent. No more mocking and jeering.

Something was happening. Something out of the ordinary. The surety of it coiled inside him, twisted his gut and Yerái reached out through the bars of his cage until his fingertips brushed over the rough bark of the tree. A woman beside him watched, eyes fixed on his reaching hand.

Yerái had no way of knowing where the Warlord would be. He had no way of knowing if his pleas would be heard or how they would be interpreted. But plead he did.

We are being hunted, tortured and killed. Something lurks underground. The Sand Lords are not alone. Help us, Warlord.

Yerái's fingers fell away from the trees and he pulled his hand back into the cage, crossed gazes with the people inside who watched him.

"Can they hear you, Listener?" asked one.

"These trees can hear. But can our Warlord?"

No one answered and Yerái looked down. No ants. Not even they dared come to this place.

They were just three days away from Abiren'á. Had it been overrun in the time he had been away? The enemy army could not have reached their borders in such a short time. This group was surely an advance party. They had come to lay traps, take prisoners but for what?

And then Yerái wondered if Abiren'á had already been taken. Gods but he had told his people to leave. Had they been caught too? Imprisoned in cages, awaiting some dreadful fate he was still ignorant of?

At least all the children and their carers had left, and he prayed they had not been intercepted, that they had made it to Lan Taria and beyond.

In the distance, a Sand Lord watched Yerái, had seen his gesture and wondered what the elf was doing. He would report it to his commanding officer, for had he not told them to watch out for mages? If this elf was one of them, he couldn't be a very powerful one else he would have escaped by now, probably wouldn't have been caught in the first place. He would have sprouted wings and destroyed their camp, or perhaps conjured some wind devil to blow them all away.

The warrior stood, gave the order to place the cages away from the trees. No point in taking risks and facing the wrath of a Nim'uán.

He flinched at the call of a hunting bird – a hawk. His skin crawled, dark thoughts of the cursed ones. Those animals were a prelude to all things bad. One look at a hawk was to suffer an injury, an invasion of lands, lose a family member or a prized cat. If he could get a clear view of the stinking creature, he would shoot it down.

He repressed another shudder, wrapped his cloak tightly about him. With a hawk somewhere close by, he was now sure that the warrior was a mage.

He approached his commanding officer, informed him of his suspicions. General Saz'nár would want this captive alive, and he would deliver, once the Nim'uán had conquered Abiren'á.

IT WAS WELL BEFORE DAWN, and still, Fel'annár could not sleep. His mind was too full of blue-eyed hawks and Ari children.

He watched The Company and Alféna's family as they slept, her twins snuggled up against Galdith. He had felt instant affinity with her family, and Fel'annár was hardly surprised. Both she and Galdith had lost their bonded to Sand Lords. The destruction of Sen'uár had led the survivors to settle in Sen'oléi and the two had spoken well into the night about the friends they shared.

Even as they slept before the fire, Alféna and Galdith had moved a little closer together, the children between them. But the little girl's zealously guarded book was just out of her reach. Fel'annár shuffled forwards, reached for it, eyes roving over the twisted cover.

He jumped when Tensári whispered beside him.

"You're restless."

He sat back down, book in his lap. He stared into the embers of their fire, leaned forward and threw a branch onto it. "I can't help wondering what it would have been like to grow as an Ari child. They look so serious, so daunting but their feet can hardly reach their stirrups."

Tensári didn't speak for a while, and Fel'annár wondered if she was remembering her own childhood. Had it been a good one?

"It's not easy for them, Fel'annár. Their training is ... unique. We are taught from a very young age not to cry when we kill Deviants. We do at first, but the training is constant, our tutors with us almost every moment of our days. We must not feel pity. We must not grieve for the pain we cause."

"But you do."

"Of course."

Fel'annár turned to her profile, said the first things that came out of his mouth. "Don't you find it cruel?"

She met his gaze, spoke softly. "Yes. Everyone does, even our tutors, our Master. It is sacrifice, the nature of our service. We fortify our minds from the age of seven, so that when we are seven hundred, we can still fight, still stand the weight of killing."

"But ... can they *play*? Do they ever *laugh*?"

"They do. Quietly, respectfully, although with the passage of time it dwindles. Our education is quite different to that of other children. Warfare is fed to us as surely as milk. We learn philosophy, of human nature and their society. We read their poetry, their adventures. We strive to understand their values, their beliefs, their gods. It is a tragic life they lead, Fel'annár. They are born to the certainty of death, bound to search for immortality. And when they do, when nature rebels and the rot begins, someone must end their lives. It takes a lifetime to prepare the mind for such a thing."

Fel'annár wrapped his blanket tighter around himself. He'd not really thought about it that way. It was as if the Ari'atór would make of their killing an act of grace, a killing of mercy and not extermination.

He glanced down at the book in his lap, disregarded the mangled cover and opened it to what may have been the first page. There, he smiled down at a beautiful illustration of a child sitting in the forest and upon a low branch, looking down on him was a squirrel – only it was a lizard, bright blue eyes watching the boy keenly.

His breath hitched in his chest, heart warning him to exhale even as his body tingled and felt far too heavy for the ground he sat upon.

He turned the page, saw a boat on a lake, a child reaching out to a water creature with a beak and laughing eyes – *blue* eyes. He turned back to the front cover, tried to align the ripped leather. With bulging eyes, he read.

Ari Myths and Legends.

Something was happening, something strange. This was not *myth*. He had seen these things with his own eyes. He turned to Tensári at his side, opened his mouth to speak and then closed it again.

"What's wrong?"

"You were raised as an Ari child. Have you read this?"

"Of course. We all do. You asked me before if we play like other children. We do. The Ari Myths and Legends is a classic, the first in a series of books about strange beasts with the souls of Ari'atór. They venture to faraway lands on exciting adventures. We call them *Arimals.*"

Fel'annár wanted to pinch himself. It was ridiculous. He searched for his pack, dragged it towards him and fumbled with the clasps. Opening it, he delved inside and pulled out his journal. He opened it, flicked desperately to one of his latest sketches. He passed it to Tensári, poked the page with his finger, hard enough to crease it.

She took it, looked down at the beast Fel'annár had drawn and then followed the arrow to its eyes, the scribble underneath.

Blue eyes.

She smiled. "It does look like an Arimal, I'll give you that." She handed it back to him, smile fading. "You think *this* is an Arimal?"

"A squirrel that's a lizard, with blue eyes. What else could it be?" Fel'annár's mutinous eyes dared her to gainsay him.

She did.

"They are *myths*, Fel'annár. What you saw was a trick of the light, perhaps some new creature that only lives in the Evergreen Wood. But to assume that this creature is an animal with an Ari soul is ..."

"Don't you think it's a bit of a *coincidence*? I mean there are more of them. Look."

"Sshhh." She leaned over as Fel'annár flicked through the pages and when he had finished, she breathed deeply, looked to the stars for a moment.

"All right. I concede only that it is a coincidence. But I don't agree. These creatures don't exist, Fel'annár. What you saw is similar in appearance only. It is much more logical to assume that the author of the books saw what you did and was inspired to create these fantastical stories. I am surprised you have never come across them. Most children I have ever met know them well."

"And the hawk? Azure? What of *his* blue eyes?"

"*Azure* is not an Arimal, Fel'annár. Aria you are tired, exhausted, you are drawing absurd conclusions because you have seen little Dera's book."

Fel'annár stood, glared down at her. "I'm going for a walk."

He stood, placed the book carefully within Dera's reach and left. He wanted Tensári to remain here, knew that she wouldn't. Still, she understood him well enough to stay away from him for a while. He knew what he had seen and to explain it away as mere coincidence was ... *logical.*

IT WAS unwise to walk too far from the camp. Still, he found a secluded spot at the base of a large oak and he sat with his back to it, heard its uneasy song, repeating the message from the north.

The enemy comes.

I know. He smoothed a hand over a protruding root.

Help us, Warlord.

He sat straighter, strained his mind.

Yerai? His hand repeated the movement, the root arcing up like a cat seeking attention. But still, there was no answer. Was Yerái in trouble? Or was he simply adding his voice to that of the trees? He heard the rustle of cloth and the creak of leather and he turned, saw Oruná standing there, watching.

Placing his hand in his lap, he watched as the Master Ari'atór approached. "May I join you?"

Fel'annár nodded. He had had so many questions before, about Abiren'á, about the Ari'atór and the northern territories. But now that Oruná was here, he didn't know where to start.

"You have come, as we knew you would. You don't have enough warriors. You know that don't you?"

"Not for sure. There are close to three thousand behind us on foot, maybe more. And it's my hope that Commander Hobin will bring a host from the east."

"He knows then?"

"That's my hope, Oruná."

The Master nodded, stared at him from where he now sat beside Fel'annár, legs similarly crossed. "You are curious."

"Yes, about many things. I wonder what it would have been like, to be one of those Ari children."

"Recruits."

"It sounds so cold."

"To those who don't understand us, yes. But to an Ari'atór, being a recruit is a high honour. It is the path the child takes, one of two that lies before her. She can become Spirit Warrior or Spirit Herder. The recruit is the servant who will sacrifice her own life for that of others, in service to Aria. There is no greater compliment to an Ari child than to be called recruit. You would have known this had you been told what you were as a child. It must have been hard for you, not knowing, feeling different."

Fel'annár smiled mirthlessly. "You remind me of Narosén," he mumbled. He didn't expect the Ari to laugh quite so loud or scandalously.

"And well I should. We are friends of old, he and I. He told me of your coming, almost a year ago now."

"Funny, I suppose. If things had worked out differently, you would have been my instructor." Fel'annár turned to Oruná, met his somewhat unnerving gaze.

"Yes, I would. I would have enjoyed that very much. I've heard of your skill with the bow and blade and ... with the *trees*. Tell me, Fel'an-nár," Oruná leaned sideways, as if he thought someone might overhear his words. "Is this your purpose? To defend the forest from this enemy? This Nim'uán?"

Bright green eyes rested coolly on the shrewd Ari'atór, wondered whether there was any point in avoiding the question.

"I'm not sure."

Oruná straightened, surely hadn't expected that answer. After a while he nodded. "Then your road is not yet complete, Ber'anor."

"No. And what of yours?"

His question didn't surprise the Master. "I am to forge the future generations of Ari'atór, prepare them for their hard but glorious road to death. But tell me, the name of your Guiding Light."

Fel'annár's smile was genuine now and he glanced at the tree in which he knew Tensári was perched, no longer angry at her.

"Lainon."

Oruná smiled just as widely back at him. "I knew he was meant for greatness. I am glad you had him to guide you."

This master had known Lainon and yet, he seemed genuinely happy that he had died, had not flinched at all when Fel'annár mentioned him.

"There is much for you to learn of your people, Fel'annár. You think me callous because I am proud that Lainon is dead. He died, yes, and that saddens me. But that was just a transition, a necessary step upon a road that goes ever onwards. You will walk it one day, as will I."

His dream was back in his mind, the Last Marker that was himself. He had managed to convince himself that it was not a sign that he would die in this battle, but Oruná gave him pause.

He breathed out, hand back on the root beside him. It stirred beneath his fingers and Oruná watched.

"They say your skill as a Listener far surpasses that of Yerái."

Fel'annár turned to him, studied the eyes he had first thought were cold and devoid of emotion. "I'm not just a Listener."

The Ari'atór frowned at him and Fel'annár enlightened him as much as he could.

"I have that ability, but I hear the trees much more clearly. And I can

... conjure them, *move* them." He watched Oruná, saw his words slowly sink past his scepticism.

"There was a rumour, I admit. But you know how things go, how words can magnify and sometimes diminish. Tell me, will they be of use to you in this war that looms?"

Fel'annár nodded slowly. "That's my hope, Oruná. If I can call on them, I must simply ensure that our army is not caught inside the forest when I do. But when I think of the Three Sisters, of the giants ... I try to imagine them, how big they are and what would happen if they were to move ..."

Oruná chuckled. "Many cry when they set eyes on the Sisters for the first time, Fel'annár. And I wonder at you, with this skill you possess. Anora – Moonsister, Golora, Sunsister, Bulora – Cloudsister – they reach to the very heavens, Warlord, and they move for no one." He smiled at Fel'annár, but it soon faded. "Does Pan'assár know to plan his strategy around this?"

"He knows. He was there, in Tar'eastór when it happened for the first time. But there is no guarantee that I will be able to do it again."

"But you must try. An army of three or four thousand is entirely insufficient to meet what we have seen on the horizon. And you know that Supreme Commander Hobin will not send many. He is cautious in his service to Aria."

"I know."

"You have met him then?"

Fel'annár turned to him, offered a smile. "I have. He shepherded me upon the road of understanding. It was a time of revelation, of things I found hard to believe."

"But you did, in the end."

"Yes. He carries my grandfather's Guiding Light."

Oruná smiled back at him. "I know." The Master stood, looked down at Fel'annár. "When you are able, you must go to Araria, learn of your people."

Fel'annár looked up at Oruná, thought he would like that and yet doubted he would ever have the opportunity.

Oruná nodded, and then left. Just as Tensári thudded to the ground close by. She wandered over to him, sunk down beside him and waited patiently. But Fel'annár said nothing.

"Why didn't you ask him about the Arimals?"

After a while, he answered her. "I'm not sure that I should speak of it to anyone besides The Company. I'm not sure it is beneficial to anyone to know about what I believe I saw."

Tensári remained silent, and Fel'annár resolved to think of it no more. There was nothing he could do here. But if he survived the war, he thought he may venture into the Evergreen Wood once more, try to solve the mystery if he could.

26

MYTHICAL CREATURES

∾

THE FOLLOWING DAY, Sorei prepared to ride out, not to war in the north but south, and to the city of Ea Uaré.

She was not happy, but she respected Gor'sadén as much as she did her king.

She wanted to fight the battle that loomed before them, but so too did she wish to create more Synth Blades, knowing now that Gor'sadén endorsed her sword as the finest he had ever wielded. Sorei's blades for this new army were more valuable to King Thargodén than her participation in the campaign.

She had chosen the fifty warriors who would accompany her, but she would leave Pengon here. She didn't need a lieutenant for so few warriors. Besides, she had Oruná.

Her eyes drifted to one of those wagons, where Fel'annár stood talking to a woman and her children.

"Take no risks. Don't stay in the villages but make for the city and find Amareth."

"I'm going with *you*." Eloran looked up at him stubbornly.

"Eloran. We have discussed this." Alféna's careful voice.

"I'm old enough, mother."

"You are not. You are still a child. You are not allowed to start recruit training for at least another year."

"I can fight. And that Isán is my age. He's already a novice!"

"He's Ari'atór, Eloran."

"I can help. A Sand Lord army's coming. I can't just walk away from it and hide."

"And you're not old enough, not skilled enough to be of help. You'll be in the way, a source of concern to the warriors. A *distraction*, Eloran."

"I can fight."

The man who was still a boy was angry, indignant at the thought of fleeing with the civilians. Fel'annár understood him well. It was the reaction he would have had, had something like this happened to him in Lan Taria.

"Alféna's right, Eloran," said Galdith. "You have your brother and sister to think of too. And you need training. Without it, death will be swift for you, my friend."

Eloran looked at the Silvan warrior, then turned to Fel'annár when he spoke.

"Listen. You and I will make a pact, or rather we will renew it. Do you remember what I said when we first met?"

"I told you I would train, and you said you would look for a novice by the name of Eloran. I saluted you," he smiled ruefully.

"You did. And I meant that. When this is over, you go to recruit barracks. You'll already be in the city and I'll be there to help you."

Eloran considered the situation, knew Fel'annár and his mother were right, not that it made him any less angry at the injustice. He tried one more time. "I can shoot a bow."

"And there are still Deviants about, Eloran. It falls to you to defend your family as you travel. Once you arrive in the city, look for Amareth. She will take care of you all."

"Amareth, Queen Lássira's sister?" asked Alféna.

Fel'annár started. "You call her *queen*?"

"We all do." She shrugged. "Just a habit really."

Fel'annár stared back at her for a moment, but Pan'assár's voice from further away snapped him back to the present.

"Ready for departure!"

"Remember, Alféna. Find Amareth. Do you promise me?"

"I do. And you take care of yourself. You have made my son a promise."

Fel'annár smiled and stepped back, watched as the younger children waved effusively and Eloran held one arm up in a more adult gesture.

Soon, they were gone and Fel'annár turned away, aware that if he died in this war, he would not be able to honour his promise to Eloran. Still, Turion would see him invested as novice and beyond. He took comfort in that.

It was time to leave, resume their march, and Lan Taria, land of his birth, would be their next destination.

IT HAD BEEN two weeks since Fel'annár had left. Two weeks in which she had thrown herself into her new role as Lestari. Only at night did she allow herself to reach out, in search of her connection with Fel'annár.

He was still there. He was still alive.

She spent her free time with Sontúr, Handir and Maeneth and now, with Amareth, who had accepted Llyniel's offer to stay in one of the many free rooms in the quarters she shared with Fel'annár. The king resided at the end of this corridor, handy for morning councils, after which Fel'annár's aunt would spend the rest of the day at the Merchant Guild with their people.

It had been a long day. She had hardly seen Sontúr at all, knew he'd spent most of it with Maeneth. Their friendship was the object of hearsay now, and Llyniel knew it was time for Maeneth to tell her royal brothers about the true nature of their relationship, supposing they had not already guessed.

Yesterday, Llyniel had told Amareth of her plans for dinner this evening. Amareth had seemed surprised, unsure at first that Llyniel even meant for her to be present at it. Her law mother could be so confident and sure in her role as councillor, but as a family member, she was wary and unsure, feelings of inadequacy all too clear to Llyniel.

But then Amareth had surprised her by offering to cook, and Llyniel was just fine with that idea. Even now, as she sat waiting for her guests to arrive, the smell of pea soup permeated the air. It was her husband's favourite food and before she could stop it, Fel'annár's smiling face was before her mind's eye. She steeled herself for the sudden flood of tears in her eyes. She held them back, clenched her jaw and smiled at the sound of a familiar knock.

She opened the door to Sontúr, who slipped inside while Llyniel poked her head around the door, looking one way and then the other.

"I have not seen Rinon all day, Llyniel." Sontúr grinned at her.

She returned it. "He could be lurking somewhere."

"Of course," said Sontúr, watching his friend closely. Llyniel could guess what he was thinking. She was more worried about Rinon finding out about his relationship with Maeneth than he himself was.

"How was the war meeting this morning?" she asked, making for the sideboard and pouring wine. Sontúr sauntered towards her.

"Worrying. It seems frightened flocks of birds migrating from north to south may be interfering with our messenger birds. We cannot bank on our missives arriving and even if they do, the birds may take longer to return with answers, if they ever do. The chiboos are wreaking havoc with them."

Llyniel faltered, eyes briefly catching Sontúr's. "Our army will be left without our allies. Only the Gods know how many Sand Lords have come."

Sontúr said nothing, surely knew that she was right but was unwilling to add to the anxiety the truth would bring. He quickly changed the subject.

"I am going to do some research tomorrow. I have taken it upon myself to look at how the effects of the Gas Lizard might be counter-acted. Many of our warriors fell before it, and poor Pan'assár was retching for days. His voice could have been permanently damaged. I also wonder if there is a way to bring that thing down – some substance that may be used to subdue it, to counter the gas. I wish Idernon were here ..."

"But you have Maeneth ..."

The prince had no time to answer her and instead, put his wine on a low table to open the door. Standing on the threshold, was Maeneth.

Sontúr's face almost split into two as he stepped aside, watched her enter. She smiled back at him and Llyniel rolled her eyes at them both.

"You can kiss or whatever in front of me. You won't shock me you Alpine twits."

Sontúr arched a brow and Maeneth grinned as she went on tip toe and pecked the prince on the lips with a saucy smile. Llyniel watched him, watched his eyes. Whatever the prince wanted others to believe, this was no mere infatuation. Sontúr was succumbing to something far deeper than that. It was Maeneth she was not yet sure about.

"Maeneth. Sontúr here has a proposition for you."

"Interesting. Go on."

Sontúr obviously hadn't missed the look in Maeneth's eyes. It didn't match her somewhat flippant tone at all. Llyniel continued to watch her as Sontúr spoke.

"I will spend tomorrow evening in the library doing some research. I wonder if it will be of interest to you, whether you might help."

"Research? Go on." Maeneth sat perched on the edge of her seat, eyes glittering in anticipation.

"The Gas Lizard. I mean to understand how it works, the substance that emanates from its gills and how it may be neutralised."

"But we have no sample. We thought them extinct until Rinon told me you had encountered one. I did not believe it at first and much less when he told me that the Nim'uán was *riding* it."

"Indeed. But I remember the smell. If we can find another gas with a similar smell, at least one of its components can be identified."

"Interesting. Count on me, then. But do you truly believe there are more? And even if there are, would they be able to make the journey over the sands?"

"Who knows? But the simple possibility is enough to try. You would understand if you had seen the destruction that thing left in its wake."

"I do not need to see to believe, Sontúr, not in this case. The fact that we have nothing to fight against a potential enemy is reason enough to find something."

Sontúr arched his now famous brow and Llyniel smiled, eyes drifting from the prince to the princess. Llyniel was enjoying herself, but the best part was still to come. Her last guest was here. Leaving the two to their conversation, she opened the door, smiled at Handir, watched his shrewd eyes travel from Sontúr to Maeneth.

She served him wine and even then, Maeneth and Sontúr had yet to realise that Handir had arrived. Llyniel cleared her throat, watched Sontúr's frown at the interruption and then how he swayed where he stood.

"Handir."

"Sontúr."

The awkward moment was interrupted by Amareth. She bowed to the royal children and Llyniel waved her hand in the air.

"None of that, Amareth. This is a family dinner. Speaking of which, is it ready?"

"It is, come," she gestured to the kitchen area and soon, they were seated. At the centre of the table was a clay pot sitting on a wooden slab, fragrant steam escaping from under the lid on one side. Next to it, a loaf of hot, crusty bread. If Fel'annár were here, he would give her that cheeky look of his, break off the misshapen ends and stuff them into his mouth.

"Now you may not like this," began Amareth. "It's Silvan fare, simple but tasty and nourishing. It's Fel'annár's favourite thing in the world, save for Llyniel here." She smiled as she began to ladle it into the bowls in front of her. Llyniel spared her a quick glance, saw the woman smile as she worked. She was thinking of Fel'annár too.

"That is the best kind of food," said Maeneth with a smile.

Her friend hardly knew Amareth and had never spoken to her. Sontúr and Handir had seen her a handful of times at the Silvan encampment, under a totally different light. And this had been one of Llyniel's objectives for the evening. She was family - Fel'annár's aunt – which made her aunt to Handir, Maeneth and Rinon.

She watched as Amareth handed the bowls to Handir, who in turn passed them to Sontúr, Maeneth and finally Llyniel. Soon, they all sat with steaming pea soup before them, glasses in hand.

Llyniel raised hers, looked around the table. "To family and friends."

"Family and friends," they repeated and then drank.

Llyniel glanced at Amareth beside her, smiled softly at the intensity in her eyes. How long had it been since she had sat at a table with family? she wondered.

But before they could start on their food, Handir raised his glass again. There was an odd glint in his eye.

"To lovers ... wherever they may be."

Amareth looked at Llyniel, and then at Maeneth and Sontúr.

"To lovers," they repeated, Sontúr's eyes fixed on those of the princess.

The thud of glasses on wood, the clink of cutlery as they settled down to eat, and then Amareth's question, innocent and curious.

"So tell me, Sontúr. How long have you been courting the princess?"

They froze, spoon halfway to their mouths. Llyniel's eyes glittered in glee, chanced a glance at Handir. She couldn't tell if he was smiling because he put his first spoonful of pea soup into his mouth as he stared at his sister. She stared back at him, took her own first taste of soup, a challenge in her eye.

And then Llyniel giggled, couldn't help it.

"Have I put my foot in something?" asked Amareth.

Llyniel's giggle turned into a full-blown laugh and Maeneth smiled as she ate. Sontúr looked between Handir and Llyniel, still hadn't tasted his soup.

Handir *was* smiling, she realised, even as he spoke to Sontúr. "Your soup is growing cold, *brother*."

Llyniel wheezed and then coughed and Maeneth thumped her on the back.

After Amareth's timely, yet unwitting question, the rest of the evening transpired amidst talk of what each of them had been doing, their plans for the following day, and ultimately, how they were going to tell Rinon about Maeneth and Sontúr's budding relationship.

As conversation flowed, Amareth caught Llyniel's gaze and in her honey-coloured eyes, so similar to her own, Llyniel saw thanks, and something else.

She saw pride for the law daughter she was only just beginning to know.

～

THAT NIGHT, after dinner with Llyniel, Maeneth and Handir found their father and brother sitting before the fire, enjoying a nightcap. She had missed these fleeting moments of family together before the fire. It suddenly felt wrong to keep her evolving relationship with Sontúr from them.

She sat in an armchair opposite and returned their gazes for a while. Handir perched on the arm of her chair and for a moment, she could feel his eyes on her, knew he was thinking the same. She already suspected that Rinon knew, it was a simple question of saying the words and Maeneth had never shied away from that.

"So, what were you talking about before we interrupted your conversation?" asked Handir, swirling the brandy around in his glass.

"We were talking about the war effort," said Rinon. "We were saying how little information we have. We were discussing the approaching warriors from Tar'eastór and how we would use them and ... we were talking about *you*."

"Oh? And what was it you were wondering about?" asked Maeneth.

Thargodén leaned forward. "We have hardly seen you these past days, daughter."

"I have been busy, yes. With Prince Sontúr's injury, him being away from his Company and Llyniel so busy at the Halls, I felt beholden to keep his company. We are planning to carry out research into the Gas Lizard so that some antidote may be found against its paralysing effects. There is also the question of how it may be brought down in battle."

"I remember we discussed this at one of the war councils. It is better to be prepared for any eventuality, no matter how remote. These things will help us to better confront our enemies in the future," said Handir.

Maeneth nodded at her brother. "I have also completed my proposals for this building for the most part. I hope to get your approval to begin as soon as possible. With new Silvan refugees arriving every day, it would be good to hire some of them to help with the construction work. They will be a great asset, and it will keep them busy while they are here."

Thargodén nodded slowly. "I would love to see your drawings and proposals, although we may have to wait in order to implement them. There are far fewer Silvan refugees than we had anticipated, and we do not know why that is. All of our craftsmen, masons and carpenters are busy repairing the city after the Battle of Brothers, and that must be a priority. It seems prudent to wait until more Silvans come before you start."

"That sounds reasonable, father. Besides, for what I have in mind, the Silvans will put their hearts into the project where the Alpines will simply do the work. They won't understand what I am trying to do, not until it is finished and they can see it for themselves."

Rinon crossed his arms. "Are you really going to make this building into a *farm*?"

She smiled as she huffed. "Wait until you see my proposal before you judge, brother. But is that what you *really* wanted to ask me?"

"Of course not," he answered.

"There is something else I wish to share with you, although I feel sure Rinon here knows exactly what I will say."

"Say it anyway."

"Sontúr and I have become close."

Her words echoed about them. Handir stared into his glass while Thargodén's brows sat high on his forehead. But Rinon's face was unreadable – even to *her*. She pressed on.

"We share many things. Our love of science, our positions as royal children. And he has grey hair."

Handir snorted. "I for one am glad for you. Sontúr is a good friend, a skilled statesman and a brother to Fel'annár. For my part, you could not have picked a better partner."

Maeneth raised her glass at her younger brother. But still, Rinon said nothing and neither did her father.

"How serious is it?" asked the king.

"We have not spoken of the future, if that is what you mean, father. For now, we simply enjoy each other's company."

Rinon finally ripped his eyes away from her and drank noisily.

"So, are you keeping your thoughts to yourself, Rinon? Or are you devising a way to kill our princely guest," asked Maeneth.

Rinon didn't smile, didn't even frown. Instead, he spoke, tone devoid of emotion. "Sontúr seems like an honourable elf. I'll grant him that."

"But you are not happy for me ..."

It took a while for Rinon to answer. "We shall see."

She knew he was holding back, was sure about what he was thinking but hadn't said. He wanted to know if there was a chance she would leave – again – travel to Sontúr's homeland in the mountains. It was just as well he hadn't asked her that, because she would not have been able to answer.

"Well then, I have a busy day tomorrow. Our patrols are due in with information on the Deviant horde to the east. If you will excuse me." Rinon stood, placed his glass on the table and bowed to the king. With a nod at his siblings, he left.

The door clicked shut and Thargodén heaved a breath. "That was not as bad as it could have been."

"Nor as good as it might have been," said Handir.

"He thinks you will leave," said Thargodén, almost to himself. And if the king were to be honest with himself, he wanted that as little as Rinon did. His gaze lingered on his daughter, wondered if she could see his heart in his eyes.

"I do not know how this will go, father. I cannot answer that question."

Thargodén nodded slowly. "Then we shall see. But know this, Maeneth. You are free to love who you will, here or in Tar'eastór or wherever your heart takes you. You must never break it, because in truth, it is all you have to fight for. If you lose your heart, you lose *everything*."

Maeneth cocked her head to one side as she studied her father's eyes. "You approve then? Of Sontúr?"

"If I didn't, what would you do?"

She smiled sadly, leaned closer to where her father sat before her.

"I would love him anyway."

Thargodén smiled, glanced at a relieved Handir and then back to his daughter. Gods but if there was anything at all that was clear in his mind, it was this one thing. His children would be free to love who they would, whether or not they would leave. Whether or not he approved.

And in this particular circumstance, Thargodén did.

"Then love him you must, daughter."

～

A CLOAKED elf leaned against a wagon, its owner sitting a distance away, eating quietly by himself. He had glared at Macurian for daring to touch his property but made a swift retreat when the former Shadow returned it, his icy grey eyes hard as flint.

He could see the entire courtyard from here, not as well as he had once been able. One of the many injuries he had received just before the Battle of Tar'eastór had left him with a slash down the side of his face. Mercifully, it hadn't caught his eye, but the skin over and around it was not in the right place, wouldn't be for a few years yet.

He had searched in the obvious places. The houses of wealthy lords, friends and acquaintances of the deceased Lord Sulén. And then he had searched in the less obvious places. In the Merchant Guild where Melu'sán reigned supreme, and then in the whore houses of the western quarter of the city, where Sulén had other acquaintances they say he frequented.

Nothing. The letter Or'Talán had written to his son before his departure to war was nowhere to be found. But he wasn't going to tell Lerita that. There were still roads to investigate. If someone had destroyed that letter, then someone knew of it - that would be Macurian's second line of investigation.

But he had to be careful. There were two people in this place who would remember him, and he had no intention of antagonising them. One would sound the alarm should she see him, and the woman could scream, he'd give her that. The other would likely kill him. Well, he could try, huffed Macurian. The fool prince had taken an injury that had left him useless from what he could see. Still, he had been shot saving the crown prince. Not a fool. Sontúr was honourable, everything he had not been.

Those days of treachery and disloyalty were over for Macurian. He wanted something more, wanted to return to those distant days in which he had believed in something, believed in a king and then lost his way, tempted by money and renown. Perhaps that was why he had come to Ea Uaré, instead of remaining in Prairie. The one person whom he admired was here, never mind that he had attempted to kill him a few times. Luckily, he had failed.

Fel'annár Ar Thargodén.

What Macurian hoped to achieve by being in the same city as his former target, he did not know. Indeed, it was dangerous. That Company of his would throttle him the moment they laid eyes on him.

Still, Lerita was known to pay well.

He watched Acting Commander General Turion stride across the courtyard, from the Inner Circle to the palace, surely on his way to the king's morning brief. He was a good general, they said, looked out for his troops. Macurian admired that.

He pushed away from the wagon, ignored the insult from the ragged merchant and made towards the eastern quarter where the darker side of Ea Uaré spent their hours of play. But Macurian wasn't going to play. He was going to find others – like him – ex-combat elves who made a living just like he did, honourable or otherwise. Because if anyone could set him on the right track to understanding what had happened to that letter, it was them.

THE AFTERNOON WAS SWIFTLY DARKENING, and so were Fel'annár's thoughts.

That conversation with the Ari Master had set him thinking about his dream in the Evergreen Wood, about what it meant. It had renewed his fears that perhaps death was his destiny in this war.

But then, who ever got to know the moment of their death? If it was a certainty, then he needed to stop fretting about *when* it would happen and simply live his life to the fullest, however short or long it may be. Oruná had said that death was a transition, a necessary step upon a road that goes ever onwards. The Ari children had surely been taught this from an early age, and Fel'annár would embrace the thought. *He* was Ari too.

He snapped out of his musings with a warning call from the trees. There was a small group of Sand Lords not far to the north and yet closer than they should have been. It was unheard of for Sand Lords to be this far south. He wondered if it was a scouting party, sent ahead by the Nim'uán to spy on them.

He kicked his mount forwards, came shoulder to shoulder with Pan'assár, eyes glowing softly.

"Sand Lords to the north. Thirty minutes. A small stealth unit, most probably scouts."

"Small enough for The Company to handle?"

"Yes."

"See to it, General."

Fel'annár nodded, and then started when Bulan called to him from behind.

"I would join you."

Fel'annár glanced at Pan'assár, saw his nod of approval. With a gesture to The Company, they cantered away from the main body of the army, even as news of the incursion rippled backwards and throughout their group.

THE COMPANY and Bulan rode through the forest, light failing around them, sky beyond the canopy a deepening blue. Fog was rolling in, covering the ground and half obscuring the trees, casting a bluish-grey tinge over everything. Fel'annár was reminded of his nightmare in the Evergreen Wood, repressed a shudder at the thought of what had been inside that fog.

"The trees don't give me numbers, but it's not purposeful. They seem distracted. I can only assume there aren't many as their alarm would be greater. Still, this close it's strange. It *must* be a scouting party."

"It would make sense," said Idernon. "They'll want to know the army that comes to meet them, our numbers and weaponry. They're strangely far into the forest, though. Surely the trees would have warned you had the main body of the enemy army entered?"

Fel'annár said nothing, his eyes drawn to the trees around them. There were deep echoes in his mind, something ancient, something not quite worldly was here. His eyes scanned the boughs, nothing but silhouettes now against the deep blue sky.

A flash of blue caught his eye.

Azure.

"There," he pointed, pulling on the reins and waiting for the others to join him.

Tensári watched as Fel'annár held his forearm out and the hawk glided down and then landed there.

Bulan and The Company gasped behind him.

"Peace. He's a friend." Fel'annár turned his head, saw his uncle's shock at the sight of a goshawk with blue eyes, Idernon's wide eyes and Carodel's gaping mouth.

"So this is why you asked about hawks with blue eyes," said Idernon. "You were referring to this bird."

"I was. As you can see, it was no trick of the light."

Bulan guided his horse closer to Tensári, leaned in to speak, so that only she could hear.

"It looks like an Arimal ..."

"But he's not, Captain. I'm sure you agree," said Tensári, glaring at Bulan, daring him to gainsay her. But the captain was too shocked even for that, his next words all too predictable.

"Of course I agree ..." he said absent-mindedly, eyes on the hawk.

Silent minutes later, Fel'annár raised his hand for them to dismount and continue on foot. He was listening, eyes reflecting the waning light like a cat watching a steady candle. Another signal later, they slowed their pace, drew their weapons. The enemy was here, not yet visible in the twilight forest. Fel'annár raised his arm, felt Azure hop onto his shoulder.

Fifty yards, closing.

Tensári's long sword was in her hand, fog swirling around it as she inched forwards, The Company around her. Fel'annár's own swords were in his hands.

They moved slowly, walking almost sideways, feet careful and silent, breath visible in the growing humidity. Bulan, spear in hand, eyes on the path ahead as much as they were on the strange bird that seemed quite at ease amongst them.

Fel'annár signalled behind him.

Twenty yards, closing.

The enemy was not travelling away from them but had either stopped or turned to meet them. Not scouts then, realised Fel'annár. If they had been, they would have fled, eager to take whatever knowledge they had gleaned back to their commanders.

One hand in the air, a signal to stop, sudden and urgent. In the distance, standing before a tree was a single Sand Lord. He was cloaked in black, but the customary silver and gold of their armour, vambraces and weapons was missing. Had there not been a light breeze that had moved the dark cloak, Fel'annár would not have seen him standing there. But why didn't he move?

Fel'annár's hand signalled for a slow advance but still, the Sand Lord remained. Elven eyes searched the branches in case attack came from above. Not normal for this enemy but as Galadan had rightly said, they had learned to expect the unexpected where the Nim'uán was concerned.

One finger up, wrist rotating.

Form a circle. Move right.

The angle opened, giving them a first glimpse of what stood behind the black-clad Sand Lord. More of them, standing utterly still and Fel'annár's eyes flared. Only now did the trees tell him the reason why the enemy simply stood there. But there was no time to explain it to The Company, just as there was no more need for stealth. He reached out, fingers grazing over the bark of a tree and he talked as he walked towards the Sand Lords.

"Faith. Charge and don't stop, *whatever* happens."

"What are you talk ..." began Bulan.

"Charge!" yelled Fel'annár, lurching forwards, the confused Company running behind, the flapping wings of a hawk now above them as Azure took flight. Feet thudded over the ground, the Sand Lords nearer and still they did not move, satisfaction on their faces. Bulan glanced at Idernon just beside him, for any sign that he knew what they were doing. He could see the Sand Lord's glee ... they were surely running into a trap.

But that self-satisfied leer he had seen just moments before, changed to confusion and then disbelief. As one, The Company yelled and Bulan shrieked as they were hoisted into the air by the trees. They sailed over the enemy and then descended from the branches on the other side. No sooner they hit the ground they turned to face the Sand Lords who were now in front of them. The trench the enemy had thought to lure them into, now lay behind the Sand Lords.

Bulan finally understood.

A flurry of muted clicks and trills struck a discordant note in their minds, like a giant insect mesmerising its prey. The Sand Lords didn't shout as they charged forwards, scimitars and swords above their hooded heads.

Two of Idernon's arrows hurtled through the air before them, hitting but not killing one of them. It was now too dark for effective archery and he discarded his bow.

Grunts and gasps, clanging metal and the thud of weapons against flesh; there were more of them than Fel'annár had anticipated. He remembered how the Sand Lords had been standing, one behind the other; the trees did not understand numbers. It was always him to interpret what they saw, and on this occasion, they had seen too little.

Fel'annár feigned right and cut through the belly of a Sand Lord and then turned to the next. He slit a throat, deftly ducked under the arc of blood that followed the angle of his blade. Back to his next opponent, he stabbed backwards and then kicked out, freeing his swords as a group of three rushed him from the left. Feign right, then left, he turned full circle, blades swivelling in his hands, confusing his enemies. All three fell and he turned to where Bulan was fighting with his spear, seeing him for the first time in battle. His enemies fell around him, the longer range of the spear killing them before they could get close enough to him with their blades. Fel'annár wanted to watch but Galdith shouted and then fell sideways, rolling out of the way of a downward strike. Galadan's sword was through its gut and the Sand Lord shrieked as he pulled it back.

And still they came. Even as he killed another, he saw Tensári surrounded by three. She was by far the superior warrior, but the Sand Lords were tall and bulky, harder to take down than Deviants. They were wearing down her endurance and Fel'annár fought his way towards her. He slashed over the back of the legs of the foremost opponent. He fell away and Fel'annár stabbed him. With the rest of The Company and Bulan occupied, Fel'annár and Tensári fought side by side but still, the Sand Lords came.

He should have brought more warriors. Pan'assár had asked him if The Company would be enough. He'd been wrong.

He blocked an incoming scimitar, the stroke so powerful he stumbled sideways, crashed into Tensári.

They fell.

Eeaaa Eeaaa Eeaaa aaaaaaaaa

Fel'annár's head snapped upwards where he lay on the ground, saw Azure's outline, dark against the slightly lighter sky beyond the trees. Movement to his left and he turned, just in time, narrowly avoiding a scimitar. He rolled the other way, heard a blade thudding into the ground beside him. He brought his long sword up, parried another blade just before his face. He caught sight of Tensári, grappling to her feet and falling, Sand Lords separating them.

Not now, not yet ... it was too soon to die. He had not fulfilled his purpose.

"To the Warlord!" Idernon's frantic call. And then Fel'annár heard flapping wings, too close to the battle. Confused, still on his back, he looked up, mind scrambling. He couldn't move, couldn't think but his eyes watched as Azure glided down from the skies, bigger than he had been before. The closer to the ground, the wider Fel'annár's disbelieving eyes. He needed to lift his swords and *fight,* but he felt boneless for Azure was growing, changing, until his fanned tail elongated and then separated and there were two legs instead of feathers.

The Sand Lords looked up in terror, pointing and yelling, swords in one hand, other arm protecting themselves.

Eeaaaaaaaaaaa aaaaagh! The bird was an elf and he thudded to the ground, swords already in his hands.

The Sand Lords stared in horror at the winged elf, while tears spilled from wide green eyes, heart hammering, lips quivering with a thousand words, a thousand emotions. Fel'annár's skin was ice and even as he scrambled to his feet, his knees were as rigid as a new-born calf.

It wasn't possible ...

"*Fel'annár!*" He turned, shocked, lifted his sword over his face to parry, felt the flat of his own blade bash into his face. He staggered backwards, Galadan flitting before his blurry vision and then Bulan, spear whirling through the air close by. He could hear the battle, as if from somewhere else, hear the shocked thud of his own heart, strained and irregular. Swords up he circled on himself, blinked furiously to clear his eyes, saw Azure fighting, all black and blue in the foggy half-light. An elf with wings, two swords slicing through his opponents with a strength that was not born of Bel'arán. He was too fast, too strong. Fel'annár searched for Tensári, saw her standing still amidst the fighting.

"*Idernon!*" Fel'annár called even as he made it to her side, fought off a Sand Lord that intended to slice her head off from behind. Soon, Idernon was on her other side, Bulan and Ramien close to Fel'annár but the distraction was too great. He dared not look at her lest the vision before him disappear. He drank of it, eyes on the face of Azure as he slashed through his last opponent and the battle was over.

Azure turned to face them, wings folding behind him.

The elf bird stared back at them, and then turned his eyes on Tensári. He stepped forward, held out a hand, the hint of desperation on his face. She took an uncertain step, held her hand out, fingers caressing the air between them, the gap between them ever smaller. The ghost of a grief-stricken smile, for Azure seemed to know something they did not. His blue eyes burned so brightly Fel'annár could hardly see his face anymore, and the closer Tensári drew, the brighter it became, until Azure was nothing but a ball of burning blue light.

But Fel'annár knew what he had seen. *Who* he had seen.

"*Noooooooo!*" Tensári's raw, wavering voice. Fel'annár could hear her indignant anger, her panic that he was leaving, her confusion that mirrored his own.

Fluttering wings and from the light, Azure was a bird once more. He flew past them, up and then away. Circling above them once, he banked away with a final squawk until he was lost from sight.

Fel'annár ripped his eyes away from the sky and to Tensári. She had sunk boneless to her knees, eyes wide and disorientated. Harnessing his blades, he covered the distance between them and joined her on the ground, knelt before her and listened as words spilled from lax lips.

"I had a dream in Araria." It was nothing but a whisper, a thought only just given voice and Fel'annár listened, in the hope that it would bring him back from the strange half-world he himself still wandered.

"I dreamt I was a bird, soaring over the mountains, searching for a path. I found it, knew it was my destiny. Ea Uaré. But then I returned to Tar'eastór, flew past it and to Araria, to Valley and to the very Source itself. I saw my Connate standing before it. He turned and although I was bird, he knew me."

Fel'annár could feel hot tears streaming down his cheeks, over slack lips. Eyes travelled upwards, from Tensári's clenched fists and to her face, her eyes dancing from one side to the other. She was thinking, piecing together a puzzle in her mind but then her eyes suddenly focussed on Fel'annár.

"It wasn't me I dreamt of. It was *him*.

"It was *Lainon's* future."

The Company and Bulan stood shocked and perplexed around them. Bulan didn't know who the winged Ari'atór was, but the rest did and Idernon turned to Bulan.

"That was Lainon, Fel'annár's first Ber'ator. Tensári's Connate. He died in Tar'eastór."

Bulan said nothing, couldn't. None of them could.

Fel'annár climbed slowly to his feet, swiping at tears, breath still coming too fast. He looked upwards, breathed in the forest around him and then looked down at Tensári. He held out his hand. She studied it for a moment and then took it, locked her knees and stared at Fel'annár, thinking perhaps that he would have an answer for her. He smiled through his own confusion.

"He came back ..."

"He left again."

Fel'annár shook his head. "He's still up there, somewhere. Alive, Tensári, alive and in *this* world."

She said nothing, but Fel'annár's mind was bursting at the seams. Azure was Lainon, but was Lainon Arimal?

"Can Arimals take the shape of their former selves?"

Tensári shook her head. "No. That is not a part of the myth."

Fel'annár had suspected as much. This was new. Azure was not simply an animal with an Ari soul. It was an entirely different being, a dead elf who had returned to Bel'arán in the shape of an animal.

Whatever creature this was, the Evergreen Wood was full of them.

27

WEEPING GIANTS

~

IN THEIR ALMOST THREE weeks of travel, a number of elves had joined the cavalry on their march north. Last Gor'sadén had counted, there were one thousand six hundred and seventy on horseback. He could only pray that more had joined the foot soldiers behind. But they couldn't be sure of that until they reached Lan Taria, their next destination.

There, the army would regroup, and the horses would stay behind. With some luck, Dalú and their supplies would already be waiting for them.

After that fateful skirmish in the woods, The Company and Bulan had returned shocked, strangely devoid of emotion and Gor'sadén knew something had happened. Likewise, Pan'assár had heard Fel'annár's report, but in it, there was nothing to warrant their strange mood. All Fel'annár had said was that the Sand Lords had dug a trench, had expected them to charge straight into it. He had then recommended that Pan'assár send out small stealth groups in search of further traps so that they could be disabled. The Sand Lords wanted live prisoners, but why they would do something so uncharacteristic was beyond them for now.

Sand Lords never took prisoners.

Was this how the enemy intended to hinder their march northwards? Slow them down with traps so that when they arrived, it would be too late to retake the city? Whichever the case, Pan'assár had heeded Fel'annár's suggestion, and small groups had been sent out to scour the land before them.

With Lan Taria just a few minutes away, they were nothing but a week away from Abiren'á, and just four days if they took the Wetwood route, which was Pan'assár's intention.

But before they could tackle the hardships of that place, they would be forced to wait for the foot soldiers to join them in Lan Taria. It was a source of distress to the warriors. Many had family in Sen'oléi, Lan Taria, Ea Nanú and Abiren'á. The very thought of their Silvan city in the north, invaded by Sand Lords was enough to send them galloping on, tear through the Wetwood itself, Pan'assár's orders be damned.

But the commander was right. They needed to wait for the army to be complete before facing the enemy if they were to have any real chance of success. The warriors knew this, but they didn't like it.

The river was half-a-day's trek to the west of Lan Taria, one of Fel'annár's favourite places as a child. To him, Ramien and Idernon, the walk to the river was like a mighty quest back when they were children. They would take their picnic basket and then spend hours watching the fishermen. To the three children, the narrow river was like an ocean, but when Fel'annár had grown, he realised it had simply been a matter of proportion. He smiled fondly at the memory, glanced at Idernon and then Ramien, rather thought they too, were reminiscing.

Home. It was here where he had been raised, ignorant and shielded from his Alpine family, even his Silvan family. He wanted to vault off his horse, find his friends, the kind people who had known him with no teeth and a shock of silvery hair. He wanted to touch every tree, remember every laugh and every moment of awe, of discovery, of whispered dreams high in the boughs.

Had they truly all known who he was? Idernon and Ramien hadn't, small mercy, he supposed. His childhood fantasies and adolescent dreams should be fond, not sour as they were now, tainted by the knowledge that his existence had been a lie, to protect him yet still, nothing but a worthless fabrication. He could feel Idernon and Ramien on either side, he sensed Gor'sadén's concern from further away but he could only guess what Bulan would be thinking. He glanced upwards, in search of Azure.

Lainon.

Even now, the thought of his brother, up there in the form of a bird seemed nothing short of ... unhinged. No one spoke of what had happened, but they would. There were questions to be asked, of how it was possible, of why Lainon had not stayed to explain. They wanted to know what he was, why he had come, if there were others like him. Was he an Arimal? Or was he something entirely different?

But Azure had not returned.

The first villagers came into sight along the main path that led into the centre of the town. They watched silently as the mounted warriors marched past them, eyes fixed on Fel'annár who rode beside Pan'assár and an Alpine lord they did not recognise.

And then Fel'annár spotted the four riders from the advance patrol and beside them, to his utter relief, was Dalú. He raised a hand in greeting, watched the captain return it with a smile. With Dalú and his unit, it meant one hundred more fighters for their cause, and the bulkier supplies they would need for the battle.

He turned back to the path before him, realising that hardly any of the villagers had evacuated. Even the children were here, sitting on their parents' shoulders and watching.

What did they want of him? These people who watched him now, were the same ones who had forged a fictitious life for an orphaned child. They had fed the story to him for fifty-one years. Now, it was time to face the consequences of that lie. Surely they knew he had discovered their deception, that he was angry? So why hadn't they left? Or was that precisely why they had *not* left?

Pan'assár leaned into Gor'sadén, exchanged murmured words and then both fell back from the front of the line. Fel'annár cast an inquisitive glance at his mentor, who gestured to the fore with his chin and for a moment, Fel'annár's eyes drifted to Pan'assár. Whether the smile was really there, or his mind had simply conjured it, he couldn't say. But the commander had yielded the honour to him. Fel'annár and The Company would lead the warriors into Lan Taria, their hometown, and at their side, Bulan, the uncle these people had never spoken of but knew well.

The three boys from Lan Taria moved into place, The Company and Bulan just behind and the tense silence began to waver, and then break. Birds took flight, flitted around the boughs as the faces of children appeared from above and Fel'annár looked up. He saw their round eyes, awestruck by the army that filed past them. They waved at him, innocent smiles that spoke of pride and excitement and nothing remotely related to the great deception that had been his own childhood. They knew nothing about that. Only that the Warlord had come, and he was from Lan Taria.

The chiboos settled and began their screeching and squawking and the children imitated them as they laughed. The bird and elf song was almost deafening, but the Silvan warriors laughed and clapped each other upon the shoulders while the Alpines looked up, just as awestruck as the children who looked down on them.

The path was becoming more populated, but unlike the children in the trees, the people did not cheer. They were unsure, realised Fel'annár. Yes, they knew that he knew. They knew he was angry and that *was* why they were here, risking their lives because they had surely believed they had done the right thing, as surely as they knew how implicitly wrong it had been.

The Company, commanders and warriors rode on to the stables and then dismounted, and soon, they were surrounded by the townsfolk. They stared at Fel'annár and the armour they had had a part in creating. The boy they had sheltered was a Warlord, strong and resolute, if not unnerving, because his resemblance to Or'Talán had only grown over the years, and his eyes were brighter than they ever had been.

Word spread through the lines of onlookers, ripples of muted voices but still they looked at him with some shared emotion in their eyes. They were willing him to speak, to say something.

To forgive them.

Fel'annár thought he understood. He saw the old baker, remembered how he used to save the crusty tips that had fallen from the bread and toss them at him so that he could eat them before Amareth could tell him off. He spotted the weapons master who had first shown him how to hold a bow, how to swing a sword and here he stood in the armour of a Warlord, the grey sash of a Kah Warrior around his middle, Master of both those weapons.

He saw Dalia, his first love, her eyes on his Bonding Braid and the sadness in her gaze. He saw Golloron, the town's Ari Spirit Herder, eyes wide in realisation, or was it confirmation? Had he known that Fel'annár was Ari'atór, that he was Ber'anor, even back then? The Ari children had.

But it was when he saw Thavron that his emotions threatened to wrest control from him. He had been close, would have been a member of the original Company, save that he had never felt the call to arms. Instead, he had stayed in Lan Taria and became a forester.

Fel'annár stepped forwards, opened his arms to the friend they had left behind. Their embrace was strong, fierce and silent and then Idernon and Ramien joined them. Four friends, four brothers.

Their circle of love was the catalyst, and the crowds began to move, voices stirring, sounds of relief and the first, tentative smiles broke through the hurt, the concern, the plea for forgiveness. Like a pot bubbling over, a dark cloud full to bursting, first drops becoming a downpour.

For Fel'annár, it was the moment he truly forgave Amareth, the moment that he finally understood what she had done. He could even forgive her for sending him into the world unprepared, at the mercy of others.

Had she allowed Bulan to take him to Abiren'á, he would have grown with a proper family, would have been happy. But he may never have become brothers with Idernon, Ramien and Thavron. He may never have met Turion and Lainon and then travelled to Tar'eastór. He would never have met Gor'sadén, called him father and Kah Master, and he would never have been able to help Pan'assár on his road to redemption.

He would not have met Llyniel.

Yes, he forgave Amareth, because he would change nothing of his road to here and now.

He squeezed his eyes shut, arms full of love, surrounded by it, filling him, feeding him.

"Hail the Warlord!" A scream from the crowds.

"Hail!" A roar from Lan Taria.

Hands on his back, on his hair, shouts of welcome and Fel'annár finally raised his head and looked about. People everywhere and instinctively, The Company and even Bulan surrounded him. Soon enough, Thavron's plea for silence was heeded and the din began to fade.

Golloron stared at the Warlord who had once sat on his lap and played with the beads in his hair. He bowed, and there he stayed until the silence was complete.

"Welcome home, Ar Lássira, Warlord. We have been waiting for this day to come. We could not leave until you came, Ber'anor."

Gasps from the crowds, from the warriors who hadn't known what he was. And there it was. Golloron had always known, or at least suspected.

"We come to you in a time of strife, Golloron. It's time to fight once more and this battle will be our biggest challenge yet. The enemy brings a mighty host from Calrazia, and its destination is our forests. The king sends our new army to meet it but you, all of you, must leave. Take the rafts down the river and to the city docks or travel the path southwards to the city. There, Amareth and our Elders await. Find them and stay there, wait for us to return in victory."

Would they listen? he wondered. He had been nothing but an untried adolescent when he had left this place yet here he was, a Warlord ordering them to leave their homes.

"We have discussed this," said Golloron. "We all wanted to wait, to see for ourselves what had become of you. We wanted to show you that we are sorry and yet not so. We wanted to express how much you and your family mean to Lan Taria. We decided that we would do whatever you bid us. You've spoken, and we *will* leave but heed me, Fel'annár. When you return victorious to the city, we will set that place alive with a Silvan dance the likes of which has never been seen. Our hearts are set on it. What we did, what you have achieved, deserves celebration."

Fel'annár looked from Golloron to Thavron, to the baker and the weapons master. He saw Dalia's understanding eyes and how the others stared back at him, waiting.

But what to say? He had no words and so he bowed his head and when he lifted it once more, the smile on his lips and the fondness in his eyes told them everything they needed to know.

Gor'sadén's chin was high in the air, as was Bulan's and Pan'assár watched in silent curiosity. Fel'annár's head whipped to one side, familiar voices rising over the murmuring crowds.

"Idernon!"

"Ramien!"

He knew those voices, smiled wide as he watched his two friends embrace their parents, desperate hands clutching at their cloaks, or in Ramien's case, to the back of his waist.

This was what Fel'annár had coveted all his life – this sense of belonging – to have a family. And then he reminded himself that he had one, back in the city. He had a father, two brothers and a sister. He had an aunt and an uncle, a grandmother and a cousin.

He had Llyniel, Gor'sadén and The Company.

He *did* have family. He just didn't know how to be a part of one. He had never learned as a child.

Idernon, Ramien and their parents turned to Fel'annár, smiled and held out a hand in invitation.

Fel'annár turned to Pan'assár, Gor'sadén beside him, silent permission to leave for a while. The commander smiled, quite uncharacteristically and Fel'annár turned back to the elves who had been the closest thing to family that he had ever had as a child. They had adopted him, and he had spent as much time in their houses as Ramien and Idernon had in his own with Amareth. It was time for a little Silvan repast, tales on the cusp of battle. They may never see each other again, but they would enjoy the moment of their reunion, one more time.

Bulan and the commanders turned away, greeted Dalú who had been watching from further away. Dusk was falling and Pan'assár sent the two captains to oversee the camp while he and Gor'sadén spoke with Golloron.

Tomorrow, they would decide their route and strategy because beyond this point, the terrain would begin to change. They needed a plan, but for any plan to succeed, they needed information, and that was something they did not have.

Once the warriors on foot caught up with them, they would step into the unknown.

IT WAS LATE when The Company returned to the camp. Bellies full, hearts full, they sat and brewed tea, quiet contemplations in the night.

Their families and friends would leave tomorrow. Some would walk, perhaps cross paths with the foot soldiers. Others would take the rafts, travel down the Calro to the docks. Golloron and Thavron would take that faster route, then make for the city in search of the Elders.

It was time to wait for the army to regroup and then plan their strategy for the final leg of their journey north. Soon, Fel'annár would finally know how many others had joined their cause. How many had been persuaded to give Pan'assár another chance?

Fel'annár frowned, looked sideways, eyes shimmering. Idernon leaned forward, waiting for him to tell them what it was he had sensed.

"That Listener is out there somewhere, his message weak, but I can sense him. He's frightened of something."

"Do you know where he is?" asked Carodel.

"Somewhere between Sen'oléi and Abiren'á."

Hot tea in their hands, some drank while others stared into the hot liquid. But Tensári looked to the skies.

Their evening in the company of family had been a blessed distraction from their memories of Lainon, of the burning questions his appearance had triggered. They had yet to speak of it. It had been too recent, too unbelievable, even though they didn't doubt what they had seen.

"Do you think he'll come back?" asked Ramien.

Fel'annár stared at him, and then turned to Tensári when she spoke.

"Yes. Even now, he is up there, watching us. I think he is waiting for the shock to clear our minds, *my* mind."

"Can you sense him?" asked Galdith.

"Yes. But there is nothing new about that. I have always sensed him, but now that I think about it, the feeling has been stronger these past few weeks."

"I have never heard of this ability to change physical form, and I am older than most here save for the commanders," said Galadan. "I know of the Ari myths about creatures who possess Ari souls. But they do not transform as Lainon did. And I have never heard of anyone who came back from the Short Road." His eyes landed on Fel'annár, drifted to the tea in his hands.

His cup was shaking.

Fel'annár felt guilty now for not telling them of the creatures he had seen in the Evergreen Wood. But now that Lainon had revealed himself, now that Fel'annár knew he had surely followed him from that place, he needed to tell them. Because what if the Squiliz and the Fibird were also capable of changing form? Were they Ari'atór who had fallen in battle?

Fel'annár felt himself teetering on the border of understanding. Was it the Evergreen Wood itself he was destined to protect? But of course, as one question may have been answered, it brought with it a whole new array of uncertainties. What were the creatures doing there? Why had they not crossed into the Source? Or perhaps they had but had come back, in which case why?

He couldn't breathe. Panic momentarily taking over. One hand came up to his still chest and then he gasped, stood awkwardly, other hand held out to steady himself.

Galadan shook his arm, the others standing around him. "Fel'annár. *Fel'annár!*"

Something crackled, a soft vibration underground and the troop stirred. Some even stood, hands on weapons. A soft breeze disturbed the leaves, and Fel'annár stood tall, hair floating around him. He tilted his head back, eyes burning as the world turned green.

A conflagration, something jolted through his body, made him weak. He felt Tensári's strong hand at his back. Scalp tingling, braids writhing, snaking around his peripheral vision, he could hear his own, harsh breaths, feel a power envelop him as the world moved too slowly around him.

To the others, he was nothing more than an outline inside the blinding light. They shielded their eyes, stepped back save for those of The Company and the commanders.

"Fel'annár!" Idernon's frantic call.

"The Xeric Wood is breached."

"Numbers!" yelled Pan'assár from further away.

"Thousands. They keep coming - an army of men and beasts."

"Beasts?"

"We don't know, Commander."

"*We?* What's going on?" asked Bulan, as panicked about the answer as he was for his nephew.

"How long until they reach Abiren'á?"

"Hours, Commander."

The Silvan troops were on their feet, preparing to leave and defend their Silvan city. They didn't doubt what Fel'annár said. The Silvans and Alpines of Ea Uaré had seen the Warlord's transformation before, as had most of the Tar'eastór warriors who had fought in that battle with the forest. But others were terrified of the spectacle and their companions tried and failed to calm them. Pan'assár turned to them, Galadan instantly at his side.

"Stop." Pan'assár's practised voice of command.

"Warriors!" Galadan's own, characteristic bellow.

Dropping their half-filled packs, they stood up, rebellious faces turned to the commander, strange sounds from the forest around them. Deep rumbling, a discordant hum and then some unearthly choir that struck dread in their hearts. It came in waves, ebbed and then started again. What was this? they asked. Was this what Listeners heard? And if it was, how could they stand to hear it, hear what seemed to them to be the voice of doom, trumpets heralding the end of all things. What message lay inside this terrible symphony?

But only Fel'annár knew the answer to that.

"Do not be afraid! We will take our city back. I promise you this. But not tonight. We must wait for the rest of our army to come, so that we can face whatever has come and strike it down."

"Our people are there. They'll be slaughtered!" yelled a warrior.

"And so will we if we run blindly through the Wetwood and to Abiren'á."

There were murmurs, heads swivelling here and there as the disturbing sounds washed over them again and again, some arcane lament from the trees.

"The commander is right," shouted Galadan. "His strategy is sound, you know that it is. We wait, as much as it feels wrong, it is the right thing to do." Galadan turned to Bulan just beside him, a steely command in his eye to help them keep their warriors at camp.

Another wave of discordant harmony and Bulan stepped forward.

"Hold fast. Obey. My people are there too and the Gods but I would charge in there and deliver them from danger. But I won't. You won't. We need to wait for the rest of our army, and then we march on those unholy bastards and we slaughter them!"

The roar of defiance from the warriors that followed Bulan's words was enough to drown the unnerving sounds from the forest, but not for long and the waxing and waning choir was back.

The troop sat stiffly at the fires once more, while Dalú explained to them how his unit had met many rafts from Abiren'á on their journey up the river, full of families and children. Many warriors held to hope that their own mothers, fathers, sisters and brothers had made it out, that they had taken the rafts. But others wondered whether their loved ones were among those who had refused to leave, despite the warnings.

A crescendo of minor notes, incomprehensible voices inside. Fel'annár sat at the fire, body shaking, eyes softly shimmering. The Company watched him. Gor'sadén watched him while Pan'assár, Galadan and the captains left to begin their vigil upon the outraged and unnerved warriors.

"What is that sound, Fel'annár?" asked Carodel quietly, so as not to startle him. He was surely still listening.

"It is the voice of the Sentinels of Abiren'á, the Three Sisters I have yet to meet."

They were quiet for a while, faces pulled into a deep frown as another wave of sound washed over the camp.

"And what do they say?" asked Galdith.

"They say nothing.

"They *weep*."

～

KING THARGODÉN STOOD upon his rooftop plateau, staring out over the Evergreen Wood, eyes tightly closed.

Behind him, Aradan stood a distance away, eyes searching the sky, scanning the forest.

"What *is* that?" he asked, resisting the urge to cover his ears.

Thargodén turned his back on the trees, faced his life-long friend, face screwed up in pain and grief.

"We are under attack, Aradan. The enemy has breached my realm."

On the floor below, Llyniel stood before the back window of the parlour, staring out at the forest beyond, arms crossed protectively before her.

In her mind, Fel'annár was anxious.

Sontúr, Maeneth, Handir and Amareth were behind her, sitting at the table and discussing what they thought was happening. Maeneth spoke of earth tremors and the vibrations they may be causing upon the wind, or even the sea. Sontúr favoured strange weather, coming storms while Handir listened and said nothing.

She wished they would speak louder, so that their voices would drown out the terrible lament in her mind. So that she could stop asking herself what was happening, why Fel'annár felt ... different.

THE GIANTS HAD WEPT throughout the night, and although the warriors had eventually slept, it had been fitful. Come morning, they were as tired as they were unnerved, the unfamiliar sounds causing them an inexplicable feeling of anxiety. They had all felt it, but it fell to the captains to bolster their troops, keep their minds busy – off the strangeness of the night before, and the worry for their families further north.

They had days before the foot soldiers caught up with them. And now, knowing that Sand Lords were encroaching upon Abiren'á while they sat here doing nothing, Pan'assár knew he had to keep the warriors busy.

Together with Bulan, Dalú and the other captains, Pan'assár set up training sessions. He and Gor'sadén would continue their instruction with the new Kah Disciples, while Dalú would prepare the Alpines from

Tar'eastór for their upcoming journey through the Wetwood, the fastest road to Abiren'á. They needed to know what they should and should not do in a rain forest: how to set up camp, store food, dodge insects – even how to walk and breathe. They would also learn about jungle warfare, quicksand, the cold and the heat, about the animals and which of them were dangerous. The natives of this land knew there were many things that could kill a warrior just as easily as any Sand Lord.

Gor'sadén continued with the basic Kah stances, demonstrating them with Fel'annár's help. It was the perfect excuse to better acquaint himself with his new, Synth Blade. And of course, he could keep Fel'annár nearby. After last night's transformation, his son was not quite himself.

Pan'assár was restless, too, and Galadan had left The Company to join him as he watched the camp from the side lines.

"Commander," nodded Galadan, coming to stand at Pan'assár's side.

Neither spoke as they watched the warriors train and learn, watched them try to remain calm when they knew that invasion was a reality, when they knew that they could not move on until their army was complete.

They were frustrated, and Pan'assár knew they blamed him for this. He hadn't missed their fleeting glances, nor had he imagined the words they murmured and thought he could not hear. He knew exactly what they were thinking. This had been a long time coming. The north had been unprotected for far too long. There should have been more outposts, more warriors, all those things the Silvans had asked for and Band'orán had argued were useless if the Silvans continued to inhabit the area. Pan'assár had allowed himself to be swept away in what he now realised was a baseless argument, meant only to empty the forest of Silvans, and then take it for himself.

He took a deep breath, turned to Galadan beside him, eyes drawn to the Golden Sun in his collar. A strange thought occurred to him then. Galadan had been his most trusted and skilled lieutenant for many decades. He was a veteran, skilled in the healing arts, quiet and effective – old. But that was all he knew, all he had ever bothered to know about the lieutenant who had remained loyal to him through his years of self-serving bigotry.

"I must thank you for your timely intervention last night. Our army was ready to take flight in spite of my orders. I think they may have, had you and Bulan not spoken."

Galadan said nothing, and Pan'assár pushed on.

"You told me many times, didn't you? Tried to tell me that I was being unfair. That I was neglecting the north. You told me about the under-manned outposts, that it was never about evacuating our people but helping them to remain."

Galadan started, held Pan'assár's gaze. "I did."

"And I never listened, just like with Silor. You told me he was not fit and all I did was condone his behaviour. I was wrong about all those things and I would ask your forgiveness."

He had surely surprised Galadan and for a while, the captain said nothing. "That is the past, Commander. You set out to atone and you have."

"But look at what I have done, Captain. How I have broken this army I was charged with leading."

"You can bring it back. You can mend it. We have already come a long way."

Pan'assár nodded slowly. "With Fel'annár's help, we will fix it. I wonder though, if *you* will ever serve with me again."

Galadan watched his commander, knew he hadn't finished.

"You are happy with The Company," he said simply.

"I am. But I would gladly serve with you again. And I believe that in time, so will the Silvan warriors."

"You have an acute sense of duty, Galadan. It is something you and I share with the likes of Gor'sadén, Fel'annár and the Ari'atór. It is a blessing and a curse in some ways, because when you fail, as I did at the Battle Under the Sun ... when you fail it is hard to forgive yourself."

Galadan nodded thoughtfully but he said nothing, surely under-standing that Pan'assár needed to speak. He wasn't wrong.

"You were always my best lieutenant, Galadan. Strange that we hardly know each other in any personal way and yet, I will always choose you to see things done. I will always trust you where I doubt others. And although I am glad you serve with young Fel'annár now, I wonder if you would do me one last favour, before I release you from my side and officially assign you to his."

"Ask it."

"Serve at my side as we traverse the Wetwood and to the doors of Abiren'á."

Galadan's wise eyes were on him once more. Thinking, analysing. "And after?"

"You will fight this war with The Company, where you belong."

Galadan turned to the training warriors, to where Fel'annár stood with Gor'sadén, speaking with the Disciples.

"It would be my honour to serve with you once more, Commander."

Pan'assár smiled, and then wider. Despite the heavy burden that still sat upon his chest and which sometimes was almost too much to bear, Galadan's words were heartening. With this extraordinary captain who he knew so well and yet not at all, he could lead them to victory.

It was twilight and Galadan had come to the river to help Carodel fill their buckets.

The captain had been pensive for the rest of that day, even quieter than he usually was. Pan'assár's moment of sincerity, his apology and his request that Galadan serve at his side until they reached Abiren'á ... it was a nostalgic favour, he realised, a door that would close on the past, open to a new and better future.

Once Fel'annár had finished training with Gor'sadén and then Bulan, Galadan had sought him out and told him what Pan'assár had asked of him. With the Warlord's blessing, Galadan would serve as the commander's second and as he did so, he would do his utmost best to help Pan'assár upon his road to forgiveness, for one last time.

Galadan breathed deeply, looked up at the waning sun and then at Carodel. They were safe from Sand Lords here at the narrowest part of the river, but not from the *local* population ...

A wail and then a screech, a mighty splash and Carodel fell into the stream, the bucket he had been trying to fill still in his hand. He sat now, on his backside, face to face with a lizard, its black forked tongue flicking in and out of its mouth, orange eyes staring, almost seeming to laugh at the wide-eyed warrior. It turned and walked away, tail swaying from side to side as it disappeared into the undergrowth and Carodel let out a ragged breath. Galadan stood over him, lips pursed, trying not to smile and failing atrociously.

"It could have *attacked* me." Carodel shivered. He had always hated reptiles.

"It wasn't going to. They only attack in groups." Galadan held out his hand and Carodel took it, hoisted himself up. Galadan tutted, looking him up and down, then shaking his head at Carodel's sopping wet clothes.

"Don't you dare ..." said the Bard Warrior, finger pointing at Galadan.

"I won't mention the lizard," promised Galadan, both hands held out before him.

Carodel held his gaze for a moment, and then took two of the four pails of water.

Back at camp, Galdith watched them approach, eyes darting between Carodel and Galadan. "We normally take our clothes *off* to swim, brother."

"Aye well, those banks are treacherous. Lost my footing for a moment," explained Carodel, avoiding his friend's eyes.

Galdith looked at Galadan, saw his veiled humour and pushed on. "That's not like you, Bard. You're swift of foot, eyes sharp like an owl ..."

Idernon and Ramien were watching, glad of the distraction, knew each other well enough to read beneath Carodel's lame excuses.

"There was an intruder," said Galadan, mindful that he should not mention *the lizard*. "It was this high, had leathery grey skin and a tongue this long. There were crinkly scales on its back. What are they called?" He clicked his fingers. He'd promised not to mention the *lizard*.

Ramien's shoulders were shaking.

"It could have *attacked* me! They eat *meat* you know." Carodel defended himself, hands on his hips.

Galdith was laughing, but then he wheezed with Galadan's next words, at his cool, calm and silky voice.

"He squealed like a boar stuck in vines, lost his footing and then came face to face with the thing."

Idernon's eyes twinkled but Carodel's face was a terrible thing as he glared back at Galadan, couldn't believe he, of all people, was ribbing him.

"City boy," murmured Galadan as he sat beside Galdith, still smiling. He rarely joked the way he had done just now, but it felt right, on this the eve of his temporary service to Pan'assár. He would grant the commander's wishes, until the battle itself when he would return to The Company once more, this time for good.

FEL'ANNÁR WALKED THROUGH THE FOREST, not far from camp, but far enough for a modicum of privacy.

He knew these parts like the back of his hand. There was a brook not far away. He used to go there as a child, look into the crystal-clear waters and stare at himself. He would wonder who he was, who his father had been, what had happened to his mother. Other times he would ask himself why he heard things that others didn't. He had learned to hide that from a very young age, understood that those voices were not something normal elves could hear.

The place hadn't changed much, save that it was all so much smaller. He walked to the same moss-covered rock he used to love, sat beside it and lay one hand over the humid green carpet.

He could still hear the giants, their strange wailing nothing but a distant lament now but still, it had made him feel sick, had affected him in a physical way. He needed to think, understand why.

His head was pounding, his body was burning, and his fingers and toes were tingling, as if his hands had been tied and just released.

Tensári thudded to the ground at his side, but Fel'annár already knew she had been in the tree above him.

"Do you feel it too?" he asked her.

After a moment, she sat in front of him, looked about the lovely place and then at Fel'annár. She saw his shaking hands, the crease of his brow.

"We all feel strange. Anxious, nervous and unsettled. Is that what you are referring to?"

"Partly. I just ... I don't feel right, Tensári. It's as if there was something in that noise that was not just words and feelings. It's as if there was a toxin, something I may have breathed in and has poisoned me in some way."

She scowled, leaned forward. "What exactly do you mean?"

He looked up from his hands. "My head is pounding, there's fire in my gut and my skin feels overly sensitive."

"Perhaps we should speak with Galadan."

"I don't think he knows what this is, Tensári."

"He might, Fel'annár. He is old enough to have seen many strange ailments."

"No." Fel'annár shook his head, held out his right hand and rolled up the sleeve of his tunic.

Tensári's eyes flickered wide and she swayed backwards, unable to speak because there, just under the surface of Fel'annár's skin, was a shimmering green light. It lent the inside of his wrist a translucency, like an emerald under a mountain pool.

Fel'annár pulled his sleeve down, far more than he needed to and she looked up, into his overly bright eyes.

"Perhaps you are right. I have no idea what this may be Fel'annár. But bearing in mind that your eyes light up like that when there is important news, it should not alarm you. This is surely the same phenomena, extended from your eyes to other parts of your body."

Perhaps she was right. This was new only in that he had never seen the lights anywhere other than in his eyes.

He reached out with his mind, to the trees around him and then further north. He felt their fear, their terror at what they knew was coming. He continued, further north, imagined what Abiren'á would look like, what the giants would look like.

Can you hear me?

We hear you.

The voice was deeper, almost hollow, as if the trees spoke up at him from the bottom of a well but it was clear, articulate. And then he started, rode the wave of ice that swept over him from head to foot.

Can you feel us?

He closed his eyes tight, knew that Tensári was watching him closely. He answered.

I feel you.

He opened his eyes, said the first thing that came to his lips.

"They are inside me, Tensári."

Her brow twitched. "Who ... is inside you?"

In spite of his aching head, tingling fingers and his fluttering heart, he smiled tentatively. This strange ailment was not malicious.

"The giants. The giant Sisters of Abiren'á."

28

DARK TIDINGS

~

DINNER HAD COME AND GONE, but Galdith had set aside two plates of food for Fel'annár and Tensári. He watched them as they ate, unwilling to speak of the reasons they had left camp, and why they had taken so long.

Tensári put her plate on the ground beside her and looked up into the night sky.

"He's here."

Fel'annár put his own plate down and joined her. Soon, they were all standing, looking skywards and a distance away, Pan'assár nudged Gor'sadén beside him. Soon, the entire camp was watching The Company, wondering what it was that had disturbed them.

And then they heard the sound of a hunting hawk.

Eeaaa Eeaaa

Galdith pointed to a dark spot above them. "I see him!"

Fel'annár followed Galdith's outstretched finger and peered into the distance. Soon, he spotted the distant bird, watched as it flew closer and closer and Tensári was on her feet. Instinctively, she held out her forearm, bracers still on. She waited as Azure glided straight for her, feet out before him, wings angled to the fore. Talons spreading, Azure landed on

Tensári's bracer, her arm dipping and then rising with his weight. There was a collective gasp from those who sat at the fires close by, but Fel'annár was too glad to see Tensári's dazzling smile and the blue eyes of Azure, which seemed even brighter today than they had been.

"I wonder if Lainon is still there, or whether he's only aware in his other form. I mean can he understand us?" Carodel murmured quietly as he peered at the hawk, barely resisting the urge to reach out and stroke the feathers of his chest.

"Lainon. If you can understand us, make a sound that means yes." Fel'annár looked around him, knew the camp was watching but could not hear his words.

But there was nothing, and Idernon shook his head. "This transformation seems to be complete. This is a hawk, one that becomes Lainon. But does that only happen during conflict? Can he change in different circumstances?"

Fel'annár shook his head. "I suppose the only way is to wait for the next fight. We need to speak with him, see ... we need to know how big this army is. We need to know where the Ari'atór are, what Abiren'á can tell us. How fast can hawks fly, Idernon?"

"The fastest can cover Ea Uaré to Tar'eastór in five days. From here, he could reach Abiren'á in an hour, the borders in under a day."

"I wish he could communicate with us. He could tell us everything we need to know. Damn it." Fel'annár ran a hand over his hair.

"Attach a message, a ribbon to show this bird is a carrier. Whoever receives it will answer our questions." Tensári watched as Fel'annár considered her words.

"I can't do this without the consent of Pan'assár. We could introduce Azure as a trained hawk that may be able to help us. But if Azure does transform into Lainon once more, the commander will need to know. The distraction to our warriors may cost lives. But how to convince him of such an unlikely thing?"

"Bulan was there; he will tell them," said Galadan.

A deep breath and Fel'annár nodded. He gestured for them to follow him and The Company walked into the centre of the camp, Azure perched on Tensári's bracer. As they passed, the warriors stood, stared at the passing hawk with blue eyes. They were surely wondering what else could possibly shock them more than the strange sounds from the night before and the transformation of the Warlord.

"This seems so unlikely. As if we play a game and yet I'm actually expecting this to work," said Fel'annár.

"No one's going to believe us," said Ramien.

"Until they see it," said Idernon.

Fel'annár and The Company were soon at the commander's fire. Pan'assár, Gor'sadén, Bulan and the other captains stood staring in disbelief, didn't even look at Fel'annár when he spoke.

"May we join you?"

Pan'assár nodded, gestured to the fire and then sat. But his eyes never left the goshawk which now sat placidly on Tensári's shoulder.

"We have something quite – *incredible* – to tell you. Something happened the night we rode out to neutralise that group of Sand Lord scouts."

"We knew something had happened," said Gor'sadén, eyes back on the blue eyes of the hawk.

Pan'assár leaned forward, forearms over his crossed legs, staring on in silence while Amon and Benat shared a baffled glance.

"I had previously heard the sound of a hawk. It had been following us for days but then it made contact." Fel'annár turned to Azure and then back to the commander. "It looks like a hawk, except that it has blue eyes, as you can see, and is not afraid to be in our company."

"Hawks don't have blue eyes," said Benat, even as he stared at precisely that.

"No. No they don't. When we engaged in battle, the hawk – this hawk – turned into ... into Lieutenant Lainon."

Lainon. The word echoed softly between them. Silence followed, save for the crackle of their fire and the creak of leather.

"He's dead," said Pan'assár, quite unnecessarily and Fel'annár searched his mind for the right words.

"He *was* dead. Somehow, he's back from the Short Road, something I didn't think was possible."

"You cannot be serious. This is some delusion, some Sand Lord trick, or perhaps a spell to make you see things that do not exist ..." Amon was shaking his head. "There are mushrooms in these parts that ..."

Bulan turned coolly to the captain, waited as his words trailed off. "I was there, I vouch for what he's saying. This Ber'ator has been sent back, for a purpose we have yet to understand."

"Captain, this is madness ..." said Benat.

"Benat. *He* is a Ber'anor," said Bulan, pointing at Fel'annár. "Tensári is Ber'ator, as was my father Zéndar. She was Lainon's Connate. This is not madness. She would know if this were some trick, some toxic fume."

Fel'annár nodded. "We have tried to communicate with him as he is now, but he doesn't answer our questions, shows no signs that he understands. But Tensári here has an idea. What if we pen a message to Abiren'á? We tell them where we are, how many are coming and how long it will take us to reach them. We ask them to tell us what's happening, what they can see. It's my hope that the hawk will carry that message and bring back news."

"Hawks don't carry messages ..." Pan'assár was shaking his head, staring at the goshawk.

"I believe *he* will, Commander. If this works, we can find out what's going on in Abiren'á this very evening. We need to know why we haven't met any warriors from the outposts. Why the people have not fled towards our position. We know the frontier is breached but where are our people?"

No one spoke. The dry chirp of grasshoppers pulsed steadily and Pan'assár took a hand to his mouth. His eyes latched onto Galadan, saw his steady regard. He believed what Fel'annár had said about Lieutenant Lainon, had surely seen this transformation, all of The Company had, even Bulan.

"A winged Ari'atór that can send messages faster than ever. If this works, Fel'annár, it will give us a singular advantage. He could overfly the enemy, observe it. But how can he convey his findings? Can he change at will?"

"All we know is that the transformation happened during the skirmish. It seems likely that he changes in order to fight. It may be the only way that we can communicate with him, the only way he can tell us what he sees."

Pan'assár nodded slowly. He glanced at Gor'sadén beside him, and then at the Silvan captains who sat pale and silent, eyes darting between the hawk and Pan'assár.

"What is the bird's name?"

"Azure," said Tensári from Fel'annár's side.

Pan'assár looked at her, wondering what she was thinking. He sipped the cooling tea in his hands, glanced upwards and then at Fel'annár. There was only one way to test the veracity of what Fel'annár claimed, not because he distrusted the Warlord, but because he would be basing his entire strategy upon such an unlikely series of events. He tried to envisage how he would explain himself in his report when everything was over, but to one who had not been here, it would sound utterly absurd.

The deeper questions would come later, once the shock had worn off. Lainon's return as Azure broke the foundations of their world. There was no return to Bel'arán from across the Veil, not until now.

Pan'assár decided he had nothing to lose and everything to gain. They needed to know how many Sand Lords were coming, what they brought with them and where the civilians were.

Minutes later, message written, he watched as Tensári tied it to Azure's foot. If the hawk returned with news from Abiren'á, then he would think about the implications of how the bird had known where to go and what to do.

He watched Tensári stand, distance herself from the others and then hold out her arm. He didn't hear the murmured words meant only for Azure.

"Safe flight, my love."

THARGODÉN'S FORTRESS city was little more than a day away. After an almost five-week journey, Sorei and her fifty warriors were tired.

They had met few Deviants on the road from Tar'eastór, right up until they had joined Commander Pan'assár's army. From there, she had been sent to the city to protect the civilians from Sen'oléi and the Ari children. That had been a week ago, and strangely, that was when the fighting had begun.

With most of Thargodén's army marching north on the Nim'uán, it seemed those who remained were insufficient to keep the Deviants from pressing further and further into Silvan territory. Even now as she sat with Master Oruná, eating the last of their supplies before the final leg of their almost completed journey, Sorei had doubled the watch.

They had been joined by more civilians on the way, some of whom had decided to stay in Sen'Garay. There were children, entire families from Abiren'á who had evacuated the city no sooner news had come from the Warlord. Others had come from Ea Nanú and its outlying hamlets, many refusing to live in the king's city of stone – not unless the enemy defeated their army and entered the Deep Forest.

And then they had heard the strange wailing from the forest, had watched throughout the night as the trees swayed and thrashed. The Silvans had sat in silence, wary eyes alert, hushed voices speaking of spirits, of the wrath of the woods and whether it was the Warlord further north. Sorei's warriors stayed alert, unnerved by the forest, disconcerted by the reaction of their Silvan and Ari charges.

But Sorei had looked to Master Oruná, watched as he had sat in calm silence together with his novice and his recruits. Whether that was because he knew the origin of the disturbance, or whether he did it to keep the children calm, she didn't know.

She repressed a shiver, turned to young Eloran and tried not to smile at him as she ate, but the corners of her mouth twitched rebelliously. Every day on the road, she had watched him obey his mother, and when his chores were done, he would roam the camp. He listened to the warriors, watched their interactions, asked if he could see their weapons. They indulged him, enjoyed his enthusiasm, told him stories of their times in the army – the good ones – not about the horrors, about the memories that sometimes still haunted. He was still a lad after all.

Hooves thundered in the distance and she stood, Oruná at her side. The scouts were returning in haste.

Three horses broke into the camp, the foremost rider on the ground before his horse could stop. He saluted.

"Captain. Deviants approach from the eastern slopes. The biggest group yet. We counted close to a hundred before we were forced to flee, but we are sure there are more of them."

"Distance?"

"Ten minutes at best."

"Birán, Taigor, Sai, Rosen."

The four warriors were around her, tightening harnesses as they listened.

"Taigor, Birán. Take twenty warriors, ride south west. Get the refugees as close as you can to the city."

"Captain. That leaves only thirty against over a hundred Deviants." Birán didn't say it was suicide but Sorei understood him anyway, knew the odds.

"Birán. This is the nature of our service. Go, and protect those children with your life."

"Captain!" She saluted back, glanced at Taigor and together, they dashed away, ran for the horses as they shouted the names of those who would accompany them.

Oruná turned to Sorei. "I cannot help you in this fight, Captain. My purpose is to protect the children."

She was disappointed, hoped that such a formidable fighter would stay to fight, but she had already suspected that he wouldn't. The ways of the Ari order were not new to her. He would not falter in his duty, even when he knew that it would surely lead to her death.

She nodded, watched him mount, and then the rest of the civilians as they grappled with the horses and climbed awkwardly into the saddle or jumped onto the back of the wagons.

They were frightened and disorientated, but the Ari children pleaded with their carers to allow them to fight. Oruná would not allow it, they were too young, had not yet taken the oath and so they did as they were told, sat in the wagon and crouched low, out of sight as Isán instructed. Within minutes, Birán and Taigor had arranged their warriors around the refugees and turned to Sorei and the remaining patrol. A solemn salute, swords before their faces and then they charged away, didn't look back.

Alféna rode with one twin while another Silvan had taken her brother. Eloran rode just beside them and on his back, a basic set of bow and arrow he had been gifted by one of the warriors. He told himself he would use it if he had to. He would kill any Deviant that thought to harm his family. But this was the closest he had been to warfare. He had never imagined he would be this frightened and he wondered, if it came to it, would his shaking hands hold the bow steady? Would his terrified heart allow him to sit still and reach for an arrow? Would his eyes remain open and dry, so that he could sight and release? That was what warriors did and for the first time he understood what his mother had said, what Fel'annár and Galdith had said. He wasn't ready, not yet.

He would learn though.

As he watched the Tar'eastór warriors gallop through the thinning trees, something in his mind clicked into place and it would never move back. Eloran *would* become a warrior, would be the best he possibly could be, and perhaps one day, he would serve in The Company with Fel'annár.

~

"Sai! Rosen! Archers up in the trees. Blades to me. Backs due south, sound the horns!"

She could smell the Deviants, hear them through the metallic blast of horns. There were too many of them, more than they could handle. They needed help and she still didn't understand how such a large number could be so close to the city.

"Archers in position!"

The first wails of the Deviants and they drew their blades while their four archers pulled their first arrow, rested it against the string, eyes straining into the distance.

More wails, louder, movement between the trees.

"Range!" shouted the head archer from above.

"Fire!" yelled Sorei, eyes like ice, long sword in hand, the band of a Blade Master catching the afternoon sun. She had gifted the first Synth Blade to Gor'sadén, but she would make this her humble blade proud, she swore.

~

ELORAN COULD BARELY SEE beyond the lunging warriors, but he heard horns behind them. Not Silvan Ashorns but he supposed they served the same purpose. He knew what it meant, and then almost cried when the warriors sat straighter in the saddle, hailed a group of warriors that galloped towards them from the direction of the city.

And then Ashorns answered the desperate cry of the Alpine horns. He heard yelled orders, saw hand signals Eloran didn't understand but a blond general thundered past their group, at least a hundred warriors behind him. Help had come and he could only pray that it was not too late for Sorei and her warriors.

A handful of the newly arrived warriors stayed behind, joined the Tar'eastór troop and began to lead them on. Eloran glanced at the darkening sky. There were no more than two hours of light left. No time to get to the city, one more day on the road. He looked back over his shoulder as they cantered on.

He liked Sorei, liked Sai and Birán and all the others. They had unwittingly sealed his fate, and the thought of them all dying made him want to cry.

But he wouldn't.

~

"CHARGE!"

Shouts and yells behind her, beside her. Blades glinted in the waning light. Gods but these Deviants were from the mountains. Large and powerful, the extent of their decay was almost unbearable, even to the most veteran of warriors.

She had heard the Ashorns, could only pray they would arrive in time to avoid their death in battle. With a mighty roar she cut downwards, slashed sideways, ducked and started again. Jostling bodies, the gnashing teeth of Deviants. Tainted blood splattered one side of her face and a blade glanced off her pauldron.

Arrows flew from the trees at the larger specimens but there were so many. Her feet stepped backwards, again and again the line retreated as the Deviants pushed forwards. A yell, a warrior fallen and then another.

"Courage! Brave warriors *fight!*"

A collective yell of determination, for a moment they did not move backwards but stood their ground. But still, more rotting bodies pressed down on them and warriors fell, one after the other.

Sorei hissed, a stinging blade cutting into flesh between pauldron and vambrace. She ignored it, whirled around and beheaded the cretin. She pushed back into the fray. She was tiring but the blade in her hand was steady, her mind on the feel of it in her hand. Thrust, slash, parry and lunge. Someone barrelled into her from the side, and she lost her footing. She crashed to the ground, rolled instinctively, protected herself with the blade, just in time to block a sideways stroke to the thigh. She pushed back, the enemy blade almost touching flesh.

And then it was gone with a mighty clash, a flash of blond hair before her face and a clean blade.

No time to look, only to regain her footing and fight. Help had come but still more Deviants ran for them. She heard a cheer from behind, heavily accented voices.

Silvans. The Silvans had come.

SUPREME COMMANDER HOBIN urged his horse forwards, as far as he dared without revealing himself to the enemy. Captain Jendal followed at his side.

He strained his eyes into the distance, heart sinking into his gut. An army of Sand Lords and Deviants had settled, a sprawling camp not minutes away from the treeline of Ea Uaré. It was easily visible from here. The Three Sisters were impossible to miss, impossible to ignore.

Ea Uaré *was* under attack.

Hobin looked to the skies. The weather was clear and hot. It would be a cold night. He made to look away but a black speck over the forest to his left caught his attention. His smile was sparing, as it almost always was, but he loved to watch hawks in flight, admired their speed, agility, their freedom from duty.

Closer now and his smile wavered. Hawks were illusive creatures, but still it flew towards them, unperturbed by their presence.

Ee Eeaaa

The shrill cry echoed around them, struck some strange chord in Hobin's chest. He held his arm out, far in front of him and Jendal watched him with disbelieving eyes.

Outstretched talons and magnificent wings flapping forwards, the bird latched on to Hobin's bracer and steadied itself. Hobin watched, felt heat behind his eyes. Zéndar's memory stirred in his mind and the hawk's gaze seemed to sharpen and widen, as if it waited for something, as if it willed him to understand.

The hawk held up one foot, and the commander reached for the ties of the string. Opening the package as best he could with one hand, hungry eyes raked over the parchment.

Four thousand seven hundred warriors would reach Abiren'á in under a week. The Warlord called for information on the enemy, but Hobin had little to offer. He realised then, that this message had been meant for the leaders of Abiren'á, not for him and yet the bird had brought it here.

The implications were as bad as they were intriguing.

His eyes turned to the magnificent hawk, watching his every move with bright blue eyes. Hobin scowled, felt Zéndar's Guiding Light ripple to the surface.

Hobin had no answers to Fel'annár's questions, but at least he knew where and how many had come from Thargodén's city, how long it would take them to reach Abiren'á.

It would take him that much time to reach the last ridges of the northern Median Mountains. But with a mere one thousand, he couldn't initiate an attack, not on an army this size. He would need to wait until the Silvan army arrived.

Such a strange moment, pondered Hobin as he sat in his saddle, half obscured from sight, a wild hawk perched on his forearm. If the bird could speak, what would it be saying to him now, he wondered. A distant memory surfaced, of childhood on his father's lap, his favourite story book open before him.

Ari Myths and Legends. Book I: Arimals.

"What is your secret, my friend? What do you hide behind those Ari eyes?"

OF THE THIRTY Tar'eastór warriors who had faced the Deviants with Captain Sorei, only twelve were left standing. The rest were either dead or wounded. Those with knowledge of healing knelt beside them, repairing the damage as best they could. She missed Pengon and his customary cloth bag, stuffed with bandages and creams and all sorts of foul-smelling herbs.

Sorei watched the blond general issue orders to his one-hundred-strong patrol, and while the dead Deviants burned, horses were collected, and the wounded mounted. The forces of Tar'eastór and Ea Uaré would leave the battle ground and find a suitable camp for the night before making the final journey to the city tomorrow.

Sorei pulled herself up into the saddle, hid the shock of pain that ran down her left arm and urged her horse towards the general.

"You have my thanks for a timely arrival, General." She saluted stiffly, endured his scrutiny.

"I am General Rinon, and you have my thanks for protecting these people."

She studied his face. It was familiar and eyes travelled downwards, over his cuirass and the skilfully etched markings over the silver plate. Acorn and emerald, house of Or'Talán. But he had not come to her as a prince.

"I am Captain Sorei of Tar'eastór. We follow the orders of Commander Gor'sadén whom we met in the presence of your commander general and army. I and my warriors are to report to General Turion."

"I will take you to him. The seriously wounded will not stop for the night but be taken straight to the city. We will make camp with the refugees and continue on in the morning."

Sorei simply nodded.

"And then you can see to that arm."

She frowned, thought she had hidden it well enough. Obviously not, and she nodded again. She knew he was watching her, thinking she might engage in conversation, but she was tired, just wanted to report to this Turion and get settled. She had a job to do, one Gor'sadén had bid her do.

The sun had set, and the light was rapidly failing. Yells echoed around them, strange sounding voices, an accent she was not wholly familiar with. There was bird call too, but she couldn't distinguish elf from beast. They were extraordinarily good at it.

The camp opened up before them. Two tents had been erected on one side and fires burned brightly. She cast her eyes around the place, took note of the sentinels she could see, knowing there would be more further afield. They were surely well protected.

A collective cry of joy went up and Sorei started. The Silvan refuges stood, arms up to the sky, smiling. They were hailing her while the Ari'atór and their recruits bowed low.

A smile pulled at her mouth, blue eyes softening just for a moment as she raised her uninjured arm in response. She liked these people; so expressive, so unconcerned with what others might think about that. From the corner of her eye, she knew Rinon was looking at her, but she didn't turn and when they arrived at the makeshift pen where the horses stood calmly, she dismounted, took a moment to quell the pain of aching muscles and exhaustion.

Righting herself, she came face to face with Oruná. He didn't smile, showed no expression at all that she could detect.

"Your devotion to duty rivals that of an Ari'atór. You have my respect, Captain Sorei."

She bowed to the Ari Master, glanced at Isán the novice beside him, and then left together with the general.

"I would see my warriors."

"When someone has seen your arm, of course."

She turned to him and for a moment, she saw the mirror image of her own eyes.

Closed to discussion.

No point in arguing and so she nodded and followed him to one of the fires. He gestured for her to sit and she obeyed. She reached for the buckle of her harnesses and pulled it loose. Slipping out of it, she released her pauldron with only a slight twitch of the brow. There, on her upper arm was a long, bloody cut.

Rinon sat beside her, not too close, waited for another warrior to clean and bandage it.

"The warriors here at camp are well enough. None of them are in danger of passing."

"Still, I would visit them, General."

"Of course. But first, tell me, what news from the north?"

"A great army of many thousands has been seen in the sands."

Rinon sat straighter, eyes moving from one side of her face to the other.

"How long ago was that? How far away were they?"

"The army was seen from a place you call the eh ... Doorway?"

"Doorway to the Sands, yes."

"You will need to ask the Ari Master Oruná for the details, but it was estimated to be at a distance of around two weeks when they saw it. By now, your borders must already be breached."

"Dear Gods ..." Rinon stood, hands on his hips, mind enumerating the consequences the news brought. Their warriors would be outnumbered, and there was no guarantee that Hobin would bring enough Ari'atór to even the odds. The night the forest had sung its discordant song, his father had said the realm had been breached. Now, Rinon knew that he was right. He needed to speak to Turion urgently, no sooner they arrived in the city.

He turned back to Sorei. "I must speak with Oruná. You will find your injured in the tents over there," he gestured to the far side of their camp. With a curt nod he left in search of news from the Ari Master, but his mind was still on the north, on Pan'assár and Fel'annár, just days away from a battle they may not be able to win.

SOREI RETURNED from the makeshift pavilions where the wounded lay.

The Silvan refugees sat at their fires, talking and eating and for a moment, she simply listened to their quiet murmurs, watched the way they sat close, touched each other often and smiled just as much.

"Being a warrior is no *game*, boy. Go back to your mother."

Sorei turned to the right, eyes searching.

"I know it's not a game. I just want to learn."

"Best you stay in the trees where you belong, little squirrel."

Snorts of amusement, soft laughter.

Sorei's eyes turned to ice. There, standing before a fire, was Eloran and with him, a group of Alpine warriors. Not hers, but from Ea Uaré. She walked towards them, watched Eloran, saw his shimmering eyes. He was upset.

She emerged from the shadows and before they could stand, Sorei stood in their midst. The laughter died, gave way to the crackling fire and the singing cicadas.

"When I was eight years old, I knew I would be a warrior. How old were you?" Her frigid eyes landed on the warrior at the very centre of the circle she stood over. She waited, didn't move at all, didn't even blink.

"Fifteen or so."

"A child."

"Yes."

"Did you dream of serving? Play with swords and bows? Did you imagine yourself saving your people? Did you see the colours of your family on your horse, the sigil on your chest? Did you feel proud?"

It took him longer to answer this time and when he did, the surety in his tone was gone.

"Yes."

Sorei's head lifted, she glanced at the stars over them and then back at the warrior.

"Did you deserve to be mocked for your vocation? For that which you wanted with all your heart?"

Again, his answer was slow to come, almost a whisper now.

"No."

She nodded slowly. "Your name."

"Karon."

She watched him closely, saw his gaze travel over her shoulder and then back. Someone was behind her, but she hadn't finished.

"Why does he belong in the trees?" Her tone was almost wistful, almost like a child asking an innocent question.

Karon didn't answer.

"Are you ashamed of the answer? Is that why you cannot say it?"

"I – was wrong."

"Had *he* been Alpine, you would have sat him down beside you and indulged him. You would have answered his questions and patted him on the back. But Eloran is Silvan – *he* belongs in the trees. Is that what you meant, Karon?"

"I – I apologise, Captain."

The wistful tone was gone, replaced by the cutting edge of the sharpest blade. "If you were a warrior in my patrol, I would put you to shame before this entire camp. I would say that you have forgotten your oath, your pledge to uphold the Warrior Code. I would say you are a dimwit, a pinhead with delusions of superiority. I would say you should apologise to *Eloran*, not to me."

The entire camp had fallen into silence. The Silvan warriors watched, the Alpines of Tar'eastór and Ea Uaré stared at Karon, remembered how he had always been unashamedly vocal in his dislike of Silvans, but no one had shut his mouth quite the way Sorei just had.

Karon stood, turned to an almost quaking Eloran who could not look the Alpine warrior in the eyes.

"Your first lesson as a future warrior of these lands, Eloran," said Sorei. "Look your opponent in the eyes, know that you are just, that you are right. Don't be intimidated. Stand tall." Despite her words, her eyes were soft when she looked at him. He straightened, turned to Karon, watched as the warrior bowed.

"My apology, lad. No offense was intended."

Eloran bowed back and Sorei offered him a fleeting smile. She walked slowly towards Karon, only slightly shorter than he was.

"You are brave. You have humbled yourself before a Silvan lad. This entire camp has seen your courage. You made a mistake, one I feel sure you will not make again."

"He will not."

Sorei turned to the blond general behind her, watched him walk towards Karon until he was so close their chests almost touched.

"No sooner we return to the city, I want you in my office," he murmured.

Karon nodded, wide eyed now, watching as Rinon turned his back on him and then left together with the foreign captain. Karon sat heavily, exhaled noisily. No one spoke to him, no one clapped him on the shoulder in comfort.

Eloran returned to his family, not far away. He sat pale and silent and his mother watched him. And when she finally caught her son's gaze she smiled.

"I am proud of you, Eloran. That warrior was wrong, and I wager he will think twice before speaking out of turn again. See how the warriors ignore him now?" Alféna searched for Sorei in the distance, watched her sit together with Rinon in the half light. "With more captains like her, those Alpine Purists will soon fade into the past."

Eloran nodded, found his tongue at last. "I want to be like her. Strong and clever with words. Fair and protective because that's what warriors should do," he reasoned out loud. "Warriors are never nasty, even to the enemy."

Alféna started, surprised at the wisdom of her son's words. He was still a child, but in some ways, he was already an adult.

With one more respectful glance Sorei's way, she smiled.

A LIEUTENANT RAN through the corridors of the Inner Circle of Ea Uaré. Those he met face on, dodged sideways, eyes on the small paper clutched in his hands. The captains slowed their pace, turned in the direction the sprinting warrior had gone.

To Acting Commander General Turion's office.

The warrior sprinted over the inside courtyard, and then hammered on the door. It opened abruptly and he almost forgot to salute.

"What is it?" Turion's urgent question.

"News from Abiren'á, Commander."

Turion stood taller, reached out for the paper and snatched it from him. Unfolding it, he read, even as the captains converged on his door.

"This is the confirmation we never wanted to receive. A great host has been seen from the Doorway. It was two weeks away when our warriors first saw it."

It took a while for anyone to pluck up the courage and ask about the date on the missive. Turion looked at the captains, and then down at the filthy, crumpled paper in his hands. He knew it should have arrived long before. The late summer migrations had indeed delayed their missives. "This was sent over two weeks ago."

Some closed their eyes while others stared at Turion as if he had lost his mind. The enemy was already inside the forest.

"It must have been that day, when the forest cried out," said Captain Henu, and Salo nodded from beside him.

No one could gainsay him. But there was still one more question to ask.

"How many have come, Commander?"

Turion held Henu's gaze, glanced at the others. "It was impossible to count. They said the midday horizon was black."

"Dear Gods, that's surely five thousand at least," said a veteran from the Battle Under the Sun.

"Too many for our army," said another. "We must pray that Araria sends aid, that they have seen this host and can arrive in time."

Turion nodded. "Call an urgent Circle, at the twentieth hour. I must inform our king."

The captains saluted, left in a cloud of worried words and conjectures. Turion knew what they were saying, what was in their minds. If the worst came to pass, if the enemy defeated their admittedly insufficient army, there would be nothing between the Nim'uán and this city. All Turion had was five hundred warriors and a constant struggle against the Deviants.

Turion had four, maybe five weeks to prepare for the worst possible outcome. His stomach turned, mind reeling with all the things he needed to do, the things he knew Pan'assár would do.

It was time to prepare for war, on the very doorsteps of the city of Ea Uaré.

29

THE FOLLY OF GODS

~

IT WAS the morning of their third day in Lan Taria, and the troops were close to breaking point. Amon had suggested they move forward, slow enough so that the foot soldiers could catch up with them in a few more days.

Pan'assár had refused. There was no way of knowing what lay ahead, beyond the Wetwood. It was a too great a risk. They would continue to wait and Amon had left, expression dour.

Just last night, Azure had come and then flown away on a mission so unlikely it was almost humorous. Except that Fel'annár was not in the mood for laughing. He had seen lights beneath his skin again but mercifully, the hammer in his head had ceased its banging and his heart beat normally once more. At least now he had an idea of what this ailment was. He had somehow communed with the giants, the Three Sisters he had yet to set his eyes on. Later, he would ask Bulan to tell him of them.

Azure's call pierced the morning sky.

The Company were on their feet, the commanders and captains converging on their fire. They watched Tensári hold out her arm, and then stared in admiration as the bird landed and then settled, bright blue eyes turning to Fel'annár's green.

Now came the real test.

How to know what Azure did? How could they find out what he had seen?

Fel'annár reached for the leather ties around one talon and pulled. Inside the small pouch was a piece of folded paper, not the same one Pan'assár had sent. He glanced at the commander, saw his nod of approval and read.

"Commander Hobin!"

"It's not from Abiren'á then?" asked Bulan.

"No. Hobin says he brings one thousand. That he will wait on the eastern flank of the Xeric Wood for our signal to start the attack. He also says there is massive Deviant activity on the eastern slopes of the Great Barrier Ridge."

"One thousand is not much, but it's something at least," murmured Pan'assár. "But we need numbers."

"What about our city? Why haven't they answered?" asked Dalú.

Fel'annár shook his head. It had been over a day since the breach. Abiren'á must have done battle with the enemy and lost, either that or for some reason, Azure had not been able to approach. But that didn't seem likely to Fel'annár.

"We need answers," murmured Pan'assár. "We are four days away from Abiren'á and we still don't know what's happening there. We need a plan, and the only way is to send out scouts. But that's risky in these parts. It is entirely possible that the enemy has taken Abiren'á and has even penetrated the Wetwood."

"Wait, Commander. If Azure knew what we needed him to do last night, he understands us, and that tells me there must be a way to communicate with him. Give us some time before you send out scouts. It may not be necessary."

Pan'assár looked between Fel'annár, the hawk and then Tensári. "You have until midday."

The group broke away, Dalú's voice calling the warriors back to training, while Gor'sadén signalled for the Kah Disciples to resume their training. As for The Company, they left in search of somewhere quieter, so that they could talk and think.

Fel'annár and Tensári sat on the ground, side by side and Idernon busied himself with the fire. With nothing particular to do except wait, the others checked their packs and cared for their weapons.

Tensári stroked Azure's feathers and Fel'annár stared at him, mind working, searching for a way to know the bird's mind.

Azure hopped from one foot to the other, bobbing from side to side. It was an endearing sight, and Fel'annár reminded himself that this was Lainon Ber'ator, not a pet. He almost laughed out loud, and then held his forearm out. Azure immediately hopped onto it.

"Any ideas, Idernon? Short of purposefully walking into a group of Sand Lords to provoke an attack?"

The Wise Warrior looked over at him, shook his head and Fel'annár sighed. He was mentally tired, even though it was still midday. His body though, was rigid, muscles too tight, shoulders hunched. He needed to relax, yearned for Llyniel's soothing hands. He leaned back against the tree behind him.

Six thousand Sand Lords in Abiren'á. Four thousand beyond the Xeric Wood. Two thousand Deviants to the east.

Fel'annár sat up, eyes wide. He half turned to the tree behind him and then back at Tensári. He held out his arm so that Azure would hop back over to her. He needed to lay both hands on the tree so that he could listen for the details. This time they had *numbers* for him, at last!

But Azure would not move.

"Tensári. *Take* him."

Azure opened his wings, flapped them and shrieked, the sound grating on their eardrums and drawing the attention of the warriors from further away. Fel'annár shook his head and Tensári spoke.

"He doesn't want to. What do the trees say?"

"The trees have numbers ..." said Fel'annár.

Eee Eee

He frowned, leaned back into the tree.

It is time for the protected one to shine.

Words from the past that Fel'annár would never forget. Shock drained all colour from his face. Those were *Lainon's* words, the last he had ever uttered to Fel'annár. It wasn't the trees that were speaking to him but Lainon, in the only way that he could.

Through the trees.

"What is it?" asked Tensári, alarmed. Idernon and the rest were on their feet, drawing closer.

"Brother?" A disbelieving, noisy breath. Realisation.

Is it you, Lainon?

Novice.

He closed his eyes, smiled, savoured the words and then he opened them, looked at Azure, urgency in his questions.

Can you survey the land around Abiren'á? Tell us how close the enemy is, what they are doing in the city, where our people are?

Already done.

He chuckled in disbelief, sat forwards, turned to an uncomprehending Company. "It's *him*, Tensári. I can speak to him through the *trees*." He could feel his smile, pulling so hard it hurt his face and Tensári, mirrored it, the last remnants of her painful grief fading, its shards scattering and then dissolving. Lainon was no longer dead. He was no longer on the other side but here, with The Company once more. He was with *her* once more. Carodel's hand was on her shoulder.

Fel'annár had so many questions for Lainon. About why he had returned, how it was possible. Had he come from the Evergreen Wood? And if he had, as Fel'annár suspected, what had truly happened that night? Had he dreamed?

Or had it all been real?

But those questions had to wait. It was time to give Pan'assár the information he needed, so that he could plan their strategy at last.

The warriors were torn between sitting and discussing the extraordinary rumour of a flying Ari'atór, and charging into the Wetwood, out the other side and to Abiren'á, Pan'assár's orders be damned. The enemy was surely already there, walking amongst their trees, eating their supplies and disregarding nature. But where were their people? Where were the waves of refugees they had expected?

But Bulan had asked them to wait.

As they spoke, they watched the Warlord and his company, hawk included, as they made for where the two commanders and captains sat.

Pan'assár stood slowly, asked his question even before they had arrived at the fire. "Have you found a way?"

Fel'annár smiled and began to explain what Azure had seen that night.

"Our foot soldiers are half a day away. Our army will be complete come the evening."

"Thank Aria," said Bulan.

"Do we know how many are coming? Whether more have joined them?" asked Dalú.

"He says he has counted close to three thousand. That's a good few hundred more than we had before."

"That makes four thousand seven hundred or so, and Hobin's one thousand on the eastern flank. What of the enemy? What numbers have they brought?"

"The enemy has broken into two. An estimated six thousand are already in Abiren'á. They carry rope and plenty of it. Azure has seen pale-faced Sand Lords and movement below ground. He says there are cages with captive elves inside ..."

A collective hiss of breath, the murmurs louder. The warriors had come closer, well within earshot now but Pan'assár was not going to order them away. They were already on the brink of mutiny. Besides, they needed to know what was going on. Better they heard it from the Warlord than from himself.

"Four thousand have stayed in the sands. They have contraptions we assume are mining towers. They are tapping into the subterranean waters and bringing it to the surface. We believe they plan to channel it northwards, into Calrazia."

Murmurs threatened to interrupt Fel'annár, but he raised his voice, held his hand up for silence.

"Azure has also seen two thousand Deviants in the same area as Commander Hobin's group. We must pray they don't interfere with his intervention on that flank."

Pan'assár nodded, the map in his mind taking shape. Even as he imagined it, he heard Bulan's words from beside him.

"With six thousand already in Abiren'á, four thousand in the sands and the threat of Deviants joining them. That could be more than ten thousand. Impossible numbers, even with our superior knowledge of the land. We cannot allow these two contingents to come together in battle. We will lose. We *will* be pushed back."

The murmurs ceased as the implications sunk in. Pan'assár nodded his agreement.

"Victory *can* be ours, but as Captain Bulan rightly points out, so long as we do not allow those two contingents to fight together.

"You mean to separate us?" asked Benat. "Won't that simply make two uneven battles instead of one?

"Five thousand seven hundred against more than ten thousand is certain defeat, Benat. But facing them in smaller numbers, in the trees, gives us a chance. Besides, we have another ally. The forest itself. If our Warlord can conjure the trees, bid them fight for us as he did in Tar'eastór, then it would not be in our favour to have a larger number of warriors inside the forest."

Pan'assár's eyes lingered on Fel'annár, even as he continued to explain his plan.

"We leave the horses here in Lan Taria, advance on foot through the Wetwood, keep the element of surprise. With six thousand of the enemy already in Abiren'á, it is logical to assume a number of them will be guarding the roads into the city.

"We must be on full alert. Smaller groups at the fore, the bulk of our warriors behind and then once we are on the other side, we make for Skyrock and regroup. It will lend us the best possible view of the terrain and the enemy's movements. With Abiren'á just a day away from the outlook, we make our final plans to regain our city, banish this scourge from our woods."

There were scattered 'ayes' from the warriors and plenty of sceptical eyes, too, Silvan eyes, warriors who wondered at the term the Alpine commander had used. '*Our woods,*' he had said. But what did *he* know of the torture they were enduring now? Abiren'á had been taken, their people held captive, caged as no animal ever should be. It was Bulan who gave voice to their thoughts.

"And what of our people? This strategy of caging them ... what is it they seek to achieve? And what, if anything, do you plan to do to free them?"

"Captain." Fel'annár took a step forward, stared at his uncle, watched him closely. He had been civil enough to Pan'assár thus far, but his patience was cracking, his perspective skewed, like so many others who now waited for Fel'annár to explain.

"Commander Pan'assár has not spoken of our people because he can't. Azure flew there with a message for the leaders. But it seems the Sand Lords are superstitious. They fired at him. He tried to hide but the alarm was raised. He barely escaped, northwards, first to the Xeric Wood and then eastwards where he found Hobin's host, hiding in the foothills."

Bulan stared at Fel'annár, nodded curtly, turned to Pan'assár. "It doesn't make sense, commander. Sand Lords never take captives. Why now?"

"I know, Captain. But had they all been slaughtered, there would be evidence of it, Azure would have seen fire, killing fields. I understand your frustration and your worry, but for now, all we can do is march, carefully and stealthily, for as long as we can without detection. Wherever they are, we will save them. You have my word."

Bulan raised his chin, and Fel'annár knew that his uncle would remember these words, in case Pan'assár didn't.

While Azure's report was being discussed in Lan Taria, Rinon and Sorei's remaining warriors accompanied the refugees towards the city of Ea Uaré.

He couldn't risk more Deviants intercepting their caravan. There were civilians, children and even though they were nothing but four hours ride away, attack this close to the city would no longer surprise Rinon.

The prince rode at the front of the long column of warriors and refugees, Captain Sorei at his side. Both were pensive, but only one was musing on the bigotry and blatant disregard some Alpine warriors of Ea Uaré showed towards the native Silvans. This attitude had led them to the doors of civil disorder, not that she knew much about what had happened after Fel'annár had arrived.

And so, Sorei asked Rinon to tell her about it.

For the next hour, the prince spoke of Band'orán's treachery and what it had led to. He told her of the nascent army that had emerged, how precarious it had been when they had ridden to war.

With Sorei's curiosity sated, Rinon indulged his own with questions he had not wanted to ask until just recently.

"Did you fight in the Battle of Tar'eastór?" Rinon kept his eyes to the fore, unwilling to show the captain he was as interested in her as he was in the battle.

She turned to him, eyes cutting. "Of course I did, General."

Rinon held his tongue, failed to see why it was so obvious. "Then you have seen this thing. The Nim'uán?"

"Oh yes. I did not engage it, but I saw Commander General Gor'sadén and General Fel'annár fight it. A formidable foe. There was a Gas Lizard too. Commander General Pan'assár cut it down, but not before it got him in the face."

Rinon said nothing further and neither did she, and after almost an hour of silent riding passed, he resigned himself to no more small talk from Sorei. He almost flinched when she spoke.

"Where are your furnaces in the city?"

Of all the things he thought she might ask, this was never one of them. "To the south of the Inner Circle, a brisk hour's walk, twenty minutes on horseback. It is a curious part of our city, not the safest, mind. I go there sometimes to watch them work although recently, there hasn't been much time. I would be happy to escort you there to watch if you like."

"I have no inclination to *watch*, General. I seek the use of a forge."

Rinon turned to her, face blank. "You are a *smith*?" Rinon couldn't help it. His stony façade was gone. He felt his eyes widen with surprise, desperately tried to hide it because she had irritated him with her somewhat forward tone of voice. He wanted to look angry, not stupid. He knew he had failed when she looked away, saw the amusement that momentarily tugged at the corners of her upturned mouth.

"I have surprised you. Is that because I am a woman?"

"No."

She stared hard at him.

"Yes. And why *wouldn't* it surprise me? Are you saying there are so many female smiths that I should *not* be surprised?"

"No. That much is true."

"Female artisans are not common, but those I know of always procure their metals *before* they begin their creations."

"What are you *talking* about?"

There it was again. That tone that said he was a fool. He took offense.

"What do you *think* I'm talking about. Your rings, your necklaces or whatever it is you make." He waved one hand in front of his own face in irritation.

Sorei's nostrils flared, eyes glinting as her gaze clashed with Rinon's. There was no apology in her eyes either.

"I am a *swordsmith*, General. I do not make *baubles*. I am searching for the perfect balance. Weight and agility, strength and flexibility. It is a synthesis I seek, one I believe I have found. Commander General Gor'sadén agrees and Commander Pan'assár bids me create as many blades as I can. It is all in his missive for Commander Turion."

Rinon felt stupid for his stereotypic assumptions, although he was still angry at her tone, even though in hindsight, he had probably deserved it. He was curious though. She was a swordsmith, good enough that the commanders had sent her back to the city to make swords. Unusual though it was, he felt the need to – apologise.

"I am sorry for my inaccurate assumptions, Captain," he said, trying not to clench his teeth as he turned to her profile.

There, a faint crack in her stony façade. She had obviously not expected him to apologise. But then again, neither had he. She nodded curtly at him and turned back to the fore.

He wanted to escort her to the forges, but she irked him. He chanced a glance sideways, observed her harsh profile set in stone, fixed on the terrain before them. She was cold as ice, hot like the molten metal she worked with. Fast and temperamental, he wanted to see her in battle again – as much as he wanted her in his bed.

THE FOOT SOLDIERS arrived that evening, to the relieved cheers of the warriors.

The army was complete and ready to move come the dawn. It was almost time to put all they had learned about the Wetwood into practice.

There was a longer but safer route to the city, but with an army that size, they would draw the enemy's attention. Pan'assár needed to get them as close to Abiren'á as he could without being detected.

The captains organised their now five thousand seven hundred warriors into small, manageable groups of one hundred. Each would be led by an experienced captain or lieutenant, who would guide them safely through the Wetwood and to the other side.

Of these groups, the more veteran warriors would take half, and march a few hours ahead of the rest, ensure the terrain was safe by marking the problematic areas with etchings and symbols for those behind.

Each group also had a number of designated runners who would cover the distance between those at the fore and the groups at the rear, and all the while, the leaders would continue to instruct their warriors on the dangers and precautions they needed to take at all times.

They would travel like this for three days, and once they were on the other side, they would regroup and make for Skyrock, where they would still be shielded from the enemy.

From there, one more day, and the war would begin.

Pan'assár and Galadan would lead one such group at the fore. Bulan would take another, as would Fel'annár with Galdith as their specialist. These were his lands, after all.

At dawn, as the first wave of warriors set out, Galdith explained to those at the front, who would then fall back and relay his words to those further behind.

"It'll be hotter during the day, colder at night. It'll be humid, the air so thick you'll struggle for it. Don't overestimate your stamina. Running in these conditions takes more energy. It'll rain and then the sun will shine. You'll sweat and then shiver but you must keep your wits about you.

"Beware the swamps that are often invisible to all but the most able of scouts. And watch for the lizards and the yellow ant."

Carodel dared not look at his brothers. Lizards terrified him, they all knew that by now, but the prospect of yellow ants horrified them all.

"Adapt your clothing accordingly but never march barefoot. Don't expose your skin to the elements and neither touch nor eat anything you don't recognise. Sleep off the ground if you can, and keep your food supplies well-sealed.

"This new terrain changes the way we work as an army. Reduced visibility means numbers are less important than strategy. Small, close combat teams can be more effective than a large patrol on the ground. And beware, the savannas and glades are the perfect place for an ambush, both from the enemy and for us to take advantage of."

Duly briefed, Idernon fell back and relayed Galdith's instructions together with others. After a while, he returned to the front with the rest of The Company. Only Galadan was missing. He was travelling with Pan'assár.

Fel'annár was speaking quietly while Galdith nodded. A hand signal later, and four archers took to the trees just in front of them. Gor'sadén watched his son as he took counsel with those more experienced than himself. It was the mark of an excellent commander and he couldn't help the surge of pride that washed over him. Still, he knew that Fel'annár's true test of fire was yet to come.

The air was suffocating, just as Galdith had said, the heat unbearable and all the while, their eyes scanned the earth beneath their feet, the trees above them, the sky now completely blocked from sight.

Fel'annár heard strange sounds from animals he had never seen, and he found himself straining his eyes and wondering if any of them had blue eyes. But none of them did. He turned to Azure, who sat calmly on Tensári's shoulder.

That night, they slept in hammocks they had fashioned with their blankets, just as Galdith and the other veterans had instructed them. All in all, it had been an uncomfortable day of travel, but tomorrow, it would only get worse as the forest grew even denser.

At dawn, Fel'annár and Galdith gathered their group as close together as they could in this enclosed place. There was barely enough light to see, and as Galdith began to brief them, his breath swirled in the humidity around them.

"As of today, there will be no more fire. Not for food, tea or even to see. It's dangerous to the forest, frightening to the animals. Camouflage starts now. No unnecessary buckles. Bright hair and pale skin must be muted." Galdith looked pointedly at Fel'annár before continuing. "Veterans please instruct the others on how to achieve this during breaks and at camp. Harnesses must remain open, bags and supplies closed tightly. Make sure there is nothing on your person that can make a noise and check your fellow warriors frequently for insects and ants. Flick them away but never swat at them."

Carodel swallowed thickly while Ramien was already checking his own clothes. Fel'annár watched them, turned to Tensári and wondered if Azure would warn her of any unwanted visitors. Or would he perhaps eat them? He shivered at the thought and then stepped up to Galdith, clapped him on the shoulder and continued with the brief.

"I want four archers in the trees every ten minutes. No talking. Bird calls and hand signals only. I want you alert, ready to fire in an instant. We may have the upper hand in this forest, but the enemy will have learned the terrain. We don't know if they've yet ventured this far south, but if we do encounter them, don't underestimate them. Be aware of their clicks and trills. Anything suspicious and you call the alert.

"Stay focussed and busy. Two more days, warriors. Two days to Skyrock and then a day of rest. Bolster your minds, remember your training, serve well and be proud of the deeds that lie before us."

They spent some time learning the art of camouflage from Galdith. He had found feathers, cut ferns and large leaves from even larger plants and brought them back for the others. He brought vines too, showed the others how to wrap their heads and then use them to secure the leaves and feathers. By the time they had finished, Fel'annár was hard-pressed not to laugh at the sight of Gor'sadén with a jungle sticking out of his muddied Alpine locks. As for himself, he didn't need the vines to secure the fauna and neither did Tensári.

The canopy here was dense but still, timid birdsong was breaking through the tense silence, replacing the sound of crickets and cicadas. The enemy was not close, or so said the trees, but there was something about their voice here that was different, more akin to the Evergreen Wood, he thought. Just like what happened with the Sand Lord incursion The Company had dealt with, they were reluctant to share their knowledge, and Fel'annár found himself constantly prodding them for information.

He was reminded of Turion's words to him back when he had been a novice on his first patrol into the north. He had said the forest was dark here, that not everyone was able to endure it for long. He could see why that would be. It was, indeed, oppressive, but there was something else. He wondered if it was the constant threat of battle, the constant skirmishes with Sand Lords and Deviants they had suffered over the years. He wondered if it was the cruelty they had seen and become accustomed to. Had they fallen into complacency? Had they given up? Lost hope for a peaceful future?

Fel'annár reached out, fingers trailing over the ferns all around them. *Where are you, Yerái? What is it that has this forest so quiet? What are we walking into?*

AT MIDDAY, they stopped only briefly.

With his back against a tree, Fel'annár asked Azure to fly over the Wetwood before them, and while he was away scouting, he watched Galdith, the way he constantly checked the troops. He had never seen him in a position of command, and he realised he would make a fine lieutenant in his new, Forest Division. He just hoped he himself would be alive to see it done.

They saw spiders the size of Ramien's hands, lizards that stood waist high and colourful birds that screeched so loud it grated on their ears.

They saw black beetles that flew around them, armoured wings clacking as they searched for exposed flesh and found none. Galdith hand signalled that they should not bat them away. The warriors had walked stoically on, rigid as they prayed the insects would not land on them, keeping their heads down lest the beetles were attracted to their eyes.

Bulan had diverted their march around a swamp. Fel'annár already knew it was there, just as he detected a pool of quicksand further ahead. Galdith had guided them around it but for all the trees had warned him of it, even as he passed it by, he couldn't see it.

There was a constant hum of insects, the incessant chatter of birds that only heightened as the light began to fade.

Funny, mused Fel'annár, because although he had not weaved the Dohai that morning, he felt infused, as if he had only just performed it.

He looked upwards, felt the pull of these trees, like an invisible rope, tensing in all directions. But then he swayed to one side, a tug from a nearby tree and Tensári steadied him.

"Someone approaches. Not the enemy."

It was hard to see the sun through the dense trees, and the lack of light cast a dreamy dark blue over everything. But there were no doubts in Fel'annár's mind. Something was coming, and they peered through the gaps in the trees.

Bird call from the archers above.

They heard them before they saw them. The thud of many feet, thrashing through the undergrowth. They could see the bushes moving, stomping running feet, frantic breaths, almost gasps and then an elf was running towards them, right past them. Had their camouflage been so good that they could not be seen, even from such a short distance?

Behind that first elf, another came, and then another. The warriors, startled at first, reached out, tried to stop their mad rush through the forest. But it was as if they hadn't seen the warriors at all. They reached out to them, but the people didn't stop.

Fel'annár managed to grab one by his clothes, jostled him until he stopped. He shook the elf until he looked at him.

"What's happened?"

The elf tried and failed to tell him. Started, stopped, scratched furiously at his scalp and suppressed a sob.

"You have to help them. *Help* them. They're not dead. They're not *dead!*"

The desperate civilian shrugged out of his clutch and ran. No use shouting out. Panic had taken hold. They would soon run into the rear guard and then Lan Taria if they were lucky. They weren't prepared for this terrain.

Gor'sadén managed to catch a woman with blood in her hair.

"Tell us! What's happened?"

"They're taking us alive. They're caging us and taking us away!"

"Where have you come from?"

"Abiren'á ... *Help* them ... They're coming!" It was almost a scream.

"Listen to me. You are safe, do you understand? You are *safe!*"

She looked at him as if he had gone insane. "We're not safe. None of us are. They're not dead ... they're not dead!"

"Who? Who is not dead?"

Silence.

"Tell me!" He shook the woman hard. "Who is not dead?"

"Us ... and then they come. They're *coming!!*" She was screaming, hysterical as she wrangled her way out of Gor'sadén's clutch and ran.

Fel'annár doubted they knew where they were going, as much as he doubted they would survive the Wetwood the way they were. He watched as the last of them ran past the warriors. One tripped and fell. No time to help him as he scrambled to his feet and sprinted away. Any moment now and they would run blindly into the quicksand and bogs they had left behind them.

"They're not dead ..." murmured Gor'sadén.

"And who's *they*?" asked Galdith.

"They're taking our people alive ..." said Fel'annár. "Making them look dead when they're not ...?"

"Azure is still out there. If there were danger close by, he would have warned us by now," said Galdith.

"Agreed. Maybe he's gone on to Abiren'á for a second try. We need to know what the enemy is doing to our people that has them so panicked they would sprint through the Wetwood and risk death," said Fel'annár. "What could be worse than that?"

No one answered, and with the heat slowly rising, the humidity became almost unbearable. They adjusted their camouflage and resumed their march through the undergrowth, their breaths so laboured they were gasping.

Fel'annár thought it was twilight, and Galdith confirmed it. With the call of a frogmouth, the perturbed warriors stopped. They were exhausted, hungry; wet and filthy. It was all they could do to climb the trees, as Galdith had instructed.

They sat in small clusters, eating nuts and dried fruit. If they were lucky, they would catch a few moments of rest before dawn and it was time to march once more.

Fel'annár climbed as high as he could, enough to see over a part of the forest, enough that it afforded him the most beautiful view of the night sky above him.

A bright ball of light stood proudly, almost at the zenith and just beneath it, another, perfectly aligned.

He watched, mesmerised by the simple beauty of nature, the incomprehensible light and how it moved, ever westwards.

So quiet. A moment of peace, even here, where Sand Lords had dared venture.

BOTH KEY'HÁN and Saz'nár were Masters of Steel – QasQeen – as the Sand Lords said in their peculiar tongue. Key'hán liked it because it was neither elven nor human. It sounded *animal*. It was harsh and wholly unexpected at times. There were trills and clicks, pops and clacking noises all mixed in with the familiar sounds of elvish and human. He liked it because it was like him, not entirely anything. Human and Sand Lord, elf – animal. That was what he was.

Key'hán walked through the camp, just outside the Xeric Wood. His brother Saz'nár, had taken six thousand inside, would already be presiding over his new domain, preparing to meet the elven army they knew would be coming soon. Meanwhile, it was Key'hán's job to oversee the mining towers and the onset of the piping that their engineers had already started to construct. Once their job was done and the Deviants arrived from the Median Mountains, they could join Saz'nár, eliminate the enemy and continue their march southwards.

The warriors quietened as he passed, unwilling to draw attention to themselves and that satisfied Key'hán. Respect was not given in Sand Lord society. It was to be earned, and earned it he *had* in these last months of preparation and travel. The price of that respect was a small number of their army who had served as examples of what happened when you defied a Nim'uán. But others were proof of what could be gained with obedience and sacrifice. Jewels, finery, a prestigious place beside the immortal generals. They would be the heroes Key'hán and Saz'nár would present to their elder brother, Gra'dón, soon-to-be emperor of Ea Uaré.

On the edge of the camp, well-guarded and barely fed, sat the cages they had filled with elves. They were mostly warriors. Key'hán crouched before them, eyes raking over his captives, enjoying the shock and the fear on their faces. A young elf in brown and green hunting gear boldly stared back at him. His were not the clothes of a warrior.

"You. What is your trade?"

The elf stared back at him, fear warring with disgust, with rebellion. Not a warrior but brave nonetheless, thought Key'hán. He liked that.

"I'm a forester."

"Oh, the trees, yes. Such veneration you forest elves have for those plants. How would it feel, I wonder, if I burnt them all down?"

The forester didn't answer and Key'hán's eyes blackened. "Answer me."

"It would be a tragedy. But you're not stupid ..." he held his tongue, looked away, courage faltering.

Key'hán smiled, enjoyed the fear and the indecision. The forester had wanted to say more, had wanted to insult him.

"No, I am not. To destroy them would be to expose the ground beneath, extend the Xeric Wood and we have come to conquer these lands, to live in them and swim in your waters. I have not come to burn trees. I have come to burn *elves* ...."

That last S was far too long, like a snake hissing a warning. The caged elves whimpered and cowered against the far railings, most of them only just past novice training.

Key'hán stood, looked down on them in pity and humour for only he knew what fate awaited them. It was time to speak with his chieftains. It was time to plan the second part of their strategy. With Saz'nár in Abiren'á, he would already be preparing the city in such a way that the elves would not dare set foot inside it, because to do so would seal the fate of their people.

He knew the elven army was close, and Gra'dón had warned them that Araria would send aid. Still, he felt confident that his Sand Lords and the coming Deviants would outnumber the elves. But superior numbers alone would not win the day, not in a place like this. Too many trees, Gra'dón had said. And if there *were* mages here, then that threat needed to be neutralised.

Gra'dón had heard of how one of them had vanquished their

brother. The Deviants called him the *Silver One*. But just how many of these mages existed? And so, the Nim'uán had instructed the warriors to search for any signs of magic. Any elf with strange eyes, any incidents involving trees were to be reported immediately. If they could root them out before the battle, they could stop the trees from turning against them.

He smiled as he continued his walk, sand rippling beneath his feet and just a few yards away, he caught sight of a scaly blade as it surfaced for just a moment, before ducking back inside, into the dark where it most liked to be. It was hungry and soon, Key'hán would oblige his ally. All that was left to do was wait for news that Abiren'á was secured and ready, wait for the engineers to complete their task. Only then, would he lead them all into the forest. With the north-west secured, the Nim'uán had all the time in the world to slowly advance southwards, to the very gates of the elvenking's realm.

He smiled wider, wagered there was a glitter of excitement in his eyes. Glory days were coming. They had their own lands and people to rule over now. And later, when they had established their paradise, they would march on Araria, free this world of the taint of mortality, exterminate the exterminators.

It was the time of the Nim'uán and the Deviant.

It was time to mend the folly of Gods.

30

AZURE'S FLIGHT

~

THE COURTYARD before the palace fortress of Ea Uaré was teaming with warriors, healers, civilians and children.

General Rinon had escorted a large group of refugees into the city, and there was no mistaking where most of them had come from.

Abiren'á.

There were Ari children, a sight seldom seen, and the people stared and talked as they pointed at the young recruits and their solemn-looking leader.

But that wasn't the only thing they stared at. There was a female captain, and with her, a small patrol of warriors from Tar'eastór.

The Silvan Elders were directing the families and the Ari'atór to the Merchant Guild, while Llyniel and Kristain directed the stretchers to the Halls. Captains Salo and Henú accompanied the Alpine warriors to barracks, save for their captain who stood together with Rinon, the Ari Master and Commander Turion.

"Report, General Rinon."

"Captain Sorei was sent by Commander General Pan'assár to escort these refugees from Abiren'á and Sen'oléi. One hundred Deviants attacked, them, just a day and half from our gates. There are ten dead and eighteen wounded."

"Has the horde been neutralised?"

"It has, Commander."

"Welcome home then, General. Captain Sorei, we are most grateful for your protection of our people. I request a report from you tomorrow morning."

"Of course, Commander." She held out the orders Gor'sadén had written for her.

Turion took the folded paper, but he didn't open it, not yet. Instead, he cast his gaze over the slowly emptying courtyard.

"Are there no more refugees?"

"My contingent was with your army, just past Oran'Dor when they arrived, Commander. I know they come from Sen'oléi and Abiren'á, your northernmost settlements."

"Yes. But there should be hundreds more."

"If I may, Commander."

"Master Ari'atór," greeted Turion.

"There are many others who took the barges with their children. They stayed in Sen'Garay, refusing to live in what they call the 'stone city.'"

"There may come a time when not even that place is safe, Master."

"But it is not now. My people are a part of the earth, Commander. They will stay in the forest until there is no other choice."

"I know. And we must pray it never comes to that. But the news is troubling. We do not have enough warriors. The enemy army is many thousands strong, and ours is not."

"But you have Captain Bulan. You have the Warlord and you have the living forest, Commander. You must hold to hope that together, they will be invincible."

"Commander General Pan'assár will see it done," said Turion, watching Oruná's eyes closely. But there was nothing, no flicker or frown. No emotion at all.

Turion looked down at the paper in his hands, opened it and read, and then he looked up at the captain, noticed the band of a Blade Master sitting high over her right bicep.

"Despite your evident skill at arms, Captain Sorei, Commander Pan'assár is adamant that you be free to create these ... *Synth Blades*. I confess I am somewhat at a loss, surprised, admittedly, that he would relieve you of active duty in favour of creating blades. Still, he is not aware of this evolving Deviant threat here in the city."

She nodded, surely wondering if he would revoke her orders.

"I will have you escorted to the furnaces tomorrow. You will be provided with the materials you need, and I will make sure you are not disturbed. Is this activity of yours to be withheld from others?"

"Indeed, Commander. I would not reveal my secrets to any other than our own military swordsmiths. Should those secrets transcend the Inner Circle, they would fall into the hands of unscrupulous merchants and then into enemy hands in weeks. Still, it is not only the composition but the method with which they are treated. Even if they had the right materials, their results would not be satisfactory."

"Then I confess to being even more intrigued, Captain. Perhaps some other day we can speak of these blades. For now, know that I reserve the right to revoke Commander Pan'assár's orders and place you back on active duty if the need arises. These are uncertain times. For now, you both must rest and tomorrow, we will get to work."

Turion led them across the courtyard and to the female barracks. It was a long stone building that had been occupied by males until recently. The recruits, not that there were many of them, would be out in the training fields, a scant few dozen.

There had been no time for recruitment, even though Turion needed all the warriors he could get his hands on. Still, he had spotted a few female warriors in Sorei's unit, wondered if that would motivate their own women to join the army.

At the end of the aisle was a door that led into a comfortable room. A bed, a desk and a chair, a fireplace and a selection of books. Sorei seemed pleased with the arrangements.

"The mess hall is yet to come into service in this barrack, but we would welcome you at the Inner Circle for meals. I will have someone escort you to the furnaces tomorrow morning and show you about the place. Is there anything else you need, Captain?"

"Commander. Where will the refugees be taken?"

"They are at the Merchant Guild, under the guidance of the Silvan Elders."

Sorei nodded, threw her pack on the bed and turned to the two generals. She saluted them.

No sooner the door clicked shut, than she released a long, tired breath. Her stony façade gone, she sat heavily on the bed and lay back. She had been sent south to protect the civilians, make her blades but now, she wondered if war would come here, to the very gates of the Silvan city.

But they didn't have enough warriors.

Turion and Rinon continued to the fortress palace, and as they walked, the commander turned to the general, taking his time before speaking.

"Well then."

"Well then what?" asked Rinon.

"Well then what do you *think* I mean?" asked Turion, half frustrated, half amused. He hadn't missed the tension between Sorei and Rinon.

Rinon's lips twitched but he said nothing. The woman was insufferable. Stony face, sarcastic, irreverent. Why on Bel'arán did she intrigue him?

"I want you to accompany the captain to the forges tomorrow morning."

"If I must."

Turion pursed his lips, smothered his smile.

That night, Rinon was restless.

His mind was working through the day's revelations, of the arrival of Sorei and the backup they had so desperately needed. But of the one thousand that Vorn'asté had sent, only fifty had come. The rest had stayed with their army and Rinon supposed that was where they were most needed.

Tomorrow would be a day of planning, in which Turion and himself would decide how best to deploy the Tar'eastór warriors. It felt like rationing one loaf of bread to a hundred hungry elves.

Yet despite the worrying news, the imminent war in the north and the growing conflict with Deviants here in the south, his mind strayed to his sister. Sontúr was courting her, and she had asked him a question, one he had not wanted to answer.

Was he happy for her?

To say no would be selfish, hurtful and he would never do that, not unless her choice of partner was one he thought may be damaging to her. But she had chosen Sontúr, and try as he might, he could find no reason to dislike the prince.

What *did* bother him was the prospect that she would leave Ea Uaré, leave *him* – again.

He pulled his weapons off, stored them and then undressed, even as he prepared his bath and then sat in it. The hot water was almost scalding, just the way he liked it. It distracted him, forced his mind to stop, concentrate on nothing but the water, the touch of it on his skin.

Sometime later, clean and changed into a simple robe, he brushed his loose hair and then poured a glass of wine. With no more hot water to concentrate on, his mind resumed its meanderings.

Turanés, Colanéi, great swordsmiths of old. Every warrior wanted one of their creations hanging from their belts or tucked inside their harnesses. But few could afford them, unless they were lucky enough to inherit one from a warrior father. His own Colanéi was a gift from his father, who said it had once been his own great grandfather's.

If this – woman – had been ordered by Pan'assár to create these Synth Blades she spoke of, then it was for a reason. The commander must have been impressed, otherwise he would have bid her stay with the war effort. She was obviously a fine warrior, a Blade Master Pan'assár could well have used in the north.

He put his wine down, left his rooms and headed to the royal library, two floors down. It was late, but Rinon wasn't concerned about his loose hair and unprincely clothing. Only the guards would see him, and they were accustomed to that.

At the open doors, he stopped and looked about the place. At first glance, there was no one here, and so he made straight for the area where he knew the books on blades were kept. Before one such shelf, his eyes swept up and down the titles.

Reaching out with one hand, he hooked a finger over the spine of a large book and pulled. It left a gap between the books, big enough to reveal two people, sitting together at a table, too far away from him to hear what they said, and yet close enough to see their faces.

He should have turned away, but he didn't. Couldn't.

Sontúr laughed and Maeneth smiled, a sea of books and scrolls scattered around the table. She pointed, spoke animatedly and he listened, nodded thoughtfully and then he reached for a scroll, handed it to her. With his arm still strapped to his side, he couldn't open it and a pang of guilt hit Rinon, for watching them – for being the cause of Sontúr's injury.

Maeneth opened it, and Rinon watched her as she read. When she finished, she looked at Sontúr once more.

Rinon could not deny the evidence in her eyes. It was as plainly written as the words on that scroll. Hers was an elven soul in love, he somehow knew it, even though he had never felt that thing they said existed.

He needed to look away, but his stubborn eyes watched as Sontúr leaned forward and kissed her lips, soft and deliberate and she returned it. He could almost feel her joy, feel his twin's soul pulse and shine in his mind. Maeneth loved Sontúr; there was no doubt in Rinon's mind, and that unspoken question was back.

Would she leave? Would she follow her prince to the Motherland?

But as he watched, he realised that he *was* happy for her. Even if she did leave, he was happy for her. All that was left to do was tell her so, because with his abrupt departure after she had asked her question, he knew he had hurt her.

Rinon's smile was joy and grief, excitement and disappointment. It was elation and it was despair. But the rapture in Maeneth's eyes, reflected in Sontúr's, was a treasure far greater than any anguish he felt at the prospect of losing her.

He turned away, book in hand and left quietly.

∾

THE FOLLOWING MORNING, Galdith called the warriors down from the trees with the cry of a nuthatch.

Once they were on the ground, they ate what little was still in their packs, and then gathered around the veterans and Fel'annár.

Another day of travel through the Wetwood lay ahead of them and Azure was overdue. The fate of warriors' families and friends was a constant cause of frustration and irritation, for many of them were from these parts. Those who weren't were equally outraged at the violation of what had once been the Silvan capital city. It was a symbol of their identity, one most of the Alpine warriors respected, would never question.

Fel'annár could see the downward spiral. So far, they had obeyed Pan'assár's orders because Bulan and the Warlord, Benat and Amon had asked it of them. But their worry was making them curt. Fel'annár glanced at Gor'sadén, saw the same worry in his eyes. They needed to keep the troop occupied, focussed, minds off the what-ifs and on the task ahead, and with any luck, Azure would return with news.

But where was he?

Amidst worried glances and apprehensive eyes, Fel'annár and Galdith led their group out on their third and final day of travel through the Wetwood.

It was midday by the time Azure finally returned.

Fel'annár took Azure from Tensári and walked to the nearest, largest tree. He leant back against it and allowed his eyes to lose focus. Minutes later, it was all Fel'annár could do to remain standing. Had he not been surrounded by anxious Silvans who needed to be kept on track, he would have sunk to the floor in despair. Still, he couldn't help his drained face and wary eyes. He wouldn't give them the details, not yet, not while they were still in the Wetwood where tempers could easily flare, where everything seemed more dire than it truly was.

"Our people are being held captive, but they are well for now. They are alive."

"The enemy is using them as bait?" asked one warrior, face pulled into a deep frown.

"That's a possibility. But we'll free them. We're almost there."

The warriors looked around them, saw Galdith and Gor'sadén, saw the Ari'atór and the Warlord. None of them had had a hand in those

decisions which had led to these parts of the forest being all but abandoned. No one to blame, they realised, and they sagged where they
stood, slowly dissipated into smaller groups and Fel'annár resumed their
march with a warning look at Galdith.

In a voice that was meant only for The Company and Gor'sadén,
Fel'annár told them the whole truth.

"Abiren'á is overrun. The Nim'uán itself is there, upon the high
talans. It makes sense now, most of it at least."

"Fel'annár." A hard shake on the shoulder from Gor'sadén and he
snapped himself out of the message Azure had conveyed to him. It was
still sinking in. He couldn't quite believe what he had heard.

"There are cages hanging from the trees. Thick ropes anchor them to
the ground but there is some sticky, white substance all over them, caked
to it, Azure says. Our people sit inside them, starving, thirsty, panicked
half to death.

"The Gods but how *dare* they. They're not warriors, they're ..."
Galdith was shaking, face red, veins in his neck bulging. Idernon placed
a calming hand on his shoulder.

"Our time will come for vengeance, brother. You'll see."

Fel'annár nodded at Idernon, and then continued to relate Azure's
findings. "He says he has seen pale Sand Lords and crates they carry
with great care."

"Pale Sand Lords. Azure already told us that, but what does that
mean? Some new race?" murmured Gor'sadén. "How many are in the
city, did he say?"

"He confirms six thousand in and around the city. He says they come
and go to the Xeric wood where another four thousand await. They are
guarding the mining towers, as we suspected. Whatever their purpose
for invading our lands, it is partly to do with the water."

"There are elves in the trees and there are strange Sand Lords, not to
mention the enigma of this *undead* business those civilians could not
bring themselves to better explain. What are we missing?" asked
Gor'sadén, turning to Fel'annár and wondering if he had heard anything
of what he had said. His face was turned upwards, eyes vacant.

"I can't conjure the trees. I will kill our own people."

Gor'sadén, Galdith and Tensári shared a knowing look, and Fel'annár gave voice to what they were all thinking.

"Have they done this purposefully, because of me?"

A soft breeze played about the ferns, leaves rustling, playing with the ends of Fel'annár's braids. He knew he was right.

"How would they know you?" asked Galdith.

Gor'sadén turned to him. "The Nim'uán will know him. Fel'annár killed its brother."

Galdith was shaking his head. "But why would that matter to a beast like that?" But even as he asked the question, he was reminded of the sketch he had seen just recently in Fel'annár's journal, the sketch of the Nim'uán with expressive eyes, the look of one who knew grief. Fel'annár had said that it *feels.*

"Vengeance?" ventured Tensári.

"Perhaps, murmured Fel'annár. "And yet I believe it's more than that. The Nim'uán are not mindless beasts. We know there's a practical purpose to this invasion – our water. But why did the Sand Lords send a Nim'uán? Why not some other general or commander? See, even if it *does* know of me, it has no way of knowing that I am *here.* It's too much of a distant possibility to base its entire strategy on my presence."

"And perhaps it *doesn't* know you're here," offered Idernon. "If one exists, why not more? Maybe they think there are many who can move the trees."

Fel'annár nodded slowly, momentarily caught Gor'sadén's gaze.

"He's right. I hadn't thought of that," confessed Fel'annár. "At least we know where our people are now, and what we need to do if we have any chance of enlisting the help of the trees." He tried to imagine getting their people down from the cages whilst battling the Sand Lords. It was possible, if the odds were even. But they weren't. They were outnumbered.

He *would* need to conjure the trees.

"There may come a time when you must think of the greater good," warned Gor'sadén. Fel'annár stared back at his Master, his father, saw the understanding in his eyes, the pity that came with it.

He closed his eyes, felt sick to the stomach. Could he invoke the trees, knowing that their people would surely plummet to their deaths? Because that was in the interest of the greater good?

He didn't know if he could do such a thing and even if he could, he wondered how he would ever be able to live with himself afterwards.

THEY WERE APPROACHING the end of the Wetwood and Fel'annár thanked the Gods they had not met any Sand Lords. It could well be a sign that the enemy was not ready to continue its march southwards. But then again, it could also mean that it was never their intention to move further south at all.

He could only pray that the panicked civilians they had come across would make it safely out the other side of the Wetwood.

The forest was less dense here, the air lighter and fresher. Boulders jutted from the ground all around them and in the distance, a high, rocky peak soared above the timberline. Halfway up it, a plateau and a single tree. This was Skyrock, their destination, a place Fel'annár had only ever seen in books.

He stared up at it as they marched, then almost lost his footing. He felt a hand under his forearm and he turned, red-faced and scowling. Galdith grinned and turned away, obviously trying not to laugh.

Within hours, they would be reunited with the other groups beside and behind them. The army would camp behind the imposing tower of rock while the captains and commanders would climb up to the highest point and survey the land, make their final plans to regain Abiren'á. And, if Fel'annár were Pan'assár, despite the urgency, he would take a day to organise their supplies and ready the troops, perhaps ask Azure to scout for them one last time.

They came to another wooded area, the trees different to the ones they had passed for the last three days. The sounds were different too, the native animals less noisy, more melodious. This was the forest he knew and loved and Fel'annár smiled.

But the smile wavered, and then it disappeared.

The familiar tingle of fine hairs at the back of his neck, the warmth in his eyes, the surge of blood through his veins.

Danger.

Fel'annár turned to Gor'sadén.

"There are two score Sand Lords just behind that crest ahead. Pan'assár approaches with his patrol from the east. Neither he nor the Sand Lords have detected our presence."

"They must be scouts. They will flee rather than fight, send news to their leader that the army has arrived to meet them."

Fel'annár nodded in agreement. "And most likely there are other groups that will hear the fight. It'll be difficult to hide our presence from here."

"True. But we can keep the size and nature of our army from the enemy a while longer. Lead the attack, General."

Fel'annár stared at his Master, nodded and then turned to his patrol.

He signalled to a small group to pan towards the east. They were to find Pan'assár, warn him to stay out of sight. Should any of the Sand Lords escape them, they would believe this was a scouting party and not the entire army.

With a signal to the rest, they set out in search of the enemy patrol.

They advanced, slowly and quietly behind Fel'annár, Azure perched on Tensári's shoulder. This was the moment of truth, the moment in which they would know whether the only way to see Lainon was in battle. And then Gor'sadén and the other warriors would see him transform for the first time. Fel'annár and The Company needed to be wary of the distraction it would cause, and he was glad he'd warned Pan'assár with time enough to brief the warriors. Many had been sceptical, others confused and unnerved. Even though they had been briefed, they would still be distracted, just like Fel'annár had been that first time he had seen Lainon returned.

He held a hand up to stop. He could hear clicks and trills, strange sounds and muted laughter. Another signal to stand low. Fel'annár reached out to the trees around him. They had still not been detected. The call of a frogmouth from the right told him that Pan'assár's group had arrived. They wouldn't intervene unless they were needed.

The trees told Fel'annár what he needed to know and he, in turn, signalled the enemy's position, their numbers, and then gave the silent order to progress, to stay low, to watch him as much as the terrain before them.

Movement between the bushes, white smoke, the smell of fire. More sounds, the Sand Lords were talking quietly. They sounded like friends, as if they joked about something as they cooked the midday meal. They must just have arrived, no time to organise a watch. There would surely be more of them soon.

It was time to move.

The signal to engage was the cry of a hawk and he turned to Azure. Lainon's bird eyes stared back at him and then he opened his wings. Gor'sadén watched, eyes wide as Tensári lifted her arm, a smile on her face, and the piercing cry of a hawk rent the air. Azure flew and the Sand Lords were on their feet, shouting and flapping their hands in the air. They seemed terrified, and Fel'annár took advantage of their distraction.

As one, they ran towards the enemy, Tensári on one side, Gor'sadén on the other and a goshawk diving down from the skies. The screech of a hunter turned into the battle cry of an Ari'atór and he landed on the ground beside Tensári, swords in hand, wings fading away.

The Sand Lords were running, not fast enough and they were forced to turn and fight or be cut down. Gor'sadén's wide eyes were on the Ari'atór Lainon and not the enemy that ran towards him. Luckily, Galdith was beside him, stabbed the Sand Lord before he got too close to the almost paralysed commander. It only took Gor'sadén a moment to call on all his training and he was cutting down the enemy, as quickly and efficiently as The Company.

Fel'annár thought it was the first time he had run into battle with a smile on his face. He felt the thrill of something powerful, almost over-whelming, pushing him to fight harder and faster.

A warning from Tensári beside him and the shadow of a flying warrior passing overhead. Lainon flew forwards and slashed at the Sand Lord who had broken away from the group. He fell dead and Lainon flew back, thudded down beside Fel'annár and again, the wings seemed to dissolve.

Metal crashed loudly, the sounds of grunts and heavy breathing, thuds and cries of pain and utter terror.

And then silence.

With no more Sand Lords left to kill, Fel'annár sheathed his swords and turned to Lainon, waiting for the transformation to begin.

But it didn't, and he simply stared, watched as the dark wings faded away once more and he turned to Tensári. The two Ari'atór approached slowly, embraced fiercely and Fel'annár's eyes filled with tears as he watched. He looked away, caught Galdith's gaze, saw the tears in his eyes, memories of his own, lost love.

Gor'sadén stood rooted to the ground, eyes wandering over Lainon's back where the wings had been just moments before. He started when the Ari'atór turned to him and nodded.

"Commander."

"Lainon."

The word sounded utterly limp, but he couldn't help it. He had never seen such a thing, never *heard* of such a thing. When next he saw Hobin, he would have his answers, supposing the Supreme Commander had any.

Lainon turned to Fel'annár. "I don't have much time. From here you must be wary. There are atrocities upon the path."

Light was engulfing him, surrounding him. Black wings materialised and slanted blue eyes became round. He turned to Tensári.

"I will see you again. Whenever there is danger or battle. I will be with you, with the Ber'anor."

He jumped, upwards and away, felt his legs melt away, tail feathers steadying his flight, arms now wings. He screamed his frustration to the heavens, damned this strange fate that had allowed him these fleeting moments of joy. He wanted to curse Aria for her cruelty, and then he reminded himself that he had been given a choice.

He had chosen this, to become Shirán – Arimal – destined to a life of the highest service, to know things that no one else could, even should. He had condemned himself to eternal temptation, for the recompense of fleeting seconds in which he could touch the face of bliss.

Lainon was proud of the elf Fel'annár had become, watched him and then Tensári's shrinking forms until they were nothing but black dots far below.

Soon, if Fel'annár survived the battle to come, he would understand his purpose, at last.

THE INNER CIRCLE stood and saluted as General Rinon and Commander Turion arrived. At their side, an invited guest, one they had all come to hear of.

Captain Sorei of Tar'eastór.

Word had spread of her deeds on the outskirts of the city. The Silvan refugees spoke of her bravery, hailed her as defender. The Silvan warriors amongst them treated her as one of their own while the Alpine warriors seemed to respect her, for the most part at least. Karon was not one of them, but his commanding officer said he had mostly kept his mouth shut, even when the others mocked him for his public upbraiding.

"The Inner Circle turns." The bang of a staff upon the floor and the captains sat while Acting Commander General Turion walked into the centre.

"I am sure you will all join me in welcoming Captain Sorei into the circle. Her deeds precede her. Know that King Thargodén is most grateful for your protection of our people."

Sorei nodded but her eyes did not waver, even though she knew others were scrutinising her.

"We gather today to discuss two pressing questions. The increasing number of Deviants to the east of our city, and the overwhelming numbers we now know the enemy army boasts in the north.

"Both these questions clearly show that we need more warriors, to defend the eastern borders and to prepare for the worst possible outcome in the north, Aria forbid our warriors are overcome."

Rinon stepped into the circle. "Commander Turion and myself have been discussing the Warlord's proposal to bring female warriors into the army. As you know, Commander Pan'assár has approved of it but so far, only a handful of them have stepped forward. And there is also the suggestion that we may recruit humans from the coastal areas and Port Helia. At present, with our army away in the north, we have five hundred and seventy warriors to protect the entire realm, north and south. There are four hundred novices and two hundred recruits. King Thargodén has called for aid and King Vorn'asté will already know, supposing our messengers have arrived successfully. But Tar'eastór is five weeks away. Any contingent from there will take another three weeks at least."

The newly appointed Silvan captain Henú stood and then stepped forward. "Commander. May I suggest a recruitment effort? There are many young elves undecided as to what their future may hold, especially after our recent toils. I could garner the help of some of our more engaging lads, venture into the squares and other places our younger citizens frequent. We could explain about the new army, the new contingents and how they might serve. It will take the more skilled of the recruits five weeks to reach the status of novice. They could be put to use here in the city for the menial tasks, which would free up our more experienced warriors for the field."

There were murmurs from the other captains and Turion stepped closer to Henú. There was uncertainty in the young Silvan captain's eyes and Sorei rather thought this might be his first intervention in the Circle.

"An interesting idea, Captain Henú. You have my blessing to try. Having said that, it will be a slow process, one we will feel the effects of later on. We have need of warriors now."

General Rinon stepped forward. "Commander. What of this possibility of recruiting humans? Port Helia is a four-day ride away. We might draw them into our ranks with the promise of monthly coin. Many have military experience, would be handy enough in a fight."

Turion nodded slowly. "With careful recruitment that is a possibility. Captain Sorei, has Tar'eastór ever had humans in their ranks?"

"Occasionally, Commander. Personally, I have not served with them."

"Very well. For now, I am approving the departure of a patrol of one hundred. They will ride east, and then follow the foothills south. Their mission is to neutralise as many Deviants as they can, as a deterrent to other local groups, and then continue their journey to Port Helia. All available warriors are to return to the city. If there are humans who wish to join us, the king offers two months of coin and housing as recompense."

Sorei's eyes drifted over the captains. They were concerned and they were right to be. She herself had been surprised at the proximity of the enemy. That they were considering drafting humans into their ranks spoke of the urgency of their situation. She had rather thought

Gor'sadén had sent her to safety and yet now, nothing seemed further from the truth.

A few more questions later, and the Inner Circle was over, and Sorei approached the young captain Henú.

She saluted, watched him return it humbly.

"Captain. I wonder if I could join you on your recruitment effort. Perhaps more of your young women will take a chance at a military life. From what I can see, there are very few at the recruit barracks." Gor'sadén had bid her create Synth Blades, but that didn't mean she couldn't turn to other worthy causes, so long as they did not distract her from her primary goal.

Henú's brows rose, and a smile pulled at the corners of his mouth. He glanced at Salo beside him and then nodded. "Your presence would be much appreciated, Captain. We start tomorrow. Meet us at barrack two at the eighth hour."

She nodded, turned to leave and the two young captains shared an enthusiastic smile.

From afar, Rinon watched her leave, alone, surely making for her forge. He had escorted her there that morning, and he found himself wanting to return. Their first talk at camp had been positive, if not somewhat cold. But then he had spoiled it with his preconceived ideas about women and forges. He wanted to mend the damage; tell her he had not meant to underestimate her.

He had though, quite unconsciously, and it did not sit well with him at all.

᠅

IT HAD BEEN a long day for Rinon at the Inner Circle.

He was preparing for the scouting mission he would lead into the foothills, but his back ached and his mind was tired. He stood, knew he was too restless to return to his quarters just yet.

Making for the door of his office, he spotted a long, dark cloak he sometimes used when he couldn't be bothered with the bows and salutes that came with his office as crown prince. He reached for it, threw it around his shoulders and pulled the hood over his silvery hair.

At the stables, he allowed the carers a glimpse at his face and then lead his horse outside. Mounting, he was soon away, to the other side of the city, beyond the Inner Circle where the smiths and artisans ruled supreme.

After a while, the streets became narrower, the buildings closer together and he dismounted.

It was quiet at this time of the day, yet still, he passed small groups of elves who stood around talking. They looked like merchants, striking bargains on goods to be imported or exported to Port Helia and beyond.

Rounding a corner, he looked up at the houses. Two and three-story buildings, mainly occupied by merchants, craftsmen, tutors and scribes. They weren't luxurious by any standards, but neither were they run down and filthy like some of the quarters he had seen once in Port Helia.

Should he turn right and not left, he would walk into the Pleasure Quarter. He'd been there a few times, although not recently. There had been no time for that. Sometimes he had partaken of the springs and spas and the able elves who massaged and pampered the body while other times he had stayed for more.

Today though, he went in search of Sorei.

There was a chance she was still at her forge. He shrugged. He would take the chance and if she was not there, then he would ride back and forget he had even tried to find her.

He remembered their awkward conversation on the way back to the city. Embarrassment aside, he mulled over the question of this project of hers. It was the way she had said it that told Rinon these Synth Blades of hers were more of an obsession than a task. The way she spoke of crafting the steel, finding the perfect balance, the perfect *synthesis*.

Rinon tied his horse to a pole and wandered through the streets. The doors were closed, windows dark and unlit. He turned down a side street, walked to the very end and then took a left turn. There, at the very end, he saw a faint, orange glow.

At the door, he knocked, waited in vain for someone to open it. He pushed it with the palm of his hand, felt it turn inwards, slight friction over the ground. Stepping inside, he pushed the door closed behind him and simply watched the spectacle before him.

Black leather and sweat-slick skin. The yellow glow of semi-liquid steel reflecting off icy eyes that sparkled and glittered in anticipation and concentration. Platinum hair stuck to her face and neck, down her arms, muscled and defined. With one, she held the red-hot sword and with the other, she worked it with a hammer, breaking the fibres of the iron ore within. A Blade Master band lay over her bicep, the evidence of it in her body, her gaze. But it was none of these things that stirred his soul. It was the strength of her mind. Something drove her, some search for perfection that overrode even her own comfort. An obsession she was incapable of letting go.

Power. He thought she could achieve anything she put her mind to, so long as it touched her. The capacity to pursue a desire, as far and for as long as it took, to whatever end. Some called it stubbornness but to Rinon, it was the essence of greatness.

Even as she continued to hammer at the sword, her head turned to the door, cool regard, as if she had expected him. But her arm did not falter, orange sparks dangerous, but never landing on her skin.

Grabbing the iron tongues with both hands, she shoved the blade back into the hearth and worked the flue. Rinon stepped closer, watched the blade glow brighter, from red to yellow and she pulled it out again, began to tap the outer edges of the sword, and he wondered at the strange technique.

"How long does it take to complete?" he asked, breaking the silence between them, barely audible over the clatter and clang of her work.

"That will depend on how many hours I have free. This sword is not yet born, General. I would, at least, create its structure."

"Rinon will do, Sorei. We are both off duty."

"Rinon, then," she said, a faint smile dancing across her lips.

"It is longer than any longsword I have seen."

"Longer yet no heavier for it."

"That is not possible."

"Oh?" She hesitated, stared at the prince for a moment, resumed her work when he didn't answer.

"Point taken."

Closer to the anvil now, the heat uncomfortable but Rinon was drawn to her like a spring shoot to the morning sun, eyes fascinated by the play of light in her eyes, the muscles in her neck as she worked.

Strength, determination, skill, she was not afraid to walk alone, rather thought she often did for elves such as she were not common. But then again, neither was Rinon.

She straightened, took the nascent sword and shoved it back into the hearth but she did not feed the flames, rather she left the tongs, wiped her hands on a cloth, drew it over the back of her neck and down her front. Rinon followed its trail and she watched him.

Before Rinon could react, two hands were pushing him backwards, did not stop until he banged into the wall behind and she was before him, body flush with his, still hot from the fires, breath even hotter.

"Why have you come?" she whispered.

Rinon hesitated, didn't want to answer in case he said the wrong thing again and she turned away. Instead, the truth tumbled from his lips.

"In search of you."

She stared back at him with eyes so similar to his own. Her gaze lowered to his mouth and a wave of pleasure and anticipation hit Rinon as it never had before. And then she was upon him, kissing him, hard and demanding. There was nothing decorous about it. It was pure desire and Rinon responded in kind, kissed her back and yielded to her searching hands, skilled hands that worked him now as they had the swords she had been forging. His own hands came up, fingers splayed as they touched shoulders and then raked down her back, followed the curve of her buttocks. Lips on his neck, devouring, hungry.

Rinon could take no more and he turned her around, feeling her body hit the wall hard. But she was a warrior and so was he. Within seconds, half their clothing had gone, as surely as Rinon's rational mind.

31

THE GRUESOME PATH

~

PAN'ASSÁR'S GROUP had joined Fel'annár's after the skirmish, and together, the army advanced towards Skyrock.

There was a stunned sort of quiet about them. They had already seen Fel'annár transform back in the city and then in Lan Taria. They had seen a blue-eyed hawk and they had heard the weeping giants the night the enemy had crossed their borders. And now, they had seen a bird transform into a winged Ari'atór and they wondered, what more could possibly surprise them on this final stretch towards the Xeric Wood? Talking was not allowed, but even if it was, Fel'annár wondered if they would be capable of it.

His dream, if that was what it had been, was replaying in his mind once more. He remembered the Last Markers, seeing himself carved in black stone, standing beside Zéndar. He remembered the green beast, how he was being throttled. And then he remembered the flutter of heavy wings and waking up far from where he had been.

Had Lainon *carried* him to safety?

He had been staring at Azure without realising and Tensári turned to him. She believed his experience in the Evergreen Wood had been real –

either that or a dream, but not one Aria had sent him. She had felt the danger, heard Aria's call to help him and been stopped by the trees. He understood her, because why would Aria purposefully scare him halfway to Valley? Why would Lainon need to save him if the beast in the fog had been a figment of his own imagination? Somehow, it didn't seem like the kind of thing she would do. It left him with only two possibilities: that it *had* been a dream, a reflection of his own thoughts and fears, or, incomprehensible though it was, it had been *real*, as Tensári had said.

He repressed a shudder of dread, didn't want to think about it, not here when they were out in the open, so close to an enemy which surely knew they were here.

After an hour of marching, a dense blanket of mist had descended upon them. Luckily, they had seen no further sign of the enemy and the trees seemed more open and willing to share their thoughts with him. Their voice was deeper here, and he wondered if those bass notes came from the Sisters. Gods but he felt like a child for the excitement he felt about contemplating them for the first time.

A wave of nausea hit him. Something was wrong and he slowed his pace. Tensári narrowly avoided bumping into him.

There are atrocities on the path ahead.

Lainon had said that before he had become Azure, and Fel'annár was about to find out what he had meant.

"What's wrong?" murmured Idernon.

Galadan moved to Pan'assár's side, whispered something and then re-joined The Company.

Fel'annár's pace had visibly slowed. He was falling back, eyes fixed on the road ahead but he was far too pale, a light sheen of sweat on his brow, breathing too fast.

"Stop. Just … stop, please."

Galdith whistled and Pan'assár turned, signalling for the troops to stop. He walked back to where Fel'annár stood, like a deer before a sharp arrow.

"What have they done …" It was nothing but a whispered question, confusion and disbelief making him sound as young as he truly was.

"Warlord?" Pan'assár's eyes were searching their surroundings, but

Gor'sadén and then Bulan were at his side, deep frowns as they watched Fel'annár, strained to hear his words.

Anguish. Torment. Agony. Horror.

Tears flooded Fel'annár's eyes and the troops began to murmur, unsettled.

"How they suffered." A sob threatened to escape him, one hand coming up to cover his mouth. His next words sounded so inadequate, but they were all he had. All the forest had.

"I can hear their screams, their begging and their pleading. I can see their confusion, their disbelief, their ..." he placed a hand over his aching chest, tears of empathy splashing onto his own arm. "Their *agony*. Gods but how long does it take to die?"

Pan'assár had no answer. All he knew was that there was something up ahead of them, just like there had been on their journey back from Tar'eastór when they had found Silor's company slaughtered.

"Fel'annár. Tell us. What lies ahead?" Pan'assár's voice was low, meant only for The Company to hear.

"Our people, our ... families ..." he couldn't say the words, turned his head away.

Pan'assár heard enough to know he needed to bolster the troops for whatever lay on the road ahead of them. Fel'annár's reaction was far beyond anything he had ever seen from him. With a signal, he invited the captains to come closer.

"Listen carefully. Whatever we come across now, keep your eyes to the fore and remember why we are here. Whatever you see, remember it is our job to put it right. This is the north, many of us here know this forest, its strange ways and the wherefore of them. Atrocities happen here and the trees see them, feel them but remember. It is our job to make it right, captains. Gor'sadén, Fel'annár and The Company at the fore. Bulan, Amon, Benat, at the rear, full alert. Warn our warriors and watch them carefully. We make for Skyrock as fast as we can. There is no way around this path."

The commanders and captains moved into place and together, the warriors resumed their trek amidst quiet murmurs the commanders were hard-pressed to quieten. Until just minutes later when the first bodies appeared.

It was then, that Pan'assár realised why they had met no Sand Lords here, so close to Abiren'á. The enemy had clearly thought *this* was a far more effective deterrent.

The head of an elf stuck atop a pole at eye level. And then another and as they progressed, more of them, until the path was lined with them, a macabre welcome to the outer limits of Abiren'á, conquered territory of the Sand Lords of Calrazia.

Warriors stopped dead in their tracks, eyes wide, shaking hands reaching out to faces they knew. Civilians from Sen'oléi and Abiren'á. Women and men, old and young. Bakers and farmers, artisans and teachers.

Some warriors ushered their friends on, almost dragging others. There were shouts of dismay, names of the dead echoing around the place. With weeping hearts, the captains shouted louder. They couldn't stop, it was too dangerous and there was no time to give these souls burial.

"Eyes to the fore. Don't stop."

Behind the road of staked heads and to either side, the trees bore the dismembered bodies of others, most of them civilians. At first, they were nothing but misshapen silhouettes hanging in the fog-laden forest, nothing but a hint of the atrocities that had taken place here. But the closer they drew, the more vivid and stark the truth became.

Headless or armless, missing legs, others with no limbs left. But they had not been cut off, rather their flesh hung in ragged gashes, as if wild animals had fed on them. But all of them had been disembowelled. Scores of them, hundreds further behind. Everywhere they looked, the bodies of the innocent were hanging, dangling, spread eagled or crumpled awkwardly in nets. They were dead, but oblivion had not come swiftly. They had been left to die, gruesome offerings from twisted Gods to those who would defy them.

How long does it take to die?

"Eyes to the fore!" shouted Pan'assár. But some did look, because they knew these people. One warrior lunged away from the column, ran for a man tied to a tree, a rope around his neck, head red and purple. He tugged and then yanked at the ropes, shouted out his frustration when they would not come loose. Others ran to him, pulled him away as he sobbed and screamed, calling out to his father again and again.

"Eyes to the *fore!*" shouted Pan'assár again.

Someone retched, another swore to the gods while others cursed the Sand Lords. But so too did they damn the Alpines for not acting sooner. They had not listened, had not created the outposts they had warned were needed so desperately – they had not cared enough about these people to protect them. Had there been more warriors in this area, this might have been avoided.

And the one who had taken those ill-founded decisions was here, amongst them. Commander General Pan'assár.

Fel'annár, just like the others, had unintentionally defied the commander's orders to look to the fore. This gruesome path was a warning he understood as well as the rest of them surely did.

And then the bodies were gone but still, Pan'assár shouted.

"Keep moving. Remember why we are here."

The captains repeated his words, their own eyes full of the horror, hearts broken but they needed to keep moving, find a place of safety and that was Skyrock. It was all they could think of now, that and how Pan'assár, ultimately, was responsible for this.

The terrain was still dense with trees, but the loamy ground gave way to rock and a singular formation loomed before them. Fel'annár had seen it in books, but he had never imagined the awe it would strike in his mind. Still, it wasn't enough to replace the sight of tortured bodies hanging from trees.

They were tired, stunned into silence as they began to set up camp and Pan'assár watched them carefully, Gor'sadén beside him.

Both were experienced enough to know the danger would not come from the enemy this night. Already he could hear angry murmurs and recriminations. This was the pinnacle of Pan'assár's torment. This was the evidence of what he had done, what he had allowed to happen.

Minutes later, the murmurs became conversations, and then the conversations were heated discussions.

"It should never have happened. Our Elders told them, time and again and all they did was sit there and sneer at our plight."

"But it wasn't *all* of them, you know that. It was the *Purists* ..."

"And those who didn't dare speak out? They're just as bad. With their silence they've brought this massacre upon us. It's a travesty!"

"Aye. Where are the outposts? They wanted us to abandon this place, our home, because they couldn't be bothered to protect us. And look at what they've done!"

"Are you not ashamed?" asked a Silvan warrior of his Alpine companion. "I can still remember how you laughed at us, how you sent us for water and put us to cooking instead of using our knowledge of the land, instead of listening to us and heeding our warnings. Gods you should be on your *knees,* begging for forgiveness!"

The Alpines amongst them held their hands out, a silent plea for them to quieten because they agreed. They understood and wouldn't argue. The Silvans amongst them had agreed to return to the army because the Warlord said things would change. But after travelling that road of death, the Silvans had been pushed over their limits. They were shouting, almost raging, and then the first fist flew into the face of an Alpine warrior.

The camp erupted.

Fists and backhands, Alpines and Silvans were grappling with each other. They punched and kicked, pulled at hair and shoved at each other. The Company and Gor'sadén moved in while Bulan tried to calm his Silvan brethren, albeit he was hard pressed not to repeat their words to Pan'assár, punch him in the gut himself.

Two Silvans dived for Galadan but The Company surrounded him, pushed them back while another shouted.

"Pan'assár's faithful Alpine hound!"

Galdith flew at him, punched his face but Carodel pulled him back and both fell to the ground.

Pan'assár jumped onto a rock and lifted his voice more than he would have liked with an army of invading Sand Lords just a few leagues away.

"Warriors!"

It was that kind of voice, the voice of an experienced commander on the battlefield, a tone that they could not help but heed. They stopped their scuffling and turned to him, hair and clothes in disarray, barely contained ire. Whatever Pan'assár said now would either inflame or douse the fire in their eyes. Gor'sadén knew that, stood below his brother with one hand on his sword.

Pan'assár pursed his lips, looked to the heavens, warm blue and soft white. A strange sense of peace descended on him then, in spite of the volatile situation he faced.

"The *enemy* has killed our people, hung them from the boughs. We have all seen it. We have all cried for them. *All* of us. The *enemy* has violated our most sacred of places, murdered innocent elves, killed them in the most atrocious of ways and left them to rot, so that we can *see* what they have done."

There were shouts of despair, sobs, insults that Pan'assár chose to ignore.

"Listen to me. The enemy is there, in Abiren'á. Not here, warriors. I – am not your enemy – not anymore."

He breathed deeply, memories coming to him fast in the growing silence around him. His admission had surprised them enough to garner their attention.

"This is not new. Some of us have seen this before, even as it happened before our very eyes, and you ask yourself. How? How is it possible that my father, my mother, my brother can die in such a way? How did they deserve such an end, after all the good they have done in life? It is unnatural, it is cruel and yet ... is this not the nature of the enemy? The *real* enemy?

"When King Or'Talán fell, *this* was the nature of his death. It was not mindless but a purposeful torment of design, meant to choke our spirit, to win their battle not with honour but with cruelty – the greatest weapon of all – and, if you will listen, I will tell you of its power."

The silence around him was complete. Because this was the moment in which Pan'assár would surely reveal what it was that had changed him, from the legendary Kah Warrior of The Three, courageous and honourable, into a bigoted, incompetent commander who had indulged the wishes of Band'orán and his cohorts.

Fel'annár had an idea of what he would say, as did The Company, where Gor'sadén knew it all, had surely thought Pan'assár would never speak openly of it as he was now.

"Cruelty draws the eye, shocks the mind, stuns your soul and then it replays, over and over. The images, the sounds, the crushing grief as you watch all those things that make a person disappear. You forget everything they were, everything they said and the times that you laughed with them because those final moments are so utterly hard to bear. They neutralise it all. The great person he was is gone, and all he becomes is a quivering, suffering heap of flesh that wishes only for peace and oblivion.

"I saw that happen to our king, my brother in all but blood. As I fought impossible numbers at the Battle Under the Sun, I tried to ... I tried to reach him. They must have realised, must have seen my desperation because I have often thought they could have killed me but didn't. It was too entertaining you see – to watch me as they slowly and methodically butchered our great king – my brother. They cut him to pieces with their bloody scimitars until he could scream no more – until *I* had no voice left."

He half turned, looked to the sky, a desperate attempt to control himself. As calmly as he could, he faced his judges and continued with his confession.

"That cruelty took me, turned me against my fellow warriors, made me forget who I was, even who the *real* enemy was. It was never the Silvans.

"It was *cruelty* – evil in its purest form.

"It corrupts, bends and twists the soul and by the Gods it will break you if it can. Don't bend before it. Never lose yourself in it as I once did."

There was a shocked sort of silence about the warriors as they stared back at Pan'assár, not the commander but the elf who had lost someone irreplaceable. He had told his story in one, simple minute of time. He had passed on the wisdom that had come to him after years of suffering, because he had faced cruelty, faced evil. They realised then, what it was that had changed him. Some had been there, at the Battle Under the Sun, although admittedly not where the great king had died. But they had heard the stories, knew the horror of his tragic death.

Pan'assár had lived it. Seen it face to face and had almost broken.

Bulan stepped forward, cocked his head to one side, eyes searching the commander's face, studying his eyes, the truth in them.

"Why did you turn against the Silvans? Why not throw yourself into battle with the enemy? Why did you not see that we cared? that we were loyal to the Great King?"

Pan'assár gave him a sad smile. "That was part of Band'orán's conspiracy. The Silvan troops we had called for never arrived. They failed to ride to the aid of their king, thanks to Huren's scheming. I blamed the Silvans for our king's death because it was the perfect excuse, you see. Because when something utterly incomprehensible happens, we strive to understand and when we can't, we invent it. I was wrong. Band'orán played me for a fool and I walked into his trap willingly. Your Warlord here killed him but if he hadn't, after reading King Or'Talán's last journal, believe me when I tell you that I would have hacked him to pieces myself, as surely as the Sand Lords did Or'Talán, as surely as they have our people."

No one spoke, because what Pan'assár confessed to, was what *they* had just done, seek to place the blame on the Alpines amongst them because they needed a reason for the mindlessness, someone to blame for the atrocity, so that they could *understand.*

"How did you find your way back, Commander?" Bulan's question was careful, aware as he was that he trod a fine line between showing his warriors that Pan'assár was worthy of their trust or risking a mutiny.

Pan'assár smiled once more but this time there was no grief in his eyes as he glanced at Fel'annár.

"Your Warlord, Captain. You see, cruelty – evil – has a counterpart. It is *honour*. But honour is not impervious. It can crack and bend and cave under the weight of suffering. But it never truly fractures, never breaks completely. Fel'annár reminded me of that, quite unwittingly. In the face of adversity, he endured. He overcame the prejudice, worked and studied hard for the Kah trial I put him through. I almost killed him that day, and the only thing that stilled my hand, was when I saw Or'Talán in his eyes. It was as if I was killing my king, my brother. And if there is one thing grandfather and grandson share, other than their resemblance to one another, it is that staunch belief that honour is the only path. That honour must *never* be sacrificed, even in the face of death.

"I used to hate the Warlord because he was half-Silvan and *they* were the enemy. But after that trial, everything began to change. I no longer despised that face of his that reminded me of those final moments,

moments in which I was powerless to stop my greatest friend from an undeserved death, one I have always believed I should have shared. I suppose I did die, in a sense. Now, all I see when I look at him is hope for this land. He is the beginning of a new era, one I welcome with all my heart."

Bulan stared, everyone did. Fel'annár smiled through his tears, for the great words Pan'assár had spoken, words he wanted to remember, so that they could be chronicled, immortalised. He glanced at Gor'sadén, still standing at Pan'assár's feet, watched as he stared at the ground, keeping his own emotions in check. He started when Bulan raised his voice, cut through the paralysed silence.

"You have led us this far, knowing what the Silvans amongst us thought about you. We have watched, I have seen our Warlord look to you in respect and now, you have seen the plight of our people. You understand, have shed tears with us, will always remember that gruesome path of horror."

Bulan turned to the onlooking troops. "I second Commander Pan'assár's words. The true enemy is out there - Sand Lords - and I for one, will not crumble and seek guilt amongst my fellow warriors. Instead, I will embrace my Alpine brothers and smash this enemy into the very ground with my fists, my weapons, with everything that I have. Where the enemy sought to break *me*, instead they have made of me an avenging spirit that cannot die, because even if I am killed, my death will fuel those behind to fight stronger, harder. No matter they are Silvan or Alpine, Ari or Pelagian. It is the soul of the *warrior* that will answer, that will return time and again."

Bulan turned back to Pan'assár.

"It took a brave man to do what you have done. It took courage to stand before these, your warriors, and confess those sins. Captain Bulan Ar Zéndar salutes you, Commander."

Gor'sadén blessed Bulan's Silvan boots, because in that one gesture, he had as much as assured the unity of their group. But it was more than that. It was the peace this moment would bring to Pan'assár, a peace his friend had not felt since Or'Talán had died.

Likewise, Galadan saw Bulan's gesture for what it was, but there was more to it than simple strategy. Bulan had meant what he said. The Silvan captain they all looked up to had forgiven Pan'assár at last.

Pan'assár stood wide eyed and rigid, watched as Bulan and then all the captains behind him saluted. A ripple, backwards and the entire group – warriors and lieutenants – gave their most formal of salutes. If Bulan could forgive the commander general, then so could they.

Pan'assár's eyes were full, of shock and humble thanks. After everything he had done, and then every gesture he had made to right his wrongs, the fruit of his contrition was finally ripe. He would pluck it, savour it but for now, all he wished for was solitude.

He returned their salute, held it for far longer than was necessary and then he jumped down from the rock and turned away. Eyes wide, chin quivering, he walked away and then he climbed until he stood breathless upon the ledge that looked out over the leagues of forest that separated them from Abiren'á.

He breathed, closed his eyes, cocked his head backwards.

One more battle. And then he would pass this heavy burden to Turion. He meant what he had said.

It was time for a new era to begin.

~

SAZ'NÁR STOOD ON A FLET, high above the central glade of the Silvan city of Abiren'á.

He was surrounded by majestic buildings, sprawling platforms interconnected with ropes and bridges. This was, indeed, a city, much larger and far more complex than he had ever imagined.

He loved this place, its art and its natural beauty, wished he could stay here once the elven army had been annihilated. In fact, he thought he would make his home in one of the giant trees that stood at the very edge of the forest. He could look north and to the land of his birth. Or, he could look south, to his new domain, his mother's home.

Six thousand Sand Lords were with him, and their first job was to fortify the city and its surroundings, secure the hostages in the trees and then meet the ridiculous army the elvenking had sent to meet them.

His scouts said there were one thousand and some on their way. But

Saz'nár was an experienced general. He knew more would be marching behind. Still, the king's army was small by all accounts. They would still be woefully insufficient to take on his Sand Lord army of QasQeen Masters.

And Reapers.

There was only one thing that could jeopardise their victory.

The trees.

The trees and the mages they said could move them.

A knock at his open door and he turned to his captain, watched him salute stiffly.

"Commander. Lieutenant Sdo may have found something on his journey back from Sen'oléi. He saw one of his captives reaching through the bars of his cage and touching the bark of a tree. He says he stayed like that for minutes."

"Does he have silver hair?"

"No, sir."

Saz'nár nodded, eyes moving from side to side. "Bring him to the glade below. He may be useful."

"Sir."

The captain saluted and left to do his bidding. If this was one of those mages, a lesser one perhaps, then he could certainly help to spread the news. He had already shown a handful of the civilians what the Reapers could do and then let them go so that they could tell the others. But if this one spoke to the trees, the fame of the Reapers would be all over the forest. None would dare come to Abiren'á. No elf would stand in their way on their march south.

Horror was a powerful weapon.

Saz'nár walked to the edge of the platform and stepped into a wooden cubicle. It began to descend as his warriors worked the mechanism from below. As he moved through the trees, he watched the elves inside the cages they had fashioned. Some of them were far away from him while others were nothing but an arm's reach from his moving lift. He watched them watch him, enjoyed the horrified silence, the fear and confusion because Saz'nár was no monster to look at. He was an elf, almost like them except that he was paler, bigger, and should he smile, the illusion would be shattered. Not elven.

He was Nim'uán.

Minutes later, he landed on the ground and stepped out into the glade. Above him, the cages looked like bunches of fruit from late summer trees. The immortals inside sat huddled together, hands clutching at the bars, looking down on him, wondering if it would be *their* turn tonight.

Behind him, the sounds of a scuffle. A brown-haired warrior struggled between two Sand Lords, hands tied behind his back. Saz'nár turned to him, watched for any sign of magic but saw none.

"Are you a mage?"

"A ... *what*?"

"A mage. Can you move the trees?"

Yerái shook his head. "No, that's not possi ..."

A hand smashed into his face. He would have fallen sideways had the Sand Lords not held him in place.

"Do not take me for a fool, Silvan."

Yerái hesitated. "I can't move the trees, but there is a rumour."

"I know." Saz'nár gestured to the cages around them, as if they were prize trophies. "There was one in Tar'eastór. He made the forest dance, and then he killed my brother. Tell me, how many of these mages are there?"

Yerái needed to say something, but he had no idea if his words would be detrimental or helpful. Caution was his only road.

"The rumour says there is only one."

Saz'nár smiled back at Yerái. "Perhaps. Or are you lying?" The Nim'uán's face was inches away as he stared into the bright eyes of his captive. "What does it matter, tell me? Even if there *is* only one, he will not move the trees now, will he?" The Nim'uán smiled triumphantly and only now did Yerái truly understand why they had done this. They were protecting themselves against the Warlord.

"But come, tell me, mage. Why do you touch the trees? Do you pray to them? And careful, now. The truth may save your life."

"I listen, to their whispers, feel some of the things they do, that's all."

Saz'nár stared back at Yerái, fascinated. "That is a wonderful skill. Tell me, can you sense others like you? Do the trees whisper about them?"

"I don't know if they're anywhere close by."

"Can you sense the Silver One?"

It took Yerái a moment to understand that the Nim'uán was talking about Fel'annár. "I wish that I could. But I've heard nothing from him."

Saz'nár had no way of knowing whether that was true or not. After all, Gra'dón had made it clear that the whereabouts of their brother's murderer was unknown. He could even be dead after the battle in Tar'eastór. Xar'dón had bitten him after all, and no one survived the bite of a Nim'uán.

But they were taking no risks because if the trees turned on them, then defeat was the only possible outcome in a place like this.

"Then let's send him a message, shall we? Let's show him the folly of coming here, of standing in our way. It is a message you will take to him *personally.*" Saz'nár smiled, eyes gleaming as he watched the mounting dread on the Silvan's face.

From the surrounding trees, a figure draped in black walked towards them and beside him, the ground moved, like a Rainbow Jumper just beneath the surface of the sea. Yerái looked from the strange undulation to the cloaked figure, its face still shrouded from sight and that, thought Saz'nár, was a small mercy. He appreciated beauty, found the Reapers' faces distasteful.

The other half of the Reaper stirred beneath the ground and Saz'nár smiled. This was the part he liked best.

A rumble and then a loud bang and a crash. A body surged from the ground, rearing up until it stood upon its tail, twice the height of its other self, clumps of forest loam pattering to the ground around it. It turned slowly, black scales clacking, head fanning out to the sides as it opened its mouth and hissed. Lowering its body, it slithered surprisingly quickly towards the first hooks and pulleys that held the cages in place.

The serpent-like creature climbed onto the thick rope and began to travel upwards, leaving a trail of something white and sticky behind it. That rope they had paid good coin for would be impossible to cut now, but that didn't matter. Once the Reaper had fed, the Sand Lords would leave the cages where they were.

Those elves would never set foot on the ground again.

The steep incline of rope was almost at an end and the elves inside screamed and shrieked and prayed to their gods. Saz'nár watched in growing glee, enjoyed the spectacle, their rising panic, how they rocked the cage, desperate to escape, to unbalance the serpent that approached them headfirst. When it finally loomed before them, one elf threw himself from the cage. How he had managed to squeeze himself through the bars was a mystery to Saz'nár. He marvelled at the things one could do when panic took over.

No need to sting then.

The serpent understood the other half of itself. The jumper was still alive, struggling weakly upon the ground, legs bent at unnatural angles. He wore the clothes of a warrior, mused Saz'nár. Had he jumped purposefully, to protect the others? The thought hummed in his veins, made it all so much more thrilling.

The serpent slid back down the rope while the elves above it cried and screamed a name.

Nurodi.

The elf on the ground stirred and then moaned. From the looks of it, he had surely broken his back, but he wasn't dead, just as the cloaked part of the Reaper had already known. He could smell life, another skill Saz'nár coveted. He watched as the Reaper approached, his armoured serpent beside him.

The cloaked Reaper fell to his knees, bent over his weakly struggling victim. Long, white hands reached for the clothing at the elf's neck, pulled the cloth apart and then bent over his exposed neck. Saz'nár watched in gleeful anticipation, breath caught in his throat. A scuffle beside him as the lesser mage tried to free himself. Saz'nár smiled, turned to him, just for a moment because he never tired of the spectacle of feeding Reapers.

He watched as one long, black nail dug deep into the skin at the fallen warrior's neck, blood welling up and then over the white hand. The Reaper bit deep into the soft flesh, pulled back on it until it ripped, careful not to break the large vein that pulsed furiously. It chewed, not ravenous but appreciative of the choice flesh. The first, agonising screams sounded around the glade.

The feeding began in earnest.

Saz'nár's eyes flickered wide when the screams became screeches and then raw, voiceless gurgling as the cloaked figure feasted on the living elf's flesh, ripping away blood-soaked muscle, savouring it and then moving in for more. But it could no longer continue to eat through this part of the body, not without killing it and so it moved lower, cut open the elf's abdomen with its long, black talons and then ripped him open with both hands. This was the part Saz'nár enjoyed the most, the very thing that struck paralysing terror in the Sand Lords themselves. No one had ever invaded the Northern Territories of Calrazia. No one dared to die a death so terrible, to watch as these beasts fed on their intestines.

The captive mage at his side was struggling again, trying to free his hands so that he could cover his ears, for the Reaper continued to feed and his victim continued to gurgle, even now as his arms flailed helplessly in a pool of blood and guts. Elven endurance never ceased to amaze Saz'nár. The elf was still alive, in spite of what the Reaper had already ingested, but soon, there was no strength left in him, throat too raw to make any real noise.

The sounds faded away, as surely as the elf had and the black-clad Reaper stood and stepped away from its ravaged victim. It was time for its serpent self to start its own feed, on dead flesh. Tearing and ripping, feasting on what was left.

Yerái fell to his knees, retched at the Nim'uán's feet. Saz'nár watched with interest. So strong of body, so weak of mind. Too many emotions getting in the way of his duty as a warrior.

"Tell them. Tell them the Reapers are come. Tell them that if they confront us, if they touch the trees, their people will die – like this – every day until they are exterminated from the face of Bel'arán. Turn away, leave these lands. You can save them, mage."

He nodded at one of the guards to cut the captive's binds.

Yerái wiped at his mouth with a shaking hand as the Sand Lords pulled him up.

"Go. Run. I can hold the Reapers for a few minutes, give you a head start but don't stop, mage. They will be behind you, the serpents below you. They hunt together. Don't let them catch you!" He smiled at the horror his words brought.

"Run and don't stop!" Hissed words and the Sand Lords' hands released him. Yerái staggered forwards, glanced upwards at the petrified faces of his people. He wanted to stay and help them, but his feet were moving towards the tree line. And then he was striding, remembering how the abomination had descended on the injured warrior, remembered the screams, the raw screeches. He felt himself running, trees streaking past him. He could hear their cries, their screams and their anguished pleas to flee and bring help.

And then he heard a wail, like a wolf hunting in the dark but louder. And then another, and another. The Reapers were coming, and tears of terror and anguish leaked from the corners of his eyes as he ran, mind screaming at him to turn and help his people, save them from such a horrific death but he couldn't. There was no one to help him, no weapons to fight with. He needed to find the Warlord, to warn him.

The trees were shouting at him to flee, showing him the path to where, he couldn't say. He answered them, mind pleading for them to tell Fel'annár, tell him what Yerái had seen. He glanced behind him, saw the ground arcing upwards.

The Reapers were coming for him.

32

SAND LORDS IN THE RAIN

∽

FEL'ANNÁR HAD CLIMBED SKYROCK, to the rocky platform that seemed to float over the forest. It reminded him of the king's plateau that looked out over the Evergreen Wood.

He could see for leagues around him, as far as Abiren'á, as yet a haze of green and brown. He was still too far away to see the giants, which stood on the other side of the tree city of old, on the very borders with Calrazia. Still his heart thumped at the prospect of seeing them for the first time. They were inside him now, under his skin, a part of his flesh and blood in a way he had yet to understand.

He rubbed the inside of his right bracer absent-mindedly, fingers tingling again, reminding him of the strange communion he had felt, the deep, echoing voice of the Three Sisters.

Gods but it was beautiful here, he mused as he closed the journal on his lap and slipped it inside his pack. He had drawn Lainon, the Silent Warrior as he had once been called, only this time with wings. Then, he had drawn Pan'assár standing upon a rock and around him, saluting warriors. He drew Bulan bowing solemnly but he could not bring himself to draw the road of death. Instead, he drew a weeping warrior, and then Abiren'á as he imagined it in his mind. But however much he had tried to conjure the image of Anora, Golora and Bulora, he had not been able.

He stood, walked to the very edge of the outlook.

Clouds were billowing in from the west, slowly stretching upwards and darkening until they were columns of teal, like the stone giants on the shores of Hager Island he had only ever read about. They leeched the colour from everything save the green canopy that stretched on, slowly rising the closer you travelled to Abiren'á where the trees were taller, the terrain higher.

It was so still up here, air heavy and hot. It was like the prelude to a dream, that same oddness in which reality was still hard to discern from imagination.

A jagged streak of molten light sliced through the teal sky, crackling with power, splitting the heavens and then a boom reverberated over the forest, like Silvan war drums on the cusp of battle.

Storms like these could bring fire, but the promise of swift rain was ripe in the air and Fel'annár smiled as he watched the heavens flicker and sing. He savoured it, marvelled at the raw, unfettered power of nature, its majesty and command.

Thunder snapped in the air once more and in its wake, distant voices. A tumult of wonder. Whatever they said they were surely thanking their gods, whoever they were, for they seemed to play a game, mimicked the thunder and the lightning, laughing and then cheering.

And then he realised.

It was the voice of the enemy.

They said Sand Lords had little water, that rain was scarce but now, as the fat drops fell swifter, the voices elevated into a choir of joy and thanks. Were they praying, he wondered? Were those hands that had mutilated their people, now open in supplication to a higher being? Did they not fear judgement for their deeds?

These were the Sand Lords they would kill, come tomorrow. They felt, had hearts and surely had families. They had invaded this forest for a reason and Fel'annár would not allow himself to dwell on what that might be. He told himself all that mattered were his own people. These were Silvan lands, holy lands he had trained all his life to protect. He had a right to kill them in battle, but he would not judge their reasons – only the manner in which they obtained their goals.

Light flickered, blinded him and the ensuing crash of thunder was just a second away. It jolted him, reminded him of everything he held dear, everything he had discovered this past year. He had found a family and he swore to himself that he would protect them, that nothing would tear him away from that path, one it had taken him so long to walk.

Existence was a delicate balance of life and death, and for the Deviants, somewhere in between. Regardless of his dream, of Oruná's words, he could die tomorrow, simply cease to exist and that was a warrior's lot.

But he had never told Amareth that he loved her. He had never embraced his father.

Footfall from behind warned him that someone approached. A Kah Warrior, he knew. He didn't turn when Pan'assár came to stand beside him.

A soft voice, contemplative, almost sad. "You and I have never spoken of anything that is not warfare, or the Kal'hamén'Ar. And yet there are things I have never said to you but perhaps should have. My atonement is almost complete save for one thing."

Fel'annár turned to Pan'assár's profile, studied it for a moment before he turned back to Abiren'á in the distance, and the storm that raged above it.

"I must ask for your forgiveness. I discriminated against you, insulted you, took everything you did in the worst possible way. I was blind to your worth, told myself you could never be better than Or'Talán because you were half Silvan."

"And you nearly killed me during my test for apprenticeship in the Kal'hamén'Ar." There was a soft smile on Fel'annár's face, one he knew Pan'assár had seen.

"Yes, that too."

Pan'assár turned back to the city they would attempt to reconquer tomorrow. "It all started with you, you and my reunion with Gor'sadén. Gods but I bless the day he met you, because without that moment of fortune, I would have driven myself to ruin." He huffed, shook his head. "Whatever happens on that battlefield, Fel'annár, it will be my last in the field. When we are home, I will hand over the command of these lands to Turion."

Pan'assár's words sounded distant, as if he had only just made that decision, but something told him it was not so.

"Then it will be a sad day, even in our victory. I would have you stay."

"My duty is to the line of Or'Talán, Fel'annár. I won't leave. But it is time for change. The return of the Warlord was the beginning of the end of The Three. I must let go now."

This ... this was the Pan'assár that Gor'sadén loved as a brother. This was the commander that Galadan had always seen, always followed.

"And I would know you as a friend, Pan'assár. Aria as my witness but I never thought I would say that. You never allowed me to see beneath the commander, not completely."

"And now? What do you see now, Fel'annár?"

He smiled, words gliding easily from his tongue. "I see a glorious warrior who has suffered the arduous passage through hell and was brave enough to come back. If you can do that, you can achieve anything, even happiness."

Pan'assár straightened, ancient eyes glittering in the growing dark, fixed on the face of his one-time king.

"Even happiness," he echoed wistfully. His smile was genuine then as he watched the face beside him smile with him. "Sleep, Fel'annár. Tomorrow will be your first command on a complex battlefield. Go, to your Company. Galadan is yours now. Tomorrow, we wage war together."

Fel'annár turned to him, offered a bow, a nod, and then left the commander upon the lip of the outcrop.

Pan'assár had once mistaken Fel'annár for Or'Talán, and now it could well have been him for the words of wisdom he had just spoken. Resolve throbbed in his chest, fed him the courage he would need. He meant what he had said. This would be his last battle in command of an army. He would step away and fulfil his duty to Thargodén, closer to home, a simple Kah Master in service to his king.

He cast his gaze out over the treetops below, to the dark, expanse beyond. A patch of clear sky amidst the towering clouds. The stars there shone as brightly as they ever had in Pan'assár's life and he afforded himself a soft smile.

He stood there for a while longer, staring at the majesty of Bel'arán. Beautifully wild, savagely immense in its naked beauty. How could he ever have hated this place? Who could deny this land of trees had its own flavour of magic? It weaved spells on the senses, sunk into the very soul of an elf and made him feel small and grateful and uplifted at the same time. This was what Or'Talán had felt, from the first time he had set foot inside these lands. He had not come to conquer them. He had come to drink of them, love them.

And he had.

By the following morning, the army had re-grouped at the base of Skyrock.

The guards upon the outlook had reported no enemy movements, and it seemed logical to assume that the Nim'uán would await them in Abiren'á.

Fel'annár listened as they prepared their weapons and their packs with only what was strictly necessary for the battle ahead. There would be food enough in Abiren'á, and healing supplies, blankets and water would be readily available. What they needed now, were weapons, arrows, shields and pikes, sharp blades and as much courage as they could muster.

Azure watched from his perch on a rock beside Tensári, while Galadan spoke quietly with Galdith. The two had always been close, even though they were so different in their ways. One was silent and introspective, while the other was impulsive and outspoken.

Ramien and Carodel were honing their blades, but Idernon watched Fel'annár, the way his hands rubbed over the inside of his wrist. He pulled at the ties of his bracer, allowed it to fall away and then his fingers were rubbing once more.

Idernon frowned, happened to catch sight of Tensári. She stared back at him and then resumed her careful whittling. Whatever Fel'annár was doing, she knew what it was, what that light was he had seen under the material of his cuff. Once they were alone, he would ask him straight.

Fel'annár sat up, like a wolf scenting its prey.

"Yerái."

The others stopped what they were doing.

"He's here …" Fel'annár stood, collected his weapons and The Company did likewise, then followed him away from the camp, under the watchful eyes of the commanders further away.

YERÁI HAD RUN through the night, his horrified mind so distracted he had fallen more times than he could count.

They had chased him those first few hours, and then the trees told him they had gone. But still, he ran.

And then he had sensed the army, felt the Warlord and reached out to the trees, his feeble attempt to communicate surely insufficient.

He was exhausted, outraged, felt sick to the stomach. He wanted to run back to Abiren'á, run away from it and try to forget what he had seen.

But he knew that he never would. For as long as he lived, he would hear those sounds and see the things he had been forced to watch. He would remember the face of the Nim'uán, its beauty and its cruelty, its curiosity and intelligence – its glee in the face of suffering.

He could hardly run now. He was thirsty, hungry but the thought of food made him gag. But the plight of his people pushed him on. They needed help.

And then he felt power, heard the whisperings from the trees, from beneath his feet.

The Forest Lord is come.

The message was clear, the words exact. He slowed to a clumsy walk, looked hopefully around him, saw nothing. He felt dizzy, crashed to his knees and bowed his head, some invisible weight holding him down. It was the weight of grief and confusion, of the knowledge that a travesty had taken place before his very eyes and would stay with him for the rest of his life.

He lifted his leaden head, saw a glint of green between the trees ahead of him. He needed to get up, draw his weapon.

Peace.

And then the Warlord was walking towards him, strange green eyes fixed on his own that felt dull and lifeless. There were others around him but Yerái somehow couldn't look away. There was power in that gaze, one he was seeing for the first time uncloaked.

"Yerái."

The Warlord hadn't raised his voice and yet his name echoed around him, in his mind, but all he could do was stare up at the vision of Or'Talán.

He slowly rose, swayed to one side and The Company rushed forwards, steadied him, clapped him on the back.

"Come. We make for camp. Our army is behind Skyrock, ready to march on Abiren'á tomorrow. You have a story to tell us."

Yerái looked at the Warlord as if he had lost his marbles. But no words passed his lips and he walked with them. Just the prospect of telling them his story was enough to evoke a bubble of hysteria, but he held it at bay; he had to. He could see their complicit glances, knew they wanted to press him, as well as he knew he needed to tell them.

But he couldn't.

Minutes later, they were at the camp, and Yerái recognised Gor'sadén and Pan'assár. But blessed gods his friend Bulan was here! A wave of joy hit him and then he realised it would be a catalyst. He couldn't greet him, couldn't tell him he was glad to see him because Yerái would surely crumble.

Bulan frowned, looked to Fel'annár for answers and found none, and so he followed them to where the commanders stood waiting.

As they passed, warriors called to him and he turned his face, searched the crowds but saw none from his own, scattered patrol. They had either escaped or been captured, perhaps even killed.

Pan'assár gestured for them to sit, and Bulan made a place for himself beside his friend, while Fel'annár sat on his other side. Still, Yerái said nothing.

Bulan handed him a skin of water and the Listener stared at it for a while before reaching for it with shaking hands. He took it to his lips, hesitated, and then sipped.

He turned his head away, coughed the water up with a grimace. He wiped his mouth with his sleeve and then took a deep breath. Fel'annár watched his desperate attempt to gather his wits, calm himself from whatever he had seen.

"Listen to me, Lieutenant," began Pan'assár. "We know something has happened that has frightened our people. We met a group of panicked civilians inside the Wetwood, but they told us nothing. I wonder if you know what it was that they saw ..."

Galadan stared at the newcomer as he rummaged through his pack. He knew the feel of what he was searching for. Pulling out a small sachet of herbs, he reached for a cup and ladled hot water into it from a pot over the fire.

"They should have left. I told them, Mavorn told them..."

"You are the one who first sensed the danger – in Sen'oléi?" Pan'assár's questions would hopefully coax the warrior into giving them the information they needed. Because left to his own devices, he seemed incapable of gathering his thoughts. Fel'annár had never seen a warrior quite as shaken as Yerái was now. But he thought that Pan'assár may have.

"Yes. Some of them left, others stayed. Thank the Gods the children went down the Calro. Thank the Gods ..."

"We met Ari children from Abiren'á, on the road to Oran'Dor."

Yerái's head whipped to Fel'annár beside him, eyes suddenly sharp. "Thank the Gods. They travelled around the Wetwood."

Fel'annár nodded, turned to Pan'assár as he continued with his carefully selected questions.

"Lieutenant. The civilians we came across in the Wetwood. Why were they running?"

Yerai stared at the commander, didn't quite seem to know how to say what was in his mind. But Fel'annár didn't think it was confusion that stayed his tongue.

"The Nim'uán let them go, so that they could tell you ..."

"Tell us what, Yerái?" asked Pan'assár carefully.

"To ... to stay away. It let me go too, on purpose, so that I could tell you, the trees ... warn you that if you enter Abiren'á, the ... the things will kill our people. They hang from the branches in cages, waiting for death ..."

"Then it's true. They have been taken captive so that I don't conjure the trees." Fel'annár had said it more to himself than the others, but they understood exactly what he meant.

"Can you?"

Yerái's question surprised them all and Fel'annár looked at him, thought he seemed more focussed now that he had spoken of it. But he was under no delusions, there was more, something horrific Yerái had yet to speak of.

"Yes."

Yerái's eyes widened. "Even the giants?" It was nothing but a whisper.

"I don't know."

Yerái nodded slowly. "The Nim'uán knows, thinks others can do the same. It's obsessed with what it calls *mages*. It searches for one with silver hair." Yerái turned to Fel'annár before he turned back to Pan'assár.

The commander was thinking, eyes moving between Yerái and Fel'annár. "I believe we can safely say they have taken our people as hostages, to protect themselves against the Warlord, so that he does not use the trees as a weapon against them. We are outnumbered, and the chances are that we will need to use that power you have, Fel'annár."

"We have to find a way to get them down from the trees," said Fel'annár.

There was something in Pan'assár's eyes that spoke to Fel'annár of pity. Did he think Fel'annár would need to call on the trees even with their people still captive? Did he think he would willingly sacrifice those people? So that they could regain Abiren'á?

Would he?

"Commander ..."

Pan'assár held up a hand. "Hear me out, General. We will get them out. Their release from captivity will be just as much a part of our attack strategy as any other. But tell me, Yerái. How many people do you think are up there in those cages?"

After a while, Yerái answered with his best estimate. "There are some thirty cages, each with around ten civilians inside. If more are not killed before we can free them ... that's around three hundred civilians."

"Commander." Fel'annár was almost angry, his tone that of an order, a warning and a plea. "We can't sacrifice three hundred people ..."

"It would be a tragedy, Fel'annár. But if we don't stop the enemy, they will kill many more than that."

"You can't be serious ..." Yerái didn't seem to care that he was speaking to the commander general of Ea Uaré, but one look from Pan'assár and his words died upon his lips, only now realising what he had said.

"I can't do that, Commander."

Pan'assár's gaze was on Fel'annár again, that same look from before, that it may come down to that. He was shaking his head, the thought almost incomprehensible.

"We will do everything we can to avoid it," continued Pan'assár. "We will plan for this, now that we know. But tell me, Lieutenant. Tell me the *whole* truth. What is the nature of this enemy? Why has a Sand Lord army shaken you so much? I have seen the Nim'uán, Fel'annár and Gor'sadén here have seen it far closer than any elf should, and we know the fear it can stir. But it is not *this*. Tell us ..."

Yerái's eyes were wide, glistening, seemingly unable to focus. Galadan leaned forward, offered him a steaming cup and the lieutenant stared at it, reached slowly and took it in his shaking hands.

Fel'annár wanted them all to leave Yerái alone, give him time to deal with his harrowing experience. But they needed the information, so that they could understand the nature of this enemy, so that they could be ready for it, bolster their minds and not be distracted once the fighting began.

Yerái knew this, was clearly trying to gather his words. He looked down at the cup in his hands. A moment of hesitation and then he took a gulp, swallowed thickly, resisting the urge to gag.

Bulan and Dalú, Amon and Benat, Eramor and Fel'annár waited patiently, as did the commanders and The Company, while Azure stood utterly still on Tensári's shoulder and further away, the troops watched, out of earshot yet knowing that some dire news had come.

"The Nim'uán wanted to show me the consequences of marching on Abiren'á. He showed me so that I could tell you in the hopes that you would turn away."

"We won't. None of us will." Bulan was already angry.

"Some might, Captain. Some *might*."

Bulan scowled, didn't understand. None of them did.

"The Nim'uán has a Sand Lord army but they have brought an ally, a creature I have never seen or heard of before. The Nim'uán called it a Reaper."

Fel'annár's eyes lost focus and the trees whispered, even as Yerái related his grim experience.

Monsters.

"I saw one, but I believe there are more. It looks like a thinner, taller Sand Lord but its skin is white, almost translucent. It has black nails and its eyes ..." Yerái's breathing was erratic. He stopped, took a gulp of air, closed his eyes and then started again.

"Its eyes are red."

The captains shared a confused glance at each other, but they were soon staring at Yerái once more, willing him to continue.

"It commands a kind of ... of serpent ... but it's armoured, like a beetle. It lives under the ground, emerges at some invisible command from the Reaper. It stings its victims, paralyses them but they are awake. They are *alive*."

They're not dead.

"That's what those civilians said. They were talking about our people," said Bulan.

"That they're alive is a good thing, isn't it?" asked Dalú, utterly confused.

Yerái stared at the captain, even as he was shaking his head. "No. It's not a good thing. The Reaper eats its victims alive. It starts at the neck, gorges on the flesh, careful not to kill, and then it rips the abdomen open with its claws, eats its fill and still, the victim is alive, forced to watch but unable to move and they scream, Captain. How they *scream*. It takes a long time to die, but when that mercy is granted, the armoured serpent eats what's left ..." Yerái was staring at his cup in his shaking hands. "The Nim'uán made me ... made me watch as Nurodi," he turned away, screwed his eyes shut, forced himself to say the words. "It made me watch as Nurodi was eaten in front of me." He took another gulp from his cup, dropped it, and then covered his mouth with one hand, swallowing thickly.

The images that Yerái's account conjured in their minds was enough to send any reasonable elf running, as far away as they could – just as those civilians had done. Bulan had known Nurodi, closed his eyes in a mixture of horror and fury at what the enemy had done to him.

In Fel'annár's mind, he saw the gruesome path they had walked, elves hanging from the trees, limbs half gnawed, flesh not sliced but ripped, most of them disembowelled. It had surely been the work of these Reapers. Pan'assár's steady voice brought them all back to the present.

"Is this thing a Sand Lord?"

"I don't know, Commander."

Insects buzzed in the late morning sun and Pan'assár cast his gaze to the heavens. Fel'annár watched him. It was surely too late to initiate an attack now. His strategy would require time they no longer had. Besides, with this new information, they needed a plan to free their people, so that Fel'annár could call on the trees.

Pan'assár wouldn't fail him. He couldn't. He felt angry, outraged at the travesty. The Nim'uán had done all this to protect himself and his army against him – Fel'annár.

He stood, a little too fast, whirled on his heels and strode away. Bulan made to follow but Gor'sadén stopped him with an upturned hand.

"Leave him for a while, then go to him if you wish."

Bulan stared hard at the commander, wanted to disobey. But he had seen the relationship between them, one of father and son. Gor'sadén knew his nephew better than he himself did. And so, he waited, and come late afternoon, he would join The Company and Yerái. He would give Fel'annár the time he needed to come to terms with the truth, with just why their people were being made to suffer so much.

WHILE THE FOUR thousand seven hundred warriors camped behind Skyrock, weapons ready for imminent battle, Pan'assár was away, thinking in solitude.

After Yerái's account of Abiren'á, it seemed clear that the enemy would wait for them in the city itself, with the Silvan people as their guarantee against the *mages*.

Against Fel'annár.

The Company and a silent Yerái sat quietly, preparing their weapons and their backpacks while Azure had flown once more, in search of details that might give them the upper hand.

They had found a tree some distance away from the others and Fel'annár leaned back against it. He took a deep breath and closed his eyes, taking stock of his body, fatigued with travel, infused with power he knew he could unleash at will. If only they could free the hostages. It preyed on his mind, weighed him down. He glanced at Bulan a distance away, knew he wanted to speak with him after he had returned to camp. But Fel'annár had avoided him, any situation which would lead to speaking of his dilemma.

Tensári watched the skies for Azure, while Galdith talked quietly with Galadan. Ramien and Carodel sharpened their weapons and inspected their remaining arrows. But Idernon's eyes were on Fel'annár. They drifted downwards and to his arm, to where Fel'annár was rubbing it. He leaned forward, spoke quietly.

"I saw you."

"Hum?" asked Fel'annár, distracted.

"I saw light under your tunic. When were you going to tell us about it?"

The others turned first to Idernon, and then expectantly to Fel'annár. Yerái watched them keenly.

Fel'annár exhaled, drew his knees up to his chest. "I was going to tell you when I understood what it was."

"And?" asked Galdith.

"I don't know. It started back in Lan Taria when we all heard the weeping giants." He shrugged.

"Have you noticed anything else? Is it just the light that concentrates there?" asked Idernon, hand scratching his chin.

"The voice of the Sisters ..."

"You said you could hear them," said Yerái. It was practically the first thing he had said since their briefing with the commander.

"I can. I still do. It's so deep I can hardly hear what they say. But I do know that they're waiting for me."

"Do you think it's related?" asked Galadan. "Their voices and that light?"

"Yes. But don't ask me how. What I do know is that the Sisters are different. They're still Sentinels but more powerful somehow."

"What's a Sentinel?" asked Yerái.

"A tree that shepherds the others. Their voices are strong, their words clearer and wiser."

Yerái was still shaking his head when Tensári asked another question.

"How are they different from Sentinels?"

Fel'annár looked at her, wondered if he should speak his mind and risk saying something that was nonsense. But at the end of the day, it *all* sounded like nonsense, not to mention there had been a shape-shifting goshawk perched on Tensári's shoulder just hours ago.

"They speak as Aria does to me in my dreams ..."

He could see their shock, Yerái's confusion, but there was none of that in Tensári's eyes. Instead, he saw suspicion.

"What is it?" he asked her.

"I'm not sure, but what you describe sounds similar to what our Divine Guards say."

"What are Divine Guards?" asked Fel'annár.

"Ari'atór who have seen much battle – our veterans. They are rewarded by serving at the Veil itself. They usher our people upon the final steps of the Long Road. Only they know the exact location of the Source, except for Commander Hobin himself. Some say they can see things across the Veil, that they know things others don't. They speak of the trees that surround that place."

"They call them Originals."

"What is the relationship between them and the Sisters of Abiren'á?" asked Idernon.

"The Divine Guards say the Originals are the mouth of Aria. They say she speaks to them through the trees. They are not Listeners," she held up a hand to stop Idernon from anticipating that possibility. "They speak of whisperings in the forest, of a voice almost too deep to perceive. I will say no more."

Fel'annár was staring at her in shock. "Are you saying the Sisters are Originals?"

"I am saying they *may* be. It is a species thought native to Valley. Perhaps that is not correct."

"How far is it from the Originals to the Veil?" Fel'annár's question was almost too quiet to hear, but Tensári heard it all the same.

"I don't know for sure. At a guess, two to three weeks."

Fel'annár's skin was crawling, tingling painfully, mind rushing through his dream, the things he had seen. If the Sisters were Originals, they were too far away from the Veil in Valley. It took months to get there. But they were only three weeks away from ... the Evergreen Wood.

Protect the Last Markers.

His mind rushed through his dream, remembered the things he had seen and heard. He shook his head, must have looked ill because Galadan grabbed him by the arm and shook him.

"Fel'annár?"

He opened his mouth to speak but snapped it shut when he saw Bulan approaching, close enough that he would hear.

The Silvan captain nodded at them and then sat. He looked around the circle and frowned.

"Am I interrupting?"

"No," said Fel'annár, before Idernon could say yes. He pushed his suspicions to the back of his mind; no use drawing hasty conclusions until he was in a position to think them out carefully, and that was not going to happen any time soon.

Bulan looked at his nephew, not really believing his answer. Still, Fel'annár wanted him to stay and so he crossed his legs, looked to the ground and then rested his elbows on his thighs. "You were right. Pan'assár *has* changed. He has earned my respect once more."

Fel'annár recalled Pan'assár's timely confession and wise words, and then Bulan's passionate speech later. He had seen how the Silvan warriors had listened, and then heeded him. He felt proud of Bulan, he realised, proud of the blood they shared.

"You had to understand that for yourself, all our warriors did. I'm glad for him." He picked at a loose thread at the hem of his cloak. "Bulan, what is Abiren'á like?"

Bulan smiled tightly and then turned his gaze sideways as he chose the words that would best describe his home.

"It's like nothing you've ever seen. A work of extraordinary engineering. There are mighty buildings aloft the tallest, thickest trees, some with platforms carved from the wood itself while others have been built outwards. From the ground you see the buildings and the semi-circles jutting from them, and from above, you see hanging ropes and stairways. You see pulleys and air lifts. The community hall is many feet above the ground and in the tree beside it, there is a music hall where the Silvan war drums sit. When patrols leave to engage the enemy, we play them so that our warriors can hear our heartbeat from afar and know their people are grateful, that they are thinking of them. When there's a celebration, they sing a different tune, of bonding, of thanks, praise to a god or for the birth of an Ari child. It is a wooden world of wonder, nephew, one I would have you see in a time of peace."

"And the Giants? I've seen them in books, and recently I've heard their voices, can even feel them sometimes, I think." He rubbed the inside of his right wrist. "Tell me what they're like."

"That's not easy. See they are larger than even *you* can imagine. Think of the tallest tree you have ever seen and triple its size. Imagine the widest trunk and multiply it by ten."

"Do people live on the Giants?"

"No. The Sisters are sacred souls, keepers of the Silvan legacy. They watch over us, some say even protect us. You must see our Spring Festival, Fel'annár, so that you can understand what they mean to us."

Bulan looked up, as if conjuring the image of the Giant sisters. "Anora – Moonsister – is the tallest. She reaches to the moon, drinks of its light and some say she grows with every full cycle. You are not fully Silvan until you have seen her bathed in the silver light of a full moon.

"And then Golora – Sunsister – the second highest. She drinks from the light of the sun, her leaves the most vibrant colour of green two hours after dawn. Her boughs light up the north with a thousand dappled lights, like fireflies around the festival bonfire."

Bulan smiled, looked to the sky. "And then, there is Bulora – Cloudsister – the smallest of the Sisters. My mother named me after her. See, her sisters reach for something they can never touch, never attain but Bulora – she touches the sky, Fel'annár. She reaches and she finds. It's what my mother Alei wanted for me, what Zéndar wanted for his son. To strive towards your goals and never stop until you reach them. He used to say that was the essence of happiness."

Idernon stood, gestured to the rest. They joined him, sensed that Bulan wanted to be alone with his nephew on this, the eve of battle. The captain nodded at Idernon and then turned back to his nephew.

"You know, I lost my wife to Sand Lords. They took her from my side, left my daughter motherless. I know their cruelty, and I know what's in your mind, how you toil with the reasons that our people have been taken hostage. You tell yourself they suffer because of you, so that you won't conjure the trees, so that we can't win this battle."

He watched his nephew carefully, knew that he was right. "Heed me, Fel'annár. Remember this. They are in those cages because they wouldn't leave. They were warned, knew the risks of staying. It's not your fault, not anyone's fault save for the Sand Lords' that they are hostage in the trees. We will do everything we can to save them, risk our own lives and die for them. But should it become apparent that there is no way to save them, then you must conjure the trees. And should they die as a consequence, they would not fault you. They would see it as inevitable. We are Silvans, Fel'annár. We are the forest, and the trees are our family. And you, more than most, know the pain of separation."

Fel'annár was staring at him, so many emotions swimming in his eyes but he smiled too, as if he had conceded something important, and he supposed he had. His separation from family since birth had hurt, but he had never wanted to admit to that.

"Of all the places we could have fought together, it had to be here, where I have never been but always wanted to. How I yearned to see those things you describe to me. The Sentinels and the Sisters, the Doorway to the Sands, the Silvan Bastion of old ... We will see all those things together, Bulan - Cloudson. You and I will return here one day, and you will show me my ancestral home. As for me, the Sisters call to me, wait for me. I must give them hope, Bulan, just as you must give me hope, that you will survive the day. We have yet to hear the commander's battle strategy, but we may not fight in the same contingent. I may not be able to look out for you."

"That you would even do so is more than enough, nephew." Bulan smiled, studied Lássira's son he had met little more than a month ago. Whatever he had thought he would find it was not this, but he found himself at a loss for words. Fel'annár had surprised him so many times, had proved him right and then proved him wrong. He had magic, or whatever it was he did with the trees. He had skill beyond his years, a natural disposition to lead and to fight, just as his paternal grandfather had. But there was a vulnerable side to him, the side that had always yearned for family.

"If this is to be the last time we speak on Bel'arán, know that I will find you beyond the Source, Fel'annár. If either of us is destined to die tomorrow, we will still be the family that circumstance did not permit in this life. You will find yourself sooner, and when I finally do, we will right that wrong."

The smile that blossomed on Fel'annár's face was a ray of sun on the cusp of battle. Bulan was touched, utterly glad that his nephew was the way he was. He was proud to call him Aren Zéndar, proud of the spear upon his back. They *would* return here, together, sometime in the future when the Sand Lords were gone and chiboos sat upon the highest boughs of Abiren'á once more.

33

THE PRICE OF VICTORY

~

IT WAS A PECULIAR MORNING.

The Evergreen Wood sounded strange and unsettled and for the first time in many years, Thargodén had closed the windows that looked out over the great plateau and the Evergreen Wood beyond.

The sun was just dawning over the land and the king sat at his desk, still in his night clothes. He heard the guards stand to attention outside his door and then the soft click of the handle. Not Rinon. He looked up, watched as Handir bowed to him and then made straight for the wall of doors that led to the king's gardens.

"What do you hear?" asked Handir, turning away from the forest and to his father.

The king stood, joined him behind the closed doors. "I hear nothing. But I feel a strange stillness, like a breath held back, like the eye of a storm. As if the sap in their branches had frozen."

Handir turned back to the forest. "Do you think the battle in the north is near?"

His son's voice sounded distant, wistful, almost sad but the words mirrored the fears in his mind. He answered without much thought.

"Yes. Yes I do. And I think Fel'annár lives."

Handir was watching him, stayed that way for a while and then turned to the chimney and the mechanism beside it. He pulled the chord and then sat at the empty hearth. Moments later, the king joined him, night clothes fanning out around him.

"Funny, but when they left, we knew where the enemy lay, knew the odds and rode to face them. Now, the Deviants take advantage of our weakness and press in from the east. We cannot wage two wars for much longer, Handir."

Handir leaned back, crossed his legs, propped his heavy head up with one hand. "There is some hope that Rinon will be able to bring back warriors from Port Helia, elven or human."

"Where *is* your brother?"

Handir turned to the king, eyes unreadable. "He will be with us shortly. He is - entertaining."

Thargodén scowled. "Entertaining who?"

The blank façade of a Royal Councillor changed so subtly that most would have missed it. The flicker in his eyes and the tug at one corner of his mouth.

"Captain Sorei of Tar'eastór."

The king's brows rose as high as Sontúr's ever had but he said nothing and instead, he leaned back in his chair.

"Good for him." The king sat opposite Handir, ran a hand down his face. "I would dine with my children tomorrow night."

Handir nodded, and then started with the king's next words.

"My children and their companions."

"Sontúr and Sorei?"

"Of course. Unless you have someone you would add to the list?" The king stared at Handir expectantly.

"No. No one to add, father."

∾

JUST DOWN THAT SAME CORRIDOR, Sontúr sat before Llyniel in her quarters, brow furrowed as he watched her remove the leather contraption from his damaged arm.

He ground his teeth, tried to look impervious to the pain Llyniel was inflicting on him because Maeneth was there, grimacing in sympathy and grinning at his brave but losing battle.

"There, you're finally free of the brace, Sontúr" murmured Llyniel as she prodded at the limb.

"Can we burn it?" said Sontúr through clenched teeth.

Maeneth snorted. "Like a sacrificial offering? We could conjure Galomú, I'm sure he would find some diabolic use for it." She chuckled and Sontúr grinned and them, then grimaced when Llyniel tied a sling around his neck and lay his arm inside it.

"All right, enough for today. After lunch, I want you to do those exercises yourself. The aching pain is good, stabbing pain is not – you know the rule."

"Yes, yes."

A knock at the door and Maeneth opened it. Handir smiled as he approached Sontúr, arm now in a light sling across his chest.

"How is the shoulder?"

"Much improved," explained Llyniel. "Light exercise is in order, I think. I'm sure Maeneth can help him with that," she said, turning to pack her supplies away, a lop-sided grin on her face. "And where's Nuthead?" She turned to Handir, face utterly straight and then grinned when Maeneth snorted again.

"In his rooms with his new friend," said Handir.

"Captain Sorei?" asked Sontúr.

"The same."

"Have you met her?" asked the prince as he stood.

"Only briefly," said Handir. "She is curt, unwilling to be drawn into conversation, at least by me. I cannot say I know anything about her at all."

"Me neither. I have seen her in passing. Gives me the chills," murmured Llyniel.

"In Tar'eastór she is a highly respected captain. She is also a swordsmith. It seems Gor'sadén has charged her with continuing her production of some new sword she has designed. She calls it Synth Blade."

"Synth as in synthesis?" asked Maeneth, intrigued.

"Yes. I spoke to her briefly about it a few days ago. She says Gor'sadén tried it, and Fel'annár sliced through a tree trunk with it."

"Well, if anyone can," smiled Llyniel

"We will all get the chance to know her better tomorrow. Father would dine with his children and their *companions*."

"Do you think it's to do with the forest? About its disquiet? I mean I assume you all felt it?" asked Llyniel.

"I certainly did," said Handir. "And I know the king did. We believe that battle may be imminent in the north."

"I think he's right," said Llyniel. "And Fel'annár is well for the most part."

"The king said the same. But what do you mean by for the most part?"

Llyniel stared back at Handir, before her gaze flickered over Sontúr and then to the window behind him.

"There is something inside him. Something new. Something powerful, beyond what we have seen."

No one spoke for a while, until Sontúr asked a question.

"Is it a *good* thing?"

She crossed her arms, repressed a shiver. "I hope so, Sontúr."

THE MERCHANT GUILD was busier than it ever had been.

A large group of refugees had recently arrived from Sen'oléi and Abiren'á, amongst them, the Ari'atór Master at arms, Oruná. He had sat next to his great friend Narosén, and explained everything he knew about the coming war to the Elders.

From what Amareth had gathered, a Listener by the name of Yerái, had warned Sen'oléi of an army approaching from Calrazia. He had then travelled to Abiren'á to see it for himself and then raise the alarm. Those with children had taken to the rafts, while Master Oruná had taken the Ari children to Lan Taria, where they had taken horses. A while later, they had met with the refugees from Sen'oléi whilst on the road towards Oran'Dor.

It was there that the two groups had met the mounted warriors heading north. They had seen Fel'annár, whole and hale.

But Amareth had seen no one from Lan Taria, save those who had already been at the encampment and she wondered if they had stayed to welcome Fel'annár home. And if they had, how had Fel'annár reacted? Was he still angry at them now that he knew of their deception? Or had he forgiven them? And would they come, once the Warlord had left for the north? Golloron would, but she wasn't sure about Thavron, stubborn forester that he was.

On the far side of the hall, Alei and Erthoron were serving food, while Lorthil was washing a cup. There was still a pile of other utensils to clean but the one in his hand was, apparently, still dirty after five minutes of scrubbing. Amareth wanted to take him by the shoulders and shake him, tell him it was already pristine. But she knew it would serve no purpose.

Her eyes drifted from one group to the next, listened to the snippets of conversation that were loud enough for her to hear. They spoke of the north, of the coming of the Warlord. They spoke of Bulan and how he had been reunited with his nephew at last.

And they spoke of Sorei.

All Amareth could gather, was that she was one of the Alpine warriors who had escorted these people into the city, sent by King Vorn'asté and then by Commander Gor'sadén. She had apparently put one of their own warriors to shame for debasing a Silvan lad.

Good for her, she reckoned.

"Lady Amareth?"

She turned, came face to face with a woman, and at her feet, two small children. Beside her, a boy who was almost a man.

"Can I help you with something?"

"Amareth Ora Lássira?

Amareth straightened, scrutinised the woman before her, wondering if they had once met. She simply nodded, watched as Alféna bowed, straightened and then smiled.

"It is a pleasure to meet Fel'annár's aunt. He told me to find you, that you would help us."

"I will help you, of course. But who are you? How do you know my nephew?"

The woman smiled again, a soft frown on her face. "We *all* know

Fel'annár, lady, especially those of us from Sen'oléi. He saved our village, saved my children here. That was more than a year ago and now he rides as our Warlord. You must be very proud."

Amareth was speechless. "Yes, yes of course." And she was. She had heard of the fires at Sen'oléi, knew from Narosén that was when Fel'annár's powers had begun to manifest. And then it hit her.

"You're Alféna? The one who gave him his honour stone ..."

A wide smile from the woman, an excited nod from the elder boy. "That was my father's."

Amareth bent her head in respect. "How has your stay been? Do you need anything?"

"To be useful, perhaps. I can farm and cook, sing and entertain children. Do you have a place for them, where they can play and learn?"

"Not yet. But *you* might want to organise that for me ..."

"Gladly. It'll be good to feel useful."

Amareth wondered if the upper floor of the Guild could be used for the children. There were splendid tapestries and luscious fabrics that lay draped over opulent furniture. She thought of a roomful of Silvan children, imagined Melu'sán's sour face. "Use the first floor, in any way you see fit. And if there's anything you need, find me. I'm almost always here, except when the war council is in session."

"I'm glad to be of help, then. It's a great pleasure meeting you, Amareth. Count on me if you need me."

Amareth nodded, turned away and smiled. She liked Alféna, would remember her offer of help. She watched for a while as the woman left and then turned to the main door. There, a blond warrior stood, watching the crowds of Silvans. She wasn't from these parts.

"Can I help you with something?"

The captain turned icy eyes on Amareth. This woman was commanding, to the extent that it made you want to take a step back. It was not a welcoming expression and Amareth wondered if she did it on purpose, to protect herself from criticism. As a female captain in an Alpine army, Amareth could see why that may be necessary. This must be Sorei, she realised, the one they were talking about.

"I am looking for Alféna."

"I'll take you to her."

They made their way through the crowds, Amareth leading the way in the direction Alféna had just gone. But not halfway towards their destination, she had to slow her pace. Sorei was no longer behind her but caught in the crowds of people who wanted to greet her.

Amareth turned back, watched Sorei as she was surrounded by smiling people. The transformation was utterly mesmerising. Where before a chill had run up her spine at the mere sight of the captain, now, there was nothing but warmth in those Alpine eyes.

"Captain Sorei!" called Eloran, misty eyes full of admiration and perhaps something else. Amareth smiled, wider than she had done in a while.

Fel'annár was alive and well, and young Eloran was utterly besotted.

RINON PEERED at a map on his desk at the Inner Circle.

The scouts had returned, and now, Rinon would make the final preparation for his patrol to Port Helia.

"You found the group here, on the eastern slopes? That's just four hours away from the city."

"It was a small group, barely past Incipient I would say. We believe they were scouts. As we speak, our relief patrol is riding past the interception point and beyond, in search of the main party."

"Good. Keep me informed."

The captain saluted and left, and Rinon was alone before the crumpled map. All these new groups were coming from the same place. The caves on the eastern foothills of the Pelagian mountains. It was a place that Pan'assár and Turion patrolled regularly. The Deviant numbers had been cut to record lows, and yet now, no sooner their army had set out to face the Nim'uán in the north, they were amassing once more. Something stirred in his chest, because he had never given Deviants much credit where planning and strategy were concerned. Not until now.

A knock on his door and he called out. Turion entered, eyes on the map in Rinon's hands.

"Same place?"

"Yes. This does not feel right, Turion. The numbers are not great as yet, but they are scouting, and they are obviously finding the information they seek. Their raids are more and more frequent; they know we are hard-pressed for warriors. Where do they mean to stop, Turion? Are they planning a larger-scale attack?"

"I do not know. Under normal circumstances I would increase our patrols on the eastern flank but there are no more warriors, damn it. Whatever happens in the north now, even if they have swift victory, they are still four weeks away from us, probably more with the wounded. I pray you are wrong, Prince, that the Deviants are not planning something like what they did in Tar'eastór, although I am beginning to suspect that myself."

"Prince Sontúr believes it. In their case, the Deviants tunnelled under the citadel. Here, there is no such geographical advantage. We know where they are, but we just cannot face them in the open, not with five hundred warriors to our king's name and no Warlord to enlist the help of the forest.

"Sontúr has sent a message to his father. Vorn'asté will send more, but that is another five weeks to hold the Deviants at bay. They are slowly but very surely whittling away at our warriors."

"What about Pelagia?" asked Rinon.

"A missive leaves today. Still, they have a small terrestrial army as you know. Their strength rules supreme upon the seas, not the land."

Rinon stared back at Turion, knew he was right.

"When can I take my patrol out to Port Helia, Commander?"

"Once the last patrol is back. Two days at most, General. You must bring us warriors, General. Pelagians, humans, anyone who can brandish a sword. This realm is on its knees."

"Have your warriors on alert for an imminent departure, General."

ABIREN'Á COULD NOT FALL, Pan'assár knew that. It would be the beginning of the end of Ea Uaré. Or'Talán had died so that the enemy would not reach that place, and although it now had, Pan'assár swore he would take it back, stamp the Nim'uán into the ground, wipe that place clean of its stain and return to the Silvans what was theirs.

Once, he had not cared about this place. Now, it was a symbol of his own cleansing.

He glanced up at the sky, knew there was only an hour of sunlight left. It was time to return to camp, tell his commanders his plan, and then pass the night in quiet contemplation, as was customary on the eve of battle.

The troops were keeping themselves busy, but he could see their apprehension, knew the conversations they were having with friends and brothers.

At first, they swore vengeance on those who had desecrated their people upon the Gruesome Path, said they would return to that place and cleanse it, honour those who had died such a terrible death. And as their anger waned, they spoke of their families, whether they had fled to safety or if they had been captured and imprisoned in these cages Azure had spoken of.

Later, as the fires burned lower and their voices were quieter, they contemplated the cruelty of war, the nature of the enemy and the Nim'uán. They spoke of life and death, of what they would do if they survived the day, and what they would have others do should they not.

But there was one other recurring conversation he had heard during his wanderings. The warriors spoke of Pan'assár, of Bulan and how he had accepted the commander they had almost turned their backs on, how the Warlord had *always* accepted him. Whether it was Pan'assár's imagination or not, he thought they no longer looked upon him with disdain, wondered if it was curiosity he could see now in place of hatred.

He was almost at the base of Skyrock and the view from here was quite literally breath-taking. The vertical needle of rock was a wonder many had speculated on over the years. How had it been formed? Had it once been a mountain that had fallen away in some tremor? It looked like a stone lance that some god had thrust into the ground, as if to mark its territory.

It was here that the captains and commanders were to gather. It was time for Pan'assár to reveal his strategy.

He glanced sideways, to where he knew The Company sat together with the Listener Yerái, wondered if the lieutenant was even up to fighting after what he had seen. He would need to warn the troops of these Reapers, but he also needed to find a balance between the practical necessity of it, and not frightening the wits out of them. If there was one thing Sand Lords and Silvans shared, it was a propensity for superstition.

Fel'annár and The Company were the first to arrive, followed by Bulan, Dalú, Amon, Benat and Eramor. Gor'sadén was soon beside him and then the rest of his captains, their lieutenants close behind. It would fall to them to inform their warriors, warn them about the cages and the Reapers.

The ground was rocky here, wouldn't allow the torches to be staked and so warriors held them instead. For them, it would be a rare glimpse at a Circle of command, one which was now ready to turn.

Fel'annár watched Pan'assár, wondered if his own opinion on how the strategy should be handled would coincide with the commander's. He was about to find out.

"We know that inside the city, there are over six thousand Sand Lords while another four thousand are in the Xeric Wood. Our first consideration is how to avoid these two contingents coming together. General Fel'annár?"

He started, hadn't expected to be included in this first part of the planning. He glanced at Gor'sadén and then stepped forward.

"We break into two contingents. Three thousand five hundred for Abiren'á, one thousand two hundred for the Xeric Wood. With Commander Hobin's one thousand on the right flank, that makes for an even fight in the sands, if the Deviant numbers don't surprise us." He looked at Pan'assár, saw his slight nod and then stepped back so that the commander could continue.

"Two contingents. I will lead the three thousand-five hundred into Abiren'á. We will be outnumbered two to one, but we have the Warlord and the Kal'hamén'Ar.

"Our main objective is not to defeat the enemy, but to free our people from the cages that hang from the boughs. As soon as that is achieved, General Fel'annár will conjure the forest and bring us victory. When that happens, we must run north, towards our second contingent in the sands."

Pan'assár paused, watched the Silvan captains especially. "Saving our people is our priority, our first duty as warriors. It is written in the Warrior Code, and we have all sworn to uphold it. Many of us will die before we can free them from the cages. But that is our pledge, our sacrifice. It is the price of taking back what is ours."

Pan'assár's gaze landed heavily on Fel'annár, waited for him to return it. He did, but the commander could see the anxiety in his eyes, as clearly as he could see the approval in Dalú's.

This was the essence of warriorhood. Understanding that your own life is second to the cause, and to the people.

"Captain Bulan will command the one thousand two hundred bound for the Xeric Wood. He must wait on the sands, for as long as he can before engaging the enemy. We cannot risk that second contingent of Sand Lords attacking too soon, overcoming our contingent and joining mine in Abiren'á. However, sooner or later, they will understand that we are outnumbered, guess our strategy and call the charge. Only then will you intervene. Commander Hobin will surely not move on the enemy until you do."

Fel'annár looked at Bulan, wondered if he had hoped to command the Abiren'á contingent. But all he saw on his uncle's face was understanding – and acceptance. Yes, he had wanted it, but Fel'annár thought he understood why Pan'assár had not given it to him. They would be sorely outnumbered in the city, and Pan'assár was a Kah Master, would be best used where the fighting would be more desperate. It was also about the chain of command. Bulan and Fel'annár were the natural leaders of this army in Pan'assár's absence. He needed to separate them in case one of them fell in the battle.

"Captain Bulan. Once you have called the charge and you are victorious, if we have not arrived, you must return to Abiren'á and secure it, with Commander Hobin's help."

"There will be no need, Commander. You will prevail. I will see you on the sands before our charge, or during it if the enemy advances sooner."

Pan'assár nodded, smiled because he had not missed the strong and confident manner in which Bulan had spoken of Pan'assár's assured victory in Abiren'á. The captain's eyes had remained steady, shown him the conviction of his words, the trust Bulan graced him with once more.

He turned to Fel'annár and nodded that he should continue. The time had come in which the Warlord needed to warn the warriors of what would happen once the captives were freed.

"There are two things you must be aware of. One of them is the conjuring. General Fel'annár?"

In the centre of the Circle once more, Fel'annár collected his thoughts. If this was anything like Tar'eastór, then he knew what he needed to say. But every forest was different, he knew that after his experience with the trees in the Evergreen Wood. He had never been here. These trees felt different – the Sisters felt different.

"Once our people have been brought down from the trees, the maelstrom will begin. You mustn't fear it, but you mustn't stay inside it. The trees will not be able to differentiate between friend and foe, not with any precision at least. There will be wind and debris. The trees will sway and thrash their boughs and branches; they'll be as dangerous as any blade in the hands of a Kah Master. This will mark the beginning of our victory over Abiren'á, a sign that you must leave, whatever the circumstances. You run towards Captain Bulan's position and together, we run this enemy down."

He observed the captains and lieutenants around him, silent and wide-eyed. He knew he had unnerved them, but there was no other way to say it. He could only warn them and then pray whoever commanded them would keep a cool head when the time came.

"The second issue we must all be aware of, is the existence of some creature the Nim'uán is using as a weapon. This creature is of a particularly vile nature, captains. I believe it is responsible for the massacre of our people upon the Gruesome Path as I know some of you have called it. It is also the instigator of the terror our people witnessed; the same terror Lieutenant Yerái has related to us. Thanks to him, we can be prepared for what he has called Reapers."

There were nervous murmurs, shared glances of apprehension.

"They are taller, thinner than the Sand Lords we are accustomed to, and they work together with a serpent-like creature. The serpent stings its prey, renders it unmoving, so that the Reaper can feed while the victim is still alive. Once dead, the serpent feeds."

The uproar was almost deafening, as Pan'assár knew it would be. He allowed them their words of horror and condemnation, their angry curses and then he held up his hands for silence.

"If they thought to terrify us with this, so that we would flee, they have done nothing more than inflame our outrage. Let it fuel your muscles, guide your hands. Let it lend you the strength you will need to blast this enemy from our forests, from these your holy lands. Don't let it defeat you. Let it infuse you, drive you to victory."

They were listening once more, eyes wide, they looked to Pan'assár for the encouraging words they needed to hear. The Sand Lords had brought horrors from the north in the hopes of whittling away their resolve. They needed to hear that they *could* defeat it, that they would be stronger than the effects of the cruelty they knew they would witness come the dawn.

"I will assign a unit specifically for the purpose of freeing our people from their cages in the boughs. As we fight, they will release our people. No sooner that is achieved, General Fel'annár will conjure the forest and we run – north, and to Captain Bulan."

"Let *me* lead that unit, Commander."

All heads turned to Yerái, overly bright hazel eyes staring defiantly at Pan'assár.

"You are not fit for active duty."

"Perhaps not. But the danger is only to myself. I know how the mechanisms work. I know what they have suffered, and those people know me. I sat in one of those cages, watched with them as our people were eaten alive. I must do this, Commander."

Pan'assár watched him. The Listener had suddenly come alive, emerged from the clouds of confusion and trauma, because the prospect of freeing those poor souls would somehow help his mind to heal. Pan'assár understood him well.

"All right. Now that it falls to you, Yerái, the success of your mission will trigger the onset of the final battle for Abiren'á."

"I can do it, Commander. I swear it."

Pan'assár nodded, would remember this warrior. "How many warriors will you need?"

"As many as you can give me, Commander."

"You have fifty. These fifty must be protected, Captains. The sooner we get those people down the better." Pan'assár walked around the circle. He thought better when he moved, always had.

"I want each contingent commander to brief his troops. You must discuss your weapons, the supplies you will need. You must designate your second, agree on your hand signals, and Lieutenant Yerái," he turned to the lieutenant, held his gaze for a moment. "Chose your fifty well. You know these warriors, know their strengths."

Yerái nodded, once more looked like the warrior he had met on the road to Tar'eastór. He was once more the indignant Silvan who had sensed the power of the Warlord, had refused to salute Pan'assár.

Only this time, Yerái did salute the commander, and in his eyes, was grateful thanks.

Respect.

~

THE CAMP WAS QUIET.

The warriors spoke amongst themselves in hushed whispers, about the Reapers, the maelstrom the Warlord said would come. They spoke of home, of their loved ones and their children, the future that awaited them.

Pan'assár sat with The Company, with Gor'sadén and with the captains that would fight in his contingent come the dawn.

"Amon. You will take the western flank into the city, Benat takes the eastern. Deploy your field bows as far ahead of time as possible.

"Eramor and Dalú will command the rear, east and west respectively. Fel'annár, Gor'sadén and myself will take the lead."

Eramor leaned forward where he sat across the fire from Pan'assár, eyes gleaming.

"You will implement the Wheel of War?"

Pan'assár stared back at him, then glanced at Gor'sadén and Fel'annár who sat beside him.

"I will. And *you* must keep your focus on the timing of our attack, Eramor. The Wheel will move down the centre of their ranks, fracture it in two, leaving Amon, Benat and Eramor to charge from three sides.

Archers will already be firing at the enemy snipers as the Wheel is turning."

The captains nodded, knew the protocols. But the odds were dire in spite of it all, and Fel'annár could see the anxiety in their eyes, surely reflected in his own. But his was perhaps a different sort of dread. The Wheel of War depended on discipline of the mind as much as it did physical skill. Fel'annár would need to bolster his resolve, not look into the boughs in search of Yerái.

"Remember, Captains. We are outnumbered almost two to one, but only until General Fel'annár can conjure the trees. Our goal is to engage the enemy, keep them away from Yerái and his unit so that they can free our people. After that, it is the Sand Lords who will be outnumbered, by many hundreds to one."

"And what happens if we are overrun? What happens if Yerái and his unit are brought down? What then?" asked Dalú.

Pan'assár stared back at Dalú, long and hard. "The Warlord will do what he must."

~

A SHORT WHILE LATER, Fel'annár had found for himself a quiet spot away from camp. Tensári was close by, Azure with her and now, another approached, one he recognised as family.

He knew what Gor'sadén wanted to say. It was what Fel'annár didn't want to hear.

Sure enough, Gor'sadén emerged from the mists that had descended on them, eyes searching the boughs above for Tensári and Azure no doubt.

"May I?"

Fel'annár gestured with his head and then leaned back against the tree behind him, knees bent, forearms resting on them. He could hear the whispered anticipation, the forest as it spoke of war. And he could hear the Sisters ...

Moon, Sun and Cloud watch over you.

Their voices were so clear in one way, and yet he had to strain his mind to hear them because the tone was so deep he could almost not make out the words.

"You are distracted."

"The Sisters speak to me."

"What do they say?"

"That they wait for me."

Gor'sadén turned to his profile, saw the shimmer of green light before his eyes.

"Will they fight for us?"

Fel'annár turned to meet his gaze. "Yes. Even now they speak of it, wonder how they can achieve it without killing our people."

"And you? Do you wonder the same thing?"

"Of course I do," he murmured. "It doesn't bear thinking. Bringing down all those cages in the midst of a battle, outnumbered as we are ... it seems unlikely they will all survive. I don't want the death of innocent civilians on my conscience. It would make my life as a warrior meaningless."

"You have sworn to serve and protect your people, even unto death. That is what the oath says. By sacrificing the few, you would save the many from slaughter and grief. I know that you understand this, that you will doubt. But you mustn't. You are no longer a simple warrior, Fel'annár. You are a commander. You are beholden to protect those civilians first and foremost, but so too are you charged with keeping your warriors alive.

"If things go ill, *if* we lose that battle, there will be nothing to stop the Nim'uán from marching southwards. It will destroy your forests, massacre the rest of your people. It will march on the city itself ... that is the price, Fel'annár, a price you must remember tomorrow. If we cannot free those civilians – if there is no other way – you *must* invoke the trees."

Fel'annár hung his head. There was nothing more to say that had not already been said.

"Last time we waged war together, we never had this moment to share – to say goodbye – just in case."

"No. The Nim'uán sprung its attack while you were out on the slopes."

Fel'annár remembered how Sontúr had run from the fight so that he could warn Gor'sadén and ready the army. He remembered how they had both almost died; how he did, and then came back. Life was such an ephemeral thing, even for an immortal.

"I'm grateful for this last year in which I met you. I've learned the ways of warriorhood, of the Kah. I've learned how to be a son, what it is to have a father. I never quite understood how much I'd missed as a child, until I met you."

He knew Gor'sadén was staring at his profile. It took courage to turn and look at him now, for one who had never really allowed his needs to surface. But Fel'annár did. And what he found was an open door to a soul he loved. It was strong and resolute. It was wise and caring. It was proud and it loved him back.

His eyes filled with the strength of a bond that had been tied in Tar'eastór, tightened in Ea Uaré, until now when that bond was complete and yet, it felt as if it had always been there, that it would never fade, even if one of them died.

"Whatever happens tomorrow, Fel'annár. I will see you again. Whether it is here on Bel'arán, or across the Veil, to wherever that leads. Our souls will find each other. We're family now, you and I."

Gor'sadén stood, almost too quickly and Fel'annár followed him, slower.

Face to face now, his father placed a heavy hand on his shoulder. "Fight well, and if you must die, then die well and remember my words. I will see you again, Fel'annár."

The hand tightened and then pulled him forwards. Fel'annár opened his arms, accepted the embrace because it could well be the last one they shared. It didn't feel uncomfortable or undeserved. It didn't feel awkward or unnatural.

It was a cloak, a shield, a balm to the soul, food for a hungry child.

They parted with one, last and resolute nod from his father. And then he was gone. Fel'annár watched him until he disappeared through the trees, and then sat back down, rested his head against the rough bark behind and closed his eyes.

He listened to the wisdom of the forest, and as they spoke words of comfort and hope, he in turn, asked of them a favour.

Help us. Help us to free our people before I – before we – must kill them.

34

WHEEL OF WAR

~

GOR'SADÉN, Pan'assár, Fel'annár and the new Disciples performed the Dohai before the rising sun, graceful dance before the slaughter.

Fel'annár returned to the still quiet camp, knowing that they watched him, lights still shimmering around him. The Disciples shared murmured conjectures as to what it was, while Pan'assár and Gor'sadén spoke of how his power was growing with every dawn.

Fel'annár already knew that, could feel the new voices in his mind. The Sisters were calling him and for all that it was exhilarating, there was a part of him that dreaded their encounter. He had seen all sorts of trees moving for him, fighting for him.

But Giants?

He wondered if they were Originals after Tensári's description of them, and if they were, the implications were worrying, if not disturbing. He had told himself not to think on that for now, that it would distract him. There would be time enough later, if he survived the day.

The mist was stubborn and as the sky slowly changed from deep blue to dark grey, Fel'annár and The Company stood in their own tight circle, Azure perched on Tensári's shoulder and a hesitant Yerái just beyond. Fel'annár caught his eye, gestured him into the circle.

"Time for war. Time to face death, accept it – if that is our lot. There will be times when I will be separated from you. But I'll be looking out for you, as much as I'll be protecting Yerái here, and those he chooses to free our people and I pray that he does." He stared at Yerái, saw the determination in his eyes, as clearly as he saw the lingering horrors of the things he had seen, things he had yet to come to terms with and perhaps never would.

"You, more than any others, know the power of the forest, once I conjure it. When Yerái is done and I give that order, it may fall to you to get our warriors out, to save them from the distraction. Galadan, Idernon – this may fall to you because Tensári and Azure here, will be with me. You mustn't stay, even when I do. You must run north to Bulan."

Fel'annár rubbed the inside of his wrist, the strange burning tingle was back but he daren't look at the skin beneath his bracer and tunic.

"Tar'eastór was a small forest yet even so, you saw what it did. Here though ... their power is almost too much to bear and I confess, I wonder, how it'll be when they join the fight. In Tar'eastór, they spoke of ousting the Deviants. In the Evergreen Wood they spoke of destroying Band'orán and here ..."

"Tell me," whispered Yerái. "Tell me what the trees of my homeland say." There was an intensity in his bright eyes, a need to know, a desperate wish to hear what he knew was there but could not quite reach.

Fel'annár looked at Yerai, then at Idernon and Ramien, at Carodel and Galdith, Galadan and Tensári, Lainon in his bird form.

"They speak of destinies. They speak of purposes yet to be understood. They speak of a taint that must be cleansed, of past horrors that will be avenged." He frowned, allowed the unexpected words to flow from his mouth. "They speak of secrets, doors that must be closed, a world far vaster than this one we live in." He shook his head, didn't understand what he was saying. "The Sisters will watch over us."

Tears spilled from Yerái's eyes. "Gods but to hear the voices of the Sisters ..."

No one spoke, and Azure opened his wings. Tensári held out her arm and The Company watched him fly. Fel'annár wondered if Lainon knew the meaning of those words, whether he understood the incomprehensible things that had tumbled from his mouth.

Ramien flinched at Dalú's call to arms and the camp was suddenly alive. Soon, it would be time for Pan'assár to bolster the troops. They were nothing but a few hours from Abiren'á, an hour more before the onset of the Xeric Wood and their warrior minds began to dominate. Today was for fighting, not for contemplation and within minutes, Fel'annár and The Company were armed and ready for battle.

Pan'assár had climbed to the first ridge of Skyrock, and he stood now, looking down on the four thousand seven hundred warriors under his command.

"Today, we take back what is ours. Today, we serve justice to those who have slaughtered our people. Today, we will fight as we never have done before because this is personal. This is about us, as elves. They have killed our mothers and fathers, brothers and sisters. They have taken our home as theirs and we will not tolerate it!"

"Aye!"

"Today, I say I am Silvan. Today, all your Alpine brothers are Silvan, stand by you and everything you love, everything they love comes together – no difference, as it always should have been. We will fight together, suffer together and die together because these lands are greater than any of those horrors we know await us. The promise of peace is worth everything, even death.

"Today, you will see things, marvels of nature which must not distract you. You will see Lainon the Ber'ator, the hawk-elf that strikes terror in the hearts of our enemies. And you will see the Warlord, he the forest proclaims its Lord. As he is changed, you will see the trees you so love, the trees you never wanted to leave as they come to life and fight for us.

"And so you see, nature is with us, warriors. The Silvans, the Alpines, the Ari'atór are joined by the Ber'anor, the Ber'ator and the trees. We are not alone, not outnumbered. All we need do is free our people and then it can begin. The forces of nature converge on Abiren'á because Aria is with us and she is Silvan, Alpine, Ari – she is the trees, the forests we live in. She fights for us and we must not fail her!"

"Aye!"

The roar was enough to wake Abiren'á in the misty distance and Saz'nár stepped out of his tree house, high enough to see the surrounding forests for leagues into the distance.

The enemy army was at Skyrock, hiding behind it and Saz'nár smiled. The day had finally come. His Sand Lords and Reapers would defeat the elves and then the second part of their plan would be a reality. Protected from the mages as Saz'nár's army was, the battle for Abiren'á was just hours away, one the elves could not win.

He looked around him, at the cages full of silent elves, hope in their once dull eyes as they peered through the boughs for a hopeful glimpse of their saviours. Let them dream, he thought, because their ruin would be all the more satisfying to watch.

He pulled out a small sketch from under his tunic. An elven woman stared back at him, soft smile on her lovely face. He smiled back at her.

"For you, mother. For the pain you could not bear."

~

"Go now, Captain. Serve well. Our king is grateful to you, and I am so glad you are with us."

Bulan faced Pan'assár, saluted and then bowed. "And I am proud to fight under your command once more."

The flicker of a smile ghosted over Pan'assár's lips and Bulan turned, ready to depart with his one thousand two hundred, bound north-west and to the Xeric Wood. But he caught Fel'annár's gaze and for a moment, he allowed it to travel over the extraordinary boy he would have raised as a son, had that been his destiny.

But it hadn't, and his eyes rested on Harvest, his father's prized spear, the one he had taught Fel'annár how to use.

Bulan raised his hand to the Warlord, a fond farewell and Fel'annár returned it. They had already said their goodbyes with words, but the fear and the love in their eyes was a testimony to just how much they had come together these last weeks.

Fel'annár was snapped out of his musings by shouts of surprise and fear, and then the flapping of heavy wings, the thud of boots on the ground just behind him. He whirled round, only to come face to face with Lainon.

"I didn't mean to startle you. I'm not quite used to landing just yet."

Fel'annár barked in laughter and disbelief while Tensári's smile was so wide she looked utterly changed.

"Brother."

"Fel'annár." Lainon turned to Tensári, offered her a grim smile.

Yerái's jaw was half open, while Dalú held his hand out before him, as if to warn the elf-hawk away from him. But there was recognition and a thousand questions in the captain's eyes.

A smiling Fel'annár glanced at Gor'sadén and then Pan'assár and the Silvan captains around them. Some of the warriors had sunk to their knees while Amon and Benat bid them stand, even as their eyes did not leave the Ari'atór whose wings had dissolved before their very eyes. He was surely an envoy from Aria herself, they said, come to defend Abiren'á, just as Pan'assár had said.

"How is it possible?" asked Tensári.

"I can stay this way, so long as there is danger to the Ber'anor."

She stared at him, asked him the question she had been wanting to ask since she had first realised who he was, the same question she knew was on Fel'annár's lips.

"Are you Arimal?"

Lainon stared at his Connate, glanced at Fel'annár beside her. "Arimals are things of myth, based on a reality. I am Shirán."

While she stared at Lainon, Fel'annár turned to her, couldn't help the triumph in his eyes. He had told her so, and she had laughed. Still, the revelation was startling to them both, their own questions forming in their minds. Were *all* Shirán like this? Able to take on the shape of a hawk?

The main body of the army was moving out, and Dalú clapped Fel'annár on the shoulder as he passed. And then Benat, Amon and Eramor did likewise, murmured words of encouragement and optimism. He smiled, returned them but his heart was thumping too hard and he rubbed the inside of his wrist, that strange yet familiar burn beneath his armoured forearm, the unasked questions safely stored for when he could speak privately once more with Lainon.

THIS WAS NOT the way Fel'annár had imagined seeing Abiren'á for the first time. He desperately tried not to look at the thick ropes which swayed in the breeze, hanging from the highest and thickest trees he had ever seen.

Even here, on the outskirts of the city, there were hooks and chains and pulleys all over, a system of transport between trees and even between buildings. There were rope bridges everywhere, connecting trees and there were buildings jutting out from the massive trunks while others were nestled inside the canopy itself. He wanted to climb, run his hand over everything but he was distracted, because large cages hung from the heights like stalactites, and inside, the captives they had come to free so that Fel'annár could conjure the forest.

As they moved closer to the centre, they heard cries for help from above, but he couldn't look. He mustn't look lest he catch their eyes. If they failed to free these people, Fel'annár told himself he didn't want to remember their faces.

He saw Sand Lords, still distant, standing in what Fel'annár assumed was the central glade. His eyes travelled upwards and to the places Fel'annár knew the enemy archers would be. He caught sight of one, just behind a cage.

"They're hiding behind the captives," he murmured to Pan'assár at his side.

"I know."

As they slowly advanced, shields thudding together, pikes clattering between them, Fel'annár glanced at Amon, Benat and Eramor further down their front line. He could see them looking, analysing, making decisions even as they covered these last few steps to where Pan'assár would surely call a halt, just beyond the reach of the enemy short bows.

The trees were swarming with black and silver, like some new species of beetle that had infested the place. But search as he might, Fel'annár saw no Reapers.

A shout, strange words, oddly grating. A Sand Lord general was surely giving his final orders to his troops.

Above them, the sorrowful moans and cries of their people served as the backdrop for Pan'assár's own words, before it was time to charge.

"Benat, Amon, Dalú, Eramor. Positions. Archers away."

As they split off from the column of warriors and headed towards the trees, the ground suddenly shook beneath them. Not enough to throw them off balance but enough to startle. Three times, like boulders falling to the ground from a height.

"The serpents." Yerái's unsteady words from behind Fel'annár. The voices from their people in the trees had fallen silent, while the Sand Lord commanders yelled, strange sounds echoing around the trees.

At the call of an eagle, the battle in the heights would start in mere moments, and the Wheel of War would turn. If they were successful – if they managed to split the enemy warriors into two – then Dalú would lead the charge from behind, while the other captains moved in from the sides, and Yerái's unit climbed up into the heights.

This would be Fel'annár's biggest battle, one he may not survive and his bond with Llyniel flared in his mind.

He saw her face, her playful smile, remembered her Silvan wisdom and her Alpine poise.

He breathed deeply, duty clear in his bolstered mind, power from the Dohai pressing on the doors of his control, the forest in his head.

He would do it for them. For Llyniel. For the family he had found and would never again turn away from.

From beside him, Gor'sadén spoke softly. "We have trained hard for this moment, Fel'annár. It falls to us to cleave their ranks in two, pave the way for our warriors to attack on three fronts." Fel'annár listened as his eyes scanned the tree city before him, awestruck even now, invaded as it was by Sand Lords.

"Remember your beating heart, the rhythm of three. Remember the three steps backwards and the reinitiation of the Triad."

Pan'assár continued on his other side. "I believe in you, Fel'annár. With this Dance of Graceful Death, you will become a Master upon our return." A warm hand that did not shake upon his shoulder. Fel'annár turned to the commander, his gaze not cold and forbidding as it almost always was, but heavy with emotions. It was almost as if Pan'assár allowed him this glimpse, past the door to his heart that was almost always closed. It was the gaze of one who had seen too much, who had teetered on the border of chaos and returned.

But it was not grief he saw. It was care, encouragement and perhaps even pride. But there was something else, something beyond his feelings towards Fel'annár. He wondered if it was joy, and perhaps closure. Pan'assár had finally come to terms with the horrors of the past because he had been forgiven, by the only ones who could give him peace.

The Silvans.

He smiled back at Pan'assár, nodded respectfully and then drew a long breath.

The Dohai was pulsing inside him, pushing upon the walls of his chest, pressure growing. Shouts from above and ahead, and then the whisper of arrows overhead. The fight for vantage in the trees had begun. Bow strings thwacked and arrows sailed and then thudded into wood, into flesh and warriors fell from the heights, dead elves and slaughtered Sand Lords but the cages still hung high above the ground. The hostages screamed, huddled together as best they could but stray arrows sailed through the bars, hitting flesh and wood and iron.

Archers moving into position.

"Archers in position." Fel'annár nodded at Pan'assár. "Commander. They'll be caught in the crossfire ..."

"You can't control everything, not in a war."

It was the second time he had been told that, but it was against his nature, this was wrong but the raw yet practised scream of a commander split through the forest, and the trees moaned and wailed, voices crazed and pleading, the bass notes of the Sisters trumpeting, like a fanfare to a victorious king.

"Bows!"

The army upon the ground notched arrows, drew, from where they stood behind the shields and pikes and then stepped into the glade.

Silence.

The cry of an eagle, shrill and overly loud. Fel'annár's breath caught in his chest.

"Fire!"

The hollow base note of thousands of arrows sang around them, bolts sailing into the air and then arcing downwards. An enemy volley followed.

"Shields!"

Arrows clattered into the rooftop of wood and brass and the first line stepped backwards, only to be replaced by another line of archers ready to release.

"Fire!"

Arrows away, they collided mid-air with an answering wave of black projectiles which sped towards them.

"Shields!"

The first of their warriors fell whilst above them, Silvan archers careened to the ground, and Sand Lords toppled from high platforms, like a waterfall of death, bodies thudding around them, like the uneven beat of the Silvan war drums.

"Ready!"

The troops around him braced. Gor'sadén turned to Fel'annár with knowing eyes, eyes that knew the exhilaration, the dread, the sheer madness of the moment in which they three would take the fore and smash into the enemy.

Fel'annár almost swayed where he stood. He closed his eyes, desperately holding on to the Dohai that threatened to burst from his body, out of control. He watched Yerái sprint away, his chosen warriors behind him until they could no longer be seen, and he prayed, as hard as he ever had.

Aria protect them. Help them to free our people.

"Amon, Benat!" shouted Pan'assár.

His voice was followed by two, an order to raise shields on the right and left of the two Masters and the one the others knew would also be a Master soon. They tilted them backwards at an angle and the warriors shuffled sideways to make room for them. A wall of wood and steel, from which pikes protruded from the junctures. Soon, that wall would split into two, no longer horizontal to the enemy but vertical.

Just behind the Kah Triad, The Company, Lainon a brother once more, wings appearing, ready to take flight if the need arose. He half opened them, like a protective cloak around The Company.

Three Kah Warriors exhaled, and then one yelled to the heavens.

"*Charge!*"

Pan'assár was running, and at each shoulder, at a practised distance, the other two ran, sashes flying around their legs and behind, the armoured line advanced at a defiant march, each step a daunting, breathy challenge to come face them.

Mere seconds went by, but Fel'annár remembered Gor'sadén's words back in the glade of the Evergreen Wood.

It is a circular formation ... three strides wide.

A sea of Sand Lords stood before them, walking forwards, black cloaks billowing around them.

The Dohai is strong and projection is high.

They were almost upon them, jewelled swords moving upwards, ready to strike.

Each Master executes the same move in time to the beat of his heart.

Whether he had closed his eyes or not he couldn't say, but for a moment, the world quietened, and someone breathed.

It was deafening.

Until he heard a single thud, then another. He had not touched the trees, not yet, wouldn't until the cages had been cut down and yet he felt power around him, brushing against his skin, heightening the Dohai.

Pan'assár lifted his long sword, short sword just behind. Gor'sadén swivelled the Synth blade and a broad sword while Fel'annár hefted his own two blades, the very same movements as the other two.

"*Kal'hamén'Ar!*"

Swords flashed in a circle, undulating upwards and downwards and it was not only the enemy that gasped as one and then stepped backwards. Behind, from the cracks between shields The Company watched in terror and awe as the three lone warriors carved a path before them. There was light everywhere, streaks of green and blue and purple, all around them, as if they danced around the midsummer ribbons. Warriors fell, screamed as they were cut down, an arc of blood splattering continuously as they advanced to a beat of three. None came close to them, even though they were already halfway into the glade. Fel'annár faltered, felt the wheel slow down.

As one, they stepped backwards, and reformed the circle. Still, in those fractions of a second, the enemy did not move in, was too confused to take advantage of the lull. Too late and the Triad span forwards once more. On either side of them, a path strewn with dead Sand Lords, lying in bleeding heaps before their army, a warning not to approach the Wheel of War.

"Fork out!"

Pan'assár's yell and the army behind them was moving left and right, pushing into the enemy with their shields, widening the breech the Kah Warriors had opened. They skewered as many as they could with pikes until the fighting became too close and they hefted swords, discarded the heavy shields.

Azure screamed a bird, yelled an Ari'atór. Wings flapped as he burst from behind the shields, two swords shining with a preternatural light, almost as blue as his eyes he rose above the fighting and attacked from above. Sand Lords skidded to a halt, terrified eyes contemplating what was surely one of the mages their leader had said would come. There were four of them, or so they had counted so far, three who cleaved through their lines and one who hovered above the elven army.

The surprise was wearing off and the Sand Lords began to move forwards. It was too close now for the Wheel of War and instead, the Kah Masters danced the Graceful Death, enemies still crumbling around them.

From high above the glade, on the largest platform that overlooked the entire city, Saz'nár stood watching the battle below. The mages *had* come, just as they had feared. There were four of them, one in the form of a hawk, a harbinger of death.

Key'hán had been right all along, knew exactly how to still their hand. He cast his eyes around the trees, to the cages filled with elves. They shouted, desperately sought a way out of their wooden prisons, even though they already knew it was not possible. The ropes that anchored them to the ground were too thick, too crusted with the slime from the serpents. So long as those cages remained aloft, the trees would not thrash as they said they had in the mountains when his brother had died. Indeed, they were utterly still as the battle raged below.

Behind him on his platform, his army of Reapers stood shrouded in their black cloaks and face wraps which covered every inch of their bodies, save for their red eyes and their hands, and that was just fine with Saz'nár. Even had he not known they were there, the stench of them was proof enough. To the Northerners though, it was perfume, the stronger, more acrid it was, the more powerful that Chieftain was.

Beside each of the black figures lay a crate, upon which they laid their possessive hands. Saz'nár corrected himself. They were not hands, they were claws, black nails crusted with detritus.

"Free the serpents. It is time to feast, Chieftains."

The scrape of wood and the thud of the restraining doors opening and Saz'nár's features momentarily distorted. It was time to descend, time to confront the mages and strike them down. Without their magic, the enemy would flee before Saz'nár's own flavour of fear.

Calrazian fear.

They would cower and beg mercy, but they would find none for behold the outcasts, those even the Sand King feared, for had he not made this pact of aid so that he would be rid of them?

Saz'nár smiled for the power it gave them, watched as the serpents travelled over the wood, down the trunks. Once on the ground they would smash into it, burrow beneath the feet of their enemies and the true battle would begin. And should any of the mages escape the Reapers, then he would serve them death with his own hand, for they were warriors worthy of a Nim'uán's killing blow.

And if one of them was the Silver One, then once he perished, nothing would stop the Nim'uán from taking this forest for themselves, as was their birth right.

YERÁI WAS HANGING from a high branch, as close as he could to one of the cages. Around him, his patrol fended off the enemy archers that tried and failed to get a clear shot at him.

They knew what he was trying to do.

Inside the cages, the people he had known all his life were moaning and yelling, hanging on for dear life as arrows whizzed past them and Yerái struggled to reach them.

"We'll get you out. The Warlord has come and Bulan fights with our army against the Reapers."

"Yerái?"

"Aio? Is that you?"

"Get us out of here, Yerái."

"I'm trying. Is there a way out – the mechanism – can it be broken?"

"No. We've tried a thousand times."

"Then we need to lower the cages ..."

"You can't. They don't reach to the ground. The rope that holds us to the branches above can be cut but not so the ones that tie us to the ground. It's stiff with some secretion from the serpents. If you cut the string above, the cage won't land on the ground. It will capsize. The only way is to cut the rope on the ground somehow and then lower us from above."

"Aio. I'll be back. I'll find a way, I promise."

"Hurry brother. If the Reapers don't kill us, thirst will, or these arrows!" Aio threw himself against the back of a cage as an arrow clattered through the iron bars but hit nothing.

Yerái scurried back to the trunk, signalled to the others to remain where the ropes were tied. As for him, he needed to find a way to sever the encrusted ropes on the ground, so that his warriors could then lower the cages. He would need the sharpest axe, the most skilfully wrought blade – a miracle – to cut them free.

HIS FEET MOVED in a circle of three, blades flashing and glinting as they arced high and low, heads rolling, blood splashing everywhere. There were hands too, swords still trapped inside frozen fists and the press of Sand Lords became closer. Just behind Fel'annár and the Masters, the Company fought and then the rest of their host and all the while, the Kah warriors did not stop and the lights around them did not wane.

From the heights, small, wooden lifts descended and inside one of them, Saz'nár, blue eyes wide in gleeful anticipation of the glorious moments that were about to take place. He tightened his vambraces, unbuckled his weapons harnesses, stretched his neck and licked his lips.

The lift shuddered and then bumped to a halt. Opening the door, he stepped into the battle, even as his feet felt the first vibrations from below. The Sand Lords before him stepped aside, cheering as he strode forwards. Their best chieftains regrouped around him, their bejewelled blades out before them. Courage bolstered, anticipation growing at the arrival of the Northern Reapers who would surely mark the end of this battle. They rallied together and then turned satisfied eyes upon their doomed enemies.

Saz'nár lifted his sword, screamed his battle cry, an unearthly sound, like a furious insect, more beast than elf, or man. A surge of fear rippled over the advancing elves and from the chaos of battle, a voice rang out, loud and clear over the rest.

"For Abiren'á!" To the answering roar of elves, Fel'annár sliced an arm off and then turned. That was when he saw Saz'nár, swivelling his swords before him and then lunging into his first opponent with the strength of a raging bear.

This Nim'uán was bigger, stronger, faster and more terrifying to look upon than his brother in Tar'eastór. To him, one elven opponent was nothing but a bundle of hay he tossed aside in a river of blood. One strike, one death and even as the beast cut its way through their rapidly depleting army, Fel'annár caught his first sight of a mighty spear, still inside the harness on the Nim'uán's back.

Someone had to take him down – now – before the Nim'uán could reap any more damage. Fel'annár was torn between helping to lower the cages and free their people, so that he could activate the trees, or confront the beast himself, because the only warriors who had a chance against this formidable foe were the Kah Masters.

WITH THE COMING of the Nim'uán and the Northern Reapers, the Sand Lords fought with renewed spirit. Strength and endurance reigned supreme now and not for the first time, Fel'annár glanced at the tense ropes that formed a part of a system of pulleys that held the cages in place high above them. Why had they not been lowered? He could see elves frantically working the mechanisms, but the ropes did not move. He fought as he made his way over to them, glanced at Tensári not far away. She moved with him, Lainon hovering over them both, stabbing downwards at any who got too close to her or Fel'annár.

He spotted Yerái at the base of one of the hanging cages.

"Why aren't they coming down?" he shouted as he stabbed a Sand Lord.

"They're caked in something. Our blades can't cut through them. My warriors are up there, ready to lower them but we can't until these ropes are cut. They're rigid, as hard as steel, damn it."

"We must sever them?"

"Yes, and then lower them from above. It's the only way!"

And then it hit him. "Climb back up! Commander Gor'sadén has a blade that can cut them. On his mark!"

"How?"

"Don't ask!"

A Sand Lord to his left, he sliced sideways, watched him fall and then searched for Gor'sadén. He was fighting three. Raising his hand to his mouth he meant to call out to him but suddenly, from the ground beside him, a creature surged, soil and roots erupting like molten rock from the southern volcanoes, smattering onto the ground around them like summer rains. The ground beneath his boots disappeared and he was falling, even as he heard the screams from The Company, from Yerái.

Their yells abruptly stopped as the beast descended into the depths once more, almost as fast as it had emerged. It had not seemed to realise it had snagged Fel'annár on its journey towards Pan'assár.

Fel'annár was nowhere to be seen. Only Harvest lay where the Warlord had been standing just seconds before.

"Fel'annár!" Tensári's scream, Lainon's wings flapping as he hovered above the ground that had swallowed the Ber'anor.

Idernon turned to the cry, Ramien, Carodel and Galdith searching and failing to find their leader. Gor'sadén was running, Pan'assár and Galadan just behind and the Sand Lords shouted in glee. One of the mages had fallen, only three left to kill.

"What the Hell!" shouted Galdith.

"He's not dead!" cried Tensári. "There has to be a way in to wherever he is!"

"Then we *find* it!" shouted Idernon, eyes desperately searching the ground for any sign of a way in. But there was nothing and despair began to take hold of them.

Nervous glances between the fighting warriors. The Warlord had fallen, disappeared beneath the ground and the Nim'uán was fighting his way towards them. It was only a matter of time before the armoured snake resurfaced and still, the cages hung from the heights and Yerái waited, for the Warlord to re-appear, for Gor'sadén to cut the ropes.

But there was no air underground. If Fel'annár had perished, then the Sand Lords had already won this war.

35

THE MAGES ARE COME

~

FEL'ANNÁR WAS SUFFOCATING, soil in his mouth, choking him. He couldn't breathe and still the ground shook and turned around him. He retched, coughed, blew out through his nose and then he felt the brush of a root across his face. Arms flailing, fingers reaching for it to anchor himself – wherever he was.

The root entwined itself around his hand even as he was tossed around in the churning soil. He covered his mouth and nose as best he could with one hand, but breathing was all but impossible. He felt faint, disorientated but the root around his wrist was pulling at him. It gave him hope that it was not yet his time to die.

And then the smell came, of decaying bodies, hot, rancid breath from somewhere nearby. His eyes were closed lest the soil blind him, but the lights were there, just as they had been in the Evergreen Wood. In luminescent streaks of blue and red, a snake-like creature materialised, its head nothing but a gaping mouth, a mouth with rows of teeth – or perhaps tentacles and at the other end of its body, a pincer.

It burrowed, scales brushing past him. Had it not seen him? he wondered as he tumbled over and over and still, the root pulled on his wrist, upwards. He saw the sun as the serpent broke through the surface. *Now.*

Light exploded in the world beyond his eyelids and he opened them, just as the root around his wrist disappeared and he was catapulted upwards, somehow landing on the back of the serpent.

He felt the beast beneath him, shrieking and clicking, twisting its way forwards, powerful muscles rippling under plates of hard scale, nail-like to touch. Fel'annár reached back to pull out his spear, but his hand met air. A moment of panic and a giant pincer stabbed forwards, searching for him, thudding into the ground around him again and again. And then its whole body arched upwards. He reached out, to anything to keep him aloft and he was flying up and down, through the air, clinging to the back of a furious serpent that was trying to shake the elf from its back.

He could hold on no longer and he was flung backwards and to one side.

He rolled over the ground, skidded to a halt. On his knees, the world spun around him as he gasped and coughed, spat soil from his mouth.

"Fel'annár!"

"To the Warlord!"

But the snake-like beast reared up before him, scales clacking as it moved, crusty flaps of skin protecting the slimy flesh below. It shrieked in its failure to sting the mage, and its head that was a mouth, opened wide enough to swallow him whole, a rush of foetid breath making him gag. And then from over its head, the pincers hurtled towards him once more. He rolled sideways, desperate and weaponless after his fall and then the winged Ari'atór was above him, at his side Tensári, brandishing her sword before the creature.

Someone caught him and helped him to his feet, pounded his back as he coughed out the last of the soil and wheezed. It was Idernon, and in his hand, Harvest. He steadied Fel'annár, waited for him to wipe his face with his sleeve, inhale deeply and nod before passing the spear to his friend with a wry smile and panicked eyes.

A cheer from those warriors close enough to have seen what had happened, and Fel'annár swivelled Zéndar's spear in his hand. It would taste battle once more, for the first time in his hands. All Bulan's teachings came to him and he felt its weight, its perfect balance.

Fel'annár lunged forwards, sliced through the tail with the double-edged blade at one end of his spear. A wet squelch and a grating shriek, it twisted on itself, rearing to its full height. Another warrior moved in to help. Too close. Mouth open with the exertion of battle, a whip-like tongue darted out of the serpent's head and shot down the elf's throat before he could scream. He choked, tried to pull the thing out of his body but it had latched onto something inside. Blood fountained from his mouth, just as Fel'annár sliced through the tongue. Too late for the warrior but it was enough to give him the advantage over the stinking creature and he cleaved the head in two, a powerful strike down the centre of its mouth. Another blow across the middle and it came apart, in two pieces.

He grimaced, wiped at his mouth again while Ramien spat.

"It stinks."

"Keep your mouths shut!"

"Glad to see you too," said Carodel as he killed a Sand Lord.

Gods but Fel'annár wanted to laugh in spite of his underground misadventure and the humongous serpent that had tried to stab them with its pincers.

He turned, spotted his Master in the distance.

"Gor'sadén. To the ropes! The Synth Blade is our only hope!"

The Company battled its way towards the two commanders, and then looked up at the cage directly above them. But the elves inside were shouting and pointing to somewhere behind The Company. Galadan spotted movement from the corner of his eyes. Turning, eyes bulging, he shouted a warning, just in time.

"It's not dead!"

Whirling around, all he could do was watch as Lainon faced not one serpent but two. With a mighty slice from the side, he cut through the two heads and from somewhere close by, an unearthly scream rent the air, almost a howl.

It had not come from the serpents.

"It multiplies in death!" shouted Lainon. "Don't cut it into two. Stab it instead!"

No time to ask questions but plenty of the warriors around them had heard, including The Company as they ran towards Gor'sadén, fighting the Sand Lords as they went. There were plenty of them around the commanders and as they fought, Fel'annár shouted over the din.

"Will the Synth Blade cut those ropes?"

"It might. But the cages won't reach the ground."

"Yerái and his warriors are waiting for your signal. Those he cannot lower, the trees will."

"You will leave yourself vulnerable to attack."

"I have The Company. Free them, Commander, and then we can be done with this!"

Fel'annár was aware of the Nim'uán, fighting his way across the battlefield, heading for Gor'sadén, Pan'assár and himself. All he needed was to give Gor'sadén the time he needed to free those cages, for Yerái to cut them from above and then command the trees to lower them to safety.

They rallied as many warriors as they could around Gor'sadén who stood before the encrusted ropes, Synth blade in hand, he swung it over his head, brought it down onto the rope, not quite all the way through. The fibres tensed, began to break and then the rope snapped as the cage swung violently to one side and then the other, like a giant pendulum, the captives inside screamed, white-knuckled hands clinging to the bars. Above them, what was left of Yerái's warriors began to lower it but it was too heavy, and the rope slipped from their burning hands.

Fel'annár ran to the nearest tree, The Company still around him, Lainon fighting from just over their heads. He reached out, touched, felt the power of the trees almost wrest control from him.

Steady the cages.

Gor'sadén looked up, leaves raining down on him and then the moan and creak of live wood. From the heights, branches reached out, wrapped around the cages until they stopped their wild swinging. In the trees above, the wide-eyed warriors released their burning grip on the ropes. It was no longer necessary, the trees had taken the weight from them and they watched, moved to tears in the midst of battle as gentle arms lowered the cages to the ground.

The wooden door burst open and the people stood there in the middle of the battlefield.

"Run through our warriors, go south. Get out of here and don't stop!"

They were away, helping each other along. Some wouldn't make it, Fel'annár knew that – they all did.

Gor'sadén ran to the next rope, and The Company followed while Fel'annár continued to touch the bark and the Ber'ator protected him. The Synth Blade cut through the caked rope with two swings, and Yerái and his team watched with a mixture of excitement and joy, cutting the ropes above, and then leaning away, so that the branches could embrace the cages, take the weight from the warriors and lower them to the ground. Some reached out, brushed their fingers over the living, moving wood in fascination.

Another cage on the ground, the civilians scrambled for the treeline, not before looking over their shoulders, watching in utter shock as the mighty trees of Abiren'á bent this way and that, lowering cages, while Gor'sadén broke the ropes and Yerái freed them from above.

Saz'nár watched in grudging respect at the power of the silver mage. With no hostages in the trees, the mage would be free to command them as he had in Tar'eastór. They would suffer the same fate as Xar'dón had, Saz'nár was sure of it. Gutting the elf before him, he strode forwards, bound for the mage with the strange sword that was capable of cutting through the caked ropes. He had thought them unbreakable by any steel he knew of. He would kill this blond mage, take the blade for himself and then kill the other mage who was touching the trees, the Silver One, bane of his younger brother.

Pan'assár saw the moment Saz'nár made for Gor'sadén.

He couldn't allow the beast to confront him, to distract him from freeing those people because if he failed, Fel'annár would be forced to sacrifice those who were still inside the cages above them.

And he would.

But the burden would be too great, too heavy for one so young. Of them all, even more than Gor'sadén, it was the Warlord who must survive the day. He was of the line of Or'Talán and Pan'assár would take his oath to the grave if that was what it took. He had failed to save his friend in the Xeric Wood, but he could not allow his grandson to perish, or worse still, to dwindle away in self-inflicted torment as he himself almost had.

He killed another opponent and then yelled a command to rally around Gor'sadén and The Company. But their numbers were dwindling and still, cages hung from the heights.

The Nim'uán was advancing on them, a host of others around him, cutting through the elves that stood valiantly before them and paid the price.

Pan'assár watched it, watched his warriors, Alpines and Silvans desperately trying to slow the enemy commander's coming. Glancing sideways, Pan'assár wondered if Galadan understood what was in his mind. But Galadan had *always* understood him, even now as he caught his gaze and nodded. The commander turned to where Fel'annár was conjuring the trees. They locked gazes, Pan'assár smiled and then looked away.

With a mighty roar, he launched himself into a sprint towards the Nim'uán, and behind him, Galadan ran as he brandished his sword.

Fel'annár's stomach plummeted to his boots. He willed them to stop, even as he continued the conjuring, looked up at another cage that was being lowered by the trees.

Just a little more time ... just one more cage ...

Gor'sadén moved to the last cage, while Idernon freed the panicked civilians and pushed them behind their slowly retreating lines. But a sudden movement to his right drew Idernon's attention. Eyes wide, panic surging from his gut, he shouted, as loud as he could, to anyone who could hear.

"Pan'assár means to take on the Nim'uán!"

"Gor'sadén has to get those ropes ..." muttered Galdith to no one in particular, but Ramien and Carodel heard him, watched as Galadan charged beside Pan'assár. But they couldn't help, because the push of Sand Lords towards Gor'sadén, towards Fel'annár and the Ber'ator was constant. They were almost overrun, needed to retreat.

"To me. Warriors to *me!*" Pan'assár's characteristic voice of command.

Gor'sadén looked up from his arduous work and through the fighting, he saw Pan'assár streaking across the battlefield. There was a wild sort of glory about him, almost reckless but Galadan was with him, as he always was. He looked up, the last cage harnessed from above and he swung his blade, bore down on the rope with one, a powerful swing.

But it would not break.

He swung again, and again but the fibres were stuck together. He needed to finish this, join Pan'assár and fight the Nim'uán. But his brother was almost upon it.

Gor'sadén would never reach him in time.

BULAN WIELDED HIS SPEAR, killed as he advanced, painstakingly slow, over the undulating sands.

Fighting in the desert was hard. Uneven and ever moving terrain, it was easy to lose your footing. Many had and paid the price at the hands of Sand Lords or worse still, the serpent creatures and their unnatural allies who stood on the side lines, waiting for the moment in which their serpents trapped their next victim.

Bulan had tried to postpone the confrontation, give Pan'assár time to retake Abiren'á, but the enemy commander had read their strategy far too easily. He must have known their army had broken into two.

They had surely been wrong. The Nim'uán was not in Abiren'á. It was here.

As Bulan's contingent battled with the Sand Lords, Commander Hobin's forces had clashed with a horde of Deviants that had amassed on the eastern flank. Even now he could see the Ari'atór fighting in the distance to his right.

But for now, Bulan and his one thousand two hundred elves were alone against the terror of the flesh eaters, the Reapers and their serpent hunters that did not kill but paralyse, and when they were cleaved into two, or three or four pieces, they came back alive, every piece a new creature. They had found that out the hard way, understood they must not dismember them but instead stab them. So far, they had killed nothing but a handful, their thick, protective scales making them almost impervious to their blades.

They were deceptively fast and elusive, capable of diving beneath the sand as if it were nothing but water. The pincer was the weapon it used to render a warrior vulnerable, so that the Reaper could feed on living flesh, so that it could eat what was left. It was a horrific sight, one that had cost lives. How they had tried not to look. Only the very bravest, the veterans amongst them, were capable of killing their own warriors, so that they did not have to endure being eaten alive. It was breaking their resolve, fighting Sand Lords and killing their own brothers.

He swivelled his spear, left and right as he moved forwards and then sliced through the face of his opponent, turned the other way and stabbed another in the gut.

There was no telling what had happened in Abiren'á. The only way was to wait and see what came out of the forest. Elves to help them in the battle, or Sand Lords to finish them off.

They were losing, and Bulan wondered, did Fel'annár still live?

He glanced sideways, roaring with the effort it took to slice a Sand Lord's head off his shoulders and then dodged the swing of a scimitar that whispered over his head. They were all tiring, had not advanced into the sands at all and from what he could see, The Ari'atór had hardly advanced on the eastern flank.

"Warriors! For Abiren'á!"

They yelled and screamed, still fighting, still strong enough to continue, their hope still there. They had to believe that the Silvan city had been reclaimed. But with every fallen warrior, with every poor soul who was dragged away by the dark ones, their spark was dwindling.

He heard a foreign yell, an answering roar of determination and the Sand Lords attacked with renewed vigour, eyes alight for they could smell victory, their commander had surely said it was coming and he was not wrong.

The Nim'uán was an impressive warrior. Many had tried and failed to bring him down, a trail of bodies behind him for he was large, broad, bigger even than Fel'annár's Wall of Stone. He was not slow for it but nimble. He had even seen it kicking in the air, twisting sideways, adopting stances which to others may seem a show of arrogance. But to him, Blade Master, Spear Master that he was, Bulan knew the truth of it. The Nim'uán was well-trained, knowledgeable in the martial arts. He could tell by the way he reacted at the very last minute, how his feet moved, how his free hand moved in time to his blade. There were only three he knew of who could ever have a chance before this beast.

But they were not here.

He heard shouts, saw the Sand Lords rearranging themselves and his heart sank. A large group of them ran to the perimeter of battle and then away, into the forest. Even with them gone the battle was all but lost. This was exactly what Pan'assár had wanted to avoid. Stop the two groups of Sand Lords from coming together.

Bulan had failed him.

PAN'ASSÁR CHARGED STRAIGHT at Saz'nár and the two formidable warriors came together, swords already attacking, defending.

From behind the Nim'uán, a serpent reared, screeching as it vied for a clear shot over its ally's shoulders. It found one, launched its tail at an unwitting warrior close by. The pincers clamped down over the side of his neck, piercing skin and muscle. The warrior fell boneless to the ground, chest heaving and yet the rest of his body utterly still.

Another warrior moved in, sliced at its belly but all it did was enrage the thing. It twisted upon itself, advancing like a dust devil as it shrieked and clacked, sticky mucus flying from its body. It bore down on a warrior, its head opening like a flower and then it rolled away, the warrior writhing and kicking until he was spat out and he lay utterly still, alive.

Pan'assár attacked, powerful yet precise strokes almost penetrating the Nim'uán's defences. He danced sideways, attacked again, this time from the side but a warning yell from Galadan and he aborted it, dodging the strike of the serpent. From the corner of his eye, he spotted one of the fallen warriors and sitting over him, the black, half-crumpled form of a Reaper.

He frowned, avoided a blow from the left, struck the Nim'uán but it was not fatal. It should have been, and he disciplined his mind to just focus on his enemy. But his eyes were once more drawn to the fallen warrior, watched in utter horror as the being turned to him. Half its face was a mouth and in it, the still steaming entrails of a now screaming and wailing warrior, fresh blood dripping from twisted lips.

Horror surged through his body. He hefted his swords above his head, anger and wrath fuelling his heavy strikes, but the Nim'uán countered them, again and again. Shock at such barbaric cruelty had rendered Pan'assár off-balance, for just one passing moment.

He stumbled.

He heard the thud of an elven arrow, and the wailing warrior fell silent, a friendly arrow through the temple. The flesh eater upon him screeched. Too late did he hear the swoop of heavy metal rushing towards him, too close. Pan'assár braced for death but all he heard were muffled cries and the scuffle of falling bodies, his own in the melee.

He crashed to the ground, something pinning him there. Warriors were moving before him – Alpines and Silvans – taking on the Nim'uán. All he could move was his head and as he turned, he came face to face with Galadan's closed eyes.

Where was he? What had happened? He struggled with Galadan's weight, managed to slide out from under him but he couldn't get his feet beneath him. He tried again, gasped at the searing pain that tore down his side, down his leg. He gritted his teeth, turned his head to Galadan.

But Galadan's eyes were still closed. He hadn't moved at all. Bloodied and still, he realised then that his best captain had thrown himself in front of the blade meant for him. He had stood distracted by the savagery of the Reaper and Galadan had saved him once more.

Feet were thudding over the ground and Pan'assár felt dizzy, had yet to understand why. And then he saw Galdith, running and yelling and behind and above, the winged Ari'atór. Dark hands snagged his cuirass, and he was dragged away, just as Galdith pulled his friend along until they were behind a tree stump, close to where Gor'sadén was slicing through ropes. He wanted to know what had happened to the Nim'uán ...

"How bad?" called Gor'sadén, but neither Galdith nor Lainon answered. Gor'sadén chanced a glance over his shoulder to where Pan'assár knelt awkwardly over Galadan, hand on his head, staring down at him as if he didn't understand.

The fallen commander felt the rush of wind as Lainon took flight and returned to Fel'annár and The Company and then Galdith's raw voice ground out, between clenched teeth and a heaving chest, reaching out for Galadan's limp hand.

"Gala?"

Bleary blue eyes cracked open, looked up at Galdith. Gods but he had thought his friend dead.

"I am honoured ... to have served ... these lands ... with you ... The Company. Protect him ... I ... no longer can." He coughed, grimaced and Galdith's eyes brimmed.

"Take ... my knife bro ... brother. Use it. Remember ... the good times."

Galdith took it, and Galadan's head lolled to the side but his eyes were still open, staring now at a barely kneeling Pan'assár.

"My privilege ... to serve ... with you."

Galdith and Pan'assár watched the once fiery blue eyes close, for the last time.

Galadan of Tar'eastór had passed and Pan'assár let out a strangled moan, as if someone had pulled an arrow from his gut. Galadan had given his life for him and Pan'assár would make it worth something, worth *everything*.

Pan'assár felt something wet trickle down his side, burning pain in its wake and an odd sensation of displacement. He needed to get up and fight. Only then did he realise he had lost his sword. He looked up at the last cage that Gor'sadén and The Company were struggling to free. He heard the screams and yells to hurry, but his eyes latched on to a young man, grasping at the clothes of an older elf. His father, he thought. His breath stilled in his chest because in those young, innocent eyes, it seemed to Pan'assár that the entire Silvan people looked back at him, pleading with him to do something. He had ignored them once. He wouldn't now.

He turned away from those begging eyes and sought the Nim'uán and his chieftains. They had killed Galadan, and now, there was nothing between them and Gor'sadén, save for The Company.

The Warlord could not die as Galadan had. He was the future of Or'Talán's dream. He was the hope of these people, the only one who could tip the balance and win this battle. He couldn't allow Fel'annár to confront it, couldn't allow the Nim'uán to stop Gor'sadén from freeing these people.

He had taken an oath to protect these people. Even unto death.

Pan'assár stood, ignored the lance of pain that threatened to topple him, the weight of grief squeezing his heart. The bleeding in his side would not stop, and he knew that it never would. He looked down at Galdith, at the small knife in his hand. The warrior was watching him.

Pan'assár held out a shaking hand and Galdith looked at the herb knife and then back at the wounded commander. He held it out, watched Pan'assár take it, and then nod at him. The commander turned to an unwitting Gor'sadén who was hacking furiously at the half-severed rope. The Commander General of Ea Uaré smiled, somehow knew his friend would overcome. He turned away from life, willingly and in peace, and then he ran towards the Nim'uán.

Only then did Galdith understand.

"*Pan'assár!!*"

Gor'sadén whirled around, eyes wide, watched his brother charge weaponless at the Nim'uán.

"Stop! Wait, damn it. *Wait for me!!*"

But Pan'assár didn't and as the Nim'uán smiled and held his sword out before him, Pan'assár of Tar'eastór and Ea Uaré ran himself through with it. Face to face with the shocked Nim'uán, he watched as shock turned to glee, triumph shining in its elven eyes. The blade twisted in his chest and Pan'assár cried out, just as Gor'sadén's scream rent the air about them.

Victory, victory was his! He had killed the elven commander, another mage. Saz'nár's smile was wide, elated, curved incisors protruding from his mouth.

Pan'assár felt his final breaths dance in his mouth and from the depths of his chest, with the last of the Dohai left in his body, he raised his right hand, and drove Galadan's herb knife into the side of the gloating Nim'uán's throat.

Glee became confusion, then pain and then panic as blood spurted from him, over his face, down his neck, coating Pan'assár with it. Saz'nár was floating away, to where he didn't know.

There was no Short Road for a Nim'uán, was there?

The screams of Sand Lords and Reapers rent the air, discordant and panicked, just as Gor'sadén brought his Synth Blade down over the last threads of rope and then sprinted to where Pan'assár and the Nim'uán still stood, bloodied and half-dead. He pulled his friend off the blade, staggered backwards towards where Galdith knelt over Galadan and then lowered his friend to the ground. He turned, watched the last cage of Silvans as it floated to the ground and the doors banged open.

Yerái and what remained of his unit, scurried down the trunk of the tree while another voice rent the air.

"Fel'annár!" Benat, or was it Amon? Gor'sadén didn't know, didn't care and he turned to his son.

Tensári and Lainon were beside him, and then Idernon, Ramien and Carodel joined them. Fel'annár looked straight at him. His eyes strayed to the fatally injured Pan'assár in his arms and then to Galadan, already dead at their side.

Gor'sadén saw the moment that wrath took over, watched as the Forest Lord's countenance changed, until he no longer recognised him.

Fel'annár turned back to the tree under his hand, his whole body shaking as blinding light surrounded him, seemed to shine from every pore of his skin, his eyes.

Rage, molten anger, it gripped his guts and wouldn't let go. It drowned the final dregs of his control, but it wasn't just his. It was the forest.

It was the Sisters.

Their fury could not be contained and the wood under his hand was vibrating, the earth beneath him trembling, ready to burst. He wanted to tell The Company, tell Gor'sadén to get out, as far away as they could from him.

But it was too late. Voice bubbled and then surged through his chest, out of his mouth and he screamed – so loud it had surely reached the very confines of Ea Uaré.

A conflagration swept over them, through them, sending friend and foe staggering backwards, sideways. All of them except Fel'annár who stood like an avenging God, cruel and vindictive, capable of anything, overcome with his fury and that of the forest, of the Sisters.

Weapons flew from hands and a wind swept everything around in circles and upwards. Sand Lords yelled in horror and panic, scrambling for their swords and daggers. Those lucky enough to escape the killing branches ran, northwards and to the sands of Calrazia.

The Silvan warriors and the last of the civilians protected their faces, terrified eyes looking upwards in denial. Their forest city was thrumming with ire, seething in wrath – they somehow knew that, felt it in the very fibre of their Silvan being. Their trees, their homes, their walkways and their mechanisms stretched this way and that, snapped and whipped around in the hurricane, and branches as large as Hager Giants crashed to the ground around them.

Branches swayed low, skewered the Reapers and hoisted them aloft, the sound of trumpets and screeching, the trees called victory with every beast they impaled.

Galdith stood, pulled on Gor'sadén's cloak but he wouldn't move.

"Commander!"

Gor'sadén looked up at him and Galdith knew that he wouldn't leave. Pan'assár was still alive and so he sprinted towards The Company, jumped over bodies, ducked under branches as they swayed low and Idernon waited for him.

He took one more look at the terrifying countenance of his friend, knew it was no longer just Fel'annár. He turned to Tensári, and then Lainon, searched for the promise he sought in their Ari eyes.

He found it.

He couldn't help Galadan now, no one could because Galdith was here, would never have left Galadan's side had he still been alive. Pan'assár would surely follow him upon the Short Road for Gor'sadén did not move, wouldn't until his brother had passed.

"Company! Warriors! Make for the north and Bulan. Get out now!"

With a final glance at Fel'annár, Idernon left him in the company of the Ber'ator and he ran, The Company fast on his heels.

It was the hardest thing he had ever had to do.

∾

TEARS SPILLED unchecked from Gor'sadén's eyes, blurring his vision. The searing pain of grief in his chest and a name, bubbling deep in his soul, rising upwards, searching for release. The ground shook, elves and Sand Lords yelling around him. He needed to get up, but Pan'assár was not dead.

He sat with his back to a tree that did not move, Pan'assár in his arms, still warm body leaning against his chest. As the wind raged faster and louder over them, some invisible pressure growing around them, Gor'sadén could not let go of his dying brother. He could feel the ragged breaths and he bent forwards, so that his ear was flush with Pan'assár's face. He could feel the soft breath brush over his cheek, barely hear his final words.

"Lead them on. Lead Fel'annár to victory, brother."

"What have you done!" A rhetorical question. Gor'sadén knew exactly what Pan'assár had done, *why* he had done it.

"What I had to. I could not save ... save Or'Talán, but I could save ... these people. I could save ... Fel'annár ... from a life of regret, of ... of guilt for forsaking them."

"You didn't even have a weapon ..."

"No difference ... I was already lost. Galadan ... saved me from instant death but the blow ... was fatal, brother. He ... he never faltered ... showed me the nature of duty ... a true warrior ... like Aren ... Or'Talán. I go with him ... again. Will see Orta ... this night."

The wind was buffeting them hard now, branches scraping over Gor'sadén's back, he could hear warriors yelling at others to get out, but he wouldn't leave Pan'assár. He felt numb. His brother was leaving him. It was unthinkable.

"Give my short ... sword ... to Fel'annár. My ... Turanés. Tell him ... to wield it ... in the Dance ... that will see him ... become a Master."

Gor'sadén looked up, desperate eyes on the thrashing boughs, arms tightening around his friend.

"Serve well. Live well, Brother. Bring ... the Kal'hamén'Ar back."

Panic, like Gor'sadén had never felt before. He couldn't let him go. There was too much to say.

"Pan'assár ..." he gasped, tried again. "Pan, wait ..."

"Gorsa, Gorsa ..." a weak smile pulled at pale lips and some strength seemed to fuel his words, whispered though they were.

"We have lived, laughed, protected our people. We saw days of glory, stood in the presence of great ones. We looked down on the world from the highest pinnacle of the world, looked up at the Hagar Giants from the heights of the Glistening Falls. We have seen wonders together. Remember those ... those things and not these ... my final gasps."

Gor'sadén nodded, held him tighter, no longer heard the howling wind and the battling forest, only the slowing heart of a great warrior. He opened his mouth, words spilling freely.

"Did you see them, brother? Standing there and saluting you. Did you hear what Bulan said?"

"I did it, didn't I? Redeemed ... myself ..."

Gor'sadén's face crumbled beside the paling face of Pan'assár, tried and failed to squeeze the tears back into his eyes. "You gave them everything in the end and I ..." he was choking, cleared his throat. "I am so proud of you."

He felt Pan'assár's hand tighten around his forearm, his only answer. And then it slackened. Gor'sadén placed a hand on his forehead. Too cold. His hand slid down to Pan'assár's chest, but it was still and Gor'sadén shook his head, tears splashing onto his own hand.

He was enveloped in blue light as it floated before his face, mingling with his tears, turning the whole world blue. Something surged from his soul, like a giant exploding from the depths of the Median Mountains. It was the colour of his crushing grief.

Pan'assár was gone and he pulled the limp body tighter into his arms, as if he could squeeze a part of his own life into it. But he couldn't and he lifted his head to the thrashing boughs above and screamed. He screamed until there was no breath left in his chest.

His hand moved to the side of Pan'assár's face, kissed his forehead and then lay him down gently, like the most delicate of flowers. He turned away, sat in a maelstrom of destruction, even as the last of the blue mist dissipated. Feet under him, hands out to the side he stumbled to the first tree and turned back, to the strange sight of Pan'assár dead on the ground, Galadan beside him.

Roots were writhing beneath him, a branch careening towards him. He ducked, looked around him. No one left save for Fel'annár and the Ber'ator at his side. He stumbled sideways and crashed into a tree. He pushed himself away and then he was striding, running, sprinting, tears streaming into his hair. He would fight until he had nothing left. Or'Talán and Pan'assár had left him alone, in a world in which he no longer belonged. He was the only one left of The Three, and if he were to join them this night, he would make his own end just as glorious as Pan'assár's had been.

36

THE MOTHER

~

BULAN WAS HANGING on to the southern flank with all that he had, which was not much.

Two thousand Sand Lords had managed to break through their defences and penetrate the tree line. They would be well on their way to Abiren'á to join their commander.

This was not what Pan'assár needed. His contingent had already been outnumbered.

Bulan killed his opponent, moved on to another, but with every Sand Lord he fought, he found himself ever closer to the tree line behind. His only hope now, was for the Ari'atór to break the Deviant lines on the eastern flank and join his warriors here, stop the enemy from advancing further than they already had.

Just moments later, a roar of victory sounded over the battlefield and his head snapped to the right. The Ari'atór held their weapons aloft. Bulan's prayers had been heard, and Supreme Commander Hobin's warriors had run down the Deviants. He watched as the commander rallied his remaining Ari'atór and made towards his position.

They still had a remote chance.

Memories of his times in Araria flooded his mind, even as he continued to battle with the enemy.

He had met Hobin on several occasions, and the Ber'anor had always managed to unnerve him. Servant of Aria, just like his own father, Zéndar had fallen in battle protecting his Ber'anor, Hobin. That had been the last time Bulan had seen Hobin. When next he looked into those blue eyes, he would do so knowing that his father's Guiding Light would be looking back at him.

As the first Ari'atór joined their ranks, the Silvans and Alpines cheered and Bulan caught Hobin's gaze from afar. The commander raised his hand in salute and Bulan nodded respectfully. If both of them survived the day, he would seek Hobin out, seek answers to the questions he had never had the opportunity to ask.

How had his father died?

A distant droning sounded from somewhere behind him. A minor note that struck dread in his heart. It reminded him of Lan Taria and what Fel'annár had said were the weeping Giants. But there was something more to it, the notes more complex, deeper – more disturbing.

The battlefield pulsed, caused a lull in the fighting as the air crackled around them and the drone became louder.

His ears popped, a distant rumble of thunder from invisible lightning. The sands moved beneath them, and a wind came from behind, hair flying about his face.

The shocked elves stood, eyes searching for the source of the disturbance. The Sand Lords' black robes whipped about them, stuck to their bodies. Their hoods fell away, revealing copper skin and copper eyes which they shielded from the unnatural wind with their hands.

For many of the elves, it was the first time they had seen the face of a Reaper. All they had seen until now, was their blood-red eyes but with their hoods down, they could see their grotesque mouths, three times the size of a normal elf, jagged teeth bloodied, riddled with shredded flesh. Some gagged, others retched, unable to forget the tortured bodies of their people, eaten alive and impaled in the trees. It had surely been these Reapers who had slaughtered them.

As the wind buffeted them, the armies continued to fight, even as their eyes watched the forest warily. From somewhere behind Bulan, an elf shouted.

"The trees. The *trees!*"

Bulan glanced over his shoulder, saw the boughs snapping to and fro, heard his lieutenant shouting over the growing din.

"Stay away from the trees! Sound the Ashorns!"

A chorus of Silvan horns came together, an order not to retreat into the trees. Some were confused, close to panic while others knew exactly what this meant. Their people had surely been freed from the cages.

The Warlord had conjured the trees.

There were cheers from those who had seen this before, upon the slopes of Tar'eastór and in the Evergreen Wood of Ea Uaré. Minds bolstered, exhaustion gave way to the last dregs of determined stamina and with all they had left, the Silvans roared and yelled as Bulan brandished his spear above his head and screamed into the sun-drenched sky.

"Kill them all!"

~

FROM BEHIND THE front line of Sand Lords and Deviants, Key'hán stood watching the distant forest. Whatever was happening inside the trees, it was time to put an end to this battle in the sands. He would kill the Silvan and Ari commanders with his own hands and then he would march to Abiren'á, help his brother to secure their new home if he had not already done so.

But above all, he would find and kill the mage who had awoken the trees. He didn't want to think about how he had been able to do that. Key'hán had seen the weakness of the elves, had been sure they would not have forsaken the hostages as any brave Sand Lord would have.

For the first time, Key'hán contemplated the possibility that Abiren'á may have fallen.

All the more reason to end this quickly, and then make haste to the city.

It was time to conjure the Mother.

IT WAS Idernon and Galdith who led the others through the trees. Behind them, less than a thousand warriors followed.

Around them, the forest was moving, but this was nothing compared to the devastation that was raging through Abiren'á behind them.

Idernon found it disquieting without Fel'annár, especially when the branches creaked and groaned, as if a weight lay on them, ready to snap them clean in two. It almost took his mind off what he had had to do, what he had sworn never to do.

Leave Fel'annár behind.

Galdith stumbled, something Idernon had rarely seen him do in this forest he knew better than any other in The Company. The loss of Galadan weighed heavily on them all but especially on the veteran Silvan. They had shared a special relationship. Fierce Warrior and Fire Warrior, they had been so different – so similar.

The tense branches snapped and then moved, slowly at first, wood bending before them, slowing their pace. They swooped down, brushed against them, warning hands holding them back. It seemed worse up ahead and they moved carefully, stealthily, hands out, brushing against the restraining boughs.

Bodies began to appear. Underfoot and under tree.

In the trees.

Sand Lords lay dead everywhere they looked. They hung from the boughs, clothes in shreds, limbs all but severed. It was reminiscent of the Gruesome Path they had traversed on their way to Skyrock. Some were still alive, moaned and whimpered in their last, terrible moments but still the trees moved around them, like taunting spirits come to avenge the dead.

Behind him, Idernon could hear Carodel shouting to the troops further behind to slow their pace. These were the Sand Lords who had managed to escape the maelstrom in Abiren'á, only to walk into the avenging arms of these trees. There were far more than Idernon had anticipated, and he wondered whether some of them had come from the sands, meaning to join the battle in Abiren'á. If that were the case, it did not bode well for their army in the desert.

He prayed they were not too late, that they could still help Bulan, stop the enemy from pressing into the forest.

Leaves fell around the Divine Servants, as if to douse the wrath the forest had just loosed on Abiren'á.

The ground around them was littered with branches and twigs, split and mangled chunks of wood the size of sea-faring ships. But above all, there were fallen weapons and bodies.

The dead lay in heaps, serpent creatures twisted grotesquely, curled in on themselves. There were dead Silvans and Alpines, some of them mutilated by the Reapers, half-eaten by the serpents, or killed by their own brothers.

But his heart bid him move on.

He tried, but he was spent, swayed where he stood. He was empty, depleted of his last stores of energy; no Dohai. His knees wavered, eyes burning, skin overly sensitive and a throbbing ache pulsed at his temples and wrists. Every cut and bruise screamed its presence.

But his mind begged him to step forward.

Not far away, at a safe distance from the Ber'anor, Tensári and Lainon stood watching him, waiting for a sign that it was over, that they should follow the others north.

But it was not over.

Fel'annár reached out, placed his hand upon the bark one more time, careful and soft.

Don't let them in. Protect our people, even in death.

His hand slipped heavily away, and he walked slowly, towards the dead Nim'uán who had taken the life of Galadan and Pan'assár. He looked down on it, on the surprised and pained expression. But it wasn't enough. He wanted to *see* its torture, its terror.

Something caught his eye beneath the bloodied armour and clothing. He crouched, reached out with a shaking hand and pulled it out. He stared down with overly bright eyes at the blood-splattered portrait of a Silvan woman. He stuffed it under his own armour and spared one, last look at the monster who had taken Pan'assár and Galadan's lives.

It didn't deserve peace.

His gaze drifted to the fatal wound at its neck, where Pan'assár had stabbed it. There, still embedded in the cool flesh, was the killing weapon. He shook his head as he pulled it out and brought it before his tired, stinging eyes.

Galadan's herb knife.

His eyes filled with grief and ire, until he trembled with it. So angry. So *bitter* ...

He stood, hand flying to the sword in his harness upon his back and with one, perfect swipe, he severed the head of the beast and again he looked down.

But nothing had changed.

It hadn't suffered enough. He wanted to make it scream and beg for mercy, plead for forgiveness for the atrocities it had committed.

But it was dead.

Tears of grief and anger spilled down his filthy face and he bent down, grabbed at the silky dark locks of the Nim'uán head. Macabre trophy in hand, he walked toward the tree where he knew the bodies of his friends lay and behind, with careful steps and sealed lips, the two Ber'ator followed.

Fel'annár threw the head on the floor, a distance away from the fallen, and then made for where Pan'assár lay next to Galadan at the base of a tree. He knelt at the commander's side.

He stared at the half-closed eyes, half-open mouth. He told himself it was not the face of a dead warrior, a fallen commander. It was the face of *bravery*. Fel'annár knew what he had done, had seen it all, could have stopped it, but then he would have sacrificed that last cage of civilians, would have delayed the maelstrom and many more of their warriors would have perished.

There may come a time when you must think of the greater good.

Gor'sadén's words had stopped him from running to Pan'assár and Galadan's aid. The Fire warrior had perished protecting his commander, and Pan'assár had seen no other way to stop the Nim'uán than to sacrifice himself. He had made his last charge with nothing but a herb knife in his hands, so that the last of the hostages could be freed. So that Fel'annár could regain Abiren'á.

Another Kah Warrior gone but by the Gods Fel'annár would proclaim him a hero, would claim him Saviour of Abiren'á. He placed a hand on the cold forehead, bit his bottom lip.

I will see you again.

But where was Gor'sadén?

Fel'annár had seen him kneeling over Pan'assár. His eyes raked over the ground, but his father's body was nowhere to be seen. He had to believe that he was still alive.

He rose slowly, painfully and then sunk down on the other side where Galadan lay. He stared dumbly at the pallid face of the Fire Warrior, the flames in those blue eyes now gone and memories flooded his mind.

He remembered Galadan's silent support on that fated first journey to Tar'eastór.

Be safe, my Prince.

He remembered his years of wisdom, his subtle guidance. He remembered the times they had fought and survived the day and he would always remember this one, when one of them had not. Galadan had taken the Short Road, just as he knew he too must, one day, just as Lainon had.

An Ari'atór crouched beside him and Fel'annár turned to look at his first Ber'ator. He had sat like this when Lainon had died in the mountains. A dark hand came to rest on his shoulder, squeezed softly but still, the Ber'ator – the Shirán – did not change back into his bird form.

Fel'annár turned back to the body of Galadan. He would take him with him in his mind, keep his memory close and one day, they would all be together, across the Veil.

He breathed, long and noisy, and then touched the bark of the tree under which his dead friends lay. He closed his still glowing eyes and for a while, he stayed there, poured his wounded heart into his plea. There was no telling what was happening in the desert, whether Bulan was holding the front. But whatever the outcome of this battle, he would keep these bodies safe.

As he stood, a root emerged from the ground. And then another, and another. They danced as they weaved together, around the bodies of the fallen. Fireflies joined the guardian roots and Fel'annár knew they would be safe, until he could return and send their bodies away, into Aria's merciful embrace.

While Lainon watched the beauty of it, Tensári's eyes were fixed on Fel'annár's clenched fist at his side. Light shimmered beneath his skin, and the longer she looked, she realised it was not random. She thought she could see runes, but then Fel'annár stood, turned to her and Lainon, and bowed his thanks. They returned it but still, they did not speak, and Fel'annár seemed grateful for that.

With no more hostages in the trees, Fel'annár was free to command the forest, free to fight as his nature allowed him to. But he had used all his strength, surely had nothing left to give.

He breathed in, looked up into the wood-strewn heavens of Abiren'á, to the broken branches that still fell from the gently swaying trees. He turned, walked back to where he had dropped the Nim'uán's severed head. He reached for it, tied it to his belt by the hair.

It was time to join The Company, find out what had happened, whether the battle still raged or whether it was over. But one way or the other, the enemy would not enter this forest.

The Sisters await you, Lord.

He opened his eyes, felt that strangeness inside him again, some new level of energy growing, expanding. The soles of his feet were burning, his hands tingling, skin crawling, not with cold needles but hot pokers.

Looking north, anger and grief steeled his nerve, strength slowly renewing, surging into him from the ground, from the air around him. His wandering mind narrowed into a thin, pulsing line, vivid and red. The path north and to the Xeric Wood would open before him and then he would face whatever was there. He would send it to the pits of torment and despair. Smash them down, strike fear in their unnatural hearts. He would show them that Ea Uaré was for the elves, for any who came in peace. And he would show them what fate awaited those who thought to take it for themselves. He would show them the consequences of killing a member of The Company. Make them understand that the forest was him and he the forest.

He turned to Lainon and Tensári.

"Prepare to *fly*."

Tensári turned to Lainon, knew that he too had seen it. Where just minutes before, Fel'annár had been utterly depleted of strength, now, he pulsed with something new. It wasn't the energy from the Dohai. This energy she could see.

It was not his own.

The strange lights were back, dancing and writhing beneath his skin, still nothing but a hint of script. He was changing, into something she had never seen before. Beyond the bright eyes that would soon flare and almost blind them. Beyond the maelstrom that would twist around him, there was something in his very body - under it. Beneath pale skin, lines were forming, emerging. Patterns from books of myth, symbols of power and magic and even as his face was changing, his flesh seemed almost translucent.

Prepare to fly, he had said, and when the first vines took hold of her, she didn't scream, and she kept her eyes on Lainon. He would always catch her if she fell.

But she knew that she wouldn't.

～

As THE FURY of the trees died down, Idernon, Gor'sadén and The Company sprinted towards the border, no longer hampered by the branches.

Gor'sadén had caught up with them, had surely been sprinting while they had been forced to a slow and careful walk through the carnage and the angry trees. Once he had reached The Company, he would surely have overtaken them in his mad, frenzied dash towards the sands. But Idernon's forbidding hand had grabbed his shoulder hard and pulled him back.

He was not himself, stunned and unable to comprehend that his greatest friend had fallen. They needed to watch him, because there was a recklessness about him that would surely get him killed if they didn't.

Idernon thought he heard Dalú's characteristic voice from somewhere behind, and he had seen Eramor briefly too. Of the others, he had no idea, and Yerái was nowhere to be seen.

He turned to his right, caught Carodel's gaze and then gestured to

Gor'sadén with his head. Carodel seemed to understand. The Commander, as he was, was a danger to himself.

It was becoming lighter, the gaps between the trees wider and the sounds of battle beyond them louder. Idernon's heart lifted, because it wasn't over. They weren't too late.

There was still a chance.

Idernon pushed his legs harder until he was sprinting, past a marvel of nature that threatened to take his ragged breaths away. He felt tears on his face, for the majesty of the Sisters, for the beauty and mystery of these Silvan lands which moved him even now as they broke through the tree line and dry soil became sand. He turned meaningfully to Galdith at his side.

Galdith met his gaze, didn't care who was in command and he opened his mouth, held his sword aloft and screamed his battle charge as loud as he ever had. And after it, another, just as savage, just as broken and raw.

"For *Galadan!*"

"*For Pan'assár!*"

They erupted into the fray, the battling elves before them cheering as they passed.

But The Company and Gor'sadén did not stop until they were on the very front line of the battle. With all their strength and all their broken hearts, they beat down on the Sand Lords and Deviants with their swords and their axes. They crushed skulls and slit throats and the battling warriors around them saw their fury, the tears that leaked from glittering, wrathful eyes. They knew the strength of their blows, fruit of their grief over whatever had happened in the city. They had heard the charge, heard the names of those who had surely fallen.

A serpent reared just beside Ramien's foot but before it could shriek and twist, Idernon stabbed through the pincer, making sure he did not sever it. It fell but another was twisting towards him, kicking up sand as it advanced. Its tail arched over its head and then a spear sailed through it. It shrieked and Idernon followed the trajectory of the weapon, to Bulan who ran towards the body to retrieve his spear.

"Idernon!"

"Captain." He stumbled sideways and Bulan span round and then slashed the throat of a Sand Lord who had meant to skewer the Wise Warrior. Separated by the flow of elves and invaders, it was all they could do to breathe as they fought, let alone talk. Idernon had wanted to tell Bulan that Fel'annár was alive. Even now as his eyes registered the field, he could see anxious glances at the trees, see how the warriors searched and failed to find the Warlord. He was surely coming, to fight for the forest.

They needed him here.

Idernon's arms were moving, feet struggling to keep himself aloft. Blood splattered all around him, the thud and clank and screech of weapons and bodies, the gasps and moans and grunts of effort. In and amongst them lay the dead and the paralysed, the black spirits swooping down on the undead to feast in their frenzy for fresh meat, unable to wait for the danger to pass. They simply knelt beside their victims and gorged.

He saw Commander Hobin to his right, but there were no Deviants to be seen. He had prevailed but at what cost?

Idernon caught sight of Gor'sadén, not far off to his left. He was surrounded. His superior skill made him a priority objective for the Sand Lords, and how he fought, thought Idernon as he edged as close as he could to Carodel, Ramien and Galdith, who were fighting closer to the commander. They couldn't lose Gor'sadén too.

Some strange sound wailed in the distance and Idernon's head whipped to the back of the enemy line. Halfway up a mining tower, an overly large figure blew into a horn, the opening pointing downwards, toward the sand.

A rumble from below, and then the ground lurched and the sand beneath Idernon's boots vibrated, softly at first until it was more violent. Whatever it was, it was surging from underground, big enough to cause this tremor that was throwing their warriors onto the sands.

Idernon looked around, frantically searching for the source of the disturbance, until the rumble became a roar and he turned to the tree line behind him. A mountain of sand reared up before the Three Sisters, bulged skywards until the sands exploded and from the mushroom of particles, the biggest monster serpent they had ever seen towered over them.

It stood upon its pincered tail, tall and arrogant, as if to show them its full height and girth, as if it enjoyed the fear and terror its presence evoked.

Even the Sand Lords cowered, moved further back into the sands, while the Reapers wailed, grew bolder as they stepped further into the fray, towards their Mother. The lesser serpents stood tall, like adoring worshippers, indeed were they not a part of her? Born of her flesh?

Key'hán watched from atop his mining tower, horn still in his hands, eyes glittering with anticipation. The Mother would feed her brood, for she was one with them and they with her and the Reapers.

"Stand firm!" yelled Bulan. "Reform the line! Ari'atór to the fore, Benat, Eramor, Dalú to the rear. We fight on two fronts!"

Gor'sadén watched Bulan, agreed with his commands, reluctantly admired the Sand Lords' strategy. The beast was cutting off the only retreat the elves had.

They couldn't win this battle, not unless the monster serpent was brought down.

Gor'sadén turned, and moved back towards the forest, where the Sisters stood tall and unmoving, and before them, the slowly twisting and screeching beast.

Bulan was yelling at his half of the remaining army to stand its ground, but they stepped backwards, again and again, for how could such a beast be brought down? It stood at least ten times the height of an elf.

But that wouldn't stop Gor'sadén, even though its head stood as high as the Doorway to the Sands, half way up Bulora.

He could hear Idernon from somewhere behind him, shouting at him to come back, and then Ramien, Carodel and Galdith joined him. But Gor'sadén continued towards the beast, feet steady over the sands. Some would call him reckless, others valiant, but his brothers were waiting for him on the Short Road, and if Gor'sadén fell, The Company would see Fel'annár through.

He lifted his Synth Blade, brought it before his face as he stepped before the Mother.

"*Gor'sadén!*" A desperate cry from behind, just as the serpent leaned forwards and opened its fang-filled mouth and shrieked. The warriors covered their ears, took another step backwards.

"Hold your ground!" He thought it must have been Bulan, but there was nothing *he* could do to take the beast down, nothing anyone could do, except one thing. And that was what Gor'sadén would do. He would sacrifice himself, as Pan'assár had done, for the greater good.

The serpent lowered its head further, jowls open wide, and then its tail sailed forwards, over the head and stabbed into the ground, sending sand high into the air, like angry waves in a storm, and with every stab the ground shook around them. The warriors were barely able to keep their footing but still, Gor'sadén did not retreat and Bulan could do nothing but stare at him, at the monster, and then at the Sand Lords who were advancing slowly from the desert, despite their commanders' orders to charge. They were terrified too, and soon, the Reapers and their serpents had taken the lead, eager to move in and feed once the stinging began.

The Mother turned, hissed at the group of warriors behind Gor'sadén who had taken up pikes. Its pincered tail stabbed into the sands, and warriors fell into the crater it left behind. The tail swiped sideways, and more warriors sailed through the air, screaming and bracing for a painful, if not fatal impact.

He could wait no longer, and Gor'sadén was striding, then running towards the Mother.

The snake turned back to him, opened its jowls wide and screeched, foetid breath sweeping Gor'sadén's hair away from his face, but this Kah Master was nimble, stood on the balls of his feet and watched it begin to turn and turn until it was a whirlwind and it moved towards him. He brought the Synth Blade out before him, saw Pan'assár's stony face in his mind.

Time to dance ...

Blade overhead, his depleted strength renewed, he darted forward and skirted the twisting beast, watched the pincer carefully. It towered over him, the scales on its body like armour, overlapping, difficult to get under.

But he would, with his blade and the sheer ire that fuelled his muscles and dulled his grief, dampened his sense of peril.

It was coming towards him, tail rearing and then whipping over its head, again and again, smashing into the sand to his left, then right, kicking up clouds that obscured his vision. Gor'sadén dodged its strikes, and then caught sight of flesh between scales. He would need to be quick.

He lunged but the beast moved, and his sword skittered over nail-like plates. Gor'sadén stumbled away but didn't fall.

The serpent changed direction, and Gor'sadén followed, eyes once more on the opening between scales. Just enough time to turn and slice through them. The monster shrieked, and the warriors cheered.

The Mother lowered her head, orange eyes close to Gor'sadén, as if she would inspect her prey before she paralysed him, curious perhaps at the reckless, fearless warrior who dared confront her. Gor'sadén was mesmerised by her savage eyes.

So very beautiful.

"Move! *Move!*" Someone was screaming at him – Bulan again – he thought as he lifted the Synth Blade over his head, swivelled it in his expert hands, watched the eyes, for the slightest hint of movement. As the beast opened its mouth to shriek at him, he saw his chance.

"I'm coming brother," he muttered under his breath. With a mighty lunge forward, he threw himself at the mouth full of sharp teeth and thrust his blade upwards, aiming for the roof of its mouth. If he could pierce the soft palate, reach its brain ... the tip of his sword almost reached its intended target, but the serpent jerked back too quickly.

He fell, and then he was soaring through the air. He heard screams and yells from afar. Moments later, he was hovering over the desert, trapped in the mouth of a giant serpent.

Time to die.

All it needed to do was snap its jaws closed and break him in two. He braced for death, felt sharp teeth around him, penetrating the metal and then leather of his armour.

From somewhere behind him, he heard a blast of trumpets, like a fanfare to a conquering king, and then the shouts and screams he had heard before suddenly stopped. Even the Mother serpent seemed to hesitate.

He brought his sword arm round, jabbed upwards, desperate to relieve the growing pressure around his middle. It was suddenly gone but he was slipping through teeth, falling out of its mouth and heading for the ground far, far below. His free hand grappled to hang on, found a jagged tooth, clung to it as best he could. Pain tore through his hand; he couldn't hold on for much longer.

The blast of trumpets sounded once more, and the serpent stilled. His arm was burning, shaking with the effort to hold his own weight aloft. Small mercy that the Mother was distracted, oblivious to his desperate fight to stay aloft.

But what had distracted her?

Below him, sand began to rise, like spray from a storm wave it engulfed him, swirled around the monster serpent. He could hardly see, but there was no mistaking a second serpent that streaked past him, taller than the one he hung onto and almost as thick.

But it wasn't a serpent. It was a *root*.

His eyes bulged wide and he looked down. From the churning red haze, more roots were rising, twisting around the serpent, meshing together, like some giant sea creature enveloping a ship.

The serpent screeched and screamed, tried to twist but the roots were closing in. It thrashed this way and that, desperate to escape the deadly embrace but the roots were all around it, growing taller and taller, impervious to its sting.

His grip was slipping, blood dripping down his hand. He yelled through the agony, squeezed his eyes shut and opened them, surely for the last time. His final vision was of a figure, balanced upon one of the rising roots, surging past him and over the head of the thrashing, writhing snake.

Gor'sadén's bloody hand slipped from the jagged tooth and he was falling, through haze, past rising roots. He closed his eyes on the world, sent a farewell to his king and his son.

Something curled around his middle and his free fall slowed. He was floating upon red clouds, through a storm of roots as they battled the monster serpent.

His boots touched the ground, roots uncurled from around his waist and then shot skywards, back to the battle above him. His knees buckled, he felt hands under his arms, pulling him away from the fury of the beast and the ever-rising roots that were cocooning it.

As he was dragged backwards, he looked up, blinking desperately to clear his vision. There, at the very top of the column of roots and scaly flesh, stood Fel'annár, his spear in both hands, high over his head. The monster tried to twist itself free, but the roots of the Sisters were too strong. Green, blue and purple lights danced around Harvest, lent some preternatural strength to Fel'annár's hand as he brought it down. It sunk through scales, into its brain and the beast screeched, so loud his ears rang.

In its death throes, the serpent reared its head, and Fel'annár disappeared from sight, into the clouds of red dust that billowed into the air, coming closer to the warriors, like a storm swell, and Gor'sadén could no longer see.

He grappled to his feet, staggered sideways and ran with the rest of The Company, the only ones who had dared to come this close. He looked over his shoulder but all he could see was a wall of sand coming towards him. They ran until they fell, and they covered their heads, felt sand raining down on their backs.

GOR'SADÉN COUGHED, turned where he lay, shook his head, saw Ramien stir beside him. Galdith stood, held a hand down to him. Gor'sadén looked at it, took it with his uninjured hand and pulled himself painfully to his feet. The Synth Blade lay in the sand, glinted under the desert sun. He reached for it, watched as the rest of The Company stood, how they stared at him and then turned to the monster serpent, lying prone in the sands, a mountain of dead flesh.

But the roots were nowhere to be seen, and neither was Fel'annár.

They turned with the first wails and laments from behind. All around them, the lesser serpents exploded from the ground, but they didn't attack. They just stood upon their pincered tails, utterly still, like hides drying in the sun. The Mother had perished, and they could not survive without her.

"Strike them down!" screamed Bulan, spear aloft, and Benat and then Eramor echoed it further afield. The remaining warriors ran towards the confused serpents and stabbed into them, watching as the stunned serpents fell, one after the other. The wails of their other selves were almost deafening as the black-clad Reapers sunk to the ground in a heap of black cloth.

They were dead.

Gor'sadén felt a hand on his bracer and he turned to Idernon. But the Wise warrior was not looking at him but at where the Mother had fallen. Galdith followed his line of sight, and in turn reached out to Ramien, who shook Carodel and soon, they were facing the still hazy tree line behind the dead serpent.

From further afield, Hobin watched Bulan's warriors, knew why they were facing away from the Nim'uán and his remaining army. They were searching for Fel'annár.

"Ari'atór!" yelled Hobin, sword in hand, gesturing for his remaining warriors to follow, closer to the tree line and the Silvan commanders. They needed to regroup and brace for the ire and desperation of the Sand Lords who had surely thought themselves invincible with this horde of unnatural beasts, with the monster serpent they had thought could not be vanquished.

He would wait and pray for a sign that Fel'annár was alive, but if he wasn't, he would wait for Bulan to rally them all together, jolt them out of the shock of what had just happened, before the Nim'uán gained the upper hand once more.

Bulan and Dalú had similar thoughts and even now, they could see the Sand Lords stirring in the near distance. But Bulan understood all too clearly what had just happened. Fel'annár had killed the monster with the help of the giant roots of the Sisters, and in doing so, had surely lost his own, young life when he had fallen from the beast, surely crushed under its weight.

He caught Dalú's saddened eyes, turned away from him, avoided Eramor and Benat.

~

KEY'HÁN STOOD incredulous before his mining tower, eyes searching the haze that had still to settle in the distance.

His most powerful ally had fallen. The Mother had been vanquished by a mage. It had to be the Silver One, the most powerful of them all, the one who had murdered his brother. The one they had tried to protect themselves from. No other could have conjured the roots, and he had seen the unnatural lights over the Mother. With her gone, so were her children and their Reapers. Their entire clan had been exterminated.

Still, the mage must have died when the Mother fell. Not even he could withstand a fall such as that one. Perhaps it had been worth it, he mused. The sacrifice of the Mother, in exchange for the death of the Silver One.

He turned to his remaining chieftains, called out his orders. He straightened his spear in his harness, gripped his long sword in one hand, drew his short sword in the other. It was time to finish this battle, join Saz'nár in Abiren'á and then continue with the second part of their plan.

March south, first, to Ea Nanú in search of family. And then further still, where the elf king resided, to the city they had come to conquer.

37

THE THREE SISTERS

～

No sooner forest loam turned to rock beneath their feet, Yerái, Koldur and Jonar threw themselves to the ground, breathless and exhausted from their wild flight out of the killing forest and here, to the outskirts of Skyrock.

The leader of Abiren'á, the head forester and Lieutenant Yerái straightened their crooked forms and turned disbelieving eyes on the Silvan city below – still rocking, thrashing, trumpeting and screeching.

Behind them, the remaining two hundred civilians who had shared their captivity, the horrors they had been forced to watch. They too, all but collapsed, gasping for breath.

"I don't understand," gasped Koldur, grimace on his face, head shaking from side to side."

"Our trees ..." Jonar, the forester, voice breaking in both terror and wonder, eyes full of tears. The very trees they lived amongst, the giants they knew so well, had moved and killed with a ferocity they could never have imagined.

Yerái looked around him, to the remaining twelve warriors from the fifty he had been assigned. "Lord Koldur. There have to be more of us somewhere out here. Those who were freed before the battle ... they may have taken refuge nearby."

"Or they are making to Lan Taria, perhaps even Sen'oléi," said Koldur.

Yerái could hear crying behind them. The sounds of desperation, of pity and terror. Many civilians had died as they had tried to run from the glade, through the battling warriors. But some had been caught by the Reapers, others killed by the Sand Lords.

"Do you think our warriors made it out of there?" asked Jonar of Yerái.

The Listener breathed deeply, reached out, felt a power so great he swayed to one side, held a hand out to steady himself.

"Most would have, yes. Pan'assár and Fel'annár knew what would happen, had warned them to run once the maelstrom began. Still, the power that was unleashed in Abiren'á endures. Whatever is happening, it's not over. What is left of our army is surely making for the northern borders where Bulan fights the Sand Lords."

The leader, the forester and the warrior turned back to the Silvan city that still swayed and yawed, caught in an invisible tornado surely none could survive.

"Abiren'á is destroyed," whispered Jonar.

Koldur's head whipped to his forester, angry, defiant eyes waiting for him to meet his gaze.

"*Never*. Abiren'á will never be destroyed. I will not *allow* it! I will wait for the trees to still and by my Silvan blood I will march back in there and I will rebuild it with my own *hands!*"

Koldur was shaking, his resolve unbreakable and Yerái felt renewed fire in his veins.

"And I will help you. Whatever happens in the sands now, we must hold to hope that our warriors will prevail. And when they do, they will return to Abiren'á."

"And we will be waiting for them, with any who will follow us."

Koldur, Yerái and Jonar turned to the civilians behind them, found them standing, staring back at them and in their eyes, anger, grief, and perhaps guilt.

They had faced terrible things, horror beyond imagining. But they also knew it had been their choice. They had chosen to stay, even when they had been warned to flee, and their army had rescued them at great cost.

But whether or not it had been the *right* choice, they would follow, go back and rebuild what had been destroyed. And they would wait for their army to return, thank them for their selfless sacrifice.

Grief and anger turned to conviction and determination.

Abiren'á would rise from the ruins, be great once more.

BULAN FELT a strong hand wrap around his forearm. He turned, started when he found Hobin's painted face just inches from his own. The Supreme Commander gestured to where the serpent had fallen and together, they watched.

Only then did Bulan register the quietness around them, here on a field of battle. There should have been screams and yells, shouts of victory and cries of pain. But there were no clanging swords, no arrows whizzing overhead.

Nothing.

From the haze that still lingered around the dead beast, the outline of a figure emerged, rising from a low crouch. Across his back, a mighty spear and as the silhouette slowly stood, a long blade glinted blue.

Distant thunder boomed over the forest, loud enough to rattle their bones, and the alarmed warriors looked to the skies.

No clouds. Not thunder.

Bulan's heart was hammering in his chest as he watched the misty figure approach, daren't believe it might be Fel'annár.

A crack, a bang, as if lightening had struck beside them and the ground beneath their feet was moving once more.

"Hold steady! Don't run!" called Idernon, even as his eyes were pinned on the figure that approached. Further afield, the Sand Lords were shouting, holding their hands up to the clear skies. Foreign commands, surely to hold their ground. They were frightened but then again, so was Bulan.

Closer now, and it was not one but three figures who emerged from the clouds of sand. Black wings open, a Ber'ator on either side of their Ber'anor. The Warlord was alive.

Fel'annár was not dead.

When at last he stood before them, the elves did not cheer or hail him. Instead, they stepped backwards, held their arms out before them as if to protect themselves from him. Shouts of fear, and Dalú's voice rose over the mounting panic.

"Do not fear the Warlord. He fights for us! Wait for his command!"

But how could they not fear him? Many had seen the power he had unleashed in Abiren'á. They had seen their trees killing the enemy, tearing them to pieces at the Warlord's behest. They had seen him ride upon the roots of the Sisters and strike down a monster serpent – live to tell the tale.

Their warriors were terrified and disorientated. Their forest was swaying in the distance and the Warlord was surely not an elf but an avenging God, come to seek retribution for the atrocities the Sand Lords and their Reapers had committed against their people

Bulan stared incredulously at his nephew, thought him unrecognisable. But the Gods he could have cried for the relief that threatened to send him to his knees. He had thought him dead.

The ground rumbled, the deep unintelligible voices they had heard in Lan Taria echoing around them. The tree line creaked and groaned and the pressure in the air around them seemed to rise.

Fel'annár had once said he had felt something different, a power unlike that of the Evergreen Wood and the forests of Tar'eastór. Gor'sadén had believed him. And now, he could see it for himself.

There was light beneath his skin, his hands and face seemed painted with runes and geometric lines that scintillated below the surface. They appeared and disappeared, changing with every coming. It was like a book, he thought, being written before his eyes. Even before he was close enough for confirmation, he somehow knew it was Old Ararian, the language of the Book of Initiates.

Movement to Gor'sadén's right and he glanced that way, saw a group of Ari'atór sink to their knees but Fel'annár didn't look at them, didn't stop because his path was clear, and Gor'sadén and The Company stepped out of his way, and then followed behind him.

A voice pierced the air, over the battlefield, unnaturally loud and much lower than Fel'annár's natural tone of voice.

"Ea Uaré!"

A cold shiver ran down Gor'sadén's back, eyes impossibly wide.

"Warriors of Ea Uaré! Of flesh and wood!"

A boom echoed once, twice and the three Sisters seemed to lean forwards, like commanders at the front line of battle.

"The trees!" shouted a warrior.

"The Sisters are moving!" yelled another, but the Warlord was calling on them.

"Form the line before the trees, before the Sisters."

There was a moment of hesitation, nothing but a second, in which they realised that the Warlord was alive, that the giant serpent had been vanquished, the Reapers were dead, and the Sand Lords were no longer overrunning their position.

They had moved from impossible odds to a chance of victory, and a second later, the elves cheered, incredulous at first, weapons held aloft. And then they roared as they began to believe it *could* be done with the Warlord at their side once more.

They sprinted away, followed Bulan's cry to arms, and then Dalú's and Benat's, joy warring with the unbearable need for vengeance, for the Gruesome Path they had walked. For all those who had died at the hands of Reapers. For the violation of their Silvan city and the loss of Pan'assár and Galadan, protectors of Abiren'á.

"Form the line! We fight with the forest!" shouted the Warlord.

And then Dalú's scratchy voice, just as loud.

"The Sisters are with us!"

Another roar, blood all but boiling in their veins and they formed the lines, ten of them. With what was left of Hobin's contingent, Gor'sadén's best guess was two thousand warriors. He ran forwards, stood on the front line with Hobin and waited for The Company to regroup.

Just behind, the Warlord and his Ari'atór came, and at their passing, the warriors bowed, fear and respect in their eyes. Apprehension for what would happen now as they watched him make to the fore.

Bulan, Dalú, Benat and Eramor, Hobin and The Company stood, Gor'sadén beside them, weapons in hand. Above and behind them,

Bulora, Anora and Golora towered to the heavens, now a part of their ranks.

Anger and joy, wonder and trepidation. Determination and courage. This was Ea Uaré's final stand, one they would remember as the day they fought with the forest. The day the Sisters took up arms together with the people who loved them so much.

KEY'HÁN WATCHED them as he tightened his harnesses and walked towards the front line.

The Silver One was alive, damn him. And those he had sent into the forest to help Saz'nár in Abiren'á had not returned.

The Gods but Gra'dón had warned them and they had prepared. How had the elves freed those cages? Nothing could break those ropes – he had checked that himself. He had gone to Abiren'á, helped Saz'nár with the final preparations. He had used the sharpest scimitar, tried with an axe and a broad sword and not one fibre had broken.

And now the Mother was gone.

Still, even with her gone, with the Deviants gone, he realised it was now an even battlefield. So long as terror did not invade his warriors, they could still prevail. Superstition was the Sand Lords' one weakness, one the Nim'uán had used to maintain discipline in the ranks during their long journey here.

One warrior babbled words of horror, of devils in the trees and those around him murmured and nodded. Key'hán lifted his curved dagger, cut his throat as he passed. Those who had been listening shut their mouths and turned stiffly to the fore, for they feared their own commander as much as they did the mages and the winged harbinger.

And they were right to do so.

Key'hán swore he would spill the mage's blood, kill he who blocked his path to his chosen home. And with the mage dead, the trees would no longer stand in his way. All he had to do was stay away from the forest until then.

Prepare to die, Silver One. This forest is mine.

THE SILVAN WARLORD STOOD, pale skin covering some green fire that churned beneath, blazing symbols appearing and disappearing on his skin.

Supreme Commander Hobin was now close enough to read them, and when he did, he turned away, eyes wide, colourful blotches floating across his vision. He shook his head, turned back, read again. Passages from scriptures, from the Book of Initiates and other words he knew were not in that book, in any book that he was aware of.

Gor'sadén watched too, but his eyes travelled downwards, and to the gruesome head tied to his belt by the hair. The macabre rictus of pain and surprise upon that face was reflected on the enemy commander in the distance.

They had been wrong, realised Gor'sadén for the first time. There had been *two* Nim'uán, not one.

Identical twins.

The Warlord strode forwards, past the ranks of their remaining army, his almost black eyes set on the enemy before him. Gor'sadén wanted to reach out, pull him back but Fel'annár stopped within shouting distance of the beast. The commander closed his eyes in relief, only for his heart to drop into his boots.

Fel'annár took three running strides, drew his arm back, and flung Saz'nár's head straight at the remaining Nim'uán. It landed with a thud and rolled over until it was face up in the sands. Fel'annár watched for a sign, some glimmer of the suffering he felt, that he knew would be consuming Gor'sadén.

And then he saw it. Trembling face and clenched jaw. Glittering eyes and steely fists the Nim'uán bent down, took his brother's head in both hands and kissed its cold forehead, anointed it with a single tear. Fel'annár's smile was twisted and vicious, but Bulan turned away, disturbed at the sight.

Reverently, Key'hán passed Saz'nár's head to a Sand Lord beside him, and then turned to the Warlord, eyes dancing over the strange runes that appeared and disappeared beneath his skin.

He had never fought a demon before.

One hand rose, arm extended, finger pointing straight at Fel'annár. All remnants of grief and despair at his brother's passing were gone, and in their place, unadulterated, undiluted wrath.

"You!"

A single word, strange accent, it echoed around them, the promise of utter destruction almost tangible beneath its tone. Fel'annár raised his head, blazing eyes all but obscuring his own expression and still, the droning pulse behind them grew.

"You killed my brother. By the blood of my Silvan mother, I will crush you into the ground, elf. I will gut you alive and feed your entrails to the Reapers. I will slice your head from your shoulders and feed your eyes to them and then I will take this forest, enslave your people. I will kill your entire bloodline, stake their bodies upon the parapets of your forest palace and leave them there for *eternity*."

Those last words were more a shriek of rage. The Nim'uán trembled, fought to keep his control but it was a losing battle and Fel'annár watched, kept his eyes on the beast and then he spoke.

"When I kill your commander, Sand Lords. Run. Run away from here. My trees will never suffer your presence, and neither will I." Fel'annár took another step forward. The power in his chest was a heaving cauldron, pressing against his ribs, his heart. He felt none of his injuries, felt nothing at all as he allowed the power to take him, possess him. His mind was not entirely his own for he could feel the forest inside him. He could feel its outrage, its wrath, even its cruelty, just as he had in the Evergreen Wood only this time, it was inside him, not around him.

But so too could he feel the Sisters, the strength they lent him, their strange messages always there, beneath the droning. They were not Sentinels. They were something far more powerful.

They *were* Originals, and they were ready.

"I have killed your people. I have set the Northern cannibals upon them, enjoyed their suffering. I heard their screams, remember their begging, their last vision of this world the jagged teeth of a Reaper. Did you see them? We lined them up for you, as a welcome from your neighbours." Key'hán smiled at the hint of emotion he had wrenched from the daunting Warlord before him.

"And for that, you will pay."

Fel'annár backed away from the enemy together with The Company, Gor'sadén and Bulan, who had come to stand behind him. As they retreated, they heard the chieftains issue their final orders and before long, Fel'annár was back at the front line of his army, his captains awaiting their orders.

He turned to Gor'sadén, saw his bloodied hand, his ripped and damaged armour, knew that he had almost died.

"Pan'assár is gone, but will you stay for me?"

Gor'sadén's eyes flickered, surely hadn't expected Fel'annár to notice his lack of regard for his own life but he had, The Company had, and his eyes filled but did not brim over.

"If I can, I will stay – for you."

The illuminated Warlord smiled, turned away from him, and to The Company. Lainon looked like any other Ari'atór save for the extraordinary light in his eyes. His wings were gone for now and Fel'annár smiled as he looked from one to the other, painfully aware of the one who was missing.

"Galadan is with us. He is here," he thumped his heart. "And here," he tapped his temple. He turned away, raised his voice over the lines of warriors at his back.

"Ready Captain Dalú!"

"Ready!"

"Ready Captain Bulan!"

"Ready!"

The fire was back in their veins, the call for arrows surely imminent. One signal, a moment of shocked hesitation, because Fel'annár had not given that order. Instead, he called on them to armour the front lines.

What was he doing?

Bulan frowned, looked to his right, saw no movement from Dalú's flank.

Fel'annár signalled again. Shields and pikes. Archers in position. Do *not* fire.

They could see the fires flaring on the enemy line, knew exactly what they intended to do. The enemy meant to burn their forest. They needed to take down the enemy archers because here in the Xeric Wood, there was no defence against fire, none except rain and they stood under a cloudless sky. They didn't understand the Warlord's strategy, and the warriors' panicked eyes sought out Hobin, Bulan and Dalú. But their own confusion was plain to see, and they turned back to the fore, blind faith pushing them on.

Fel'annár knew what they would be thinking, but there was nothing he could do to reassure them. He could feel the Sisters, reading his strategy in his mind, forming their own. Whatever they intended, they didn't say, or rather wouldn't.

But he trusted them.

He raised his hands and signalled to his captains one last time, even as he watched the Sand Lords draw their flaming arrows.

"Stand firm at the tree line. Shields overhead. On my order."

Behind the Warlord, anxiety was growing, for this strategy made no sense. And yet Bulan, Hobin and Dalú were obeying those orders. They hoisted their painted shields skywards, desert sun glinting off them, a fleeting moment of relief from the sweltering sun.

The deep droning was back, an undertone at first but it grew louder, and the choir of voices was back, minor tones lifting, moaning and wailing while the droning became all but unbearable.

Key'hán watched, triumphant smile revealing pointed incisors. The fool mage had no defence against his fire archers. Nothing but a handful of wooden shields and a world of wood at their backs. He would torch them all, burn their flesh, their wood, raze it to the ground and step on the burned remains of those who would defy him.

"*Fire!*"

He watched with eyes that reflected the flames of hundreds of flaming arrows as they sang across the sands between armies, bright streaks of molten destruction arcing into the sky.

Fel'annár raised a hand, palm to the fore.

Stop.

An echoing boom sounded above and behind them, hot air slamming into their backs. The burning projectiles were thrown off course, away from the elves and back to those who had fired them.

Sand Lords screamed as they held their hands over their heads, fire raining down on them. Some ran, robes and hair in flames while others fell to the arrows of their fellow archers.

Ramien turned to Idernon. "What was that?"

Idernon answered, eyes still on the chaos on the front lines of the enemy. "Some sort of shock wave," he murmured.

Enemy commands were barely audible now as the chilling forest choir waxed and waned, a crackling, snapping noise overhead and the desert sun was blocked from sight. Fel'annár looked up, at the branches that were reaching out above them, meshing together like a wooden net, a sheltering sky under which all the elven races of Ea Uaré would fight, united against the Nim'uán and his Sand Lord army.

The Sisters were ready to fight.

"Swords!"

The warriors drew their blades, eyes on the darkening sky above them and the Warlord's sword, high over his head.

"*Charge!!!*"

The Company, Gor´sadén and Hobin sprinted after Fel'annár, while the captains screamed their own charge. The warriors held their blades before them as they ran, eyes on the three Sisters that were leaning over them, boughs reaching, branches like claws, like the talons of eagles searching for their prey.

The disorganised Sand Lords before them were still reforming the line but it was too late. The elves were upon them and the two armies clashed together.

Fel'annár, Gor'sadén and The Company cleaved into the front lines. The Synth Blade wreaked havoc on the enemy, while Bulan used his own sword. The fighting was too close to use spear. As for Lainon, his mere presence was enough to send the Sand Lords running in the opposite direction and so he stayed at Fel'annár and Tensári's shoulders, hovering above them and stabbing down at any who came too close.

Around them, branches smashed into the ground, skewered Sand Lords or swiped low over the sands, flinging them sideways and amongst them, the elves dodged them as they fought.

Fel'annár saw the Nim'uán retreat, further behind the enemy ranks where the trees could not reach. It was shouting something unintelligible, orders to his chieftains, he supposed. He couldn't let it escape, allow him to regroup his warriors further inside the desert where the trees could not reach.

Around him, the battle was raging, Sand Lords fighting the elves before them and the trees from above. Gor'sadén was always surrounded, a target for the Sand Lords who surely thought him a mage for the way he wielded his blade, each strike a killing blow.

Fel'annár glanced at Tensári, nodded, and then caught Idernon's gaze. He looked up, to the sun peeking through the boughs. With his decision made, he carved a path for himself, out from under the protection of the Sisters and towards where the Nim'uán had disappeared behind its army's ranks.

He fought those who stood in his way but with The Company's help at his back, he pushed forwards. After a while, only Tensári and Lainon remained with him.

A horn sounded somewhere off to his left, not an Ashorn but some Sand Lord contraption and a number of enemy warriors converged on the Ari'atór. He could hear them fighting behind him, but he had to keep going, find the Nim'uán before it escaped.

Beware the traps.

He stopped, eyes raking over the sand for any sign of a mechanism. He saw nothing but he slowed his pace, eyes searching the rear of the Sand Lord camp. It had been damaged by the shockwave from the Sisters. Half-destroyed wagons, mining towers and the construction materials they had been using lay strewn about the place, as if a storm had pulled it all up into the air and then released it from above.

He looked over his shoulder, saw Tensári and Lainon in the near distance and then The Company further away, still fighting under the boughs of the Sisters. He wondered if the Nim'uán had ordered its warriors to keep them from Fel'annár's side.

Danger.

From his left, a long plank of solid wood was hurtling towards him. He twisted away, just in time to avoid it crashing into him. He moved in the same direction, to where he now knew the Nim'uán had taken refuge.

Arms out, eyes everywhere. Another warning and then a wagon was careening towards him. He ran, dodged it and then staggered in the deepening sands. He fell to his knees, rose to his feet again and still, he could not see the Nim'uán.

Look up.

He did, only to see the Nim'uán flying towards him from atop a mining tower. Fel'annár barely dodged the oncoming blade but his foot slipped, and the two warriors crashed into each other. They rolled, grappled in the sand but it suddenly gave way beneath him and he was falling together with the Nim'uán.

He was choking on sand and then he slammed into the ground far below him.

"Fel'annár!" screamed Tensári as she battled and then killed a Sand Lord, but another came, and then another. Lainon stabbed down at an overly-large warrior and then spread his wings, ready to fly to where Fel'annár had disappeared.

But he couldn't. A Sand Lord had thrown a rope around him, pressing his wings to his sides. Angling one wrist upwards, he sliced through it, freed himself but no time to fly because another rope was hurtling towards him.

More Sand Lords were breaking away from the rear of the battle, sprinting towards them as rope after rope was thrown at Lainon. Tensári knew they were being targeted, so that they couldn't help Fel'annár.

As she fought, she yelled over the din of battle, louder than she ever had.

"*Company!*"

Idernon killed his opponent, whirled around to where the desperate cry had come from.

"Ramien, Carodel, Galdith. To Tensári!"

SAND IN HIS MOUTH, in his eyes, arms and legs flailing in it as it slowly settled around him. He looked around desperately, saw a halo of light.

He had fallen into a cave, flat on his back. It was a miracle he had not hit his head on the rocks that poked out of the ground, but his body hurt, in spite of the sand that had cushioned his fall.

Movement above him and he saw the Nim'uán, climbing down the rocky wall of the cave, long spear across its back. It must have known the cave was here, pushed him into the precarious sands while he had held on from above. It must have thought the fall would kill him but it hadn't. Fel'annár staggered to his feet, only for a sharp pain to lance up his leg, from the sole of his foot to his knee.

Damn it.

Sand still falling from his hair, his clothes, he reached for the buckles of his cloak and weapons harnesses, releasing them and then pulling out Harvest. This would be his first battle with it and he wondered at the Nim'uán's skill.

But there was no time. The Nim'uán jumped to the ground with a loud thud and was striding towards him. Fel'annár straightened himself as best he could, weapon out before him. He needed to get away from the back of the cave, angle himself around so that he had a chance of making it outside.

He took a step sideways, knee almost buckling but he remained aloft, tried and failed to ignore the pain.

"Pity you didn't break your neck in the fall. Now, it is just you and me."

Fel'annár watched, eyes gritty with sand as the Nim'uán circled him, spear horizontal before his face, guarding it.

"You can't beat a forest. Even if you kill me, you can never live in my domain. Do you think forests are peaceful?"

The Nim'uán lunged at him, spear shooting forwards, a probing strike that Fel'annár met with Harvest, and then staggered to one side.

The Nim'uán smiled at the show of weakness. "Not peaceful, no, not when you are near. But when I kill you, they will offer no resistance, will they?"

Key'hán launched another attack, faster and more powerful than the first. The arrowhead of his spear grazed past Fel'annár's temple as he dodged sideways, staggered backwards, slamming into the wall of red rock behind him.

"These are my lands too. I have a right to live in the trees. I am part Silvan you see."

Fel'annár's brow flickered.

"My mother was from Ea Nanú, but I never knew that place. I *will* though, when I have slaughtered you and staked your head before your pathetic army. I will find that place and make it my own."

"I will not allow it."

"You will be *dead!*" Key'hán struck an attack stance, stood ready to launch himself at Fel'annár once more.

With a testing flex of his leg, he didn't think the bone was broken, and he called on the Dohai, willed it to dull the pain so that he could fight. Warmth rushed into it, feeding the surrounding muscle and strengthening it.

"If your mother was Silvan, she would be ashamed of her son," taunted Fel'annár. "She would run from you, monster, unearthly beast. *Abomination*, she would call you." He remembered the portrait he had found on the body of this one's brother.

Ankelar.

He launched himself at the Nim'uán, Bulan's words in his mind.

Jab forwards, feign left, right, under sweep. Wait for your opponent to jump

...

And the Nim'uán did.

Fel'annár was behind it, arrow tip before him, he stabbed out. But the Nim'uán was quicker than he had given it credit for, and his spear was smacked to one side. He held onto it, danced sideways and out of the way of a counter strike.

It moved fast, spear almost impossible to follow, a blur before his eyes and then a lance of pain across his arm. He hissed, moved out of the way, felt the rush of air over him, jabbed upwards and twisted sideways.

The Nim'uán landed before him, excited smile on its face.

"You can't beat me, injured as you are, and there are no trees here. Just me and you, no harbingers to protect you now, mage."

Fel'annár inched sideways, towards the light and the desert beyond, could feel the sun on his face. Above him, he could hear the thud of boots, voices calling to him and the Nim'uán's head shot up.

Fel'annár swivelled Harvest in strong hands. He flipped it, held it behind his shoulder with one hand. With his other hand, he marked the position of his enemy.

Key'hán smiled, mimicked his movements and stepped forward side-on.

With one, sudden movement, Fel'annár whirled the spear over his head, feet swift as they turned his body full-circle and he was before the Nim'uán, the fabric of his undertunic still settling but not so his braids.

The beat of his heart, the wind in the distant trees. The soft patter of sand spilling underfoot and the rush of air into his lungs. No pain, nothing except for the opponent before him and the spear in his hands.

You must hear your heartbeat in battle.

And Fel'annár did. Steel flashed before him and he darted sideways, turned and slashed forwards. The Nim'uán ducked, faster than his bulk should ever allow. He was well-versed, nimble. This adversary was better than his brother in Abiren'á. Better than the other in Tar'eastór.

A pointed tip hurtled towards him. Spear in both hands, Fel'annár pushed it upwards and away, deflecting the fierce lunge. He brought the blade of his spear down, and the beast sidestepped, mimicked his move, testing skill, observing strength, just as Fel'annár was doing and all the while, his feet took him further and further to the entrance to the cave.

The Nim'uán's next move was as sudden as it was vicious and power-ful. His spear paddled forwards, tip on one end and then blade on the other, flashing in succession but where would the weapon fall?

Wait for the last possible moment to move ...

Fel'annár dodged to the left, slashed through leather at the Nim'uán's armoured waist. It turned, corrected its stance. Anger breaking through the mask of concentration.

Wood clacked, metal tips and blades clanged together, their spears a blur of movement. They were now outside the cave, knew there were elves and Sand Lords around but he daren't look and distract himself from the bubble he had created, so that he couldn't feel pain, so that he could use all his skill, the Dohai that was still inside him.

There was no clear winner in this fight, but the Nim'uán's step upon the sand was sure, better than his.

The enemy spear hurtled towards his knees – his weak spot - and Fel'annár jumped, and then ducked under it, but as fast as a lizard's tongue, the enemy spear was careening towards his legs once more.

He jumped over the oncoming blade and rolled in the sand. One leg anchored him, and he moved into a crouching position. He stood slowly, injured leg shaking, saw the satisfied smile on the Nim'uán's face, heard the collective gasp of warriors still upon the cave above them.

Just to his left, Fel'annár saw a small ridge of rock that protruded from the sand. He ran for it. Stepping on it, he jumped into the air, feet tucked under him, spear angling downwards, searching for the juncture between shoulder and neck. The Nim'uán deflected it and their strokes came fast and vicious.

Clack after clack, up, down and sideways. Feet kicking out, almost too fast to follow and then Fel'annár felt something strike his face. He swivelled away from his opponent, watched him from afar, ignoring the pain and then moved in once more. Spears swirled around each other and then locked, forcing their wielders' bodies together, faces just inches away. A cruel, twisted smile appeared on the Nim'uán's face, jowls opening wide, reaching towards the tender flesh at his neck. Memories of the terrible bite he had received from its brother flooded his mind. In that split second, he jerked to the side, deadly fangs grazing his skin. Projecting the Dohai, Fel'annár headbutted the Nim'uán, heard the satisfying crunch of bone, the howl of pain that followed.

The Nim'uán pushed away from him.

Fel'annár staggered backwards, heard shouts from above the cave, around it, but the Nim'uán was already careening towards him and their spears were in motion once more.

But that headbutt had thrown the Nim'uán off balance and Fel'annár saw an opening to his opponent's left. He jabbed forwards, felt his spear pierce armour, sink into flesh but the beast was twisting away even as it roared in pain, blood flowing freely from its shattered nose and side.

Key'hán backed away, scrambled to put distance between them, give himself time to stop the world from spinning around him. He swayed, crashed to one knee.

It was now, or never.

Fel'annár ran, and then he sprinted. He saw Galadan and his herb knife, he saw Pan'assár and his rare smile, saw their dead faces and breathless lips. He pulled his right arm back, spear behind him, hand holding it at the very centre of balance. Three running strides and he threw it with all his wrath and his grief, all his power behind it, landing in a deep crouch.

The black and gold wood sailed through the air, through the Nim'uán's chest, the tip smashing through its back and then into the sands. Key'hán was pinned backwards where he knelt, blood flowing like a river from the fatal wound.

Fel'annár approached the macabre spectacle, looked down upon the face of the beautiful monster.

"You have failed."

The Nim'uán smiled softly, blood trickling from one side of its mouth.

"Have I?"

Fel'annár stood over him, watched as the beast stared at the sun, bent backwards and spread-eagled, fading away yet even now, unwilling to admit defeat.

Fel'annár glanced to one side of the cave mouth where he knew Gor'sadén was standing, Synth Blade in his hands. He looked at the blade and then at the commander. Nodding, he stepped away from the brother of Pan'assár's nemesis, knowing that Gor'sadén knew his mind.

The commander strode forwards, stood over the gruesome sight of the impaled Nim'uán. He lifted his weapon, eyes full of unshed tears. His blade severed the head completely.

Fel'annár watched as Gor'sadén bent, took the head by the hair and held it up to the onlooking elves.

Silvans and Alpines shouted as one, and more came, looked over the ridge and downwards, at the headless beast that had thought to take their forests. They cheered again but they didn't smile. It was sheer satisfaction, vengeance, sweet and just.

Fel'annár grimaced, the last of the Dohai spent. He sat heavily on a rock and looked down at his hands, at his wrist that no longer burned. The scintillating runes were gone, even before he could understand their meaning. He felt light-headed, utterly drained, and every ache and pain in his body began to pulse and throb. His searching gaze landed on The Company, who were sliding down the sands to one side of the cave. They approached together with Tensári and Lainon, dishevelled and beaten but alive and on their own two feet.

Idernon's sharp gaze raked over Fel'annár, and then he turned to Ramien. He nodded towards the cave, and moments later, the Wall of Stone reappeared, Fel'annár's weapons harness and cloak in his hands. He held them out to the sitting Fel'annár, who garnered a lop-sided smile and then looked up, at what was left of his army, standing upon the ridge of rock above him.

He saw Bulan, his shock, tears heavy in his eyes, a myriad of strong emotions that had touched them all. The monster serpent, the charging Sisters, the magic of the Dohai, and the duel in the sands.

But there was relief and pride in Bulan's eyes too. Fel'annár still lived after a masterful display with the spear, with Harvest. With that trial, the Warlord had truly earned his Spear Master band. Bulan would see it done on their return.

"Hail the Warlord!" he shouted, and the warriors echoed it, again and again.

Something broke just then. The years of decline under the onslaught of Band'orán's indoctrination. The revelation of his treachery against Or'Talán and the Battle of Brothers. All the hatred and the frustration, all the shame and the regret rushed to the fore, no longer willing to be swallowed back or banished from their minds. Some invisible force pulled them together, stronger than anything they had ever felt.

They turned to each other, embraced whoever was closest. As for Fel'annár, he stood at the centre of his own circle of brother and sister-hood. The Company embraced and Galdith murmured.

"Galadan is here with us."

They shed tears of awe and grief, of pain and victory, stayed there for as long as their hearts bid them.

The promise of rest and comfort was calling, but first, they must clear the battlefield of the enemy, and send their warriors on their glorious way upon the Short Road. Later, they would light their own fires, speak of the war, of the inconceivable things they had seen, strive to understand them.

There were no shouts from the enemy. Their leaders had perished, all their dark allies gone. The Mother was dead, the Nim'uán commander was dead.

Those Sand Lords who had managed to back away from the distracted elves were now upon the sands, running away, to anywhere that was not this cursed forest and Fel'annár watched them until they were nothing but dust on the horizon.

38

WHISPERING SISTERS

∾

THARGODÉN STOOD at the very tip of the plateau that jutted out over the Evergreen Wood.

Robes billowed around him in the soft breeze, but he stood utterly still, watching as the trees swayed and thrashed, as boughs flexed and shifted, weaving into and then away from each other.

It was not just the Evergreen Wood, but the entire forest that had been doing this since yesterday. Some tilted sideways, yawed this way and that, like a strange dance, to a music others could not hear. But to Thargodén, it was drums and it was primal screams. It was wails and it was tribal war charges. It was all things earthly and Silvan, and he knew there was one who could hear it *all* – the same one who had surely instigated this atavistic ritual.

In his mind he heard whispers of war, whispers of grief and ire. He felt despair and he felt wrath. He felt wonder and shock.

He felt *magic*.

And then the earth tremors had come, and Rinon and Llyniel had been needed at the Inner Circle and the Halls of Healing. And so, their family dinner had been postponed.

His people were unsettled, many afraid of the moving forest, and come the morning, there had been a steady stream of Silvan refugees coming into the city from Sen'Garay and beyond.

Some believed it was a good sign, that the Warlord had activated the forest, was fighting for them, for their lands in the north. But others wondered if the enemy had overcome their army and was marching southwards, while the forest tried to stop them.

Whichever the case, there was no guarantee of safety, and so as one, they had taken the decision to shelter behind the closed gates of the king's stone realm.

Thargodén would visit the Merchant Guild later, see Amareth and make sure the refugees had everything they needed, and then later, if circumstances permitted, he would dine with his children.

Tonight would be the last he would spend with Rinon for a while. Tomorrow, his son would ride to Port Helia and bring back as many warriors as he could. Desperate times none of them had foreseen the day their army had marched north, and yet here they were, scratching at the base of the barrel, retreating into the city and sending urgent pleas for help to their allies.

They would soon be forced to close the gates and pray the army returned victorious. And when that time came, he would do so knowing that the Silvans had come to the city at last. There was no telling how long they may be forced to remain behind closed gates, prisoners in their own city.

Aria lend you speed, my sons.

~

As THE SUN set behind the trees on the western horizon, the boughs were bathed in red and orange, as if a mighty fire raged behind them. But it was a fire that warmed and soothed and for all the warriors wished only to throw themselves to the ground and stay there, there was work to be done.

They had won the war with Sand Lords and Deviants. The Nim'uán had been brought down in battle and their lands were safe, after years of incursions and then finally, invasion.

But the cost had been great. Of the more than four thousand seven hundred who had congregated at Skyrock, less than two thousand remained. Their people had been slaughtered by the Reapers, caged and hung from the heights. They had seen things they would never forget, things that would forever linger in their minds when darkness fell, and the world waxed silent.

Fel'annár limped away from the cave together with The Company and Gor'sadén. Behind him now, the corpse of the Nim'uán, bent over backwards in the sand. Harvest was no longer pinning it down but safe in Ramien's hands.

Fel'annár wished he could just sit and breathe, calm his aching body and quieten the questions in his mind, but he was content that at least The Company remained silent. He needed to think, process everything that had happened.

He cast his gaze over the battlefield, saw Dalú and Bulan as they made their way to him. From the opposite direction, Benat, Eramor and Hobin. They came together, expectant eyes watching, waiting for Fel'annár to issue his orders.

Pan'assár was dead. *He* was in charge now.

He felt weak. His skin was no longer translucent, and the lights beneath had dissipated. Fel'annár wondered how much longer he could hold himself aloft. He had used up all his strength in Abiren'á, and then the Sisters had restored it before the battle on the sands. But now that it was over, that preternatural strength had waned. They were still inside him, but the power that had fuelled him had gone.

Rest, Lord.

He looked at his captains, at the commanders. Some were limping, like him. They were bloodied, exhausted, shocked at the things they had all seen. But it was too recent, too incredible for questions. They would surely come later, but for now, he knew his priorities.

"Are you all well enough for command?"

"We are, sir. Nothing that can't wait for later," said Bulan. "Benat has cracked his wrist, Eramor here, took an arrow through his upper arm." But there was no mention of Bulan's own evident injuries, of Dalú's crooked gait.

"We lost Amon in Abiren'á."

Fel'annár nodded at Benat, had already guessed.

"And you, Warlord?" Bulan looked at his obviously exhausted nephew, searching gaze landing on Fel'annár's injured arm, blood dripping from under his sleeve. He frowned, and then his eyes drifted to the bleeding cuts at his neck.

Fel'annár's hand shot up, felt the shallow lacerations where the Nim'uán had tried and failed to bite him. He looked at his now bloodied hand.

"Nothing that can't wait, Captain. How far to the nearest water source?"

"Abiren'á," said Dalú. "But in the growing dark, injured as we all are and with our path strewn with bodies, it's not wise to risk it. I could organise a ..."

"Wait," said Idernon. "We have water, right here." He pointed to the mining towers the Sand Lords had erected some distance into the sands.

"Are they even working?" asked Dalú.

"I can find out. If I can be spared a number of warriors, I can try to make them work."

Fel'annár nodded. "Excellent thinking. Bulan, take Idernon as your lieutenant, see to our water supply and organise the wounded. We'll make camp here at the treeline tonight. Benat, scour the enemy camp, find whatever we may use. Materials for stretchers, food, anything. Eramor, gather our dead, prepare them for their journey. Dalú, gather the enemy carcasses, you know what to do. We must also gather weapons and light fires, forage for food if none can be found in the enemy camp."

The captains saluted, and Idernon turned to Fel'annár. "I'll send a few buckets of water your way," he said, knowing eyes lingering on the bleeding wounds at his neck. He was soon gone together with Carodel and Ramien, and Galdith placed a hand on Fel'annár's shoulder.

"We all saw what happened during the fight. The Nim'uán missed but not completely. You need to sit and take the antidote, or all your other injuries are not going to heal, especially that arm."

Fel'annár turned to Galdith's pale face, felt his own draining. "The Gods ..."

"What is it?" asked Galdith.

"I left it behind ... I ..."

"But you said Llyniel had given you a sachet. You packed it, I *saw* it."

"Skyrock ... I left it ..." The world flickered and turned grey. He swayed on his feet. Hands grabbed him, alarmed voices called out, but his vision was fading. The last thing he remembered was Tensári's voice.

"Find the Junar, Lainon. Fly, my love."

FEL'ANNÁR STIRRED, wondered if he was dreaming.

He was listening to the Sisters. He could hear the rumbling of their deep bass voices, hear their thoughts, their gentle whispers for him to awaken.

Awaken? Why was he asleep? What day was it? He tried to remember. And then reality slammed into him and his eyes flew open. He sat up too quickly, and pain shot through his body. The whole world spun around him, and he closed his eyes, felt a strong hand pressing on his chest, pushing him back down.

"Be still, Fel'annár. The battle is over. We won, in case you cannot remember. And you are a bit hurt." He thought he recognised that voice. Not a Silvan accent.

"Pengon?" He cracked his eyelids open, saw the Alpine lieutenant kneeling close by, and beside him, Galdith's relieved face. Just behind, Tensári and Lainon looked down on him, equally relieved.

Fel'annár had fond memories of Pengon. The Company had served under him in Tar'eastór when they had ventured into the mountains with Captain Comon.

"The very same. Glad you are awake, you were unconscious for a few hours though," said Pengon as he began to check on Fel'annár's wounds.

He was lying on a makeshift bed of leaves, next to one of the Sisters - Bulora, he thought. In fact, his hands were resting against a gigantic root. No wonder he had been hearing them in his dreamscape.

Peace.

"Ramien insisted on laying you here," explained Galdith, watching as Fel'annár moved his hands over the roots while he looked up at the Sister. "He carried you here himself, told us to remember the potted plant and the Sentinel back in Tar'eastór. We thought it the best place for you, given the circumstances."

Fel'annár smiled faintly. "Ramien knows best."

"Good, the bleeding seems to be finally stopping. The Junar is starting to do its work." Pengon nodded approvingly as he carefully re-wrapped the bandages.

"How did you get hold of the Junar? I thought I had left it at Skyrock..."

"You did," said Tensári.

Fel'annár's brows rose and he turned his head to the side, to Lainon who wore a rare smile, subtle though it was.

"I'll go tell the rest that you're awake." Galdith strode off and Fel'annár turned back to Pengon who was still hovering over him.

"Since when have you become a healer?" asked Fel'annár as he sat up slowly, wincing at the pain in this back, leaning against Bulora with a sigh of relief.

"After the battle of Tar'eastór, Arané saw just how important it was to have warriors who were trained as healers out in the field, as our Prince Sontúr was. He asked for volunteers to come forward to be trained, and I volunteered. About twenty others here did too. They have their work cut out, let me tell you."

Fel'annár recalled his sarcastic, witty brother from Tar'eastór who had come to Ea Uaré with him. Gods how he missed having Sontúr riding with the Company. He made a mental note that he too, needed to build a team of warrior-healers in his Forest Division. Sontúr could help to train them.

"How many Tar'eastór warriors survived the battle?"

The hands that fussed with his bandages did not waver. "About half of us. We count ourselves as lucky, having survived *two* battles with Nim'uán."

Galdith returned with the rest of the Company in tow, all sporting bandages in various places. The two commanders followed, and Gor'sadén looked especially relieved. Fel'annár knew why. He had just lost Pan'assár, had thought he might lose Fel'annár too.

The rest of the Company clapped him on the shoulders, and he hid the pain it caused; it was nothing in comparison to the realisation that they were all truly well, in body, at least.

"Your whole back is badly bruised, moving will be painful for the next few days. There's a deep cut on your arm that will need stitching, cuts on your neck and a multitude of bruises all over you. Your leg is not broken but sprained - I have wrapped your knee to give you additional support when you walk. And you are beyond exhausted. While you don't have any serious wounds, the cuts are many. Until the bleeding stops entirely, you will suffer bouts of light-headedness. Galdith here will help to give you another Junar dose tonight, and three times a day for the next two days. Lestari Llyniel was *very* specific with the instructions she left in those sachets." Pengon stood as Gor'sadén spoke.

"You have done well, Lieutenant Pengon. Thank you." Pengon saluted his commander general, then left to help the other injured warriors.

Fel'annár shifted his position so he could see the camp and post-battle activities better, absently stroking the root of Bulora next to him with one hand. The Company and commanders arranged themselves around him on the ground.

"Tell me what happened while I was ... away. It looks like Bulan and Dalú have everything well in hand."

Idernon nodded, and then began to explain.

He told Fel'annár how he had finally managed to put the mining towers into use. The water the Sand Lords had planned to channel into the desert was now a saving grace to this tired and decimated army. They could drink, flush wounds, wash blood from their faces and hands. Fel'annár would put the pumps to use so that the new northern outpost he planned to create would not have to depend on Abiren'á.

Idernon then told him of how Dalú's elves had piled the carcasses of Sand Lords and the foul, dark things that had gorged on elven flesh. Even the serpents had been dragged away. Piles upon piles of enemy bodies still burned in the distance, the wind mercifully carrying the stench away from the warriors. Once this task was completed, they would usher their own dead onto the Short Road, upon the pyres that were already being constructed.

Bulan had led his warriors to the enemy camp that had been

partially destroyed by the shock wave from the Sisters' during the battle. They had scoured the ruined tents, the boxes and smashed crates for anything that could be re-used by the elves.

There were poles, planks of wood, canvas from the tents that could be fashioned into stretchers for the wounded. They found flour and salt that could be used to make flat bread, and Bulan had found a book which he had then given to Idernon. Fel'annár's eyes looked down at it, where it sat at the Wise Warrior's side, one of Idernon's hands resting protectively on the worn leather.

It was Ramien who explained how they had found an enormous bank of food which had clearly been raided from Abiren'á. The Wall of Stone had hoisted a generous sack of honey nuts over his head with a triumphant bellow. The scavenging elves had cheered at the recovery of it. In that same place, they found cheese, dried herbs and even raspberry jam.

Others had recovered healing supplies. Bandages and ointments the more knowledgeable had smelled and identified for the most part, except for a jar of some liquid that smelled like the very devil. They wouldn't use it, but Idernon had taken it all the same, wrapped it in a cloak so that it wouldn't break. He would give it to the healers in Abiren'á, in case it was something useful, or perhaps something new that they had no knowledge of.

Conversation continued while the fire before them burned steady and brighter as the light began to fail. The smell of baking bread was slowly infusing the air, and Carodel unwrapped a cloth full of cheese. Galdith uncovered a small sack of honey nuts while Lainon made flat bread. Of them all save for Tensári, he was the most familiar with the recipe, one that was strikingly similar to the bread they made in Araria.

They ate quietly, grateful for the unlikely feast they enjoyed as they watched those at the other fires. From time to time their eyes were drawn to the wooden pyres that would soon be set alight.

Fel'annár's eyes looked up, to the distant canopy of the Sisters, high above him. He tilted his head backwards, up the trunk and to a platform that jutted out over the sands. The Last Lookout, he thought, the Doorway to the Sands. He wondered where Yerái was, whether he had survived the day.

"You want to go up there," said Lainon. Fel'annár turned to the Ari'atór. His wings had dissolved and Fel'annár wondered how it was that he was still in his elven form. He didn't need to ask the question, Lainon could read it in his eyes.

"There may still be danger, and you are not well yet. I don't think I will fly until tomorrow."

Fel'annár offered him a half-hearted smile. "Yes, I want to go up there. But not now, brother. There's too much to do this night, too many warriors to farewell, so many injured."

Hobin and Gor'sadén stepped into their circle, sat quietly. After eating, they had been to the healers, and Gor'sadén's hand had been treated and bandaged. Fel'annár was sure he had other injuries, but so too was he sure that his father wouldn't speak of them – wouldn't speak of anything just yet.

"There are three hundred of my Ari'atór left," said Hobin. "They have basic training in field injuries and are helping the Tar'eastór warriors with the wounded."

Fel'annár started. Hobin had lost two thirds of his contingent. He nodded his thanks, closed his eyes as pain shot up his back. "Thank you, Commander. We will need them. More than half of this army has perished, and from what I can see of Bulan's sector, the injured lie in the hundreds."

"It is the price of victory, Warlord. The Short Road is full of friends this night," said Hobin.

Fel'annár looked to the ground, glanced sideways at Gor'sadén. He thought of Pan'assár and Galadan, lying side by side in Abiren'á, two amongst the thousands of warriors who had perished in their fight to regain their land. But then Lainon and Tensári were still behind him. Fierce Galdith, Wise Idernon, Strong Ramien and poetic Carodel were with him. Gor'sadén – his chosen father – still drew breath and Bulan was leading this army while he himself could not. They had survived, and for all the grief Fel'annár felt, he couldn't help but give thanks for the living.

～

WITH THE PYRES now burning brightly, it was the Warlord the warriors watched the most. They had been concerned about his collapse earlier, were glad to see him on his own two feet again.

Those who were able to stand, joined him and The Company, at the pyres. Three armies, or what was left of them. Alpine, Silvan and Ari - no difference between them. No pyres were higher than the rest. No warriors stood further forward than the rest. They were all the same in death – wonderfully diverse in life, and many now wondered how they had allowed someone like Band'orán to lead them so badly astray.

But those days were gone, they said, as they watched the Warlord. They had seen him falter on occasion, seen the Alpine lord's hand as it shot out to keep him aloft. And as they stood with him to watch their brethren depart from the world, they asked Aria for forgiveness, promised to atone for their part in it, even if it had been mostly their silence in the face of discrimination.

With the moon now low in the east, Fel'annár limped back to their campsite together with the Company. They saw many warriors on their knees before the Sisters and there, they prayed to Aria, despite their aching bodies and confused minds. They knew what they had seen during the battle, knew there were no words to describe it, not yet. But they were thankful that they had won.

They knew they were alive because of the Sisters' intervention.

Fel'annár did not kneel. Instead, he stood there for a moment, head cast upwards to the skies and the towering boughs of the Sisters, no longer leaning forwards, spreading outwards but standing tall, reaching for the clouds, the moon and the sun once more. He stepped forward, over a carpet of broken branches and twigs, reached out with one hand and the warriors stood slowly, wondering what flavour of magic he would conjure now.

Fel'annár's fingers brushed over the rough bark of Anora, the highest of the Sisters, yet there were no lights, no booming skies or thrashing boughs. Still, some would say they heard a soft sigh in the wake of his touch, a breathy whisper of relief, a gentle rustle of leaves meant to soothe.

But Fel'annár heard more than that.

He heard their thoughts, lucid and articulate, wise and unassuming, despite the majestic spectacle of strength and power they had manifested that day. It was a day he would never forget. It was the day he began to understand what Aria had been showing him this last year, and yet there were still so many questions that needed an answer. And they were there, just beyond his ken, ready for when he was free to ponder them.

Now was not that time.

Fel'annár continued on, back to their small camp beneath the Sisters. He sat, closed his eyes, leaned his head against the giant tree behind him. Tensári handed him a cup of liquid, his next dose of the Junar and he drank it, watching as Galdith replaced the bandage on Gor'sadén's hand with a long strip of cloth he had found. He reached into his belt, holding the bandage in place as he fumbled for his dagger.

Fel'annár reached under his own tunic and pulled out a small herb knife. He offered it to Galdith. "He would want you to have this." His voice was soft, almost a whisper and Galdith's eyes focussed on the object, stared at it for a while. He looked up into Fel'annár's eyes, his own filling and glimmering in the flickering, agitated light from the fire. He reached out, took it in his hands and brought it to his eyes. Around the handle, minute etchings, something he had not noticed before.

With love.

The tears in Galdith's eyes spilled over his bottom lid, fingers enclosing around the blade, head falling to his chest. He hadn't cried since the loss of his family because nothing had ever moved him enough after that.

But the rest of The Company did not succour him and neither did Gor'sadén. It was too soon, their own emotions too raw. And so, they sat in silence, watching as Galdith cut the bandage with Galadan's herb knife and then slipped it into a pouch at his belt.

A sad smile played about Fel'annár's lips as he slowly lost the battle to remain awake. Sore body, smarting head, aching back, and exhaustion battled with grief at Galadan's passing, at Pan'assár's loss. There was anxiety too, for the things he had been capable of. The runes under his skin, the charge of the Sisters, the cruelty he had shown against the Nim'uán. He would have to live with that, understand it if he could.

There were questions about his purpose, too.

But Fel'annár was so tired, beyond rational thought and so he shuffled backwards against Bulora, turned on his side and lay down. As he closed his eyes, someone placed a cloak over him.

It was his last memory of that extraordinary day.

An hour later, Bulan approached the small circle. Most of them were asleep save for Lainon and Idernon who poked at the fire and Gor'sadén who stared at nothing at all. Bulan's eyes landed on a sleeping Fel'annár, seeing but not registering the roots that had entwined themselves around one hand. He turned questioning eyes on Idernon who stared back up at him coolly.

"What is he?" whispered the Silvan captain as he crouched painfully beside the Wise Warrior.

Idernon's stony countenance softened, and he even smiled and then shrugged his shoulders. There were a thousand things he could say, but only one that truly mattered in that moment.

"He is my brother."

Bulan hadn't expected that but still, he thought it fitting and he returned the smile with the surety that his extraordinary nephew was in the best possible company.

In the company of friends who were closer than family.

THAT FIRST MORNING after the battle, Fel'annár woke to a different world.

He had never seen cruelty as he had those last few days. He had never *been* cruel himself. He had, though, and now that he knew he was capable of it, somehow – the world had changed.

The sun shone timidly through the trees, breeze almost inexistent. Birds sang in the boughs for the first time since he had stepped into these parts. Everything was as it should be, except that Pan'assár and Galadan were dead.

Someone shuffled beside him, sniffled then coughed. The sound of liquid falling into a cup and then hot steam before his face. He turned to Galdith and then looked at the cup in his hands. Slowly, he sat up, grunted at the shock of pain in his knee and then took it, wrapped his hands around it.

As he drank, he registered his surroundings. The Company sat around him. Bulan sat at an adjacent fire and for a moment, their gazes crossed. Bulan regarded his nephew for long moments before he nodded, and then turned away. He looked worried.

Fel'annár wondered what he was thinking, and then allowed his eyes to continue their journey over the solemn troop that stretched out along the Xeric wood. In the distance, the charred remains of the enemy, and closer, the pyres they had constructed for their own.

He reached out to the trees, knew that Gor'sadén had sought solitude away from the troop. He would seek him out later when time permitted. He had hardly said a word since the battle, except to thank Pengon for his help with Fel'annár's injuries.

Sleep had done his mind good, but his body felt worse than it had done yesterday, save for the dizziness, which was slowly dissipating. The only way to remedy the aches was to move. He was about to get up, but his wandering eyes latched on to a group of Ari'atór. They sat around a large fire, talking quietly as they stared at him.

"What do you think they say?" murmured Fel'annár to Lainon just beside him.

"Many things. You are Ber'anor, sit in the company of two Ber'ator, one returned from the Short Road. It's not a common thing."

Fel'annár huffed, half-turned to his friend. "Not common, no. But I wonder, if you will ever answer my questions."

Lainon leaned forward. "I can't answer your questions, brother. But I can accompany you on that quest for the knowledge you seek, in whatever form I may take."

"Will you tell me at least, what those runes under my skin meant?"

Lainon spared a glance at where Hobin sat with a number of his warriors and then turned back to Fel'annár.

"They were mostly passages from the scriptures, from the Book of Initiates."

"Tell me."

The Company leaned forwards as Lainon spoke.

"Servant of Aria. Aria commands you."

Fel'annár stared at him for a moment. "What else? You said mostly they were passages."

Lainon nodded slowly, lowered his voice until it was nothing but a whisper.

"A land at war."

Fel'annár frowned, while the others shrugged. He didn't understand why Lainon would think that important. But the Shirán had not finished.

"A failing king."

Fel'annár's frown deepened. He shook his head but Lainon was speaking again.

"A light in the forest."

It referred to the light inside him, the one that lit up his eyes when he Listened. *He* was the light in the forest. But Idernon's words from beside him gave him pause.

"It sounds like a prophecy."

Fel'annár turned from the Wise Warrior to the Silent Warrior. Lainon stared back, said nothing and turned away.

More questions, no answers, and no time to pursue them. If Lainon wouldn't speak, perhaps Hobin would. But that would have to wait.

Fel'annár stood, arranged his filthy clothes. Even his weapons were dirty and that was the way they would stay until they reached Abiren'á in a few hours. His injured leg shook under his weight, and the agony in his back made his eyes water. He steeled himself against the pain and then glanced at Dalú, Bulan and Hobin in the near distance.

He knew what he had to do. He wouldn't fail Pan'assár.

"Make ready to break camp!"

Dalú smiled, crossed gazes with Bulan, the worry in his eyes gone, replaced with the light of relief, excitement, and pride.

They stood, echoed Fel'annár's order down the line, watched as the remaining warriors stood and made ready to leave.

The Warlord was back, changed and older, wiser and sadder for it, perhaps. But none of this had broken him and Dalú pledged to himself that he would follow this leader until the end of his warring life.

As Bulan made his way back to his warriors, he pondered on the magic of Fel'annár's coming, the power of his presence and the victory he had brought them. Bulan and his Silvan fighters would follow him now, not because he was Ar Lássira, Ar Thargodén or Aren Zéndar. It was not even because he was the Warlord.

It was Fel'annár, Green Sun who they would follow. Alpines, Silvans and Ari'atór would march behind him, as proud as they once had been standing behind the Great King Or'Talán. No decrees, orders, beliefs or customs would command them now, for a leader had risen from the very earth of this land.

This day marked the Rise of *the Silvan* and behind him, the forest entire would follow.

39

CARODEL'S SONG

∿

SOREI WASN'T sure what serving under Rinon would be like, but she knew herself, knew that her relationship with him would change nothing. She was a disciplined captain, demanded the same discipline from her warriors – expected it of her superiors.

She looked up at her black charger, his noble eyes looking down on her in anticipation of the ride ahead. She smiled, smoothed a hand down his velvety nose and turned to Rinon, smile gone as she watched him watch her.

"Something wrong?"

"No. Why should there be?"

"You're staring."

"Is that always a bad thing?"

She frowned, turned back to her horse, answered as she checked the reins and saddle.

"Often times, yes. Men stare at women when they are judging them, which is most of the time."

It took Rinon a while to answer her, but when he did, his tone was calm, curious.

"Is that what it is like, to serve as a woman in the army?"

She turned to him, stepped closer. "Oh yes. That is what it is like. It took me years to gain their respect and their trust. Strangely, it is not so bad here. Your Silvan warriors show no bias, only curiosity and a touch of playful mischief. It is the Alpines amongst you that are wary and mistrustful."

"Women warriors break their moulds while in Silvan culture, in the times before the colonisation, they were commonplace in their tribal groups. Each house had its own force of men and women, but when the Alpine army took control of the forest, that same mistrust you speak of all but eradicated the Silvan women from the military. Only now are they beginning to return, slowly as I am sure you have noticed."

"Yes. They say the Warlord had plans to include them, but with him away in the north, they had thought to wait for his return before stepping forwards."

"But you have inspired them, Captain," said Rinon, closing the gap between them. "Just as you have inspired our warriors, gained their respect even before you stepped into this city."

"I'm no heroine, Prince. Just a simple captain with a love for steel."

"You are much more than that, Sorei. There is nothing *simple* about you."

He stared at her, wanted to take her in his arms and embrace her, melt the ice in her eyes. Strange, because the people had once called *him* Ice Prince, thought him cool and unfeeling and perhaps he had been. But that was the past, before Fel'annár and Band'orán. Before Maeneth's return.

Before Sorei.

Sorei frowned, placed a hand over his heart. "Guard this well, Prince. I am not a romantic woman. I am practical and rational. I enjoy your company, but I am sworn to Vorn'asté, not Thargodén. I am here only for as long as Commander Gor'sadén bids me stay." She patted his chest, turned away from him and mounted, looked down on him as if she dared him to gainsay her.

Rinon stared up at her, read those cool eyes far better than he knew she was comfortable with. He wasn't convinced of her words, yet his own had confused him even more. He snorted as loudly as any horse as he mounted, and Sorei watched, a fleeting grin on her face.

What did *he* know about love? Nothing. All Rinon knew, was that he would have her stay, enjoyed her company and he would miss it if she were ordered home to the Motherland.

He should have smiled, frowned instead and then kicked his horse into a gentle walk, out of the stables and into the front courtyard. There, one hundred mounted warriors stood waiting. It was time to ride to Port Helia, call back all those warriors who could be spared, and any others who would come, from Pelagia, or beyond.

IN A SECLUDED GLADE, not far from the Inner Circle, Maeneth and Sontúr stepped apart, swords in hand while Handir and Llyniel stood from the bench they had been sitting on. Handir had been watching his sister and friend as they sparred gently, while Llyniel watched closely for any signs of discomfort from Sontúr.

He was progressing, she thought. He could heft his sword well enough, but his movements were slow, and she could see the signs of discomfort when he blocked Maeneth's gentle attacks. Still, he had come a long way. All that was left was to build up the muscle he had lost and regain the mobility he once had.

From afar, they watched Rinon lead the patrol through the main gates, Sorei just behind. They had all said their goodbyes just this morning. It was a short mission, one of the utmost importance because if the final battle had already been waged in the north, then their army would not return for another month. The way things were going, it was time the city of Ea Uaré did not have. They would be pushed southwards, into the city within a week, imprisoned behind their own walls because there would be insufficient warriors to keep the hordes of Deviants back.

Rinon's patrol may be the last before they were forced to close the gates and wait for their army to return. There would be far-reaching implications. They would need to stock up their supplies to provide for the many Silvans who were now swarming into the city from Sen Garay and further afield.

Llyniel picked up her bag. It was time to return to the Halls, to the many wounded that lay there, not only from the constant attacks from the Deviants but from the tremor that had rocked the city.

Handir reached for his book, tucked it under his shoulder and together, the four friends made back to the palace.

Maeneth prayed that her new-found brother would return victorious, while Sontúr willed it in his mind, told himself The Company would prevail, had faced impossible odds before and survived.

Handir's heart was heavy. He had come to love Fel'annár as a brother, a friend closer than any other he'd ever had save for Llyniel. He had to come back.

His gaze drifted to Llyniel, looked hard at her profile.

She didn't grieve, but she *was* confused. She had said that she could feel Fel'annár, that he was surrounded by a presence she did not recognise. Handir didn't understand that, but he was content for now that Fel'annár lived, and although he was not one to pray, he willed his Silvan brother to stay strong, to come back to a family he had searched for all his life and had finally found.

Fel'annár led the army towards Abiren'á.

They limped, leaned on each other, bore stretchers with the more sorely wounded, while around them, off the path and in the trees, others worked to cut down the Sand Lords and Reapers who had been slaughtered by the forest.

Fel'annár had not had to assign warriors for such a gruesome task. There were more volunteers than he could count. They were soiling the trees, they said, and no Silvan from these parts would stand for it. They had gone ahead an hour before the main body of the army had begun its trek to Abiren'á and now, the warriors hailed them as they passed, shouting words of thanks and praise. But they didn't smile, and their eyes were dull.

"What will we find in Abiren'á?" asked Bulan from Fel'annár's side at the front of the line.

"A place of death and destruction. The bodies of friends and foe. Broken branches, smashed cages, severed bridges. We will find Pan'assár and Galadan's bodies resting under a Sentinel."

"What happened?" he asked quietly, hoping that Gor'sadén couldn't hear. But truth be told, the commander didn't seem to hear anything. He just watched the world with bleary eyes.

"Pan'assár gave Gor'sadén the time he needed to free the last cage. Thanks to him and Galadan, our people were rescued. He fought and killed the Nim'uán. Galadan shielded the commander from a blow. Both died shortly after."

Bulan nodded, while Lainon turned to Hobin, walking just behind him. The Ari commander looked at the returned Ber'ator, a hundred questions in his mind about how it was possible that he was here. But there was something in Lainon's eyes that gave him pause. It was a question, one he wagered Lainon would not ask until they were alone. He frowned, watched the elf-hawk turn away. He would seek him out later, ask his own questions and he wondered if the elven hawk would answer them.

If he *could* answer them.

The closer they drew to the city, the more bodies they came across, and another unit was assigned the task of clearing the path ahead. The dead were carried or dragged sideways, depending on whether they were friend or foe. Their cremations would have to wait until they could be transported to a place where the flames would not pose a threat to the trees.

The dead were dead, they said, and now, it was time to care for the living.

But there were so many. Yesterday, Fel'annár had been numb to the devastation, but today, his dull eyes registered everything. The dead bodies, the pain on his warriors' faces and their expressions, the way they sometimes looked at him that Fel'annár did not quite understand. He chose to believe it was reprobation and resentment.

Pan'assár had devised their strategy. It had worked, brought them victory, but at a price far greater than Fel'annár could ever have imagined.

How does a commander lead warriors into war, knowing that so many will not come back? How can he know that he made the right decisions?

For the first time, Fel'annár wondered if it would not have been better to conjure the trees from the very beginning; sacrifice the three hundred civilians so that three thousand warriors would not die. Had he been weak? Was he capable of command? Did he truly deserve the parallel lines in his collar?

Closer to their destination, the bodies marked their path into the Silvan city, and a banging, thudding and cracking sound grew louder and louder.

Fel'annár stepped into the central glade where he had danced the Wheel of War with Pan'assár and Gor'sadén just yesterday. He stopped, held up his hand for the column behind him to do likewise.

The people of Abiren'á had been imprisoned in wooden cages, hung from the heights. They had suffered at the hands of the Reapers, been fed to their serpents, had watched each other die. And, as logic would dictate, he had thought Abiren'á would be an empty place of death where the echoes of terror would keep the citizens away, perhaps for years to come.

But he was wrong.

Amidst the post-battle haze, scores of ragged figures moved here and there. Some held axes, hacked at the ruined cages that had fallen from the heights while others carried the smaller pieces of wood away. But the giant branches that had fallen during the maelstrom were too big, too heavy and so the elves moved around them in their search for bodies and discarded weapons.

They stood now, frozen in their tasks as they began to realise that the army had returned. One of them made towards Fel'annár, the misty haze swirling about him. This elf was a civilian, his clothes blood-stained and ripped, filthy from the detritus he had immersed himself in, so that he and his people could begin the reconstruction.

The elf stared, as if he didn't understand something, and then his eyes wandered over Gor'sadén, The Company, and the haggard army behind.

"I am Koldur, of the clan of Three Sisters, leader of Abiren'á."

"General Fel'annár." His voice echoed about the place, sounded as small as he felt. He suddenly realised he didn't know what to do. He started at a familiar voice behind him.

"Lord Koldur."

"Bulan?" The elf peered into the mass of dour warriors, found the one he sought. "Aria be praised you live!"

Bulan stepped forward and Fel'annár watched as the two embraced, and all the while, his mind was working through the priorities. He finally found the wherewithal to speak, prayed he would not make a fool of himself.

"Lord Koldur. Where can we take our wounded?"

The leader turned back to Fel'annár. "We are working to erect pavilions. Lestari Dengar will lead the way. Our dead have been taken to the river edge. Weya is in charge. The ruined wood is being taken there too, supervised by Jonar, our forester, but these branches cannot be moved. There are more of us on the way but for now, I suggest you make your base camp right here, in the central glade. It's cleaner here, and small fires can be lit. The river is two minutes' walk that way. Bear with us and our field kitchen will soon be up and running."

He paused, as if his mouth had run away with his thoughts.

"Are we safe? Are the Sand Lords vanquished?"

Fel'annár stared back at him. They had battled Deviants, serpents, Reapers, a Nim'uán – and Sand Lords.

"Yes, we are safe."

Koldur closed his eyes, turned a little too quickly to the civilians behind him.

"The north is ours once more. *Victory* – is ours!"

The roar that followed was visceral, raw, violent in its intensity and Koldur closed his eyes, and then sought out Jonar and Yerái amongst the people. He smiled, nodded at them, and then turned back to Fel'annár as he began to issue his orders.

"Eramor, take fifty and help Weya with the dead. Dalú, take your fifty and help Dengar with the wounded. Find Pengon and any others with knowledge of healing and take them to the pavilions. Benat, to Jonar and the wood. Bulan, oversee the camp and report to me with our needs. Rotate our duty shifts every two hours; we're all tired."

As his captains made to carry out his orders, Fel'annár glanced sideways at Gor'sadén. A slow nod of approval and he turned back to Koldur. But no words would come. He felt awkward, unsure of himself, out of his depth. He was untried in circumstances such as these and yet, he had already lost so many of his warriors. Half of those who had survived were injured, needed water, food and attention, he himself could hardly stand.

But he had to. He was the leader of these warriors. He would not rest until they did, he swore.

With the three contingents now joining the scattered citizens, one side of the glade was soon cleared enough for them to make camp amongst the fallen tree branches. With a signal from Fel'annár, they broke rank, drifted off into small groups, but Fel'annár stood for a while longer, knees locked lest they buckle.

He observed the captains, their cool command, minds focussed on the task he himself had set them, no sign of the horrors, of the losses they had suffered. Their minds were on the living, as it should have been, and yet Fel'annár could think only of the thousands of dead warriors. Why were his fighters dispensable yet not the civilians – those who had refused to leave despite the warnings?

Bulan was shouting orders, had surely arranged for water bearers to provision the camp. Fel'annár caught sight of a swinging rope and looked up. He could hardly see the end of it, so high up in the boughs where just yesterday, the cages had hung, and their archers had cascaded to their deaths.

It was then that he spotted Yerái for the first time after the battle. He held a hand up to him, and Yerái approached, his battered face watching the pale and limping Warlord closely.

Fel'annár felt genuinely relieved that his fellow Listener had made it. His had been a central role in the liberation of these people yet more than this, he liked the messenger from Abiren'á, even back when they had met on the road from Tar'eastór.

"How? Why have they come back, after all they've endured?" But even as he asked the question, Lord Koldur joined them.

"In answer to your question, I say we are all warriors. We all fight the battle of life, whatever it places in our way. The citizens of Abiren'á are fierce in their love of this land, bold with their lives when the trees are endangered. We fled the battle, not Abiren'á."

The slightest of proud smiles flitted over Yerái's face and Koldur returned it. "Your warriors saved my people, General Fel'annár. And for that, Abiren'á honours you, and them. There are mighty tales to be told in the days to come, of the war that has been won. It was so, long ago after the Battle Under the Sun. Back then, it was your grandfather we lost. Today, it was his greatest friend." Koldur breathed deeply, was surely reliving those days in his mind. But it was strangely comforting to Fel'annár that this elf, at least, knew what he was doing, what needed to be done, even as he himself did not.

"Let my people help your warriors. It's time for you to rest, Warlord."

Fel'annár tried to smile, knew that it had been only half successful. His body was screaming at him to rest, leg and back aching fiercely. "I'll rest when my warriors do, those alive and those who have passed."

"We're collecting the dead upon the banks of the Calro. We're constructing pyres there. The first will surely burn this evening, but there will be many more nights of fire and prayers, Lord. We lost so many."

Fel'annár felt his eyes fill, but he forced the tears away, and turned to the Sentinel where he had left Pan'assár and Galadan. Koldur followed his line of sight.

"We did not touch the Protectors."

Fel'annár started. *The Protectors*, Koldur had said. It was fitting and once more, his emotions pushed back against his resolve. This was, perhaps, the hardest part of war. To behold the price of it, contemplate its consequences, deal with the crushing pity it brings, and even then, be the commander his warriors needed him to be, even though it had been *him* who had brought this about.

He felt Idernon's hand on his arm and he half turned, but when he spoke, it was to Koldur once more.

"Then our farewells begin today. The Protectors will lead the way for the rest, their light a beacon to the others upon the Short Road. At the twentieth hour, Lord Koldur, I and The Company will carry them to the river."

Koldur nodded. "Then we will gather here, follow your lead. I must return to my work, but later, you and your Company will stay at my residence."

"That's not necessary, my Lord. We can camp here with the rest."

"I insist, Warlord. Let it not be said I did not succour you in your time of need. When the dead walk the Short Road, make for Star Dome. There is no destruction up there, at the pinnacle of Abiren'á, strange though that may seem."

Star Dome. It was an enticing name, as enticing as the thought of a soft, warm bed and shelter from the elements. Fel'annár felt guilty accepting such luxuries while the rest of his warriors were out here, camping on the ground. And then had he not just told himself that he should have sacrificed these people? With what justification could he now accept their humble hospitality?

"They'll want for nothing, Warlord. We know what to do. Bulan and I have done this before. They'll be well looked after, my word."

Fel'annár stared back at him, and then caught Gor'sadén's gaze. The commander nodded slowly. He too, knew what to do. Fel'annár was surely expected to accept Koldur's hospitality, even though he didn't deserve it.

"All right. We are most grateful, Lord." He bowed stiffly, watched Koldur and Yerái leave, and then spoke to no one in particular.

"Let's find a spot to sit." Fel'annár's eyes drifted over the busy glade. Everything was in motion, and the trees whispered words of assurance. There was no danger; he could sit, even if it was just for a short while. He spotted a tree that had not been occupied and limped towards it, Lainon and Tensári close behind.

He tried to sit but couldn't, felt hands under his arms, lowering him to the ground. He tried and failed to keep his knee straight, sat with a grimace. He breathed through the pain, lent back carefully and rested his head on the bark behind while The Company and Gor'sadén settled.

There were people moving between the groups of warriors. Some carried buckets of water, others kindling or dried food. Idernon raised his hand, and Fel'annár watched a young man trot over to them, eyes pinned on him and then on Gor'sadén and the Ari'atór. His eyes were not dull but sparkling with excitement and youthful curiosity. If only he knew, mused Fel'annár.

"Water, fire and food, sirs?"

Idernon opened his mouth, hesitated. "Yes. Thank you." He turned back to Fel'annár. "You need a healer, and a dose of the Junar. After, I suggest a trip to the river. I've seen people handing out clean clothes."

"You go. I'll wait."

"Why must you wait? You're injured, you can hardly stand, and that arm needs stitching."

"Let the healers tend to those worse off than me. I *can* stand, Idernon." It had come out much harsher than he had intended, and he held up an appeasing hand. "Brother, if I stop now – if I accept the aid of a healer and bathe – I won't get back up. I need to say goodbye, Idernon. Only then will I deserve to rest."

The Wise Warrior frowned, caught a glimpse of Gor'sadén sitting off to his right. The commander stared back at him, but he said nothing, hadn't all day.

Idernon turned away, and for a while, they just sat there and contemplated Abiren'á in the aftermath of war.

A young lad placed a pail of water to one side of their circle, and handed out the dried food, while another set to lighting a small fire. Soon, it was smoking and then burning timidly and Ramien took over from him. Galdith half-filled a cup with water, and then rummaged through his pack, in search of the Junar that Lainon had given him. He sprinkled a dose into the water, swirled the mixture around, and then passed the cup to a silent Fel'annár. He watched as he drank it down with a grimace and then a gasp at the bitter taste it left.

Time seemed to pass far too quickly for Fel'annár. He was sat upon the ground, body and mind like lead, but still his eyes continued their detached scrutiny.

Koldur had indeed, done this before. It was organised chaos, he thought. Thousands of Silvans and Ari lived here, but for now, it was the few hundred who had survived the cages who strove to succour an injured army of thousands.

He could see the lines of warriors, a steady stream to and from the river edge, where the healers were working, and warriors were surely washing away the filth of war. It would be madness to go there now, not that he had any inclination to do so. He meant what he had said to Idernon. When Pan'assár and Galadan had been sent on their greatest journey, when the first pyres with their dead lit up the sky, only then would he rest, if he could.

FEL'ANNÁR REALISED he must have dozed off.

He could feel his back against the tree behind him, head bent backwards against the rough bark. He swallowed thickly, reached for the cup that someone held out before him and drank.

Idernon was looking back at him, but he said nothing and Fel'annár's eyes scanned his surroundings in the rapidly failing light.

There were no dead bodies around the glade, and the scattered remnants of wood had been cleared, save for the giant branches that still littered the glade. They would need many more hands to drag them away.

He looked up at the severed ropes that hung from above. He saw pulleys and air lifts, most in need of repair, but what lay beyond his vision, high up in the canopy was still a mystery to Fel'annár. He knew there were buildings up there, a place Koldur had said neither the Sand Lords nor the trees had destroyed.

The distant beat of a drum resounded through the glade, and for a moment, warriors and civilians looked up. Someone was playing the war drums, a slow and steady beat that filled the silence of the warriors, somehow seemed to bridge the gap between their hurt and confused minds, and the real world around them. Fel'annár felt as if he was floating just above reality, like a lost spirit unable to comprehend the finality of death, the crippling pity it brought.

To one side of the glade, the field kitchen Koldur had promised was bustling with activity. Ramien, Galdith and Carodel had taken their turns in the many lines of hungry warriors, while Tensári and Lainon had gone to the river for more water. Now, they sat around their timid fire, eating as they watched the glade, memories of other afternoons, sitting around a campfire with Galadan and Pan'assár.

But this was no time to *feel*, not for Fel'annár, and so he looked away, brought the drums to the front of his mind as he finished his meal.

"I need a crutch, and we need two pallets for our dead brothers. I would carry them to the pyres."

"Not you."

"*Me*, Idernon. You, Ramien, Carodel, Tensári, Lainon and Galdith – Gor'sadén. *All* of us, and my step will not falter as we carry Galadan and Pan'assár upon our shoulders, give them the full honours they deserve."

Idernon glanced at a despondent Gor'sadén, but still, he said nothing, and so he stood and approached Lord Koldur, who was discussing something with Yerái and two others. Fel'annár was hanging by a thread, he knew. They all were, wished for nothing but sleep, but he was the Warlord and they his Company. Their task was not yet complete. Idernon understood that, as well as he knew that Fel'annár was struggling with the weight of his command, and perhaps something else.

"Lord Koldur. Can you arrange for two pallets to be brought to the Protectors? It is almost time to send them on their way."

Koldur nodded solemnly, gestured to an elf nearby and then turned back to the lieutenant. "How is our Warlord?"

"Adamant that he can carry our brother to his pyre. His priority is his warriors. He won't rest until he's sure *they* can. He will need a crutch, and perhaps a miracle."

"I have a crutch," said Yerái. "Broke my ankle once in a raid. It'll take me a while to retrieve it."

"Quicker than making one from scratch I wager."

"Oh yes. And more comfortable, let me assure you."

"Thank you, Yerái."

The lieutenant jogged away and Idernon turned back to Koldur. "He's not well, Lord. But we must allow him this one duty. After though, we would gladly accept your hospitality."

Koldur nodded kindly, eyes drifting to where the Warlord sat. "I look forward to it, Lieutenant. He will have all that he needs. Your loyalty is noted."

With a nod of gratitude, Idernon made his way back to where The Company sat, Gor'sadén still silent, gaze lost. He tried to imagine himself as the commander of this army, tried to imagine it had been *he* who had been involved in making decisions that had cost thousands of lives.

This, he knew, was what tormented his friend.

Idernon knew Fel'annár better than most. All this was new to him. Yes, he had commanded warriors in battle before and lost hundreds. But this was beyond anything any of them had lived through. The enormity of it, the magnitude of death and the manner of it.

No, he couldn't feel what Fel'annár did at that moment, but he did understand it, knew that his friend would need help in the days to come.

NIGHT HAD FALLEN, the pyre was ready, and Yerái had given Fel'annár his crutch.

He stood, leaned heavily on it, pain warring with determination, and a newfound need for atonement.

"Let's go and get them, brothers." He daren't look at Gor'sadén, lest his own resolve shatter and so he pressed on, limped towards the guardian Sentinel, while Lainon and Tensári stayed close to his side in case he fell.

Those still gathered around the Sentinel stepped away but did not leave and instead, they watched.

Fel'annár's heart shuddered in his chest, almost stopped at the sight of his two friends. He stared down at their shining faces, and although they had died yesterday, their flesh seemed flushed, as if blood still rushed through their veins, and although their eyes were closed, he thought that should they open them, they would be bright and alive.

A soft mist lingered above them, like the finest of silk, shimmering and translucent, and Fel'annár reached out, brushed over it with his finger. The light flickered then brightened, and the onlookers gasped softly, whispering as they watched, drawing others to where they stood.

Fel'annár had asked the Sentinel to protect them, but it had done far more than that. It had cared for them like an indulgent mother.

Fel'annár knew that it did not mourn. Instead, it sang a song of renewal and of thanks. But the elves did mourn, especially Gor'sadén, who looked down on Pan'assár, expression utterly straight as he began to work.

Two pallets had been laid down beside the dead, but whoever had brought them had not wanted to touch the Protectors. Gor'sadén, Carodel, Lainon and Tensári took Pan'assár's body, carefully depositing him upon one of the pallets, while Fel'annár struggled to put his crutch in his weapons harness. Ramien helped him, ignored the answering glare he received as recompense. With Galadan's body prepared, the two groups raised their charges into the air, rested the weight upon their shoulders while their other hands steadied the bodies they carried.

To the rhythm of a sole drum beat, they marched as one, slow and solemn despite their injures. Fel'annár limped only slightly, teeth gritted, hands shaking and all the while, the drum sounded like a heartbeat, the hearts that should never have stopped, hearts he wished with all his might that hadn't. Galadan had guided him on his first steps as a lieutenant, had once called him prince when others called him bastard. He had treated his injuries, given his staunch loyalty, his years of wisdom to one so much younger than himself. Galadan had been the epitome of a warrior, one who had inspired him upon his own road. Fel'annár willed the pain in his body to come back, so that it would dull the agony in his mind.

No one spoke as the two bodies were carried towards the river, warriors and citizens behind.

It was time to say goodbye.

Fel'annár didn't feel the ground beneath his trembling legs, nor the pain in his knee and arm. He couldn't feel the sting and ache of bruises down his back, for his mind was screaming. Pan'assár was gone. *Galadan* was gone because he had believed in Pan'assár, had believed in *Fel'annár.* They were dead but he was still alive.

It didn't seem right.

He had seen them, sprinting side by side, charging at the Nim'uán, no doubt on their faces, no hesitation. And Fel'annár had watched Galadan fight, and then watched him fall, never to get up again.

He hadn't helped them, had instead chosen to save the last cage of civilians. He had all but sacrificed them.

So fast. So final. It reminded him of Lainon's passing, wanted to turn, assure himself one more time that he was here. But he couldn't.

They crested the last hillock that led to the shores of the Calro, and before him, an endless line of pyres emerged. One after the other, the rectangular boxes lay like tombstones, and upon each one, four dead warriors had been placed. Beside each pyre, a flaming torch was staked into the ground, waiting to be used by whoever would come forward.

The Company and Gor'sadén marched on, the drum now distant but still there, the only sound save for the softly lapping ripples upon the shore and the crackle of torches.

Captain Dalú stood before the only empty pyre, one hand out towards them, a gesture to lay down their charges and on they marched, just as slow, just as silent on the outside.

They lay their charges down, one beside the other. Though there was room for two more, no others would lay beside the Protectors. Koldur had ordered it, and Fel'annár thought it fitting.

They straightened clothing, reverently took the swords, daggers and bows they would no longer need.

Gor'sadén slid Pan'assár's Colanei long sword and his Turanés short sword into his harness, beside his own, while Galdith took Galadan's bow and sword, even though his friend had no one to bestow them upon.

Fel'annár watched as Gor'sadén tucked Pan'assár's hands under the purple sash of a Kah Master, his own hands resting lightly over them for a while. But Gor'sadén's face did not crack and his dull eyes held no tears.

One by one, they said goodbye, whispered words meant only for the dead and then they stepped away. Lord Koldur held a flaming torch in his hand, and Fel'annár met his gaze as he took it from him.

This was the moment he had not been able to witness in Ea Uaré, after the Battle of Brothers. He had not had the chance to say goodbye, to say thank you to those who had followed him and died for it. His eyes drifted from one pyre to the next and he opened his mouth, willed his voice not to waver or falter.

"There is no higher sacrifice than this. To give your own life, in service to the people, protect them from harm with our most precious possession. Their selfless duty will be remembered. It is *our* duty to remember them. Every commander, general and captain, every lieutenant, warrior, novice and recruit will learn of their deeds and marvel at their bravery, exalt their loyalty, for they charged at the enemy that would have killed our brothers and sisters, our children. We live, and they now follow the Protectors upon the Short Road. May their eternal light guide them all, into the arms of Aria."

He breathed deeply, closed his eyes for one moment, and then turned to Gor'sadén, offered him the flaming torch. He watched, thought that perhaps this was his father's greatest battle. To say goodbye to one who had meant so much to him, through long centuries of war and peace, friendship and hardship.

Yet still, no tears fell from Gor'sadén's eyes as he reached out, took the torch and turned to the pyre. To their left and right, others took up their torches: Bulan, Dalú, Benat and Eramor, Koldur and Yerái, others they did not recognise. But they all looked to Gor'sadén, watched him step forward and insert the torch into a gap at the base of the pyre. He stepped back to join The Company, watched as smoke began to rise, timidly at first, until the flames were higher, and the crackle and pop of wood joined the solemn beat that still sounded in the distance.

As the other torches were placed into the pyres, a single voice rose above the crackle of fire and the whispering river beyond.

It was soft at first, just loud enough for The Company and Gor'saden to hear, and Fel'annár whispered as Carodel's song began.

"Farewell, Galadan of The Company. Fire Warrior. We will meet again."

Gor'saden said nothing, that blank expression still on his face, even now as the flames grew higher and the voice grew stronger. And then a flicker of blue eyes, a twitch of the brow as the beauty of the Bard Warrior's voice, his poignant words cut through the many layers of Gor'saden's grief. It resounded throughout the glade, rose higher when the fireflies came. The golden lights flitted over the flames, dancing upon the currents of hot air, turning the orange light to golden and the people that watched gasped in wonder at it.

And Carodel's song grew stronger, moved as they all were, by the spectacle that nature bestowed upon the dead, lending his voice a depth of sorrow and grief that left none unmoved. It was the clarity of it, a certain timbre that softened the heart, broke through those walls they had all erected, so that they could make it through the day.

It was a song of forgiveness. A song of past wrongs and atonement, the meaning of those lyrics lost to none of them.

Carodel sung of friendship, of a bond beyond understanding, brotherhood that transcended reason. Every phrase was like melting honey, mellow browns and then clear, crisp greens and blues, words like echoes from the highest peaks of Galadan and Pan'assár's mountain home of Tar'eastór, a place they would never again see.

They cried, for those who had died, wept for the beauty of song and the power of Aria, and when the tune finally rose to its bitter-sweet conclusion, Fel'annár thought of Pan'assár, of the tiny part of himself he had allowed Fel'annár to see, the elf behind the commander that Galadan had always seen so clearly, understood as no other had save for Gor'sadén.

Fel'annár looked up to the stars, swiped at his wet eyes, adjusted his grip on his crutch and with his other hand, he saluted.

The warriors followed suit, just as they had done at Skyrock, when Pan'assár was alive and had asked forgiveness.

Later, days into the future, Pan'assár and Galadan would be upon the tongues of them all, their place in the annals of the Silvan Chronicles assured, together with the thousands who had died in this, the Battle of Abiren'á.

But for now, with the flames burning lower, the crowds floated away. Yet Fel'annár was not quite ready to leave.

He felt The Company closer around him. He felt their hands on his shoulder, raised his own and placed it on Idernon's. He couldn't help the words that tumbled from his mouth.

"I'll miss his stony face and fiery eyes, his quiet, unassuming wisdom."

"I'll miss his careful instruction, his long years of knowledge," said Idernon.

"I'll always remember his guiding hand, his soft, rare smile," said Carodel.

"I'll miss his cooking and his quiet whittling at the fire." Ramien sighed.

It took a while for Galdith to bolster his courage, say the only words that came to him with shining eyes and a wandering gaze.

"I will miss my friend."

Fel'annár squeezed his eyes shut, and when he opened them, he looked to where Gor'sadén had been just moments before.

But the last of The Three was nowhere to be seen.

TRUE TO FEL'ANNÁR'S WORD, he had not faltered as he carried Galadan to the pyres, nor had he stumbled as he had said goodbye to his dead warriors upon the banks of the Calro River.

But with every step he took, the more Fel'annár's crutch shook and the paler his face. Idernon shared a conspiring glance with the rest of The Company and Bulan who stood further away. Even so, he hadn't missed the signs either, nodded at Idernon and watched as they ushered him along the shore, bound for the glade and the comfort Lord Koldur had offered them.

Their path back to the centre of the city took them along a quiet stretch of the river. In the distance, on the farthest jetty, sat a solitary figure. Fel'annár turned to Idernon, gestured for him and the rest to give him a moment. The Wise Warrior's eyes drifted to Gor'sadén at the very end of the pier, and although he nodded, Fel'annár could see his disapproval. He was sorry for that, sorry that he had snapped at his friend on more than one occasion that day. But he needed to speak with his father, needed to know that he would be all right. And although Gor'sadén had yet to utter a word, Fel'annár wondered if he would answer the question that had been plaguing him all day. It was a question only Gor'sadén could answer.

He struggled down the wooden pier, crutch banging far too loudly but he couldn't help it. He could no more pretend that it didn't hurt.

Moonlight reflected off the gently rippling water, and only now did Fel'annár realise there were no boats. They had all surely been taken weeks before by the families who had mercifully evacuated southwards with their children.

He was almost at the end, knew Gor'sadén had heard him but he did not turn, and he still did not speak, and so Fel'annár carefully sat beside him with a grunt and then a groan. Collecting himself, he admired the beauty of the woodland river, unsoiled here by the aftermath of battle.

He turned to Gor'sadén's profile as he sat there, gaze lost, feet dangling over the edge, boots not quite touching the surface of the water.

He turned away, to the gently flowing river and for a moment, allowed his mind free rein. As he did, words came easily, flowed unchecked, straight from the heart. His doubts tumbled from his mouth unchecked.

"How do you do it? How do you live, knowing that you led so many warriors to their deaths?"

Movement in the corner of his eye, told him Gor'sadén was looking at him, but Fel'annár didn't turn, in case he faltered.

"You remind yourself that they followed you into war. You remember the Warrior Code, the oath we all take when we evolve from novice to warrior. That oath is taken freely, gladly. We serve, even though our duty may lead to death."

Even unto death.

He had said that himself, heard others say it when they had accepted their promotions. "But how do you know that your choices were the best ones? How do you know they didn't die because you made a mistake?"

For a while, Gor'sadén said nothing. Fel'annár wondered if he was thinking of the past, perhaps of the time he and The Three had taken their oaths as young warriors.

"Look at me, Fel'annár."

He turned, met Gor'sadén's eyes for the first time. It almost broke him, knowing that his father could see his guilt, as clearly as Fel'annár could see the grief and understanding in his.

"Had you made mistakes, I would have told you, and I know you would have heeded me. I said nothing because there were no flaws in your judgement. Pan'assár would agree with me, and there was no better strategist than he. He made you general, awarded you the Forest Emerald. He showed you the art of strategy, listened as you gave your opinions. He believed in you."

"But they're still dead, and that makes me feel - inadequate. It makes me wonder if I could have done something differently. If only I had conjured the trees from the very beginning, sacrificed three hundred in exchange for three thousand lives. If Pan'assár had my power, what would he have done? Tell me?"

"If there had been no other way, Fel'annár, then that road would have been open to you. But there was another way. You cannot know if more or fewer elves would have died but even if you knew the cost to your lines would be great, that is the nature of your service. We serve the king and his people – this is what the Warrior Code states. We serve the *people*, Fel'annár. *We* take the oath, not them. It is our job to protect them with our lives. If it takes ten warriors to save one elf, then that is the price."

Gor'sadén breathed deeply, cast his eyes over the steadily flowing river.

"I will never discourage you from asking yourself if you did the right thing. But don't let the 'what ifs' turn you bitter, Fel'annár. Ask only so that you can learn. And all commanders must learn, sometimes the hard way, but there *is* no other way. That you even ask the question is a measure of your heart."

"It is a weakness I have ..."

"*No*. The heart is never a weakness, Fel'annár. *Hiding* it is a weakness. Swallowing those feelings of pity and remorse will only exacerbate them, turn you bitter. Only excellent commanders feel what you do. It is what makes you as great a leader as Orta ever was.

"Feel. Think. Reason. Act. In that order. But never lose the heart, because that is what moves everything. You must allow yourself to grieve for those we lost, and in doing so, you honour them, remember them. But never turn away from your feelings."

An owl hooted somewhere off to the west, and water lapped at the wooden quay. Gor'sadén's words were wise, heavy in their own way, and as they settled in his mind, the burden in his heart eased. He had doubted himself since the end of the battle, and only now did he begin to wonder if he had been wrong, if he *had* done the right thing.

He turned back to Gor'sadén's profile, wondering if he would take his own advice and allow himself to grieve. He didn't expect him to speak again.

"He knew ... that this would be his final battle, the end of his warring days."

Fel'annár nodded slowly, remembered Pan'assár telling him that.

"Once he had relinquished his command to Turion, he intended to help me to re-establish the Kal'hamén'Ar, and then escort your father on the Long Road, when that time comes."

"He told you that?"

Gor'sadén nodded, eyes on the river and Fel'annár's on his profile. "The king is leaving?"

Gor'sadén turned to him, caught the glint of fear in Fel'annár's eyes. "Not yet perhaps. But Pan'assár did say he didn't think he would stay for much longer. A century or so he reckoned. Now, he cannot carry out that final act of duty to the line he swore to protect." He breathed out slowly, shook his head minutely.

"It is times like these that show you the true nature of the world, Fel'annár. It puts things into perspective, shows you the things that really matter. All Pan'assár wanted was atonement. He had it in the end, died with that thought in his mind, with the knowledge that he had achieved it, in the end." He huffed, shook his head. "This might seem strange to you, but it was almost as if Pan'assár was *meant* to die in the Battle Under the Sun with Or'Talán. I know he thought that, felt guilty for living. Strange twist of fate that he should die here, so close to the Xeric Wood, fighting with Or'Talán's grandson, buying him the time he needed to win the day."

Fel'annár looked down, past the edge of the jetty and to the inky waters below his boots. He started when Gor'sadén spoke again.

"In those final moments ... some ... some of his last words were for you. He told me to lead you to greatness, he who once hated you, and then came to love you, in his own way." Gor'sadén reached behind and to the ornate pommel of Pan'assár's Turanés short sword. He pulled it out, presented it to Fel'annár in both of his hands. "He asked me to give you this."

Fel'annár looked down at the beautiful weapon, didn't bother to hold back his tears. He took it gently from his father's hands, brushed a thumb over the hilt. He sniffled, slipped it into his harness, swiped at his eyes and stood awkwardly.

He looked down, at a still sitting Gor'sadén as he looked out over the Calro in silence. Fel'annár reached out, squeezed his shoulder.

"I still need you, Gor'sadén. I have so much to learn of leadership. Promise me *you* will stay a while longer."

Gor'sadén looked up at Or'Talán's grandson, no doubt in his heart.

"I will stay for you, son."

Gor'sadén saw his relief, his uncertainty about leaving him alone with his grief, but the commander smiled, gestured to the distant camp with his head.

"Go and rest. I will see you in the morning."

"I'll be at Star Dome," he shrugged. "Whatever that is. Look for me there."

Gor'sadén watched Fel'annár limp away, join The Company on the banks, and then he turned back to the softly flowing river. His charge had passed an important test, one every commander faced, sooner or later. Some cracked under the weight of duty, became bitter, lost their hearts. But not Or'Talán.

Not Fel'annár.

They had risen to the challenge and won.

He remembered his own baptism of command, and then that of Pan'assár and Or'Talán. The Three had done everything together, and once more, Pan'assár's death flooded his mind.

A sudden memory made him want to dip his toes in the moonlight water, as he had so many times as a boy together with Orta and Pan, brothers of The Three.

Three boys swung their legs over the quayside, fishing boats bobbing on the water below, ropes flexing and sagging.

Orta stood, took off his shirt and boots, threw them recklessly to one side. With a toothy grin, he took a running jump and curled into a ball. With a mighty splash that sent shock waves all around him, he sunk below the water and then exploded from it. A squeal of laughter and Gorsa and then Pan were on their feet, tugging at their own boots, leaving them neatly to one side. With a graceful dive, they slipped under the waters.

Youthful faces, innocent and free, unaware of everything except their own joy. Gor'sadén stood, unbuckled his cuirass and laid it carefully on the ground. Strange to think of those two boys, the gruesome wars before them nothing but playful stories. Two of them were dead now.

Race you to the buoys and back. First one plays Commander General!

He opened the ties of his undertunic, folded it and laid it over his damaged cuirass, patted it carefully. The water would wash away the grime on his body, the grief in his mind.

"Second one plays Master Strategist!"

A smile tugged at Gor'sadén's lips, but it was a desperate kind of smile. He pulled one boot off, then the other, placed them in perfect alignment with the rest of his things, looked down at them for a moment. If only he could remember the sweet taste of innocence.

"Third one gets the last honey cake!" Giggles and gasps as they kicked their short legs and paddled with their arms, a ferocious battle to the buoy and back, white water splashing all about them.

Gor'sadén ran, and then dived into the water. Below the surface there was nothing but swaying reeds and scattering fish. He surfaced yet still, the memory lingered, pulled him forwards, faster and faster.

Gor'sadén had won the honey cake that day, had eaten it in two gulps but he would never forget that extraordinary friendship, that brotherhood of three. He was the only one left now and he swam, kicked hard as he soared through the water, memories of The Three flitting through his mind.

Their promotion as novices. Their ascension to command. The Blue Mountain and the victories they had won over the enemy of the Motherland – and still, the waters rushed by, arms straining, stroke after powerful stroke propelling him to the other side, to the end of the path.

He remembered Or'Talán, reading of the distant forests of the Silvans, incessant obsession and he knew that should his friend venture there, that Pan'assár would follow.

It was the day The Three had parted. Now, they had all but disappeared, nothing but memories.

The tips of his fingers brushed over rock and he floated to the river edge, stood and then made for the bank. He sat, sopping breeches, knees bent, elbows leaning on them, propping up his heavy head and there he remained, at the end of the path, silent tears mingling with river water as it pattered to the sodden ground beneath him.

There was no going back to the innocence of youth, nothing that could cleanse his mind of the grief, the weight of centuries of brotherhood gone. And even though he knew they would return, alive on the other side, those memories brought pain. All he could do was ride its cutting, frigid waves and know that with the passage of time, those very same memories would one day bring him joy.

40

PINNACLE OF THE WORLD

~

STAR DOME, Koldur had said, and Idernon asked a passing elf for directions. She smiled, pointed upwards, seemed to enjoy their shocked eyes as they travelled from the ground and upwards, until all they could see was a blur of green and brown.

At the base of the towering tree, two elves gestured to one of various air lifts. Fel'annár could see some damage, thought this tree would have been used by the Nim'uán, for it was surely the highest of all the trees here in the city. It would have afforded that beast a spectacular view over the lands it had thought to conquer.

Only three were allowed into the airlift at the same time, and with no one else available to work the others, they took turns. Idernon and Galdith helped Fel'annár inside, and as they were hoisted up, he looked around him. With the gigantic trunk blocking his view to the right, he looked ahead and to his left. Far below, warriors sat in motley groups where small fires would surely burn throughout the night. He saw the tarpaulins that covered the area where the healers worked without respite. If Llyniel were here, that was where she would be. He thanked the Gods that she wasn't, that she hadn't been forced to see what he had seen and done.

Above him, thick branches sprawled left and right, pathways that led to different buildings, some small, some large, some with doors and others without. On each side of these branches, rope railings added extra security, not that any Silvan elf would need them under normal circumstances.

But these were not.

The journey skywards continued, and still the canopy was thick. He saw bridges, sitting areas nestled in leafy corners, oiled cloth stretching over boxes and bundles, and even figures that had been carved out of the wood itself. It was like a village, he mused, all in one tree, and perhaps that was exactly what it was. He turned to Galdith.

"Do all trees have a name?"

"Yes. Although we refer to them as *settlements*. They're self-sufficient. They have their own transport systems for provisions, leisure areas, work areas. Everyone who lives here works together, shares everything, cares for the tree under the auspices of the foresters. This is what many Alpines don't see, what they can't understand. Although I admit ... I've never been to a settlement quite *this* big."

Fel'annár was humbled at the size of the tree, by the sheer complexity of what lay inside. If only his body would obey him and he could enjoy it, get out and touch everything. But it wouldn't. It was all he could do to stay on his own two feet, just a little while longer.

It was minutes later that the airlift jolted to a halt. Fel'annár didn't see Lord Koldur and three others upon a sprawling platform. Instead, his gaze was cast upwards and to the open night sky, full of glittering, winking stars. A rush of air left him, his bewildered eyes unable to take it all in, understand the wide, wide world that had opened up to him in the blink of an eye. He stood dazed, overwhelmed, humbled almost to tears at the beauty above him, of its incomprehensible vastness.

He was standing upon the pinnacle of the world, he mused.

He turned to Koldur, saw his indulgent smile.

"Star Dome is a phenomenon of nature, not for the weak of heart, mind."

"No," he whispered. It was all he could manage.

"Welcome, Fel'annár Ar Lássira. We have prepared a cabin for you and your warriors. Captain Bulan has sent a message in which he respectfully requests that you stay here. He says he and Captain Dalú are seeing to your warriors."

Blessed Bulan, thought Fel'annár, as he put one foot in front of the other, limped forward and grit his teeth. It had worked before, when there were pyres to tend, warriors to farewell, something to distract him from the voice in his mind and the pain he felt. But it wasn't working now, and he stopped, breath caught in his throat. He could walk no more.

Idernon and Galdith took hold of his arms, held him aloft and walked him across the platform to a cabin which sat nestled inside the topmost branches of the giant tree.

His blurry eyes distantly registered a room with a fire, and beyond, another room with a bed. Their journey came to an end in the bathing room which stood to one side of the bed chamber. There, a bathtub awaited, and beside it, a dark-haired healer stood, red sash around his waist.

Fel'annár would accept the comfort, only because he had come to the end of his endurance. There was no more fight in him, only clumsy surrender as he was half-dragged to the bath.

They must have cleaned him, put this long shirt on him but he couldn't remember. All he could feel was Idernon and Galdith's hands under him as they walked towards a bed. He reached out for it with his good hand and all but fell onto it.

It smelled of spice and resins, all things Silvan and how he wanted to forget everything, sink into dreamless oblivion and forget the battle, the dead faces of his warriors.

But he couldn't.

Idernon and Galdith must have left, but he couldn't remember that either. He turned to the healer who was looking down at him with an expression he had seen on Llyniel's face so many times. But this elf seemed old, had that same air about him as Galadan once had.

He pushed the thought away, watched the tall healer as he set to mixing herbs at a table at the foot of the bed.

"How you managed to walk with that knee is a marvel of nature, Warlord."

Fel'annár blinked at the unexpected voice. "My warriors were waiting to take the Road."

Dengar glanced at his patient as he worked. "You shouldn't have walked on it. You've done more damage to it."

"Then so be it."

Dengar frowned, and then wandered to the side of the bed, offering Fel'annár a cup. He took it, drank it down and handed it back. He could taste the Junar, mixed with other, familiar herbs. Galdith must have explained about the antidote, he realised.

The healer bent, took Fel'annár's leg and carefully moved it this way and that, watching his patient's face, sometimes blank, other times pulled into a grimace of pain.

"Have a care, Warlord. Your warriors need you whole and hale."

Fel'annár's eyes wandered over the black robes, the red sash tied at his side and the equally black headdress that held his dark hair from his face. "You are Lestari ..."

Dengar nodded slowly. "Yes."

"Then why are you here? Why aren't you at the pavilions, caring for those who need you most?"

Fel'annár's tone had been harsher than he had intended, but Dengar did not falter in his work. Instead, he looked down on his patient with eyes that were kind and wise. Gods but it could have been Galadan standing there.

"Who decides where I am needed most?"

"Logic, Lestari. I'm not going to die."

"Logic is sometimes surprising, Warlord. Besides, I have spoken to your Galdith. He tells me you have a penchant for hiding injury. It's a common thing with warriors. Or'Talán was famous for it."

Fel'annár said nothing, watched as Dengar rubbed some foul-smelling cream over his knee and then wound it in a clean bandage. Arranging the pillows on the bed, Dengar helped Fel'annár to lean back on them. He slathered a different liquid on his arm wound, and then took a needle to it. Fel'annár barely felt it, knew there must have been pain-killing herbs in the medicine he'd drunk earlier.

"They say an army needs a leader, so that the correct decisions can be made, so that lives are not lost unnecessarily, and the warriors are emboldened so that they can fight. If this is true, and you are that leader, then you must be fit enough to command. That makes healing you a priority."

Fel'annár's face hardened, nostrils flared, and eyes glittered. "I led them to their *deaths!*" His voice was nothing but a furious whisper and he turned away, ashamed at his outburst. Hadn't Gor'sadén gone through this with him earlier? Had he not told Fel'annár that he had acted correctly? That he was not responsible for the thousands of deaths? Fel'annár had heard the words, but he had yet to release himself of the guilt and self-loathing.

Dengar continued to stitch Fel'annár's arm, face serene. "Many decades ago, when I was a novice healer, I found myself in this very situation. Our king – your grandfather – had died, his body unsalvageable, and the warriors had burned him in the Xeric Wood. It was General Pan'assár who lay injured here back then, he and Captain Bulan. I remember your uncle's words, his lament. Yes, he had seen *battle* and plenty of it, was no stranger to losing warriors. But the Battle Under the Sun was *war*, Fel'annár, on a scale similar to this one. We lost thousands then too, and Bulan was angry at himself. He said his contingent was dead because of *him*, because of the decisions he had made, because his warriors were loyal to *him*. He thought he didn't deserve the attention of others. His guilt ate at him for days, until someone offered him wise words."

Fel'annár listened to the tale, anger at bay, curiosity prevailing. "What ... what did they say?"

"He said warriors die in war because they follow orders, from leaders they are loyal to, leaders they look up to and respect. They *choose* to follow, Fel'annár, and in that choice, they decide their own fates."

Fel'annár remembered how Gor'sadén had spoken of a warrior's oath, the one they had all taken.

Even unto death.

"You are not responsible for their deaths. You are responsible for the victory you brought us. You are the reason we are here now."

Fel'annár looked away, unwilling to accept Dengar's words of praise. Then he frowned, half-turned to the healer. "Who said those things?"

Dengar smiled. "It was Captain Bulan's father, Zéndar. Your other grandfather."

Fel'annár squeezed his eyes shut, felt tears leak from the corners of his eyes but he was too tired to care. He felt Dengar's hands on his arm, bandaging his stitched wound.

"Command came so easily to you; so say the warriors in the pavilions. But I suppose you never can understand the weight of it, until you understand the true price of war. But should you ask them – would you have charged into Abiren'á, even knowing that none of your loved ones were hanging from the heights – what do you think your warriors would say?"

Fel'annár stared at Dengar, intrigued by his question.

Dengar smiled. "They would say 'yes'. They would say that it could have been *their* mothers, *their* fathers, their brothers and sisters, friends. No matter it wasn't. Today for you, tomorrow for me, is that not how brotherhood works?"

Fel'annár blinked, looked away. "You're not a warrior..."

"Oh but I am. Not on the same battlefield as you. But I treat warriors, know them well. I battle with the injuries to their bodies and their minds. Your doubts are not unique. Every commander I have ever treated has those same misgivings. You must stop punishing yourself for a crime you did not commit."

Dengar stood, replaced the corks of his bottles and vials and Fel'annár watched in silence for a while, allowed the wise healer's words to sink into his defensive mind, mingle with those Gor'sadén had offered him at the river. They spread, began to push past his futile anger and self-pity.

Dengar, Gor'sadén, even Zéndar had offered sound words of advice this night, through those who still lived, and they were far older and wiser than he was.

Were they right?

Words sounded distant to him, his body heavier in the bed, even as his heart felt just a little lighter than it had.

"Turn over."

He half-turned, felt pillows being re-arranged, hands on his shoulder and thigh. He was vaguely aware of something cold on his back, not enough to bring him back from his wanderings. The pillow under his head blurred and then faded to grey.

The last thing he remembered was the weight of a blanket, the warmth it gave, and the quiet voice of the dark-haired healer, humming some ancient tune as he worked.

GOR'SADÉN HAD SLEPT in the forest, alone with his thoughts.

He shrugged into his dry but crumpled clothes, buckled on his dented armour. He thought Pan'assár would laugh at him for his pathetic appearance. He tried to smile but couldn't and made his way into the city.

His tired feet took him to the place where Pan'assár had rested under the Sentinel, remembered Carodel's extraordinary voice at the pyres.

No one walked where his brother had lain in his final hours in this world, but as they passed, they reached out, fingers brushing over the bark of the Sentinel that had protected him and Galadan.

He felt a presence beside him and turned. Two elves stood there, one much taller and older than the other.

"A great elf lay here," said the elder, and Gor'sadén looked from him, and then down to the honey-coloured eyes of the younger elf.

"Your son?"

"Yes. Alive thanks to Commander Pan'assár. He looked at us you know – when we were still inside that last cage – before he ran for that beast and killed it, killed *himself* ..."

Gor'sadén flinched, but then he wondered at the strength of this grateful father, a Silvan forester who had surely once hated Pan'assár.

"We will call him Protector. He freed us so that the Warlord could bring victory. The Silvans will remember, Lord Gor'sadén of The Three."

Gor'sadén pressed his jaw together, suppressed the tears that threatened to overwhelm him. "And so will the Alpines. *I* will remember him. Always."

With a nod, Gor'sadén left in search of Star Dome. He would find

Fel'annár, make sure he was well, and then he would bathe and sleep, try not to dream of his glorious past with The Three.

Along the way, he met Bulan in the company of Hobin. He saw their surprise at his appearance, hardened his features. He didn't want their pity.

"Commander, Captain. Where is Star Dome?"

"We were just on our way there, if you'll join us?"

Gor'sadén nodded at Hobin, ignored their concerned glances, and together, the three warriors made their silent way to the air lift. He didn't know what Star Dome was, but by the time he was at the very top of it, he understood.

Hobin was as taken with the place as he himself was, while Bulan simply smiled at the beauty of his home. His own house was outside the city, closer to the western mountains but as a close friend to Koldur, he'd been here plenty of times.

As the air lift jolted to a halt, Lainon stood waiting for them upon the platform. Hobin peered at him, was surely thinking the same as the others. Why was he still in his elven form? The war was over. Still, the mystery of Lainon's return had not been discussed, not yet at least.

They followed the silent Ari'atór to the wood cabin. The first room was empty save for Tensári at the fire who stood and bowed. Gor'sadén made for the only door that was open and stepped inside.

On the bed, fast asleep, was Fel'annár, and standing beside it, was the Lestari.

"How is he?" asked Gor'sadén as he stepped inside, followed by Bulan and Hobin.

"He sleeps." Dengar turned from his patient and faced Gor'sadén, eyes roaming over his dented armour and pale face. "He needs some rest and recuperation, but it is his mind that needs to heal now."

Gor'sadén stared back at the tall healer, saw the years in his eyes, knew exactly what Dengar meant.

"He won't wake for a while, but come to the pavilions if you need me, my Lord."

Gor'sadén nodded slowly in respect and thanks, watched Dengar make for the door but he stopped and turned.

"I am sorry for your loss, lord."

Gor'sadén steeled himself. He had broken down in solitude and silence last night, and since then, it was all he could do to contain his tears. He nodded curtly, turned away and Dengar's gaze drifted over Bulan and Hobin, a silent reminder to call him should he be needed.

Hobin placed a hand on Gor'sadén's shoulder. "Come. There is a room for you too, with a bath and clean linens."

Gor'sadén nodded slowly. He would bathe, change into something clean and then come back here, concentrate on Fel'annár, so that he wouldn't think of Pan'assár. But before he left, he bent over Fel'annár and placed a hand on his warm brow, mouth close to his ear. His words were nothing but a whisper meant for his son.

"They *chose* to follow you, even unto death. You led them to *victory*."

He stood, turned, and followed Hobin out of the room. But Bulan lingered a while longer. He had heard Gor'sadén's words, understood them all too well. Dengar had said his mind needed to heal, and well he knew its ailment. This war had been Fel'annár's baptism of command, just like his own, so many decades ago in this very same place.

His own father stirred in his mind, memories of his quiet, commanding presence surfacing, comforting, and he wondered, where his father was now, what he was doing or thinking. But one thing was certain. He would be proud of his grandson, as proud as Bulan was to call him family.

Bulan had gone to the city of Ea Uaré in search of a nephew. Instead, he had found the greatest commander these lands would ever know.

It took a while for Fel'annár to realise that he had been dreaming.

He had been standing in the main glade, naked save for his two blades, and above him, a waterfall of bodies fell from the heights, rushed past him and thudded to the floor. On the other side of the fall, Pan'assár and Galadan stood riddled with arrows, the tip of a sword poking out of Pan'assár's chest. They stared back at him in anger and in pity.

The thwack of an arrow, and Lainon's body fell right in front of him, landing face up on a rocky riverbed, water running red, his vacant eyes staring straight up at him accusingly.

Fel'annár squeezed his eyes shut, felt tears slide down his face. He tried to remember where he was.

He turned his head to the foot of the bed. There, with his back leaning against the footboard, was Lainon.

He instinctively recoiled, scrambling back up against the headboard, eyes wide while he tried to get his breathing under control. He forced himself to remember where he was.

He was in Abiren'á, on Star Dome at night, in a room with a door. He had commanded an army and lost half of it. Pan'assár and Galadan were dead, while Lainon had returned from the other side.

"I am *real*, Fel'annár. I'm not a houseless soul. I am sorry that I startled you."

Fel'annár stared back at him, reality slowly sinking in. He breathed in, then out, settled himself against the pillows, legs stretched out before him.

"Tell me of your dream." The voice was quiet, tone inviting.

Silence. A deep breath, a whispery sigh.

"My warriors were dying, their eyes full of reproach. And then you died in front of me."

Silence.

"Did you see Galadan too?"

Silence.

"Yes. And Pan'assár."

Silence.

"We need to talk."

Silence.

"About what?"

"My death."

Fel'annár could no longer sit still. He told himself he didn't want to hear what Lainon would say. He felt trapped and he stood, reached for the crutch that had been placed beside the headboard. He leaned heavily on it, and then staggered towards the door. He needed to get out, didn't want Lainon to accompany him, but he knew that he would.

He felt so weak and he wondered just how long he had slept. It had been night time when they had arrived here, and it still was.

Outside the door, he passed Tensári, watched her glance at Lainon, knew that she wouldn't follow, and soon, he had made his noisy, clumsy way out onto the platform, not too close to the edge lest he slip and fall. He wondered if the trees would catch him if he did.

For a moment, he just stood there, looking down on the meandering river and the pyres that still smoked. He should have been there, but his own body had conspired against him. Still, he knew his captains would have carried out the rites in his place.

Fel'annár turned to a quiet corner off to his right where a bench and two chairs sat around a small table. Lainon was already there, waiting for him. He knew there was no avoiding the conversation, indeed it seemed strange to him now that they had not spoken before. He supposed it was the shock of Lainon's return and then the dizzying sequence of events that had followed.

He felt better here, under an impossibly open sky. He felt sheltered beneath these stars, felt more at home than he ever had in Lan Taria.

He sat beside Lainon on the bench, and a memory assailed him, almost overwhelmed him. He and Lainon sitting on an outcrop, looking out over the Downlands. It had been the day that Fel'annár had embraced the Alpine side of himself, and Lainon had said something that he had never forgotten.

I choose you as a brother, if you would have me.

Fel'annár remembered the joy those words had brought, and then the pain when just days later, Lainon had died in Tensári's arms.

He bent forwards, leaned his forearms on his thighs. When Lainon spoke, it was soft, almost distant.

"Tell me. Did you feel guilty when I died?"

Fel'annár stared back at him, wanted to deny it but he couldn't. Lainon had thrown his life away to save him.

"Yes."

Lainon smiled only slightly as he too, leaned forward as he listened.

"I failed to understand my gift, and that led to your death. Tensári would not have lost her Connate and you would still have been at my side. Days ago, I failed again, I should have conjured the trees earlier and not waited for thousands of warriors to die. I could have rallied The Company to face the Nim'uán, save Galadan and Pan'assár, I ..."

"Stop."

"It needs to be said, Lainon. I'm not ready for command on this scale. I'm too young, too foolish to lead warriors in battle. Look what I have done! So many warriors dead! I am responsible for Pan'assár and Galadan's deaths, responsible for *your* death." He was shaking, eyes full of unshed tears. Images from his dream came back to him, the waterfall of bodies, his dead friends staring at him, blaming him. He wanted to scream it, demand that they stop calling him Warlord because he was nothing but a foolish child.

He started at Lainon's voice, because he sounded angry. He had hardly ever heard him use that tone, except for once when he had publicly scolded him after his first skirmish with Deviants.

"Yes. Look what you have done, Fel'annár. Behold, for we sit here in peace! There are no Sand Lords, no Reapers and their vile serpents. No Nim'uán. We have not lost our lands and we are free. *Look* ... what you have done. You have brought victory and the price was high. But you did not set that price. The enemy did. It was not your *fault*."

Fel'annár stared back at the Ari'atór. There was something about the moonlight that illuminated his black hair, something about his steady blue eyes. Lainon was not a spirit, but the Gods he felt like one. In the ensuing silence, Lainon's words began to reform in his mind.

It was not your fault.

"You took the right decisions, not the easiest decisions, Fel'annár. You need to accept that. If you had conjured the trees without rescuing those elves in the cages, would you have been able to live with yourself?"

"I asked myself that before Pan'assár decided our strategy. But in hindsight, three hundred lives in exchange for three *thousand,* Lainon ..."

"What do you think your warriors would have wanted you to do? Save their lives at the expense of those they had sworn to protect? Or let them help you try to save the lives of innocent civilians, even if it meant sacrificing theirs? Each of your warriors swore an oath to uphold the Warrior Code. That meant saving innocent lives at the expense of their own. They *chose* to do it."

Fel'annár was silent, and Lainon pushed on, willing the despondent Warlord to see what *he* saw so clearly.

"If you had hesitated before conjuring the trees, even had you managed to save Galadan and Pan'assár, who might we have lost in their place? Bulan? Idernon? Me again? And you ask, what has this to do with my death? The answer is plain."

Fel'annár lifted his heavy head, forced himself to look at the first elf he had ever looked up to. The first leader who had inspired him, believed in him, had become a brother to him.

"Once, I took the right decision, not the easiest decision. I took that arrow meant for you and I died, so that you would not, so that you could become what you have. I never regretted it."

Fel'annár looked at the stars, reminded himself that he was a part of something much bigger than himself. Lainon had given his life and yet here he was, by some miracle he would surely never understand. He *had* felt guilty then, but he realised that it was because Lainon had thought him worthy of his sacrifice.

It was a hard thing to accept, but then Lainon was right. It had been his decision, not Fel'annár's. He remembered Gor'sadén's words once more.

That oath is taken freely, gladly. We serve, even though our duty may lead to death.

"And neither should *you* regret anything you have done – because *everything* you did was the *right* thing to do. I was watching you, as was Gor'sadén. Your father, your brother, both of us proud of the things that you have done. If you had chosen the wrong thing, we would have stepped in. We would have told you, and this pride you see in my eyes would not be here."

Had you made mistakes, I would have told you, and I know you would have heeded me. I said nothing because there were no flaws in your judgement. Pan'assár would agree with me, and there was no better strategist than he.

Fel'annár remembered Pan'assár, sprinting over the battlefield, side by side with Galadan. He was buying time for Gor'sadén to break the ropes, so that Fel'annár could conjure. Had he not invoked the maelstrom when he had, then Pan'assár's sacrifice would have been for nothing. Galadan's death would have been futile. And if Pan'assár had thought it necessary to conjure the forest before Fel'annár had, he would have ordered it.

But he hadn't. And Fel'annár trusted Pan'assár's judgement.

He made you general, awarded you the Forest Emerald. He showed you the art of strategy, listened as you gave your opinions. He believed in you.

He closed his eyes and exhaled loudly. "So... I didn't ... you think I was right to wait?"

"I am sure of it."

"I made all the right decisions?"

"Yes."

"Yet still, I couldn't save Pan'assár nor Galadan. I couldn't save the thousands of warriors who died in this war. I ... couldn't ... save *you*, brother."

He watched Lainon stand, turn to him, look down on him with nothing but love in his eyes.

"No."

The guilt Fel'annar had been harbouring was leeching away. He had done nothing wrong, had made all the right decisions. He couldn't have done anything more to save his friends.

Maybe, just maybe, he could then believe the other things they had said. Could he be the commander Pan'assár believed he would become? That Gor'sadén thought he already was?

Could he finally believe in *himself*?

"I missed you so much, brother." It was nothing but a whisper, as if Lainon were not there at all but still somewhere across the Veil.

Lainon held out his hands, palms up. "We will always be together, in some shape or form." He smiled softly at the irony of his own words, and Fel'annár returned it. And then he caught sight of something he had never seen before. It was a mark, on the inside of Lainon's wrist, a short, wavy line and beside it, a single dot. But then his brother saluted someone and Fel'annár turned.

"That is the way of the Ari'atór, is it not?" A new voice from behind, and Fel'annár made to stand with Lainon. But Hobin gestured for them to remain seated.

"May I join you?"

"Of course," answered Fel'annár, watching as the Supreme Commander tilted his head backwards and looked skywards.

"It's good to see you finally awake, Fel'annár. I myself once slept for two days straight after a particularly gruelling week of battle."

Fel'annár's brows rose at that. Had he been sleeping for two days? He turned to Lainon, but he was already speaking.

"I will take my leave." He stood, nodded resolutely at Fel'annár and then bowed to Hobin. He had not given the commander time to protest, and Fel'annár wondered if he was avoiding Hobin for some reason. Perhaps he knew he would have questions, questions which, as Shirán, he could not answer.

With Lainon gone, Hobin watched after him for a moment and then sat where he had just a moment before.

"Will you tell me of your first reunion with Lainon Ber'ator? Of how he returned from the Short Road?"

Fel'annár turned to him, remembered that Hobin had been there when Lainon had died in Tar'eastór. That was the first time he had met the Supreme Ari Commander. But before he answered that question, he had one of his own.

"Have any others ever returned from the Short Road like Lainon has?"

"Not to my knowledge, no. Which doesn't mean they haven't. I suppose if anyone would know, it would be the Shirán."

"The secret order?"

"Yes."

Fel'annár remembered how Tensári had told the guards in Port Helia that they were Shirán on a mission for Araria, remembered the fear he had seen in their eyes. That had been the first time he had heard of them. The second time had been just recently, when Lainon confessed that *he* was Shirán.

"Why are people scared of them?"

"There are few of them, selected by the head of the order for reasons which sometimes seem arbitrary. I have always assumed there must be something they all have in common, but I have spent years wondering what it might be. Once chosen, they undergo training not even I am allowed to see. Their leader is Ber'anor, but unlike us, his purpose changes, and he is free to deploy his Shirán in order to achieve those goals he says Aria places before him."

"What's his name?" asked Fel'annár.

"Ket'subá. If you ever come to Araria, you will meet him."

Fel'annár nodded. "Hobin. I asked Lainon if he was Arimal. He said they were myth, based on a reality. He said he was Shirán."

Hobin turned slowly to him, said nothing, and Fel'annár finally answered Hobin's first question.

"I first saw the hawk on our journey north, although truth be told, I believe our first meeting was ... in a dream." He shrugged, turned back to the view over Abiren'á. "Or perhaps it wasn't a dream."

Hobin started, waited for him to continue, watched the Warlord slowly straighten his crooked body with a grimace, visibly gathering his thoughts.

"Do you know of the Evergreen Wood, Hobin, the one that Or'Talán forbade to the elves?"

"I have heard of it."

"I asked permission to go inside, only as far as the place I knew I would be tolerated. Given my affinity with the forest, the king granted permission and I set out to that place alone. That night, I dreamt that I passed that place I knew that I shouldn't. I couldn't help myself. I came across ... across the Last Markers, Hobin. Have you ever been there?"

"Yes."

"I know that you can't speak of it, that you won't, but I need to know, whether it was a dream or whether it was *real*."

Hobin was shaking his head. "Where were you in this dream?"

"I was in the Evergreen Wood, Hobin, not in Araria."

"Then it was a dream."

"It felt real. I saw Zéndar, Hobin. And I saw ... I saw myself standing next to him."

A breath of ragged air, as if it had escaped Hobin without his permission. Eyes wide, head moving from side to side.

"What did you say?"

Fel'annár stared back at Hobin, dread in his gut at what he thought it might mean. "I said I saw myself." It was nothing but a whisper and Hobin turned his face away from Fel'annár. But he didn't speak and Fel'annár pressed on.

"Only the dead are Last Markers, I know that. I thought my dream a forewarning of my death, that this war would end my life."

At this, Hobin turned back, face inscrutable. "Go on."

"Should I?" Fel'annár stared at his fellow Ber'anor, watching his eyes for any sign of doubt. But he found none.

"Yes, I believe you should."

"I reached out and touched the spear on Zéndar's back, and ... something exploded from the mountain behind, an unnatural mist and inside, a huge green beast – a wyvern, I think. It came for me, wanted to kill me. I fled into the forest, following the sound of a hawk that was guiding me to safety. But the green mist followed me, caught me and then strangled me to death. The last thing I recalled was the loud flapping of wings. The next morning, I woke up to find myself back at my campsite. It had all been a dream, but as I left the Evergreen Wood, a hawk followed me to the gate, seemed to be watching over me. I believe it was the same hawk that saved me from death in the dream. Now, I believe that hawk was Lainon. That was the first time I ever met him, without me knowing who he was."

Hobin tried to school his face, but Fel'annár could see the shock in his eyes as he listened, lowering his head at the end, obviously pondering deeply about what had been shared.

"I wanted to ask Lainon whether that was a dream. But he seems reticent to speak. Tensári says it wasn't a dream because she felt the danger I was in."

After a while, Hobin–lifted his chin, could not quite seem to meet Fel'annár's gaze. "The statues you saw. You are right – in that only dead servants are carved into Last Markers. They are mostly Ber'ator, but there are some Ber'anor too."

"But – but I'm alive. I'm still alive."

Hobin nodded slowly. "Perhaps it wasn't *you* that you saw, Fel'annár."

He frowned, shook his head as he stared back at Hobin. "It was *my* face ..." He stopped mid-sentence, the truth dawning in his mind.

"*Or'Talán?*"

"I – we believe so."

"We?"

"Lainon and I."

Fel'annár's eyes filled with tears of shock as he stared at Hobin, tried to process what the Supreme Ari Commander was saying.

"You've spoken? Wha ... how can you be so sure of that? How can it be possible?"

"Fel'annár, Lainon said something you should know."

Fel'annár breathed deeply, waited for Hobin to continue.

"He saw something while you were conjuring the trees in Abiren'á. He saw the moment Pan'assár died in Gor'sadén's arms."

"I know how he died, Hobin." He turned back to the stars.

"You don't understand."

"What don't I understand?" murmured Fel'annár.

"Lainon saw Pan'assár's Guiding Light as it left him and entered Gor'sadén."

Hobin's words echoed in Fel'annár's mind.

Pan'assár's Guiding Light.

He felt dizzy where he sat and he slumped forward, rested his hands on his thighs, eyes squeezed shut. A strong hand grasped hold of his arm, grounding him. Fel'annár's stunned mind was racing as understanding slowly dawned.

A Guiding Light could only mean one thing – Pan'assár had been Ber'ator, *Or'Talán's* Ber'ator. It meant that they too, had been *pale* Ari'atór, like himself. His head was spinning at the flood of questions, the implications, the growing surety that it was true.

Gods but how had he not understood before?

41

THE FAR SIDE OF THE FOREST

∽

"Pan'assár was Ber'ator," said Fel'annár. "That's why he could never overcome the severed link between him and Or'Talán, his *Ber'anor* ... did they even know?"

The Supreme Commander was shaking his head slowly. "I do not think Pan'assár knew. I have not had much dealing with him, but he must have had dreams of revelation, Fel'annár, dreams he may have failed to recognise. As for Or'Talán, he forbade access to the Evergreen Wood but for what purpose?"

"He must have known, Hobin. And I think he knew his purpose. It was the same as mine ..." Fel'annár's voice dissipated as he wondered at the words coming out of his own mouth. He felt faint again. Breathing deeply, his eyes wandered far south and although he couldn't see it, he knew exactly where it was, the forest he had been born to protect, for the precious treasure which lay inside.

"What ... what is that purpose, Fel'annár? This battle against the invading army - something that Or'Talán did too – it was not your purpose, was it? You once told me you knew that you were to unify Ea Uaré, but I remember you were unsure as to whether that was your ultimate goal. Now that you have achieved that much, still, I can see the question in your eyes.

"What is your purpose?"

Fel'annár opened his mouth once more, forced himself to speak the words, so that the stunning conclusion he had just reached in his mind would make sense. But all that came out was a whisper, just loud enough for Hobin to hear.

"I had to unite Silvans and Alpines, so that we could come together against the Nim'uán. I had to defeat the Nim'uán and we have. All this, Hobin, because I am to defend the Last Markers."

"I don't understand. The Last Markers are in A..."

"There is another Source, Hobin. In the Evergreen Wood. Another Valley, another doorway to a second life, another Long Road and I am its keeper, as you are the guardian of Araria."

A light in the forest.

Lainon had told him of the words that had appeared beneath his skin. It wasn't *him* who was the light. It was the *Source* ...

"It's not ... it's not possible ..." It wasn't really a statement, more a failed attempt to tell himself that Fel'annár was wrong. He *had* to be.

Fel'annár reached out to the Sisters.

Are you Originals?

Soft whispers, deep voices in the distance and Fel'annár strained his mind to understand what they said.

The Ber'anor's purpose has been understood.

Then tell me.

We are Originals, first defenders of the Source.

His eyes flew open, blazing pools of green light and despite the shocking revelations the evening had brought, Fel'annár smiled.

"Or'Talán knew what he was, as well as he knew his purpose. Defend the Source. It's why he rushed off to war, so that the Sand Lords would not invade Ea Uaré because sooner or later, they would have found that place. He was Divine Servant, but he never said anything to anyone, not even Pan'assár ..."

"This revelation brings with it many questions, Fel'annár. The reasons why there is another Source that is secret."

"During my trip into the Evergreen Wood, I found other things I have spoken about only with Tensári."

"That is well. She is Ber'ator."

"Yes, but still, she didn't believe me – until Lainon came back."

"What do you mean?"

"I saw many animals like Lainon – Azure – animals that should not have blue eyes. I must ask myself if they too, are Arimals, if they are Shirán."

Hobin said nothing, but he was shaking his head, as if he didn't understand, but Fel'annár knew that he did.

"I know that Azure - Lainon - was there in the wood, that he saved me from ... a beast I thought was a figment of my imagination but now I must question that too. But ... but what if ... what if that Source is for the Ari'atór – specifically the Divine Servants – Ber'anor and Ber'ator who, for some reason, must return to this world ..."

"Stop. Fel'annár this is ... it is too much."

"I know. But tell me my reasoning is flawed. Tell me I have not thought of something that would deconstruct my conclusions. I know for sure that Azure came out of that place. I know there are other creatures, based on the myth of the Arimal, that are likely elves. I have seen them, Lainon himself is here, defending me so that I can defend the Evergreen Wood, so that those Shirán can do ... whatever it is they do."

The silence between them stretched on. Fel'annár ran a hand down his face. He wanted to go through his own reasoning again, catch the flaw that was surely leading him to false conclusions. But the weight of uncertainty had lifted from his soul and in its place, what he knew was the truth began to settle. Or'Talán had died defending the Evergreen Wood, and Fel'annár had been charged by Aria, to continue his legacy.

A long sigh, he closed his eyes and then slowly opened them, Hobin's deep yet soothing voice beside him.

"It's cold out here. It's time to go back to your fire to rest and heal, Fel'annár. There will be time enough to speak more, on our journey back to Ea Uaré."

Fel'annár turned to him, wondered if he had misunderstood.

"You're coming with us?"

"I am now. Jendal will return to Araria with a missive for Ket'subá."

"You think Ket'subá may have answers?"

"He is the head of the Order of the Shirán. If anyone knows of the existence of these creatures, it will be him."

Fel'annár nodded, allowed himself a smile. "I'm glad you're coming with us, Hobin. I can't speak of this to any save for The Company, but only Lainon can go into the Evergreen Wood. You though, are Supreme Commander. You are Ber'anor. You could surely accompany me, Hobin, see this place for yourself."

"And I have every intention of doing so, unless Aria tells me otherwise. I will have my answers. But for now, do not speak of this Source to anyone."

"No. But Gor'sadén needs to know about Pan'assár."

"Does he?"

"Yes. I won't keep that from him. He won't reveal it without my permission."

"You must be cautious, Fel'annár. Until you are sure of the existence of this second Source and what purpose it serves, no one must know."

"The Company, Hobin, and Gor'sadén. They must know."

"I will trust your intuition then. Now heed me. You must rest and your Company will see that you are not disturbed."

Fel'annár nodded and together, the two Ber'anor made back to the Cabin.

"Hobin. About this ... beast that I saw behind the Last Markers. I won't ask you the question but tell me. Does it surprise you to hear of this ... guardian?"

Hobin didn't look at Fel'annár when he answered, one word, strong and resolute, no surprise at all.

"No."

FEL'ANNÁR WOKE up to a radiant morning.

He could feel the sun's rays warming his cut and bruised face. He felt warm, comfortable, didn't want to move but he knew that he had to.

There were things he needed to do, people to speak to, decisions to be made. He rolled over, grimaced with the pain that came with the movement. But not even that was enough to snap him out of the strange mood that had taken him.

He had come to understand his role in the war, accepted its weight, resolved to never again question himself in the destructive way that he had. Analyse, correct, try harder, these things he *would* do. But he would not wallow in self-pity, would not grind himself down into the mud and tell himself it was all his fault. Lainon did not blame him. Pan'assár and Galadan would not blame him; Gor'sadén had told him that. Not even the warriors nor the civilians would blame him, according to Dengar and Bulan.

And then he had heard of Bulan's own baptism of war, his ascension to command. It had been Zéndar who had put him straight, who had put *Fel'annár* straight, through Lestari Dengar.

And who was Fel'annár to question The Three? Zéndar or Lainon Ber'ator?

Ber'ator ... it was only then, that last night's revelations came back to him, the shocking truth of his grandfather's prohibition, the *real* reason why he had barred entrance to the Evergreen Wood. There was surely a second Source, one he was meant to guard. It lay in a forest of colour, where the Shirán were free to roam.

But then, if all that were true, had his dream been real? Did wyverns exist? Was it an Arimal? A Shirán?

There was only one way to be sure. Return to Ea Uaré and seek the truth.

He needed to speak with Gor'sadén, and then The Company, because this changed everything. It changed him and Gods but although his body still ached, some new resolve surged from the depths, lent him strength.

He turned once more, started when he saw Idernon sitting in the chair beside the bed.

He pushed himself up with his good arm. "You look fresh."

Idernon cocked a brow. "And you look ... hair raising?"

Fel'annár snorted and Idernon seemed happy that he had. Who could blame him? He had snapped at Idernon, slept for days, had hardly spent time with The Company after the war. But he would today.

Ramien poked his head into the room. "Good to see you finally awake," he said cheerfully.

"Exactly how long have I been sleeping?" He looked from Idernon to Ramien.

"All in all, three days. Long enough for people to travel here from Sen'oléi. We were about to shake the living daylights out of you, thought you'd gone down with the Nim'uán poison. But Lestari Dengar assured us you hadn't."

Fel'annár nodded. Three days was too long, immersed as they had been in the aftermath of war. But he had needed it – needed *everything* that had happened last night. He turned to Idernon.

"Brother, get a message to Commander Gor'sadén, the captains, to Lord Koldur, Commander Hobin and Yerái. I would hold council on the platform. And can you arrange for some breakfast? I'm starving."

"We're returning then?"

"Soon, but first, there are things we must do." Fel'annár pushed the bedclothes back, sat up with a grimace. "Pass me that stupid crutch."

Idernon hid his grin, did as he was told and watched as his friend stood on shaky legs. While Ramien went in search of The Company, Idernon entered the main living quarters in search of food. He found Gor'sadén standing with his back to him.

"Commander."

Gor'sadén turned.

"Fel'annár has awoken and has called for a council."

The commander nodded slowly, glanced at the open door as if he were debating whether to enter. "Who would he call?"

"You, our captains, Lord Koldur, Commander Hobin and Lieutenant Yerái."

"Leave it with me, Idernon."

"Commander, I can do it, I didn't mean to ..."

"Leave it with me. Go with your Company."

Idernon smiled, bowed his thanks, watched him leave.

He turned to the platters of food someone had left on a side table and grabbed the largest of them. He walked carefully back into the room and placed it on the table at the foot of the bed. Moments later, Ramien,

Carodel and Galdith entered, arms full of packages, clothing and weapons.

Galdith straightened his back with a grimace. "It's chaos out there, brothers. More people have returned from Sen'oléi, and the foresters have finally allowed all the dead wood to be carried to the shores of the Calro. Still, it's going to be a feat, moving those giant branches and trunks. There's no room to roll them. They'll need to be carried."

Fel'annár listened as he watched them sort through their effects and separate them into piles on the bed.

"And what do the people say? The warriors?" Fel'annár reached for the hot bread, tore a generous piece off and began to eat.

The Bard Warrior glanced at Ramien, Galdith and then Idernon. "They're all tired, exhausted from the days of cleaning, of mourning. The civilians worry for the future, that this will happen again, and the warriors tell them that it won't. Still, I can see their wary eyes, as clearly as I hear their words. They speak of you, Fel'annár. They say you will come. They say you will fix it but I can see them falter."

Idernon nodded, turned to Fel'annár. "They need to see you, hear you." He braced for his friend's denial, some comment that perhaps they shouldn't be so sure, that he was not worthy of their trust.

But Fel'annár smiled, and in his eyes, Idernon saw strength. He saw determination and he saw something else, something he had only ever seen in Gor'sadén and Pan'assár's eyes. He battled to find words to describe his impressions.

"What did we miss, Fel'annár? You have come back from the pits of torment and there is a reason for it."

No sooner had Idernon said the words, than Lainon and Tensári entered, eyes on Fel'annár as he spoke.

"Dress, and then stand at my side today, brothers, sister. It's time to descend Star Dome, show these people, our warriors, what the future holds for us. We will join the lines, carry the timber to the shores and we will tell them – show them – that change has come, at last."

And change *had* come, not only to the forest, but to Fel'annár. He had fallen beneath the murky waters of nascent leadership and had emerged a commander. And so command he would, and then later, he would speak with The Company, tell them of Pan'assár and Or'Talán. He would tell them the road he must now walk and ask them, one more time, if they would follow.

"Tonight, we will sit and drink while I tell you of the revelations and questions that have come to me. I will tell you what may lie at the end of this path, the road we have always walked together."

"And always will," said Idernon."

"So you're going to make us wait – as usual – to tell us about this mystery. I mean I don't know why I'm surprised but can't you just come out with it?" Carodel's arms were out to the side, a questioning stance, face a terrible scowl. Ramien rumbled with laughter, but they all looked at Fel'annár. He smiled back at them apologetically.

"Some things are best said in the silence, Carodel. Later, when there's wine and we are free to roam this Silvan paradise, I'll tell you what's in my mind." Fel'annár's eyes drifted to Lainon, thought they looked brighter than they had just moments before. His smile faltered, but The Company was collecting their things. It was time to dress and prepare.

He turned to the pile of belongings he knew were his. His clothes and armour had been cleaned, his weapons cared for and his boots polished. He smiled, picked up his shirt. Beneath it, the portrait of the elven lady he had found under the Nim'uán's cuirass.

Ankelar.

He remembered the name written on the back, wondered if this was the mother of the Beautiful Monsters. A wave of grief and pity washed over him, for what she must have suffered, what her children must have suffered, before they had turned. But then, had one of them not kept this portrait? Had they not still cared, even though they were Nim'uán?

He turned to the door, watched The Company leave to dress. But Lainon lingered. Perhaps he knew that he would need help with the buttons and buckles of his uniform. And of course, his hair! He smiled, mind somewhere in the recent past, of a time when Lainon had first shown him what to do with his unruly locks, even though he hadn't known he was Ari'atór at the time.

He placed the portrait in his open pack and sat. Lainon smiled, sat behind him and began to weave the Ari twists in his hair, collecting them at the crown of Fel'annár's head, one more time.

Minutes later, Fel'annár and Lainon emerged into the main area, one a general of Ea Uaré, the other, his original Ber'ator. Yerái's crutch banged over the wooden floors, not quite as loud as it had done yesterday.

The Company waiting, splendid in their clean uniforms.

"Is everyone here?

"They are waiting outside."

Fel'annár nodded at Idernon, raised one hand over his heart. "And Galadan is here, carried in the hearts of those who remain."

The others covered their own hearts, and after a moment of silence, The Company stepped from the cabin and onto the platform.

Under the late morning sun, Koldur stood in fine robes of green and lavender. Hobin stood utterly still, bright blue eyes moving between Fel'annár and Lainon. Gor'sadén stood tall, eyes unusually bright. Yerái, Bulan, Dalú, Eramor and Benat watched as Fel'annár and The Company spread into a circle.

Fel'annár stepped into it, saw no reason for preamble and asked his most pressing questions.

"Captain Bulan. How many dead?"

Bulan unfolded the parchment in his hands, looked down at it. "All in all, 1,903 warriors from Ea Uaré are dead. Of Captain Sorei's contingent, some five hundred. Captain Jendal reports some seven hundred Ari'atór have departed. Civilian bodies are still being collected and counted."

If anyone had expected Fel'annár to grimace, close his eyes and look away, they were wrong. Bulan shared a hopeful glance with Gor'sadén.

"How many seriously injured?"

"Some five hundred. Most will make it, I'm told. As for the rest of us, we're wounded but able."

Fel'annár nodded slowly. "After the battle, the *war*," he corrected. "After the things our warriors have seen, the people they have lost, these ... devastating numbers ... can I truly tell them that we won, Bulan?"

The veteran captain stepped forward, resolute eyes unwavering as he looked at Or'Talán reincarnate.

"We *did* win, Fel'annár. We saved this forest. We stopped a monster and his unholy brood from slaughtering our people. We *did* win. Never doubt that."

Fel'annár's eyes lingered on Bulan, and then drifted to Dalú's resolute eyes, Benat and Eramor, pride and respect in their steady gazes. They did not doubt their victory, and so neither would Fel'annár. Not any more.

Fel'annár's eyes wandered to Lainon. A soft smile graced the Ari'atór's lips, and his eyes were even brighter than they had been. He frowned, turned back to Bulan as he continued.

"You brought us victory, Fel'annár. On the heels of Pan'assár's command, you rose above it, beyond it. We the captains of Ea Uaré came back to this army because you asked it of us. It was our choice. It was our *privilege*."

Fel'annár's eyes misted far too quickly, and Bulan smiled because he had, indeed, been where Fel'annár was now, understood him all too well.

"Do we know how long before the injured can travel?"

"The Lestari says a week at best," said Dalú.

"Then we have one week to rebuild this city. After, most of us will return to Ea Uaré."

"Most?"

Fel'annár nodded, turned to Yerái.

"Lieutenant Yerái."

"Warlord?"

Fel'annár limped towards him. "I have no Golden Sun to place in your collar. But with Lord Koldur, Commanders Gor'sadén and Hobin – these captains as my witnesses – I say you are Captain Yerái, commander of the new Silvan outpost of Abiren'á. Do you accept this duty, as a captain of the Inner Circle, *even unto death*?"

Fel'annár's eyes drifted to Gor'sadén, saw his soft smile, and then he faced Yerái once more.

His fellow Listener stared back at him. "I accept – *proudly*, Warlord."

Fel'annár smiled, held out the crutch Yerái had lent him, nodded his thanks and limped unaided, back into the centre of the circle.

"Captain Yerái will select three hundred from our ranks and create the northern outpost in the Xeric Wood. You have the mining towers, the water supply you need. All you must do is build your barracks. Within the year, I will return." Fel'annár glanced at Bulan further along the circle. "I have a promise to keep."

Bulan smiled as he nodded, and Fel'annár returned it, knew that

Bulan had not forgotten. He *would* return here, in a time of peace, with his family. He turned away, to where Lainon stood, found him staring back with eyes that were glimmering.

Too bright.

He stepped closer, searched those Shirán eyes. "You're leaving."

"For a while, Fel'annár. But I will be back, I think."

"When there's danger?"

"Who knows? Perhaps, perhaps not. But this is not a second goodbye, Fel'annár."

He nodded, knew that Lainon was surely not at liberty to discuss what he was, how it worked. Still, there was one, final favour he would ask of his brother.

"Lainon. Can you take a message to the king for us? Tell him of our victory, of how many return, and that we lost Pan'assár. Can you wait for me to pen it for you?"

"No need," said Lainon, a hand out before him. "I will find a way."

Fel'annár didn't understand. There was no way that Azure could write with talons, but the light in Lainon's eyes was growing. They were out of time but still, he could see Lainon's face.

"We will meet again, Fel'annár, upon your path of understanding."

Fel'annár smiled tentatively. "Until then, brother."

Lainon stepped backwards, turned towards Tensári but Fel'annár called him back.

"Lainon!"

The elf that would soon be a hawk looked over his shoulders, eyes almost blinding.

"You will always be a brother of The Company."

Lainon smiled, as broad and as bright as Fel'annár had ever seen him smile and he watched as his brother's hand reached out to Tensári. They touched for one last time and then Lainon stretched his arms and stepped over the side of the platform, disappearing from sight.

Koldur cried out, but Bulan grabbed his arm, smiled reassuringly. The leader turned back, watched a black hawk fly upwards and then around Star Dome, crying out his farewell. And then it banked steeply, turning south and to the city of Ea Uaré.

Koldur and Yerái gaped in utter shock at the hawk that had been an elf just moments before. Hobin held out his hand in farewell, while The Company smiled, pulled Tensári closer to them and then watched Lainon fly away, until he was completely gone from their sight.

Fel'annár turned to face the commanders, captains and the leader of Abiren'á.

"Lainon is the first to depart, but soon, many of us will ride back to the southern city. But first, there are things I would say, to your people, Koldur – and my warriors."

Koldur frowned, turned to Gor'sadén, to Bulan, but they seemed equally confused.

"Today, we begin a new cycle, a new reality. Follow me, see its birth with your own eyes."

Fel'annár walked towards the air lift with the remaining Company and began their descent.

None of them knew what Fel'annár was up to, but they would soon find out.

~

MID-DAY, and Abiren'á was full of people.

Many more had come from Sen'oléi, while others had returned after fleeing the traps of the Sand Lords.

Civilians mingled with the able-bodied warriors, their uniforms clean but their eyes were wary and their smiles sparing. Too many memories of friends lost, of the horrors they had seen. But so too were they shocked by the magic they had witnessed, overwhelmed by the power and the majesty of The Sisters. The Warlord had invoked them, and they did not understand. Confusion warred with doubt and apprehension for the future.

They watched him now as he walked in their midst, joined the ranks of warriors as they made for the fallen logs and branches that had been dislodged during the maelstrom and which still littered the ground.

They said he had been injured, could see that he still limped, but wherever he went, he exuded strength, some surety that made him smile and his eyes shine. Some remembered Lássira, others Zéndar. Some even spoke of Thargodén and his silvery-blond locks. But it was Or'Talán they remembered the most, the Alpine king that the Silvans had loved so much, the king who had died in a war so similar to this one. After the Battle Under the Sun, Ea Uaré had turned dark, its new king absent in the face of growing hatred and discrimination. They asked themselves what would happen now?

Aren Or'Talán walked with The Company. They were closer than family, said the warriors, loyal to each other like none others, save perhaps for the stories they had heard of The Three, tales from foreign lands, so great they had transcended the boundaries of Tar'eastór. Yet one of those legends followed the band of brothers with none other than Hobin, Supreme Commander of Araria.

They stopped to watch, murmured in curiosity and then their words spread, like the smell of baking bread, the aroma of burning resins wafting through the boughs at a midsummer dance. The Warlord and his elves had come with Koldur, joined the steady flow of elves who made for a mighty branch that had splintered and fallen away from a giant tree. There was no room to roll it to the river so that the timber could be used for boats. It needed to be carried.

The foresters had already cranked it up from the ground at different places, as high as their mechanisms would allow. Still, they had to crouch low to get under it, place it over their shoulders.

Warriors and civilians, lords and commanders, bakers and farriers stood side by side, and when the foresters called on them, they braced, and then roared with the effort it took to lift.

With one elf on either side of the mighty limb, they marched in unison to the shouts of the foresters. Their arms shook, but the determination on their faces did not waver. This wood was much more than a fallen branch. It was the symbol of unity reborn. Alpines and Silvans, Ari'atór, men and women, old and young, pale and dark. They all carried the burden.

They were close to the river now, the trees further apart and with a yell from a forester who could have been a commander, the mighty branch was set down.

The elves stood, stretched their backs and grimaced, but they smiled at the feat they had achieved, and their eyes once more turned to the Warlord and his Company.

His smile was gone but not his determination, and he looked around him, at Idernon and The Company, at Gor'sadén and Bulan, at Hobin and Koldur. His other captains, Eramor and Benat, Dalú and now, Yerái. They all looked back at him, even as others came from the glade, until the push of elves was so great they could hardly move.

Word had spread. With his descent from Star Dome, it seemed he had stirred a city steeped in grief and shock, and now, they stood waiting, for what they did not know.

Fel'annár limped to a junction in the wood and stepped on it, felt Idernon's steadying hand at his back. This wood had come from a giant, the branch just as big as any normal tree. He could see everything. The sea of people around him, those on the quayside to his right. The construction of the pyres had stopped, and healers and warriors had stepped out from under the tarpaulins of the pavilions. With the water at his back and the trees around them, Fel'annár remembered Gor'sadén's words.

Never lose the heart ...

And so he would speak from the heart.

"Behold the far side of the forest," he shouted with a smile, lifting both arms. "They tried to take it from us."

Green eyes watched his growing audience. Those too far away to hear had come closer, vied for a better spot, so that they could see the Warlord, for the first time after the pyres, hear his words directly and not depend on the recounting of others.

"My grandfather perished in the Xeric Wood, at the cruel hands of Sand Lords. Some of you were there, at the Battle Under the Sun.

"And now, at this the Battle of Abiren'á, Commander General Pan'assár gave his life to save us all, and at his side, Captain Galadan of The Company protected him, so that we all could live.

"We have all suffered, have all lost those we love. We have shed tears before the pyres, for the thousands of souls we have lost. The Nim'uán and their Sand Lords took their lives, but they did not take their *freedom!*"

"Aye!" The warriors shouted, the citizens nodded, and then the crowd settled for the Warlord had not finished.

"And so, mourn we must. But so too must we celebrate. The greatness of our lost warriors, their sacrifice is testimony to the goodness in this world, because we remain a free nation thanks to them. And so I say, on the twelfth day of the eighth cycle, we will remember those who fell to protect us."

There were murmurs from the crowds, conversations begging for freedom, but the Warlord had still not finished.

"We who lived to see this day will feast, lift our glasses and remember the Protectors, the glorious dead and the bold who lived to tell their tale. This we will do, on the twelfth day of the eighth cycle of the year! On the day of the Battle for Abiren'á!"

Voices screamed to the heavens. Grief and determination, courage and relief, Fel'annár's words had inspired them and still, they looked up, wanted more of Or'Talán's grandchild.

"You are no longer alone, not anymore. I as your Warlord promise you this. A new outpost will be created here, starting today. Lieutenant Yerái is now Captain. He will fortify our northern territories with three hundred of these warriors who wish to stay. They are already home, and once I am back in the city and there are warriors to be had, I will send more, so that we have outposts in Sen'oléi, Lan Taria and Oran'Dor, as it always should have been. And when I return, in a time of peace to this my ancestral home, I and whoever will follow me, will rebuild our lost village of Sen'uár."

A mighty cheer rent the air and Fel'annár sought out Galdith's pale face. He saw surprise and he saw gratitude, as well as he saw the lingering grief that the Fierce Warrior hid so well.

Fel'annár breathed deeply, forgot he was standing before thousands, felt the breathy sigh of the forest that looked down on him. That sluggish, cold disregard he had sensed on his arrival here had gone.

"I feel these lands from the inside. I know the mind of the trees, as well as they know mine. I have heard the Sisters and they charged with us into battle. Gods but you have seen terrible things and you have seen wonderful things that you don't understand. Some call it magic, are afraid because they don't understand it. Yet think of plants as they lean to the sunlight. Think of leaves unfurling in spring and flowers that grow from the grassy plains beyond the Wetwood. Is this not magic too? The magic of a rising sun and a setting moon, the passage of stars across the sky. It is the same force that shines in my eyes, that conjures the trees. We all live inside this world of magic and I am nothing but its wielder."

He smiled, unaware that his eyes let off a soft glow, not enough to startle. Enough to press his point.

"So let this be a new day. A day that was bought by the sacrifice of the noble warriors of Ea Uaré, of Araria and Tar'eastór. We shall speak of Captain Amon!"

"Aye!"

"Of Captain Benat!"

"Aye!" Benat smiled as he was clapped on the back from all sides.

"Captain Eramor!"

"Aye!"

"Captain Dalú!"

"Aye!"

"*Brave* captain Bulan!"

The crowds erupted, hands in the air, weapons flashing in the dappled sunlight as Bulan was swept off his feet and Fel'annár laughed. And then he jumped from the giant branch and almost fell. Ramien steadied him, just as a yell from the crowds rent the air.

"Hail the Warlord!"

"Hail!"

"Hail Fel'annár Ar Lássira!"

"Hail!"

He was surrounded, by people, by warriors. They reached out to touch him as he stepped down, only to disappear into a sea of thankfulness. When at last it was over and he was left standing alone, messy hair and crooked cloak, he turned to Gor'sadén and The Company.

No words left their mouths, but Fel'annár felt their love, felt their loyalty, returned it in equal measure.

The young lad who left Lan Taria with a pocketful of dreams, the one they called *The Silvan,* had risen to command. He had finally understood where his path must lead, and all those feelings of lingering foreboding that had once plagued him had gone. In their place, an almost unbearable curiosity to be home and in the Evergreen Wood, so that he could see for himself what Aria had bid him protect.

~

IT WAS a sultry day in the city.

There wouldn't be many more of them to come. In a scant few weeks, the leaves of the Great Forest would change their hues from green to orange and brown. But not so the Evergreen Wood.

Fel'annár had said there was something not quite friendly about it, but Thargodén had never felt anything but comfort from it. Today was no exception.

Rinon had left on his mission to Port Helia, would be away for the next week and he had taken Sorei with him. His son had yet to tell him of the nature of their acquaintance, but if Thargodén were to guess, he would say there was more to it than either were willing to admit.

With Maeneth though, he had sensed something deeper. Sontúr had counselled him for long enough for Thargodén to see his worth, know him honourable – suitable for his daughter's company but it was far more than that. He liked Sontúr, found him intelligent, witty, compassionate and entirely compatible with his academic yet pragmatic daughter.

A steadying breath, the scent of pine and resin collecting at the back of his throat. He savoured it – the smell of home. All he needed was to keep the enemy at bay for three, maybe four more weeks and if he was lucky, the army that had left five weeks ago, would return with sufficient numbers to fight the Deviants back, show them they were no longer defenceless.

If they had won the war.

He glanced upwards. It was still warm, but the light had changed. Summer was slowly merging into autumn. By the time Fel'annár was back, the leaves would be shedding, and everything would be awash in golden browns and fiery reds. Except for here where it would always be green.

One finger stroked over the emerald hanging from his hand.

Evergreen wood, evergreen love – tell me – have you found yourself, Lássira of Abiren'á? Should I leave, will I see your smiling face on the other side of the Veil?

He would wait, wait for his children to find their paths. He would wait for the promise of sustained peace and returned prosperity. Once he could be sure that the follies of his long years of wandering had been mended, then he would take the Long Road.

The road to happiness, at last.

He smiled, cast his face to the sun, felt its warmth. A hunting bird squawked in the distance, flew overhead and he watched it, wondering briefly what had diverted it from its path in the forest.

The black hawk rested on the highest peaks of the Academic Guild and Thargodén turned away, back to the woods, back to his thoughts of Lássira below a late summer sun.

~

THE EX-SHADOW MACURIAN ducked inside the Academic Guild, in search of Lerita.

He found her sitting in her library study on the first floor of the Guild, sipping on liquor and staring at nothing.

"Lerita."

"Macurian." No surprise, even though he had appeared in her room unannounced. She had left the door open and he was an ex-Shadow.

She turned, looked up at him. "Sit."

The woman was no taller than his tits, but every time she spoke, her words sounded like orders. He respected that, wondered if she'd learned it somehow, or whether it was a natural skill she'd been born with.

"You found nothing, did you?" She poured a glass of whatever it was she was drinking and then slid it across the small table between them. Macurian reached for it, took a large gulp and waited for the fire in his gullet to die down.

"No."

She hung her head, drank again as Macurian explained.

"I don't think it exists anymore. Or'Talán gave it to Lord Ileian, who may have destroyed it. It's unlikely of course, because in the hands of a traitor like him, it was a hefty prize. If Sulén knew of it, he hid it away. It seems he had a penchant for collecting items of historical importance."

"Like Or'Talán's final journal."

"I've caught wind of that, yes," said the ex-Shadow, drinking again and then looking appreciatively at the finger of liquid still left inside the glass.

"And Sulén is dead, as is his son Silor. Who else could have inherited such a thing?" asked Lerita.

"Ras'dan, but he died and his own son remained in Tar'eastór. According to sources, he is in the military, plays no major role in society, not since his father's death. The possibility that he has it is remote. And then we have Band'orán, but Analei was destroyed and if he did have it, that letter perished along with everyone else."

"As surely as Or'Talán," murmured the strange woman. Macurian had never seen her like this, introspective.

"Why is it so important to have this letter? Surely it was just a good-bye, to a son who was crown prince."

"Who knows what a king would say to his son on the eve of battle, Shadow? But now, it seems we will never know."

Macurian frowned, gulped down the last of his liquor. "You think there was something important in it, don't you?"

Lerita looked at him, and then past him, to the painting over her fireplace. The Evergreen Wood, painted by one who knew that place well – as well as she herself did. A soft but sad smile played about her thin lips, and for a moment, Macurian was drawn to her overly bright blue eyes.

She turned to him, smile gone. "Nothing that need concern you." She stood, made for her desk and the drawer on one side. Pulling it open, she retrieved a small but heavy pouch. She returned, stood before Macurian and held it out.

"You have done well. Here."

Macurian stood, took it and tossed it in his hands. Heavy enough a recompense for his efforts. He nodded, decided that he liked Lerita.

"There's one last possibility. Remote, but maybe worth a try."

"Speak it."

Macurian's shifty eyes travelled the expanse of the room, as if he thought someone might be watching. "Draugolé," he murmured.

Lerita's frozen face cracked a little and Macurian watched in fascination. "Explain."

"Well. Every time I investigated a lead. Sulén, Ras'dan, Silor, their families and acquaintances, that name came up time and again. Think about it. He was Ileian's apprentice, as was Sulén. He was Band'orán's right-hand man. No one knew more about him than Draugolé. If there's anyone who may know something about that letter, it's him."

Lerita nodded slowly. "I will need permission from the king. He sits in the dungeons, in isolation."

"Is he that dangerous?"

Lerita stared back at Macurian. "He cannot wield a blade. He is the most dangerous elf I know."

Macurian's curiosity was piqued. "Then if you get that permission, I'll pay him a visit."

"And you will enjoy it, I wager," said Lerita. "I'll be in touch soon, Shadow."

"You know how to find me."

And she did, would see the king tomorrow.

She watched him leave, and then turned to the hearth and the painting above it. One hand reached out, a finger glancing over an area painted in greens and greys. Tree and rock and amidst it, her true home on Bel'arán.

Soon, their army would return, and if the Warlord had survived, she would seek him out, know whether he had understood, at last.

Lerita raised one hand, turned it palm up, brushed one finger over the short wavy line and dot on the inside of her wrist.

She was startled from her thoughts by the call of a hunting bird.

She smiled.

∾

RINON AND SOREI led their patrol along the hillside. Below, the Calro Estuary was widening. Just over the next crest, they would see the silver sea and Port Helia in the distance, hazy in the late afternoon sun.

It had been years since Rinon had last come this way. He hadn't seen the sea for years and even then, he had felt nothing. He had been numb, angry and foolish then and yet now, after the Battle of Brothers, the war raging in the north, and Maeneth's arrival, everything seemed to have changed. He would allow himself the indulgence of exposing his mind to the outside world, to feel it without worrying that it would weaken him, or that it would make him seem lesser in some way.

But it was more than that. It was the return of his father, of the king. It was the discovery of Fel'annár and the coming of Sorei.

He had told himself so many times over the past few days that she was a delightful distraction to the growing difficulties of rebuilding a kingdom and an army, assuming his responsibility as a general and crown prince even as they battled the growing numbers of Deviants.

But he was old enough to know that was a lie. She was becoming a necessity to him, a part of his life he was beginning to depend on like a drug. But he hadn't told her that, not yet.

He held his hand up to the patrol. They would stop here for a while before descending the hills and entering Port Helia. Sorei oversaw the camp, watched as Rinon walked towards the edge of the hill, knew the sea was just beyond.

She repressed a smile, walked away from the camp and to where Rinon was standing. The green horizon was slipping lower and lower, until it was replaced by the hazy silver of the sea, and then the fleet of white-sailed ships approaching the outer isles of Pelagia.

She frowned, covered the final steps towards the edge until all she could see was a white-dotted ocean, an armada of warships before a city bathed in fire.

She whirled around, to Rinon's frigid profile, to his trembling face and disbelieving eyes, heard his breathy whisper because that was surely all that he was capable of.

"Holy Gods."

A horn sounded in the distance, and then another. The Sirens of Dan'bar. Pelagia - the greatest sea-faring nation on Bel'arán - called for help.

Had Rinon and Sorei been closer, they would see mighty serpents painted on those sails, jowls open, amber eyes wide and ready to strike. They would see Sand Lords prepared for war, and beneath their armoured boots, under the decks, creatures that roared and screeched and clawed at the confines of their cages.

Those creatures could smell freedom, land beyond the sulphur of their own breath. It was the promise of green pastures and space to run and climb, the surety of fresh meat.

Upon the very prow of the largest, foremost ship, a formidable warrior stood, an unbeatable force of nature, the greatest of the Nim'uán - he who would be Emperor.

Gra'dón was home at last.

The End.

FROM R.K. LANDER

I hope you enjoyed this instalment of The Silvan Saga. Writing is currently underway on the sixth and final episode, coming soon.

Please consider reviewing on Amazon. If you are a member of Goodreads or Bookbub, you might consider leaving a review there, or perhaps a recommendation.

Why not join my Reader's Club? You'll get exclusive access to the The Silvan: A Reader's Guide to the Silvan Saga. This is an ongoing project and you'll receive regular updates as a member of my Newsletter list. You can join and download your free copy here:

https://dl.bookfunnel.com/6p8l8xvan1

Another way to keep updated with my releases is to follow my blog at:

www.rklander.com

ABOUT THE AUTHOR

www.rklander.com

f   facebook.com/rklwrites

🐦   twitter.com/rklwrites

📷   instagram.com/rklanderwrites

BB   bookbub.com/profile/r-k-lander

ⓐ   amazon.com/R-K-Lander/e/B06XWDLZ8X

ACKNOWLEDGMENTS

As always, my unwavering gratitude to the mighty M.Y. Leigh. There is no better developmental editor in this world!

I would like to thank my incredible team of ARC readers over at R.K. Lander's The Company. What a wonderful job we have done together.

Special thanks go to Ana Pérez, Jen Smith and Leone Marais for their incredible and painstaking proof reading. I would also like to thank Marilyn Wilkinson, Kirsty Kilpatrick, Sharon Willis, Lesley Walsh, Donna Navarro, Adrian Lee, Bruce Sutton, Claudia Linquanti-Sue, Sherrin Eiffler, Singa Nga, Joanna Duggan, Ken Edmondson, Adrian Lee, Natalia Glinoer, Greg Dietrich, Evelyn Ziegenhagen, Claire Eleanor Stewart-Wilson and Meinir Michael.

Another special mention goes to Christopher Edwards, Warrior (USAF retired), for his input in all things military. Thank you for your invaluable insights and unwavering encouragement.

Thank you Simon Prebble, for your help with all things technical. We couldn't have done this without you.

And to the rest of The Company. Thank you for reading and encouraging. For helping and advising, for being there when a humble writer needed your wisdom and enthusiasm.

David Witko, Kadie Gotcher, A.J. Fraser-Brown, Carolyn Langen, Charity Wiggins, Dale Whitley, Devin Vandermeer, Ellen Roddy, John Melton, Paul Zawacki, Susan Peters, Tim Carter, Tim Allen, Maria Fuess, Katie Goetcher Michaelis, Rob Thompson, Jesse Elizabeth, Beth Austin, Donnette Briggs, Lola Berry, Patricia Onório Merens, Sylvia Armijo, Nura Mascarenas, Allen Lavering II, Reg Corney, Anne Rounding, Kyna Robinson Woollery, Carmen Gerrits Nelson, Kim Wehrung, Claire Marie Soria, Tim Carter and Victoria Luna

Made in the USA
Middletown, DE
09 September 2022